The C

Victor Canning, a native of Devonshire, was born in 1911. His first novel *Mr Finchley Discovers His England* was published in 1934 and since then writing has been his full-time occupation. He has worked as a script-writer in Hollywood and many of his novels have been made into films, notably *The Golden Salamander* and *Venetian Bird*. He has also written plays and serials for television and radio, and many of his stories have been published in the principal magazines and news-papers of England and America. During the Second World War he was commissioned into the Royal Artillery, serving in North Africa, Italy and Austria. He has written over thirty novels, some of the most recent being *The Painted Tent* (1974), *The Mask of Memory* (1974), *The Kingsford Mark* (1975), *The Doomsday Carrier* (1976), *Birdcage* (1978) and *The Satan Sampler* (1979).

Victor Canning

The Crimson Chalice Trilogy

Penguin Books

Penguin Books Ltd, Harmondsworth,
Middlesex, England
Penguin Books, 625 Madison Avenue,
New York, New York 10022, U.S.A.
Penguin Books Australia Ltd, Ringwood,
Victoria, Australia
Penguin Books Canada Ltd, 2801 John Street,
Markham, Ontario, Canada L3R 1B4
Penguin Books (N.Z.) Ltd, 182–190 Wairau Road,
Auckland 10, New Zealand

The Crimson Chalice first published by William Heinemann Ltd 1976
Copyright © Victor Canning, 1976
The Circle of the Gods first published by William Heinemann Ltd 1977
Copyright © Victor Canning, 1977
The Immortal Wound first published by William Heinemann Ltd 1978
Copyright © Victor Canning, 1978
The Crimson Chalice Trilogy first published in Penguin Books 1980
Copyright © Victor Canning, 1980

Typeset, printed and bound in Great Britain by
Hazell Watson & Viney Ltd,
Aylesbury, Bucks
Set in Linotype Pilgrim

The Crimson Chalice

The Circle of the Gods

The Immortal Wound

Contents

The Immortal Wound 441

The Crimson Chalice

For my wife, Diana, with love

Forest Meeting

As the sun tipped the eastern reaches of the forest and fired the pewter sea to silver at the far end of the valley, the May morning was full of song. Through the belling of tits, the monotonous sawing of the chiff-chaffs and the melodious pealing of thrushes and blackbirds, Lerg, the big grey wolfhound, caught the clatter of a distantly falling stone on the valleyside path. Except for a slight lift of his muzzle from his couched forepaws, he made no move; but his grey-flecked green eyes watched the turn of the path where it entered the wide glade. To his right Aesc, the water dog with the long drooping red-furred ears, had heard the stone fall some few moments after she had caught the human scent coming up on the morning breeze from the sea. On the left of Lerg, Cuna, small, short-legged and wire-haired, neither heard, nor saw, nor smelled anything. Not long out of puppyhood, he was curled into a ball and, empty-bellied now for twenty-four hours, dreamt of vole and rat and hare and the dark tunnels of fox earths and badger sets.

Above them the body hung. The hide thongs about the ankles still bit tight, but those about the wrists, which held the body suspended from the stout horizontal branch of an oak, had stretched so that the balls of the tied feet just touched the ground. But it had been twelve hours since there had been any power in legs and feet to take advantage of earth's touch to ease the dragging weight of the body on shoulder muscles. Bluebottles, and a small cloud of midges and early gnats, clustered over the crisp-curled head of hair and the brown, sweat-dried face. An hour before sunset a pair of red kites had spiralled down, forked tails splayed, to roost on the upper branches of the oak. Bran, the raven, had given an angry *carp, carp* and had flown at them, chasing them away inland over the rolling green sea of forest.

Bran sat now on the oak top and watched the newcomer moving up the path towards the glade. Twice during the night a lone wolf, ancient and pack-exiled, had come to the glade's edge and Lerg had driven him away. Now, five miles away to the east, the wolf fed on a calf among the slaughtered cattle in a stock-yard close to the fire-black ruins of a homestead, and had for company cohorts of crows, kites, buzzards and eagles. In the dust of the forecourt an old woman sat holding her long grey hair over her face to keep the day away, keening and moaning softly to herself, numbed and half-crazed by the memory of the horror which had filled the last two days.

The newcomer turned the swing of the path and came to the edge of the glade. It was a girl grown close to young woman-hood. The hood of her short brown woollen mantle was pushed back on to her shoulders, leaving her fair hair free. Around her waist, over a white, dust-streaked linen tunic, she wore an embroidered belt with a bronze clasp in the shape of two dolphins. On her feet were leather sandals held by a cross-gartering of red-dyed doe-skin thongs which ran up her bare legs and were tied beneath her knees. Over her right shoulder she carried a bulky sack made by the knotting of four corners of a bed cover of green and yellow striped silk.

Standing at the edge of the glade she saw the three dogs, saw the rapid mouse-movement of a tree-creeper work up the rough trunk of the oak, saw the raven at the top of the tree, and breathed with a slow, anguished tightening of her face as she saw the body. For a moment she closed her blue eyes against memory. A low rumble from Lerg startled and frightened her. To turn away she knew, for she was no stranger to animals, might bring the dogs after her. To go forward, too, she reasoned, could start the trio of guarding beasts into a violent, rushing attack. She stood where she was and waited, her eyes on the dogs and the bowed head of the body that hung from the tree, ringed with a moving halo of flies and gnats.

Lerg growled low again and Cuna, awake now, slowly sat up but knew better than to move past Lerg. Lerg was the leader. Aesc and Cuna waited.

The girl waited, too, her body trembling under the swift assault of her fears. The strengthening sun burned against the skin of her right cheek. Across it ran a dark smudge of black ash, and above her right eye, dark against the fair skin, was a bruise as large as a crab-apple. She waited and watched and saw the quick flirt of a red squirrel into the top of a young ash tree, saw the bending of the slim branches whip back into place, the silver grey bark flashing in the sun. Lerg growled again and then slowly rose to his feet. The other dogs made no move. Long-legged, lean-bodied, the grey coat shaggy as lichen, he stood as high as a month-old calf and she knew his kind, for they were highly prized now far beyond Britain for their speed and courage in the killing of wolf and deer. And the other dog, too, she knew, with its red coat and long ears – a kind that loved water as much as the otters and wild fowl they hunted. Then, remembering that her father had often said, 'There is no dog which cannot read the cast of any mortal. Feel fear and they scent it and give no trust. Harbour villainy and they will return it. Offer friendship and they will accept it – but at their own gait', she forced herself to stand where she was and watch the slow movement of the hound towards her. He came, not directly, but on an arc which took him away to her right where she lost sight of him. Without words, the cry locked silently in her mind, she pleaded with the hound . . . *your master suffers . . . there is suffering with me, too . . . leave me free to help him* . . . She stared ahead at the hanging body. Its top half was covered with an undershirt, its front open, stirring slightly in the morning breeze. The lower part of the body was sheathed in tight-fitting leather breeks reaching just below the knees. On the feet were heavy, metal-studded, thick-soled sandals fastened by thongs at the ankles.

The hound paced back into her view and circled to her left, but this time halted within her sight. He raised his head, looked back at the oak tree and the other dogs, then swung his head slowly round and eyed her. Her instinct was to make some move, some show of friendliness, but she held still. Fear ran steadily in her, but it was a fear now which she fought to control. Slowly swamping her own misery and recent griefs there rose in her a warm compassion for the being who hung from the tree, who might still live and need her help. The hound lowered his head and moved towards her, stiff-legged, hackles part risen. He stopped close to her and reaching out his muzzle sniffed at her left hand which hung against her side. She felt the warm breath on her fingers and caught the strong, rank dog smell in her nostrils. Suddenly the hound licked her hand, gave a low, easy growl and turned from her. Lerg walked back to the other dogs and sat on his haunches, his eyes on the girl.

Then, as though possessed by some strange power never known to her before, the girl felt her trembling ease, the quick beating of her heart die down and without hesitation she walked forward. The dogs' heads turned as she came up to them, passed them and went to the body. There was no fear in her now. She eased her bundle to the earth and unknotted the covering. Reaching inside she fumbled around for a while and brought out a small sharp-edged dagger. She put the haft in her mouth, then crouched and jumped for the overhanging branch. She got two hand holds, then swung her legs up and worked herself to a prone position on top of the branch. She eased herself along and began to saw at the thongs of the left wrist. As she cut the last one the body lurched sideways, spun slowly on the stretched thongs of the right hand and the bound feet dragged across the earth.

The dogs watched but made no sound.

She wormed herself further along the branch and with a few quick slashes cut the thongs of the remaining hand. The body fell in a heap to the ground. As it hit the earth there was the sound of a long-drawn moan. On the oak top Bran called sharply *carp, carp* and launched himself into the air in a clumsy spiral.

The girl dropped to the ground. The body lay face down-

wards. She cut the ankle thongs and rolled the body over on to
its back. For the first time she saw the face clearly. It was the
face of a youth of about eighteen, a lean, strong, tanned face,
streaked with sweat and dirt, a young tawny-red beard growth
fuzzing the square chin. Across the right side of his face was a
jagged cut over which the blood had dried in a hard crust.

Oblivious now of the dogs which had accepted her, she went
back to her bundle and brought out a small bronze cooking
cauldron. She ran across the glade and along the path by which
she had arrived. A little way down it a small spring sprang
from the hillside feeding a shallow cress-covered pool. She filled
the cauldron and went back to the youth, and pulling a small
earthenware beaker from her bundle, squatted on the ground
and lifted the youth's head and shoulders up on to her knees.
With a firm hand on his chin she forced his mouth open and
poured water between his cracked lips. He moaned a little and
choked, the water spilling over his face and neck. She tried
again and this time eased only a little water into his mouth, her
hand shaking, chiding herself, 'Gently, Tia, gently'.

Slowly she fed him water and when she judged he had had
enough, she lowered his head to the ground, cushioning it on a
woollen blanket from her bundle. She tore a long strip from the
edge of her linen tunic and bathed his face, keeping the water
away from the hard crust on his wound as much as she could
since it was a better protection than any she could devise. His
wrists were raw and bloody with the thong-marks so she tore
the linen face cloth into two strips and bound them around the
wounds.

The sun was climbing higher in the sky. In a little while she
knew the glade would be in full, hard sunlight. She would have
to find shade for the youth and – since the times were what
they were – some kind of concealment. There was little charity
abroad these days. There were men about who would murder
for a worn pair of leather breeches and a pair of old legionary
sandals.

She hurried away to the edge of the glade. As she went Lerg

moved to the youth and lay down at his side, but the water dog, Aesc, followed her and, after a moment's hesitation, so did Cuna.

Not far from the edge of the glade she found a stunted yew with a tangle of wild clematis in fresh leaf trailing over its lower branches to form a narrow bower. She went back to the youth, took off her cloak belt and, looping it under his arms, began to drag him into the forest. Within the hour she had him in the bower, resting on a couch of old bracken growth and fresh branches, his head and shoulders propped up on her travelling bundle. She refilled the cauldron, fed more water to him, drank herself and ate part of a wheat cake she carried. She undid his wrist bandages, laid dock leaves around the wounds and replaced the bandages. Then she covered him with her mantle and sat by him, looking down at him. In all the time she had been with him he had never opened his eyes, but now and again he had given a long groan. He was young, strong and hardened, and tight-muscled and there were no wounds on him except for his wrists and the cut cheek. She sat patiently watching him, knowing that time and the water she had given him would do their work. A spear's length away from her Lerg lay couched under a bush. Of the other two dogs there was no sign. Unknown to Tia, Bran sat high up in a nearby ash tree on a roost which gave him a view through the forest's canopy of the dark fringe of the yew bower and Lerg's shadowy couched form. Before roosting Bran had robbed a magpie's nest of its two blue-quilled fledglings and had eaten well. Somewhere Cuna and Aesc were hunting. Only Lerg lay still and close to his master and would not eat until he knew that it was safe to leave him.

And Tia, elbows resting on her knees, chin cupped in her hands, remembered the night which had passed and the days before it, and knew that there could be nothing in the future which could replace all that had been lost ... her brother and his wife dead, the villa and the homestead huts plundered and burned, cattle slaughtered, and most of their own workpeople turned against her and the family. Only the devotion of her maid's husband, Tullio, had saved her from the savagery of the estate steward who had laid a drunken claim to her from which she had been saved by the dagger thrust of Tullio's old service *pugio*. She began to sob. In a few short hours the peace and ease of her life had been shattered, her loved ones killed and the security of her sheltered, rich life destroyed. She covered her face with her hands and her body shook with quick spasms which she could not control.

Lerg gave a low whine and Tia straightened up, the spasms passing. As she did so the youth stirred and opened his eyes. He stared without moving at the dark roof of the yew branches overhead, and she saw that his eyes were a dark, shining brown reminding her of the colour of the closed sea anemones that studded the low water rocks of the beach that marked the estate's southern boundary. She reached to her side and dunked part of the hard wheat cake in the water of the cauldron. Cradling his head on her arm she tried to feed him, but he closed his eyes and turned his head away. She filled the beaker and offered him water. With his eyes still closed he drank, and this time he swallowed the water avidly. When she lowered his head and shoulders back on to the bundle he sighed. She sensed the slow ease taking his body as its strained muscles relaxed. He slept and his breathing, which at first was heavy and troubled, took on a regular, slow rhythm.

The sun climbed higher. Aesc and Cuna returned and settled a few paces away. Cuna slept, curled into a ball, but Aesc lay couched, her eyes wide open watching the youth. Somewhere, Tia guessed, the two dogs had discovered food. There was plenty to be found in the ruined huts and the yards and fields with their slaughtered cattle and poultry. Stirred by the tongues of the rabble-rousers the country people had proved themselves as ruthless as any of the Saxon sea-folk on their sudden, summer raids. Soon they, too, would be back. Each year they came earlier and in greater force, and each year more and more of them stayed to swell the ranks of their kinsmen who had made the Saxon shores and the rich corn lands and settlements east of Anderida their own; each year moving farther west with no true leader bold enough to raise arms or banner against them.

The youth beside her began to talk in his sleep. At the sound of the voice Lerg's ears half-cocked and Aesc raised her head. It was difficult for Tia to understand anything of what he said. He spoke sometimes in her own tongue, but it was the rough, slang-filled language of the army auxiliaries, the old language of the barrack blocks and camps, and sometimes he spoke in the true language of the country of which she knew only a few words and phrases. In his voice there was, too, an accent and burr which was strange to her. After a while he slept without talking. Tia sat with him. At midday, feeling hungry, she ate some more of the wheat cake and a piece of the goats' cheese which Tullio's wife had put into her bundle. The smell of the cheese woke Cuna. He stood on his stubby legs and came to her. She broke off a piece for him which he ate and then settled at her feet.

Tia lay back on the grass aware suddenly of her fatigue and her own despair. She had travelled all night blindly across-country fighting always the panic in her thoughts. Within a few moments she was asleep.

When Baradoc woke and came to himself, the sun was half-way down the western sky. He lay for a while watching the dapple of sunlight through the yew branches, aware of the wrack and soreness in arm and shoulder muscles. He raised his hands and looked at the bandages on his wrist. A confusion in his head cleared slowly. Above him appeared the head and shoulders of Lerg. The hound gave a low whine. Baradoc fondled the grey muzzle and then, gripping the dog's neck, eased himself to a sitting position. For a moment his head swam and he shook it to clear his vision, seeing through a blur Aesc and Cuna standing beyond Lerg. Then, as his head swung slowly round, he saw the girl. She was sleeping on the grass, her mantle flung open, the torn edge of her white tunic rumpled above her knees and suntanned legs. Her short, fair hair was breeze fanned across her temples and she lay with her cheek couched in her hand. He looked from her to the dogs and then half turned, wincing with the pull on his strained muscles, and saw the cloth-wrapped bundle on which his head had been resting. Looking again at the girl he saw now that close to her side a small dagger lay on the ground ready to her free hand. He smiled to himself, guessing much of what must have happened, and knowing gratitude; knowing, too, from one look at her face that she was not one of his people. Her red-thonged sandals would have cost more sesterces than any working country girl could have afforded. Unexpectedly his head began to swim violently. He leaned forward, holding it with his hands, fighting off the vertigo. The attack passed and, as he straightened up, he realized that he must have groaned aloud. The girl was awake and, half risen, was resting on her knees and facing him, dagger in shaking hand.

For a moment or two they faced one another without words, and Baradoc knew that, even though she must have cut him down and looked after him, she could have no surety that such an act of charity would be met with friendship or thanks. There were plenty of men in the country today who merited being left to hang for the crows and ravens to pick clean. He looked down at the small dagger which she held in her unsteady right hand, and said, 'You won't need that.' He spoke her tongue. 'The gods were good to send you, and the dogs marking your goodness let you pass. I owe you a life. On my people's sign I swear it.' He pulled the edge of his loose shirt aside and touched his left shoulder.

Tia, fear dying, saw that tattooed on the brown skin was a small, black, crow-like bird with red beak and red legs. She guessed then that he must come from the far west or north for there lived the only tribes who marked their skins so.

She said, 'Who are you?'

'My name is Baradoc. I am from the far west where the land falls into the sea in the heart of which the father of all the oceans sleeps. Who are you?'

'I am Gratia. But mostly I am called Tia. My father was Marcus Pupius Corbulo. He and my mother are long dead. I live with my brother Priscus and his wife . . .' She broke off for a moment or two and then went on, 'That is, I lived with them

23

until yesterday. They are both now dead – killed by our own farm workers.'

Baradoc let his eyes rest on the bruise on her forehead and then they moved to the bundle on which his head had been resting, to the water-filled cauldron and the beaker by its side and on to the half portion of the flat wheat cake and the broken piece of cheese which lay on a large leaf alongside it. He said gently, 'These are bad times. Men easily turn against their masters. Some do it because there has been a fear in them ever since it was known from General Aetius that there will be no Roman help for us from Gaul. And others because a new fear is growing with every longboat that brings fresh crewmen to join their brothers along the Saxon shore. They fear the new masters and turn against the old.'

Listening to him Tia was surprised at the masterly manner of his speaking, as though his knowledge and authority admitted no questioning. Before she could stop herself, she said, 'When you lay there sleeping you talked in the speech of the camps and the barracks. Now you talk as I do.'

Baradoc smiled. 'I have known many old legionaries, and I talk as they did. But also I was for years a servant of a retired Chief Centurion. With him if I did not speak correctly I felt the weight of his vine staff. I am the son of a tribal chief, taken as slave when I was twelve years old. My master took my education seriously.' He grinned suddenly, deep creases bracketing the sides of his mouth, and added in soldiers' speech, 'My belly grumbles for a taste of that cheese.'

Tia laughed at the sudden transition and, in the midst of her laughter, wondered that she could, with all the darkness which still clouded her life. She handed the cheese across to him. As he stretched out his hand and arm for it she saw him wince at the flex of his stretched muscles. She said, 'When you have eaten I will massage your shoulders and arms. This was something I did often for Priscus in our bath house.'

Baradoc nodded, his mouth full of cheese. Tia, watching him, was sure now that she had nothing to fear from him. There was, too, she sensed, a strength and self-confidence about him which she guessed he could readily muster against trouble.

She asked, 'This master of yours, is he alive still?'

'No.' Baradoc scowled and his face suddenly turned grim. 'The Saxons killed him a month ago. But long before that he had given me my freedom.'

'You are going back to your people?'

'Yes.' Baradoc reached for the water beaker and drank.

'You could have gone before. Since you were free.'

Baradoc smiled. 'I could have done easily. But my master was good to me, and there were many things he taught me. To read and write and speak his language. About farming and fighting, and how to read the stars, and to understand about building and mathematics and geometry and history and about the rest of the world out there.' He waved the empty beaker vaguely southwards. 'So I stayed. I am the son of a chief. One day I shall be the leader of my people. It is right that I should know more than they do and then teach these things to them.'

Tia smiled. 'You will be a very important man, I see.'

Baradoc chuckled. 'Thanks to you, yes – since you came along and cut me down.'

'Who hung you up like that?'

Baradoc frowned and said stiffly, 'Two – that called themselves friends. One day I shall kill them both. But that is no business of yours.'

Tia stood up, suddenly angry at his words and his abruptness. She said sharply, 'True. Perhaps, then, I should have passed the tree and left you hanging there since that, too, was no business of mine!'

Baradoc reached out quickly and caught the edge of her mantle and said, 'Hold now! Don't fly off like a hen disturbed from her night roost. I meant no rudeness. It was just the thought of those two that stirred me up.' He let go of her mantle and grinned, his tanned face creasing. 'You are full of Roman fire and guts aren't you? But that's good – especially in these days. But not good enough to take you safely through this country alone the way things are. So calm down and tell me where you want to go and I will see you safely there.'

'Even though you go west and I should say Eburacum?'

Baradoc laughed. 'Why not? Even though you should say Vindolanda on the North Wall – though that might give us a little trouble. I owe you a life. The longest journey would only be a little paid off the score. So, stop scowling, and tell me where.'

Tia slowly sat down. She said, 'My brother and sister are dead. All that I have in this country now is an old uncle who lives near Aquae Sulis. It is in my mind to go to him.'

'Then let it rest there. I will take you. And I won't pretend that I'm not glad it's on my westward road. But first there are two things to do. Give me your hand.'

'What on earth for?'

Baradoc sighed. 'I shall have trouble with you, I can see, for you are not easily led. Give me your hand.'

Slowly Tia held out her right hand and Baradoc, smiling, took it by the finger tips. Then he turned and said two words in his own language to Lerg. The hound rose from the ground and came slowly forward and stood at Baradoc's side. Baradoc raised Tia's hand and placed it over the eyes of the hound, palm down, and he spoke again to Lerg in his own tongue. This done he called Aesc forward and repeated the ritual. Then, ignoring Cuna, he gave an order to the three dogs and they turned and disappeared quickly into the forest.

Tia said, 'What does all that mean?'

Baradoc answered, 'You will see. Now remember always this word.' He paused and then said softly to her, '*Saheer*. You have it? *Saheer*.'

Tia nodded. '*Saheer* – but what is it?'

'It is my word, and now, for Lerg and Aesc, it is also yours. Whenever you are in trouble, call it as loudly as you can.' He grinned. 'Go on – shout it now. As loud as you can.'

Tia hesitated for a moment and then, taking a deep breath, shouted, '*Saheer*!'

Almost immediately there was a crashing in the low forest thickets and Lerg and Aesc came rushing to her and settled one on either side of her, alert and on their legs ready for action, growling and barking. A few seconds later Cuna arrived and began to imitate the action and growls of the other two.

Baradoc gave the dogs an order and they relaxed into sitting positions around Tia.

Tia said, 'They will come – always like that?'

'At any time, anywhere – if they can. And the gods help any man who is near you.'

'Why didn't you give my hand to the other, the little one?'

'Cuna? Because he's young and still a little stupid. But the others will teach him. Some time as we travel I will teach you the other words they know.'

'These are words of your language?'

'*Na* – these are our words. There is a magic in them because only the dogs, myself and soon you will know them. Can you whistle?'

'No, of course I can't.'

'Then you must learn because there could be times when you might need Bran.' Baradoc put his forefingers to his mouth and let out a sudden blasting whistle that made Tia jump.

Within a few moments a shadow swept across the sunlit patch beyond the bower. Then with a noisy beating of his great wings and a raucous calling of *carp, carp* Bran, the raven, swept under the spreading branches of the yew. He circled twice around Baradoc and then settled on his shoulder, eyes alert, the great ebony beak weaving from side to side.

Drawing back a little Tia said, 'That's Bran?'

'Yes. And when he attacks he goes for a man's eyes. So you must learn to whistle him.' Baradoc reached up his right hand and Bran jumped to his wrist. 'Take a piece of cheese and throw it into the air for him.'

Tia broke off a piece of cheese and tossed it high into the air. Bran made no move to take it and the cheese fell to the ground.

'He's not hungry.'

Baradoc laughed. 'Oh, yes he is. Bran is always hungry. But he will take food from no one unless he, too, is given the word. Throw it up again.'

Tia took the cheese and tossed it into the air once more and, as she did so, Baradoc called gently, '*Aka, Aka!*'

Bran swooped from Baradoc's wrist and took the cheese low to the ground as it fell and then flew off to the top of a nearby ash tree.

Tia said, 'So now he knows I am allowed to feed him?'

'Yes. Though he fends for himself even better than the dogs. When you can whistle he will always come to you.'

Baradoc stripped off his under shirt and rolled over on to his stomach, couching his head on his arms.

Tia asked, 'What now?'

Baradoc grinned sideways at her. 'You promised to massage me. My muscles are as stiff as salt-dry ropes.'

After a moment's hesitation Tia went to his side and knelt by him. For an ex-slave he had an abrupt way of treating her at times, but she guessed that this came from his self-confidence and his pride in the fact that he was a chief's son. The women of the remoter tribes, she knew, were of little importance except to do the bidding of their men. Leaning over him she began to massage and work his shoulder muscles in the way she had often done for Priscus. As she worked she pushed from her mind as much as she could the thought of her brother and his wife. In a handful of savage hours her whole life had changed. Her grief belonged to her. Nobody could share it. The gods had been good to them all for a long time, and now the gods had turned away from them. When she got to Aquae Sulis she and her uncle would make their devotions to the gods of the shades and set up a stone for Priscus and his wife and then . . .? What would she do then? Her uncle was old and would not last much longer. This country – her country for she had known no other, but not hers in the way it was Baradoc's – was falling apart. Priscus had often talked of selling up and moving to Gaul. But things were not much better there. There was a darkness falling over the land. She could feel the coldness of its shadow touching her heart.

Easing and working the stiff arm and back muscles of the youth, she said, 'How long will it take to get to Aquae Sulis?'

'Who knows? There is no marching these days along the west road like a century of legionaries, quickly knocking off the miles. We've got to take the old tracks and steer clear of towns and villages. It's taken me three weeks to come down from Durobrivae and there's not been a day without smoke in the sky from some villa or homestead going up in flames. Tell me, Tia – what have you got in your bundle? My two good friends, whose throats I'll cut one day, took all my stuff and the pack horse as well.'

'There's not much. Some food. Some clothes. A few cooking things. A little money, the dagger, and a brooch that belonged to my mother.'

'I see. Well, we'll need to acquire a few more things.'

'Acquire?'

'Yes. Steal if needs be.' He rolled over and away from her suddenly and, looking up at her, he said firmly, 'But one thing you've got to remember – if I tell you to do something, you do it – fast! Any bush or thicket can hold a cut-throat. Understood?'

After a moment's hesitation Tia said, 'Yes.'

'And we must cut your hair even shorter. You've got to look like a boy, even if a pretty one. So don't pull a long face about it.'

Although she hid it, there was a flare of anger in Tia at the way he spoke, treating her over-familiarly. Sarcasm edging her voice, she said with a little shrug, 'If that's what the great Baradoc, son of a chief, orders – then yes.' On her knees she made a mock bow.

Baradoc grinned and said, 'Don't give me any of your sauce.' He stood up and began to flex his arms and shoulders and then bent over and touched his toes, loosening up his body. As he did so, he went on, 'You must know this part of the country well?'

'Yes.'

He jerked his head towards the glade. 'Where does the path lead?'

'To the sea. It's not far.'

'Is there a village down there?'

'There was until last year. A longboat raided it and it was burnt. But there are still a few old huts the fishermen use when the shoals come along the coast.'

Baradoc bent and threw open her bundle. He took out a thin woollen blanket, slung it over his shoulders and tied it about his neck. He smiled at her. 'I'm going scavenging. You stay here.' He turned and said something in his own language to the dogs and then walked off. Lerg and the other dogs watched him go. Cuna whined for a moment and then was silent. As Baradoc disappeared through the trees Tia saw Bran lift himself from the ash tree top and slide away on the sea breeze, slanting low over the forest towards the coast.

Tia moved to the open bundle and began to tidy the things which Baradoc had left in disarray. She arranged them neatly in the silk cover but left out the small cauldron and the beaker and her dagger. Before tying the ends of the coverlet together to contain her possessions she unwrapped from a piece of linen her mother's brooch. It was a small gold oval set on a strong pin. On its face, worked in relief, were clasped hands. Around them ran the inscription – *To Januaria Hermia, my dearest. Marcus.* The brooch had been given to her mother on her betrothal by her father.

Holding it Tia was struck by a sense of desolation. Alone now, with no need to cosset her pride or hide her feelings from anyone, she suddenly felt a swift grief and the strange dark knowledge of utter loss possess her. Resting back on her heels she put her hands to her eyes and wept silently, her shoulders shaking, her head bowed.

After a while she felt the warm lap of a tongue caress the back of her hands. Looking up she saw that Aesc had come to her and licked her hands. Behind him Lerg sat upright on his haunches, his great tongue lolling from his mouth as he watched her. She fondled Aesc's silky head and, as she did so, Cuna gave a little whimper, came to her and flopped his head into her lap.

She wiped the tears from her eyes, sniffed a little, and then fondled Cuna's head, setting his stubby, docked tail wagging.

The gods took, she thought, and the gods gave. There was no questioning their ways. Yesterday was one life; today another – and one for which she was utterly unprepared or fitted. Well, so what, she thought with a moment's heartening defiance? She must learn to live a new life. And then, almost as though she could hear his voice, a favourite saying of her brother came back to her. *The blackest night must die under the fiery wheels of Apollo's golden chariot.*

She wrapped the brooch in its linen and began to pack up her bundle. Grief for those lost, from now, she would keep locked in her heart. As for herself . . . well, she must count herself lucky. Had she not the son of a chief to guide her westwards to Aquae Sulis? And three guardian dogs and an eye-piercing raven to watch over her? Cocksure and abrupt Baradoc might be at times, but there was, she sensed, far more than that to him. There was a temper and a strength which would hold him to any course he set.

It was close on sunset when Baradoc returned. He came with the blanket slung over his shoulder, bulky with his findings. He carried in his right hand a long, wooden-shafted fishing spear, its socketed three-pronged iron head missing a tang and the two others badly rusted. He dumped the bundle on the ground and, squatting by her, laid out his pickings from the fishing huts. There were some rusty hooks of different sizes; a length of worn hempen rope; part of a circular throwing net with some small stone weights still attached to its skirts; a tangle of old catgut lengths; a sail-maker's needle with a broken point; a small wicker woven bird cage with the bottom missing into which he had stuffed odd lengths of cloth; two wooden platters, both badly cracked; a large lump of beeswax; a raggedly shaped piece of goat's hide as stiff as a board; a thick woollen fisherman's shirt, with a slit down the side, half a sleeve missing and the front coated with tiny, dried opaline fish scales; a well worn piece of striking flint, and a small length of tallow candle with a rush wick.

As he laid all these out, Tia watched in silence. He took no notice of her until he pulled out the last of his finds, a pair of long coarsely woven leggings that reached down to the ankles, stained with rust and pitch marks and with a great hole in their seat. He dropped them on the pile and looked at Tia with a grin of satisfaction.

'What do we want with all that rubbish?' she asked.

Baradoc frowned quickly. He shook his head and said, 'I know the kind of place you come from. Like my old master's. You had servants and maids, fine clothes, and fine table furnishings. Aye, even glass in your windows and worked mosaics on the great room floor. Baths and hot rooms and a home farm that gave you all everything you wanted for the table. You've probably never done a real hand's turn in your life. You've lived soft, wench – but now the world is upside down.'

Tia jumped up and said furiously, 'Son of a chief you may be, but call me "wench" again and I walk from here and find my own way to Aquae Sulis. My name is Gratia. As a mark of friendship, Tia to you. Name me so and not as a herd or kitchen girl.'

'Whooah! Rein back! I meant no rudeness. Tia it shall be.' He reached up, took her hand and pulled her down. 'Should we fight now – whose side would the dogs and Bran take since they have been given the word for you?'

'I'm sorry. I have a quick temper.'

'No – 'tis pride and that is a good thing. I shall not offend it again – except by mischance for which I ask forgiveness now to save further trouble. So, let's get back to our rubbish which is no rubbish. What one man throws away another can use. A fish spear with two prongs is better than no fish spear. Fish can be eaten but first they must be caught. So, I brought the spear, the hooks, the gut, and the piece of net. I can sharpen a new point to the needle and with threads pulled from the cloth and waxed you can repair the shirt and the long hose.'

'Who are they for?'

'The shirt is for me. The hose for you.'

'I wouldn't wear those filthy things!'

Baradoc was silent. For all that she had recently suffered Tia was far from realizing what change had – if only temporarily –

come over her life. Never before had she ever had to think of black tomorrow, of a tomorrow which would be as full of want as all the yesterdays. In this wilderness of place and evil times she was no more able to survive alone than a fledgling, unfeathered, pushed from its warm nest. He could have wished that it had been some simple herd girl who had saved him and who would have needed no teaching. Still . . . she was not. He must learn patience. He said with good humour, 'As you know, the world is upside down and will stay so for a long time, Lady Tia. The clothes can be washed first and mended after. In long hose and the legs gartered you will be a handsome young fellow. And don't frown at me – it must be so for your own safety. Now, do I have to explain the rest as though you were a raw recruit, goggle-eyed in barracks for the first time?' He took the flint and holding the spear head jabbed into the ground struck the stone against one of the iron prongs and brought brief, blue sparks spurting to life. 'Raw fish or fowl cheer no belly. Fire we must have to cook. And have I not brought two cracked platters to go with your cooking cauldron and that wicked little dagger you keep always close to your side?'

'And this – this stinking piece of hide?'

'It's a long way to Aquae Sulis. Those fancy sandals of yours could need new soles in a week. Now – let's get packed up and moving. And Lady Tia – leave the rest of the cake and cheese near the top of your bundle. We shall need them before the night is out. Tomorrow we'll lay up somewhere safe and make a proper meal which will –'

Baradoc broke off in mid speech as Lerg suddenly gave a soft growl. Lerg growled again and was silenced by a sign from Baradoc. At the same time, he took Tia's arm and drew her down flat on the ground so that the screening bushes hid them from the nearby glade. His face close to Tia's, Baradoc whispered, 'Keep down and don't move.'

Pressing herself to the ground alongside him, Tia saw the three dogs slink quietly away from them to disappear into the trees and thickets between them and the glade. At that moment she heard the distant noise of people shouting and singing and the faint thud of horses' hooves beating on the hard ground of the distant pathway.

She lay there with Baradoc's hand gripping her arm. His breath faintly touched the side of her cheek. A few moments later, across the small length of glade path which she held in her view, Tia saw a strange procession pass.

First came two horses ridden by men in loose working smocks. The men carried large leather drinking skins which, as they passed, they up-ended to their mouths, guzzling greedily, wine spilling over their cheeks as they swayed unsteadily on their mounts. Behind them came a rabble of working men and women, shouting and singing. Many of them carried mead and wine jars, and all of them were laden down with household loot and bulging sacks of pillaged goods. Some of the women wore fine silken scarves and pearl-beaded billowing robes while their wrists and necks were strung with loops of amber and coloured glass beads, twisted gold-wire torques and silver and enamelled bracelets. A short, fat, perspiring man stumbled along wearing an old and rusted legionary's helmet topped with a spray of elderberry branch stuck into the plume holder. About his body was wrapped a long white toga sweeping to the ground over which he tripped and stumbled as he pranced by clasping to his breast a large round cheese. An old man hobbled along with a wooden household kist balanced on his bowed back. Children, half-naked, ran wildly in and around the mob, at the rear of which came four youths leading two milk cows and two draught oxen, astride one of which sat a drunken man, shouting and singing who, as Tia watched, fell to the ground and lay there unconscious as the mob passed, abandoning him.

Watching the crowd disappear Baradoc knew that somewhere another villa had been sacked, another farmstead pillaged by these workpeople and servants in whom the quick flowering of long growing envy had been forced by the fast blaze of fear spreading from the east. He twisted his lips in disgust, knowing well the thought that held all these people – *take what we can now before others far stronger come to take it.* Knowing, too, that such a mob had sacked Tia's brother's villa and homestead, he put out a hand and held her wrist, not to restrain her from any rash action but to give comfort. He caught her eyes for a moment and saw them mist with tears before she turned her face from him. One day, he thought savagely, there would arise a leader from his kind who would halt and crush the savagery from the east and bring this country to peace and to a strength and power greater even than had ever been wielded by the Romans.

Slowly the tumult of the mob's passing died away down the valley towards the coast. The drunken man lay in the glade, flat on his back, snoring in a stupor of wine.

When the last sound had long died Baradoc stood up, motioned to Tia to stay where she was and went out into the glade to the man. After a while he came back, followed by the three dogs. In his arms he carried a fine cloak of woven goats' hair, a broad leather belt with a bronze buckle which had strapped to it a leather scabbard that held a two-edge dagger, and a small sack half full of oven-dried corn.

He fastened the belt around his waist and handed the cloak to Tia, saying, 'The nights are still cold. Your mantle is a pretty thing but no proof against rain and wind.' He dipped his hand into the sack, showed her the hard corn grains, and smiled. 'Tomorrow I promise you hare or deer meat stew with this to thicken it. A full belly makes a light heart. Now, let us be on our way.'

The Black Raven

During that night's march Tia felt that she was living through a dream. Tired and racked by the want of sleep, her leg muscles stiff from the hard going, there were times when she felt that in a while she must wake from a dream in her own bed in Priscus's villa. She would hear the morning sounds of cattle and poultry from the homestead, the chink of bridle and bit as Priscus saddled up outside to make his early morning rounds, and the creak of the bedroom door as her maid, Tullio's wife, Sabata came in carrying her breakfast of fresh-baked bread spread with honey, a beaker of creamy milk and a dish of fruit all borne on the silver tray which had once been her mother's, a tray embossed with the figure of the god Neptune, the rim decorated with fishes and writhing sea creatures.

The first time they stopped for a rest, she dropped to the ground, pulled the warm cloak close around her, and was asleep almost at once, just conscious of Cuna snuggling up against her side, relishing the softness of the woven goats' hair, before oblivion claimed her. Almost at once it seemed that Baradoc was waking her, his hand firm on her shoulder.

She pulled herself to her feet and swayed a little until he steadied her. For a moment she wanted to protest against being wakened so soon, but the impulse died in her as she saw that while she had slept a full moon had begun to climb the eastern sky and the forest now was a black and silver maze of shadow and light. Baradoc handed her the beaker full of water and she drank gladly, saying nothing but knowing that somewhere near he must have found a spring. To speak was forbidden unless he spoke first. This he had made clear the moment darkness came. She handed the beaker back. He tucked it into the top of her bundle. The bundles had been tied, one to each end of the fishing spear which Baradoc carried fore and aft over his left shoulder, leaving his right hand free to reach for the dagger at his belt. The only thing he had let her carry was the half empty corn sack whose weight as she now set out after him she knew would increase with every step she took.

Her mind clear now that she had slept, she felt a sudden dissatisfaction in herself. She had thought she was fit and strong, but she knew now that real strength and hardihood lay at some point far beyond her experience. Baradoc had it. He carried his load with ease and seemed tireless. She realized that without her he would be travelling much faster. There was a strangeness, too, about him. Some kind of magic in him which worked without words. Not once since they had started had he spoken to the dogs, and not once since Lerg had gone ahead and Aèsc had slid away to their left flank had she seen either dog. Only Cuna – she smiled to herself remembering Baradoc's words, 'a raw recruit, goggle-eyed in barracks for the first time' – stayed with them, trotting between them. Ahead the hardened campaigner, behind the two raw recruits. And, she was sure, somewhere up above Bran would be scouting on sable wings. Priscus had often said that there were men of the tribes who had a power over animals which was beyond belief. Baradoc the magician. Out of her tiredness, she giggled aloud.

Baradoc stopped and swung round, staring at her and in the moonlight she saw his face scowling and full of displeasure. She made an apologetic gesture with her free hand and he turned away and began walking along the track. And that, too, she thought must have something of magic in it. He could not know this forest – the great forest that ran league after league westwards along the south shore – yet he moved through it as though he had been born in it. Always they were on a path or track of some kind, deer run or one of the ancient trackways made, long before the Great Caesar had come to the country, by the Britons and still used by many of them. And – since the times were now what they were – to be used more and more by them in the days to come.

The days to come ... The days to come ... What kind of days would they be? She thought of her uncle in Aquae Sulis. Long, long ago he had been a Chief Centurion in the Second Legion and finally its Camp Prefect but had retired and settled in the country a few years before the Legion left for good. Uncle Truvius, always a bachelor, well over eighty, living for many years now in a villa just outside Aquae Sulis and still hoping that one day its waters would cure his rheumatism. Surely the country would not be so unsettled as far west as Aquae Sulis? She would live with him, look after him. Times would be good again, and one day she would marry. Returning fatigue flighting her mind to wild fancies, she began to think of herself married and with children and the times brought to order again. What kind of man would she marry? A pure-blooded Roman? Blood as pure as her own, though she had never seen Rome? There were not many of such blood left now. No full legions stationed in the country for years. And now only a handful of discontented auxiliaries left. No young men, proud legionary tribunes, no tall, dark handsome cohort commanders or dashing cavalry officers ... Well, maybe she would have to settle for some nice Romano-British type. After all, that's what Priscus had done, and who could have been sweeter or kinder than his wife, Martina? But then Martina had been born and bred in Londinium where her father had been a wealthy merchant. Who would want to marry, no matter how important his own people considered him, a Celt or – even worse – a Pict or – the gods forbid – a Scot? Fatigue lightening her head and heightening her sense of the ridiculous she giggled silently to herself at the thought of being mistress of some mountain boothy, wearing wolf and bear skin and when the fire failed in bad weather chewing on a strip of dried fish.

At this moment, unmindful of her step, her right foot caught in a half hidden tree root across the path. She tripped and fell forward flat on her face, the corn sack shooting from her hand and catching Cuna on the rump, drawing a sharp bark of protest from him.

Before Tia could stop herself she let fly loudly a round of her father's favourite army oaths. Baradoc swung round and said low and furiously, 'You stupid, clumsy wench! We might as well march with lighted lanterns and singing! Pick up your feet and watch the path!'

On her knees, half-risen, Tia retorted in sudden fury, 'Oh shut up and don't be so bossy! And I told you not to call me "wench".'

For a moment or two Baradoc was silent and then he reached down a hand and pulled her to her feet, saying, 'All right, Lady Tia, I'm sorry I was disrespectful. Am I setting too fast a pace?'

'No you're not. I can keep up.'

'Good.' He picked up the corn sack and handed it to her, saying, 'For a high-born lady you've a nice choice of barrack room oaths.'

They began to march again and Baradoc, without making it too obvious, slackened off his pace a little. In this part of the country there was always by day or night the chance of a dangerous encounter. At any moment one could stumble into the sleeping camp of a party of rogues and thieves or pillaging, cutthroat workers who had taken to the easy pickings that came with the breakdown of law and order. When they got farther west, into more open and, perhaps less unsettled country they might be able to travel by day. But at the moment the forest was best crossed at night. He had Lerg out ahead and Aesc on the seaward flank to give warning of danger. And danger was not only to be feared from humans. There were wolves still in the great forest. True, the packs had grown smaller with hunting, but there were still times – as food grew scarce – when they hunted boldly. Thank the gods that at the moment there were plenty of easy pickings for them amongst the slaughtered and straying cattle.

Hearing Tia moving behind him, he smiled to himself as he remembered the oaths she had let fly. Those he guessed must have been picked up from brother or father. Then, the smile dying, he wondered what lay ahead for her with only now an

aged uncle living in Aquae Sulis. The great days of the long
Roman settlement of the country were gone. New conquerors
were coming in from the east. To be Roman soon would be to
be in danger, to be Romano-British little better. The new invaders and the scum and riff-raff of Britons who had served the
old masters would have no pity. To curry favour with the new
lords, the workers and low born were already turning against the
old masters. Only in the west and the north were men true to
themselves and their race and determined to hold their own.
And amongst them new leaders would be needed. Men who
understood what was happening in the world and could shape
their courses to meet the thrust of new methods, new weapons,
and a new way of life. How many times had he listened to his
old master on the subject? A wise old man, wise in wars and
learning, who had read to and talked with him, laying out (he
could see his stick now, tracing countries and battle formations
in the loose sand of the courtyard) the rise and fall of emperors
and empires, the onthrust of the races from beyond the Rhine
and further east, a great wave rolling slowly but steadily across
the western world. Had he not known from some instinct that
he had much to learn from him he would have escaped four
years ago. His old master had known this, too. He remembered
him sitting in the sun one afternoon after he had finished reading a chapter of Caesar's great book on the conquest of Gaul
and Britain, and saying, 'The world will always have its Caesars,
boy. Some good, some evil. One day this country will spawn
one ... some Celt living or yet to be born who knows that in
the heart and the brain there is no true man who can live and
be called slave. It is because of this that I know if I freed you
today you would not yet turn westwards with Lerg and Aesc.'
And that had been the truth. But now the old man was dead and
he was going westwards – even if it were with a Roman girl
dragging at his heels. *Aie!* that was ungrateful since but for her
he would have still been swinging from an oak all spark gone
from him and his carcass drying up like an empty, sunbaked
wine skin. The gods give her thanks, her gods and his gods. He
had made her a promise. To Aquae Sulis. Long before she got

there she would be marching twenty-five miles a night without turning a curl of her pretty fair hair which tomorrow would have to be cropped as close as a boy's.

Marching, he watched the moon and the stars in their slow swings, and shaped his course, but even in pitch darkness the magic compass in his mind would have served him, though less finely. Once or twice he heard an owl call, and now and again came the harsh screech of a hunting nightjar. The forest was alive with Nature's hunters whose skills were more precise than any man's. Now and again either Lerg or Aesc would come from the darkness to his side for a few seconds and then disappear to their posts once more. Towards morning, with daylight like a grey wash of cobwebs through the eastern trees, he sent Cuna out to the right flank. Of all the dogs he and his old master had bred for export abroad, there had been none to touch Lerg or Aesc. They had been kept jealously for the household. Cuna would learn the wordless signs in time. Of all animals the gods had gifted dogs with a magical kinship with man, but only to some men the gift of the words and signs that held them coupled in understanding and loyalty.

It was almost mid-morning before Tia woke. There was a fresh westerly wind blowing and the sky was full of low, rolling grey clouds. She sat up and looked around her. She had only the vaguest memory of the last stretches of their march and the moment when Baradoc had halted and said they would make camp. She had been conscious of him stirring around in the moonlight and shadows, unloading their bundles and spreading covers on the ground, of herself dropping to the ground and the last memory of him throwing the warm goat-hair cloak across her.

She stretched her arms, yawned and rubbed the last of sleep from her eyes. The camp had been made on a high bluff which rose clear of the forest, in a small ravine whose sides were a jumble of broken stones. Behind her the rock face rose sheer and smooth like a fortress wall. The sound of running water reached her ears. Away to the left a thin stream dripped down

41

a moss-covered cleft of the rocks and was gathered into a small gravelly pool from which it seeped away down the hillside in a marshy slope bordered by primroses and blue-starred periwinkle growths. There was no sign of Baradoc or the dogs, but Bran sat on a spur of rock above her beak-combing his flight-feathers and scratching himself about the head as he made his morning toilet. Tia smiled to herself and decided to follow his example. Her tiredness was gone but she felt dirty and tousled.

She went to the pool, stripped off her tunic and took off her sandals. Wearing only her short woollen drawers, she splashed and washed her face, the top half of her body and then her legs. There was a blister on her right foot where the sandal had rubbed her during the march. She wiped herself with a corner of her bundle cover and dressed, and shivered a little until her clothes began to bring back warmth to her body. For a moment or two she thought of the villa bath house, of hot water and Sabata bringing her clean clothes after her toilet. Soft living . . . those days were gone for the time being.

Then, seeing close up against the rock face the contents of their bundles which Baradoc had opened up, she picked up the dirty old seaman's shirt and the filthy pair of long hose. There was no sign of the fishing spear. Baradoc, she guessed, was away with the dogs hunting for the pot. At the thought of food, she felt her belly empty and hunger bring saliva to her mouth, and she knew that she had never been so hungry before. Well, Baradoc must see to that. Each to his own duties.

She took the shirt and the hose to the shallow scoop of pool, threw them in and then began to tramp and knead them underneath her bare feet. The water flowed away muddy.

From above Bran watched her. She pounded away with her feet, and then knelt at the poolside working the clothes with her hands, spreading them out and beating them with a small heavy length of stick, talking and grumbling to herself. Bran turned his head away. He had seen many women pounding and beating away like this before. His eyes followed the dark-crested, rolling spread of the forest top away to the south. Distantly there was a glimpse of a thin arc of the sea, iron grey and still, and away to the west a sudden fall in the trees to a narrow edging of marsh and grasslands biting up into the forest. Through this valley coiled and looped a wide, slow moving river.

Moving slowly up the river, a good five miles away, was something else which Bran had seen before, a longship, the oar blades dipping and flashing rhythmically. The saffron coloured sail had been half-struck and loosely furled. Bran watched the swing of the rowers' backs and arms, saw three men standing in the raised stern, and a solitary man perched high in the prow who now and again swung a weighted sounding line overboard to read the depth of the river. As the long ship moved into a broader reach of the river, the stern steering oar was put hard over and the ship slowly swung round in a half circle and in to the left bank. Oars flashed with waterruns as they were lifted and shipped, and from stern and bow men jumped ashore with mooring ropes. As the ship was made fast a party of men moved out from the forest that fringed the river meadow and made for the ship. There were ten or twelve of them, helmeted and armed with swords and spears, and with them came four pack horses laden down with loads slung across their backs. That, too, Bran had seen before. Had he been free he might have launched himself on his broad wings and swung down valley, quartering against the cross wind, and taken a closer look, for anything that moved excited his curiosity. But the freedom was denied him because he had been given the word to mark his place by Baradoc before he had left with the dogs and the fishing spear. Bran ruffled and then ordered his feathers, shuffled to a new grip on the rock ledge and settled down to wait.

Below him Tia wrung out the shirt and the hose and spread them over the steep rock face, weighting them down with stones. They were a little cleaner, she thought, but not much. Looking at the roughly woven hose she made a wry face. Before she got used to them they would probably chafe and rub her legs raw. Still, Baradoc was right. For her own safety she had to turn from a well-bred young lady to a ragged country youth – but, thank the gods, only until they got to Aquae Sulis. She stood for a moment thinking of her uncle's beautifully furnished and decorated villa, and the soft silk and cotton covered beds with their mattresses of swan and duck down. Then she put the thought from her and, taking her dagger, went back to the pool which had now cleared. Leaning over it, she began to saw and hack at her fair hair. The wind took strands of it away like floating cobwebs and some fell into the water, drifting away on the slow current. Once as she worked, the dagger slipped and the sharp edge nicked the side of her thumb. Without thinking she used her father's favourite curse word and sucked her thumb. Then she grinned to herself. Why should she not curse and condemn the bloody knife and the bloody times to the darkness of bloody Hades? They were a man's words and she was now a man – albeit a very good-looking one.

An hour later Baradoc arrived back with the dogs. Tia was sitting with her back to the rocks, pulling threads loose from a piece of cloth and drawing them through the lump of beeswax which she had warmed in her hands. One moment she was alone, frowning over her work – and then there was Cuna at her feet, Lerg by the pool and Aesc on a rock ledge above him, with Baradoc at his side. The suddenness and silence of their appearance startled her, making her heart thump quickly. But almost immediately she realized how glad she was to see them all, feeling the comfort of their presence warm her, admitting to herself for the first time that she had not relished being alone.

Baradoc said something softly to Bran, and then jumped down to the poolside and came across to Tia. Bran lifted himself from his perch, beat upwards in a slow spiral towards the grey sky which was now showing an occasional break in the clouds, and then he drifted away southwards. He was free now to do his own foraging. There would be something to be picked up down by the river where the crewmen of the longship were now busy setting up a shore camp. Such men ate until they were full and then tossed their leavings over their shoulders to make easy prizes for any ready scavenger.

*

44

From his shoulder Baradoc dropped the hind of a young deer to the short grass. Then, from the inside of his shirt, he pulled out a handful of different fungi.

Squatting on his hunkers he took out his dagger and began to skin the leg, looking at Tia for a moment with a smile and saying, 'Fill the cauldron, Lady Tia, with water, and then search around for dry grass, dry twigs and some of that crumbly dry moss from the rocks.' He paused and nodded at the clothes she had washed. 'I see you have been busy. Turn your head.'

Tia slowly turned her head so that he could see her cropped hair. She said with a note of sarcasm in her voice, 'I hope it meets with the great Baradoc's approval.'

'*Aie!* but 'tis a pity to see such a fine flow of golden locks go. Still, a few weeks in Aquae Sulis will see them back and you'll be able to look in your mirror and admire yourself again.'

Rising to get the cauldron, Tia said, 'You are in a good and teasing humour.'

'Why not? The hunt was quick and easy. The dogs have already eaten and I brought only what we might need for a while.'

'How did you catch it?'

'One day soon when your wind and legs are stronger I might show you. Now fill the cauldron and tip into it a few handfuls of our corn and the toadstools.'

'Are they good to eat?'

Baradoc sighed. 'Would I have brought them else?'

Tia filled the cauldron and did as she was bid by which time Baradoc had skinned the meat and cut off four fair-sized portions. Then he gathered the little heap of kindling and tinder-moss together which Tia had gathered and carried them to a dry flat stone at the foot of the rock face. As he arranged them he said, without looking at her, 'Bring me the spear and the flint and your mantle.'

It was no order. He just said it as though it were the most natural thing in the world to order her around without thought of resentment from her. So, she told herself, if she wanted to get to Aquae Sulis it must be. When he did something he did it whole-heartedly, his absorption in his task leaving him no room for niceties to others.

He took the spear and jammed the two prongs into the ground at the edge of the stone, easing the dry grass and moss close to it. Then, taking up the flint, he said, 'Drape the mantle over me and hold the edges so that no wind comes in.'

Tia, knowing this was no moment to resent being ordered around, drew the mantle around the spear haft and covered Baradoc, holding the edges of the material close together to keep out the draught. Standing there she heard him begin to strike the flint against one of the tangs. Again and again she heard it strike and sometimes she heard Baradoc muttering to himself in his own language. The thought crossed her mind that he was probably swearing to himself in his own tongue. Once or twice she heard him blowing gently, only to break off with another bout of mutterings. It was then that she realized how much she had taken fire for granted in her own life. Fire and light at night had always been with her, fire for the room braziers, fire for the furnace that fed hot air into the house warming system, fire for the corn drying racks and the cooking holes of the raised hearths, and light from the tallow candles flickering in their lanterns and from the oil-soaked wicks of the elegant wall lamps of the villa. But the gift of the great god Vulcan, maker of Jove's thunderbolts, once let die had to be won from the earth again by the clash of flint and metal. Suddenly, the thought of meat stew thickened with corn and fungi made her mouth water, and there was an impatience in her for Baradoc to make fire.

At last when her arms were aching from holding the tented mantle around Baradoc she heard him blowing gently without stopping. Then a thin trickle of fine blue smoke seeped through the edges of the mantle. Baradoc lifted away his covering and put aside the spear. On the flat stone little tongues of flame were working through the dried grass and twigs.

Baradoc, face covered in sweat, said, 'Now build it. But remember only dry wood. We want no heavy smoke from damp stuff. What little there is this wind will whip away from the top of the bluff. The fire and the cooking is all yours.'

'All mine?'

'Why not?' Baradoc was genuinely surprised. 'Did you think you would ride the whole way to Aquae Sulis lolling on a litter and not a hand to lift for any comfort or food?'

'But I've never cooked in the open. In fact I –' She broke off.

Baradoc grunted. 'In fact, you've never cooked at all. Well, a late start is better than none. I've brought you the meat and the flavouring and made the fire. Would you sit by and see me do woman's work? True, I owe you a life. But at the moment you owe me a meal.'

'And what are *you* going to do?'

He held out his blood-stained and dirt-streaked hands, and said brusquely, 'Take a bath, of course. It's a habit my master beat into me. When that's done, I'll grind a new point to the needle, and wax some more threads – so that you won't be left idle after we've eaten.'

Tia looked at him in silence for a moment or two, and then said evenly, 'What you say is fair, though not gently said. But –' her voice began to rise, '– don't think, son of a chief, Baradoc, that I can't do as well as any tribe woman with greasy hair and dirty face. I will do all you ask of me, but speak me fair – or I will set Lerg at your throat and claim the life you owe – barbarian!'

Baradoc stared at her round-eyed with surprise. Then he burst out laughing and said, 'I am sorry. I was wrong to give you offence. Now, *please*, do as I ask. And also –' a twinkle came into his dark eyes, '– since I don't want to offend you again keep your eyes from the bath house. I haven't washed for three days and I'm going to strip.'

He strode away towards the pool, and Tia turned back to the fire and her duties. As she worked she heard the splashing of the pool water and his cheerful low whistling as he washed himself. There were times when she liked him, and times when she could kick him for his cocksureness. Still, whatever he was, she needed him to get to Aquae Sulis. How many more days would that be? Already the moment when she had come into the forest glade and seen him hanging from the oak seemed an age away. She fed the fire with more sticks and picked up loose stones and rocks to build a guard around it which would hold the cauldron. Her belly grumbled suddenly with hunger. As she crouched there Cuna came up and pushed his head against her thigh. She fondled his muzzle briefly and then smiled to herself. The raw recruits . . .

Two hours later they ate. When they had finished Baradoc cut the rest of the raw deer flesh into flat strips. Laying them on the hot cooking stone, he put another flat stone on top of them and then raked the hot embers over the stones and covered these with slabs of turf cut with his dagger. By the time they were ready to move off at night the meat would be cooked dry and easily carried as emergency rations. Then, in the fitful sunlight which now came between the lifting and breaking clouds, Tia began to mend the shirt and hose with the waxed threads while Baradoc with a piece of grit stone – on which he had repointed the needle – began to burnish and hone the tangs of the spear to put an edge and point on them.

As they worked, in answer to a question from Tia, he explained that in normal times they could have walked the distance to Aquae Sulis easily in six or seven days. But now the journey would take longer because they must pick their route to avoid large towns and settlements and the old Roman-built main roads. He said, 'The only people on these high roads will be armed parties, able to look after themselves, and not always to be trusted to give a true greeting to a couple of strangers.' As she sewed, his spear head finished, he drew in the loose gravel for her a map of the southern and western parts of Britain, marking in roughly the towns, rivers and forests and the areas of bare downs. He showed her where they were now – to the west of Anderida, a quarter of the way towards the next coastal town of Noviomagus. He stabbed the gravel with a stick, reciting the names of the towns like a litany . . . Portus Adurni, Clausentium, Venta, Sorviodonum and Lindinis. Tia smiled to herself for, though she recognized most of the names, she knew that quietly Baradoc was showing off his knowledge. As she sat now, so must Baradoc have sat many times at the feet of his master learning the geography of his own country.

She asked, 'And where is your country?'

Baradoc's stick swung far to the west, and he said, 'Down here, beyond Isca, beyond the Tamarus river, on the north coast two days' march from the Point of Herculis, in the valley of the great rocks. Away further, right at the end of the land, is Antivestaeum where the sea stretches away to the edge of the world.' As he finished speaking Baradoc reached for the unwashed cauldron and ran two fingers round the inner rim to collect the grease gathered there. Without looking at her, he reached for Tia's blistered foot and spread some of the grease over the red, chafed skin. Then he tore a piece from one of their collection of rags, bound it round her foot and tied it in place with a couple of waxed threads. This done he looked up at her and smiled, saying, 'In the days of the legions a man would get a beating and lose a week's pay for neglecting his feet.' He stood up, holding the cauldron, and began to move away.

Tia asked, 'Where are you going?'

'To scour the cauldron for you.'

'Woman's work?' Tia grinned, pulled a thread tight and bit off the end.

'I see no woman around here – only a crop-headed Roman lad sewing up a rip in the backside of his long hose.'

Tia watched him kneel at the pool and begin to scour the cauldron with sand and pebbles. He could be angry and bullying at times – perhaps that came from an exaggerated pride in his own powers and the knowledge that he was the son of a chief and destined for high office one day. But a little while ago his hands had been gentle and adroit, salving and bandaging her foot. There were two Baradocs. She liked most the gentle, thoughtful one. But she knew that at this moment it was the other Baradoc she needed most for he was the only one who could take her safely to Aquae Sulis.

Baradoc brought back the pot and said, 'I leave Aesc and Cuna with you. There is something I saw early this morning which interests me.'

He turned away and began to climb up to the top of the bluff and was soon lost to view. Although he spoke no word nor seemed to make any sign, Lerg went with him. The other dogs remained, stretched out beyond the fire. A dark shadow swept across the ground and Tia looked up to see Bran come to roost on one of the high rock points.

At the side of the river stood a lone alder tree, its lower branches still festooned with the jetsam and flotsam of the past winter's floods. Baradoc was wedged in the fork of the trunk close to the top where he commanded a clear view of the river downstream. Below him the banks were broadly fringed with reeds that gradually gave way to the new growth of this year's meadow grasses. Lerg sat at the foot of the tree. Below Baradoc the muddy river flowed southwards, looping and coiling its slow way to the sea. Along the rush fringes coots and grebes busied themselves with their mating and nest building. A flight of duck went downstream, the air whistling with the cut of their pinions. A marsh harrier dropped from a slow hunting foray into the reeds and rose holding a large water vole. The air was full of bird song. Out of the corner of his eye Baradoc caught the high crescent-shaped silhouette of a falcon poised for the stoop and kill. But his real interest lay downstream, a quarter of a mile away.

There, moored against the same bank as the alder tree, was a longboat. The saffron sail had been lowered and was now stretched the length of the mid-deck over its own boom to make a tented canopy. There was some large black design painted on the canvas, but because of its folds Baradoc could not make out what it was. He had seen longboats before and he knew it would be some device to give recognition of its sea warrior master to others of his kind, green, red or black raven, a whole gallery of sea eagles, sea dragons, rising suns or silver moons, great hands holding aloft broad, two-edged swords, and sometimes multi-coloured serpents coiled in great circles over the whole spread of sail.

It was no Saxon ship. It was the long keel of a far north sea-raider, of a race that sought no foreign soil to hold, no land to conquer. These men looked only to plunder and slaves and to the easing of the deep salt itch in their blood which was only stilled as the seas rolled under their keels and the winds of all seasons filled their great emblazoned sails of finely dressed skin. These men loved colour and bold designs as they loved the sea and their bloodthirsty raiding, as they loved fighting and, after the slaughter, loved eating and drinking until they fell from their boardseats bloated and stupefied.

On the bank two hide shelters had been set up and the smoke of cooking fires rose into the air Men were carrying supplies and loot aboard and other men worked round the fires. When the work was done the feasting would begin. Somewhere along the coast or in the leagues of forest that rose beyond the water meadows, he knew, there would be ruined huts and homesteads, burning barns and byres, and the fly-clouded corpses of men, women and children.

That morning, returning from his hunting, he had seen one of their raiding parties moving down the river path and with them they had been leading four sturdy ponies carrying their bundled loot. The loot meant nothing to him. But the ponies had made his eyes glisten with desire. With one or, better still, two of them, he and Tia could make faster time to Aquae Sulis and – when he had delivered her to her uncle – a pony would bring him home that much quicker; and home he longed for now with a longing which was a great thirst in him.

The ponies were in his sight now. The four of them had been loosely hobbled and were grazing in the meadow grass not more than a spear's throw from the first slopes of the forest. Within an hour all the crewmen, he guessed, would be drinking and feasting and soon have no thought in their minds for the ponies which they probably planned to slaughter for meat to ship aboard with them the next day.

Baradoc watched as the sun began to slide down the sky. The

shipmen had stowed their gains aboard and were now gathered ashore around the cooking fires and the rough tables set up outside their skin tents. Their voices, as they ate and drank, became louder and were broken by great gusts of laughter and now and then the lusty, roaring of a song. Baradoc marked a spot on the westward crest of the forest and, when the sun touched it, and the alder threw a long shadow across the rushes and the meadow, he slid down from the tree. He picked up the fishing spear which he had left at the bottom with the length of salvaged rope. He looped the rope about his waist and, keeping to the rushes, he went back up the river side with Lerg following him. When he was safely out of sight of the ship he swung away across the meadow grasses and into the skirts of the forest at the bottom of the hill. He worked his way through the trees until he was almost opposite the place where the ponies grazed. The shouting and drunken singing of the men came clearly to him now.

He wet a finger and tested the wind. It was quartering up stream and towards him. He made a half circling hunting sign to Lerg and the hound moved off into the tall grass. It was the sign he used when he wanted to send Lerg or Aesc upwind of deer or game to drive them down to him. Marking the slight crest movements of the long grasses, he watched Lerg's progress until the hound was between the ponies and the longship and upwind of the animals.

Baradoc slipped to the edge of the forest and crouched behind the dark cover of a holly bush. For a moment or two the ponies grazed peacefully. From the river came the sounds of the feasting men. Then Baradoc saw first the farthest pony and then the others lift their heads and cease grazing. Coming downwind to them was the scent of Lerg, and the body smell of Lerg from near ancestry was more wolf than dog, but not so much wolf that it immediately panicked the ponies. It made them restless and puzzled them so that they moved slowly away from it, awkward in their gait from the hobbles they wore. Then they settled to graze again. But after a while their heads went up as

Lerg, belly to the ground, slid nearer to them through the grasses, and they moved closer to the trees.

Three times Lerg moved the ponies forward and the third time the leading pony, a sturdy, rusty red mare with a pale golden mane, was almost within spitting distance of the holly bush. Gently Baradoc began to make soft clicking noises with his tongue. The pony looked towards the bush. Baradoc began to talk softly to it in his own tongue, calming it with words whose magic lay not in their sense but their sound. *Aie! you red and gold beauty ... Aie! who is it with the eyes like dark crag pools and the soft mouth, softer than the dove's breast? 'Tis you, my handsome, my proud, with the taste of sweet grass like honey on your breath. Come away, then, come away ...*

As he spoke the mare came to the side of the holly bush and Baradoc, talking low still, rose with an unbroken, slow movement, stepped smoothly forward and put his hand on the pony's muzzle and then ran it up the long cheek and caressed one of its ears. The pony stood for him as it might have stood for its unknown master.

Baradoc, talking to it still, unslung the rope from his waist and looped it over the mare's head making a rough halter. He drew his dagger, crouched, and cut the hobble between the forelegs.

He led the pony slowly into the shelter of the trees, took his spear from where it rested against a tree, and turned to lead the pony up the forest track. As he did so, a man stepped from the cover of an oak trunk less than six paces ahead of it. Baradoc halted and checked the movement of the pony with his hand on the halter. He cursed himself that he should have been caught with the fishing spear in his left hand.

The man standing slightly above him on the slope of the narrow track smiled, swayed a little, and then said gently in the Roman tongue, ' 'Twas well done, lad. And bravely done with my crew only a few cables' lengths away and you, risking your guts to garter their trews if they'd spotted you – and all for the sake of a pony! You understand my talk?'

Baradoc shook his head.

The man gave a low, tipsy laugh. 'Your ballast has shifted, lad. Your brains must be lopsided or you would not shake your head to say *No* if you did not understand my talk. O brave lad who can talk strange love talk to a part-broken forest pony, a lad who wears a soldier's cast-off sandals, and a lad who has not turned tail in fright like a startled hare, and even now stares me boldly in the eye when one sight of me would make most Britons void their bellies with fear. Speak me fair, for you understand me, or I will take your head off and fillet you from throat to vent like gutting a cod. Why do you steal my pony?' He hiccoughed.

From his manner and speech it was clear to Baradoc that he was someone of authority, someone who was used to command and to be obeyed. The odds were that he was the master of the longboat. He was bare-headed, a tall, powerfully built man, wearing a saffron-coloured, flared tunic with a wide whale-skin belt from the left side of which hung a broad sword in a decorated scabbard. His thighs were bare to his knees and his legs were wrapped in saffron-coloured cloth and bound with black thongs down to his black sandals. Across the front of his tunic was embroidered a spread-winged black raven. But the most unexpected thing about him was that he was no ruddy complexioned Northman. His skin was black, as black as the Aethiop auxiliaries who had been with many of the legions. In his right hand he held a short-hafted throwing axe. The whites of his eyes rolled now, as he hefted the axe in his hand and said impatiently, 'Answer me!' and hiccoughed again.

Baradoc said, 'How can I steal from you that which is not yours?'

For an instant the man's face tightened with sudden anger. Then, unexpectedly, he smiled, and said, 'By Odin, you've a bold tongue to speak so saucily when in the blink of an eye I could split your skull.' He tossed the throwing axe lightly in the air and caught it deftly.

Baradoc answered, '*Aie!* You could throw your axe and kill me. It is a skill I know your kind have. But you would not live long. There is one who stands behind you who would tear your life out by your throat before you could shout for your men.'

The man's smile broadened and he shook his head, swaying a little. 'Oh, no, my gamecock. You think that I, Corvo, master of the Black Raven, am to be fooled into turning by such an old trick, and give you time to use your spear? Now, toss down your spear and turn the mare shipwards. We've lost two men. We can use a good pair of slave shoulders and hands on the rowing benches. The rope's end and leg and neck irons will soon take the fire out of you. Around with you, and thank your country's good mead that you still live.'

Baradoc who, under his courage, knew fear and was not fool enough to fancy yet that any advantage was his, said, 'No, Captain Corvo, my way lies past you. And I do not try to fool you.' He threw his spear to the ground. 'Now, look behind you.'

Corvo blinked at Baradoc for a moment or two, and then slowly turned. Five paces behind him stood Lerg, the great, grey shaggy body tensed, the powerful, long head lowered, jaws parted showing his long fangs, the breath easing from him in a sudden low growl as his eyes watched Baradoc. Slowly Corvo turned back to Baradoc. Anger and admiration fought a battle across his face. Baradoc guessed that the temper of this man was not to be trusted. Anger and drink might spur his recklessness and he might risk all. *Aie!* and might succeed. The thrown axe could take Lerg first and the sword himself after. Few along Britain's coast had not heard of Corvo and his reckless courage. With drink that courage would have no limits.

Suddenly Corvo gave a loud laugh, spun the axe again into the air, caught it, and said, 'Bacchus is on your side, lad. The drink runs smoothly in me and your daring teases my humour. Take your pony. That marks the two of us as thieves. But since you must know who I am, it is just that I should know who you are.'

'I am Baradoc, son of a chief of the Dunmonii. I travel far westward beyond the Tamarus river and for this need the pony.'

'Which you now have got. Aye, I know your country and have sailed beyond it, past the Blessed Isles where the natives eat only fish and sea birds and their women have scaly tails and from the rocks sing songs of love to tempt wife-and-sweetheart-hungry crews. So, what think you of the great Corvo now you have spoken face to face with him?'

Baradoc said, 'First, that it is well that you were no Saxon for I would have put the hound at your throat long since. I hate them all.'

Corvo laughed. 'Aye, and so do I for they are land-grabbing coast-crawlers that risk the sea only on summer waters. You do well to hate them for they mean to swallow this land. Now, answer – what think you of black-skinned Corvo?'

For a moment Baradoc hesitated, then with a frank grin he said, 'That he is a man with a dark skin and a darker reputation, but that there is a goodness in him which comes not from drinking mead.'

Corvo shook his head. 'You are wrong, boy. Two horns less of mead or two more and I would have chopped you and the horse for dog meat and forced your great hound to eat it. Now go, lad, before my gentle humour leaves me.' He stepped back off the path and made way for Baradoc to pass. 'And when you next pray to your rough gods, make your thanks that you found me mellow at the time of our meeting.' With that he turned his back on Baradoc and went down through the trees to the water meadows, singing quietly to himself.

Baradoc, knowing there was no certainty that the man would not send a party after him, led the pony quickly up the rough track through the woods to return to Tia. But when he got back to her he knew that he would say nothing of his meeting with Corvo. What she did not know of the dangers around them could not upset her. As he marched, he recalled the many tales that were told in the country about the man. It was said that his mother had been an Aethiop slave of a wealthy British family near Lemanis who had been captured while a young girl by the sea-raiders and taken to their country where she had conceived Corvo by her master. Corvo, born coloured, had as a youth saved the life of his master and father and had been given his freedom and thrown in his lot with the longboat men, raiding, pillaging and fighting with his father's people, but choosing for crew ex-slaves, outcasts, any riff-raff of any race that caught his eye and earned his accolade for their valour, seamanship and ruthlessness. He called no man chief but, while he still lived, had grown into a legend. Half the stories which were told of him came from the fearful fancies of the eastern and southern tribes he plagued along the Saxon shore. Baradoc smiled to himself as he remembered his old master speaking of Corvo; *Child of a black slavegirl, fathered by a seawolf. The gods gifted his birth with the stuff of legend. The destiny of such a man can only be dark for his spirit seeks always to revenge his birth, and to forget it in the heat of battle or drink.*

Well ... either from drink or some lingering goodness the man had attempted him no harm.

Hunter's Dream

That evening they made a start long before darkness came. Baradoc gave Tia as reason for this that it was a bad part of the country and the sooner they crossed it the better. It was on the tip of Tia's tongue to point out that if this were so, surely it would be better not to move until night came. Something in Baradoc's manner made her hold back the words. She was no fool. Not for a moment did she believe that he had found the pony wandering loose in the river meadows. He had stolen it, she guessed, and in the stealing there had been trouble which made him anxious to be on his way. It was a sturdy pony with a mild nature and gentle manners, placidly taking a handful of their corn from her as it stood to be loaded with their two bundles slung as saddle-packs across its back by the hempen rope. Since Tia now had her goats' hair cloak they folded her mantle over the rope to make a small riding pad to prevent her being chafed.

'When it gets dark,' said Baradoc, 'you can ride and we shall journey faster.'

Meaning, Tia knew, faster than if she were stumbling and tripping along at the pony's heels in the dark. Well, why should she grumble? The pony was strong and would take her weight easily.

She said, 'The pony should have a name now that it has joined the party.'

Baradoc, standing at the animal's head, ready to lead it off, smiled and said, 'Then, as you're going to ride it, you name it.'

'Well, she's red and gold, so it is no hard thing. She shall be Sunset.'

Baradoc nodded. 'It's a good name. Come on, Sunset!' He

gave the halter he had made for the pony a jerk and began to move off.

Without any sign or sound from Baradoc Tia marked that Lerg and Cuna moved ahead of them swiftly and disappeared over the rocky bluff top that sheltered their camping place. Aesc dropped back at her heels, and Bran flapped lazily away out on to their left flank and was soon lost to sight.

They travelled for two hours and in all that time few words passed between them. Baradoc stayed at the head of the pony and Tia brought up the rear with Aesc. Their path lay through high woodlands which every few miles dropped into steep little valleys cut by narrow streams and rivers. Tia noticed that Baradoc kept their course as much as he could into the eye of the westering sun. North by west, away from the coast, that was the way to Aquae Sulis. At least, Tia – her memory now of Baradoc's map a confused one – hoped it was. Once there this Baradoc of many moods, this son of a chief of a half-savage tribe, would leave her and go on to his home grounds, perched on the edge of the endless seas where Neptune and his conch-roaring son Triton ruled, and she would never see him again. That would be no loss. Still, when he brought her to her uncle safely, she would get the old man to reward him well, and after she might for a while remember him in her vesper prayers.

She walked behind Sunset letting her thoughts roam idly, banishing them only when they turned to the cruel things that had happened to her brother and his wife and the villa and farm. The air grew chilly as the sun dropped and she pulled a fold of her great cloak over her head because the breeze cut coldly around the nape of her neck where her hair had been shorn. Her rough hose, cross-gartered up her legs, was still slightly damp and the harsh material made her skin itch. Although she had washed the garment as well as she could, she hoped that she would not catch some skin disease from it.

Ahead of her Baradoc halted the pony. She saw that he was looking at the loose sandy soil of the track they had been following through the trees. On his knees he examined the ground for a moment or two. Then he rose and led Sunset on. As she came to the spot Tia stopped and looked at the ground. Part of it had now been disturbed by one of Sunset's hoof marks. But, still clear in an untouched part of the track, was the imprint of a sandal. It was obviously a man's heavy sandal from the depth of the print, the outer edges of the sole showing a rim of deep stud marks. In the centre of the sole, studs which had been hammered into the leather made a pattern of a five pointed star in the sand. Well, that was not unusual; many sandals, for men and women, were often soled with fanciful stud patterns. But somehow she had the feeling that Baradoc's attention had quickened as he had examined the print. When he had risen he had glanced back at her and his tanned face had gone wooden, signalling emotion even as he sought to show no trace of it. Why did he have to be like that, she thought crossly? So self-important and secretive. If she let herself forget some of the nice things about him, she could easily bring herself to dislike him completely. Well, she supposed some people were like that. They tried to make themselves impressive by keeping things to themselves. Something, she was sure, *had* happened when he had found Sunset. He had come back grim-faced and had just started packing up, hardly throwing her a word until they were ready to go. Well ... if he thought she cared a fig he could go to Hades. She pushed all thought of him from her mind and began to think about Aquae Sulis and her uncle's villa which lay a few miles outside of the town. She had stayed there many times with her father and then her brother. Always she had the small room with the wall paintings of naiads bathing in splashing brooks and waterfalls. The real sound of falling water came from the courtyard outside. Here, her uncle had planted flowers and grape vines and cosseted two olive trees which had been grown from the stones of olives eaten at his farewell banquet when he had retired from his prefecture of a cavalry cohort. She sighed at the thought of it ... a lovely villa, full of treasures acquired by her uncle in his many campaigns all over the empire. Part of the covered walk beyond her room was an enclosed aviary where he kept his collection of exotic birds. Having no children, he treated them as such so that they came to his hands to eat and their colours flashed through all the hues of the rainbow as they flighted free about the great courtyard when the weather was fine . . . And the food at the villa! By the gods, it made her belly feel empty to think of it! And the soft, soft bed with the alabaster-carved lamp at its side!

Her left groin began to itch and she scratched at it, Aquae Sulis going from her mind. Fleas or lice for certain, no rough scrubbing with cold water killed them. Or, maybe they had come from one of the dogs. Aesc was always scratching. Well, it was no good complaining. Baradoc would probably tell her that a flea had every right to take its living where it could. For certain he and his greasy tribespeople would never give them a second thought.

Baradoc halted Sunset suddenly. Tia, engrossed with her thoughts, walked straight into the pony's hindquarters and was brought to the present by the sharp switch of its long tail against her face.

Without thought, she shouted, 'Pluto take you! Why don't you give warning when you're going to stop?'

Baradoc turned, eyed her, and said mildly, 'Why don't you keep your eyes on where you're going instead of day-dreaming along? And shout a little louder, then if there's anyone around they'll get a real chance of knowing we're here.'

Cross with herself for her show of temper, Tia mumbled, 'I'm sorry.'

'That's all right.' He chuckled. 'Nobody likes walking into the backside of a horse.' He patted Sunset's neck. 'Luckily, she's good tempered or she might have kicked out.'

He began to re-arrange the bundles on Sunset's back into a saddle pack.

Tia asked, 'What now?'

'It's getting dark. It's better that you ride. Up you get.'

He bent down and made a cup of his clasped hands for her to mount. Tia climbed on to Sunset and made herself as comfortable as she could with her legs dangling behind the bundles, her hands taking a loose loop of the halter. She looked down at Baradoc through the darkening gloom and said, 'There was a print on the path some while ago. Does that mean someone is close ahead of us?'

'No,' said Baradoc. 'The print was not made today.'

'I had a feeling the star pattern meant something to you.'

'You're right. You have quick eyes. But for now, stop trying to read my thoughts and hang on tight.' He moved forward and Sunset followed with Tia swaying on her back.

The next few hours were mild agony for Tia. Baradoc set a good pace. The going was rough, up and down the forest and valley tracks, with the occasional switch of a loose branch flicking across Tia's face so that she had to pull the cloak close about her head to protect herself. Within a mile the inner skin of her thighs was chafed, all feeling had been bumped out of her bottom, and her arms ached from hanging on to the halter. Curiously enough the hardship – since nothing could be done about it – served to lift her spirits, making her forget the biting of the fleas which attacked her from the old hose. Aquae Sulis lay ahead – hot rooms and warm baths and her uncle's old maidservant to massage her body with oils and perfumes ... and clean clothes. To reach all that comfort and security, what could a few days of dirt and discomfort matter?

When the moon rose, long past midnight, they stopped in a small clearing where years before the trees had been chopped down and the ruins of a woodman's hazel-latticed shelter still stood.

Baradoc helped Tia down from the pony. As she stood bow-legged he smiled at her and said, 'The stiffness will soon go. Did you never ride before?'

'Yes, of course. But not bareback.'

'In a couple of days you will think nothing of it.'

He took the cold deer tack from one of the bundles, the last of their cheese and wheat cake, and they ate, lying on the ground with their backs propped against a moss-covered fallen tree trunk.

He said, 'There's no water nearby. But we'll drink at the next stream we cross.' Then, as though she had asked him a direct question, he went on, 'The star pattern comes from the sandal of one of the two who strung me up to the oak. He is of my tribe – my cousin – and journeys westward as I do. The other was a wanderer who had joined us. They could have killed me but that, because of the laws of our tribe, is forbidden to the wearer of the star-sandals. So they strung me up to let death come without any dagger thrust.'

'Why is it forbidden?'

'Because I am the seventh son of my father. The last son, too. None of my brothers is living. The gods will give no gifts, nor long years to any who kills, except in fair fight, the seventh son of a family. But to leave me to die was different.' He shrugged. 'It's a nice point of morality. But when I reach home there will be a fair fight and a killing of my cousin – thanks to you.'

'So, I save one life in order that another shall die.'

'The gods have thrown their dice. They fell that way. I tell you this much to excuse a hardness that is sometimes in me. The two ahead will soon take a different path from ours. I'll take you to your uncle and then my debt will be paid. He smiled and rubbed his hand over his beard-fuzzed chin. 'Maybe your uncle will give me the use of his bath house and the loan of a razor to smooth my chin. With my people no man may grow a beard or long moustache until he is married.'

'Is there a chosen girl in your tribe that you will marry?'

'No. My cousin and I were only twelve and gathering shell fish along the shore when we were taken by sea-raiders and sold together as house slaves, first to a Phoenician trader and then to my master in Londinium – where he then lived.'

'Your people must think you are dead?'

'No – the word was passed many years ago. But under the law there was no way of buying our freedom. Nor did either of us need it, for we are much alike in many ways and knew there was much to learn and a sheaf of years ahead.'

'But this cousin –'

'No more of him.' Baradoc sat forward and tossed a piece of deer meat to Aesc.

Tia, not wishing to break their talk, said, 'What are the girls of your tribe like?'

Baradoc laughed. 'Like all other girls. Some fat, some thin. Some beautiful, some plain. At your age many of them are long married and have children. Sometimes I see in my mind's eye the girl I will marry.'

'Tell me.'

'How can I since the picture changes so often? Sometimes her hair is a dark flame, richer than the stag's coat when he stands in the full light of the new morning's sun. Sometimes it is blacker than the raven's wing spread against the year's first snows. And sometimes her skin is warm and polished, brown like a harvested hazel nut, or creamier than the finest goat's milk and blushing with the glow of a bright ember.'

Tia teased him. 'Her eyes, too, will be no ordinary eyes?'

'Why should they be? Dark as a black sea pebble with the green of waving tide-wrack reflected in them. Or bluer than the brooklime flower and dancing with a brightness as clear and crystal as a hill stream over white sands.' He turned to her and, matching her mood, said, 'You wish me to go on? Her teeth, her arms and legs? The way she walks and runs and swims? Her voice like a dawn blackbird's when she sings.'

'Spare me. I've had enough poetry.'

'*Aie*, that is true. But there's always room in each day for a little – otherwise living is as flat as stale wine. We're not barbarians, my people. We have our songs and our stories, and there's not one of our kind who doesn't learn them from first talk and pass them on. So, even with death, they are not lost. Their magic cannot die so long as men have ears.' He stood up, sucked noisily at a fragment of deer meat lodged in his teeth, and said, 'It's time to move.'

He turned away from her abruptly and went across to the woodman's shelter. He came back after a while carrying an armful of bracken which he had found there, the remains of a rough bed. He bound it into a soft roll within their piece of fish netting and then wrapped it in her mantle to make a large, soft saddle. Without a word he helped her to mount.

Riding after him Tia was touched by his rough, silent courtesy. Yet when he needed words he could find them. Then, thinking of his dream of some girl waiting for him, she was amused that he had given no place in his thoughts for a fair-haired girl like herself. Maybe there were no fair-haired women in his tribe, but she doubted it. Amongst the Britons of the south and east there were plenty. Strange Baradoc, rough and kind, withdrawn one moment, then easy with talk the next. And one day – for she guessed the intent lay in him as hard as a stone – he meant to kill his cousin for the wrong done to him. She shivered a little at the thought. There was too much of killing already in this land.

Early the next morning they made camp beyond the fringe of the forest in a small willow grove on the edge of a clear stream that flowed down from the distant line of the almost treeless uplands which rose away to the north. They ate and then slept while the dogs kept watch. When they woke Baradoc went down to one of the stream pools and with willow stakes fixed their piece of net across the narrow gullet through which the stream fed into the pool. Then he called to her to help him, telling her to take off her long hose and sandals, and to roll up the skirt of her tunic and pin it tight with her mother's brooch. Tia noticed that although he was concerned she should keep her leg-hose dry, he seemed heedless of wet or discomfort. He just walked into the water wearing his leather short trews and his shirt. Rain or shine, wet or dry seemed to make no difference to him. A few paces abreast they waded up the pool, beating the surface with branches. The trout and grayling in it went upstream to escape through the gullet and some of them were entangled in the stretched netting. Baradoc pulled them out, killed them and tossed them on to the bank.

When they waded out together, Baradoc picked up the fish, strung them on a slip of branch through their gills and handed them to her, saying, 'If you have not done it before you cut their heads off, slit them down the belly and shake or scrape their innards out. The ones with the big fin on the back are grayling and smell of dried thyme. The others are trout. We'll eat them before we move off.'

'Women's work, my lord.' Tia said it with a straight face.

Baradoc nodded, unsmiling. As Tia took her dagger and started work, Baradoc went to one of their bundles and ferreted about in the pile of old rags he had found in the fishermen's hut. He sat down and laid out a long narrow piece of cloth before him.

Tia, her hands slimy and scale-covered as she gutted the fish, asked, 'What are you doing?'

'Making a throwing sling. There are duck farther downstream which I can kill and Aesc will retrieve. The fish will serve us for today. The duck we can cook and carry for tomorrow in case nothing else turns up. I will make a fire when I come back.'

He rolled the long ends of the cloth into thin grips, binding them with pieces of catgut. The centre of the cloth he thickened into a pad by sewing on top of each other three squares of extra cloth. Then he gathered a handful of smooth small stones from the stream verge.

Coming back to Tia he dropped a stone into the padded loop of the sling and said, 'Watch. The top of the far stake I set up for the net.' He swung the sling gently in a circle at his side to get the feel of the weight of the stone. 'It was with such as this that the first of my countrymen over four hundred years ago gave a welcome to the great Caesar.' He whipped the sling around and let the stone fly.

'You missed,' said Tia.

'I expected to. With a new sling one must get the feel and the balance.'

He slung another stone and this time only narrowly missed the stake. With the third stone he hit it a hand's span from the top.

Tia clasped her slippery, fish slimed hands and said mockingly, 'O Mighty Baradoc!'

Baradoc shook his head at her, smiling. 'You should not be too pleased. When I come back you will have a duck to pluck and gut.' He tucked the sling into his belt, thrust a handful of stones into the front of his shirt and walked off downstream with Aesc following him. Tia went on with her work. Sunset, tethered by a long head rope to a willow, cropped at the young grass. Bran flew down from a willow perch and took one of the trout heads. Cuna lay sleeping in the sun, and Lerg lay on the ground, head raised, watching the direction in which Baradoc had disappeared.

When Tia had finished the fish, she covered them with leaves against the sun and then washed her hands in the stream. She took off her tunic and spread it in the sun to dry. Wrapping their woollen blanket about her she wandered around the willow grove collecting dried wood for the fire, and gathered a small pile of dried leaves and grasses so that Baradoc should have tinder for starting a flame.

Half a mile downstream Baradoc crouched, hidden in the rushes at the riverside with Aesc lying at his side. The river was broader here and ran in two channels around a long island fringed with mace reeds and low alder growths. Coming downstream he had put up several pairs of mallard and teal, but with no chance of hitting them. This was the courting and mating season and he guessed that the island would be a favourite nesting place, for the weed-thick shallows around it made good feeding grounds. He and Aesc crouched, still and watchful, hidden in the rushes. A dog otter came upstream, rolled like a porpoise, sun and water silvering its flanks, and dived to appear in a few moments with a large trout in its forepaws. It lay on its back and let the current drift it downstream while it ate the trout. A kingfisher fished from a low, overhanging branch at the top of the island. The life which Baradoc had disturbed when he took up his hiding place began to come back. Grebe and moorfowl fed and went through their courting rituals below the island while overhead a pair of buzzards circled high, their mewing calls coming faintly to him. Beyond the river and the far grassland, the forest trees rose in long swelling waves of changing greens. Distantly, above the farther tree crests, Baradoc marked a thin plume of blue smoke coming from some solitary fire. He guessed it to be some hours' march away. Now and again the smoke thickened to a dark, breeze-ragged plume. Whoever tended it, he thought, was well-armed or foolish. These days men and women held close to their homesteads or villages for safety. The forest held only the spoiled or the spoilers. The dark face of Corvo came back to him and with it a quick stir of concern about Tia. Yesterday he had left her for a while and there had been trouble, trouble which he had kept from her. He decided that if no flighting duck came in soon, or mating pair appeared from the island reeds, he would go back. Not even Lerg could protect her against some odds.

He smiled to himself as he thought of the way she teased him now about 'women's work', and the flashes of angry spirit she showed from time to time. He guessed that she must long for the security and comfort of her uncle's villa at Aquae Sulis. That was her kind of life. She had lived sheltered and lived soft, her family wealthy and with servants to come to her call for all her needs. In his time with his master he had known many such families and households. These Romans, most of whom had never seen Rome, lived in the dying radiance of the empire's glory, and called this country their own. And so many of them, even now, did not understand that it had never truly been their country and that slowly now the strong hand of another race was closing in on it. Tia, he thought, might find lasting shelter and plenty at Aquae Sulis, a haven that would last out her days maybe, but he doubted it. Men like Corvo were only carefree raiders who lived from day to day and for each day's plunder and each night's drinking and feasting. But back in the east, now far beyond Tanatus and Rutupiae, spreading north and south of the Tamesis river, encircling Londinium, their eyes looking ever westwards to the rich lands of the Atrebates, to Pontes, Calleva and Venta, were the Saxons, driving forward slowly and holding every mile of ground they took and making serfs of common folk and culls of British chiefs, Romano-British merchants and town dignitaries, all those of power and wealth who had lived soft too long. Only among the men of the north and west on mountain and moor and wild cliff top and deep river fronts the dream still lived of dominion over all the land. It lived with him, too, like a slow peat-burn waiting only the right wind and the right season to start the hidden embers to flame. His old master had known his dream

but had denied its truth, saying that there was no going back
to old glories, old times, that the gods gave men dreams but
shaped their destinies, and the fate of their nations, into patterns
the human mind could not foresee.

Aie, if he believed that, then he would never have stayed
slave to learn and listen and watch for so long. He would have
run and been back with his people years ago . . . back and married to some maiden who would have given him other dreams
and other cares to fill his days. Thinking this, he smiled again
to himself, remembering Tia asking him about the girls of his
tribe and how – although there were fair-haired ones amongst
them – he had described no such maiden, knowing he held back
yet not knowing why in truth. Bright hair like the gold of the
marigolds in the marshes, and eyes under pale lashes, their
colour misted as the faint sea-haze softened the sheen of the
turquoise slow-heaving seas of summer.

Two heavy splashes brought his attention back to the river.
A pair of mallards, duck and drake, had planed in, furrowing
the water as they landed. Baradoc watched them as the drake
began to display to the duck. Beside him he felt the faint
tremble of Aesc's body as the dog watched too. Under the sun the
drake shone as though it were a jewelled bird, yellow bill and
glossy green head flashing as it bobbed and dipped, the great white
and purple wing patches opening like a fan as it preened its
wings and rattled its quills while the duck, head lowered, slid
away pretending lack of interest, but never going far. Baradoc
fingered the set of his stone in the sling and slowly stretched the
length of cloth even, held in both hands at his side ready to
throw when he rose. *Aie!* it was a pity to kill when the day was
so bright and the birds moved to the dance of love. But an
empty belly drove all thought of beauty and poetry from the
mind. The slate-backed peregrine would rove and stoop and
kill untouched by sentiment, and the questing vixen would
scatter the bronze and green and white feathers as she shook
her clamped jaws to break the long neck to carry food for her
cubs. The gods gave dreams of a paradise where none killed,
man nor beast nor bird – but they shaped the destiny of them

all differently. Taking a deep breath and holding it, Baradoc
tensed himself for the move which would bring him upright
with the long sling already circling to take the drake, his left
hand already holding the second stone for the duck.

He stood swiftly, smoothly, and the sling stone hummed like
a hornet as it sped across the water and took the drake with a
vicious blow on the right shoulder, breaking the wing joint.
Baradoc whirled the sling again and aimed at the duck which
with a beating of wings and strong thrusts of its webbed feet
had jumped into the air for flight. The stone narrowly missed
the duck which disappeared up the river calling with alarm.
By the island the drake circled helplessly on the water, thrusting uselessly with one wing to find flight. Aesc, knowing her
moment, slid into the stream and swam to retrieve the bird.
She brought it back to Baradoc who killed it quickly with a
twist of the head which broke its neck. He pushed it into the
front of his under shirt, looped the sling over his belt and
turned to leave his cover, to hunt further downstream away
from the disturbance he had caused.

As he reached out his hand to take the fish spear which he
had thrust into the mud of the bank a voice said, 'Touch it –
and you get this through your head.'

Standing full in the centre of the break in the reeds through
which Baradoc had made his way to the river was a tall youth,
dark-haired, his skin brown from dirt and sun, a straggling
growth of beard covering his chin. He wore old, tattered woollen breeks to the knees, the rest of his legs bare. From his
shoulders hung a brown cloak held tight about his waist with a
broad leather belt from which hung a deep fringe of rusty,
finely linked ring-mail to form a short skirt. On one side of the
belt was looped an unscabbarded short broad sword, rusty and
blunt-edged. Hanging from the other side was a leather quiver
full of short arrows. His arms raised, he held a charged bow,
the arrow aimed at Baradoc. He was flanked on one side by a
lank-haired young woman with a long, ill-humoured face, an
old scar deeply marking her right cheek. She wore strings of
coloured beads around her thin neck, the long loops falling

across a dirty, ragged, long-sleeved white stole striped with red and green diagonal bands. At his other side stood another youth who, small and sturdy, dressed in a belted tunic of furs, heavy sandals on his feet, carried a light throwing spear.

Baradoc, making no attempt to touch the fish spear, said calmly, 'You need not hold the arrow on me. I mean harm to no one. I hunt and kill for the pot alone.'

'You live around here?' The tall youth spoke with the flat accent of the eastern Cantii. Many such, dispossessed, roamed the country now.

'No. I make my way west to join my people. I have been working up-country.'

'You had a master there?'

'Aye. But he is now dead.'

'He was good to you?'

'He was. He gave me my freedom.' To name himself once a slave, he thought, could do him no harm with them.

The youth spat suddenly. 'No masters are good. So you were a slave?'

'I was.'

The young woman said impatiently, 'Leave him, Atro. Take his spear and sling if you will.' She laughed. 'His clothes, too. And those good sandals and trews and the dagger at his belt. But leave him. We have better work at hand.'

'Shut your mouth, Colta.' Atro spoke roughly without looking at her. Then to Baradoc he said, 'Come here.'

Baradoc moved through the reeds on to the grass and Atro stood back from him, the arrow still levelled.

Colta said, 'Now what is in your mind, Atro?'

'That we have to live. That he means nothing to us. That there is no tie between us except poverty. These days that tie is a cobweb broken by a breath. So –' his mouth twisted angrily, '– he is a freed slave. But who should take his word for it? There are those in Clausentium and Venta who will buy without questions – and crop his ears to mark their property. Enghus, tie him.'

But for the arrow tip a few feet from his head Baradoc would have made an attempt to escape. The iron-tipped arrow could not be denied. It would split his skull like an eggshell. Then the thought of Tia left alone stirred him to make a plea which came hard to his lips. This Atro spoke of poverty with hard, personal anger. Yet under his ruthlessness there might be some common sentiment to wake good feeling.

Baradoc said firmly, 'Shared poverty holds no value these days. But we are of the same country and we have the same enemy. If you sell your own kind to slavery what can you expect for yourself when the new masters come? And come they will unless we hold together in a kinship bigger than this country has ever known since the old queen put Verulamium and Londinium to the sword and flame.'

Atro shook his head. 'Now you talk big and fancy. Such talk means nothing. Old kings and queens or new ones mean nothing. Today it is each for himself. Bind him, Enghus.'

Enghus, giggling, danced round behind Baradoc while Colta knelt to a travelling bundle that lay on the grass at her feet and brought out rope lengths. She handed these to Enghus. Then, taking his light spear, she pressed the point against Baradoc's neck, saying, 'Now, Big Talker of the good times to come, put your hands behind your back and stand calm. What matters it to you if you are sold as a slave?' She scratched the tip of the spear lightly across the skin of his neck and laughed. 'There is always escape to another freedom.'

Baradoc put his hands behind him. Enghus bound them tight and with another cord roped his arms to his body, grunting as he jerked at the knots.

Atro lowered his bow and withdrew the arrow. He reached forward and jerked the dead mallard from the inside of Baradoc's shirt and tossed it to Colta.

'Take it. Tonight you shall roast it at the shrine keeper's fire. Eh, Enghus?'

Enghus gave a giggle of pleasure and jerking his head to the west said, 'But not until we have roasted him first to make him sing. The old fool, he burns his garden weeds, filling the sky with smoke as though the whole world moved at peace.' Then he shook his spear and pleaded, 'But first, brother Atro, promise, let me tease him a little with this to put him in the way of true speaking before the fire touches him.'

Atro laughed. 'Maybe, Enghus, maybe. Just to make you happy my little blood-thirsty brother.' Then, to Baradoc, he went on calmly as though there could be no hard feelings between them, 'Enghus is my brother. When he was born the gods touched him with a happy madness. Even when he feels like weeping he laughs. He laughs at his own pain and the pain of all others. But my wife Colta, my beautiful Colta, she is gentle and good – unless the mood takes her otherwise! Then sometimes even a kind word will have her turn on you like an angry adder. Now, since you know us all, tell us your name.'

'My name is Baradoc.'

Colta, now holding the fish spear, came up to him and touched his cheek and gave a sudden sharp tug to the beard growth on his chin. 'If you were my slave I would beat you daily to take that proud look from your face.'

'Enough of that,' said Atro. 'We move.' Then looking round, he asked, 'Where is the dog?'

Enghus said, 'It moved off a while ago. And such a pretty colour. I could have made myself a hood from its skin and a belt pouch from its ears.' He laughed to himself, jerking his head up and down.

Atro said to Baradoc. 'Call the dog.'

Baradoc shook his head. 'It would not come. It is a stray that joined me company only this morning. But someone has trained it well.'

'So I saw when it took the duck. A dog like that could have been useful.'

Baradoc shrugged his shoulders and made no answer. Atro turned abruptly away and began to walk down the river bank. Before Baradoc could move he was pricked none too lightly from behind with the point of Enghus' spear. He began to follow Atro with Enghus giggling behind him.

Baradoc knew that Aesc would return to Tia. What she would do now that she was alone he could not guess. But one thing was certain. If he did not manage to escape from this ragged, broken-down band soon and return to find her the dogs would leave her after a few days and come seeking him. Beyond that point he shut his mind to her fate. Before he could help her, he must first help himself.

Ahead of him Atro marched now with his bow slung over his shoulder, the ring-mail skirt swinging about his thighs, the rusty links making a soft whispering music, the battered old broad sword bumping at his side. The sword was Roman and uncared for, and the bow, an old one, but serviceable still, was of the kind which in the old days the Parthian auxiliaries had used, cunningly made of alternate strips of wood and bone. To have been taken by these three wanderers touched his pride sharply, but he could understand how it had happened. When a man hunted all his mind was on his quarry. Lost in a hunter's dream, he had crouched in the reeds, all his senses concentrating towards the moment of the kill – even Aesc had shared that dangerous isolation – and had allowed Atro to move up behind them.

He raised his eyes to the far side of the river valley, where the forest rolled upwards in green sweeps. Over a distant crest rose a plume of yellow and purple smoke to be taken by the wind and swept raggedly away.

When Aesc returned, still damp from the river, Tia expected Baradoc soon to follow. But time passed and he did not appear. She got up, walked out of the willows, and found a rise in the ground where she could look down the river. There was no sign of Baradoc. She went back and carried on with the work she had taken in hand which was to repair a large slit in one of the bundle cloths made by a broken branch or thorns during the previous night's march. But when Baradoc still did not appear, she began to grow uneasy and troubled. For the first time the black thought touched her that something might have happened to him.

Almost as though this fear, newborn in her, had been some mysteriously understood signal for which the dogs were waiting, she heard Aesc whine. She looked up from her sewing.

Lerg had risen and stood near her, his head low, the grey-brown eyes full on her. Aesc moved restlessly to and fro behind Lerg, whining gently, while Cuna lay still on the ground his eyes watching the other dogs as though he were trying to read the meaning of their change of mood. Only Sunset seemed untouched. Tethered to a slim willow trunk on a lengthened head rope, she cropped the sweet green grass, flicking her golden tail occasionally against the flies. Tia saw that Bran had flown down to the ground and sat now on an old mole hill, plumage fluffed out raggedly, head and beak drawn down between his shoulders, a picture – so her imagination prompted – of unhappiness.

Resolutely, pushing her fears from her, she went on with her work. Almost as though in protest Aesc gave a sharp bark and moved to the edge of the willow glade and back. Lerg waited, unmoving, his eyes on Tia.

Tia went out of the willows and began to walk down the river. Aesc ran ahead of her, nose to the ground, and she turned to see that Lerg and Cuna were following her. She walked a couple of bowshots down the river but could find no sign of Baradoc. When she turned back the dogs came with her reluctantly. It was this behaviour that put firmly into her head that they knew that something had happened to Baradoc.

In the willows, she stood undecided for a while. The afternoon was wearing away. It was not often in her life that she had had to make important decisions for herself. Always there had been someone to turn to, someone who would decide for her. The conviction came strongly to her that something *had* happened to Baradoc. Without him she would never get safely to Aquae Sulis. The selfish thought made her immediately angry. Baradoc might be in real trouble . . . even dead -- and she thought only of herself. She had to find him. If Aesc had not come back alone she would not have been worrying. But Aesc *was* back and all the dogs were uneasy and had returned to the willows reluctantly. Suddenly she decided that there was no sense in just staying in the glade while fears mounted in her.

She began to pack up the camp. It took her some time to stow all their possessions and lash the bundles across Sunset. As she did so Aesc and Cuna fretted around her, but she threw them a sharp word and quieted them. When, finally, she led the pony out of the willows Lerg ranged himself at her side and Aesc, followed by Cuna, ran ahead. Tia followed the line which Aesc took.

Half an hour later Aesc stopped at the break in the river reeds where Baradoc had taken the mallard drake. Tia saw at once in the muddy soil the marks of footprints.

As Aesc sat whining in front of her she waved the dog on. Aesc, head low, began to move down the river bank. There was no doubt in Tia's mind that the bitch was following Baradoc's scent. A little later she found proof that she was following Baradoc and that he was not alone. From that moment the anxiety in Tia changed to a real fear, but not a fear that robbed her of resolution. She had to find Baradoc for her sake and for his.

She stood on a sandy beach where the stream shallowed to a ford. In the damp sand at the edge of the water were the clear marks of the studded sandals which Baradoc wore. With them, some confused and some clear, were the marks of other prints though she could not decide by how many people they had been made.

Across the river was a narrow strip of wild meadow and sedge-land from which rose great terraces of dark forest.

Leading the pony Tia forded the river which nowhere came more than knee high. Cuna alone had to swim in places. On the far bank were more confused prints.

Aesc, head lowered, was already moving across the marshy meadow towards the woods. As Tia followed Bran came flying up from behind her and with a sharp *cark, cark* beat his way over the trees and disappeared.

The climb through the forest was hard and slow going. Aesc was clearly following a trail which was fresh. But the way, while it led sometimes along narrow tracks where the going was fairly easy, often headed off into the low tangle of scrub and bushes under the trees where Tia and Sunset had to force a path. That others had done the same before her was obvious from the broken branches and downtrodden growths. Sometimes Aesc disappeared ahead of her, impatient with her slowness, but always she came back whining gently and insistently. Lerg stayed with Tia all the time, content to match her pace. Looking up at the sun, Tia realized that the afternoon was fast wearing away. The thought of the coming darkness frightened Tia. And the thought that she might never see Baradoc again, perhaps never get to Aquae Sulis put a dryness in her throat and a weakness in her body that made her despise herself. Silently she cursed herself for her weakness and her selfishness for she knew that the strongest desire in her was to get safely to Aquae Sulis. If she could have been magically spirited there now, leaving Baradoc to whatever was to be, what would she have decided, she wondered? She escaped any answer from herself by cursing, stringing together all the old army oaths she could remember – and finding a strange comfort in them.

She stopped twice to drink at small streams and to rest herself. Her arm ached from tugging and leading Sunset who faced some of the thickets reluctantly, and there was now a persistent nagging pain in her right thigh where she had slipped and twisted her leg.

The sun was tree-top low in the sky when Aesc, who had disappeared ahead, came back and lay down on the track before her, panting, her long tongue lolling over the side of her jaws. She waved the dog on, but Aesc refused to move.

Puzzled Tia looked ahead along the narrow trail they were following. The trees had begun to thin a little. Twenty or thirty paces ahead the track disappeared over a thicket-crested outcrop of stony ground. Looking up Tia realized that the tall plume of smoke which now and again she had glimpsed in her march was very close. As her eyes came back from the smoke Lerg, who had never gone more than a couple of paces ahead of her so far, slowly began to walk away on his own. When he reached the bottom of the rocky rise, he stopped and sat back on his haunches.

Tia hitched Sunset's halter round a branch and walked forward. Neither Aesc nor Cuna made any move to follow her. The behaviour of the dogs puzzled her. Yet at the same time there was a strange comfort in their behaviour. She had a feeling that they knew – even Cuna – what lay ahead and, by their actions, obeyed some sure instinct. Tia moved up towards Lerg. When she was with Lerg she stopped and looked back. Aesc and Cuna lay on the ground close to Sunset who was cropping at the low leafy branches of a tree. Bran, who had shown himself only now and again during the march, dropped through the trees and settled on the ground near the dogs and began to peck at the dirt and grit of the narrow track.

Tia had an uncanny feeling that the dogs and Bran now waited on her, that in some way they were all linked in an understanding into which she could and must enter. Between them and Baradoc, she knew, there was always a silent flow of knowledge and command which linked them magically even when they were not in sight of one another. With a quick pulsing of blood and nerves, she felt suddenly that somewhere close ahead was Baradoc – and that he knew they were all here, close to him, coming to help him.

At this moment from beyond the outcrop there came a high half-groan half-scream of pain that was followed by a burst of almost demoniac, giggling laughter. Lerg's hackles stiffened and the long ridge of his back was furrowed with the slow rise of his pelt. The hound turned and he looked at Tia.

As fresh laughter and a cackling of voices came from beyond the ridge, Tia, full of fear, but refusing to let it hold her, began to move forward.

The Keeper of the Shrine

Baradoc lay on the ground on his side. A few feet behind him were the nearest trees. His hands were still tied behind him but now, too, his legs were bound at the ankles. Before him, sloping in a shallow bowl, was a clearing which rose on the far side to a crescent-shaped ridge with large rock outcrops showing through a growth of brooms, gorse, and brier tangles. At the foot of this ridge, and cut into it, was a narrow doorway framed on either side by upright slabs of stone with a thick wooden crosspiece at the top. In the centre of the clearing a large patch of ground was cultivated, the dark earth now marked with new bean growths, rows of young cabbages, a line of vines, a patch of young barley and a bed of glossy green-spiked spring onions. Beyond the garden an apple and a fig tree stood close to a low-roofed, long wooden-framed hut, the roof and sides thatched with rush bundles. At one end of the hut was a small wattle enclosure in which a cock and half a dozen hens foraged. Nearer Baradoc a small spring welled from the ground and ran in a thin rill through a marshy channel to the far slope of the forest. Between the stream and the hut a fire burned, a fire piled now with new kindling so that fresh flames leaped from it and the blazing wood crackled and spat sparks and black ash that rose in the air like a cloud of flies. Close to the fire stood Atro and Colta, each holding an arm of a tall, thin-bodied old man whose long, girdled brown robe had been stripped from the top half of his body. Standing in front of the old man was Enghus, holding the light spear. Already he had scored the man's bare chest with the spear point and now he thrust the spear head almost fully into the man's left hip. Both arms already ran with blood from previous thrusts. From a new-found fortitude or numbness from shocks already received the old man made no sound.

Baradoc watched, sickened and angry with disgust, as Colta striking the old man's face with her fist, spat at him, shouting, 'You old fool – talk!'

Enghus raised the spear to thrust again, crying, 'Yes, talk, talk, talk! Where is the treasure?'

Atro swung his free hand and sent Enghus spinning away. 'Enough, Enghus! Enough!' Then to the old man he said, 'Listen, father, be sensible and talk, and then we will leave you in peace. But if you don't we will surely kill you.' He reached out, took the old man's long dark beard in his hand and jerked his head up. 'Talk! Where is the treasure?'

Baradoc saw the slow bracing movement of the man's thin, bony shoulders as he drew breath. His dark eyes opened and he stared at Atro and his lean, weather-bitten face was stony with stubbornness. He said nothing.

Enghus lowered the spear point and held it against the old man's belly. 'Let me, Atro. Let me!'

Atro shook his head. 'No, he's had his chance. But now – you shall make him talk.' He laughed gently. 'Roast him a little. That'll start his tongue to wag.'

'Yes, yes, roast him a little . . .' Enghus dropped his spear and began to dance around, beating his hands in joy, like an excited child, chanting, 'Roast him! Toast him! That'll make his old tongue waggle!'

At this moment, long before he caught the downwind scent of the hound, Baradoc knew that Lerg was close to him. And with Lerg would be the others . . . Yes, even Tia, for he knew the dogs would never have left her so soon. He slowly turned his head and looked back at the near trees. The group around the old man were too busy with their own business to pay any attention to him now.

Enghus had taken a dry branch and was holding it in the fire, the end of it flaming in a great yellow and blue tongue. He whipped it from the fire and swung it around to kill the flame and fan the thick end into a living red coal. The moment it glowed well Enghus danced in, cackling with delight, and drew the red end slowly across the old man's chest. The old man, his body jerking violently, threw his head back and screamed, the echoes of his cry beating back from the surrounding woods, setting pigeons flighting from the far tree-tops.

Near him on the fringe of the trees Baradoc heard the shaking of a bush and a quick breathing as someone moved behind it. Slowly he turned his head. Momentarily the sunlight flashed on a scrap of fair hair. As another scream from the old man rang in his ears, Baradoc sat up so that the top half of his body would cover any approach from behind. All he wanted now was to feel the dagger thrust at the thongs of his wrists, and then to have the dagger in his free hands to slash his ankle bonds.

The old man screamed again. Baradoc watched Atro and Colta supporting the long, thin frame and Enghus dancing back to the fire to heat up the brand for a fresh assault. Anger burned in him at the wanton savagery of the three. Then he felt his left arm grasped, heard Tia's heavy breathing, and took the warm body smell of her into his nostrils. He strained at his wrists to stretch the thongs tight as, lying full length, hidden behind him, she sawed at them with her small dagger. When they came free, he said quietly, 'Stay where you are.' He took the dagger from her and brought his right hand round quickly and began to cut away at his ankle bonds.

Across the clearing Enghus stepped back from the fire, whirling his brand to make it glow. Colta was pulling at the old man's beard while Atro supported him as his legs sagged. The light spear lay on the ground, unheeded. Atro's bow was slung across his back, the quiver and broad sword hanging at his belt.

Baradoc's ankle binds came free. Dagger in hand, he began to rise swiftly. The movement caught Atro's eye. He turned full towards Baradoc, let out a loud warning cry, and began to fumble to free his bow from his back.

Through the courage Tia had forced into herself to crawl to

Baradoc raced a sudden surge of fear as she saw Atro beginning to unship his bow as Baradoc ran across the clearing. Then Tia heard the racing Baradoc shout, '*Saheer! Aie! Saheer!*'

Lerg leapt from the thicket behind her and with him went Aesc and Cuna. Before Baradoc could reach the group at the fire, Lerg was past him and leaping at Atro as the youth freed his bow. They went over in a roaring, growling mêlée of arms and legs and twisting grey body. A long shriek of pain cut through the air. Colta let go of the old man and he fell to the ground. Enghus threw his burning brand at Aesc as the dog rushed in and bit and snapped at his legs as he tried to reach his light spear. Colta raised her fish spear and ran at Baradoc, but before she could reach him Bran dropped from above in a threshing of spread wings, his talons raking at her head, his beak thrusting at her eyes. Colta screamed, dropped the spear and ran for the woods covering her face with spread hands. Enghus ran after her, away from the snapping, savage attack of Aesc and Cuna, abandoning hope of gaining his spear.

Baradoc shouted to Lerg and the dog drew back from the fallen Atro. Baradoc picked up the light spear and stood over him as Colta and Enghus disappeared in the woods. Tia ran forward and, hardly knowing she was doing it, pulled the old man away from where he had fallen so close to the fire that the hood of his gown was burning. She beat out the flames with her hands.

Baradoc stood over the fallen Atro, spear and dagger in hand. Blood was pouring from the side of the youth's neck where Lerg had taken him.

'Make one move,' said Baradoc, 'and I'll put the hound on you.' Spear poised for action, he bent down and picked up the Parthian bow and threw it behind him. Grimly, he said, 'Stand up and keep facing me.'

Holding his hand to his neck, Atro rose to his feet. Then with a slow shrug of his shoulders, he smiled and said, 'What need is there for all this? The talk of selling you as a slave was not in earnest. You should join us. Together nobody could face us.' He nodded towards the old man. 'There is treasure here. Everyone around knows it. We have only to make him speak and then share it.'

Baradoc pressed the point of the spear against Atro's breast, pressed it hard so that it reached his skin and made him wince away. 'Undo your belt and let it drop. And give me no more talk. After all I've seen – a wrong word could yet move me to kill.'

Slowly Atro brought his hands to his belt buckle. The belt fell to the ground, an arrow slipping from the quiver, the heavy sword ringing against the stones.

'Now go,' said Baradoc harshly. 'And remember this – you are marked by me and by the hound. To see you again means a killing. Go!'

Atro, tight-lipped, faced him for a moment or two and then turned and began to walk to the trees. Behind him stalked Lerg and when Atro passed into the trees Lerg still went with him.

They took the old man into his hut, stripped the gown from him, and laid him on his bed which was made of long, rough-hewn boards without over or under covering. He lay there, breathing faintly, making no move, his eyes shut.

Baradoc nodded to an earthenware jar by the door. 'Get some water. Wash his spear wounds and find some cloths to bind them. Don't touch the burns.' He went out of the hut, gathered up all the weapons and brought them back. Then, carrying only the light spear, he went towards the low crest above the hillside doorway.

Tia filled the jar with water. As she did so she noticed that Aesc and Cuna had stationed themselves on the forest edge of the clearing. Back in the hut she washed the old man's wounds and bound them as well as she could with some of the rags which Baradoc had found in the fishermen's hut. Since the rags were dirty she tore strips from her short undershift, which was reasonably clean, to go next to the wounds. When the dressings were done she made a pillow from the old man's gown, propped his head up and fed water to him from her beaker. The old man, eyes closed, drank a little and groaned sharply when her arm touched one of his burns.

Baradoc came back after a while carrying two handfuls of leaves and herbs. With a stone he began to pound some of them into a pulp on a platter and said, 'There's a hen run at the side of the hut. Get some eggs.' He said it without looking at her, pounding away at the leaves. As she went out she was glad that he was there. He knew what he had to do and acted swiftly. For the moment she existed only as someone to help. The old man was all his concern. She found four eggs in a bracken nest in a corner of the run and brought them back. She saw that Lerg had returned.

Baradoc broke them over the pulpy herb mass and stirred them into it to make a paste. When the paste was well mixed he took handfuls of it and spread it over the old man's chest burns. Although he did it gently the old man twitched and groaned at his touch.

Over his shoulder Baradoc said, 'Find something to cover him.' Except for a rough loin wrapping, the old man had been naked under his coarse woollen robe.

'There's nothing here. I'll have to fetch Sunset.'

'Then get her. There's no danger. They won't be back to face Lerg.'

Leaving the hut, there was no resentment in Tia at Baradoc's brusqueness. There was still burning in him the anger and contempt which Atro had raised. He had held back from a killing with difficulty, she guessed. His cold look, stern and rejecting, she knew would live for long in her memory. Tribesman, exslave he might be – but the moment had ennobled him with authority and power . . . the power of life or death.

As she left the clearing, Lerg rose and went with her without any sign or word from her.

When she came back with Sunset she unloaded the two panniers and freed her brown mantle from the saddle rope. In the hut she spread the mantle over the old man, covering him just short of the lowest burn on his chest.

Baradoc said, 'We must take turns to watch him. He's not in his proper mind and may try to pull the salves away.'

'How do you know about such things?'

'By not running away from my master. From his words and from his books. And much from my own kind. Although the old man burns, water will not put out his fire. It is the air which gives us life which feeds a fire. The burns must not be allowed to breathe. Did you not know this?' He looked up at her and then, unexpectedly, smiled

'There are many things I don't know. And some things I have only learnt in the last few days. It seems there is much that is missing in me.'

Baradoc stood up. 'But much that I am grateful for. You can be fearful but not lose your courage. I owe you a life already. And now I owe you my liberty. Those devils would have sold me to slavery and this time my ears would have been clipped and I would have been shackled.' He reached out, took her hand and held it between the palms of his own, pressing it firmly.

'Why do you do that?'

'As a sign. While we stay together nobody can harm you until my own power is broken.' Releasing her hand, he grinned. 'There is nothing missing in you that cannot be easily learned. And there is much in you that many will never have. You came to me here, and I am free. Because of you, too, the old man lives and will live.'

Tia shook her head. 'I came because the dogs brought me.'

'No. Without them you would have found a way. There is the mark on you. I know it and the beasts know it. They read your thoughts and know your heart. Before we reach Aquae Sulis I will teach you how to speak to them without words. Already the gift is in you. Now –' he turned to the hut door, '– let us get unpacked and settled in. It will be many, many days before we can safely leave the old man to himself.'

'Many days?'

Baradoc laughed. 'Now your face grows as long as Sunset's.

85

But 'tis far prettier. Do you think the old man will recover by tomorrow? He will be long on his couch and longer before he can work his garden and care for himself and his shrine.'

'But that means —' Tia broke off suddenly, ashamed of her own selfishness.

Baradoc said easily, 'Aquae Sulis will not run away. A little more rough living will make it seem like paradise. But if you wish you are free to go and to take Sunset with you.'

Tia's face stiffened angrily. Then putting out her hand, she said, 'This hand you took in gratitude has an itch to smack your face!'

Baradoc shrugged his shoulders. 'Good. That means you will stay. Now, let us get things to order.' He laughed, took her arm and tugged her gently towards the door, saying, 'You have forgotten to bring the fish and I have lost the duck you were going to pluck. But don't be disappointed. We will wring the neck of a hen and you can prepare that. The old man will be better for a good broth to help him heal.'

Looking back at the old man Tia said, 'He's very old. Might he not die from the burns?'

'He is old, yes. Just skin and bone. But he will not die.'

'How can you know that?'

'Because we are here. Because Atro took me in a hunter's moment of dream. Because you found your courage greater than your fear. Because the gods, yours and mine – *Aie*, and his – joined together to weave the pattern that way. Now, come and I'll show you how to twist a hen's neck.'

For the next few hours as the tree shadows lengthened across the clearing they were both busy. Baradoc killed the hen and Tia sat outside the hut and plucked it. The dogs drew back to the fire, and Sunset was tied on a long halter to one corner of the hut. Baradoc carried all their belongings inside and emptied the bundles. He made up two rough beds on the floor with cut rushes from a pile he had found behind the hut. Tia's bed was at the far end of the hut, next to the adjoining fowl run. Baradoc set his just inside the low doorway. All the arms were laid out in readiness. Holding Atro's broad belt with its sword and arrow quiver, Baradoc promised himself that the next day he would sharpen the sword and make himself familiar with the bow. It was a long time since he had used bow and arrow and he looked forward to it. The bow was an old one but strongly made and Atro had fitted it with a new drawstring. Atro and the others, Baradoc guessed, would not come back. By the time they had found new weapons their minds would be set to fresh mischief. There had been a moment when he could easily have killed Atro. He was glad now that he had held back, not only because he sensed that there was some hidden goodness in Atro which, given time, might grow to mastery in him, but also for the old shrine-keeper's sake. He would have wanted no killing, no matter the injuries done to him.

Sword in hand, standing over the old man, he looked at the wall above the bed. Hanging there was a rough tablet made of three pieces of board held in a frame. Painted crudely on it was the portrait of a beardless young man with a halo round his head. Above his head was the Christian Chi-Rho monogram. The shrine in the hillside was a Christian one, and the old man its keeper. There were many now in Britain who held to the new religion, worshipping the Nazarene and his holy father. Baradoc felt that it was the religion of slaves, no matter what its virtues. For him the gods of his people could never be replaced. Anyway, the world and the hereafter were wide and big enough for all religions. There was room enough for all the gods to live in peace. That most of the wealthy landowners and merchants of Roman and mixed Roman and British blood and their servants and workpeople had adopted the new religion meant nothing to him. The old gods were his gods and would always be so. Unholy and unlawful it was to kill for one's own gain. But if any sought to take one's life or to conquer one's country then it was simple justice to kill them. The fast dying Roman Empire had long made the new faith its own, but here in his own land there were few among the proud tribes of the far west and north who had turned from the true gods of their fathers.

He went out and began to help Tia around the fire with the cooking of their meal. They ate it in the fading light outside the hut doorway. Tia fed the old man with some broth, but he took little, most of it spilling down his chin and neck, matting his beard so that she had to wash it clean afterwards.

Coming back to Baradoc and sitting cross-legged on the grass near him, watching the hawking flight of martins across the darkening clearing, the sky paling to a faint marigold glow from the dropping sun, she said, 'Why did they treat the old man so badly?'

'Because they believed he had a great treasure hidden here.'

'Has he?'

'Who knows? He is a Christian shrine-keeper. A holy man. The country around will know him. He probably wanders about preaching. His kind are always talking of laying up treasures in heaven. Simple people get things mixed in their minds.' He took a chicken leg from his platter, chewed at it until it was near clean, and then tossed it to Cuna. He went on, 'Tomorrow I must hunt for the dogs and ourselves. There is a little store of old corn in the hut and a grinding quern. You can mill it and we can bake bread. If we are to stay here we must make a store of provisions quickly so that we won't have to go far afield each day.' He smiled at her. 'Once the old man starts to recover he will heal quickly. Although he's all skin and bone there is a strength and health in him like seasoned oak. A few weeks will see you in Aquae Sulis.'

They went to bed by the light of the small length of tallow candle which Baradoc had found in the fishermen's hut. Lying in the darkness Tia now and again heard the old man moan, and from time to time he talked to himself briefly in some language she could not understand. The dogs slept outside. Once in the night she woke to hear the far-off howl of a wolf. In the silence that followed there came the restless padding of one of the dogs circling the clearing. There was no fear in her. The hut around her seemed a fortress. Baradoc guarded the door and the dogs stood sentinel. She drifted into sleep again.

She woke to the sound of the cock crowing in the hen run.

First light came weakly through the open door. She got up and ran her hands through her hair. The old man slept, and his breathing seemed easier. Baradoc's bed was empty.

She went out and saw that only Cuna remained in the clearing. He trotted behind her as she went to the spring and washed herself. The fire she noticed had been banked with new kindling. The wood was dry and burnt low and bright with little smoke. She collected eggs from the run, filled the little cauldron with water and set it by the fire to have warm water to dress the old man's wounds. Some of the herb plasters on the man's chest had cracked and fallen away in the night. Baradoc would have to renew them and would need the eggs. She would also hard-boil some for themselves. In the hut she tidied their beds and then began to take stock of the place for the first time with real attention.

It was poorly furnished but clean. A hazel twig broom for brushing the floor stood inside the door. On a shelf rested the few simple items of the shrine-keeper's crockery and earthenware. There was also a big bronze skillet pan. In one of the earthenware jars she found three round goats' cheeses. Another robe like the one the keeper wore hung from a peg at the end of the bed, but it was much cleaner and the edges were trimmed with the white fur of winter hares. The grinding quern stood on the floor in a corner. Looking at it she was taken back to the great kitchen of her brother's villa. For a moment a pang of grief touched her, but she pushed it away. Grief would come back when she reached Aquae Sulis and there, with her uncle, it would be given its full term and they would make the obsequies. Until then she lived another life.

She stood in front of the bed and looked down at the shrine-keeper. Outside the forest was stirring with bird calls. Blackbird and thrush she could pick out but none of the others. Baradoc, she guessed, would know them all. The sunlight, strengthening, flooded through the door and lit up the painting over the bed. She had seen many such portraits and mosaics in the houses of some of the friends of her brother. The young face with the shining halo, and the Greek letters behind it, had a tranquil yet slightly sad expression. Although none of her family had adopted the new Christian faith, she had sat often through the talk of her brother with others when they had discussed religion and had been without real interest. In fact, it seemed to her now, that she had sat, or walked or idled through many times, great stretches of her life, without interest in anything except herself and her pleasures, taking to herself only the lightweight knowledge which girls of her class came by easily in their idleness and luxury. She looked at her hands with their now broken nails and the grained skin, and her mouth twisted wryly. They were fast becoming the hands of a servant . . .

The old man stirred and she saw that his eyes were open. For a moment the shadow of a smile touched his lips. With a slow movement he raised a hand. She took it gently in hers and felt his grasp tighten.

He said hoarsely, 'You are?'

'Gratia.'

'And the other?'

'Baradoc.'

'In my memory their sounds are ever joined . . . like the links of a golden chain . . .' His voice faded and his eyes closed. Tia lowered his hand and turned away.

When Baradoc came back he brought with him, slung over his shoulders, a young roe buck which Aesc had hunted downwind into the reach of Lerg who had caught and pulled it down, holding it until his master had come to kill it with a spear thrust to the heart. In his tunic front he had a store of fungi and roots which he had gathered on the way back. As he gralloched and skinned the deer, he nodded at the fungi and roots and said, 'There's little in the old man's vegetable patch yet ready for pulling. Today I will show you where to find the fungi and roots which are good to thicken broth. We must make a hanging bag for the meat we do not eat today. Even so –' he grinned, '– a few bluebottles will find a way in, but their eggs can be washed away.'

Tia made a grimace of disgust. 'You say that to turn my stomach. And so you do.'

Baradoc shook his head. 'There's much that goes into a rich man's kitchen would turn anyone's belly. But at table it is eaten with pleasure. How is the old man?'

'He sleeps. But for a moment he came back and asked our names. I have dressed his wounds, but some of the plasters have fallen away.'

'When this is done I'll make fresh salves.' Baradoc went on cutting up the carcass. He threw each dog a portion, and each dog carried its share apart and fell to eating.

So began the run of their days in the clearing. Baradoc hunted when their meat and game fell low, and Tia learned the herbs for the plasters and tended to the old man's burns and wounds. She cooked and looked after the poultry, opening their run in the morning and closing them in at night. Between them, with an old wooden hoe and a rusty mattock, they kept the weeds from the garden; and all day long and at night the dogs watched and roamed the edge of the forest. Bran, who was sociable only when he could find no food for himself, was seldom seen but never far away. Nobody now came to make offerings at the shrine or to bring small gifts to its keeper. The nearest homestead and village was some miles away. Honest people hugged their own hearths and stayed together for safety. This was not the first wave of unrest and violence which had swept across the south reaching as far west as the fringes of the countries of the Durotriges and the Belgae. Many said that it would pass and times would settle again and people would be at peace to travel the roads without fear. That was the hope of most. Something in Baradoc told him that already that hope was an addled egg no heat could hatch, but he said nothing of this to Tia who now worked hard and learned fast and who, at night, often stiff and sleep-logged, would think of Aquae Sulis and carry the thoughts into her dreams.

But it was true that she learned fast. She knew soon the herbs and roots and fungi. She knew how to broil and roast and baste meat with wild boar fat (a young sow of that year's early farrowing, run hard by the dogs, had been killed with two bow shots from Baradoc) and to mill the corn between the quern

stones and to bake the bread in the small stone oven Baradoc
built and over which the hot fire embers were scooped and piled
using flat slabs of shale for shovels. She learned to ignore the
weather, going lightly clad in the sun and meeting the rain with
indifference if her work took her into it, finding that the best
way to dry wet clothes was to go on wearing them.

Also, and this pleased her most, she began to learn how to
talk to the dogs without word or look. As Baradoc had guessed,
there was in her a little, waiting for growth, of the magic he
commanded so easily. She learned how, without seeing Cuna,
Aesc or Lerg, though they rested nearby on the forest edge, to
put one of them into her mind like a small picture. Then with a
concentration, almost like holding her breath until she would
choke, though she went on breathing easily, she would force
herself into her own mind, making a picture of herself within
herself and there give a silent word of command or direction.
Not always it worked, but as the days went by it became easier
and more often successful and she knew that with practice she
would soon always be able to reach them. But with Bran she
could do nothing, though Baradoc could. When she questioned
this he laughed and told her that Bran, named after one of his
people's gods, would only serve a woman when it suited him
and that was not often in simple day by day matters. Only
danger stirred him to chivalry.

With each day, too, the old shrine-keeper grew better, but it
was to be seven days before he could safely take to his feet. For
those first days Tia dressed his wounds, plastered the healing
burns, nursed him and helped him with his washing and toilet
as though he were a baby, often wondering to herself that she
could do this, the work of the lowest slave or infirmary servant.
But slowly she came to think it of no more account than serving his broth or changing the rushes on his bed boards. The old
man, she guessed, however, had a shame from this. Although
he was clear in his head now, he spoke little, withdrawn from
them both into some other world, as though to escape the
humiliation his body put on him. Yet each night as Tia settled
him comfortably for sleep, he would take her hand and squeeze

it gently then turn his head from her. With Baradoc, when Tia was not there, he was a little freer and made his thanks for all they had done and were doing, and told his name, saying 'Asimus is my name. Not Father or Brother, but a simple servant of our Lord Jesus Christ who sent you to me, knowing I waited for you but –' he smiled faintly, 'choosing the moment of your coming to remind me of my own weakness and pride.'

On their first day Baradoc and Tia had gone into the shrine. Beyond the rough stone and wood door with a plaited hanging rush curtain covering the entrance was a small, natural cave which ran a few yards back into the hillside. Hanging from the rock face at the end of the cave was a long wooden cross. Below it stood a table made from a wide slab of loose rock raised on two rough boulders at either end. Worn in the loose earth of the floor before this simple altar were two shallow depressions where Asimus and his visitors had knelt for prayer. On the table itself was an odd collection of gifts and tokens which had been placed there in thanksgiving: a string of blown birds' eggs, bronze and iron nails, a folded linen napkin, a small wooden model of a farm cart drawn by two yoked oxen, a little statuette of an angel made from beaten lead, some curiously shaped stones with coloured veins of quartz and minerals running through them, a bunch of dried thistle heads, an old slave whip, the worn leather thong-tails spiked with rusty iron studs, their points broken and blunted, some cheap wire bracelets and bead rings ... a dusty, odd collection but each object, Baradoc guessed, symbolizing or commemorating some accident or turning point in the lives of the givers which had brought or linked then with the worship of the Christian god. So, too, did his people lay their like tokens before the gods as gifts and the value of the gift lay not in itself but in the heart of the giver and in the all knowing mind of the god.

Tia said, 'It's cold in here.'

'True, were it not a shrine it would make a good place to hang our meat.'

Shocked, Tia said, 'You shouldn't say that.'

'Why not? 'Tis but the truth.'

'But this is a holy place.'

'Then there is room for truth here.' He smiled. 'Now – if I *were* to hang the meat here then there would be blasphemy, and that I offer to no god, mine or any other's.'

At the beginning of their second week when Tia woke one morning it was to find Baradoc already away hunting, for their store of meat had grown low. She washed herself at the spring and then went to the fire and began to warm up some broth for Asimus's breakfast. Squatting on her heels by the fire as she watched the pot, she listened to the steady sawing notes of a chiff-chaff coming from the top of a tree beyond the clearing. With help from Baradoc she was now coming to know more and more of the bird songs and calls, and through him, too, her eyes were becoming sharp and observant. The way the wind swayed the tall grasses or the hanging branches of bushes she knew as natural, but any break or change in the rhythm awoke an instant awareness in her. She could pick up the overhead passage of a squirrel or the quiet foraging of Cuna in the sedges and rising bracken growths of the shrine hillside, and sometimes the overbowed tip of briar or hogweed where some harvest mouse or wren or bluetit swung unseen at first searching for insects and grubs. Until now, it seemed to her that she had passed through life hardly aware of this ever-present stir and change of colour and shade, of animal and bird movement and the shifting cloud patterns. She had begun to have a nose for the smell of rain and even a developing sense of coming wind changes. More than that, too, the sense had grown in her of knowing when she was being watched. This had come first from Baradoc who had sometimes returned silently to stand hidden just inside the flanking forest growths to watch her work, staring unseen at her until slowly she had become aware of the feeling of eyes on her. Because of this, one day she had looked up slowly and, after a while, had made out the sharp-pointed features of an old dog fox, drawn by the smell of meat she had been cutting up for the pot, merged against the background of last year's russet bracken growth. Her ears had sharpened, too, so that at night she could tell the clumsy sound of an arrogant wild boar noisily pushing and rooting his way through the hillside tangles of the forest slopes a bowshot away, knew when a dog padded round the clearing which one it was, and when a little owl or nightjar called suddenly sensed at once from where and from how far the cry came. She was learning fast to know also the differences that marked real from imagined danger. Going to the spring early one morning she had cried in alarm for Baradoc at the sight of a snake sliding through the small pool. When he came he had picked up the snake by the neck, its long length curling like moving bronze clasps round his brown arm, and told her it was a harmless grass snake, pointing out its markings to her and, later that day, bringing her a viper he had killed and showing her the difference.

Sitting now by the fire, the broth almost ready, she was suddenly aware that she was being watched from behind. But there was no fear in her. She turned her head and saw Asimus, his brown habit drawn closely about him, standing in the hut doorway, leaning a little sideways as he supported himself on a staff.

He smiled at her, waved her down as she started to rise, and then began to walk towards her, stiffly but steadily. He came and sat down near her, upwind of the thin fire smoke.

He said, 'The smell of the broth gave strength to my legs.'

'You should have let me bring it to you.'

'No, it is time I began to fend for myself again.'

Tia filled a bowl of broth for him. He held it in his hands, blowing at it for a while to cool it, and then began to sup with an old horn spoon which Tia had found in the hut.

He said, looking at his garden which they had tended, 'The beans have grown, and the weeds are hoed ... all while I have slept and dreamed and found strength. You and the young man have been good to me at a time when there was little goodness to hope for in this land. Is he your brother or perhaps betrothed to you?'

Tia laughed. 'Neither.'

Asimus frowned a little. 'There is no tie between you?'

'Only that we are now both making our way to the west. He

goes back to his tribe and I to my uncle in Aquae Sulis.' Without emotion, for the recent past was a memory now imprisoned as surely as a fly in amber in her mind, Tia went on to tell him what had happened to her and how she and Baradoc had met. She finished, 'When we get to my uncle, he will go on to his own people. I shall never forget him and my uncle will reward him well. But there is nothing between us.'

The old man shook his head. 'You saved his life and now he guards you to your uncle. Such acts of charity put ties between people which can never be broken, neither by time nor distance. While I live there will be no day when my prayers will not include you both. Thus, you see –' he smiled gently and the dark eyes were soft in the bearded face, '– you will always be linked together by me until the good Lord closes my days.'

Made a little embarrassed and uncomfortable with this talk, Tia asked, 'Is it true that you have treasure hidden here?'

The old man finished his broth, set the bowl down and then, shaking his head at her move to help him, rose awkwardly to his feet with the help of his staff. He looked down at her, one hand gently teasing his beard, and there was a slow twinkle in his eyes.

'You are a practical, forthright young woman. That is there for all to see. So, to talk in riddles to you would make you perhaps impatient. Each day that God gives us – or that your gods give you – life and freedom to worship them is a treasure. Is that not enough?'

Tia, puzzled, shrugged her shoulders. 'That kind of talk is beyond me. You know what I mean by treasure. The kind those people would have wanted to find. Silver, gold and jewels.'

Asimus laughed quietly. 'Practical and frank. Then so will I be because a dream and a prophecy have come true. Yes, I have treasure here, treasure you could sell in the market place for a few gold coins. But their weight set in the scales against it would be nothing. You would need the whole weight of the world against it to make the beam tilt. But when you go, you and your friend shall take the treasure with you.'

Tia, feeling he was teasing her, grinned and shrugging her

shoulders said, 'Well, I just hope it won't be too heavy. We have to travel light.'

Asimus shook his head at her, giving her up, and then turned and began to make his way slowly towards the shrine.

Tia filled a bowl of broth for herself and sitting cross-legged watched the old man go into the shrine. Priests and holy men were all the same, she thought. Riddles and mysteries – particularly when they were faced with awkward, straightforward questions. She tipped the bowl to her mouth to drink and, over its edge, saw Bran sitting on the top of the hut slowly preening his flight feathers. It would be good, she thought, to be a bird, to be able to spread wings and fly to Aquae Sulis, to hot baths and fine table ware, to soft sheets and clean, comfortable woman's clothes . . .

The Centurion's Cup

From that day Asimus made an ever-quickening return to health
and he would take no more personal service from either Tia or
Baradoc. He gathered and pounded his own herbs and worts to
make into salves for his burns and he kept his half-healed body
wounds clean but refused all dressing for them, preferring to sit
in the clearing by the fire letting the air and the sun work on
them. If Tia had not fought him over it he would have insisted
on helping with the preparation of food and cooking. But she
stoutly scolded him away from the fire and such tasks and he
would retreat chuckling gently to himself. At night, depending
on the weather, they would sit outside the hut or just within
the door to catch the last of the light and talk.

It was, at first, unmarked by Baradoc or Tia that the talk was
little about himself, but always brought around to one or other
of them talking about the past, of their homes and experiences
and – more often from Baradoc than Tia – the way their minds
worked about the state of the country, of the ills it suffered and
the remedies they could suggest for shaping the new times coming into an acceptable and civilized form. He was never without
questions to Baradoc about his old master and the things he had
taught him. His face would be masked with a grave, yet almost
amused cast when Baradoc (who never lacked words or wild
flights of fancy) turned towards the east sometimes in his excitement, shaking his clenched fist as though he held a sword in
it and with one swing could annihilate the threat from the
Saxons who sought to swallow up the whole land, and bursting
with emotion cried, '*Aie!* their time will come!' and Tia noticed
that he showed no shadow of his own thought, no sign of
whether he agreed or disagreed with Baradoc.

It was this that one evening made her say quietly in a pause, as Baradoc stopped talking, 'Master Asimus, these last nights you have turned us both inside out as though we were chests stuffed with trifles and odds and ends of our lives and opinions that serve only to brighten your eye like a magpie's or to raise a smile under your whiskers as though you were a cat who had been at the cream. Is your own chest empty?'

Baradoc said sharply, 'Tia. That is no way to speak to a holy man.'

'No, no,' said Asimus, 'she is not to be scolded. First, because I am not a holy man. Only an indifferent servant of our Lord, Jesus Christ. Also, too, it is true that I am like a magpie or a well-fed cat, for the brightness and richness of your minds give me joy ... aye, and hope. Though none of these can escape the shadow this world casts on them from time to time. So –' he smiled at Tia, '– you would know what I have to show? And so you shall and so you should. I was born in Antioch. My father was a steward in the household of a general officer in the Imperial Army. Later, I worked in the household too and became the personal servant of a young son of the house. He was called John and was ten years younger than myself. He wanted none of the Army and studied law and I went with him when he left his father's house. But when he was little over thirty he turned from the law, became a Christian and joined the clergy in Antioch. I became a Christian, too. We had bad times and good times, and with the passing of the years my master became archbishop of Constantinople and people named him John Chrysostom, John of the Golden Mouth. And his mouth was golden always with words in defence of the needy and in condemnation of the intrigues in his own church. Aye ... he had a mouth with a tongue of gold when he praised and preached the teachings of our Lord, and a tongue like the whip of a fiery lash when he faced wickedness. I will not empty the whole of my chest for it would take too long. My master, the good John, died well over twenty years ago at a place you will never have heard of, near the river Irmak in Asia Minor, and I was with him at his death, which was a lonely one.'

'Then how did you come to this country?' asked Tia.

'Because of a gift he gave me the day before he died, and because of a dream he sent me after his death.'

'If all this happened over twenty years ago you must be very –' Tia broke off suddenly embarrassed at her own impetuousness.

Asimus smiled. 'There is no shame in age. I have seen far more than eighty summers. My only sadness is that I did not come earlier to the service of the Lord.'

Baradoc said, 'I believe in dreams. But the understanding of them is often difficult.'

Tia said, 'Bother the dream. Tell us about the gift first.'

'Tia!' Baradoc frowned at her.

Asimus smiled. 'There is no call to scold her. She is the practical one. Things must be clear and in the right order in her mind. It is no scolding fault. I will tell you about the gift when I give it to you, and then of the dream – but neither until the day you leave for Aquae Sulis for that too was part of the dream and –'

At this moment Baradoc jumped to his feet. Turning his head towards the forest, he said sharply, 'Listen!'

For a moment or two the three of them were silent, listening. The fire burned low like a small red eye. The feet of the trees around the clearing were lost in black shadow, and beyond the fire the three dogs were alert, facing away from the hut, watching the forest. Through the stillness of the evening came the sound of a low, long sighing throat rumble from Lerg and then Cuna whined sharply once. Then suddenly from beyond the stony, bush-clothed rise that held the shrine came a sharp, racking burst of deep roaring. There was a silence for a while, and then the spasm of roaring broke through the night again and this time it was much closer.

Baradoc turned to Asimus and Tia and said quietly, 'Get inside the hut.' He reached down and pulled Tia up and then helped Asimus to his feet.

As they moved to the hut Tia said, 'What is it?'

Asimus put his hand on Tia's arm and led her to the door

saying, 'There is a time for questions – but it is not now.' Then he turned and said to Baradoc, 'I have heard the sound before – twice. The only thing you can use is a bow. A spear would –'

Baradoc broke in impatiently, 'I know. Now, into the hut.'

He went in with them and took up his bow and strapped on the belt with its quiver of arrows and went back into the clearing, closing the rough door behind him, though the door, he knew, would hold no protection against the attack to come. That had to be met and held before the bear could move across the clearing to it. The racking, angry roar split the still night again and the dark wall of trees sent back its thunder in searing, pain-filled echoes. Only once before, while hunting with his old master, had Baradoc ever heard the sound but the memory lived with him and he knew that the beast which was coming their way moved now in a frenzy of pain and hatred for all of the kind who had lodged that pain with it. Somewhere in the forest recently, he guessed, a party of hunters, eager for meat, for the rich bear fat and the warm skin which would ward off winter cold, had attacked one of the last few of the great brown bears that roamed the southlands. Avoided and left to themselves they were no threat to human life, content to live on honey from wild bees' nests, on leaves and forest fruits and grubs and insects. But attacked and not killed, escaping with broken spears and arrows in its body, such an animal turned killer, savaging with blind anger and pain-goaded fury anything that crossed its path, following the scent of homestead fire, of any human or animal body that came downwind, seeking only a berserk killing to assuage its own agony.

Baradoc went to the fire and stood with it between him and the rocky rise. He called the dogs to him. Only in desperation would he send them in against the bear, and then only to harry and not to attack for not even Lerg could stand against such an animal. He slipped two of the short arrows from the quiver, held one in his mouth and fitted the other to his bow. When the bear came over the rock rise, following upwind the smoke and human scent, it would be outlined clear against the sky. The bear would see him and come straight for him . . . and he knew that he would have to wait until it reached the foot of the rise before he loosed the first arrow at the farthest killing range.

Behind him Cuna whined gently and from the corner of his eye he saw Lerg stretch his great jaws in a slow, wide defiant gape and he knew that while fear ran in him, drying his mouth and lips, there was no fear in Lerg. One silent signal would send the hound in.

The bear roared and as the sound beat into the air, the animal appeared as though by magic on the crest of the rise. It stood for a moment on all fours, its great head weaving and swinging. Then it rose on its hind legs, raised its head to the sky and roared its anguish and fury once more. It stood almost twice as high as Baradoc and against the long line of its belly he saw the heavy milk-full dugs . . a she-bear, her cubs now killed to swell her fury . . . and from the right side of her thick, pelted neck stuck out the splintered shaft of a great spear, and another broken spear shaft showed in her left flank, the blood from the wound thickly matting her fur.

The animal, seeing Baradoc and the dogs, dropped to all fours, roared, and began to lumber down the slope. As it did so Baradoc saw that an unbroken spear shaft stood upright in its back. He raised the bow and drew it, sighting along the arrow, knowing exactly where it must lodge, through the long fur a hand's span in from the top of the left foreleg to smash through bone and sinew and find its heart. To shoot at its head would have been to shoot at a rock. As he covered the lumbering downhill approach of the bear the pony tethered to the back of the hut whinnied and neighed suddenly with fear and then Baradoc heard the thud of her hooves as she reared and bucked in panic. At the foot of the rise the she-bear, hearing Sunset, stopped and swung her great head towards the sound. For a moment the beast's left shoulder was wide open to Baradoc.

He let the arrow fly, heard its hornet flight across the clearing and saw it bury itself deep in the bear's shoulder. The animal roared with pain, rose full height and, its jaws flecked with white foam, the red mouth gaping, the great teeth flashing ivory dull in the lowering sunlight, came on in a lumbering run towards Baradoc. And Baradoc stood his ground, for there was only death in flight; and standing his ground he cursed himself that he had not practised more with the bow at close range. It pulled to the left but the nearer the target the less it pulled. All this swept through his mind as he stood, marking the spot which the bear must reach before he fired again; and, as he held the tensed bow, he prayed to the gods that they would put virtue and cunning into his hands and eyes to humour and direct the arrow in a true flight to the small target inside the left shoulder.

When the bear was two spear-lengths from the fire, Baradoc loosed the second arrow, saw it find its mark, heard the heavy sound of its strike as the short length of shaft bore into the beast's body until the flight feathers were only a finger length from the rough pelt. The bear roared, dropped to all fours, and still came on. It charged across the small patch of garden and through the low burning fire, scattering ashes, red embers and hearth stones, and Baradoc, as he fitted another arrow, knew that the gods had deserted him, for there was no time to draw and fire.

At this moment Cuna barked sharply and ran in at the bear. He ran from the side, jumped for the furred throat of the animal, and got a grip on the side of its neck. The bear, pausing in its forward movement, rose to its hind feet and with one sweep of a forepaw brushed Cuna from its neck like a fly. Cuna flew through the air, yelping high, and landed in the soggy ground around the pool. Then, as the bear still came on and the signal was moving from Baradoc to send Lerg in, the great beast swayed sideways, halted, roared to set wild echoes ringing around the clearing, and then dropped to all fours and collapsed on its side on the ground at his feet.

Baradoc stood unmoving. From the poolside Cuna barked sharply and then came limping towards Baradoc. Lerg went forward slowly and his great muzzle dropped to the bear's head. He stood, hackles risen, and then turned away. Baradoc knew that the bear was dead, the second arrow had done its work. Then, feeling Cuna rubbing against his leg, he bent and picked him up, fondled him, and then felt his limping leg and found that no bones were broken. Silently he thanked Cuna because but for the pause the bear had made to brush Cuna away he might have been crushed and mauled beneath the bear in its dying seconds.

He went towards the hut and Tia and Asimus came out to him. Tia ran to him and for a moment held his arm, anxiety still high in her.

'You are all right?'

Baradoc nodded. 'But we have lost Sunset. The smell of the bear made her panic and she broke loose. It is growing too dark now to go after her. If she doesn't come back I'll search for her tomorrow.'

Asimus, looking at the bear, said, 'God give you good days for your courage.'

Baradoc said, 'Those who hunt should always kill. To leave a beast alive and full of broken spears would mark the name of any of my tribe with shame. A man should fetch fresh spears, take the trail and finish the killing. But now the bear is dead it is your gain, father. I will skin and butcher it and Tia can smoke the meat and fill your jars with bear's grease, and the skin you can use for a bed cover on winter nights. So do the gods, out of their wisdom, arrange bad and good into their own patterns.'

Suddenly Tia said woefully, 'Without Sunset I shall have to go afoot to Aquae Sulis. I give no thanks to the gods for that!'

Baradoc and Asimus, seeing the half angry, half rueful look on her face, eyed one another and then burst out laughing.

Asimus, chuckling, said, 'Maybe your gods, seeing into the future, have their reasons.'

And Baradoc said, 'Sunset did not break the tethering rope. The knot was pulled free from the hut post. Who was it that tied the knot?' He looked at Tia.

Sunset did not return and the next day Baradoc went with Aesc in search of her. He found her in a small valley under the craggy face of a cliff that blocked its end, but before he saw her he knew that she was dead. When he was half a bowshot from the foot of the crag with Aesc well ahead of him a cloud of carrion birds rose into the air. For a while the valley was full of calling and wheeling birds, the wide ranging, keen-eyed scavengers who came to pick clean the killings of man, wolf and fox, the air patterned with the spiralling sweeps of kite, buzzard, white-tailed eagles and a ragged black swarming of crows and ravens. Standing over the fly-swarming carcass Baradoc could guess that a hunting wolf – for the packs were broken now for cub-raising – or a rogue band of dogs had driven her up the valley to make their kill under the crag. He left the halter rope length on her and when he returned to the clearing he told Asimus and Tia that he had found no trace of her. The lie was guessed at by Asimus but he knew that it was told for Tia's benefit. That Baradoc should have this consideration for the young girl pleased him and heartened the faith he had in the dream he had dreamt so many years ago, lying under the cold winter stars by the river Irmak, waking with the sound of his beloved master's voice still alive in his memory though his master lay dead in the small riverside chapel outside which he, in keeping vigil, had slept.

A few days before Tia and Baradoc left Asimus two young men from the nearby village came to the clearing to have news of the holy man to take back to the village. They brought with them bread and a milch goat which had long been promised to Asimus, and brought also the news that the country roundabout was quiet. For days there had been no sign of sea-raiders and the rebellious town and country bands had moved away along the coast towards Clausentium and Portus Adurni in the hope of stirring up more of their kind there to a new rage of plunder and destruction against the masters and merchants and estate holders. It was this news that made Baradoc decide that, when he and Tia left and headed north-west beyond Venta and to the more open country that ran from Sorviodunum almost to Aquae Sulis, they would travel by day. When the two saw the great bear skin with the head still on it, pegged out on an upright frame of poles, the inside of the skin already three-quarter scraped clean by Baradoc and Tia, their jaws dropped.

After they had gone, Asimus, who had sat by as Baradoc had told the story of its killing, said, 'Now the story will grow in their minds with every step they take towards home. So begins the rise of a legend. Baradoc and the bear. In years to come in Venta and Noviomagus ... aye, and Calleva, there will be a drinking house or hostel called the Bear of Baradoc. Some too will come here to see the skin on my bed and to hear the story. And when they have heard it –' he smiled gently, '–maybe some will stay to hear the story of Jesus, the holy one, who died on the cross for the sins of men and the salvation of their souls.'

Tia, running her fingers through the hair on the nape of Cuna's neck as she sat by the fire said, 'Here is the real hero, little Cuna. The drinking shops should carry his name too. I take no praise from Baradoc, but Cuna should have his share.'

Baradoc grinned and said, 'Give him no praise. It will turn his head. He is so foolish still that he thinks he is a Lerg. But when I tell the story to my people he shall have more than his full due.'

'You see that you do.'

Looking down at her, her short golden hair stirring in the breeze, her blue eyes alight with the pleasure she took in teasing him, the glow of the lowering sun touching her cheeks with the soft blush of a blooming peach, Baradoc said without thought, 'If you doubt that I will – then journey west with me and do the telling yourself.'

Tia rocked on her heels with sudden laughter. 'The gods save me from anything like that! No power on earth will get me further west than Aquae Sulis!'

Baradoc laughed, and Asimus, smiling as he turned away to go to his shrine to make his evening prayers, thought that there were many gods, hers and Baradoc's, and his own. And had not the Son of his own said that in his father's house were many mansions? Perhaps there they all met together from time to time to sort and settle the destinies of mankind.

On their last evening with Asimus, after they had eaten, Baradoc and Tia were sitting by the low fire when the old man came to them from the shrine where he had been saying his evening prayers. In his hands he carried a well-worn doeskin bag gathered at the mouth with a draw-string. He sat down with them and put the bag on the ground at his feet. Then, quietly and without any emotion, he began to speak to them.

'In this country, as you know, there are many people who are Christians. And in the old Empire which is slowly dying there are many many more. Neither of you are Christians. And both of you, as I have learned while you have been here, know little of the martyrdom of the Lord Jesus Christ who was crucified at Golgotha. Before he died a centurion of the crucifixion guard dipped a sponge into a cup of vinegar and sprinkling it upon a spray of the hyssop plant put it to His mouth before He died. And when He was dead, but to be sure of His death, the same centurion thrust a spear into His side and the life blood ran from Him. The blood ran down His body and some of it dripped into the vinegar cup which had been put at the foot of the cross. All this happened long over four hundred years ago and the story changes and changes in the mouths of men as they retell it, but the real truth never departs from it. It is said that as He hung on the cross two black birds, common in the country and around its shores, perched on the cross and their feet were covered with the blood from His pierced hands. When they tried to preen the blood from their feet with their beaks then they too were covered and the bloodstains have stayed with all their kind since. There are many such birds all around the eastern Mediterranean.' He reached forward and pulled back the opening of Baradoc's rough shirt and exposed the tribal tattoo on his skin. 'You are marked with such a bird.'

'It is our tribal bird,' said Baradoc; 'and it is the bird of our sea cliffs. We call them choughs, but there is a secret tribal name which I cannot speak to you. It means the red crow of enduring. To kill one is punished by death, for as long as the choughs live so will our people.'

Tia said, 'What is in the bag, father?'

Asimus picked up the doeskin bag. 'It is the gift I have promised you. It is the little cup or chalice which stood at the foot

of the cross holding the vinegar. It is made of silver, now old
and battered, and it has been lost and found many times, and
by some is still much sought after. The good John Chrysostom
gave it to me on his death bed. It is said that warmed in the
hands of a man or woman who is marked for great and noble
duties, someone whose name will live forever, to be praised by
all true and just people, the inside of the chalice, though now
unmarked, will slowly begin to glow with the crimson stains of
our Lord's blood.'

'Have you seen that happen?' asked Baradoc.

'No. Nor have I tried it myself for I know my own worth. But
it is my gift to you both, for that was the command I received
from the good John in my dream.'

'You mean you dreamt about us ... all those years ago?' Tia's
brows furrowed with a frown.

'So it would seem.' Asimus smiled, knowing her scepticism.
'My master's voice said that I would be in a wild place, in a
country far to the north and in a moment of great peril to
myself there would come two people to save me. One would
be a youth bearing the sign of the red crow and the other
would be a fair-haired maiden dressed as a youth who wore as a
fastener on her torn tunic a silver brooch bearing a design of
clasped hands.'

'You really dreamt that?' asked Tia. 'Before we were born?'

'If the good father says he did then he did,' said Baradoc
sharply. 'Why should not the gods and the spirits of the departed send such dreams? How else speak to us and be sure
that the memory of their words lasts long and true?'

'But,' insisted Tia, 'what's the good of giving it to both of us?
We part at Aquae Sulis. To whom does it belong then?'

Asimus smiled and shrugged his shoulders and then handed the
doeskin bag to her. 'I do not know. You will find some way to
settle that. I obey only the dream, and now tell you the last
words of my master. The gift being made the bag must not be
opened before me, and the dream being told must not be told
again until one comes to hold it and the inside glows crimson
with the ghost of the Saviour's blood.'

'Does that mean it won't glow for either of us?' asked Baradoc.

Tia laughed. 'Poor Baradoc – did you want to be marked for great and noble duties, your name to be praised for ever?'

Before Baradoc could speak, Asimus said with a smile, 'She teases you, Baradoc. That you must bear, for that is the duty and nature of women.'

Baradoc said stiffly, 'For the work I have to do I need no magic chalice. One needs only –'

'Spare us!' cried Tia. 'Father, by now you should know that he goes back to his tribe to be an important man, to do great things. And so I hope it will be – but I wish he wouldn't talk about it so much.'

Baradoc stood up. He was getting used to Tia's flattening remarks now, and could see, too, that they were often deserved. Though what could a man do if that were his nature and destiny? Then, with a warning look to Tia not to interrupt, he said to Asimus, 'Father, we thank you for your gift and for your words. How the gift will be settled between us at Aquae Sulis I do not know. The gods will decide. But this I say for both of us, will be cherished and protected until the right hands come to warm it to crimson life again.'

And Tia watching and listening to him thought, the certainty strong in her, that one day he would lead his tribe, the dignity and strength and courage now in him would grow ... and perhaps, now that so much of the old life was falling apart, that was a good thing. The power and protection of her own people who had taken and civilized this country over four hundred years ago was dying, almost dead. Only Baradoc and his kind were left now to gather their forces in the west and north and then to turn eastwards to meet the waves of savagery and conquest reaching farther and farther across the country. She suddenly shivered against the cold night air ... Aquae Sulis at the moment would be safe. But for how long?

The morning of their departure from the clearing a soft drizzle was falling, the slow swathes of fine rain swaying before a mild southerly breeze. From his hut Asimus watched them go, taking the narrow path around the northern edge of the rocky bluff and soon disappearing into the massed trees of the far reaching forest. Both of them carried heavy bundles over their shoulders, the heavy sword thumping at Baradoc's side, his bow tied on top of his bundle and in his hand the heavy fish spear. Tia carried the light spear and the cowl of her mantle was hooded over her fair hair against the rain. Asimus smiled to himself as he watched her ungainly walk. The soles of her light sandals had worn and Baradoc had repaired them with pieces of hide, stitched on with sinews taken from the dead bear. Cuna stayed at her heels, the two other dogs went ahead and, for a fleeting moment, Asimus saw Bran the raven, with the southerly breeze under his tail, swing high into the rain and disappear over the far crest of the trees.

Asimus turned away and went into his shrine to pray for them and for a safe journey to Aquae Sulis. As he knelt to the ground and bowed his head he saw at once that there was a new offering on the stone table. It was the arrow which had killed the bear, the head and part of the shaft brown with dried blood. Tied in a small bow just above the feather flights was a piece of bright braiding which he knew Tia must have cut from the loose end of the belt that she wore about the waist of her tunic. He closed his eyes and began to pray.

The soft drizzle lasted until nightfall. Tia and Baradoc marched through it and their clothes and bundles grew heavier with the weight of water soaking into them with each hour that passed. A quiet misery took Tia as she plodded along. But it was a misery she could carry with the same fortitude as she carried her bundle because with each step she told herself that she came nearer to her uncle. But marching was at first awkward because she had not become used to the weight of her new-soled sandals. Now and again she would trip and sometimes curse aloud only to hear Baradoc give a soft chuckle from up ahead. At midday they ate cold meat and hard corn cake, washed down with barley mead that Baradoc carried in a small leather skin slung at his belt – a present from one of the young men who had visited the clearing.

Through the afternoon the country began to change a little. At times the forest broke away into bare heathland over the high tops and the path was overhung with tall bracken growths and drooping new-flowered switches of broom. Here and there were patches of long-stemmed foxgloves, the lower buds on their towering stalks already in bloom. Once or twice Tia heard a cuckoo call and she remembered, but held all feeling down, how often she had stood on the terrace of her brother's house and heard the same call from the hazel copses that lined the near fields, and how from those same hazels – where she had so often gathered the filberts in autumn – she had heard at night the liquid notes of the nightingales. All that seemed now a lifetime ago.

Late in the afternoon they came to a main road. It was banked up on a small causeway. As they came up on to the road Baradoc stopped and Tia halted behind him. A bowshot to the left a man and woman stood on the high agger crown of the road. In one arm the woman carried a child wrapped in a blanket and with her free hand held the halter of a small pony. Below the shoulder of the road, in the broad scoop ditch from which the material for the road had originally been taken, was a small two-wheeled cart lying on its side. Thinly through the drizzle came the cry of the child which the woman held.

Baradoc said, 'Stay here.'

Tia dropped her bundle and sat on it, and watched Baradoc move down the worn surface of the road. It was, she knew, for she had seen many in her life, one of the old military roads. But it was many years since anyone had bothered to repair it. With Baradoc went Lerg. Aesc and Cuna sat at her feet and she fondled the stiff wet fur of Cuna's nape. She watched Baradoc go up to the couple and begin to talk to them. After a while he turned and beckoned to her. Tia plodded down the road, splashing through the puddles in its broken surface. No legions, she thought ruefully, would ever swing down this road again, the eagles carried high, the studded shoes of the legionaries thudding out their heavy rhythm.

The woman was young, wrapped in a russet-coloured gown, its skirt edges torn and muddy. Rain shone on her long dark hair and her face was drawn and thin and she held the child to her right breast suckling it. The man was much older with a rough skin surcoat belted over a green tunic, his legs and feet bare. In the belt about his surcoat was thrust a small axe. He held his left forearm with his large dirt and work engrained right hand, his face twisted with pain. But as Tia came up and Baradoc said something to him in his own language the man laughed briefly and there was a flash of pleasure in his dark eyes.

Baradoc said to Tia, 'They are from Calleva on their way to Durnovaria. He is a fuller but there is no work for him in Calleva and he goes back to his people with his wife and child.'

'What happened?'

'He slept as he drove and the cart went off the road. His left arm is broken. Even with his wife he can't one-handed get the cart back on the road. They are good people – but maybe a little stupid to take the risk of travelling the old road.' He smiled. 'It is all right. They do not speak your language.'

Tia said, 'You and I can get the cart back, can't we?'

'Easily.'

They went down into the ditch and cleared the cart of the few goods still in it and then between them they righted it in the ditch. With Tia pushing from behind and Baradoc setting himself against the cross bar of the yoke pole which was designed for two horses or oxen, they ran it up onto the road. While they did all this the man and woman stood on the road and watched them as though they were rooted to the ground by some numbness of spirit which froze their bodies.

As Baradoc took the pony and yoked it to one side of the pole, he said, 'I think they both still live in a nightmare. They say Calleva has been half burned. They fled at night. They have a son of six but lost him before they left. If they ever reach Durnovaria it will be only at the gods' wish.' He patted the lean flank of the pony and then dropped down into the ditch and began to hand up the couple's belongings to Tia who put them in the cart. As she did this Tia, eyeing the two who watched them, suddenly felt angry with them for their helplessness. She felt like shouting at them to wake and stir themselves from their apathy ... but then the feeling went. She saw a town burning, flames arching over the night sky, people screaming and shouting, panic reaching through the streets and houses and, somewhere, a small boy lost and frightened, crying for his parents. And she remembered her own panic, numbness and helplessness as Tulio and his wife had done everything for her, sending her blindly off into the night from her brother's burning villa.

Before the two drove off Baradoc made a rough arm sling from a strip of cloth for the man. He made a remark in his own tongue and the man smiled and laughed again and now Tia realized that it was truly the laugh of the simple-minded. The man said something and then the woman laughed.

As they drove away Tia asked, 'Why do they laugh?'

Baradoc shrugged his shoulders. 'Because they have gone beyond tears and weeping.'

'Was his arm truly broken?'

'It felt like it. But it will heal with time and Nodons' help.'

'Nodons'?'

'Yes, Nodons'. He is our god of healing, the god with the silver hand.'

'Did they say who burnt Calleva? Oh ... it was such a nice place.'

'They don't know – but not the Saxons. There are plenty of loose-footed tribal bands in the country who would be greedy to loot such a town simply out of old hates against your people and the legions that made it. I think maybe they could have been people from Cymru, from beyond the Sabrina river ... kinsmen of my own people who would do better to keep their spears and swords sharp for the real enemy. One day –'

'Oh, no.' Tia laughed. 'Not that again, Baradoc. This is no day to stand in the rain dreaming and speech-making.'

For a moment Baradoc frowned, then he smiled and said, 'You're right. Let's content ourselves with the day that is.'

As they left the road, however, he was thinking to himself that one day these old roads would serve again for the marching of armies, but for armies from the west and the north. The men who had built them had long gone, but they were good men, true soldiers who knew discipline and purpose. Men with such qualities were needed again, but next time they would carry no imperial eagles, they would come under the banner of Badb, the goddess of war, and with the blessing of the great father Dis.

They slept that night in a charcoal burner's open-fronted lean-to. It had been built between two ash trees facing a small dell in which were the remains of the old slow fires which had not been used for months. Weeds and grasses grew now over the litter of charcoal shards and stick ends. It still drizzled and the rain dripped through the broken bracken-and-twig thatched roof. It was too wet to try and make a fire. They ate cheese and brittle bread, fed some of their meat to the dogs and then lay down on the hard-packed floor making themselves as comfortable as they could on their bundle covers and piling all the spare clothes they had over themselves. In a very few minutes Baradoc was asleep, but Tia, the dampness of her clothes and coverings reaching right through to her skin, twisted and turned for a long time before she drifted off. She woke some time during the night and felt, before true consciousness came back to her, that she must have fallen asleep in her brother's warm room while bathing. Her body was damp and hot and, for a moment, she felt too that someone had bound her arms and legs. Then she realized that to her left Lerg and Cuna had stretched close to her, and on the other side Baradoc and Aesc had moved up against her. She was being baked with the press of bodies. She lay for a while debating whether to struggle free. It rained still, and the roof drips fell monotonously through the darkness. If she moved away there would be no escape from the wet that reached her body and she would grow cold. It was better to stay warm. Before sleep took her again, she smiled to herself.

The whole mass of dogs and humans must be steaming in the dark like a mass of dirty clothes in a washing cauldron. She turned over to give herself a little more room and Lerg grumbled in his half-sleep and, his back to her, Baradoc muttered something in his sleep. Tia drifted into sleep herself.

When she next woke it was daylight. The rain had gone and a pale sun showed now and then through a drift of high clouds. She sat up and rubbed her eyes with her hands to clear the last of sleep from her, then yawned and stretched her arms. Her body was wet and stiff and she shivered a little against the freshness of the morning. Looking round she saw that Baradoc and Lerg had gone. Aesc sat outside the lean-to and Cuna slept at her side. In the dell there was a sudden yellow and green flash as a woodpecker flighted across it. A blackbird called from the trees and a yellow butterfly with brown tips to its wings went erratically across the grasses like the moving reflection from a broken mirror. The bright movement made Tia groan to herself as she thought suddenly of mirrors and combs, of warm scented baths, of her body's stiffness being massaged away by the skilful hands of her maid . . . of comfort, cleanliness and clean dry clothes. Let Jupiter, she thought, throw his bolts and strike every Saxon in the land dead. She said it so fiercely and loudly that Cuna woke with a start and was immediately on his short feet, pugnaciously prancing to the front of the lean-to and barking his head off. The dog's reaction was so sudden that Tia laughed and Cuna, giving her a puzzled look, came to her and she fondled his ears.

At this moment Baradoc moved into the clearing with Lerg. He came over and squatted before her. In his hands he held a rough platter made of large dock leaves on which was a large piece of honeycomb.

He said, 'Honey for breakfast.'

Tia looked at the crushed mass of comb-wax and honey and then said, 'Look at the grubs in it. I couldn't eat that!'

'You don't have to eat the grubs. Take them out.' He picked out some grubs from the honey and then crooked his finger into it and sucked it.

Tia, after a moment's hesitation, did the same. The honey tasted delicious. Then, grinning, she said, 'You look like a Nubian. Your face is covered in charcoal dust.'

'What do you expect if you sleep in a charcoal burner's shed? Your face is the same. But we'll have to stay dirty. There's no water around here. Later in the day we'll find a place to wash and clean ourselves.' He looked up at the sky. 'The clouds will soon lift and the sun will dry all our stuff.'

Tia, taking more honey, suddenly greedy for its sweetness, said, 'How did you find it?'

'I followed a honey bee. The nest was in a hollow trunk of an old willow.'

'But didn't you get stung?'

'Why should I? I told the bees that we were hungry and that the goddess Coventina would bless them.'

'So, they didn't sting you?'

'No.'

'Then what are those red lumps on the side of your face?'

'Ah, those. Well, those came from a few hasty bees who attacked me before I mentioned Coventina.'

'And who is Coventina?'

'The goddess of wells, lakes and springs and of all things that fly but have no feathers.'

Seeing the humorous twist to his mouth, Tia said, 'Son of a chief Baradoc your words are as crooked as the finger you dip into the honey. But if you are so close to this goddess then ask her to lead us to water soon. I'm as grimy as a bath-house stoker.'

Baradoc shrugged his shoulders and said nothing, but the smile on her face and the way she tipped her head at him and the light in her blue eyes reminded him of a girl he had known in Durobrivae ... the handmaid of a visitor to his old master, a girl who had brought a lump to his throat and a bumping in his heart every time he had looked at her, and a girl, sadly, who had taken no notice of him at all.

The Circle of the Gods

Midway through the morning they left the forest and moved into a country of heath and smooth downland, some of whose slopes were cut with the long rectangles of fields and cultivation. Some of the fields were being worked and from the hollows of shallow valleys there rose here and there the smoke from the hearths of homesteads and villages. But although the land seemed at peace here Baradoc kept always to the high ground. Behind the face of peace there was no telling what might be hidden. Even honest folk could give a hasty, hostile greeting to strangers. To pass through or near such places these days travellers had to stand and call from a distance, to show themselves and then wait while the men gathered and came to question them. There were many that travelled these days who carried a hunting horn to blow when they came down the road to a settlement or moved out from a forest fringe above a valley farm or village and, the horn sounded, stood and waited to know whether their way would be barred or opened.

Topping the smooth crest of a down they saw the land falling away below them to a river valley. Alders and willows fringed the river and the grass grew long and lush in a ribbon of pastures along its banks, and nowhere was there sign of human beings or their work.

The rain had stopped now and from the clearing sky the sun's warmth beat down against their damp clothes. Seeing the river below and the sheltering groves of trees that marked it here and there, Tia thought longingly of stripping her wet garments off and plunging into the water to clean herself. Never in her life had she felt so damp, dirty and stiff. But she said nothing to Baradoc. He was the master and he would decide.

As he moved down the slope a few paces ahead of her he stopped suddenly and waited for her to catch up with him. He dropped his bundle and put a hand on her arm.

'Listen.' He stood looking up the narrowing valley.

Tia looked in the same direction. At first she could hear nothing unusual.

'I can't hear anything.'

'You will soon. Look at the birds.' Baradoc pointed up the valley. Clear to his ears was a faint rustling noise overlaid with a thin half-squeaking, half-grunting, almost complaining sound. A couple of bowshots up the valley the air was slowly filling with the movement of birds, circling and wheeling low over the ground and gradually edging their way down the valley.

Tia said, 'I can hear it now. Like a lot of tiny puppies whimpering in their sleep. And what are all those birds?'

'They follow the army of the little furred ones. Have you never seen the march of the shrews and mice and voles before?'

'No.'

'Suddenly they all move. Nobody knows why. Perhaps the seasons have been good to them, the litters have increased and then, one day, there are so many of them they begin to move, looking for more living room, more food. As they move all the hunting birds follow them, the birds of day and the birds of night. Look, see them!'

He pointed up the valley and picked out for her the birds that wheeled and hovered and stooped and dropped into the tall grasses. Tawny, brown and barn owls swept low on silent wings. Kestrels hovered and drifted along the line of the march, sparrow hawks, merlins and hobbies cut and dashed through the air, and above them hung a ragged cloud of kites, ravens, crows and peregrines, and all of them in their own fashion dropped from the air to plunder and ravage the advancing army.

And now Tia could see the vanguard of that army and hear clearly its noise as the small brown and grey bodies rustled and squeaked and chattered through the grasses. It passed them on a wide front a few paces below them and stretching down almost to the river edge; voles, mice, shrews, all leaping and scuttering forward, calling and complaining in tiny voices that melded together grew into a low, surging of sound like the slow roll of a wave over fine gravel. Like a wave itself the brown and grey mass flooded over the ground, twisting and breaking and overleaping itself, moving always onwards; and as it went it left the tall grasses broken and flattened and filled the air with a sharp, pungent smell. Following, overshadowing and harrying it, went the preying birds of the night and the day and now they struck and killed but never stopped to feed as though, already long sated, some of the madness in the little creatures below had taken them so that only the instinct to kill was left alive in them.

Together Baradoc and Tia stood on the high slope and watched the living flood pass, and with them stood the three dogs, set back on their haunches, quivering, their eyes on the moving mass. No sound came from them, except from Cuna who, his body trembling with excitement at the sight of an occasional rat that fled by, whimpered as he longed for the chase. Of Bran – the lone one – there was no sign but Tia could guess that he was with the other birds and would stay with them until he tired of the sport. As though Baradoc had read her thoughts, she heard him say, 'The gods have linked all dogs with man. But the fish that swims and the bird that flies choose always their own paths.' He nodded at the last stragglers of the passing horde, and went on, 'They move like a people driven from their own worked-out land by hunger. So move the Saxons seeking new tilling and cattle grounds – and there is none to stop them among our peoples until the day of the new leader comes ... until the day when that god-gifted man arises and turns sword in hand to face the east and its fury. May Dagda, the lord of perfect knowledge, send that day soon and Tentates, the god of war, strengthen every sword arm.'

Tia smiled to herself as he spoke. At that moment she knew that he was oblivious of her. He spoke seeing himself as the leader. She was well used now to these sudden heroic moods which carried him away. She suspected that underneath it all he enjoyed the fine passion of his own oratory. Maybe his old master, too, had smiled at times without showing it. Maybe the old man had divined something in him that even rhetoric and speechmaking could not hide. Son of a chief, Baradoc, one day to be the leader of the people of the enduring crow, one day to be ... what?

She said quietly, 'That day will come. But at the moment it is this day that has to be lived. I want to get these wet clothes off. I want to swim and clean myself in that river – and then I want to eat cooked food and not hard-tack cold meat.'

Baradoc turned and grinned at her. 'As the good Asimus said – Lady Tia, the practical one. All right, so you shall. We'll catch some fish and maybe, I can find a clutch of duck's eggs in the reeds.'

At a place where the river divided into two channels they waded across the shallows and set up camp on the small island between the streams. They took off their clothes and laid them with their other possessions in the sun to dry. In the cover of a low willow Tia wrapped her shift about her loins and knotted it at her waist and then bound a cloth about her breasts before she joined Baradoc, naked except for a loin cloth. The far channel was deep and they swam together enjoying the mild bite of the river's spring-fed water on their skin. Tia washed her face and body with a piece of cloth, shutting from her mind all thoughts of warm bath houses, and scrubbed her hands with the fine river-bed gravel and then sat in the shallows and cleaned her broken nails as well as she could with the point of her small dagger. But even when she had finished they looked, she thought ruefully, like the hands of a kitchen servant. Massaging her feet to clean them she felt the soles harder than she had ever known them, and the sore place on her toe had healed to a hard callus.

Between them they caught three of the thyme-smelling grayling and a fat trout. Baradoc made fire and they broiled the fish on a green willow branch over the fire into which Baradoc threw wild sage and water mint leaves to flavour the flesh. All that was lacking, thought Baradoc, was salt to spark the full taste of the flesh and in his mind's eye he saw the salt pans cut in the flat land at the side of the river estuary near his home, with the white crystals glistening like frost as the sun evaporated the water. There had been some seasons when the traders would give almost the weight of silver for the harvest in his tribe's salterns, and other seasons when no traders came and the salt rotted. And thinking of the traders he did not know whether to be happy or angry, for it was a Phoenician trading captain who had taken his cousin and himself from the lonely beach and had sold them as slaves in Lemanis to a dealer from Londinium. Which would he rather have had happen – to stay free with his tribe and be there now with so much of the world's knowledge closed to him still or to have known slavery, albeit he had been kindly treated at the last, and the teachings of his old master? Only the gods knew, for he had no answer. He smiled to himself, watching Tia at the fire. Without slavery he would never have met her, never be here now and never seen the slight raising of her eyebrows and the look of mocking amusement on her face when he became too self-important and full of himself ... *Aie!* she was not like any of his tribe's girls or women. Her beauty came truly from her own race. He eyed her now as she squatted by the fire dropping pale bluey-green mallard eggs into the pot to boil them hard for the next day's journey. Her face and arms had browned, but the rest of her body was as white as a swan's and her loose, short hair shone under the sun like the rich gold fire of his own cliffs' ragged tansy blooms.

At that moment a dragon-fly hovered close about her face and she put up a hand and brushed it away. The dragon-fly darted jerkily away and began to hover and hunt over the running silver of the river. Without thinking Baradoc spoke aloud in his own tongue.

Tia turned and asked, 'What did you say?'

Embarrassed for a moment Baradoc answered, 'It was nothing.'

'If it was nothing why say it in your own tongue?'

'You would laugh if I told you.'

'Then make me laugh. There's nothing wrong with that.'

Baradoc shrugged his shoulders. 'If you truly want to hear.'

'I do.'

'Well, seeing you wave away the dragon-fly I spoke poetry in my own tongue.'

'Then speak it to me in my own tongue – if you can.'

Baradoc hesitated a moment and then, as well as he could, he spoke the poetry in her tongue.

> Over the silver stream hunts the four-winged fly
> Each eye holds a thousand eyes
> But he sees not your beauty

Tia was silent for a moment. From Baradoc, she thought, always something new. Then, turning to drop more eggs into the boiling water, knowing that she was hiding her face from him, she said, 'Which of your tribal bards said that?'

Baradoc laughed. 'None of them. There is no man of my people who cannot say such things. The tongue speaks what the eye sees.'

Tia, her eyes on the boiling eggs, said, 'And did you hear me laugh?'

'No.'

'Nor should I. The words were good.' She turned to him and her mouth was wreathed momentarily with a teasing smile. 'And poetry is a change from warlike speeches about the future of this country. Now come and eat.'

But after they had eaten and Baradoc had gone off with his bow and Aesc at his heels to get a wildfowl for the next day's pot, Tia lay back on the grass and let the warmth of the sun flood across her bare body and thought about Baradoc. Even against his tanned face she had caught the flush of his embarrassment when he had spoken his lines. In herself there had been not embarrassment but a quick flush of pleasure to which she was no stranger. At her brother's villa there had been many visitors and friends from the neighbourhood and among them young men that she knew were attracted by her. Some she had liked and some she had avoided but, like or dislike, she was always pleased when she was complimented, when she was feasted with a string of flattering words. Why not? She was a woman ... well, almost, and one day she would marry ... Dreamily, she tried to imagine Baradoc as one of her own kind. But it would not work. Dress him in no matter what clothes or uniform there was something utterly unRoman about him. Not even could he be taken for Roman-British. He was a Briton, a tribesman, and it stood out all over him like the true grain of his own country's oaks. Chance and tragedy had brought them together. She liked him and was grateful to him and she thought nothing now of the roughness of some of his ways, but in his heart she guessed that there was only one love, greater than any he would ever give to any woman. She sat up shaking her head in silent sympathy with that woman somewhere in the future who would be his wife. He would honour, protect and cherish her – but she would never have a full entry to his heart. One thing above all others ruled his mind – to be a man and with full authority and the might of a united people behind him live for that day when with a great shout the swords of the tribesmen were raised eastwards and the dust began to rise under their marching feet.

She leaned forward and picked up from the ground, where their belongings were spread to dry, the doeskin bag which held the chalice Asimus had given them. Baradoc, she guessed, since he knew that it would never glow with the soft crimson of the ghost blood for him to mark him for greatness, had no interest in it. Not once since it had been given to them had he mentioned it or shown any care for it.

She opened the bag and took the silver chalice out. It was no larger than a drinking goblet with handles each side curved and worked in the form of rams' horns. One of the horns was badly bent. The bowl itself was pocked here and there with dents and there were scratches on the fluted base. Around the outside rim ran a continuous Greek key pattern and on one side of the body of the bowl, worked in relief, was a large round boss in the shape of an almost circular wreath of bay leaves enclosing the simple outline of a human eye. For a moment or two Tia was tempted to encircle her hands about it to see what would happen. Then she put the thought from her mind. If it glowed for her – even though Asimus had said it would not – she would be scared stiff because she had no wish to become a great leader. Anyway, there was no true belief in her heart for his story. Still, if Baradoc did not want it ... well, cleaned up – for it was dirty and tarnished inside and out – it would make a nice ornament for her bedroom in her uncle's villa, and would look pretty with flowers in it.

She rose and went to the river carrying the chalice. She had nothing to do until Baradoc returned and they started on the rest of the day's march. She squatted in the river shallows and scooped up a handful of the fine silver sand and began to clean the bowl, working the sand lightly over it as she had often seen servants working fine pumice stone dust over her brother's silver. As she worked a dragon fly came upstream and hovered low over a drift of white-starred water crowfoot. Tia smiled to herself. *Each eye holds a thousand eyes; but he sees not your beauty.* One day, she thought, some woman, some tribal maiden, would be won by his poetry and find herself only a shadow against the power of his dreams and ambitions.

For the next two days the weather was fine and they travelled north-west at a leisurely pace. Now and again, and always approached with caution, they met singly or in small groups travellers like themselves, some going north, some south and some west, but none going east. From them they heard many stories whose truth it would have been idle to try to unravel. This year the Saxons were coming ashore in even greater strength and spreading and settling through the eastern countries. And with their coming all over the country many of the common folk, touched with a madness born of their fears and their deep-seated, generations-old resentment of their masters, had turned to pillage and murder. It had happened in other years, and it would happen again in the future, for as each wave of invaders swept farther through the eastern breeches and across the country so the fear and resentment would strengthen. They told, too, of rumours that the far western Cymric hill tribes, the Dobunni and the Ordovices, and the Silures from beyond the Sabrina were moving down from the mountains in raiding parties, bolder even now than they had ever been in the days when the ranks of the legions had thinned in the garrisons and forts, eager to take and hold what they could before the tide advanced to the foothills of their own homelands. The rumours, Baradoc knew, would be exaggerated, but the truth beneath was ugly enough. Until this phase passed, safety now for ordinary folk lay in the bigger towns where law and order still held, where men still kept to their businesses, paid taxes and travelled well armed and in strength, and where slaves still served them because there was no true freedom to be found in running away. Much of all this came to him in his own tongue and much of it he kept from Tia or trimmed down in the telling. Although Aquae Sulis lay on the banks of the Abona river which flowed north-west little more than twenty miles to join the Sabrina, the place was large and would be well-organized. No raiding party of free-booting tribesmen could touch it. All these tribes were tied by blood and history and common origins to his own people, and like his own people they were torn and divided by internal rivalries and feuds and had long forgotten how to stand together against a common enemy. Although they sang the virtues and valours of their ancestors who had faced the Fourteenth, Twentieth and Second Legions in the early days of the coming of the Roman invaders, they were a rabble now under many quarrelling chiefs, their destiny to be conquered unless they learned to hold rank and order disciplined battle skills against the new invader and dedicate themselves and their swords to a single leader and follow him without question or greedy turning aside for private plunder and rapine.

Of the people they met there were many he sensed, particularly among the women, who looked at Tia and must have guessed that she was no youth. Their eyes would turn back to him full of questions to which they gave no words, for curiosity about others was dangerous and their own plight swept such curiosity quickly from their minds. Tia, he knew, thought no farther ahead than Aquae Sulis and her uncle. When he left her the months and years would shape her and her life the way the gods willed. By then the gods would have shown him where his way led. Tia would live only in his memory, fading into the grey mist of the years, and be as hard to picture in fine detail as was now the image of the laughing handmaiden who had made his heart beat fast in the house of his old master.

On the evening of the second day they came up from a river valley, followed the track of an old ridgeway for a while and then climbed the bare, grass- and thorn-covered shoulder of a rising down full into the light of a low westering sun. Black against the blood-red glow of the sun were silhouetted the circular double ranks of great rising stones, three times the height of a man, many of them joined together across their tops with long stone lintels and caps. A handful of wild sheep cropping around the stones galloped away from them as they came near.

Tia said, 'What is this place?'

'A great henge of stones. There are some in my own country but not as big as this. This may be a place my master often talked of.'

'Men raised these stones?'

'No. They were raised in the days before man – when only the gods walked the earth. They raised them as a temple for man to use when he came, as a place for worship and sacrifice. Only priests are allowed to go inside the circles.'

'I don't believe all that.'

Baradoc smiled. 'I don't ask you to. But I do. And we do not go inside. We can camp on the far side, away from the ridge road.'

Tia, looking at the stones towering from the ground, their shadows long and black across the grass, gave a little shiver and said, 'I don't want to go inside anyway. All I want to do is to put up our shelter and sleep.'

That night, before they slept, as they lay under the meagre cover of a canopy made from their goats' hair cloak and a blanket, tied over hazel poles which Baradoc had cut, Tia said, 'How many more days before we get to Aquae Sulis?'

'Three or four. Tomorrow or the next day we should come to the headwater of the Abona river. Then we can travel down it. Does your uncle live in Aquae itself?'

'Oh, no. In the country. About two miles outside.'

'Which side?'

'I don't know. Just outside.'

Baradoc sighed. 'You mean once we get to Aquae you still couldn't find your way to the villa?'

'No, of course I couldn't. I've only been a few times and I was taken by my brother. We used to go in two carts with servants. But I remember the road. Up to Calleva and then down the legionary road through Cunetio – we used to stay there a night – and then on through Verlucio and so to Aquae.'

'And when you got to Aquae – was the villa this side, or did you go through the place to the south, west or north?'

Tia yawned. 'Oh, we always went into Aquae, but after that ... how would I know which direction? But it makes no difference. All you have to do is to ask for the villa of my uncle and anyone will tell you. Everyone knows him.'

Baradoc said nothing. It was useless to expect too much of a woman. But how could you go anywhere and not afterwards remember the road you took? How could you, even if the gods whipped you up and set you down in the dark of the darkest night without stars to see or wind to smell, still not raise your hand and point to the north? To do that was as natural as breathing.

Suddenly out of the darkness Tia said, 'You think I'm stupid, don't you?'

Baradoc laughed quietly. 'No, I don't. You learn fast. You can shoot a bow well, you can silent-talk the dogs, you can make a day's march and carry your load, and you can now strike fire from flint and iron. But you only learn when you have to. You don't learn because it is good just to learn.'

'Women aren't supposed to. Anyway, what a lot of fuss over

my uncle's villa. It is called Villa Etruria, and that because he was born in Etruria. In Aquae we just ask for it and we shall be told. And the sooner I'm there the better. And for you, too, because my uncle will show his gratitude for the way you have looked after me. And anyway, you wouldn't like it if women were as clever and good at things as men. Though sometimes I think, the way things are now and man having made them so, it's a pity that they aren't.'

Indignantly Baradoc said, 'The gods made man to fight and rule and to reason, and they gave him woman to bear his children and to keep his hearth, though sometimes, when a nation needs it, they give a woman the heart and brain of a man and then we have queens like Boudicca who your people –' He broke off for from Tia had come the sound of a gentle snore. But he knew that it came not from sleep but from good-humoured teasing and to stop his speech-making. He lay back with his head on his hands and watched the night sky through the front of the shelter and, seeing the shapes of the standing stones against the pale night sky, he knew what he must do at first light. He had not known that they would come to the great stone henge. Surely the gods had directed his feet this way with a purpose, maybe to show that they were with him. He heard a dog fox call across the downland beyond the stones, and a vixen answer and felt Cuna, who lay against his leg for warmth, quiver aggressively in half sleep. Then from his left came the genuine sound of Tia's slow, long-paced sleep-breath as night claimed her.

Baradoc woke at first light. He slipped quietly out of the shelter without waking Tia. He strapped on his sword belt and moved away over the dew-drenched grass followed by the three dogs. He turned and looked at Cuna and the small dog, after a moment's hesitation, went back to the shelter. Northwards from the stone circle the downs rose and fell in gentle swells, marked here and there with clumps of wind-twisted thorns. A light breeze came full into his face. In a little while the sun would be rising, but now the light was a pearl-grey, muting the colours of trees and grass. A couple of bowshots away to his right he saw a flock of great bustards. For a moment or two he was tempted to go after them, but then he knew that he must have a truly ritual animal. The bustards, seeing him and the dogs, moved away, running awkwardly, and then took off heavily, flying low, their slow wing-beats stirring up the dust and dead grasses below them until they gained height and wheeled away out of sight over the crest of the downs.

He sent Lerg and Aesc ahead and for a while they were lost to his sight. Then downwind came the clear sharp barking of Aesc. Baradoc whistled and dropped to his knees on the ground. After a moment or two he heard the thud of hooved feet and he whistled again. Over the low swelling of downland ahead of him suddenly appeared the close-packed ranks of a handful of wild sheep, heading downwind towards him, moving fast away from the dogs who had circled behind them.

As the dogs appeared over the sky-line behind the sheep, Baradoc stood up and marked quickly the beast he wanted. Seeing him the small flock swerved caterways across the face of the down. Before Baradoc could whistle, Lerg raced along one flank and turned them back on their old line and Aesc came in on the other flank. The flock slowed, made an attempt to break away, but was held by the dogs. The old ram leading them stopped and the rest of the flock bunched behind it. The ram lowered its head and stamped angrily with its forefeet, the thuds ringing across the hard ground.

While the dogs held the flock on the flanks Baradoc moved forward slowly. The closer he came the tighter they bunched with the old ram at their head. Baradoc went step by step without hurry towards them, his eyes on a young ram he had already marked as the wanted beast. He whistled gently to Aesc with her own slow trilling call and she crouched watching the flock. Lerg moved in closer from the other side. The sheep, packed tight now, moved uneasily, waiting for the signal from the old ram to break from the flock pattern and scatter in all directions. The young ram pushed out to the side of the flock and faced Lerg. Following the fashion of the old ram, it lowered its head and stamped. From the way the sheep stood and their slowness in breaking into a wild panic rush in all directions Baradoc knew that they were not truly wild. This was a flock made of strays and abandoned animals, the sight of dogs and man still without the full force of danger for them. As the young ram stamped again and tossed its head in threat towards Lerg, Baradoc whistled high and shrilly and made a quick movement of his hand.

The flock broke wildly in all directions and Lerg moved in fast and leaped at the young ram, knocking it over and then holding it down by the grip of his great jaws on the loose neck fleece and the weight of his body.

Baradoc ran in, pulling a long hide thong from inside his shirt front. Seizing the immature horns of the ram he swung the beast on to its back, clamped his knees around its forequarters and with a few quick movements looped its front and hind legs together and knotted them securely. The ram lay on its side, its back arched, its feet pinioned. Baradoc picked it up, slung it over his shoulders, the strong, aromatic smell of its dew-wet fleece sharp in his nostrils, and turned back towards the stone circle.

As he neared it the lip of the sun came over the eastern ridge of the downs and the dew on the grass was suddenly fired with its red glow, the shadows of the stones reaching long and black over the ground.

He carried the ram up to the circle. To one side of the entrance a grey, lichen-stippled stone lay on the ground. Baradoc dropped the ram on to the stone and stood back with Lerg and Aesc on either side of him. He drew the broad sword from his belt and holding it before him by point and hilt looked up at the great arc of the stones, their eastern faces flooded by the fiery sunrise, and began to speak aloud in his own tongue the call to the gods for their favour and guidance, the sacrificial prayer of his tribe, of the people of the enduring crow.

This, he knew now, was why his steps had been directed here. Never in all the years of his people had any of them made this sacrifice in the first morning light at the great stone henge, the temple made by the gods for man ... *Aie!* never; for if any had then it would have been honoured in the tribal memory never to be forgotten no matter how many seasons and years should pass. He had been sent here because the gods had marked him as surely as he had marked the young ram that lay with wide-staring eyes and heaving flanks on the stone slab at his feet. Over the levelled sword raised before his eyes, he called the prayer and then began to name the great gods so that none should be missed and work against him and his dreams ... Father Dis; Taranis the thunderer; Teutates; Esus; Coventina of the sacred grove of Nemeton; Cernunnos the horned one; Epona the hooved one; Nonus the wise and forgiving one who, when his wife deceived him with another, because he loved her, claimed the child for his own; Dagda; Nodons of the silver hand; Badb the goddess of battle who had flown high above the chariots of the great queen, and Lug the fair-haired who stirred the corn seed to life and set the blossoms of all flowering trees to swell into fruit ...

He chanted the litany of names as the great rim of the sun began to wheel above the horizon. When he was done he reached down, took one of the ram's horns in his left hand, drew the animal's head back, and with one fierce slash of the sword cut its throat. The ram kicked in its death agony and its blood ran dark over its tawny fleece and moved darker still across the rough face of the stone slab. Baradoc watched the ram die. Then he stepped back and looked through the great stone archway at the linked twin circles of raised stones over and through which the swifts were screaming and hunting the insects raised to flight by the new sun; and he looked for some sign that the gods had heard him and were pleased with his offering. Always the gods gave some sign but it lay in the eyes of man to discover and read it. And the gods gave him their sign.

There was a flutter of wings from the top of a small thorn which grew close to one of the far stones. Baradoc, catching the flash of red wings and the blue-black head, saw that it was a shrike. The bird settled on a side branch of the shrub. In its mouth it held a limp, dead wren it had killed. As Baradoc watched he saw the butcher bird with a quick stabbing twist of its head impale the wren on one of the long thorns to rest there among the dead beetles and bees of its larder until hunger should bring it back to feed. For a moment or two he was sure that this was his sign, but his mind had scarcely turned to the reading of its message for him when from the top of one of the far stones a bird, at first a slatey-blue shadow against the darkness of the stone, winged down fast. It streaked low over the sheep-bitten grasses towards the thorn, the sun metalling its dark wings with a high gloss and lighting the pale, rufous patch of its gorge with a golden glow. The shrike seeing it coming rose with a cry of alarm from the thorn and flew away, hugging the ground and swerving in and out of the thorn patches. After it in fast pursuit, swinging and turning, and fast closing on the shrike, went the other bird, and Baradoc watched, knowing now that this was the true sign for the other bird was a merlin, the smallest of his country's falcons. On the lip of the down beyond the great henge where the land began to fall away to the river valley Baradoc saw the merlin strike and kill in mid-air, saw a great puff of feathers spread in the air and then, as the merlin disappeared below the crest, heard its distant exultant killing call. The gods had spoken plainly to him, filling him with a deep and exulting pleasure and pride. Was not the bloody butcher bird the Saxon threat from the east and the swift, sudden killing of the merlin the vengeance and victory which would one day come from the west?

He turned away from the stones towards the shelter. He saw that Tia was standing outside watching him, and he knew that if she began to question him, maybe to mock or tease him, then he would be hard put to hold his feelings back. These things had nothing to do with women. He was no child now, no youth, but growing in stature and strength to fit the manhood that was closing about him.

Tia said nothing. She had seen him make the sacrifice, but the killing of the shrike had been to her no more than part of the morning stir of nature. As he came towards her she saw his face set brown and hard and the dark intensity of his eyes and she guessed that he moved with his dream of the future glowing and blood-stirring within him. For the first time then it came to her that of all the people she had known in her life none had had this fire in the heart and brain. Her brother and his neighbours and friends, the well-to-do, and the country people, the farm and estate workers, the shopkeepers and traders, British or mixed-blooded, had carried no real anger and resolve, no dedication to any cause except the small concerns of their day-to-day existence. Her brother had longed and had still half-believed that the legions would return from Gaul even in the face of the truth which was there for all to read. The great Empire, already split and split again was, like many a stranded jellyfish she had seen on the sands below the villa, fast shrinking to an ignoble death. That she could now have such thoughts surprised her, but she knew that it was being with Baradoc which had begun to open her eyes and her mind to such things. She had seen her brother and their neighbours make offerings and small sacrifices to the gods, had herself revered the lares and penates, and she knew now that the gods were not to be deceived because there had never been in her face or the faces of the others that which made Baradoc as he came towards her now a figure who for face wore a bronze mask in which only the eyes lived.

She gave him the morning greeting and then, while Baradoc began to strike their shelter and pack their belongings, went to their fire. Overnight they had banked the pile of red embers with new wood and dry grasses and covered it with turves. She pulled the turves aside and blew the slow embers into fire and fed brittle, dead thorn kindling on it. She put bear grease in the skillet and began to cook the last of the fish which they had caught the previous day. While they were cooking she mixed some of their ground corn with water and beat it into flat cakes with her hands to fry when the fish were done. The dogs sat and watched her and she threw them the last of their dried meat which had gone rank and high. They ate it with relish.

The pattern of their days was set now. They ate well in the morning and then travelled until the late afternoon or evening when they would eat again. Water for drinking they carried in their leather skin. Water for washing they took as they travelled using the first spring or river. A wind eddy blew smoke into her eyes and mouth. Weeks ago it would have made her cough and her eyes water. Now she was hardly aware of it. All could be borne because Aquae Sulis came nearer each day. Irreverently as she cooked she thought that it was a waste to sacrifice a young ram. She held in her mind the thought of a shoulder or leg being spitted over the fire. Not for a while yet could she even dare to make a joke of it because there was still a silence in Baradoc which she guessed would not go until they had eaten and begun their march. At this moment Baradoc came to the fire, carrying their two wooden platters, and squatted down on his hunkers. He smiled almost shyly at her, as though there were only a few hours gone since they were strangers and said, 'We should travel well today. The country is open and we can keep to the ridgeways.' He nodded to the westerly sky. 'I think too these parts are more peaceful. No scavenging birds, crows, ravens or kites wheel in the sky and the wind is free of rolling smoke clouds.'

Wiping her sticky, floured hands on a cloth Tia, her words surprising herself, quietly said, 'Since I've been with you it seems to me that my body and my brain have been wakened from a kind of sleep. Not so long ago I took my pleasant life and ways for granted. Other people were shadows that moved around me. I had no curiosity about them and little about myself. Now my mind is full of questions.'

'That is the way it should be. Without questions there are no answers. And without answers no truth, no progress, no future.'

'Then I am free to ask questions?'

'Why not?'

'About you?'

'If you choose.'

'You have a living dream to free your country. Once your forefathers had that dream and turned it against my people. Time has settled that struggle. Now your enemy is a new one ... the Saxons.'

'And your enemy too.'

'True. But tell me, why do you hate the Saxons with a hatred that is fiercer than a smith's furnace? Why do you have an anger in you that is harder than iron against them, so unbending that it must come from more than a love of your country and your dream for its future?' She leant forward and turned the frying fish in the skillet to brown their sides, hiding her face. 'What did they do to you?' She looked up slowly after a while and saw his face unmoving, the mask set over it again.

Baradoc, each word a chip struck from an icy mass, said, 'I had a father and was taken from him into slavery. I had a master and was his slave. But even while a slave he became my father. He taught me the arts he knew. He even taught me things about my own and other tribes I did not know. Everything I am and will be is forever marked by his wisdom and kindness. He gave me my freedom and understood, since I did not leave him at once, that there was more I wanted from him. And then the Saxons came. He hid me in the roof loft and, sword in hand, met them in the courtyard of the villa. I saw it all through a gap in the tiles. They ringed him and taunted him and baited him. Age made his movements clumsy. Slowly and savagely they speared and axed him. They made his dying long and a drunken sport. And when he was dead they hacked with their blades at his body, danced on it and kicked it, defiled and degraded it. That night I swore to the gods that I would take the sword against them so long as any rested in this land, and I made a vow that the first Saxon I ever killed I would dedicate to him.' He paused for a moment, the mask slowly faded from his face and the thin edge of a smile wreathed his lips as he went on, 'So that is the answer to your question – and Lady Tia it is not one which I expected ever to come from you. From today the people around you will no longer be shadows.'

And Tia, serving his food, wondered at this love in him for his dead master and for his country, and there was pity in her for the woman he would some day take to wife for she would have to live in the shadow of those loves.

The Villa Etruria

For the next two days, the country being open and untroubled, they travelled easily and finally reached one of the small branches of the headwaters of the Abona river. The valleys of the downland with their clear chalk streams held small settlements and farms The southern slopes were worked with terraced strip fields, the greens of sturdy growths of wheat and barley and oats patchworking the land. Now, too, they came across flocks of cattle and sheep herded and guarded by family groups who lived and slept under rough shelters on the downs. Sometimes they talked to these people and bartered the game which Baradoc killed for cheese and milk. Money none of these people would accept as payment. True value lay in barter, goods for goods.

With the days an easier relationship sprang up between Baradoc and Tia. Something had awakened in her which gave her understanding and a growing admiration for his character and strength of purpose. In him, too, grew an acceptance of her which discounted all her race and breeding. She was a travelling companion, the two of them bonded in a growing friendship. Since the going was easier now, she marched mostly at his side instead of trailing behind. As they journeyed they talked more because she seldom had any urge to tease or mock him. Instead she was full of questions about his people and his life and about his days with his master. One evening as they sat beside the slow moving Abona where they were camped for the night she asked him about his cousin who had been made a slave with him and why he had betrayed him and left him hanging from the tree in the Anderida forest to die.

Baradoc said, 'When he was given his freedom he left my

master but he stayed in Durobrivae and worked there for a smith and armourer. He has a cunning in his hands as great as the cunning in his mind. And he heard from meeting travellers who came to the smithy that my father had died. At the moment his father is head of the tribe – but only until I return. What he did to me in the forest he did first for his father, and then for himself. With me dead then one day he would lead the tribe.'

'What's he called?'

'Inbar, and our tribal name is Ruachan. After the Saxon raid in which my master was killed he came to me with a friend and we all travelled together. Not until they strung me to the tree did he tell me that my father was dead.'

'And you mean to kill him?'

'We shall fight and when he lies on the ground with my sword at his throat his life will belong to me. Then I shall give it to his father, who is a good man, and he will choose whether the sword strikes or is sheathed.'

'And what do you think he will say?'

Baradoc gave a dry laugh. 'Lady Tia, the questioner. How should I know? But if the word is to kill, then I shall kill him and he will be laid in the burial grounds on the cliff hill. But if the word is to spare him, then Inbar must rise and go from our lands forever. Whichever way the loss is great – for Inbar has many skills and his dreams are mine and his hatred of the Saxons is mine. With so much craft and cunning and courage it is a great grief that the gods at his birth flawed him.'

Tia lay back on the grass and stared at the evening sky. High above she could see the black shape of Bran wheeling slowly on a rising air current and then, suddenly in a moment of play, falling quickly, twisting and turning, the searing sound of the wind against his wings coming clearly to her. Cuna came and sniffed at her face and she raised a hand and fondled his muzzle. Tomorrow or the next day they would reach her uncle's villa and this episode in her life would be closed. But, although her meeting with Baradoc had sprung from tragedy, she knew that for her too – even as the gods had flawed Inbar to bring her to rescue Baradoc from the oak – they had fashioned time and movement to give her this period with him so that her eyes should be truly opened and her mind truly awakened. For a moment or two the thought of Aquae Sulis had no pleasure. All that she could look forward to there as the years passed would be of little importance. Menfolk, she thought were the lucky ones . . . they had a freedom to dream and then to act and create . . . Women were only shadows against them. In her reverie she heard the low, soft growling of Cuna as he played with a broken stick. Then she heard him yelp loud and Baradoc suddenly laughed.

She sat up to see that Cuna in play had attacked the loose roll of their fishing net which lay near the shelter and was now tangled in its meshes. As he rolled and twisted she laughed too. Leaping and jerking inside the web of net Cuna lost his balance and began to roll down the slope of the bank. Before she could move he had gone over the edge and landed in the river.

Laughing still Baradoc jumped up, took the long fish spear and lifted the netted Cuna out of the river. He held him up and Cuna yapped indignantly until Tia reached for him and sitting down began to disentangle him from the net. Free, Cuna shook himself, spraying her with water and then, as they both still laughed, began to race around in wild circles leaping from one to the other in mock attacks, delighted with the attention he had brought on himself. While Lerg and Aesc looked on impassively, Tia caught Cuna and held him to her breast and calmed him down.

Baradoc, watching her and the dog, said after a moment or two, 'Of the dogs he's the one you like best, isn't he?'

'Yes, yes I do. He's so small, but so brave, and he makes me laugh.'

'Then when I leave Aquae Sulis he stays with you. He is yours.'

'Oh, no I couldn't –'

'He is yours.' Baradoc stood up, his eyes turning away from her. 'The gift is made. Now I will cover the fire against the morning.'

He moved away to gather turves and grasses to damp down the fire. Watching him, holding the wet Cuna in her arms, Tia, flushed with the pleasure of the gift, knew how great a gift it was, for of all the dogs she had long guessed that Cuna, the droll and the bear-baiter, was first in his affections. She knew, too, that as long as Cuna was hers so long would the memory of Baradoc be strong and green with her.

The Villa Etruria was two miles to the west of Aquae Sulis. It stood on a gentle river-bank slope, well above the winter flood line. From the main arched entrance to the courtyard, stone steps ran down to a small landing place on the Abona. They had come to it by the road which ran west to the small port of Abonae near the mouth of the river, reaching it in the late afternoon, the lowering sun striping its red tiles with black ridge shadows while the breeze rippled the branches of a row of mixed limes and poplars that flanked the slopes on either side of the building. Part of the bank had been cut away and the villa had been built into it. A covered way ran round the large courtyard, backed on one side by the kitchen, servants' quarters and store rooms. On the other side was a small bath house with the hypocaust that served it. Between these wings the main rooms of the villa faced square across the court to the river. In the centre of the courtyard was a spring-fed well, encircled with a carved stone parapet and roofed with an ornamental canopy from which hung a large bronze bucket. A little beyond it giving shade to the yard grew a tall sweet chestnut tree, a tree, Baradoc knew, which the Romans had brought to his country in their early days When corn was short the old legionaries had milled the chestnut fruits to add to their scanty cornflour issue. Flowers were everywhere, growing up the pillars of the covered ways, spilling over the tops of tall red urns and rioting from the beds which lined the pathway around the yard.

Lying on his couch that first night it was a long time before Baradoc could find sleep. Lerg and Aesc slept outside his door, and outside Tia's bedroom not far away he knew Cuna would be lying. Thinking of Tia he smiled to himself. When he had asked her where the villa was she had said nothing about the river. She had lived until now without her eyes being truly opened. When they had come down the river into the bowl of hills that held Aquae Sulis he had been surprised to see how small the town was. He had imagined it to be much larger. There had been no sign of trouble or past disturbance and although they had drawn some curious looks from people, mostly because of the dogs and Bran on his shoulder, they had been met kindly and given directions to the villa. But although the town was small he saw, on their way to the villa, that there were many more like it scattered along the Abona and on the hill slopes.

The villa itself had not surprised him. As a slave he was used to such places. But for the first time in his life, because of Tia, he was a guest. When they had arrived he had insisted that Tia go by herself into the villa to her uncle. He had sat on the river steps with the dogs, watching the swallows making water rings as they dipped to the river surface and the flight of the bronze, green and blue dragon-flies hovering and darting above the yellow flag blooms.

Finally, with his steward at his side, Tia's uncle had come to greet him. Ex-Chief Centurion and Camp Prefect Truvius Corbulo was well over eighty. He walked now with slow, awkward steps because of his rheumatism, helping himself with a long vine staff, old and polished with use, probably a relic from his army days. His hair was white and he was a tall man, a little bowed at the shoulders but carrying himself with a natural and professional dignity. His eyes were blue, a deeper blue than Tia's, and although they looked warmly on Baradoc he could guess that in the past many an erring legionary had quailed before them. It was easy to imagine Chief Centurion Truvius of the Second Legion in the days of his prime ... plumed helmet, armoured in mail cuirass and strapped shoulder plates, a pleated leather kilt, a senior officer's highly decorated boots, sword hanging on his left side, his staff of rank in his right hand and, sweeping from his shoulders, the folds of a red paludament, the cloak of authority.

He had greeted Baradoc and in a short, but friendly speech, thanked him for all he had done for Tia and had then put him in the care of his steward. For a moment as they had moved into the courtyard the steward, his eyes on the dogs and Bran, had begun to say a few words ... a mumble about should the animals go to the stables and the young Briton ... Truvius had jerked his old head round, eyed the man without words and had moved on. From that moment Baradoc had been looked after as a highly privileged guest. He was taken to the baths where he stripped and – as he had often done in his old master's house and in the public baths at Durobrivae – passed through the cold and tepid rooms to the hot room where, once the sweat had begun to break through his skin, he lay and was shaved and then his body scraped and curry-combed by the bath servant, relishing the man's skilful strokes with the curved bronze blade of the strigil.

When he had come to dress it was to find a fresh-laundered tunic and under-shirt awaiting him with highly polished sandals of soft green leather, the leg thongs worked with a running design in fine silver thread.

Lying now with the silence of the house about him, a soft down-stuffed mattress giving him the feeling of floating on air, he realized the shock it must have been for Tia savagely to have been thrust out of the luxury of her old life into the wilderness with him. And this house *was* luxurious, though small. It had been built of the local limestone. Even the pillars supporting the roof of the open corridors that ran around the courtyard were of stone. The wall openings of the reception room and the dining room were glazed with green and yellow squares of glass. The dining room floor was covered with a large mosaic, six hanging bronze oil lamps gave light and on plinths along the walls stood family busts. One angle of the courtyard corridor where Truvius had his collection of birds had been faced, too, with glass, a rough, green whorled glass through which the light came broken and uneven as through water. But of all the things in the villa none had surprised him more than Tia when she came into the ante-room before dinner where he and Truvius waited for her, drinking a fine white wine the like of which he had never tasted before and which he guessed must have been imported from Gaul – the grim thought passing quickly through his mind that he hoped the old gentleman had a cellar well enough stocked to last him his days because there would be little more fine wine from Gaul until the country grew settled again, and only the gods knew when that would be. It was with this thought in his mind that he had turned to see Tia enter.

In the darkness now the picture of Tia glowed bright and vivid in his mind. Her short hair, combed and arranged in tight curls, shone like a gold flame and was trapped by a red velvet band that ran across her clear brow and behind her ears. From one shoulder hung a blue silk robe, leaving the other shoulder bare. A transparent, diaphanous short mantle fell in light, moving folds to her waist, while on her feet were soft blue-dyed slippers worked with a close pattern of small seed pearls. The sight of her had made Baradoc catch his breath. Gone was the forest-and-downland, dirty-faced youth who had travelled with him. Here was a beautiful young woman, perfumed and elegant, a young goddess coming into the room like a vision. The contrast shook him. For all his life with his old master, all his experience, he had felt suddenly that here was a new world. A memory of his tribe's settlement had gone darkly through his mind ... the men in their rough skins, the women, young girls and children, sun-and-weather bitten, who worked over the cooking pots, hands greasy and calloused, and tilled the hill plots and on the feast days could only find for finery a mantle or cloak of cheap wool, for ornament some solitary armlet or neckpiece, some brooch set with coloured stones ... *Aie!* it was another world for the people of the enduring crow, but not another world which could never change. It must change ... Rome had gone ... another realm must rise and no invader from the east was going to create it. He had come back to the present as Tia, teasing mockery in her eyes, had said, 'Well, Son of a Chief, Baradoc – do I get no greeting? Did you lose your tongue as well as the dirt and sweat of travel in the bath house?'

Baradoc had smiled and said, 'What could my tongue say,

Lady Tia, that could match what my eyes see? Can the beauty of a bird be told by counting the colours that paint each feather, or the silver glory of a salmon be known by the tally of its scales?'

Tia laughed and turning to Truvius, had said, 'I should have told you, uncle, that Baradoc is a poet as well as a warrior who one day dreams of sweeping the Saxons from this land.'

Truvius, handing Tia a glass of wine, had answered, 'When a man sees beauty and cannot find poetry in himself then he is a man, too, who finds no courage in himself when he faces danger. And now – stop your teasing. You have kept us over long waiting to eat.'

For the first time in his life – for not even in his old master's house had this happened to him – Baradoc ate in Roman fashion, reclining on one of the three sloping couches set around the low table and waited on by the steward. Although Truvius showed little hunger, shifting often, too, in discomfort from his rheumatism on his couch, he and Tia did full justice to the stuffed olives and preserved plovers' eggs, the cold lobster – which had been brought upriver from Abonae – and the young broad beans and carrots, followed by slices of grilled venison, their appetite lasting right through to the dessert of dried figs and walnuts. Throughout the meal the steward had hovered round, refilling their wine glasses, bringing fresh napkins and water bowls for them to clean their hands, and watching always over the comfort of Truvius, ready to help him turn, prompt with a fresh cushion to ease his stiff body.

At the end of the meal Truvius, giving them a wry, humorous look had said, 'Twenty years ago I could have matched your appetite. Forty years ago, when I was still in service, after a day's march I could have eaten and drunk you all under the table.' Then looking at Baradoc, he said, 'So – you go to the west to rouse your people? And why should you not for my own have forsaken you? But remember this when you come of age to lead and fight ...' He coughed a little, shifted stiffly on his couch and sipped at his wine. When Claudius sent General Aulus Plautius with the Second, Ninth, Fourteenth and Twentieth Legions against your people, the Cantiaci, the Regnenses and the Atrebates, then man for man, courage for courage there was no difference between defenders and attackers. There seldom is. But there was this difference in Plautius's men – discipline, one leader and one plan of battle. He wins battles who makes the enemy fight on his terms, on his chosen ground. Remember, boy, for so with kindness I can call you from the mountain of age on which I now sit, that your tribes must find a leader, just and severe, whom men will love and he must find for himself new battle skills and tactics that these barbarian Saxons have never known and ...' He had broken off in a fit of coughing and the wine spilled from the glass in his shaking hand, but when the steward came to him, he waved him away testily and, after a while went on: ' ... I would ransom my soul if such a thing were possible to be your age again, and to fight for this country, for it has been good to me and I have grown to love it more even than my native Etruria ... Aye, I would gladly fight without rank as a simple bowman or spearman if the gods would will it. But the gods give but one portion of life to each man. When his eyes close for the last time they wait on the other side of darkness to greet him with his reckoning and his reward or punishment.' He was silent for a long while, his old head nodding, his mind wandering, then he looked at them and a smile lit his lean face and he said, 'Would that I had died in battle. I find old age a bore to myself and a burden to others ...'

In bed now, hearing an owl cry by the river and catching the stir of Bran who roosted on the ledge of the window, Baradoc could remember every word the man had said, and he knew that the memory would never leave him. One leader and each man disciplined, and new battle skills and tactics that the Saxons had never known. Then, driving those thoughts away, there came into his mind the picture of Tia, a daughter of the house of Corbulo, a young woman who stirred his heart but who, now that their journeying was done, was as far above him as the stars. Somewhere he knew there was a woman he would marry and make his own .... but already she had been betrayed ... *Aie!* the heart was a house of many chambers and the doors of some once shut could never be reopened.

The next morning as he stood outside the kitchen quarters and saw to the feeding of the dogs and Bran, Tia came to him and when the dogs had eaten they walked down to the river.

With a brusqueness which he did not intend Baradoc said, 'You are safe with your uncle, and this part of the country, too, seems settled. I must go on my way. Today.'

For a moment or two Tia was silent. Then she said sharply, 'You cannot leave today.'

'Why not?'

'Because it would offend my uncle – and it would offend me. Would you treat him as though he were an innkeeper? And myself as a ... a sack of corn you deliver for the kitchen?'

'I meant nothing like that.'

'He is old. The steward tells me that he has suffered two heart attacks in the last few months. There are times, too, when his mind wanders and he is like a child. His days are numbered, son of a chief Baradoc. You will not shadow even one of them with the discourtesy of leaving so soon. You are a guest. We both owe you a debt of honour. That cannot be paid quickly as you toss a coin on to a tavern slab in return for a beaker of beer. This country will not fall apart, nor your dreams vanish for the delay of a few days. And stop scowling. It puts ugly lines across your brow.'

Baradoc laughed and shrugged his shoulders. 'I meant no rudeness. But you're right to scold me.'

So Baradoc stayed on at the villa for the next three days. On one of these days Tia and her uncle travelled to Aquae Sulis and made their prayers at the temple for the spirits of her brother and his wife, and Truvius gave orders to a stone mason for a slab to be carved commemorating them. When it was made he intended to place it in the wall of the villa overlooking the river. Baradoc travelled with them but did not go to the temple. Instead he wandered around the town. Many of the wealthier people had already left it and from the shopkeepers and working people that he spoke to it was clear that there was a deep feeling of unrest in them, a shadow of the fear which already clouded the east. But their chief anxiety centred on the Cymric tribes beyond the Sabrina river, and the tales which each new traveller brought that the hill tribes were moving. The Silures, Demetae and Dobunni who had never been truly under the old rule, saw the prospects of easy and profitable pillage, the pleasure of wielding firebrand and sword, and the prospect of slaves to sell or to work their mountain farms and herds. Rumours flew like bats at night. So, Baradoc guessed at Isca in the west, on the moorland borders of his own country, there would be the same rumours. Bands of his own people, the Dumnonii, would be moving or gathering to move, small chiefs eager for the quick pickings, and in their greed never dreaming that, creeping mile by mile over the years, their own destruction or bondage was seeping westwards. In those few days he realized, too, that many of the outlying villas around the town and along the Abona had been closed or left in the care of servants.

Sitting with Truvius that evening in the courtyard, the dogs lying before them, the sun firing the plumage of the birds in their aviary, the steady movement of worker bees about the flower urns and beds, the old man said to him, 'Sulis is a town of shadows, and many of the villas around here hold nothing but ghosts. Some of my friends have gone to Londinium and some to Gaul. But wherever they go they will find no real ease. There is no making terms with an enemy full of land hunger. Some will pay a tribute for their own safety, but each year the demand will be greater. In the end everything will be taken from them. The gods have called a term to the bright days of glory and now we begin to enter the darkness of a changing age. A man can do no more than to cherish his own honour, to fight for it and to die for it. The rest is in the hands of the gods. I have lived by war, and I would that I had died by war ...' His words trailed away, his eyes closed and his head dropped to his chest. He had drifted away into sleep, maybe into a dream of the bright, hard days of his manhood. Then one of the birds from the aviary screeched loudly. Truvius's head jerked up, his eyes blinking. Then he cocked a grey eyebrow at Baradoc and smiled. Nodding at Lerg he said, 'In my young days with the legions I would have given you a handful of gold for a dog like that. Aye, and I would rather travel with such a dog for companion than many a man I have known. My Tia was lucky to find you.'

Baradoc shook his head. 'I was lucky that she found me.'

'You were both fortunate. She says that you must be well rewarded.'

'I want nothing.'

'This I know. But I make a gift from an old soldier to one who still has to face his first battle.' He raised his right arm letting the folds of his toga fall away from it. On his wrist he wore a thin, much worn gold armlet. He slipped it off and handed it to Baradoc. 'This is the first battle decoration I won ... when I was little more than your age ... others and greater came later, the torques and discs and silver spearhead. But this was the first for no great act of bravery, more a moment of youthful rashness. Wear it.'

Baradoc took the thin, worn armlet and slipped it on. For him it would always hold the memory not only of the old Chief Centurion but also of Tia and would always rest on his right arm.

Each evening they sat in the courtyard talking before the time for bathing and dinner came; the three of them and the three dogs and the steward bringing them cool drinks and small dishes of salted nuts and sugared fruits to eat. It was an oasis of well-being and peace – which was shattered on the evening of the day before Baradoc was to leave.

They were sitting in the courtyard in the shade of the tall sweet chestnut when Cuna sat up and whined. At the same moment Lerg and Aesc rolled to their feet from where they were lying and both of them turned their heads towards their master. From a branch on the chestnut tree Bran launched himself, his shadow racing across the flower beds, and he rose into the air and began to circle over the villa.

Tia said, 'Why are the dogs uneasy?'

Baradoc stood up. None of them were armed. He signalled the dogs to keep their station. As he did so there was the sound of footsteps from behind him. He turned and saw the steward and his wife and the house servants come through from the reception room to stand in a close group at the top of the steps leading down into the courtyard. From the room behind them six men appeared and ranged themselves along the face of the covered walk, six men with long hair and bearded or moustached, six men wearing belted tunics of skin or wool, the cloth crudely striped in greens, reds and yellows. All of them were armed with spear and sword and all of them were weather-browned and hard-muscled, short wiry mountain men. Before the three in the yard could make any move or sound, the man beside the steward, taller than the rest, a bronze torque about his neck, raised a hand as though commanding silence and then pointed beyond them to the archway that framed the top of the steps leading down to the river.

Baradoc swung round quickly. The dogs held their station, waiting some sign or command from him. But he gave none. A tall man stood inside the archway carrying sword and spear, a throwing axe thrust in his belt, a short cloak hanging from his shoulders over a finely dressed deer hide tunic, his legs bare of sandals or gartering. From behind him, rippling in like shadows, without sound, like some flawless movement of a dream, came six other men in hillmen dress and they split on either side of him in even ranks, and each man carried a heavy hunting bow, raised and arrowed, the bows partly drawn and each arrow head pointing at the group in mid-court. For a moment or two it seemed that the invasion was part of a dream, and the dream a spell which held the whole company frozen in a coloured frieze that a word or movement could erupt into violent life.

Cuna broke the spell. With a sudden, short bark he raced forward to the man in the doorway. Before Baradoc could stop him, he leaped up and seized the edge of the man's tunic and hung on to it, swinging from its folds and growling. The man looked down at Cuna, then laughed, and putting his spear behind him against the archway wall, reached down and lifted Cuna by the scruff of his neck, pulling him free of the tunic skirt. Laughing still, he held Cuna aloft, yapping and growling.

Baradoc moved forward quickly, seeing the arrow points swing to follow him. He went up to the man who stood smiling still with amusement at the suspended Cuna.

Baradoc said, 'Put the dog down. He is young and bold and not yet fully broken to command.' Without thinking he spoke in his own tongue. The man, no smile on his face now, tossed Cuna to him. Baradoc fondled the dog's ears for a moment and then dropped him to the ground ordering him to go to Tia.

The man watched Cuna trot to Tia, eyed her briefly, and then turned to Baradoc and said quietly, 'You speak my language, but not with a Cymric sound. You dress like a Roman landowner's son, but your hands are marked with hard work and you have the gift of silent, talk with your dogs. Tell the big hound to come to me in peace, but say it in words, words that only I know in my tribe, words that in all the tribes are only given to the few.'

From behind Baradoc the voice of Truvius came testily, angrily but bravely, 'What does he say? What does the ruffian want? By the gods – that I should be so old and feeble . . .' He broke off suddenly in a fit of coughing.

Without turning Baradoc said in Truvius's tongue, 'These are hillmen from beyond the Sabrina. Their leader could be a man who prefers reason to force.' Then, turning briefly, seeing Tia holding Cuna, the old man bowed forward, head doddering, in his apple-wood seat, he spoke briefly to Lerg.

The great hound moved forward slowly, the sunlight sliding over his rough pelt. He went up to the man in the archway and sat back on his haunches. The man put down his hand and with the back of it gently touched the black wet nose of Lerg. Lerg sat unmoving. The man withdrew his hand and said to Baradoc, 'What did you say to the old man?'

'That you could be a man who prefers reason to force, a man who does not use the sword or spear without true cause.'

'You speak their language well?'

'Yes. I served a Roman master as a slave for years.'

'And still keep their company?'

'I did them a service. I go home to my own people beyond the river Tamarus.'

'*Aie* . . . now I know the strange notes in your words although they are mine. There is more sea than mountain, more fish than fowl, more fog than snow. That you speak their tongue is good. You can speak for me and save the legs of old Machen who nurses a mead-skin downriver with the rest of my men.'

As the man was speaking Baradoc studied him. He was taller than most hillmen and he had a full handful of years more than himself. When he smiled there was no guile behind the eyes, but when he frowned there was force and authority in him. That he would not leave the villa empty-handed was inevitable, but if he, Baradoc, could hold him to fair speaking then Tia and Truvius might be spared any personal violence.

Baradoc said, 'I will speak for you.'

'Good. But first I would know who you are.'

'My name is Baradoc. I am the only son of my father, the son of great Ruachan, chief of the tribe of the enduring crow.' He pulled aside the shoulder of the light tunic he wore and exposed the tattoo of his tribe's bird. He went on, 'I return to my people to raise them and all our kind against the Saxons and . . .'

'Enough!' The man cut him short. 'Such talk is everywhere among the tribes but it is no more than the empty chatter of house-safe sparrows as the hawk flies over. My business is of today – and here in this villa.'

Anger was so strong in Baradoc that he had to hold down the words he would have spoken. Prudence alone moved him, as he said, 'I have named myself. Who are you?'

'I am Cadrus of the Ocelos.' The man touched his right shoulder. 'I bear their mark here. We are from the hills beyond Gobannium, and Eurium. But this day we are from Abonae which my people hold after crossing the Sabrina.'

'You go to Aquae Sulis?'

'No. We are not enough.' He looked around the courtyard,

smiled and said, 'We are content to take the straying goslings. The fat goose can wait until another time.'

Baradoc knew the joke had been made for him alone. The mark he carried on his shoulder was of the goose with the golden feet and bill, the Ocelos tattoo.

'And from here? What do you take?'

'All weapons, save yours. All treasure and money. And some of the household for slaves. All this without force unless force is offered. Go to the old man and tell him this, and then stay with him and the girl while my men do their work. Who is the girl, his daughter?'

'No, his dead brother's daughter. She came with me from beyond the Anderida forest. She lived with her brother and his wife. Their villa and homestead farm were burnt and pillaged by their own people . . . the ones who fearing the Saxon coming turn in madness on their own kind. The brother and his wife were killed. She escaped into the forest and I brought her here.'

Cadrus nodded, and said, 'Go tell the old man and then the three of you hold your place while my men do their work.'

Baradoc went back to Tia and Truvius. Cadrus began to give orders to his men. Four were left spaced around the courtyard, their bows held ready, while the others began to go through the house. Cadrus stood in the archway and as the house was sacked, the weapons and looted treasures were piled alongside him, gold and silver plate spilling on to the stones, small leather pouches of coins from Truvius's room, a casket of jewels . . . nothing of good value was overlooked down to the smallest bronze brooch, the tiny hand lamps of beaten copper – and amongst it all the silver chalice given by Asimus which had stood in Tia's bedroom.

Baradoc told Tia and Truvius what Cadrus intended. The old man heard him in silence until the end and then he raised his grey head and said, 'So it must be, for the man who holds the sword and the spear is master. What they take from us is nothing. The years have made me helpless, and the times have made victims of the innocent. All my servants are free people. Now they go to slavery in some wild hill fortress.'

Tia said firmly to Baradoc, 'The man is of your kind. He holds you in good faith. Go to him and ask him to spare the servants.'

Looking down at Tia as she sat on a stool at the old man's feet, Cuna resting against her leg, Baradoc said nothing. But the shadow of unease which had been with him from the moment that Cadrus had glanced towards Tia was now grown blacker in his mind. Truvius lived now in a dream of old age. The world about him had long lost meaning. His life lay in the past, his days now were a crawling serpent of slow hours that wreathed about him and found him impatient for the final sting. But Tia was at the beginning of her days. Cadrus's face had been un-moving as he had glanced at her, but his eyes had mirrored the quick stir of his emotions. The silver and gold and spilled treasures on the archway floor were bright with colour under the sun, but the westering evening sun also quickened the sheen of Tia's golden hair, the jay-blue depths of her eyes, the plum red curves of her lips and the smooth soft nut-brown warmth of her bare arms and legs, bold against the creamy fall of the wide-skirted tunic which she wore.

Baradoc said, 'This is no moment to ask for a favour which will not be granted. The hillmen have no bellies for field or farm work. Fighting and hunting is their work. A slave is a high prize, to be put to the plough or the cattle folds, or to be sold to the coast traders from Erin.' But the more he could have said he kept to himself for a woman slave who was fair in all men's eyes was a treasure not to be passed by. *Aie* ... even in his own tribe it happened. Tia stirred angrily and began to speak. He broke in sharply and said, 'Stay here and say nothing. One wrong word could put Cadrus out of humour.' And then, as Tia looked up at him tight-lipped, he saw her face slowly change and he knew that she had read his thoughts.

From behind him Cadrus called sharply to the man who guarded the servants outside the reception room. Prodding them with the butt of his spear the man moved them down into the courtyard and across to Cadrus. They halted before him, the old steward and his plump wife who worked the kitchen, the strong middle-aged man who kept the bath house and stoked the hypocaust for water and house heating, and a younger man who did general work about the villa and kept the small stable of two horses which drew the old man's four-wheeled carriage when he drove to Aquae Sulis or went to visit friends.

Cadrus raised a hand and beckoned Baradoc to him. He nodded at the group and said, 'I take the two younger men. They are full of years and work. The old man and the woman would not be worth the food they would eat. They can stay.'

Baradoc turned to the servants and told them Cadrus's decision. At once the steward and his wife moved quickly to join Truvius and Tia. Of the two men the elder stood passive, but for an instant the head of the other turned, sweeping round the courtyard, and he half moved as though to escape. The movement was halted by the sharp hiss of a flighted arrow loosed by one of the men near Cadrus. The arrow bit deeply into the ground at the man's feet, the long shaft vibrating savagely. From the men on guard around the courtyard and from the others who had now come from the building rose a roar of laughter. Only Cadrus was silent. He watched as his men, needing no signal from him, roped the hands of the servants behind their backs and then fastened heavy leather collars about their necks, each one joined to the other by a long length of strong, plaited hide rope. Cadrus watched all this done and not until they were led away through the archway towards the river did he turn to Baradoc.

He said, 'What is the girl's name?'

'Gratia.'

'You speak grudgingly. Tell her to go gather a warm cloak and strong sandals and any woman's things she needs. Tell her that in obedience she can walk free and unshackled but if she kicks like a young heifer and would escape from the path then she will be roped to the others for she now belongs to Cadrus.'

There was no surprise in Baradoc. No tribesman would have left her free. He had now long known in his heart that this moment was coming, had faced the dilemma and had known only one answer to make to it, an answer with the strength of tribal custom behind it, an answer with which all of his own race would keep faith, but an answer which Cadrus, his eyes trapped now by Tia's grace, might sweep aside with a single sharp word to bring a flight of arrows to destroy him. No matter to Cadrus that the breaking of tribal faith might some day turn the gods against him. Tia's beauty shining in his eyes had blinded him. As he paused now and faced Cadrus with a stony face, Baradoc knew that with a single lie he, too, could be forsaken by the gods and they might let Cadrus have his way without marking his future.

Baradoc said coldly, 'She cannot go with you. She is betrothed to me. Not even Cadrus of the Golden Goose can take the future wife of a man of the tribe of the enduring crow as a slave. The gods would mark your tribe forever with shame for the crime. Your women would be barren, your hunting grounds empty and your hilltops a waste land where not even the eagle or the fox would harbour. She is promised to me, she stays with me.'

Without hurry, no movement of muscle in his face to betray emotion, his eyes steady, Cadrus raised his sword and held it out point forward so that the sharply honed tip just touched Baradoc's breast. He said evenly, 'Your tongue is swift in the battle of words and cunning. You are distantly of my blood and we share the same gods. If the feud fire had been lit between our tribes I would kill your father, slaughter your house and burn your huts and there would be no shame for you would do the same to mine. There is no feud, and you speak fair that I cannot take for slave a woman who has promised herself to you.' His hard face creased with a quick smile, and there was a touch of mockery in his voice as he went on, 'But it is in my mind that you speak falsely for her sake. I would know from her without any word from you whether you speak the truth. From this moment you stay dumb as the slow-worm. And, if she denies you, then I kill you as I would slaughter a young bull for the sacrifice!'

Without taking his eyes off Baradoc, the sword point always against the loose fall of his tunic, he called to one of his men,

'Fetch me Machen here for I need one who speaks the bastard tongue.'

From the outer side of the archway he was answered at once by a slow, lilting voice, touched with the edge of lazy laughter. 'Who sends for Machen when Machen is here fresh from mead sleep?'

A tall, thin middle-aged man, his face grizzled with long copper-coloured stubble, dressed in a rough habit of brown, its ragged skirts swinging as he walked, the loose cowl hanging down his back, came through the arch and stood alongside Cadrus.

With hardly a glance at Machen, Cadrus, sword never moving, pointed with his free hand to Tia and said, 'Tell the girl to come here. I would take her as slave, but this young bull of the tribe of the enduring crow denies me the right, saying that she is betrothed to him. She understands not our tongue but you will ask her the questions I give you in her own bastard language. If she denies the young bull, then he dies.'

'She knows you want her as slave?'

'No. They sit there knowing nothing – the ancient eagle of the legions and the sleek young falcon – and their world spins dying under them as yours spins when the mead takes you. You know their language and the gods have given you an ear for the music of song and the music of truth. If you tell me she says that he speaks the truth she can be no slave. If you hear the false note of a lie then she becomes my slave and this one dies.'

Baradoc felt the point of the sword prick him briefly as he finished speaking, and from the corner of his eyes he saw Machen move across the yard to Tia and Truvius.

Tia watched the man as he came to her. He moved slowly but easily and there was the ghost of a smile about his lips. Beside her sat Truvius, his hand in hers, mumbling to himself, staring straight ahead, his eyes blinking slowly with the fixed rhythm which marked his periods of withdrawal. Disaster had taken the villa. He had faced it for a while and now was lost to it, sheltered by the blind comfort of mindless senility.

In her own tongue Machen said gently, 'Leave the old man and come with me. Speak no word to your young tribesman friend.'

Tia rose. Of all that had gone on between Baradoc and Cadrus she had caught only a few of the words she had come to know of their language. They gave her no grasp of the trouble between them, except that her own instinct and her knowledge of the ways of tribal raiders told her that there was some argument about slaves and herself. She went with Machen across the yard and up to Cadrus. He looked at her boldly, his gaze moving over her from head to foot, and she saw his mouth tighten, his shoulders tauten as he drew sharp breath, and a sudden glitter fired his eyes. From her deep woman's instinct she knew at once that in some way she was a prize that Baradoc had disputed with him.

She stood at the foot of the semi-circular steps rising to the archway and Machen stood with her, translating for her the questions which Cadrus made in their own language, and all the time Cadrus spoke and then Machen translated, Cadrus kept his eyes on her.

Machen asked her, 'Cadrus would know how you met this young man?'

'In the forest of Anderida after my brother and sister were killed and I was making my way to Aquae Sulis ...' There was a nervousness in her which she held down but not entirely could she keep its note from her voice as she described how she had cut Baradoc down and they had then journeyed together.

'For how long have you travelled?'

'A month or more.'

'Cadrus and our people have made this raid for weapons, treasure and slaves. He takes two of your good men and also he would take you.' Machen paused, expecting some quick response or outburst from her. Women spoke or cried out before thought or common-sense could govern emotion. This young woman said nothing. Her forehead slowly creased and her mouth tightened into a thin line. He waited and when she said nothing, he went on, 'This man of the tribe of the enduring

crow disputes his right by tribal law. He says that you are betrothed to him. If this is so then you cannot be made slave.
Speak truly – are you promised one to the other and one by the
other?'

With the question, Tia, although she could not see him fully
from where she stood and there was no sound or movement
from him, knew the full reading of Baradoc's mind. It came to
her now as it came from him to Lerg and the others, not words,
not direct sense, but wholly in a magic that by its force turned
the body and the brain to paths of understanding. Yet she knew
that, without this, she would have known, for to save her there
had been nothing else Baradoc could do.

She said firmly, 'It has been a secret between us which I was
to tell my uncle this night. Yes, we are betrothed.'

Machen turned to Cadrus and said, 'She says he speaks the
truth. They are promised to one another.'

Without emotion Cadrus asked, 'Does she speak the truth, my
Machen? Tell me and swear it by your faith, by the gods of the
sacred oak groves, by the white purity of the tree-suckling
mistletoe, and may your soul shrivel and there be no after-life
for you if you swear me false.'

Machen without hesitation said, 'I swear that she speaks the
truth which is in her.' But to himself, because the mead was
still warm in him and there was a respect in him for the girl's
bold and quick-witted response, he had no fear of imperilling his
soul and his life hereafter. There were truths that grew between
people which they could not know themselves until some sharp
moment of destiny brought them to light. Even now the girl did
not know the full truth in her, but one day she would.

Cadrus, his face suddenly softening to a smile, shrugged his
shoulders and said, 'Oh, Machen of the mead-breathing mouth,
may the gods rack you if you lie because of her gorse-bloom
hair and pretty forget-me-not eyes.'

'I speak not falsely. There is no truth that lies so deep that
my ferret-mind cannot unwarren it.'

Cadrus said, 'Ask her if she knows what it is to marry a tribesman. She comes of high Roman blood. She knows only one way

of life. This —' he waved his hand around the yard. 'It is in me that she has deceived you, good Machen.'

Machen turned to Tia and said, 'Cadrus doubts you. Aye, he even doubts the truth in me. Answer now his question.' He put to her the demand which Cadrus had made.

Tia, confidence growing in her, speaking as though some outside power and intelligence answered for her, replied, 'I would marry him because I love him and he loves me. I would go to his people and their hard life because this country which my uncle and my father and all their kin before them helped to create now falls apart in misery. My uncle will not live long. I am ready to follow my love to find a new people and a new life.'

She stood watching Machen and Cadrus as they spoke together, no more than an odd word of their talk having any meaning for her, and she kept her eyes from Baradoc who stood wooden-faced with Cadrus's sword still at his breast. Then as Machen turned to her to speak again, she saw Cadrus lower the sword and slide it into the leather and wood scabbard that hung from his belt.

Machen, now smiling openly at her, said, 'Cadrus whose heart can be softened by a woman's ready wit as mine by good mead, salutes you. He accepts my word that you speak with a frank and true tongue. Now do as I say and he wishes. Go to the treasure which we take with us —' he nodded towards the piled weapons and household loot which lay heaped on the top of the broad archway steps, '— and choose any one thing you value and bring it back here to me. Go now.'

Tia walked across to the piled loot and looked down at it. What of all she possessed was of great value to her? What of all the life she had had until now was dear to her? Her family were all gone except Truvius and his days were few. These hillmen would go and the house would echo like a shell as she moved about it and the day would come when she would be alone in it. Baradoc would have gone to the west, and the lie she was living at the moment would have gained her only an empty freedom. Tears misted her eyes and almost without knowing it she bent and picked up the silver chalice and walked back to Machen. She gave it to him and he passed it to Cadrus.

Cadrus stepped up to her. He raised the chalice, touched his brow with it and then handed it to Tia. 'Tell her,' he said to Machen.

Machen, the dying sun threading his beard with copper glints, looked Tia deep in the eyes and said, 'There is a long skein of kinship between the Ocelos people of the mountains and the people of the enduring crow. Before the wedding kinsmen bring gifts. This is Cadrus's gift to you. If times were different we should stay and make feast after the marriage. Now we stay only to make the gift and to join the ceremony. I am a priest whose power and authority no tribe, not even in the far north or the west, not even over the sea with the Scotti or beyond the first of all the great walls with the Picts, can question. Take now the hand of this man of the enduring crow and go both of you to your uncle, and stand before him for his blessing so that I may join the hand of husband to wife.' Then with a quick flicker of laughter in his eyes, he added, 'This must be so because the good but still doubting Cadrus to know truth to be true would see it sanctified in deed.'

Cadrus turned to Baradoc and, his eyes now friendly, said, 'There is one in the mountains with such a fire in his belly as you have against the Saxons. In a few more years come to me and I will take you to him. but first you must grow to full manhood and have sons to follow you should you fall in battle. Go now – take your Roman filly, but think not that she will be easily schooled.'

Without a word Baradoc moved to Tia. And Tia, with a nervous shiver as though her body moved in the spell of a vivid dream, turned and took his hand. They went across the courtyard towards Truvius and the tribesmen with lowered bows and rested weapons watched them. Long evening shadows striped the paving and flower beds. The aviary birds took the last of the paling light on their enamelled wings, and the sound of the worker bees about the shrubs by the running spring water of the well made a heady droning. They walked, neither looking at the other, and behind them came the three dogs and from the end of the red-tiled roof Bran, his sable plumage lacquered with the sun's last glow, sat still and graven like a carved corbel. They stood before Truvius who sat, his head sunk on his chest in sleep, his old vine staff resting across his knees. Tia reached out a hand and touched him. Slowly he raised his head and blinked the weight of sleep from them, then smiled and said. 'What has happened? What is it my Tia?'

Tia, her hand in Baradoc's, said, 'We come to you, my dear uncle Truvius, for your blessing.'

The Flood Riders

Tia woke just before first light. As she lay in the darkness she heard Cuna whine gently from the foot of her bed. She spoke quietly to him and he was silent. About her the ravaged house was still and the memories of the previous day flooded through her mind, bright and dark pictures each stirring emotion. She saw the eyes of Cadrus on her as she had faced him. There was good and bad in the man. Her body shook with a spasm of remembered fear as she thought of the life which would have been hers had she had to follow him as a slave. Baradoc had saved her from that, but she could not guess at what cost to himself, to his pride and his deep sense of tribal customs. True, Machen – who for some hidden reasons of his own had taken her part – had guided and shielded her as she stood before Cadrus, and then had carried out the simple pledging ceremony in the courtyard, joining her hand with Baradoc's after Truvius had given them his blessing. Dear uncle Truvius. . . . Sometimes she wondered whether there were not, as well as his true lapses into senility, also times when he pretended them either to cloak his own helplessness or from a deep wisdom which compensated for the vigour and mastery of his old days now long denied him. And Baradoc? By his quick thinking he had saved her, had stood by her while Machen joined them, his face giving no sign of any emotion he felt. Strange Baradoc . . . with his burning dream of the future. As he took her hand, he would have been already rejecting the picture of himself leading a Roman woman into the homecoming gathering of his people . . . their wild and noisy greetings turning to silence as they eyed her? Well, he need have no worry. He had saved her from slavery. She would not nor could not make any claim on him.

When he got back to his people he could say that she had refused to follow him, refused to be a wife and one of his own holy men could with a few words break the tie that bound them.

Cuna whined again, louder. In the silence that followed Tia heard two sounds, the brief protesting *cark* of Bran from somewhere in the courtyard and the sharp note of metal momentarily striking against stone. Cuna whined again, a low muted note and swiftly there was an understanding clear and vividly all-embracing in Tia. Baradoc was going. Sword or fish spear had swung against the stone parapet of the courtyard well as Bran, from the ironwork canopy over it, his favourite night-time roost, had hopped to his shoulder; and Cuna had whined because ... poor Cuna, who had been pledged to her, sensed that the others moved away and longed to go with them.

Tia got out of bed, wrapped a cloak about her shoulders, and went barefooted from her room into the open corridor. Part of the yard lay washed in moonlight as pale as the underside of a willow leaf and the chestnut's shadow was dark as a thunder-cloud over the archway that led to the river. Baradoc, Bran on his shoulder, the two dogs at his side, dressed now in his rough clothes, the old sword at his side, his travelling bundle slung over his shoulder from the head of the fish spear, stood in the tree shadow at the foot of the archway steps. For a moment Tia was tempted to stay where she was, to stand and watch and let him go. The thought was in her that, if at any time since their marriage he had asked her whether she would have travelled with him, she could not have known what true answer to give. There was much between them, but nothing of lovers or man and woman. At her side Cuna whined and she knew that for Cuna's sake she could not let Baradoc go without a move from her.

She walked down the corridor, past the aviary where the bright birds were now, as they roosted, dark, strange-shaped fruit on the shrubs and twisting creepers, and out on to the uncovered terrace by the archway. Baradoc heard her, and was still as she came up to him. They stood in the tree shadow and their faces were stiff masks as though they wore them like the theatre players of some high drama.

Tia said quietly, 'So you go?'

'Yes.' Baradoc's voice was thick as if some inner anger half strangled it.

'At night and without farewell?'

'Because of what has been and the way it has been, yes. I come from a different world. There is no place in it for you even if we truly loved one another.'

'You would be ashamed to bring a Roman before your people as a wife?'

Baradoc was long in answering. Then he said, 'Be content, Lady Tia. What was done was to save you from Cadrus. Not to gain you for myself. When I reach my people the priest will set all aside.'

'You do not answer my question.'

'No, I would have no shame before them. Now, tease me with no more questions for you know that our paths no longer lie together. I take the ford across the river and the mining road west to the hills.'

'Then you shall take Cuna with you. I give him back.'

Baradoc hesitated briefly and then, with a small shrug, he said, 'If you so wish.'

With an abruptness that surprised Tia, he turned sharply and moved through the archway, his bundle swaying on the spear, the dogs at his heels. She stood in the shadows, watching him, now in full moonlight, move down to the reed-fringed river and turn along the bank.

When he was gone from her sight she went back into her room and lay in the darkness, seeing him moving through the night, the dogs around him, and Bran on his shoulder. Although she was restless with the stir of many mixed emotions she told herself firmly that Baradoc was right. What had been done had been done to save her from Cadrus. There was nothing more between them. He had his world and she had hers ... though the gods knew that hers was changing shape and meaning rapidly and she could see little of promise in it. With Truvius she belonged to the past.

When morning came, as she had done every day since she had arrived, she gathered flowers from the courtyard and went to Baradoc's room after the servant had cleaned it to refill the small earthenware jar on the table by the window. She knew that, until some new guest used the room, she would do so every day because this until then was Baradoc's room and much of him lingered there for her still.

As she arranged the flowers and stepped back to look at them she saw on the end of the table one of her uncle's flat ivory writing tablets, and she knew that Baradoc must have taken it from the reception room where her uncle kept it at hand to make notes of household affairs as they occurred to him, no longer able to trust his errant memory. She picked it up and held it under the light from the window. The smooth wax bed was stylus-scored with writing in her own language. She read the words and at first there was a confusion in her mind through which they slipped, almost avoiding capture. Then she read again. This time, although her eyes were slowly touched by tears, nothing of the message was lost to her.

> I would have built for you a house with a
> roof of green rushes and a flower-pied floor.
> A thousand sea-birds would have greeted the
> golden girl with a brow like a lily, the
> young queen who rode the perilous paths
> without harm or hurt.

And as she stood there Truvius, leaning on his staff, came into the room. She turned and ran to him and he put an arm around her and held her as she wept.

A spear's throw from the rough road Baradoc sat with his back against a rock, facing the west, eating a handful of dried grapes and a piece of hard cheese. The sun was shrouded in a low, rolling mantle of grey rain-promising clouds. There had been little morning movement on the mining road, a few carts making for Aquae Sulis with country produce, a handful of miners on their way back to the lead mines in the low limestone hills over which the clouds now were close-wreathed. The men had given him news of Abonae. The hillmen had taken it some days before and most of the people from the settlement had fled into the country to hide. Cadrus and his men would go back across the river in their hide-sheathed boats taking their spoils with them. There would be no putting the place to flames. Cadrus would leave it like a lean cow to fatten and calve again until it was time for another raid. Cadrus was not like his ancient forefathers senselessly sacking and plundering with no thought of the future. There would come a day when Cadrus would cross the river and take Abonae to stay, and then move on to take Aquae Sulis and stay ... all the Cymric tribes would do the same, moving eastwards until the day came when they would have to face the real enemy. One day someone would have to arise with the strength and power to command Cadrus and his kind, to shape and wield their courage and skills and make of them an army with a mission and a true faith. He broke the cheese into small portions and tossed a piece to each dog and Bran and he smiled to himself as he realized that to Cuna he had tossed the largest piece. The gifted dog. The twice gifted dog. Against his right hand he could capture still the bodily memory of Tia's hand in his as they had stood before Machen and had listened to his ritual words ... Aie, one day if the gods sent the chance his way he would meet Cadrus again and he would –

The thought of Cadrus was driven from his mind as Cuna suddenly leapt to his feet, barked and began to run towards the road. Baradoc called sternly to him, but the dog took no notice. At the same time, although Lerg and Aesc held their place, Bran from the top of the rock against which Baradoc leaned, took off, dropped low, his great wings almost sweeping the seeding heads of the long grasses, and then rose, beating his way above the road. In those few moments a wild hope swept through Baradoc which shook his body as though a swift fever had gripped him, firing his blood. He jumped up and ran towards the road. Far down it he saw a low cloud of dust racing away like wind-flattened smoke. Clear to him came the sound of horse-hooves beating against the hard ground.

Standing by the road, watching her ride towards him, he knew that this was what he had wished for but had cherished only as an idle dream that defied all sense and reason. No matter the manner of their joining he had no claim on her. Only she was free to turn the ceremony of duress into the truth or denial of love. Now she came riding the single horse, which being free at grazing, Cadrus's men had overlooked, and he knew that even had he left the road earlier and moved without benefit of track or path to the hills she would have found him because, no longer to be denied, the heart had its own knowledge of human courses as the swallow went unerringly south in autumn to return to the same hut eave each spring.

With Cuna barking around the horse's legs she halted before him, her growing hair free and shining in the wind, her eyes smiling but uncertain with a soft shyness. Behind her a travelling bundle was packed across the horse's back and she was dressed as he was in her old travelling clothes. Going to her and looking up, he took her hand, feeling it now in truth as a little while before he had felt it in memory. With a touch as brief and light as the wing of a passing moth he kissed her palm, and the shyness went from Tia. Her lips, up-turned with a faint touch of mockery, she said, 'O, son of a chief Baradoc, who was too cowardly to speak the truth, but wrote it on wax in the night – is that how your love will be? Easily scribed and as easily wiped away?'

Baradoc raised her hand, touched his brow with it, and then kissing it again, said, 'No, Lady Tia. What I wrote on the tablet was the shadow of a dream which I thought would die at daybreak. Come down now from your mount.' He held her arm as she slipped off the horse and stood by him, and he went on, smiling, 'Now we both have our feet on the ground and live no dream.' He raised her hand and kissed it. 'This is the kiss of my true love and the true pledge that joins us. From this day, as there is only one royal sun, so there is only one queen in my life. Your honour is my honour and any who misnames it shall have only the swift charity of my sword.'

For a moment Tia said nothing. Then, the teasing in her eyes masking her joy, she said, 'O son of a chief Baradoc, your old master gave you a skill with words that snares my heart ... Aye, and did so, I know now, from our first day together. But this day, I have ridden hard and far and without food. If you would not hear the belly of your love grumble then feed me.' She leant quickly forward and kissed him on the lips. Before he could hold her, she bent and picked Cuna from the ground and began to fondle him.

Baradoc led the horse to the rock and made Tia sit on the ground on the goats' hair cloak and he fed her from the small store he had brought from the villa with him. He fetched water in a skin from a nearby spring for her to drink and, when she had finished, he poured water over her hands that she could clean them. There were few words between them and when their eyes met it was as though a light passed between them too strong and too strange yet for them to endure its flame but briefly. Man and woman they would be but until that time came there lay ahead of them the groves of courtship to be threaded hand in hand, and a sweet and slow discovery of one another which would bring their love to full term.

They slept that night in a dry cave on the lower slopes of the hills, lying so that in the darkness they could reach out and touch one another. Until sleep took them, it was mostly Baradoc who talked, both to ease his own shyness and joy and also to have her begin to know about the journey ahead and the life that waited for them with his people. He told, too, about these hills which they must cross, where now most of the mines were worked out or abandoned, and the great stretch of marsh-and-lake land that lay beyond which must be crossed before they would reach the coast where the barren moors ran down to the sea in steep headlands, and then of the long following of the shore line westwards which would at last bring them to the country of his own people, until finally he heard Tia's breath-

note slow and her body stir briefly to find comfort as she fell
into sleep. Then as he lay awake he thought of old Truvius who,
Tia had told him, had sent her after him with his blessing, of
Truvius who had once said to him as they talked in the courtyard together, 'All countries are greater than the people who
take them by the sword. They shape conquerors to their ways
and work in them a new love which is a mystery above any
human love. I came with the legions from Etruria. I shall die
here content to be of this land ...' And as with Truvius so it
would be with Tia. One day she would know herself to be not
only his wife, but one of his people, and their children would
be of his country.

The high summer rain fell steadily the whole of the next day.
Because there was no hunting with success through the slow
driving swathes of rain as they climbed the long scarp to the
crest of the range, they turned aside to the road and found a
small mining encampment of meagre huts and a rough tavern
where they bought cheese and oat cake and dried fish, and six
eggs for their evening meal. The tavern keeper told them that in
the last weeks there had been few travellers coming or going
through from the west because the marsh people would boat
none across the lakes and swamps. He advised Baradoc to take
the long route round to the south but Baradoc's mind was set
on crossing the marshes for it would save them two or three
days' travel and there was a growing eagerness in him now to
reach his own people.

They crossed the top ridge of the hills in a grey shroud of
rain-cloud and picked their way slowly down the steep westward face through rocky ravines and sides of loose stones where
the horse, laden with their goods, had to be led and sometimes
forced to keep the track. That night on the lower slopes they
found a herder's hut, its wattle sides and bough-thatched roof
half burnt away in some old accident or act of pillage. Baradoc
cut fresh branches from a nearby thicket of alders and repaired
enough of the roof to give them shelter. Even so, the rain
drifted in upon them and they passed the night with more dis-

comfort than sleep, but because they were together and their shyness was easing they made light of the hardship. Baradoc said, half in joke and half in earnest, 'You could be lying warm and comfortable and clean in your bed at the villa, Tia. Even now I would take you –'

With a suddenness that startled him, Tia suddenly reached out and put her hand across his mouth, stopping his words, and she said without anger but with a sharp note of command, 'Never talk like that again. I belong with you.'

As she withdrew her hand Baradoc took it and said, 'Then I never will. When you command I obey.' He chuckled. '*Aie* from that first moment after you had cut me down and I opened my eyes to see you I became your slave.'

Tia smiling, shook her head. 'You talk, and your tongue runs away with you, my brave heart. You will never be anyone's slave.'

When they awoke the next morning the rain was still falling, driving before a strong southerly wind in dark, swaying curtains. They ate a scanty cold breakfast of dried fish and were wet through to their skins before they had travelled half a mile. The western slopes of the limestone range eased and finally levelled out at the fringe of the great river-and-lagoon scored stretch of marshes that lay across their path. Skirting the first stretch of towering rushes and reed-mace growths they came across a well-used path. In places the path had been firmed and strengthened with faggots of cut withy branches and bound bundles of reeds. Frogs called from the dense growth on either side of the path, bearded tits and sedge warblers flew up in alarm before them and once a marsh harrier came drifting over on great, silent wings and cried harshly as it turned away from them. After a time the path brought them to an opening in the marsh growths and they stood on the edge of a small piece of cultivated ground, the tilled dark marsh soil green with lines of growing vegetables and lank rows of still unripe barley. Beyond the cultivated ground was a narrow lagoon inlet. Built on wooden piles a little way out in the water was a reed hut which was joined to the land by a rough wooden causeway. From raised poles along the causeway and at one side of the hut fish nets were strung. From the eaves of the roof hung plaited osier cages and coops in which fowls and pigeons were penned. Tame ducks and geese swam free about the hut piles, around which rising flood water from the rains swirled fiercely.

Baradoc halted at the edge of the cultivated ground and gave a loud shout. He shouted three times before any movement came from the hut. Then a short thickset man appeared and came to the head of the causeway.

Baradoc, giving the horse's halter to Tia to hold, walked forward slowly a few paces holding his hands above his head. The man on the causeway made no movement.

Baradoc drew the sword from his belt and thrust it upright into the ground and then walked forward further. At this the man came slowly down the causeway.

Baradoc watched him as he approached. In one hand he carried a light spear and his other hand rested on the haft of a long knife which was thrust into the belt at his waist. He was bearded and long-haired and dressed in a sleeveless tunic made of otter skins roughly thonged together, the garment worn and greasy and ripped in places. The man stepped off the causeway and walked to within a few paces of Baradoc. He stood in silence for a while eyeing him suspiciously The skin around his right eye was red and swollen. The rain ran off his bare arms and legs and the sour smell of his body came strongly to Baradoc. The man's gaze went from Baradoc to Tia with the horse and dogs standing at the fringe of the reeds.

He said gruffly, 'What do you want?'

The words were in Baradoc's tongue, but heavy with the marshmen's accent and surly with suspicion.

'We go to my tribe in the west. The people of the enduring crow. We have money and will pay for a passage across the marsh lands.'

'Who is the woman?'

'My wife.'

'The word has been given that none can cross the marshes.'

He gestured to the south. 'You must go round. Besides I have nothing that would take your horse.'

Baradoc said, 'We want to cross quickly. To go round will take many days. The word was not given against your own kind. Marshmen have eaten in my father's hut many times. We have the same tongue, the same country.'

'Maybe. Show me your mark.'

Baradoc pulled his cloak and tunic aside and showed his tribal mark of the crow. 'We want to cross now. If this rain lasts another day not even you could take us against the floods.'

The man pursed his lips. 'What do you know of the marshes and the rains? Nothing. This is the rain of Latis who weeps for the return of her lover.' A smile briefly touched his dirty, weather-marked face. 'She could weep for a day or a week. No man can tell.'

Baradoc, who knew of the goddess of bogs and marshes, Latis, who was worshipped only by the marsh people, said, 'Then let us leave Latis to weep long if she must. You could have us on the other side by nightfall. Also –' he paused, for he had seen the man's eyes stray more than once back to the horse which Tia held, '– as well as paying you we would leave the horse. Two people with one horse travel no faster than a man alone.'

The man was silent for a moment and then, grinning, nodded his head, and said, 'Leave me the horse. I need no other payment.'

From that moment there was no trouble. The horse was handed over to the man, who told them his name was Odon. From his hut appeared his wife and son who was a sturdy boy, his face still smooth and untouched by any beard growth. At a word from Odon the boy dived off the edge of the causeway and swam across the lagoon inlet to the fringing reeds. He disappeared into them. In a short while, he reappeared poling a strong, light-draughted boat made of overlapping hides stretched over a framework of willow poles. The inside had been roughly daubed with a mixture of marsh mud and chopped straw and sedges, all set hard by baking in the sun, and then given a coating of fish-glue whose rank smell still persisted.

Between them they loaded up the possessions which Baradoc and Tia carried and the dogs. Tia sat forward in the blunt bows, while Baradoc was in the middle of the boat and Odon stood in the stern to pole the craft. At his feet lay a broad-bladed wooden paddle which he would use in deeper and more open water.

At first the boy wanted to go with his father and he refused to leave the boat. After a few angry words between them Odon swung his pole menacingly and the boy jumped over the side and waded ashore, shouting defiantly at his father.

As Odon poled off he laughed and said to them, 'He's as wild as a wolf – but he's a good son. I had two others but they died of marsh fever.' He shook his head to free his hair and eyes of the rain which still fell, and went on to Baradoc, 'There's a baling pot near you. The boat is sound. But with this rain it gathers water. You'll need to use it.' He dipped the pole and they began to move down the narrow inlet.

For the next two hours Tia sat in the bows, the thick woollen cloak draped around her growing heavier and heavier with the rain which soaked into it. Now and again as Baradoc and Odon talked in their own language she could pick up a scrap or two of what Baradoc said, but Odon's words because of his accent escaped her altogether.

Sitting there she was, although wet and uncomfortable, surprised by the calmness and happiness of her feelings. She had no true idea of what lay ahead. This was no journey on which she could combat hardship by the thought of some haven like Aquae Sulis ahead. Now the future was almost unknown to her, but she had no dread or concern about it because her spirit was content with the calm knowledge that whatever happened now she and Baradoc were together, not as strangers held by chance, but as man and wife tied by love. The discoveries they had yet to make about each other held no fears either because in the end they had come together freely, neither disaster nor expediency forcing them.

She sat with the dogs at her feet as the boat slid down the

inlet and, after a while, Bran who had been circling overhead dropped down and perched on the low prow of the boat. Odon, seeing the raven, said something to Baradoc who answered, but Tia could not understand what they said. Odon, now that the bargain had been made, seemed pleasant enough but there was something about the man which she did not like, something that had nothing to do with his dirty, unkempt appearance or the strange cast given to his face by the constantly twitching, diseased eye. Baradoc had told her that the marshmen had long grown apart from all the other tribes. Travellers who were ferried across the marshes by them, even though well-armed, always did so at their own risk. They were men more at home on the water than on the land, and were almost as much at ease in the marsh channels as the fish and wildfowl on which they lived. It was odd, she thought, that in this country – now her own country – which had long been civilized by her ancestors there should still be wildernesses like this which had rested unchanged and untouched by the legions. Nearly five hundred years of Roman rule had left places like this and the wild mountains from which Cadrus came much as they always had been. Beyond Isca and the mining hills which they had crossed no great military roads ran. Westward was an almost unknown land and it was westwards that she was now going. Just for a moment the thought of all the strangeness that lay before her touched her with a sudden stab of wonder at her own impulsiveness in accepting the challenge of the unknown which her love for Baradoc had provoked Then, looking up, she found Baradoc's eyes on her. He smiled quickly, wrinkling his nose at her and a quick flush of warmth spread through her, making her oblivious of the pouring rain and her own discomfort.

Hour after hour they moved through the marshes, sometimes crossing wide stretches of lagoon, sometimes snaking through narrow channels that were overhung with high reeds and rushes, sometimes sliding out into stretches of river where the brown waters rolled and swirled so strongly with the rain flood that Odon had to fight his way with strong strokes of the paddle to ease the boat out of the main stream and into a side channel to keep his course. There were times too when Odon had to force the boat across lagoons thick and matted with weeds: water parsnip and tangles of water-lilies, and yellow spiked flags and white-starred clinging crowfoot, so thick that Odon sweated and grunted as he poled them along.

Tia grew used to the sudden up-flinging of a fishing heron disturbed by their coming, to the quick fire-flash of kingfishers arrowing away from them, to the noisy alarm calls of mallard, teal and widgeon rising from their feeding grounds, churning the water to a creamy spume with their thrusting feet and beating wings, to the sudden shocks which she had had at first when the weird booming calls of bitterns rang through the rainy air. Now and again Baradoc pointed out to her an otter sliding through the water, or the white marked head of a water snake as it curved sinuously away from them, and, so often after a while that she became used to it, the fierce turmoil of the water's surface as shoals of small fish flung themselves into the air to escape the rush of some great hunting pike or perch. The rain came down steadily. Odon sweated at pole and paddle. Baradoc baled now almost without let. Bran sat huddled on the bow of the boat. Cuna shivered and whined, and Lerg and Aesc crouched without sound or movement watching Baradoc, withdrawn into some immemorial dream of their own which banished time and discomfort.

In the early afternoon they came to a wide weed-free lagoon. Near the shore stood a small group of huts built on poles over the water. From the causeways and platforms around the huts a group of marsh people watched them pass and Odon gave them a wild, ringing cry of greeting as they swept by. Sometime after this they entered a tract of swamp land where alders and willows crested the reeds of little islands and the shallow stream they followed closed until the rushes at times overhung the boat. The air was fetid with the bubbling marsh gases that broke from the water as Odon's pole disturbed the thick mud of the channel's bed.

After a while the stream began to broaden and eventually the boat slid out to a small lake into which a river ran from the south and emptied from the north end. Nearly half-way across this lake, short of the main river flow which coursed through it, a solitary hut stood on poles. It had no causeway because it was too far from the shore, but there was a wooden platform around it. Odon, taking the paddle, swung the boat towards the hut.

He said to Baradoc, 'The hut is empty. We rest for an hour and eat.' He looked up at the sky. 'Soon I think the rain will stop. By nightfall I can put you on a safe path to take you through the far side of the marshes.'

Odon edged the boat into the side of the hut platform, dropped his paddle and held on to the timber frame of the platform. He held the boat steady as Tia climbed out and the dogs jumped up with her. To Baradoc he said, 'You go up. There's a rope in the bows you can make fast. I do the same here.' Holding on with one hand he took a hide rope from under the seat on which he was sitting.

Baradoc climbed on to the platform, walked to the bows, and knelt to take the bow rope. As he did so, and before he could reach the rope, Odon dropped his rope and giving a strong push on the platform's edge sent the boat gliding away from the hut. As it drifted away he picked up the paddle and turned the boat back in the direction from which they had come. Over his shoulder he shouted, 'The word was given that none should cross. I would have taken you for you are a tribesman. But I take no woman who is not of the blood and who speaks only the foreign tongue.'

Turning his back on them he began to paddle strongly away. Baradoc and Tia, taken by surprise, stood and watched him. He was going and taking with him all they possessed, leaving them stranded in the middle of the lagoon. Then, angrily, Baradoc swore loudly, and the anger was at himself for his stupidity. The rain and the monotony of the journey had dulled his wits. For a moment his instinct was to dive in and swim after the boat, but he knew at once that Odon could easily outpace him.

All their weapons and belongings were in the boat, except for the sword which he wore. Even if he got to the boat Odon had a spear ...

Then, the dullness clearing from his mind, he turned to Tia, unbuckling his belt and beginning to strip, and said, 'Give me your dagger.'

'But Baradoc, you can't —'

'Give me your dagger!' he cried harshly as he stripped himself naked.

Tia handed him the dagger which she always carried. Baradoc took it and then turned towards Bran who had flown up on to the rush roof of the hut. He called loudly, 'Saheer! Aie! Saheer!'

Without another glance at Bran or Tia, the dagger between his teeth he dived into the water and began to swim as fast as he could after the boat.

From the platform Tia, her heart thumping, watched him and she saw that he would never catch Odon. The man, seeing him coming, was paddling hard for a reed channel at the northern end of the lake. No man swimming could ever overtake the boat. Then, harsh and seering through the rain, she heard the strong wing-beats of Bran. Bran came down through the wind-driven rain and flew low over the water after Baradoc. Tia heard Baradoc whistle to Bran as the bird hung at his side. The raven wheeled away from him and began to beat quickly towards the boat.

Standing on the hut platform, the dogs about her, alert and quivering as they watched, Tia saw Baradoc swimming as fast as he could through the dark waters, saw Odon paddling towards the reed channel, and Bran moving after the boat on strong wing-beats The raven rose in the air behind the boat and then came down in a slow, heavy stoop at Odon, passing over the man's head, raking it with his talons and then swung back to hover and beat with talons and great beak at Odon's head and face.

Odon raised his paddle and swung at Bran. The bird slid away from him only to come back at the man, first from one angle and then from another, forcing him to twist and turn on his seat as he struck upwards with his paddle. Again and again Bran dived at Odon, baulking and side-slipping to avoid the paddle blows. Once as Odon slipped on his seat, Bran landed on his shoulders and drove rapid thrusts of his great black beak at the man's neck and face.

Odon screamed with sudden pain and Bran, hovering away from him called loudly *cark, cark*. As Bran came in again Odon dropped the paddle and picked up his light spear. He stood up in the boat, blood running from his face, and slewed and turned as Bran attacked him, but Bran now kept well clear of the quick spear thrusts, circling and diving and calling loudly all the while.

As Odon could no longer paddle, the boat lost way and drifted, and Baradoc rapidly began to overhaul it. He saw Odon glance round to mark his progress. When he neared the boat he circled away to the bows, well clear of any spear thrust that Odon might make, safe in the knowledge that Odon would not risk throwing it for a frenzy now had taken Bran who whirled and swooped at Odon. One unguarded opening given to Bran and the raven would strike for Odon's eyes. Baradoc caught the side of the boat and with a great thrust of his arm and shoulder muscles lifted himself over the side. The boat tipped as he rolled aboard and water swirled over the gunwale. He heard the hoarse bark of Bran and a sudden fierce cry of pain from Odon. As he scrambled to his knees Odon, with blood running down his neck where Bran had struck him, raised the spear and hurled it wildly at him. Baradoc threw up an arm to protect himself and the blade of the spear scored the length of his right forearm and flew past him into the water. Then Odon, to escape Bran as the bird came swooping at him, dived overboard and disappeared. Oblivious of his wound, Baradoc stood, dagger now in hand, and watched the brown waters while Bran circled slowly overhead. Odon he knew would swim like an otter. And Odon now without a weapon, he knew, would not return to attack. Suddenly Bran called and went downwind through the rain wreaths towards the distant fringe of reeds about the channel opening through which they had come into the lake. Odon's head and shoulders appeared above water, but as Bran dived at him he sank quickly below the surface and Baradoc knew that when he surfaced again it would be in the safety of the reeds. He called to Bran and the raven, after a slow circle over the waters of the mouth of the channel, beat back to him upwind and dropped to the bows of the boat. Baradoc went to the stern, picked up the paddle and began to work the boat back to the hut.

The wound in Baradoc's arm, though long, was not deep. Tia, tight-lipped, tore strips of cloth from an undershift which she had brought with her and bound it. They had unloaded their possessions from the boat which was now securely tied alongside the hut platform. Above them the rain beat steadily on the weathered and decrepit rush roof. The hut was empty except for an old pile of reeds laid out as a bed in one corner. Seeing Tia's anxious, drawn face Baradoc raised his free hand and touched her on the cheek. He said, 'Don't worry about Odon. He won't come back.'

Tia, knowing now more than she had done at the time how fearful she had been for Baradoc's safety when he had climbed into the boat, said, 'You could have been killed.'

'Left here without a boat we would both have died.' He smiled. 'We've got his boat, and that's no bad bargain for the horse – and we can find our way out in time.'

'Why didn't he keep his bargain? You are of the same blood.'

Baradoc hesitated. To tell her the truth, that it was because of her and her race, was impossible. The same prejudice would arise again in the future but this was no moment to bring it to light. He said lightly, 'The same blood, maybe – but his has become diluted with the fever water of the marshes. He was over greedy for a good bargain.' He looked up at the leaking roof, the sound of the rain beating on it mingling with the noise of the flood water rushing against the piles below them. He went on, 'Odon was wrong or lying about Latis. She still weeps for her lover. I think we should stay here the night. In this rain and with darkness coming on we should be helpless. We can make an early start at daybreak. I'll see what food we've got.'

Tia shook her head. 'You do no woman's work. Sit and rest your arm. And while I do it you can tell me about Latis ...' Her voice trailed away. Impulsively she moved to Baradoc and pressed her face against his breast, holding him. She felt his arms move around her and slowly the comfort of his embrace eased the shaking in her own body and killed the fear she had known for him when she had seen him climb into the boat and Odon had flung the spear She raised her head to him and Baradoc touched her cheeks gently and then bent and kissed her on the lips.

They slept on the old bed of rushes that night, moving it below a sound piece of roof to escape the rain drips. While she lay in the darkness before sleeping Tia thought of the story of Latis which Baradoc had told her as they had sat eating and sharing their cold and short commons with the dogs and Bran. Beside her, his arms ready at hand, Baradoc slept. She drew close to him to find the warmth and comfort of his body to join with her own. Latis still wept ... Latis who, sitting by the side of a river had seen a great silver-armoured salmon swimming in the waters below her and had fallen in love with it. To please her the gods had changed the salmon into a young warrior who had stepped from the waters into her arms But each year in the winter the warrior lover moved back into the waters, became a salmon, and swam away to sea not to return until the next year's floods brought him again up-river to step silver-armoured into her arms. Latis who sits beside the drought-starved waters and weeps, flooding the rivers with her tears to bring her lover back from the sea, hastening to her up the spate-filled stream ... thinking of this Tia smiled to herself as she lay warm and relaxed against Baradoc, remembering his words, 'Latis's memory is a pebble, smooth and round, taking no mark. She weeps in and out of season without knowing why until the great fish leaps the last fall and into the pool at her feet.'

Latis wept all that night and was weeping the next morning. When they looked out the flood waters had risen so much that the boat floated level with the hut platform and would soon be in the hut itself. A brown torrent, carrying drift and flood debris, swept through the lake and the fringing rushes stood now with only their flowering tips above water. One look made two things obvious to Baradoc; they could not stay in the hut and in this flood there was no hope of finding a way across the miles of marsh they still had to cross. There was only one course open to them They must follow the river down to the sea and then make their way westwards inshore until they were clear of the marshlands.

They loaded the boat with their belongings. Baradoc pulled one of the framework timbers from the hut wall and with his sword and knife fashioned a rough second paddle so that they both could sit in the stern and handle the craft between them. With the animals sitting up forward and their belongings stowed amidships they went downstream on the summer spate-filled river, a rolling flood of creamy brown water running so high now that they could see far over the marsh stretches on either side. Great skeins of wildfowl wheeled in the sky above them, disturbed and made restless by the flood. Above them hung the birds of prey, the hawks, the sea eagles and the peregrines while like dark ghosts the harriers flew over the green tops of the almost submerged rushes. They had no need to use their paddles except to keep the boat on course. When Tia had got used to handling her paddle, Baradoc now and then left her to hold their course while he baled the rain water out of the boat. By mid-morning, the simple-minded Latis gave up weeping. The wind shifted round into the east and slowly the sky began to clear of the low, heavy clouds which had dominated it for so long.

The farther north they moved down the river, the larger it grew. At noon they came to a wide lagoon. To one side of it they saw a hut with the water well over its platform. They paddled out of the main stream and across to it. When there was no answer to Baradoc's shouts, they eased alongside the platform, tied up and Baradoc splashed along the flooded boards and into the hut. The marsh family who inhabited it had clearly left from fear of the rising waters. Such stores as they could not take with them were lodged high up under the roof or on the rough shelving either side of the door.

Baradoc found dried fish, a basket of wild duck eggs, a hard circular slab of bread, three smoked eels, a water skin half-full of thin, barley beer and a small wicker cage in which sat three miserable looking hens. He loaded them all into the boat and left payment for his takings with some of the money which Tia had brought with her. As he got back into the boat and they pushed off, Tia said, 'Look, the flood must be going down.' She pointed to the wattled side of the hut where a dark, wet band showed a hand's breadth above the water.

Baradoc scooped some of the lagoon water into his hands, tasted it, and spat it out. 'No – the flood's still running high. The tide is going out. We must be nearing the mouth of the river. The water's salty here.'

By mid-afternoon they were running down the looping estuary of the river. Mud-flats were showing above the dropping tide and echelons of gulls and waders were beginning to work them. On either side of the estuary the marsh ground spread dense and high with reeds. To the westward, over this sea of moving greenery, they could just make out, like a brown mist in the distance, the hazy rise of the first low hills beyond the flatlands. A little while later they were free of the mud-banks and the bordering marshes, moving into the sea on the breast of the river waters that curved like a dark ribbon across the turquoise and jade waters of the sea, a ribbon that thinned and faded and frayed as the sea slowly took it and made it part of itself. When they were well clear of the land the tide, running hard, took them and swept them westwards.

Tia, stiff and tired with the labour of their river ride, dropped her paddle and rubbed her sore hands. A handful of black-headed terns wheeled and dived around them. A seal surfaced briefly and watched them with lustrous eyes. The sun slipped free of the clouds, the slow roll of the waves ran musically under their keel and, now and then, threw silvery fans of spray back from their bow. Latis's mind had wandered from thoughts of her lover and she wept no more. Baradoc cut portions of the hard bread and smoked eel and handed them to Tia. As he did so he held one of her hands, raised it to his mouth and kissed the rough palm. Neither of them said anything. The sea birds wheeled and called above them and the sea was a run of coiling bright green and blue, its slow parading waves feathered and foam-laced as the steady wind caressed them.

The Fortress of Birds

That night they paddled ashore to a sandy beach walled by high dunes. Climbing the near dunes Baradoc saw that they were backed by a wilderness of marshes which stretched inland and away to the west. They pulled the light boat ashore, well above the high water mark, and tipping it on its side, propped it up with their two paddles to make themselves a shelter in whose lee they could sleep After some difficulty Baradoc made a fire, starting it with dried grasses from a mouse's nest which Cuna dug out of the dune side. They killed a hen and boiled it in a mixture of their thin, musty beer and some rainwater which Tia had baled from the bottom of the boat to fill their own water skin as they came down the river. The duck eggs from the hut they found were already hard-boiled so they cut them up into the cauldron to thicken the broth and added some mussels which Baradoc foraged from the low-water rocks. As soon as their meal was cooked Baradoc smothered the fire with sand for while they were in the marshlands he knew it was wise not to attract attention to themselves.

Even so, as they ran the boat into the water at first light the next morning and began to paddle away, four marshmen came over the dune tops and ran into the water after them, shouting and waving their spears. Seeing that they could not stop them, they went back to the beach and began to throw stones at them from their slings. For a while, until they moved out of range, the water around them was pocked with the splashes of the stones which came flying towards them humming viciously like hornets. They paddled well out and then turned along the coast pushed by the tide which had just ebbed and was running out strongly westwards. All that morning as they worked at their paddles they now and then saw small parties of men, women and children come over the dunes and down to the water's edge to watch them, all the men armed and from their manner hostile. Odon clearly had passed the word about them.

'But how could he do it so quickly?' Tia asked.

'They have signal fires and other ways. Some say they have trained birds like the pigeons they keep to carry messages, and some say they shout to one another across the marsh stretches, like the booming of bitterns and the word travels. I don't know. The marshmen have always lived apart and they have a magic which they never betray to outsiders. No matter that Odon betrayed us – we have taken his boat and that means more to him than his wife.'

With a smile Tia asked, 'And what in your tribe do you value higher than a wife?'

Baradoc smiled too. 'You know the answer for it is the same with Romans. Your honour and then my honour.'

They paddled all that morning while the tide ran. When the water finally slacked and began to turn they were clear of the low stretches of dunes and marshes and moving along a coast where now the cliffs began, rising higher with each mile they passed. The cliffs were topped with trees and green hanging valleys, some of which held a few huts and they could see the patchwork of small fields.

They turned in at low tide to a small beach, cliff-buttressed and with no sign of habitation, and they ate and filled their water skins from a small cascading stream that came down the rocks. It was here that they decided that as long as the weather, which had now set fair, lasted they would stay with the boat and work their way along the coast by water. Ashore the travelling would be hard because they were reaching that part of the coast where beyond the ever-steepening cliffs the land ran back in a high moorland plateau, full of bogs and running streams, and without roads, a place of desolation which travellers avoided by travelling far to the south. On the sand with a stick Baradoc drew a map for Tia showing the river which rose on the moor and ran south to the old legion fortress of Isca and then on to find the sea which separated Britain from Gaul. Then he outlined the other great moor which lay west of Isca where two other great rivers ran northwards rising not far from Nemetostatio, an abandoned legionary outpost, to join each other before meeting the sea in the great bay guarded on the west by the high promontory of Hercule beyond which the coast ran away sharply to the south-west towards his own homeland.

Watching him as he talked, the sunlight glinting on his new growing beard, marking the line of the fast healing cut on his bare arm, Tia was aware that it was almost as though she had never really looked at him before, that the Baradoc she had cut down from the tree and with whom she had travelled to Aquae Sulis had been more boy than man. But this Baradoc before her now suddenly seemed to have sprung across the threshold into manhood. This Baradoc was her husband He was leading her into a strange land beyond the Tamarus river, to a life which would close around her and claim her for the rest of her years – and she was not only totally unprepared for it, but had hardly given it any serious thought in the happiness which had flooded her as she had galloped away from the Villa Etruria to join him. Searching to make some amends for this, to put her immaturity and unpreparedness to a proper test she said quickly, 'From this moment we speak only my tongue in the morning. The rest of the day we use yours. I should be a wife without honour if I go to your people and cannot talk to them freely. And each night before we sleep you will tell me about their history, their legends, and their beliefs and their gods. I would not shame you with my ignorance or my dumbness.'

Baradoc said nothing. No matter all they had gone through together, no matter that out of the forced nature of their betrothal had come the truth of their love for one another, there had been a curtain between them through which they could speak and see, but through which no warmth greater than the even glow of comradeship had passed. As though the curtain were tangible, he reached out now and pulled it aside. He put his arms around her and drew her to him, both of them half upright, kneeling on the soft ground. He kissed her and felt her lips move with his, felt her arms fold about him as his held her tight to him. And they held together so moulded to one another until Cuna suddenly barked and jumped up at them, and then they collapsed sideways on to the sand map. To Cuna's barking, as Baradoc looked down into the even depths of her blue eyes, Bran added his harsh hunting call and above him the gulls, disturbed by his black, wheeling shape, began to scream and wicker in a fierce chorus that came echoing back from the tall cliffs. From that moment there was no longer any Lady Tia and no longer any son of a chief Baradoc, nor any curtain between them.

The following days moved to a pattern which was brightened by settled fine weather, and the quiet swell and fall of the summer sea imposed on them something of its own easy rhythm. They moved with the tide when it began to ebb westwards whether it was day or night. They slept sometimes in daylight, sometimes under moonlight, sometimes on the warm sands, sometimes in the boat as it rocked under the stars Tia began to learn Baradoc's language fast, and she lay often with her head against his shoulder as he told her about his people and their history, spoke their poems to her and taught her their songs. One night they slept in the summer hut of a friendly old fisherman at the head of a small beach at the foot of a gorge through which tumbled and roared a swift moorland river. Behind the hut were wooden racks on which the old man hung his gutted and broached catches to dry. When autumn came he would take the dried fish loaded in the panniers of his pony over the moors, along the heather tracks to sell or barter to the people in the settlements in the valleys south of the moor. He was an old man who knew nothing of the world outside his fishing station and the small settlements he served. From him they bought hooks, gorges, lines and a small net so that they could do their own fishing, and when they left he gave them a great slab of heather honeycomb which they wrapped in dock leaves and kept cool in their cauldron.

Before they left the old man, nodding at their boat, said, 'The gods have been good to you with the weather. Not for many years have I known it so settled. But when you come to the mouth of the Two Rivers, even though the gods still smile, take to the land.' They left him and idled along the coast for many days, working the tides, or sometimes passing whole days sheltered on secure cliff-guarded beaches, wrapped in the laziness and bliss of the sun and their own happiness. Then came a day when the high cliffs, their tops flaming now with purple heather bloom, dropped away and before them was the wide bay of the Two Rivers curving southwards in a great arc to the estuary mouth where the river waters moved over the bar in a welter of foam to fight the sea. Beyond the river mouth the land was shrouded in a heat haze, but Baradoc knew that somewhere close in the haze was hidden the great promontory of Hercule and suddenly there was in him a sharp urge to idle no more. He decided that they would cross the bay, abandon the boat, take to the shore, and follow the coast westwards to his homeland. But as they crossed the bay, although they had the tide with them, they met the spew of the strong waters of the Two Rivers. Paddle as they might they were pushed farther and farther out to sea and the pearl-grey heat haze, thickening over the distant shore, slowly began to roll in a cloaking mist over the water towards them.

Within an hour they were wrapped and lost in veils of heavy mist and the sea which had been kind for so long stirred and strengthened and began to run in a long swinging swell, deep and powerful, carrying them up its dark slopes and then drawing them down into wide valleys of foam marbled water. Through the mist came now and then the cry of some solitary seabird and sometimes a glimpse of the black-winged, surface-hugging passage of shearwaters and shags.

The three dogs, hating this new movement of the sea, huddled together miserably in the bows. Bran, plumage bedewed with mist drops, sat bedraggled on their piled belongings amidships, Baradoc and Tia now having no sense of direction sat in the stern, the boat drifting and rising and falling. Within an hour

Tia was violently seasick and Baradoc made her lie down on a couch of their spare clothes in the bottom of the boat. Although he spoke cheerfully to her, he was worried by this sudden turn in the weather. In the past days he had always been careful to hug the shore as closely as possible and only to journey when the tide was with them on its westerly course. Now, because of the mighty outpouring of the river waters, they were farther out to sea than they had ever been and in the mist he had no idea of the direction of the boat's drift. Worse still, he knew that in a couple of hours the tide would turn, and in a few more hours it would be dark. By morning they could have drifted far out to sea, maybe out of sight of land. The prospect was not a happy one, but he kept his anxieties to himself. So far they had seen no other ships but he knew at this time of the year that the foreign trading vessels from Erin and Cymru would be on their way west and south – about to clear the great toe of Britain around the promontory of Belerium to avoid the autumn storms, heading for Gaul, Iberia, and the Mediterranean. If they met one of them there was every chance that they could be taken up as slaves. Silently he put up a prayer to the gods that the mist would clear soon ... but the gods gave no answer, except for Latis. As the mist darkened with the coming of night she began to weep again and her tears were almost as fine as the mist, thickening it and wrapping it about them in a damp, clinging cloak.

By the time full darkness was with them Tia had recovered, but she had no desire for food and Baradoc would not eat by himself. They fed the dogs and Bran and put down water for them in the frying skillet. Then the two of them sat in the stern, their cloaks drawn over them, pressed close together for warmth, the darkness now so thick that although they could hear the occasional stir of the dogs forward they could not see them.

Tia slept, leaning against Baradoc, his right arm about her. She dreamt that she was back in her brother's home and riding with him as he made his morning rounds, seeing the oxen drawing their ploughs across the long strips of lynchet fields, hearing the laughter from a shearing party as men clipped the early summer coats from the sheep, riding through the beech woods on the down tops where the swineherd watched his beasts rooting through the dead leaves for the last of the past year's mast, and looking forward to the moment when they would turn down the long home combe to the beach where they would strip and take their swim. Coming back through the fishing village they would buy fresh lobsters and crabs, carrying them across their saddle fronts, alive and moving in their straw-plaited skeps. And as they turned from the beach they would rein in and watch the fishing boats, riding high on the combers, come in from their early morning netting with crowds of gulls and terns wheeling and calling noisily above them. . . . In her dream the screams of the gulls rose until she was slowly drawn from sleep to find that the noise had followed her. For a moment or two she had no idea what had happened or where she was. Then slowly memory and the present came back to her.

She stirred stiffly and sat upright. The darkness of night had gone, but the mist was still with them. She could see the dogs sitting in the bows, their coats dewed with the fine rain which still fell. But the sea no longer rose and fell in the swinging motion which had made her sick. It lay around the boat flat and calm. Not far from them came the screaming and calling of unseen seabirds.

Baradoc, seeing her awake, said, 'Take your paddle. The gulls are crying from cliffs, I think. A little while ago the sea calmed as though we had come into the shelter of land.'

They dipped their paddles and began to move the boat towards the sound of the crying gulls. After a few moments a rock, fringed with waving seaweed, appeared close on their right. They paddled on and suddenly Aesc rose from the bows, shook her coat and began to bark.

Tia said, 'Aesc smells land.'

Almost before she had finished speaking the bows of the boat grated gently on shingle and the mist ahead of them darkened, then swirled apart and briefly they had a glimpse of grey rocks footed with a small stretch of pebble beach. Baradoc went to the bow, slid overboard up to his waist and then began to drag the boat forward. Lerg and Aesc jumped over and swam to the beach and disappeared into the mist. Baradoc let them go. If there was any danger close at hand they would soon give warning.

Tia, as the boat slewed sideways to the beach, jumped over. Between them they drew the boat up on to the beach clear of the water.

As they walked across the narrow scallop of beach Lerg and Aesc came to them out of the mist. The morning light was strengthening quickly and the air, which had been still and heavy, was slowly touched with the breath of an awakening breeze which began to shred away the veils of mist. They saw that the small beach was flanked closely by rocks on either side and backed by the steep broken rise of a cliff.

Baradoc said, 'The mist is lifting fast. We'll make the boat safe and then find out where we are.'

They took all their possessions out of the boat to lighten it, carried them above the high water mark of sea-wrack and drift wood, and put them safely on a wide shelf of cliff rock. Then they pulled the boat well above the tide mark and to make it safe Baradoc tied the long bow rope to a heavy boulder. As the mist about them slowly thinned they ate and drank some water. Then, wearing his sword and carrying his spear, Baradoc sent the dogs ahead and they followed them up a narrow, over-grown track which zig-zagged and curled up the cliff through screes of loose shale and shillet and patches of scrub and low wind-shaped thorns. Sea thrift padded the rocks and patches of brown seed-headed foxgloves, willow herb and gorse filled the small gulleys and gentler slopes. Before long they were above the last, dying trails of mist and out into the strong sunlight. The cliff line ran far to the north-east and the rocks were covered with colonies of seabirds, the air full of their cries. Here and there on the higher slopes they could make out the movement of grazing goats and sheep. To the south-west the cliff line, much shorter, ran sheer for a while and then dropped sharply to the sea, ending in a small island joined to it by a line of rocks which the dropping tide was now uncovering.

Without a word to Tia, Baradoc turned and began to climb higher and after a while they came through a narrow, twisting valley to the top of the cliffs. Before them stretched a wide run of grass and heatherland rising gently to the north. Just below the skyline stood a group of round, stone-walled huts roofed with weather-browned turves. Baradoc dropped to the ground and pulled Tia down with him, his eyes never leaving the huts.

Tia said, 'What is it? Do you know where we are?'

'Yes, I think so. We're on the island of Caer Sibli – the fortress of birds. Only a handful of people live here and they don't welcome strangers. Look –' he turned and pointed southwards where the haze over the sea had cleared '– that's the main coastline over there.'

Tia saw, away across the growing sun sparkle on the sea, a faint hazy line of shadow against the lower sky. Then looking back at the huts she said, 'I don't see any smoke from cooking fires or any sign of life. We're short of food and we come in peace. Why should they harm us?'

'Because they are the Lundi people.'

'Lundi?'

'That is their name for their tribal bird. The birds you saw on the cliffs as we climbed, the ones with solemn faces and painted beaks that others call puffins.'

'But why should we fear them?'

'Because nobody ever knows what is in their minds. The sea-raiders and the trading captains know this island. They land and rob them and take those who do not hide in the cliff caves for slaves. Sometimes, too, when there is famine on the mainland the tribesmen come out in their boats and steal their sheep and goats and take their maidens. Once there were many of them. But over the years they have become only a handful.

Maybe their huts are empty now because they are at the far pastures with their cattle. Wherever they are we would risk too much by meeting them.'

Baradoc rose, took her hand, and began to lead the way down to the beach where they had left their boat. Tia went with him without question, her legs aching from the long climb to the island top. The sea and the cliffs below them were alive with the movement of birds, puffins and guillemots, cormorants and gannets moving in restless colonies on the rocks or fishing the waters. Above them, soaring and preying, hung sea eagles, ospreys, great black-backed gulls, kites and peregrines and ravens. She had never seen so many birds at one time. Half-way down when they stopped to rest Baradoc said, 'The tide is running out and the wind is in our favour. We can cross to the mainland by nightfall. The little food we have will serve us.'

He was happy, as he moved on, for if the gods were good to them, a handful of days would see them back with his people. The thought of return, as it always did now, made him picture the scene. He would come down the valley to the great rocks, to the place of his people, to the stone and timber-framed houses, past the hillside plots, to the noise of shouting children and barking dogs whose strangers' greeting would be muted as he and Tia walked into the stone-paved, walled meeting place overlooking the sea, with the wind blowing the drying nets and the boats drawn safely up from the long strand, and he would stand with his hand in Tia's and the other holding his sword and he would call aloud for Inbar . . . *Aie*, even before he called for his own mother if she still lived, he would call for his cousin and before he entered his dead father's house or took meat again with his own people he would settle the score which had to be settled.

Walking behind Baradoc, her clothes dry on her now from the strong sun, Tia watched Cuna snap at a butterfly that crossed the track before him and thought of the Lundi people who lived on this island whose hard life had taught them that there was danger in greeting any stranger. She smiled fondly to herself as the memory came back jewel-bright to her of Baradoc talking his day-dreams to her one evening as they lay close together on warm sand, his dream ... maybe his only dream ... of a Britain proud and free of all Saxons, where one day any man might walk its length and breadth unarmed and unafraid ... Baradoc the dreamer of peace – but also the warrior husband, the man she loved, whose sharp spear tines shone from the whetstone and whose sword never lacked its bright edge.

So they came down together, jumping the sea-smoothed beach boulders, on to the tiny crescent of sandy shingle, growing now as the tide ran out – and both of them were suddenly robbed of all movement.

Their boat was no longer on the beach. The large stone to which the bow rope had been tied lay in its place, and from it the shingle and sand were scored with the broad mark where the craft had been dragged down to the sea, pulled by the stern for there were no footprints showing. Tia looked out over the waters. There was no sign of the boat, only the winging and diving movement of the myriad sea birds and the long, lazy rhythm of waves breaking over the rocks and washing up on to the shore, seething and hissing softly.

Without word or cry they ran together to the mooring stone and then walked, as though in a dream, down the scored mark to the water and stared out at the diamond glitter of the sea. Then, with an anguished cry, Tia turned and ran back up the beach to the rock ledge where they had left all their possessions. None of them had been taken. They rested, piled on the ledge, just as they had put them there.

'Why take the boat and leave these,' cried Tia angrily.

Baradoc said nothing, but he stepped closer to the rock face below the ledge. On its flat face writing had been freshly scratched with the sharp edge of a piece of shillet.

Baradoc said, 'Read the writing. The answer is there if you can understand it.' Then the passion of frustration in him burst and he struck the rock with his fist and cried out bitterly, 'What have I done that the gods make sport of me like this?'

On the rock face was written in Tia's own language:

Cronus in the dream spoke thus
Name him for all men and all time
His glory an everlasting flower
He throws no seed

Tia turned slowly to Baradoc, a frown marking her suntanned brow. 'What does it mean?'

'Ask the gods!' he said angrily.

'Who is Cronus?'

'He, too, is a god, but not one of ours. From my old master I know about him. He was the god of all Time, the god of the Golden Age and the father of Zeus.'

'Why should someone steal our boat and then write that?'

Stifling his rage, Baradoc said, 'How can I tell you? But it is said that many of the people who live here, because of their close breeding, are strange in the head.'

'To take our boat and leave our belongings they must be mad. What are we going to do?'

Baradoc, catching the trembling note of anxiety in her voice, put his arm around her and said calmly, 'Accept what the gods have sent and face it. The boat must be hidden somewhere around the island shores. But we can't go looking for it without being seen by the islanders. So there is no choice left us but to go to them.'

'But they're dangerous, you said.'

'So they are. But if they had meant us harm they would have waited in ambush for us here and killed us and taken our boat and our possessions.' He pointed to the rock ledge. 'Look, the boat is stolen but the bow and the arrows in their quiver are left. That is either a sign of madness or a sign of peace.' He tightened the buckle of his sword belt, handed Tia his spear and picked up the bow and the arrow quiver, and said, 'I leave you with Lerg and if anyone –'

'Baradoc!' Tia interrupted him, her face taut, 'You leave me nowhere! Where you go I go. Until we read the truth of this mystery my place is by your side.'

Baradoc hesitated. Then seeing the firm set of her mouth, the stubborn tilt of her chin and the light of defiance in her eyes, he shrugged his shoulders and said smiling, 'What kind of wife have I taken that she overrules my words? The women of the enduring crow are meek and lower their eyes when their men speak.'

Tia said, 'So they should when the time is right. But that time is not now, though –' she grinned '– the gods know I will take no pleasure in climbing that cliff track again.'

She turned from him and began to make into a bundle such food as they had left. As she picked up the almost empty water skin Baradoc said, 'There will be no need for that. There will be water on the high heath land.' He turned and looked at the writing on the rock again. The words had been scribed by someone who knew the Roman tongue well. No wild Lundi islander could have written them. Maybe marooned on the island was some priest or learned hermit, his brains addled with the fancies that solitude had brought him.

That day, their first on the island, was a strange one. The mist long gone now, the sky bright and clear with a warm breeze blowing from the south, the sea a maze of serpentine currents below them, the air pierced with the cries of the seabirds, they climbed the cliff track. Near the island top where a small stream ran down a narrow valley they stopped and drank at a pool overhung with ferns, the rocks padded with vivid green moss.

When they reached the plateau they hid for a while and watched the nearest group of huts. They saw no sign of life. Before moving Baradoc sent Lerg on ahead to the huts. He looped away across the rough grasses, lost now and then in the tall patches of bracken, and they saw him move around the huts and disappear into one of them. After a while Lerg came out and sat on his haunches in the doorway.

Baradoc and Tia went forward with the two other dogs, while Bran circled in low flight above. There were four huts and they were all deserted. Their walls were made of piled stones, the roofs of driftwood poles – for there were few trees on the island – were thatched over with layers of heath bundles and turves. For protection against the strong sea winds the thatch was held by a network of twisted heath ropes from which hung large stones. All the low doorways faced south-east to cheat the fierce westerly winds that swept the island top in the autumn and winter gales. Outside each hut was a pile of old limpet and mussel shells, fish and animal bones and other cooking debris. Each hut had a stone hearth in the centre, long cold now and the ashes blown about the floor. Above the hearths was an opening in the roof to take away the smoke. Each hut, too, had a raised platform away from the door which served for bed, and three of these still held piles of sewn seal skins and rough woollen coverings. And each hut looked as though the owners had suddenly, in the midst of their normal life, just walked out and left everything. Earthenware pots still held stale, dust-filmed water; skillets and cauldrons stood by the cold hearths, some with dried and rotten fish and porridge in them; a string of coloured clay beads lay on the floor by one of the beds and from the walls hung fishing lines and nets. In niches were set scallop shell holders full of congealed seal oil with rush tapers for lighting. The floors were covered with soft, dark peat earth which still held the footprints of the people who had lived there.

Beyond the huts was a large granite-walled enclosure for cattle penning, the gateway of driftwood and latticed rushes broken and lying on the ground. In a sheltered corner of the outside wall stood two wind-crabbed and twisted damson trees on which the fruit was slowly turning colour.

All that day while the light lasted Baradoc and Tia explored the island, moving always with the three dogs well out ahead of them and Bran – disturbed by the myriad bird life – was soon lost to his own devices, but came winging back to them from time to time calling hoarsely. The island was almost four miles long and in its widest part towards the southern end a mile broad. It ran narrowing to the north like a roughly shaped flint dagger, the cliffs on the westerly side so steep and sheer that Tia drew back with fear as she looked down at the breaking waters and the white stippling of seabirds on the rocks and coasting above the sea. On the easterly side the land was gentler, sloping through bracken combes and small hanging valleys to much lower cliffs.

It was in one of these combes towards the tip of the island that they came upon another group of huts, lying below the crest of the plateau, the doorways looking out to sea and to a great rock outcrop far below where a colony of gannets roosted. All the huts were deserted, but here the insides showed signs of violence. Some of the roofs had been burned, the cooking vessels about the hearths were smashed, bed platforms broken and the nets and fishing gear strewn on the floor. Grain storage pots lay broken and cracked and corn and flour lay yellow and mouldy over the trodden peat. Behind the huts a walled field held crop strips, long neglected, the pods on the rows of beans now black and split, the barley in full ear smothered with poppies and weeds and thrusting bracken growths.

On the seaward side of the field, in a small marshy hollow from which a stream ran thinly, a great rock outcrop thrust up from the short turf before the fall of the true cliffs, and here Baradoc and Tia found some of the islanders.

They were all men, and there were eight of them, and they lay as they had fallen in battle with their backs to the craggy face of the rock pinnacle. Sun and weather had worked on their raggedly clothed bodies, and rats and foxes and seabirds had picked their bones clean. All their weapons had gone except for a broken spear, a sword snapped short almost to the hilt, and two round padded bucklers, skin-faced over wooden frames, their centres crowned with wide bronze bosses. One of them had been split almost to its centre by some weapon stroke, and in the bleached skull of the skeleton alongside it was wedged the iron head of an axe with the wooden handle broken off short below the socket. Bracken and yellow rag-wort had grown up around the men, mildew had spread over their rough tunics and the rain and sun had stiffened board-hard their cloak skins. They lay there in the sunshine, the bees working the new bells of the heath blossom, butterflies zig-zagging across the gorse and brooms at the rock foot, and the meadow pipits and larks calling from the streamside and sky above them.

Without a word Tia and Baradoc turned away from the scene of violence. They knew what must have happened . . . Tia seeing it all in her imagination, though she would have wished to close her inner eyes on the sight: the long keels of sea-raiders or traders who would barter and sell human or any other goods ghosting into the island by night, the sudden assault maybe at first light when all the men, women and children would be in or close to their huts . . . and here, this handful of men who had found time to snatch their weapons and make their stand, choosing death to the slavery which would await them in far places.

Suddenly Baradoc said vehemently, 'What kind of thing is man that he does this to other men? What kind of gods watch over this land that they delight in such savagery and the slavery and slaughter of the innocent? To kill in a true cause is a just thing. To kill and enslave for a handful of gold is an evil, a poison which must be stamped out as a man brings the sharp of his heel down on the head of the adder in the path before him.'

Listening to him Tia felt her body strung with a cold tremor of pity for the women and children of the island huts. In her memory was suddenly the vision of Cadrus's face as she had stood before him and his eyes had gone over her, the look searing her as though it had been a fierce flame. She felt Baradoc's arm move around her shoulders and he began to lead her away.

They passed that night in one of the huts at the southern end of the island. The three dogs kept watch outside and Baradoc lay on the sleeping platform with Tia, awake and with his weapons close to him. Tia slept and sometimes talked in her sleep and Baradoc guessed that she was haunted by dreams of the men who lay, bleach-boned and fleshless under the tall rock. Every little while he went out and joined the dogs. The night was clear and the great stars of Orion's belt blazed in the heavens. To the north a curlew called and occasionally an owl came drifting like a lost spirit over the land. Southwards, hidden in the darkness, lay the mainland. Anger stirred in him as he thought that in a handful of days they would have been back with his people ... and now, until they found their boat, they were trapped on the island. Tomorrow, although he would make a closer search around the whole shore line, his common-sense told him that there were a hundred places among the tall cliffs and rugged bays and inlets where the boat could be hidden without much hope of discovery. Maybe, too, whoever had taken it had set it adrift and it was now miles away. But – and his anger and frustration flared in him at the thought – *some-body* had taken it and, unless that person had left the island in the boat, he was here to be found. That thought, because all anger seeks a firm hold, filled his mind with a desire to find the person and, mad or sane, to face him with the bitterness that ran so strongly in him. He wanted to be back with his people, to present his wife to them, to take his place with them, to deal with Inbar, his cousin, and to be free to take up the true cause which stayed ever with him, like an always open wound when he thought of the Saxons and of the night they had circled his master and hewn him down, shouting and jeering and laughing in their drunken sport.

But the gods, as he slowly came to acknowledge as the days that followed slipped from the coil of time, were against him. By himself he searched the island, climbed down the sheer cliffs, risking life and limbs, swam across inlets and gullies that boiled with surging, foaming waters to explore caves and clefts, and lay sometimes motionless for hours on a commanding rock point watching for some betraying sign of human life, until with the passing days the fire of his impatience died.

They settled in the largest of the huts and furnished it with their own possessions and pickings from the other huts. They lacked neither for shelter, food nor water. There were fish to be netted or hooked from the rocks, and wild on the island roamed the animals of the islanders, sheep, goats and pig. After a few days a handful of the islanders' fowls made their way back to them to scavenge their scraps and stayed to lay eggs for them. Now and again Baradoc, stalking with his bow, shot a seal bask-ing on the rocks and they had its flesh to eat, its pelt to repair clothing and its blubber to render down to oil for the lamp sconces in the hut's wall niches. There was peat to be cut and driftwood to collect for their hearth fire and as the year waned they took the islanders' abandoned short-handled sickles and cut the weed-choked grain crops, and they collected the hard beans from the rows of blackened pods and Tia ground them on a stone quern to add to their flour when they made bread or to thicken their fish and seal broth. As autumn came in they found a small valley where blackberry bushes grew and feasted on the fruit and pulped some with the meagre crop of damsons and stored it in earthenware jars to sweeten their bread in the days to come. Salt they scraped from the dried hollows of the sea rocks where storm pools had long evaporated.

While the good weather lasted they both kept their eyes alert for any sign of ship or passing craft and often looked longingly at the distant mainland, and wherever they were along the island coast they searched always for some sign of their boat or of the stranger who had taken it. They wore little clothing, swam together from the rocks and hid from each other the core of longing they held to escape from the island, and only Baradoc ever went into the combe above the gannets' rock where the dead island men lay.

Against the coming of winter they laid up in one of the other huts a store of cut peat turves, dried strips of goat and sheep flesh, smoked fish and the small harvest of grain they had garnered. Baradoc repaired their hut thatch and twisted new ropes to hold more stones so that when the first gale did sweep over the island the hut stood firm and secure.

It was after this gale that Baradoc, hunting with his bow at the northern end of the island, had his first glimpse of the stranger. Lying in the bracken watching a herd of goats, waiting for them to crop closer so that he could take one, he saw them suddenly scatter and move quickly away. Distantly over the skyline close to a sheer cliff drop a brown clad figure appeared and stood looking out to the western sea approaches.

Aesc raised her muzzle as the scent of the stranger came downwind and from the throat of Lerg at Baradoc's side came a low rumble. He gave the dogs the word and they went upwind fast and steadily. Baradoc held his place, knowing that once they reached the stranger they would hold him until he arrived.

The two dogs raced across the plateau to take the stranger from either flank. Whether the man – for he was clearly such – was aware of their coming or not Baradoc could not tell. As the dogs closed silently on the man Baradoc rose and began to run after them. But before he was within two bow shots of the man, he saw him drop quickly below the skyline.

When he reached the dogs there was no sign of the stranger. The land dipped away into a small bowl that stood at the head of a great landslide of rocks that ended in a cliff face that dropped sheer and unbroken by path or by any ledge or shelf wider than would give scant roosting or breeding place for sea-birds.

Far, far below, the long westerly swells of the dying storm rolled and thundered against the cliff foot, sending great spouts and fountains of grey water creaming into the air. Yet more surprising than the sudden vanishing of the stranger who could have had no escape route it seemed than over the cliff was the behaviour of the dogs. They stood a few paces apart where they had come to a halt to hold the man and when Baradoc commanded them to the search they ignored him. Aesc, the wind ruffling her long coat, gave a tired yawn, then sat and began to scratch her flank with a rear foot, and Lerg, under Baradoc's angry gaze, lowered his head and avoided his master's eyes. For the first time since he had trained them they were refusing to obey his command ... a high wave of anger swept through him and he would have shouted at them, berating them, but he checked himself. Some power greater than his own held sway over them. There was no fault in them which merited his anger.

He left them and searched about the bowl and the cliffside, but could trace no way by which the stranger might have escaped him. In the end he gave up the search. As he walked away the two dogs turned and followed him. When he found the flock of goats he sent the dogs in to cut one out and they obeyed him. Back with Tia, not wishing to worry her, he said nothing of having seen the stranger.

Two mornings later Tia, rising early while Baradoc slept, went out to collect eggs from the hens. On the threshold of the hut she found an earthenware crock, a looped thong handle about its neck, full of goat's milk and by its side wrapped in broad dock leaves a large piece of goat's cheese.

The Island Parting

When Tia told Baradoc about the milk and cheese, he said, 'It must be a gift from the stranger. Some days ago I saw him, but he slipped from me by casting a spell over the dogs.'

After Tia had got the full story from him, she said, 'Although he may have taken our boat and destroyed or hidden it, I can't thing he means us any harm. Why leave such a gift otherwise?'

Baradoc shrugged his shoulders impatiently. 'What you say is true. But he has stopped us from reaching my people. Even if we had the boat it would be dangerous now to put to sea. At this time of the year a single cloud in the sky which would be the pride of a summer's morning grows to a storm before hot broth can cool. With a good wind and a good tide and a fair sea it is all of a day's hard paddling to reach the mainland. By myself I would take the risk, but in winter I would never put you in such peril.'

For a moment or two Tia was silent, looking down at him where he sat on the edge of the bed platform pulling on a pair of rough goatskin sandals he had made and binding the broad thongs about his sun-browned calves. For her he had made soft sealskin sandals on which with his own hands – for when he needed he could work as fine and surely as any woman – he had sewn a beaded outline of the enduring crow, the bird of his tribe, now the bird of her tribe, and a bird which haunted the island's cliffs in pairs, their jet wings flashing in sun and rain, the scarlet of their legs brighter than rowan berries. The sun glinted on his tawny beard which she had close cropped for him with her finely honed single-edged dagger. As he looked up at her, his dark eyes warm and as lustrous as bloom-free damson fruits, she knew that she loved him and could love no other.

And knew, too, that he loved her as he could love no other woman, but that a greater love which she made no claim to rival lived with him – his love of his country, his passion to see it free and to bring all men to the peace of a just and honourable life. She moved to him, put down a hand and lightly touched him on the cheek and then softly ran her finger across his rough, weather-cracked lips, and said, 'You would not only put me in peril, my brave heart.'

Baradoc tugging at a thong, raised his head to her, kissed her finger, and asked, 'Who else?'

'You do not know?'

'All I know is that this spell-weaving stranger acts out some madness which, with so much waiting to be done elsewhere, holds us here till spring comes. *Aie* ... we are well set enough with food and drink and shelter, but time passes without true action and golden hours are lost forever.' He struck his hand irritably against his head and went on, 'In here I have already schemed the way and the means. We begin small, smaller than a mustard seed, but the growth will come. First, with my own people, and then gathering a good company of men of reason and courage from other tribes, we must train and learn to love discipline as did your people's armies. We shall need men with the grain of your old uncle Truvius as he was in his prime and –'

Amused, well used to this kind of outpouring, Tia suddenly pressed her hand across his mouth. Holding it there, she said, 'Crow man – cease your clifftop croaking and listen. Maybe this stranger acts out some madness. But in my mind it is more a wise magic, far beyond that which you hold over Lerg and Aesc. Milk we have not had for many weeks. And for long now there has been in me a craving for milk, aye, and cheese. Does that mean nothing to you, that a woman should have such cravings?' She took her hand away, and laughing said, 'Now you look moon-faced at me, empty-eyed and empty-headed like some simple wit sitting on the Forum steps understanding nothing but that the sun shines and he is warm. Did your great master teach you nothing about women and their terms? Did you think that lying on warm beaches at night after the marsh crossings, happy in one another's arms to escape the cold before dawn there would not follow one day the slow flight of the white stork?'

Baradoc frowned at her. 'Now you talk in riddles.'

Tia shook her head and reaching down held his tawny hair, gently tugging at it. 'You, whose eyes are like a hawk's and can mark the stir of the far grasses as a vole makes passage foraging, it seems are blind when you look at me. Do I have to grow as round-bellied as a full moon before –'

'By the gods!' Baradoc leapt suddenly to his feet and grasped her shoulders. 'You're with child!'

Smiling teasingly at him, but trembling with her own happiness which she had had to contain until there was only certainty in her, Tia said mockingly, 'My lord Baradoc, my brave heart, I have never met anyone so quick at understanding. Yes, I am carrying your child and have done for these last few months.'

Baradoc drew her to him and, holding her, smothering her face against his shoulder, hugged her. Then he kissed her and stood back, looking at her, his face creased with joy, and said, 'It will be a boy, won't it? It must be a man child, to grow to arms and courage and honour and –' He broke off abruptly, shame-faced, and took her hands gently in his. Then, his voice low and shaking, he went on, 'Tia, my Tia ... boy or girl, it matters not for there can be no shadow of difference in my love for either, and no shadow ever over the love which binds you to me and me to you.'

'That I know. But I know, too, and you need have no shame in it, that you would if it were possible bribe the gods with ambrosia, nectar and high sacrifices to grant that our first-born be a son.'

Shaking his head, Baradoc put his hand about her cheeks, and said, 'You tease me and for my slowness you are right to do so. But you are wrong. I go now to make a sacrifice to the gods, but I shall ask them for one thing only – that when the day comes they keep you safe for you are the bright bird of my life.'

From that moment there was a fire and an impatience in Baradoc which made even the shortening days of winter seem long. To ease the itch in him for action as the old year rolled slowly towards the new, he set about building a boat which would carry them to the mainland when the spring came. He took drift wood and poles from some of the huts and slowly thonged them together with hide strips to make the framework of the hull. All this he did on a slope above the beach where they had originally landed, well out of reach of the highest tide or winter gale. He worked sometimes from first to last light, and the hours he had to lose to hunting for their pot he grudged. Most of the seals had moved away from the island now that the breeding and rearing seasons were gone, but he killed them whenever he could and scraped and cleaned the skins until, with other skins which he foraged from the bed platforms of the abandoned huts, he had enough to fashion an outer and an inner skin about the framework of the boat.

There were times at night as he sat in their hut lashing the skins together with thin strips of hide and sinew when Tia would rise and deliberately blow out the sconce lights and scold him to bed. There were nights, too, when he woke in the darkness and thought about the child which Tia carried and saw them returning to his people. Yet more often he lay working out some problem in his boat building. He had no pine pitch or clay to caulk it. Between the inner and outer skin, he decided, he would pad the space with a mash of chopped up reeds and rushes to be gathered from the bog patches in the middle of the island, working into the cut rushes pig fat and seal blubber rendered down in a cauldron over a fire. The mess would harden after being laid on and should make the boat water-tight enough to take them to the distant coast. Not a day passed, except in the fiercest gales when to step outside the hut into the shrieking wind and rains was to be buffeted to the ground or on those days when the island was wrapped in a windless sheet of thick mist that made the climb down to the boat too dangerous a task, that he did not labour at the boat with knife or axe or a small broken saw which he had found in one of the huts.

While he worked his mind flighted to the future. The child would be a son, the gods must grant him that. The task that lay ahead when he finally returned to his tribe would be more than the years of one man could achieve. He would gather and train the tribes of the west, they would in the end come to his way of thinking and acknowledge him, call him Pendragon, swear faith and follow him, the dragon head leader. In full time the years or death in battle would finally take him, but not without the comfort of knowing that a son stood at his side ready to step into the leadership and go forward with the fight.

As Tia grew bigger with her child, he made her keep close to their hut and he took from her all the work he could. He grew even harder and leaner of body, but his spirit flamed bright and steady, and Tia, knowing and understanding the passion in him, made no complaint. She loved him, knew his love for her, and knew the truth of him that under the warrior he would be lay also the poet and dreamer. There were few mornings when she woke to find him gone in the dark to catch the first light by the time he reached the boat that she did not find scratched with a stick on the smoothed out peat and earth floor some message from him. On a rainy morning he wrote, *The day weeps its sorrow for the summer suns that are gone, but in my heart like a wren in its moss bower my love for mother and child is warmth of a hundred suns.* And on a morning of rare frost which white-laced the grasses and dead bracken, she read, *Three things that are wondrous fair – winter silver on the spider's web, the moon's broken gold on the moving waters, and the smile which is a rose on the lips of my sleeping love.*

There were times after the turn of the year when Baradoc sensed often that he was being watched as he worked on the boat. Whenever the feeling struck him he would see, too, that the dogs had marked the scent of another, but they would stand near him and make no move of their own or at his command. Although he searched the cliff sides and the rocks he could see no one, but he knew that the one who watched must be the stranger who still occasionally left small gifts outside the hut, a stranger who clearly meant them no harm and who – although he must have taken their original boat – showed no concern that he should be making another for one morning he had left outside the hut a sharp-pointed stout thonging needle for which Baradoc was grateful because he had been sewing his skins together by making a hole in them with the point of Tia's dagger and threading the thongs through by hand. But no sight of the man did Baradoc ever see, though sometimes on moonlit nights, unable to sleep, he would wander the cliff tops and northern plateau land, bow in hand, to shoot wild pig or goat or to pick off from a grazing flock one of the grey geese which had come to the island to winter. Knowing, too, that the man must eat and would have fire for warmth and cooking, his eyes were always alert for the signs of smoke along the cliff tops and rock pinnacles but he never saw any.

Sometimes, lying warm under their skins, holding Tia in his arms before they slept, he talked about the man and once Tia, who needed no words from him now to read his mind, said, 'Since he means no harm and by his gifts shows kindness why do you worry about him?'

'Because I don't like mysteries. I have seen a man walk to the edge of a cliff five hundred feet high and disappear over it where none but a seabird could know safety. He takes our boat ... *Aie*, and I'm sure cast it adrift to keep us here. Yet now he does nothing to stop me building my boat. Even helps me with the gift of the needle. Is he mad or is there purpose in this?'

'I don't know.' Tia stirred in the darkness to ease her burdened body. 'Maybe he's someone like Brother Asimus. A priest or dreamer, someone perhaps who has been shown the future. Asimus had a dream and waited for us to come. Maybe this man had a dream too From his writing on the rock it would seem so. The gods use such men.' She gave a little chuckle. 'It is no good you saying you don't like mysteries. The gods won't change their ways for you. If Asimus had said that his god had sent him a dream to say that one day all that you dream and long for would come true – well, you wouldn't question it. You'd have no bile against mysteries then, would you?'

Baradoc was silent for a moment and then said, 'Why would I? I would understand it. But the riddle written on the rock, and a man who walks out into space over a cliff ... well, such things tease me even in my sleep. Like someone tickling my nose with a straw, not waking me but breaking the peace of my rest. If I were not so busy with the boat and the hunting I would find him and speak boldly with him because the child you carry would have been born amongst my people, and there would have been women to serve you when the time came.'

'I would have liked that, yes. But I am not frightened. You are here. That is all the comfort I need. Birth is a natural thing, a tide which takes a woman so that she needs do no more than drift with it. Now sleep.'

She lay in the darkness when he was asleep, listening to the sough of the wind over the thatch and the singing notes it made through the ropes from which the great stones hung. She felt Cuna jump slyly in the darkness to the foot of the platform and curl against her leg and there was suddenly a bright picture in her mind of the child – boy or girl, no matter which, though she prayed always for a son out of duty to Baradoc – a child tumbling and playing with the dogs, their child. Would it have her eyes and Baradoc's hair? Then, feeling the child move within her, she put her hand to it and drifted into sleep.

In the end it was the stranger who revealed himself to Baradoc. The year had long turned and spring was moving and awakening. The migrating birds were flocking back from the south and Tia made Baradoc take down the old bird-catching nets left by the islanders for there was sorrow in her with each small bird that got caught in the narrow meshes. Some days now the wind blew gently from the south and the air was so clear that the mainland shone as in a crystal, and the smoke of distant settlement fires rose like dark threads against the dunnock egg blue of the pale sky. The seabirds were nesting, and the boat-work was finished except for the making of two paddles, and there was a fire of impatience in Baradoc to haul the boat to the water so that he could lay the flat stone ballast in it to settle its trim.

One morning as he sat in the sun outside the hut shaping the last of the paddles from a length of rough plank, the flotsam from some ship's wreck, Tia came to the doorway, her long hair caught back with a piece of braided wool, a loose robe, leaving her arms bare, sweeping almost to her feet, and said the wish was in her to eat fresh eggs. During the winter of their few hens three had died, two had been killed by a fox, and the last had been taken by a golden eagle which had coursed it across the cattle fold, made kill and was away before the dogs could reach it.

Baradoc absorbed said, 'I'll get some gulls' eggs when I go down to the boat.'

Tia, her chin set stubbornly, reached down and took the paddle board from him. 'I want eggs now, my brave heart. A dish of beaten eggs and herbs. The desire is with me and with the babe.' She smiled, putting her hand to her front, 'He kicks from the need and greed for eggs. And we want not gulls' eggs but the eggs of the lapwings on the north land heath.'

'But I have work to –'

Throwing the board from her, Tia cut him short, 'You have no work that will not wait. We need eggs. If we do not get them the babe will kick me to death.' She eyed him teasingly for a few moments, and then went on slyly, 'He kicks as only a man child could kick. Would you have me tell him some day that the first time he asked his father a favour it was denied him?'

Baradoc sighed, stood up, put his hands on her shoulders and kissed the tip of her nose. 'Lady Tia, I am your servant. Should you ask the eggs of a phoenix I would find them for you.' Then looking across the bright waters to the mainland and the distant shoulder of Hercule's promontory, he went on, 'If the weather holds, then we shall soon be across. You have enough time to run yet to see us with my people and the babe born where he should be born.'

'The child will be born where he is born – and that is in the hands of the gods. Now fetch the eggs.'

Baradoc went north with the dogs to the downland where the lapwings flew, their cries sharp and wailing as they circled and tumbled close above his head, their broad wings cutting the air with a hissing and searing sound like water steaming and spitting from red hot stones. But before he could find any of the nesting hollows Lerg growled and Aesc gave a sharp warning bark.

A bowshot away Baradoc saw the stranger, and saw him more clearly than he had ever done before. The man stood on a hummock beyond a shallow, marshy depression which held a broad pool whose waters flowed in a stream to cascade thinly over the nearby western cliffs. He wore a long brown coarsely woven habit, its hood lying back over his shoulders, while about his waist was wound a thick rope girdle.

Forgetting his quest for eggs, without giving any command to the dogs, Baradoc began to hurry forward. The dogs went with him. The man turned and walked from him and, without a glance backward, his pace kept measure with Baradoc's so that the distance between them remained the same. Something told Baradoc that this was no pursuit, that the man had decided that he no longer wished to avoid him.

The man moved across the downland towards the edge of the western cliffs and passed out of sight over a rocky rise in the ground. Baradoc following, crested the rise in the ground and hurried down its far slope along a goat path he had often used. Old bracken growths with the first green of the new crosier heads breaking the earth covered the slope and amongst them lay a scattering of large weather-and-lichen marked boulders. There was no sign of the man, but to the left of the path Baradoc saw at once a large flat rock which was tilted at one end towards the sky. Since his memory held now a familiarity with this place and many others on the island, he knew that the rock had never so pointed skyward before.

He ran to it and saw that the rock, working on a natural pivot against other rocks buried in the ground, had been swung upwards at one end and downwards at the other to make a pent over an opening in the ground, a cavity with a stony floor away from which, through a boulder-framed archway, ran a tunnel almost the height of a man.

Baradoc lowered himself into the hole and looked through the stone archway. Light seeped through it. Leaving the dogs at the top of the hole Baradoc began to move down the tunnel which after a few paces grew in height so that he could stand with ease. He moved forward, hand on the hilt of his sword, through a light which grew stronger and stronger. From ahead there came to him the growing sound of the call of seabirds and the low thunder of waves breaking at the foot of the cliffs. The tunnel ended with a down-flight of wide steps.

Baradoc stood at the top of them looking down in amazement. Below him was a wide rock-vaulted chamber, lit by sunlight that came through a great fissure in the rocks on the far side. On one side of the fissure hung a long heavy curtain of skins, thong-looped to a pole along which it could be pulled to close the entrance. The floor of the cavern was strewn with dried bracken and rushes and a wall embrasure held a bed close to which stood a rough table flanked by a long wooden form. Around the walls rock ledges and ships' timbers formed shelves and cupboards. To one side a turfed-damped fire smoked feebly on its hearth. Near the curtained opening a goat, her udder milk full, was stalled in a pen made of rough drift-wood timber. Standing by the pen, one hand scratching the head of the goat, was the stranger.

Before Baradoc could take in more, the stranger moved across to the foot of the flight of steps and looked up at him. He was of no great height, but stoutly and strongly built and, Baradoc guessed, had seen twice the years he had. Jet black hair hung to his neck and he wore a close-cropped beard. His eyes were friendly and had the wet brown shine of closed sea-anemones.

Baradoc, his anger against this man stirring anew, said, 'Who are you who stole my boat? And why at last have you brought me here when at other times you disappear like a wild goat

over the cliffs, or watch hidden and cast spells over my dogs so
that they take no heed of my commands?'

The man smiled and the whole of his face was briefly
wrinkled and lined like the skin of a hoarded russet apple.

'I give no name in answer to a question. But the questions
not asked are answered. Between these two lies the virtue of
patience. One sees the fire and the smoke at a distance but the
warmth is not felt until the hearth is reached. But since questions stir always in your mind like angry wasps and there is an
impatience of desire in you like the unending breaking of sea
waves against a rock, I give you some ease of the mysteries.'

'You talk in riddles.'

The man nodded affably and began to unloop from his waist
the thickly plaited girdle until he held in his hands a long length
of stout rope. He walked to the rock cleft overlooking the sea,
saying, 'Come and see a mystery answered.'

Baradoc crossed the cavern and standing at his side looked
out. For a moment he half-drew back to kill a sudden stab of
vertigo. The cliff face fell sheer to the sea hundreds of feet below where the long swell thundered and crashed at its foot, the
waters, foam and current marked, heaving and moiling were
alive with the swimming and diving seabirds and over-traced
with the flying lines of others as they passed between their
feeding grounds and the roosts and new season's nesting places.

The man said, 'A rope is no mystery. You double it, put the
loose loop over a cliff-top rock and then move down it to swing
like a spider at the end of its thread and enter. Then you pull
on one end of the rope. The whole comes to you – and the
mystery is dead.' Smiling, his eyes mischievous, he turned and
put out his hand towards the hearth. 'I breathe the fire to full
life at darkness. Only the eye of the night owl could see the
shadow of smoke against the sky and the stars. Learn, then, that
a question is answered not by speaking it for another to answer,
but by seeking the truth of it in yourself.'

Momentarily Baradoc, though the man was being friendly
enough, felt higher anger spark in him at the manner of the
man's approach to him, as though he were some pestering child

intruding on the time and talk of his betters with idle questions.

He said brusquely, 'I am no child to be teased with idle riddles, nor plagued first with the theft of my boat and then puzzled by your gifts and spells. You chide me without cause.'

To his surprise the man said, 'Why should I not chide you gently as a father to an over-eager son? I speak for your own good because I have read the runes and dreamt the dreams.'

'Forget the runes and dreams. You took our boat. Why?'

'Because it was written so. Listen – for many years I lived here with the islanders. When they were killed or taken by the sea-raiders I alone escaped for the gods in my flight led me to this cave, and here at night they speak to me. But I am no islander. My feet have trod many countries from Asia to Gaul and Erin. But this is my country and there is no part a mystery to me from Vectis to the far north to the lands of the Cornovii and the Carnonacae, to the far Orcades and Ultima Thule. I have read the papyrus rolls of Londinium, Lutetia and the Great Empire City. I have talked with devils and demons and magicians and sorcerers and taken no harm but much wisdom. And in sleep and in full eye-wake the gods have shown me the past and the future, and I have learnt that while the past is a jewel fixed forever in its setting the future is a river which the gods have set in its course but which time and man's works can loose from its bed to new courses. The gods have dreamt it, but man with his waking dream of power, conquest and greed mars all.' He paused and the red gleam of his lips showed through his beard as he smiled ruefully. 'Keep faith with the true dream. Mis-shape it not by impatience and greed for false glory. One day men will call you Pendragon as many before have been called. But the true king comes to meet glory and betrayal and then to sleep until all lands groan with the labour and distress of chaos and he comes again and the true march of the centuries begins anew . . .' He broke off and moved slowly to one of the cupboards on the cavern wall.

Listening to him Baradoc knew that for all his quiet speech, his sober, even manner, that the man was mad; not mad with any violence of talk or manner, but mad with the innocence of one touched with the disease of the gods, one for whom the air was full of voices and for whom the shape of solid things, a bush, a rock, a tall pine, a running stag, wavered always as though seen through water and became the fabric and fancies of a phantom world.

He said stubbornly, 'You set our boat adrift.'

'I did. But now you have built another.' The man spoke without turning as he opened the cupboard door. 'But if you would leave this island safely with your woman and child, put it not to the water until the first red-gorged swallow comes winging north, and until that time comes say nothing to your wife of our meeting.' As he finished speaking the man turned and came back towards Baradoc. In his hands he held a shallow basket made from woven heath stalks and lined with a soft bed of moss. Resting in it were eight mottled lapwing's eggs and a slab of soft, creamy goat's cheese set about with a thin garland of snowdrop blossoms, the white petals flushed with faint green like new grass breaking through melting snow. He gave the basket to Baradoc and said, 'Take these to your wife. And remember, the war steed, which is the heart of man, smells the coming battle and stamps for the charge, but the warrior, which is the wisdom of man, must check the reins and draw the curb until the horn is sounded high and clear. Now return to your woman and wait for the first swallow to come hawking and winging over the cliffs of Hercule.'

Baradoc said nothing to Tia of his meeting with the stranger. This, not so much because of the man's injunction, but because as the child grew in Tia she had moods that flighted from periods of high gaiety and laughter over small things to times when she sat silent, touched with some hidden anxiety which she would deny if he questioned her. He guessed that at such moments her thoughts were on the day of labour and birth to come, when from wife she would become mother. Often that anxiety was turned towards him, making her reluctant to have him leave her to hunt or to put the finishing touches to the boat. To tell her of the stranger and of the nonsense he had talked would only give her food for brooding. When he gave her the gift basket, he said that he had found it nearby on the wall of the cattle fold.

'But how could he have known I wanted plovers' eggs?'

'He didn't. There was only the cheese in it. The eggs were the ones I collected.' It was the first time he had ever lied to her, but though he did it for her sake there was an unease in him for the rest of that day.

On the day he finished the shaping of the last paddle, the fine weather withdrew. For three days a gale blew from the northeast with a wind so strong that the spindrift from the waves breaking over the rocks sheeted across the high island top in swirling veils of salt mist and spume. Unable to make a trial of his boat and settle the ballast stones, unable to hunt, Baradoc sat around the hut full of impatience. He wanted the child, which they both had decided had a full month yet to reach its time, to be born amongst his people. The warning of the stranger that he should not try yet to make the crossing he had quickly put from his mind. Although some birds were already in passage, it would be weeks before the first swallows came skimming across the sea. Once let the weather settle and they would make the crossing. Since he would then be in country he knew and with people who were friendly and near to his own tribe in faith and kinship he would take loan of a quiet mare and Tia could ride in comfort.

After a few days the gale wore itself out as the sun went down. When Tia woke in the morning and sat up on the bed platform sunlight was streaming through the open door and Baradoc was away. She smiled to herself, knowing exactly where he would have gone. His impatience to try the boat had been like an itch covering his whole body while the gale had blown. She rubbed the sleep from her eyes and stretched her arms. As she did so the child kicked hard within her and a swift pain shot through her stomach of a kind she had not known before. She put her hands on her swollen flesh and spoke aloud to the babe so that Cuna, who never left her now, turned his head and looked at her. She slipped off the platform, threw off her bed gown, and went to the wooden tripod holding their shallow washing bowl. Baradoc had long ago made the tripod for her and before he had left he had roused the fire and put the cauldron on it full of water for her washing. As she bent to fondle Cuna's ears she saw that Baradoc had scratched a message for her on the peaty floor. It read :

The gods raise the door-latch of night
To let the silver morning in
Sleep veils the brook-lime blue of your eyes
The gay bird of love in my heart begins to sing
Returning, I will lay a chaplet of purple vetch about your hair
And, kneeling, call you queen.

She smiled to herself, but even as her love for him stirred her she relished the wifely pleasure of knowing that in the reading of his lines she could read also through his love the small guilt behind the offering. She liked him near her these days but the pull of his boat was strong. Stripping to bathe herself, the sunlight through the door gilding her brown body, the fine down of her arms and legs trapping its brilliance in a soft golden mist, she said to Cuna, 'Our master Baradoc weaves a net of fine words to hold us content while the gay bird of love in his heart sings of his dreams.' The child kicked hard in her again and she leant forward to ease the quick pain that flared in her loins.

On the beach Baradoc placed lengths of trimmed tree trunks he had beach-combed along the shores to make rollers over which he could run the heavy boat down from the sloping bluff on which it had been built and across the shingle to the water. Stripped to a loin cloth he hauled the boat down, watched by Lerg and Aesc, while the seabirds wheeled and called about the little cove and a colony of painted-faced puffins watched him, shuffling and nodding. The sea was gentle with the last of the dying swell from the storm, and for the first time that year the sun was almost summer-fierce on his body.

He slid the boat into the water and holding it by the bow rope let it float free. It swung gently on the swell, riding high but listing to one side. He pulled it half out of the water and packed stones in it to trim it even. Three times he pushed it out, and then pulled it back to make the balance just. Finally it floated on a level trim and with enough freeboard to take himself and Tia safely out to sea. But before he could risk that he knew that he must prove its caulking sound. They could not safely leave the island in a leaking boat. He climbed into the craft and taking up a paddle began to work along the shore. A bowshot to the south was the small island promontory that sheltered the cove from the westerly winds. As he moved the dogs followed him along the rocks. The boat answered true to the paddle and a surge of pleasure filled him as he thought of the long days of work he had spent on it, and, now, here was the reward of his labour and determination. If the weather turned fine and steady, then in a few days they would be moving to the mainland, to the place of his people, to the birth of his child and then to the days and weeks ... *Aie!* ... months and years if need be which it might take to rally all men against the coming enemy.

As the little island drew nearer he swung the boat away from the shore on a tight turn to take it back to the beach, but the bow came only partly round and then fell away against the push of a current that curved along the shore and swept seawards along the projecting island. Fighting the thrust of the current with his paddle Baradoc turned the bow of the boat into it at last, only to find that the thrust was so strong that the current still took him, sweeping the boat stern first along the island shore and dragging it out to sea. For one wild moment he was on the point of abandoning the boat and swimming ashore. The thought of losing all his past labours held him. He decided to round the island point, find calmer water in its lee and beach the boat in the first cove or inlet he found.

At the moment when Baradoc cleared the point of the island, Tia was sitting in the sun outside the hut plucking a mallard duck which Baradoc had taken with a sling stone in the marshy hollow around the mid-island pond. The light breeze set the soft breast down floating into her face. She sneezed suddenly against its touch in her nostrils and, as her stomach muscles contracted, pain hit her so hard that she dropped the bird and clamped her arms about herself tightly. The child kicked and the pain came again and then again quickly. Tia groaned from the force of it and Cuna came and touched her cheek with his wet muzzle as she bent forward.

As the pain went she heard the sound of footsteps over the hard ground between the huts. She looked up quickly thinking it was Baradoc. A man came up to her, walking slowly. He was dressed in a priest's brown habit and as he came to her he smiled. There was no fright in her. She guessed he must be the stranger for he carried in his hand a thong-looped jar down the sides of which ran goat's milk that had slopped free as he walked.

Straightening up as the pains left her Tia said, 'My husband, Baradoc, is down at the beach with his boat. It would be another and great kindness from you if you would fetch him.' She smiled. 'I think my child has his father's nature and is impatient of the long wait.'

The stranger looked westwards to the sea which ran like beaten silver to the hazy line of the horizon, and for a moment his eyes closed as though the glare or some remembered grief overpowered him. Then he turned back to Tia and, smiling, said, 'All will be well with you. Your husband will come in full time. But now it is written that it is your term and there is no waiting for him. Go to your bed and I will stay by you. Yours will not be the first child I have brought into this world. You need have no fear of me, nor have any shame that a strange man helps you. I give my name, which is Merlin, freely to you and so all strangeness dies.'

He took her by the arm, led her into the hut to the bed platform and put the milk pot down at its side. Then he turned to the hearth fire and began to fill the cauldron with water from the hanging skin.

Tia said, 'You could go to the cliff top and call my husband. It is better that he comes.'

Merlin shook his head. 'There is not time enough. Be brave and be patient. Baradoc will return and when he does it will be to be greeted by his son. Now undress and lie beneath the covers. Your son as you say is impatient like his father. He will not wait for him, for there are many who already wait for the child's coming.'

As Tia began to strip Merlin went out of the hut and although she could not see him, she could see the shadow of his body cast across the doorway and, without knowing why, the sight of it was a great comfort to her.

As she pulled the bed covers over herself the sharp pains came again; and then began for her a time when all thought and feeling and the march of all her senses lost shape and sequence, a time when she lived in a dream through which loomed always the calm and comforting face of Merlin and the touch of his hands on her were those of a woman, and the sound of his voice as peaceful and lulling as the rustle of aspen leaves under the breath of an idle breeze until finally, as though from a great distance, came Merlin's voice with a high note of happiness in it, saying, 'Take your son in your arms. He was hard on you in birth, for the birth of great ones makes the gods jealous of losing them to this world, but in life your son will never be less than gentle with you.'

At the moment that Merlin placed the child in Tia's arms, Baradoc saw the vessel bearing down on him. It came riding towards him on a freshening north-easterly wind. The great main sail was set and curved like an arching yellow shield as the craft ran free before the wind At the bows the white foot waves creamed high and flared in a great spate along its sides, below the long row of lodged war-shields that lined the gunwales. At first Baradoc had thought it a trader coming down from some Sabrina port, but as it drew nearer, the island from which he had long drifted, low on the horizon behind it, he saw from the sail and the shields that it was no peaceful ship. Racing down on him, already fetching a little from its course to reach him, he knew that it brought no hope. Black anger was added to the misery already in him as he sat, naked except for his loin cloth, watching the ship overhaul him, seeing the long line of multi-coloured shields hung over the freeboard, and clear now the two men at the great stern oar and other men in the bows, their heads all turned his way, the sun and sea glitter reflected on spears and swords, and above them, swollen and straining in the wind, the wide curve of the saffron-coloured mainsail blazoned with the wingspread of a great black raven across its full breadth. From the bitterness of despair in him rose the memory of the stranger's words ... *If you would leave this island safely with your woman and child put the boat not to water until the first red-gorged swallow comes winging north.* What kind of black sorcery, what fine cunning with words from the gods or the stranger's madness was this? He had put the boat to water, but not to leave the island, only to ready it for leaving ... *Aie,* but face the truth, there would have been no waiting for the swallow.

There was no virtue in trying to escape. If he had taken to the water they would have filled him with arrows or harpooned him like a seal or porpoise. He waited for them and the anger was so thick in him that it cloaked all other thought and he let it rest, a curtain between himself and the guilt and shame which would come in time.

The great ship passed him, an order was shouted loud, ringing across the waves to him, and then it came about sharply. The high sail boom was lowered quickly and the fine leather sail gathered safely by the crew. The ship ghosted up to him and three long-handled boat hooks grappled him to its side. Looking at the men, leather and wool jacketed and tightly long-hosed against the weather, he knew that they were none of the kind he hated, the land-hungry Saxon men, but Viking sea-raiders who had probably over-wintered in Erin or Cymru.

They took him aboard, cast his boat adrift, and marched him, held securely between two crewmen, to the high carved bows where stood a man he had met before, a tall powerfully built man wearing a silver-winged bronze helmet, a saffron-coloured tunic with the raven device, and a broad sword swinging from his whaleskin belt. His face was black as sea coal.

The man looked at him unmoving for a long while as the

wind whistled softly through the rigging and the waves slapped idly at the ship's sides. The man smiled and bit his under-lip with fine white teeth in pleasure, and then he said gently, 'By Thor, what day of omens is this that out of the sea is thrown up an old friend, my young horse-thief with the great wolf hound?' He laughed and cried mockingly for all to hear, 'Have you turned then penitent and paddle now to Erin to join a Christian monastery?'

For a moment Baradoc was silent, mouth and chin set stubbornly and the blackness stayed sourly in him, but through it came now the dim touch of hope. He said, 'I go to my people beyond the point of Hercule, a few hours' sail for you. Put me ashore, Master Corvo, and you can name your ransom money. I am the son of a chief.'

Corvo was silent, while the crew watched and the ship rolled gently. None moved except the two men at the stern oar who kept the bows dead up into the wind with their strokes. Then the man spoke and he said savagely, 'The son of a chief? And what am I? The son of a black slave woman begotten by a drunken sea-raider – and gold means nothing to me until we reach the warm south lands to spend what we have. But this trip death has trimmed our crew and I need men – not money.' His voice rising fiercely, he called, 'Put a collar on him and chain him to the rowing benches!'

Baradoc was led aft. As he went he saw far, far to the north-east the sun gilding the green tops of the island and to still himself against useless violence and the black passion of regrets and lost happiness he clenched his hands and bit his lip until blood flowed to hold back the anguish that engulfed his heart.

Envoi

Grief had paced out its first fierce measures, encircling her heart and shadowing her mind with the heavy folds of its sable mantle. Baradoc's boat at the whim of the tides and the caprice of the veering winds had drifted back to the island. Merlin had swum out and brought it in to the little cove where its keel had first touched water. When Tia saw it and wept Merlin told her that Baradoc still lived and would return to her for he had seen the future in the dreams the gods gave him.

Now with the passing days warming the rocks and all the island balmy under the touch of growing spring, the young bracken a foot high, the sea samphires and the thrift pads moving towards bloom, and the sureness of Merlin's faith that one day Baradoc would return becoming her courage and strength, Tia found a peace and a fortitude that served her strongly.

She lived now, for safety against sudden raiders and for human comfort and companionship, in Merlin's cave where Lerg and Aesc slept each night under the boulder entrance and Cuna at the foot of the child's small wicker crib, while Bran roosted on a rock spur outside the curtained fissure opening. At night the brazier glowed like a red eye and the fat tallow candles, their light flickering in the draughts that idled through the high curtain, cast moving shadows over the rough vault of the cavern's roof. Sometimes before she slept and Merlin moved to finger snuff the lights she would look down at the child in the crib at her side and find him awake, his dark eyes, dark as his father's, watching the shadows play on the vaulted roof. She would put out a hand and gently touch the warm cheek and smooth the down of his pale, mouse-coloured hair already flecked with the copper glints he drew from his father, and the down-soft touch under her fingers always brought back the

morning of Baradoc's going and she saw the rough writing on
the peat floor . . . *Returning, I will lay a chaplet of purple vetch
about your hair and, kneeling, call you queen.* And she remembered again the moment when bearded Merlin leaned over her
and put her son into her arms, the early born, the longed-for
son, and standing back from her said after a while, 'How shall
he be named?'

Without hesitation, for this had long been settled between
herself and Baradoc, she said, 'He is named after the father of
his father, and is called Arturo.'

Merlin nodded, smiling, and said, 'It is a good name. A name
for all men and all time.'

And so she lived now, cared for and protected by Merlin,
waiting for the time when Arturo should be grown enough to
make the crossing to the mainland. She would go to the people
of the enduring crow and claim her place among them and
rest with them until Baradoc returned. So, while she waited for
Merlin to name the day of the crossing, she lived with him as
she had once lived with her brother, in openness and companionship. He knew her mind and learnt of her past and the story
of her meeting with Baradoc. But the one thing she kept locked
in her mind, hidden even from Merlin, was their meeting with
Asimus and his gift to them, because the true ending of that
story belonged only to her and to Baradoc.

She used for the first bathing of Arturo the silver chalice to
hold the warm water with which she sponged his body and
cleaned his apple-bloom cheeks. When the child was a month
old, sitting cradled by her arm on her knee, his naked body
shining in the sunlight through the sea entrance, the cry of the
seabirds and the slow booming of the swell against the rocks
echoing around the cavern, it happened that Arturo, crowing in
baby delight, reached out his small fat-wristed hands and put
them on the sides of the chalice. Through the water, seen only
by her, the ice-bright silver of the bowl was misted and clouded
with a crimson flush as pure and unflawed as the rosy gorge of
the swallow which had made its nest above the cavern's sea
opening.

Postscript

In this book – the first of the trilogy – I have made no attempt to follow strictly the lines of the accepted Arthurian legend – largely because I do not think it bears much relation to truth. What the truth was nobody knows. That there was a truth is indisputable. King Arthur and the Quest of the Holy Grail are unshakably part of our national heritage.

Although there are no incontrovertible facts about King Arthur, the renown of his life and deeds in the Dark Ages was lodged for over six hundred years in folk memory. And folk, being what they are, invariably alter and embroider a good story. William of Malmesbury, Geoffrey of Monmouth and then Sir Thomas Malory were landed with the result. Lesser as well as better writers have followed them. Acknowledging that I come in the first of these two categories, I feel no shame in entering the lists poorly armed but securely mounted on a horse I have ridden for years called Imagination.

The Circle of the Gods

Affectionately for
Diana Charnock Smith

The Brooch of Epona

Aritag sat in the sun looking down over the village, its huts stone-walled, the roofs, turf-and-heather thatched, weighted with boulders against the winter gales. The river running down from the distant moorlands was low with late summer drought. Where the river met the sands of the small cove it fanned out in a shifting web of shallow channels. Some of the younger children, naked, their brown bodies gleaming like polished oak wood, played in the water, watched by a small group of women who sat in the shaded lee of the tall rocks which ribbed through the white sands at the foot of the cliffs. Now and again he caught the sound of their laughter as they worked at their spindles, teasing the wool of the moor sheep into yarn. At the edge of the sea, docile under summer zephyrs, older boys and their fathers were working on two of the fishing curraghs. From time to time, despite the summer's heat, he coughed and shivered under the striped cloak drawn close about his shoulders and, with each cough, felt the chest pain stab him, a pain which had grown fiercer with the passing of each year.

Among the women he marked the fair, gorse-bloom hair of the one named Tia who had come to them with her babe claiming it to be the child of Baradoc – the son of his long dead brother; Baradoc who – if he lived still – was chief of the people of the Enduring Crow. With her had come Merlin whose word no man doubted, Merlin who with one eye looked into the past and with the other into the future; Merlin who had said that one day Baradoc would return and speak the truth of the villainy which the woman Tia had laid against Inbar, his own son. But, since he, Aritag, now stood in Baradoc's place, he had refused any judgement until Baradoc should come himself and, amongst them all in the boulder-flagged village circle, should speak the evil to Inbar's face. *Aie* . . . but in his heart he, Aritag, knew the truth already for he knew his own son.

A shadow stretching over his shoulder from behind darkened the close-cropped grass and the scent of crushed marjoram and thyme rose briefly in the air as Merlin sat down cross-legged. Merlin ran a hand over the jet black hair which fell long to his shoulders and then scratched at the tangle of his thick beard. Short and strongly built, he had the look of a man of forty, but it was said, Aritag knew well, that he had more years than any other human man would ever have since Nodens of the Silver Hand, in return for some great service, had given him the gift of endurance.

Merlin said, 'The corn is ripe for gathering, the fleeces are stacked and the heather ready to cut for winter. All that lacks now is the silver shoaling to fill the great jars with salted fish against the winter.'

Aritag was silent for a while. Then, stifling a cough as pain wracked his chest, he said, 'If the gods are good I shall live to see it.'

'You will see it, Aritag.'

Aritag smiled. 'How many times?'

'Only the gods know that. That a man will die in bed or battle they sometimes proclaim, but they set no day in the foretelling for they often alter the pattern of men's destinies to meet the changing times.'

Aritag nodded and said, 'I would live long enough to see Baradoc return. Do the gods tell you about that, my friend?'

'He will return. That I know.'

'Then let it be before I die. Without me here, when Inbar is chief he will take the woman, Tia. There is a heat in him like a peat fire for her. He longs for my death to give him that freedom.'

Merlin picked up a ladybird from the grass and watched it crawl across his palm. 'No man has the freedom to take a woman against her will, or if she is another man's wife. Strength and arrogance he may have, but not freedom. Because of this woman it is written that he will come to his death.' He blew gently at the ladybird and it took clumsily to the air.

'Say more.'

'I cannot.'

'Will not?'

Merlin laughed. 'You think I live in the belt pouch of the gods? Good Aritag, when in my dreams I play cupbearer at their feasts, there is too much laughter and noise to catch more than scraps of their talk. Anyway, I came not to talk of the future. I came to say that my time here is ended and I go this day.' He stood up and briefly brushed dried grass and dust from his loose trews and long tunic.

Aritag smiled. 'For a man who can hear the beat of a moth's wings above the roar of the wind and the waves in gale time it is strange that in dreams the laughter and noise of the gods' feasting makes you so deaf. But I press you no more. Go to Bada and he will give you all the stores you need and a moor pony to carry you.'

Merlin shook his head. 'I need none of these.'

'You will be back one day?'

'One day.'

'But I shall not be here to greet you?'

'If not –' Merlin nodded his head westwards to the great run of the sea that met the horizon in a silver haze, '– there will be a greeting one day in the Blessed Isles.'

He raised a hand in parting and turned down the grass slope, following the narrow path to the cove. He walked through the shallow river channels and across the white sands to the rocks where the women sat working. Before he reached them Tia saw him coming and left her companions.

Merlin halted and waited for her to come to him. In the years since he had brought her with her babe to the people of the Enduring Crow she had grown a little taller and her body had lost some of the slender suppleness of a young girl and found the beginning of the dignity and maturity of a woman. Her hair, short like a boy's when he had first seen her on Caer Sibli, was long now, worked into gold braids that hung loose over her shoulders. Watching the movement of her body under the belted working smock of dyed coarse linen he knew how Inbar must feel when he saw her. The gods, he thought, gave men their desires and had created women to inflame them. The gods, he felt, sometimes expected too much of mortals. *Aie* ... but then, who was he to question the gods who now and then amused themselves with him by tossing him his occasional scraps of foresight, even directing him to Caer Sibli, the island, lost now in the northern sea haze beyond the Point of Hercule, where Tia had given birth to Baradoc's son, Arturo; a son never yet seen by Baradoc who had been swept away by the currents from the island in his small boat.

Tia came up to him and he briefly set his hands on her shoulders in greeting.

Tia said, 'You are going.'

He smiled. 'How could you know?'

She nodded at his feet. 'The whole village walks bare-foot, but Merlin wears his sandals. You travel light?'

'Yes. And far.'

'And leave the boy and myself – and no man to stand by my side?'

'While Aritag lives you need have no fear. And he will live long enough. You will come to no harm.'

'How can you know that?'

'It is written.'

Tia gave an impatient shrug of her shoulders. 'No, do not comfort me with such words. You are like Baradoc. Something calls you and you must follow it. To excuse yourself you say that the gods have decreed it. But that is not true. You use the gods for your own ends. You put words in their mouths.'

Merlin laughed. 'Or they in mine. I have done enough for you. Now you must do everything for yourself.'

'And Inbar?'

Merlin nodded at the leather belt that girdled her smock. 'You carry a knife.'

'And would use it.'

'Then, if needs be, use it – with no more thought than in gutting a sea-bream.'

For a moment or two Tia was silent. Then she said in a softer tone, the hint of a plea in her voice, 'I am strong and can look after myself and Arturo so long as Aritag lives. And without him I have friends who would stand by me. But friends may not be enough. If you can ... then, before you go, give me some word of comfort.'

Merlin shook his head. 'When the seafolk murdered your people you ran into the forest like a hunted deer without thought of comfort. When you cut Baradoc down from the tree where Inbar had hanged him in the great forest of Anderida you cut him down and gave comfort. When he took you to your uncle at Aquae Sulis you could have stayed in comfort, but you left all the pleasures of a Roman villa to follow him westwards and be his wife. For you comfort lies in the giving, not the receiving.'

Tia laughed suddenly. 'Oh, Merlin, whose tongue is as twisted as a unicorn's horn, sometimes I think that from the moment the gods made you their occasional cupbearer you have mourned the comfort of being as other men.' She gestured to the far group of working women in the shadow of the rocks and went on, 'Look – there are single women there who would join their lives to yours and give you comfort. I have seen you eye them with the eye of a man. Stay here and wait for Baradoc's return.'

Merlin, grinning, shook his head. 'Not for me, my Tia. My feet grow restless, my ears grow tired of talk of crop and catch and my eyes weary of faces grown familiar. I must move as the seasons and the stars move.' He gestured with one hand down the beach to where the five-year-old Arturo, naked and brown, was rolling in mock fight with old Lerg the great hound, splashing in shallow water and scuffling up the white sand, and said, 'There is another who will never be content at any hearthside for long, nor ever be full held by any woman and will rouse wrath in men before he gains their love. Take the withy switch to his brown hide when he offends for there is an arrogance in him which ill fits the young but will serve him well when the gods open his eyes to his destiny.'

Tia shook her head, her eyes narrowing with mockery. 'You talk like a man who has been at the mead too long. One word begets another and you spawn fine phrases careless of whether they die or live in the memory – or even make sense. Now be on your way, for I see your feet shuffle the sand with impatience. But take with you my gratitude for all you have done for me.'

Without a word, laughter in his eyes, Merlin half-bowed his head, touched his forehead in salute, and turned away. Tia watched him go across the sands and up the narrow path that climbed the cliffs to the north while above him the seabirds wheeled and called in the bright air, among them the black choughs, red billed and red legged, the tribal birds of the people of the Enduring Crow. She watched him until he reached the cliff top and his figure dwindled and finally disappeared over the headland.

When she turned it was to find Inbar standing behind her with Arturo squatting on the sand beside him, digging into it with his hands to build a barrier across a small rivulet of the spreading river.

He was taller than his cousin, Baradoc her husband, and darker of hair and colouring. His bearded face was long, strong, and pleasant so that it was hard to believe any villainy of him. Yet Lerg, the old hound, and the other two dogs Aesc and Cuna never followed him as Arturo did. Maybe, she thought, because they had seen the moments of villainy when Inbar and his companion had strung Baradoc to the oak tree to die so that Aritag, his father, should become chief and he, Inbar, chief after him of the Enduring Crow. He stood looking at her, smiling, showing the edges of his white teeth, his lean, hard body, sea and sun-tanned, bare except for the rolled up trews, held by a leather belt which carried a short sword in a whaleskin scabbard.

Inbar said easily, 'So Merlin goes. What mad dream does he follow now?'

'Only the gods know.'

'He makes too much of the gods, and fills people's heads with nonsense.'

'You don't believe in the gods?'

He laughed and putting out a leg rolled Arturo over into the rivulet with a flick of his foot. Arturo laughed and threshed the water with his hands and feet like a stranded fish. Inbar said, 'I live in this world. The gods in theirs.' Then nodding at Arturo, he went on, 'Baradoc will not return. Merlin cossets you with that dream because he is against me. But one day soon you will be my woman, my wife, and I will give you sons as strong as this one.'

Tia said evenly, 'There are plenty of unmarried women over there.' She nodded at the group in the rock shade. 'None would deny you.'

Inbar smiled. 'Show me one with hair like the turning wheat, with eyes like the blue flash on a jay's wings, with the body of a goddess and the pride of Rome in her blood and I might be tempted. There is none, and no need for you to tight-draw your red lips into a bow of contempt. I am a patient man. The tribal law sets you free by summer of next year if Baradoc does not return. By then I shall be chief for my father has little time left in him, and the tribal law says that no woman may turn away from the honour of being the chief's woman.'

'To marry her husband's would-be murderer?'

'It is a lie.'

'If Lerg, Aesc and Cuna could speak you would be proved the liar. But more, I have Baradoc's word for it, and there is no standing against that.'

Inbar shrugged his shoulders and smiled. 'Baradoc has no true love for this tribe. His eyes have always been fogged by his own dreams of greatness. He would have come back here to gather what young fighting men he could. He would have turned back to the east, impatient for battle against the Saxons, impatient for his own glory ... *Aie*, maybe for a kingship which lies for the taking beyond our Dumnonia and Isca. He needs no hearth fire or woman for warmth, only the heat of battle and the red embers of power to cloak him against the bite of winter frosts and ice. He made you his woman, his wife, because he wanted sons to carry his name and glory after him.'

'And you?'

Inbar scraped a rough line in the soft sand with one foot, his head lowered momentarily, his eyes hidden from her briefly. Then raising his face to her, a wooden, expressionless face, he said quietly, 'I want no more than to be chief of the people of the Enduring Crow with a woman of my own choosing to bear me sons, a woman whose love for me and mine for her will forever be lodged in my heart like a wren in its moss-bowered nest.'

'A woman you would take by force?'

'*Aie* ... but not the force which you picture.' He stared at her boldly for a moment or two and then a slow smile bloomed faintly around his lips. He turned abruptly and began to walk away across the sands, following the river channel upwards to the long hanging valley between the cliffs towards the huddle of huts and village buildings from which rose the blue haze of hearth fires.

Tia turned and went back to the women working on the rocks and Arturo followed her, clutching at the hem of her belted smock. Following them came the three dogs, Lerg the big grey wolfhound, ageing now, his muzzle whitening, Aesc, the water dog with the long-furred red ears, grown stout and limping on one fore-leg a little from an old bite from a sea otter, and Cuna, small, short-legged and wire-haired, now in his prime.

Joining the other women, taking up her hand spindle, Tia watched the dogs settle close to Arturo as he curled up on the sands and dropped into the quick sleep of childhood. For a moment Tia glanced up to the sky as though, circling heavily up there, she might see the black, diamond-tailed shape of Bran, the raven. But Bran had gone on the day that Merlin had brought her here with Arturo from Caer Sibli, now lost in the summer haze far out to sea. The dogs had held to her as once they had held to Baradoc. But Bran had gone. And Baradoc had gone. Maybe when Baradoc returned then Bran would come winging back.

A shadow fell across the sands at the rock foot and Tia turned to see Mawga settle herself in the lee of the limpet-covered rocks.

Mawga was her own age, dark-haired, red-lipped, her summer shift leaving one sun-browned shoulder bare, her long body large-breasted, her eyes dark and shining like closed sea anemones. From a rush basket at her side she took cheese and a flat wheat cake, broke them and passed portions to Tia. When they worked on the beach or at the tilling or cattle watching on the slopes above the village they always ate together and they shared the same hut where Mawga lived with her mother. Her father and only brother had put to sea four summers ago to follow the mackerel run and had never returned.

Mawga said, 'I have an uncle, Ricat, who is horse-keeper to the Prince of Dumnonia in Isca. He is a good man and would welcome a woman to manage his house.' She smiled. 'No more. He has but one love and that his horses. When he next comes here you could go back with him.'

Tia smiled. 'You think of me – or yourself?'

Mawga laughed. 'Both. Before you came Inbar was always at my heels, and there was an understanding. Now ...' She shrugged her shoulders.

Tia put out a hand and touched Mawga's bare shoulder. 'I stay here until Baradoc comes.'

Mawga sighed. 'When Aritag dies, you will see a different Inbar. Ever since he was a boy there has been a madness in him which breaks like a summer storm without warning. If he did what you say to Baradoc, hanging him high and leaving him to die, it was in such a quick rage that it overcame the friendship between them. You would be safe in Isca until Baradoc comes back. Think about it. Think also – Baradoc may never come back.'

Tia shook her head. 'He will come. Merlin has said so. But more than that –' she touched her breast, '– in there I know so.'

Mawga shrugged her shoulders. 'Then the gods grant that it is before Aritag dies.'

At that moment from the high cliffs behind them came the slow wailing of a horn, three long drawn-out blasts that echoed back from the crags and sea-lapped rocky heights.

Mawga leaped to her feet, spilling cheese and wheat cake, and cried, 'The shoaling! The silver shoaling!'

From the cliff top the horn rang out again, but this time calling and echoing in fast, quick notes that set the seabirds clouding into the air from their roosts and perches and turned the long run of sandy beach into a scene of frenzied activity. Men and boys abandoned their boats at the water's edge and ran for the village, and the working women left their spinning and joined them, and as they ran the cries of 'The shoaling! The shoaling!' rose and mingled with the now sharp imperative blasting on the bull's horn.

High on the cliff edge above the village Aritag stood by the horn blower and watched the scene below. Men, women and children were all running from the sea, boat work and net-mending abandoned, running fast up to the tribal huts, and from the huts came the old women and the old men leading or carrying the very young babes. For a while he watched them as the trumpeter filled the sunbright day with fierce horn blasts. Then Aritag's eyes turned to the sea. A bow shot off-shore he could see the movement of the fish, countless sprats swinging in great silver swathes as they twisted and curved through the water. Shoal after shoal came crowding into the shore until the sea began to hiss with spume and froth like a great cauldron boiling. The bright bloom of the fish hung in an eye-dazzling mist over the sea as they flung themselves into the air to escape the marauding mackerel and herring that followed them in. From above the gulls and seabirds, the diving gannets, guillemots and razor-bills, the black shags and the blacker shearwaters cried and wailed so that at times they drowned the noise of the in-sistent bull's horn, as they dived and flung themselves into the feast of the waters.

Aritag raised an arm and the trumpeter lowered his horn and

wiped his aching lips with the back of his hand. Aritag turned
and went down the path to the great stone-flagged circle around
which the huts were grouped.

Inbar came to him, the tribespeople crowded behind him,
carrying rush baskets and panniers, old cloaks and earthenware
pots and bowls, throwing nets, anything and everything which
could be used to scoop and take the harvest of fish which now
boiled along the surf edges and thrashed to creamy spume all
the waters fringing the shore. This was a harvest which none
could gather until Aritag should walk into the sea waist-deep
and scoop the first cropping in the bowl of the hide-faced,
bronze-bossed ceremonial tribal shield of the people of the
Enduring Crow. For any to take the smallest sprat, the puniest
fry, of the great shoaling before the tribe leader would be an
offence to the gods and bring ill-luck to them all.

Inbar handed his father the shield and Aritag, slipping his
left hand through the thonged arm-crotch and gripping the
short cross-bar, began to walk to the sea, following the fall of
the shallow river, splashing across its sandy shallows, while the
tribe followed him in silence, watching the leaping waters
ahead. Behind them came some of the youths, pulling the great
wooden sleds into which the shoaling fish would be loaded to
be drawn up to the drying and salting grounds about the village.
Two good shoalings in the worst of poor corn cropping years
could hold off starvation, while more meant salt fish for bartering inland as far afield as the markets of Isca.

Aritag walked into the sea, the spray and splashing of the
shoal rising about him like a mist. Merlin, he thought, had said
that he would see the shoaling again, but not how many. Merlin,
he thought wryly, would probably say anything that came into
his head that he fancied might feed his reputation and then rely
on chance to prove him right – yet, whatever men might say,
there was something in Merlin that tied him to the gods. Some
even said that he was the son of the great horned stag god,
Cernunnos, born to a mortal maid in the far past. The edge of a
smile touched his thin lips. More than likely Merlin might have
spread the story himself.

Waist deep, he turned in the sea and faced his tribespeople who lined the strand. All about him was the clamour of the feeding seabirds and the hissing and seething of the sea as the shoals silvered it into a mad turbulence. Slipping his left arm free of the shield he held it like a great bowl in both hands above the water. He dipped it into the water and raised it up full of the living, leaping, writhing fish. A great shout went up from the tribespeople.

'The shoaling! The shoaling!'

Then, as Aritag began to wade slowly to the beach, his back bowing beneath the weight of the shield and its living load, all the men, women and children rushed into the water and began to scoop up the catch, filling baskets, cauldrons, looped kirtles, tunic skirts, nets, and lengths of cloth. Between sea and shore they rushed, shouting and laughing, to fill the great wooden sledges. Aritag handed his shield to Inbar to empty and then walked up the beach towards the village without looking back, followed by the horn blower.

As they breasted the steep path a spasm of coughing took Aritag. The attack was so severe that it made his head swim with a giddiness he could not control. Bada, the horn blower, caught him as he swayed.

'Sit and rest,' said Bada.

Aritag breathed deeply and fought the giddiness in his head, slowly forcing it from him. 'No,' he said, 'it passes.'

He walked on, feeling the spell move slowly from him. His time was not yet, he sensed that. But it was not far away. This year there would be other shoalings. He would see them through. But the first shoaling of the year was the most important. Maybe the good god Nodens of the Silver Hand would give him time to see another. He had no fear of death, but he had a love of life, and he would wish to see Baradoc back. From all that came from Isca it was clear that there were even worse times ahead. Inbar would shut his eyes to trouble for he loved pleasure too much. But Britain now needed men who knew how to meet trouble and make danger work for them; and

Baradoc, his brother's only surviving son, and rightful head of the tribe, was such a man.

There were two more shoalings that year before summer passed and Aritag lived to see both of them, and the winter that followed was mild and there was no hunger among the people of the Enduring Crow. It was during this winter that there sprung up between Aritag and Arturo an affection which Tia found pleasing. Generally the children of the tribe were in awe of Aritag and came to him only when bidden. But Arturo, in his sixth year, had a boldness which in other children would have been greeted with a quelling look. Even when Aritag sat in a circle talking with the other men Arturo would work his way to his side and squat or stand by the old man, listening to the talk without fidgeting or drawing attention to himself. And when Aritag walked the cliffs with Bada, Arturo would join them or, if the weather were too bad, slide into Aritag's hut and squat across the fire from him, so that the time came when Aritag, growing used to his company, favouring him above all the other children because he was the son of Baradoc, would talk to him and tell him the tales of the people of the Enduring Crow and of the other peoples of Dumnonia, tales that went back over the years into the mists of past times.

There were hundreds of these tales and Arturo began to learn them by heart, a frown or a disdainful spitting into the red heart of the turf fire by Aritag marking any deviation from the strict form of their wording. The boy had a quick mind and memory and learnt easily. He had, too, a quick temper. If any of the other boys teased him about being Aritag's favourite, calling him nose-wiper, toe-licker, he would waste no words but take to fists and feet no matter the odds against him. Seeing his bruises, and scratched arms and face, Aritag would smile to himself and say nothing.

But in Mawga's hut Tia would scold him sharply for his quick temper, though her anger never lasted long. She was privately proud of his ready learning and quick mind and tongue. During the long winter evenings she began to teach him her own language; not only to speak it but to write it, filling a shallow osier basket with fine beach sand and tracing the letters with a stick. As Aritag gave him the history of his father's people, so she gave him what she knew of the history of her people. Always, too, before he slept he had to be told – though he knew it all by heart – some part of the story of the way she had met Baradoc in the far eastern forest of Anderida in the land of the Regni and had journeyed with him to Aquae Sulis to the villa of her only surviving relative, the aged, long retired Chief Centurion Truvius of the Second Legion; and how she had finally married Baradoc and journeyed westward with him.

'Tell me the bit about the bear and how Cuna helped to kill it. How big was it really? As tall as a rearing moor stallion? Like this?' Excitement building in him, Arturo would leap to his feet, arms stretched high above his head, brown fingers curved into raking claws, and prance around the hut like a pain-maddened bear, growling and roaring so that Cuna, sleeping by the fire with the other dogs, would leap to his feet and, barking furiously, would circle around him.

There was, however, one part of the story of her travels to the people of the Enduring Crow which Tia had not told Arturo yet, knowing that he was too young to understand it fully. This was the story of the silver chalice which she kept, wrapped in an old piece of doeskin, in the ash-wood chest which stood at the end of her bed platform. One day she would tell him of the good Christian hermit Asimus who had given it to her and of the prophecy he had made about it ... but it would be many years yet she knew before Arturo would be ready for the tale. Sometimes, looking down at the boy as he slept, her longing for Baradoc would rise to a high peak, a longing now which was often – despite Merlin's word – shadowed with a growing doubt about his return. He had built a boat to take them from Caer Sibli to the mainland, had put to sea to test it and had never been seen again, and the boat had drifted back to the shore empty. He could have been drowned, but Merlin said no, and she held firmly to her faith in Merlin's word. Arturo showed only a little interest in Baradoc. His world was too full of the people and things around him to leave room for concern over a figure as remote as an unknown father.

On a night of wind and rain towards the end of the year Inbar, heavily cloaked against the storm, came into the hut where she sat by the fire thonging a small hide jerkin for Arturo who slept in his bed. His entry set the flames of the oil lamps in their wall niches briefly wavering and guttering. Mawga and her mother were away for the night, death-watching round the body of one of their relatives in another hut. Inbar, she knew, was well aware of this. He stood for a moment smiling at her, his cloak rain-beaded, his dark hair rain-plastered to his head like a moleskin helmet.

He said, 'I come from the beach watch. There is a cold in me which fire and a beaker of mead will warm.'

'Both of which you could find in your father's house a spear-throw from here.'

'True ... but he holds a council there, haggling with Ricat, the Prince's horse-master, and the elders over the tribute of young stallions from the moor.' He slipped the throat clasp open at his neck and dropped the wet cloak across the rough beech-wood table. The flame from the wicks of the lamps steadied and the light lay across his bare brown arms, gleaming like polished bronze.

Tia rose and went to fetch the mead jar from the store room at the far end of the hut. She passed close to him but he made no move to touch her. Coming back she set the mead and a slab of goat cheese before him. He cut himself some cheese with his dagger, ate, and washed down the food with a draught of mead. When his mouth was free, he said, 'Ricat and his men go tomorrow. It is known that he has asked you to join him, to keep his house in Isca. You go with him?'

Tia shook her head. 'No. My place is here.'

Inbar shrugged his shoulders and grimaced. 'Any woman of this tribe in your place would have gone.'

'This is my tribe. But my blood is my own.'

'And good blood, too. Proud blood. But Isca is a fine place even these days, and Ricat is an honourable man who has given all his love to his horses. So why do you stay? Baradoc will never come back and next year is the seventh of his going, and you know that the need in me for you grows stronger every day.'

'Baradoc will return. I shall never be bed-warmer, wife or bearer of your children.'

He finished his mead and then, shaking his head, laughed and said, 'No other woman would ever dare say that to me.' He stood up and, reaching out suddenly, took her by the right wrist. With his other hand he pulled free from its sheath the small dagger she wore in the belt about her working shift. Still holding her wrist he held the dagger in the flat of his palm. 'You would kill me with this on the night I took you?'

'If not you – then myself.' Tia looked down at the hand that held her wrist, and said quietly, 'Free me.'

For a moment Inbar hesitated. Then he released her wrist. In a quiet, almost puzzled voice, he said, 'Why should you not like me? When the seven-year term is spent I would come to you in honour to take you to wife. You would have silver and bronze dishes in your house, the finest furs for the sleeping couch, and silks and linens of the best from the sea-traders ... *Aie*, and gold torques and enamelled clasps for your robes, and a table that would never lack for food. My father is a rich man and hoards his riches to no point. After him I shall have his riches and would shower them on you like the wind-fall of hawthorn blossom in Spring.'

'You would be kind, no doubt. But there is no gift you could give me great enough to make me forget that once you hanged Baradoc high and left him to die slowly.'

A smile suddenly flashing across his lean, handsome face, Inbar said lightly, 'Then let it be understood that when the time comes I shall take you and tame you to my ways and my love.' He flicked Tia's small dagger downwards suddenly and it lodged, quivering a little, in the rough wood of the table. 'And you will find that you have no heart for dagger work.'

He picked up his cloak, flung it about his shoulders and left the house.

Tia picked up the mead jar and the remains of the cheese and took them back to the store room. When she came back Arturo was awake, though still fogged with early sleep.

He said, 'I thought I heard Inbar talking.'

'You did. He came for mead and cheese.' Tia paused and then, following a prompting suddenly alive in her, went on, 'Do you like Inbar?'

Arturo rolled over, stomach downwards on the soft fleeces of the bed, and resting his chin on his hands said, 'Only for some things. The things he makes me like spear and bow, and the things he shows me how to do ... like ... well using a stone sling and how the wind takes off line spear or arrow in flight.' He yawned. 'Oh, yes ... he's good to me. But I would drop a boulder on his head from the clifftop if you told me.'

Tia frowned. 'Why do you say that?'

'You know why. All the boys know he wants you to wife if father comes not back and –' He broke off, turned directly to her, and grinned broadly.

'And?'

Arturo scratched at his tousled fair hair. 'And that you do not want him.'

'The boys know too much and talk too much.'

'So do the girls.' He rolled over on his back and yawning rubbed his eyes. 'So when you want a boulder dropped tell me. To kill your first man in your mother's honour would be a great killing.'

Suddenly out of sympathy with his precocity, Tia snapped, 'Arturo – talk not like that!'

Arturo made no reply. Eyes closed, limbs loose in returning sleep, he snored gently, yet although Tia knew that he could fall into sudden sleep she was far from sure this time that his sleep was genuine. But she was sure that, despite Aritag and Inbar's care, he needed the harder hand of a father. He was growing fast and over-knowingly.

Before Ricat left he came to see Tia. She was in the great

cave in the hillside above the village where the rush panniers and earthen crocks of wheat and barley were housed and with three other women was labouring at the two large milling querns grinding into flour the oven-dried ears. When he called to her she came to him at the cave entrance, her working shift looped up at one corner into her belt, her face flushed, her hands and bare arms powdered with flour.

A short, stocky man with the wrinkled face of an over-wintered apple, his belted tunic and gartered trews of the finest wool, the short red cloak of a chief servant of the Prince of Dumnonia open over his shoulders, Ricat laughed, and said, 'If your uncle Truvius were alive to see you now he would not believe it.'

'You knew Truvius?'

'I did. He often when he first retired to Aquae Sulis came to Isca to buy horses and would have none of the moorland breed, only those still bred of the true Cavalry strain, though few of those are with us now. Give a moorland stallion freedom and he will mount any mare he can find. You knew Truvius was dead?'

'No. But I long since guessed it. The gods have gained good company.'

Ricat nodded. 'He once did me a favour that put me in good standing with my Prince. *Aie*, at a moment when I needed it. I would return that favour through his kin. I say again that there is now or at any time a place for you and your son in my house at Isca – and a safe passage there though you should travel alone if you show this token.'

He reached to the scarlet fall of his cloak flap and unpinned from it a brooch which he handed to Tia.

'What is it?'

'It is the badge of the Prince's master and keeper of horse. Once you are over the river Tamarus and out of the lands of the people of the Enduring Crow not even Inbar would touch you – and,' he smiled, '– the headwaters are a day or a night's march to the east from here. Show the brooch – there is none other like it – and safe passage will be given.'

Looking down at the brooch, Tia, who over the years had learned much of the beliefs and customs of her husband's people, said, 'It is the goddess Epona.'

Ricat nodded. 'Truvius would have known that, too, as would any legionary cavalry commander in the old days.'

On the bronze brooch, inlaid in silver gilt, was the figure of the goddess holding in her arms a wide bowl full of ears of corn. Behind her stood an arch-necked horse. Around the rim of the brooch were set garnets backed by thin gold-leaf foil to give added lustre to the stones. It was a beautiful piece of work, worth many head of cattle. Tia's eyes misted momentarily at the thought of the man's kindness and concern for her. To part with the brooch, his sign of office, would mean a lot to him.

She held it out to him. 'No. I cannot take it.'

Ricat reached out and closed her fingers over the brooch. 'Keep it. I need no such sign to mark my rank. Every man in Dumnonia knows my standing. An honourable welcome awaits you in my house whenever you find the need for it. And remember this of Inbar. There is good and bad in him and the two are always at war. If Aritag should die soon Inbar's impatience will lead him to break any tribal law to gain his desire. I say this for I think you should come with me now. Put aside the pride which comes to you from your Roman blood.'

Tia shook her head. Ricat eyed her for a moment or two and then, giving a little shrug of his shoulders, touched his forehead in salute and turned away.

Late in the afternoon Tia carried up to Aritag's hall a shallow, straw-plaited basket full of flat bread rounds. Pulling the leather draw-cord thong to lift the heavy inner door bar, she went in to find the living quarters occupied only by Inbar who sat sprawling by the turf fire from which a lazy spiral of smoke curled away to the roof opening. From one of the sleeping booths at the far end of the hall came the sound of heavy snoring Beside the booth Bada, the horn blower, sat on a small stool keeping watch over his master.

As Tia set the basket down on the long table Inbar slewed towards her and, smiling, said, 'Ricat has gone.'

'Yes. He is a man of great kindness – and honour.' Tia made no attempt to mute the edge in her voice.

Inbar laughed. 'I agree. I rode with him a while to see him off the tribal grounds. He wore in his cloak a plain bronze brooch.'

'So?'

'So – you have the goddess Epona to give you safe riding to Isca should you ever need it.'

'If I ever need it, yes.'

Inbar shook his head gently. 'Your eyes are the mirror of your temper. Now they are the bleak blue of ice under a clear winter's sky. But then, who would want a woman whose eyes never betrayed her feelings. You will have no need of the brooch.' He nodded towards the far booth where his father snored in sleep. 'When my good father dies you will come to me willingly.' He eyed her for a moment or two and, when she made no reply, turned slowly to the fire, resting his elbows on his knees, cupping his chin in his hands, and stared into the red heart of the slow-burning turves.

Tia, as she left the hall and walked towards Mawga's hut, felt for the first time the chill beginning of fear. This country and the world outside it, she knew from her own experience, and the tales which came with the travellers and merchants from Gaul, were in a turmoil where none now knew the security which had marked the days of her father and even her own early days. For the first time, no matter what Merlin might have said, she faced the numbing fact that Baradoc could be dead, that the life ahead of her might have to be paced out without him. She could admit to herself now that she should have forsaken her pride and ridden to Isca with Ricat.

The Moorland Meeting

The following Spring came reluctantly. Cold winds and gale-raised seas lashed the northern coasts of Dumnonia. Leaf buds were salt-blighted by the fierce drift of spray on the high winds, the young corn blades were yellow tipped and the inland pasture grounds were slow to growth so that there was no good early grazing for the over-wintered cattle and sheep. The peregrine falcons returned late from their southern migration and mewed about their eyries showing no sign of courtship displays. Although the high nets of tallowed, fine wool thread were set on the cliffs to trap the migrating flocks of small birds moving up the coast there was little need of them because after each gale the boys of the tribe could gather panniers of exhausted or dead birds of passage. The tribal huts were redolent with the spit-roasting of warblers, finches, waders and pipits whose flesh now eked out the dwindling stores of dried fish and salted meat. Of fresh fish there was little for the sea was too fierce on most days for the small boats to risk a passage to even the nearest fishing grounds.

But the weather did not stop the Spring raiding of the Scotti bands from Erin for they came in their large boats, indifferent to the rage of the sea, making their camps on the wild coast of Demetae across the Sabrina sea, and also on Caer Sibli, and raided near and far for loot, slaves and food. Three times before the seas began to grow calm, the sun to find cloudless skies to pour warmth on the cold earth, and the first of the choughs to begin to brood a full clutch of eggs, the Scotti came to the settlement of the Enduring Crow and Bada's horn wakened the settlement to arms. The men and older youths sprang to their weapons and swept down to the beach and formed a barrier across the narrow valley mouth leading to their homes and cattle.

The first time, although they were beaten back, they took with them two youths as slaves. The second time the valley mouth defenders broke against their pressure and, before they could reform, the Scotti looted and then burned three huts and bore away the wife and young girl-child of Garmon the chief cattleman who was away with his beasts on the inland pastures. The third time they came unwisely on a night of full moon and the cliff watchers saw them long before they landed. An ambush was set for them and a third of their force was slaughtered and one of their long boats captured. It happened that on this night Tia was one of the two women whose turn it was to sit at the couch side of old Aritag who had fallen ill and could no longer look after himself. Inbar had left the long hall on the first alarm for he was commander of the tribe's fighting men and lacked no courage in facing the Scotti.

Not long after the sound of Bada's horn had filled the valley with the sharp calls that signalled the retreat of the attackers, Inbar returned to the hall. His short cloak was thrown back and blood ran from a deep cut in his sword arm. He sat himself at the long table and called for water and cloths and the woman with Tia rose and went to look after him. As she began to clean his wound he turned to Tia and said, 'This time the Erin dogs were mastered. Those who live will tell the tale and leave us free next year. Twenty now lie dead on the sands that are black with their own black blood. And we have a fine boat, planked and masterly built, which they must have plundered from some sea raider for there is none in their parts who could make such a craft.' He smiled at Tia. 'When the summer comes you shall ride in her on a down-stuffed siken seat and –'

At this moment a small figure slipped through the partly closed hall doorway and Arturo, clad only in a coarse short shift, rushed towards Tia. He stood before her, his eyes shining, his arms and legs bespattered with blood and sand, and holding up his right hand which held a bloodied single-edged knife, cried, 'Look! With my own hand I have killed a man. *Aie! Aie!*

I've killed a man!' He began to dance around, shouting and waving his knife in excitement.

Tia jumped to her feet, seized his wrist and shook the knife from his grasp. With her free hand she hit Arturo across the cheek, abruptly quietening him, and as Arturo froze, his face clouded with sullenness, she said sternly, 'Back to the hut, clean yourself and go to bed!'

Arturo made no move, his lips tightening stubbornly. Before Tia could make any move or speak, Inbar said firmly, 'When your mother gives an order, obey it.'

For a moment Arturo still made no move. Then with a slight shrug of his shoulders he turned and walked slowly from the hall.

Tia turned to Inbar and asked coldly, 'Was this your doing?'

Reaching for a beaker of mead that the other woman had set at his side, Inbar drank and then said slowly, 'That he was on the sands? No. There were other boys his age. There always are when the fight goes with us. How else do they get their first sight of battle and their first smell of blood?'

'And the killing of the man?'

'A kindness the gods would approve. He was already dying of a spear thrust. I told Arturo to cut his throat to hasten his passage to the Shades.'

'And you gave him the knife?'

Inbar laughed. 'Now your eyes have the blue flame of burning seawrack wood. No, I gave him no knife. It was already in his hand. Where he got it it would be idle to question. Theft, barter? What boy of his age in this tribe has not a knife hidden somewhere and longs for his first killing?'

That night when Tia, her spell of vigil over Aritag finished, returned to Mawga's hut she stretched herself out on the bed platform alongside Arturo. From the single night light of the wall lamp she could see that he had washed himself. He slept with the even breath of the young. Looking down at him, his face smooth and unmarked, it was hard for her to believe that his hand had helped a man to death and that already there was in him a growing impatience to reach manhood. Lying back, she drew him gently to her, holding him in her arms. In his sleep Arturo made a few puppy grunts of protest and then turned and snuggled against her.

The first silver shoaling of the following year was still to come when Aritag died. Spring was fast giving way to summer. There were new-feathered young in the seabirds' nests, the sea samphire and patches of thrift along the cliff edges were moving into bloom, the cattle and swine were fattening, and the early lambs of the now scanty sheep flock were well grown and long past all urge to frolic and sport about their elders. There was little news of the rest of the country for there were few travellers, and no trading ships came creeping along the now storm-free seaboard. From the few passing travellers there was no more to be gained than rumours that King Vortigern who had married a Saxon princess and become the pawn of the men of the long keels now faced the threat of a rival, another Ambrosius whom some said was the son of the old Ambrosius, the Western king who had once held the long line of the Sabrina river and the lands and hills about it. Only one thing held with certainty and that was that the young Prince of Dumnonia still held Isca firmly and that while no man could claim that peace reigned in the east along the Saxon Shores or through the long, looping valley of the river Tamesis, the old Roman road that ran north-east from Isca, through Lindinis to Aquae Sulis and on to Corinium was once more safe to travel in well-armed company.

Aritag died as dawn broke with Tia sitting beside him, and while Inbar with the night patrol kept the cliff watch. He died quietly and peacefully as the tide began to ebb. Bada came in, looked at him and then, blank-faced, turned and left. A few moments later all through the still air of the early summer dawn came the notes of his horn, wailing the passing of the leader of the people of the Enduring Crow. Tia held the still hand of the old man and prayed to the gods of the Blessed Isles far out in the Western Sea to welcome him with the honour he deserved and to give him good life in the Shades and fair greeting from his friends and fighting companions who had made the passage before him.

Two days later Aritag was carried in procession on a bier of three shields supported on long shoulder poles up the valley to the first slopes of the near moors to the tribal burial ground. They laid him in a shallow grave and piled it with rocks and boulders to stay the burrowing of foxes and wolves. No grave goods were buried with him for he had already gone to another life and needed nothing there. The earth held only the husk of his manhood in this world. The Druid priest, Galpan, who lived a hermit on the moor, placed a fresh-cut oak branch on the pile of stones and spoke aloud for him to the gods, naming them in turn and linking them with the different virtues of the departed Aritag; Taranis the sky-thunderer, lord of heaven and prince of light, the course-setter of all human lives and the giver of signs, Esus, son of Taranis, the god of skills and crafts and trading and the protector of all single travellers, Coventina, the guardian of springs and wells and rivers and all waters which were the life blood of man, and ended with an invocation to the great Dis, the father of all the gods and the ruler of all the stars and planets that spun their courses through the heavens. When he had finished the priest placed a sprig of mistletoe with the oak branch and turned and moved away up to the moor top. Inbar, without arms, followed him while the rest of the tribe turned away and walked back down the valley to the settlement.

Mawga, alongside Tia, said, 'In seven days Inbar will return. Seven years have gone now since Baradoc went from you. You are free to be wife to any man who pleases you, but Inbar will not wait upon the trifle of your pleasure. Bada will find you a good mount. You have but to pin the Epona brooch to your cloak and ride away.'

For a moment or two Tia was silent. She knew that Mawga spoke nothing but good sense, but there was a stubbornness in her which hardened her against flight. Baradoc lived and would return. Merlin had said so. Her place was here with Baradoc's people and Arturo's people. Inbar had stolen Baradoc's birth-right. Although she could claim no common-sense for her stubbornness, to leave would be a betrayal. Inbar would use no force with her for he knew that she would kill him no matter how long she had to wait for the moment to do it. Death in battle would do him honour with the gods, but death at the hands of a wronged woman, forced to his bed, would condemn him to the dark wandering of endless time.

She said, 'I am a freewoman by tribal law. I stay because my heart says stay although there are times when my mind urges the comfort of cowardly flight.'

Mawga shook her head. 'You are wrong. You are a young wife who has been seven years without her man. Your heart and body have become strangers to your mind. They seek comforts and means which they hide from you. But when the time is ripe they could betray you.'

'You talk in riddles and I have no time for them.'

'Then I talk no more of this, except to say only that Bada will always find you a good mount.'

They walked in silence from then on back to the settlement. As they crossed the rock-paved circle before the long hall where Inbar would now rule as chief, the three dogs Lerg, Aesc, and Cuna came to welcome Tia followed by Arturo, naked except for a loin cloth. Lerg thrust his grey muzzle briefly against Tia's hand, but Cuna barked and leapt around her and then made mock savage attacks at first Arturo and then Aesc. Arturo, shouting with laughter, grappled with Cuna and rolled in a fighting heap with him on the ground. Watching them Tia thought of the time, eight years since, when she had walked into the Anderida forest glade and seen Baradoc strung by his wrists to a tree, left there to die by Inbar, and the dogs silent and watchful below him. Her lips tightened in scorn at the thought of Inbar's treachery, her whole body suddenly strung with anger and her heart full of contempt for the man. *Aie*, she knew well enough what Mawga had meant by her heart and body now being strangers to her mind. What woman with seven years of barren love-ache would not? But for her, let it be seven times seven, it would be an ache of which she was always mistress.

At the end of seven days Inbar came down from the moor and in the long hall there was a great feast for all the men to celebrate his chieftainship. At the end of the feast all the men rose one by one and swore faith to him. Tia, who had been helping in the serving and cooking for the feast, watching them knew that had the womenfolk been called upon to swear the same oath, no power on earth could have made her step forward.

Two days later when Tia carried the weekly store of fresh-baked bread to the long hall Inbar, his beard freshly cut, his long hair trimmed to his ears and wearing a white linen tunic over soft doe-skin trews, was sitting at the table. Before him was a jug of mead and two beakers. He gave her no greeting as she came in, but when she returned from the store carrying the empty rush pannier, he nodded to the bench on the far side of the table and said, 'Sit.'

Because he was the Chief and to be obeyed Tia sat down. The slowness and reluctance in her movements made him smile.

He said, 'So far you obey me. You force your body to pay respect, but in your heart there is the stiffness of denial.' He filled the two beakers and handed one to her. 'No matter. A woman's pride can come to unexpected flowering. Drink.'

He raised his beaker and drank and slowly Tia did the same. Baking was hot work and she was glad of the drink. For that alone, she told herself, she took it. As she put the beaker down she said, 'I thank you for that.'

Inbar nodded and then half-speaking to her, half-musing aloud, he said, 'Before I come to what is topmost in my heart, there is a matter I would speak about first. Baradoc and myself were taken as slaves from the long beach over the headland. We were cousins and friends. We were sold into slavery together and we came in the end to serve the same master.'

'This I know.'

'But much you do not know. We had a good master, a retired soldier, a Roman, a man of learning, of good grace and many parts. Before I left him with my freedom I learnt many things ... your tongue, your people's ways. I came back here because

257

I would bring the knowledge of the things I knew to my tribe
... the knowledge of a way of life, of skills and arts which, if
they would accept and learn them, would make their lives fuller
and less crude. Now that my father has gone I can begin that
work. If it indeed were true, do you know why I would have
strung Baradoc to a tree to die?'

'String him there you did.'

Inbar shrugged his shoulders. 'I am tired of denying the fact
– and you slip my question. But I give you the answer. From our
master Baradoc loved only the knowledge he gained of warfare,
of arms, of fortifications and of handling troops and horses, the
care of men and the provisioning of baggage trains and the way
to look at a valley or fertile plain, not for its beauty or the crops
it grew, but for the way it could be held or seized in battle or
night attack. Baradoc would have brought back a dream of
conquest and strife, of raising all men into troops and battle
parties to turn eastwards and fight the Saxons –'

'And what is wrong with that?'

'Alone nothing – except that in his heart there is less hatred
of the Saxons than there is lust for military glory and power.
Baradoc would be a *dux bellorum* – nay, more than that.
Baradoc – another Caesar. He would have left you here while
he went east again. Or dragged you hither and thither in the
end with less thought of you than his baggage train or the well-
ordering of his men.' He paused for a moment, his eyes steady
on her. Then quietly he went on. 'You saw none of that in
him? Nay, your brain is too sharp not to have guessed at it.'

Tia stood up slowly, her mind host to two truths; one, that
the truth of Baradoc was much as he had drawn it, though she
had known it and accepted it when she had married him, and,
two, that for the first time this man had made plain to her a
truth in him which she had never expected to find.

She said evenly, 'There is nothing you can tell me of Baradoc.
I am his wife of choice and whatever way of life he brings me
I accept out of my love for him.'

Inbar stood up and slowly shrugged his shoulders.

'No. The laws of this tribe make you a free woman. Each

week when you bring the new bread – and I have given orders that it shall always be you – then, as now, I shall ask you to become my wife and work with me for something my people need more than the arts of ambush and the naught-gaining perils of distant campaigning. They fight best who have most to lose. When in the long years ahead the first Saxon warbands reach the borders of Dumnonia there shall be no lack of sword hands to rally to the Prince – just as there is no man tardy to the beach now when the Scotti come raiding. Be my wife. Help me to bring to the people of the Enduring Crow a way of life which when the time comes will be worth death in battle to preserve. This I ask out of true love.'

'No. I am married to Baradoc, and he will return.'

For a moment or two Inbar eyed her. Then he laughed and, picking up the half-filled beaker before him, drained it. He walked to the doorway and said, 'I could pull the latch thong of the door in and none could enter. I could use force and school you to love and scorn the danger of a hidden knife, but I want no golden-crowned dove to keep in a wattle cage.'

He opened the door and stood aside for Tia to go out. Standing in the doorway he watched her move down the path slope. With her went the three dogs, Lerg, Aesc and Cuna, who had been waiting outside for her. The sight of the dogs took him back to the day in the forest when with a companion he had strung Baradoc up to the oak. The dogs had been away hunting for their own food or they could not have laid their hands on his cousin. That day he had acted on impulse, sudden, unthinking and swift. But now he knew the real truth which had been in him, forcing him to unpremeditated violence.

That night as Tia lay abed with Arturo and Mawga snoring gently on her couch on the far side of the hut, she found Inbar strong in her thoughts. So far she had only thought of him as a treacherous man who had tried to kill her husband in order to ensure that he, as now, eventually became chief of the tribe. That his treachery held any more motive than a desire for power and self-gratification had never occurred to her. Yet now, though she could never condone his act, she could acknowledge that behind it lay a worthy motive. The tribespeople, roughly housed, and beyond a few badly organized efforts to make store of one season's crops, cattle and catches against the want and barrenness of another, lived simply from day to day. Bred to hardship and lean times they were almost unaware of these. Each house had its midden heap outside of bones, the empty shells of mussels, and other cast-away refuse amongst which the dogs and swine rooted and the flies bred in summer. The narrow river ran pure and clear down from the moor, but through the settlement it was polluted by seepage from the middens, by the women who washed the family clothes along its length and by the cattle and horses who drank and wallowed in it. There were no privies. Men, women and children disappeared behind the shelter of rock, bush or reed patch to ease themselves. The pottery they made was crude and coarse. The clothes they wore were of roughly cured skins and badly woven wool. The grain milled on the big quern stones in the cave was seldom properly oven-dried and its flour quickly grew a blue mould in the wet winter gales. Thinking this ... remembering the well-ordered, civilized life and economies of her father's and uncle's villas, the baths and piped water, the fine table ware and the clatter of pots and pans in the spotless cooking quarters, the store rooms well-aired and damp free and, in winter, the gentle heat that flooded each room through the wall and under-floor ducts from the furnace, she suddenly realized that in her few short years here she had not only passed from one world to another, but had accepted this crude, insanitary life as though she had never known other. But this had not happened to Inbar. As a boy and on into young manhood he had, no matter if as a slave with a good master, lived the life she had once known, and conceived the passion to bring some part of it at least back to his people. No man, she felt, who nursed such a desire could be wholly bad.

At this moment Arturo stirred in his sleep. Then, not even half-awake, rolled over her and slipped to the floor. By the light of the single wall sconce light she saw him pad in his short shift to the door, fumble with the latch-bar and go out. He stood framed against the pale night sky in the doorway and, yawning, piddled over the threshold. He stumbled back into bed and was fast asleep in a few moments, held in the crook of Tia's arm, the hut door left wide open. From up the valley came the long churring call of a night jar, a pendant of pale stars was framed in the doorway against the summer light sky and the flame of the wall light wavering in the faint night zephyrs set strange shadows dancing around the hut. And in her heart Tia found, too, a strangeness of movement which she had never known before and there arose in her, unbridled, a passionate, body-trembling longing for the return of Baradoc.

In the following weeks Tia took the bread batch regularly to the long hall, and always Inbar awaited her there and they sat and drank their beaker each of mead and talked – and talked with growing easiness for there now was a slow dying of open hostility towards him in Tia. And because there was, almost unconsciously, a growing nostalgia in Tia for her old life, she was always glad when he spoke of his days in service with his old Romano-British master. He made no movement to court or woo her, though he always went through the ritual of asking her to marry him and she without feeling always refused him. When she left he would always open the door for her and, unfailing, before she passed out would pay her some compliment that arose from his desire, phrases that reminded her of the way Baradoc, too, had found a poetry to match his love ... *My heart is a bird without song because there is always winter in your smile ... I walk the moor through the blaze of gorse bloom and know that, like yours, it is a beauty masking a snare of thorns ... What man needs a summer house of laced ash boughs and a seal skin couch if the calm of the night knows not the love sigh of his beloved?*

Apart from these brief meetings he took no notice of her when he saw or passed her in the business of daily life. But slowly more and more he kept Arturo close to his company as he worked with the other men, and openly favoured him above any of the other boys as though he would say 'One day this will be my step-son and more to be favoured than any son of my own loins.' And once he said to her over their mead, 'Be my wife and have my children, but know that I will swear before the tribal priest in open company that he shall follow me as Chief of the Enduring Crow people.'

Yet, for all he favoured Arturo, he had no hesitation in punishing him, for Arturo in his eighth year was already growing in thought and deed beyond his age. There was a small cove, not far from the main settlement beach, which was the place where twice a week the women and young girls bathed naked and washed themselves and sported with one another. One day Arturo, who could now swim like a fish and dive like a cormorant, covered his head with sea-weed and drifting offshore let the tide take him down to the cove so that he could watch the naked girls and women and was discovered by Mawga's sharp-eyed mother. He was taken before Inbar and Inbar beat him with a hazel switch and raised weals across his rump. Watched by everyone Arturo made no cry. When the beating was done he drew up his ragged trews and pulled down his tattered shirt and walked from the open space before the long hall and up the river towards the moor without word or look at anyone.

As he lay at Tia's side that night, Arturo out of the darkness said quietly, 'One day I shall kill Inbar.'

Tia smiled and turned to him where he lay face downwards to avoid the smart of his weals against the bed boards: 'Why? Because he beat you for a deserved reason?'

'No. I think nothing of that.'

'Then why?'

'For the same reason that you will not marry him. Because – be my father dead or alive – I should one day be Chief of this tribe. If my father does not return to kill him, then when I am grown the duty becomes mine.'

For a moment Tia was silent and then she asked, 'If your father never returns and I should marry Inbar as he wishes – what then?'

'I would still kill him – and find you a worthier man.'

Tia laughed quietly, but as she did so it came to her that this was the first time she had ever put in words to anyone the thought that Baradoc might never return and that she might marry Inbar. To cover the confusion in her she said sharply, 'Sleep and put such thoughts from your mind.'

But from that day on Tia noticed that although Arturo behaved as usual with Inbar he spent less time with the other boys and was always ready to go up to the moor and take provisions to the hermit Druid priest, Galpan, who lived alone in a turf shelter, and that there were nights when she woke to find him gone from the bed alongside her and to answer for his absence would only say, teasingly, 'I could not sleep so I sat on the clifftop and watched the rock foxes dance.' Or, 'I lay by the Big Bend pool and the king salmon who waits there for spawning time put his great kype from the water and taught me a song the mermaids sing.'

'Then sing it for me.'

'Nay – it is not fit for the ears of my gentle mother.'

Galpan, the priest, meeting Tia on one of his rare visits to the settlement, stopped and said to her, 'Your Arturo has the gift of memory and the fault of imagination. When he comes to me with bread and meat I teach him all the stories of this tribe and the other tribes of Dumnonia and of our country and he learns them word perfect, for so only should they be remembered less time and man's memory abuse them. He learns fast and accurately but sometimes, to anger me so he thinks, he will tell them in his own fashion. Would you know what that fashion is?'

'You would have me know or you would not be speaking to me.'

'True. He retells the stories and always the great priest, the great warrior or prince he calls Arturo. And always the feats of bravery or acts of piety are more wonderful than they were in life, and always – which is why to my shame I allow him the licence – his words are, even for such a child, golden with the gift of the true bards and his phrases so beautifully wrought for one so young that I forget to be angry.'

'Yet still, you do not tell me why you say all this to me. All children embroider a story in the telling.'

'As children, yes. As men only the truth must be spoken. But as a man, unless my years and wisdom already fail me, your Arturo though he act with valour and skill will make of his acts and the feats of others a false wonder.'

'Then he should be curbed or beaten free of the failing now.'

Galpan shrugged his shoulders and rubbed one bare foot against the dusty ground. 'No. The cock crows to the rising sun. The lark cannot soar from the bare heath without song. There is no altering them. Your Arturo will become what he will, but few men will ever learn from his own lips the full truth of what he is, or does, or dreams. For my own peace – and despite my liking him well – I have told him to come no more to me for I would not have my calm and meditation corrupted by his bright fancy and golden tongue.'

'He has shown none of this to me or others here.'

'Why should he? Until its wings are flighted the young plover is a stone among stones.'

So, Arturo stopped going to the priest and instead attached himself to Garmon, the chief cattleman, and became herd boy spending his days and many nights on the high moor slopes, and since Garmon rode his distant rounds on a spirited mealy-mouthed pony it was not long before Arturo was riding some of the rounds for him and for this Garmon was well content. He grieved still for the loss of his wife and daughter to the Scotti raiders and often his grief found comfort in a goatskin of mead or barley beer. He was content to lie fuddled in the sun and let Arturo do his rounds and always with Arturo went Cuna, alone, for the other dogs, Lerg and Aesc, were now too old for long days and hard going. There were times even when Arturo had to lift Cuna to the pony's back and ride with him uneasily couched against his crutch.

But although Arturo had joined Garmon mainly for the chance to learn to ride and for freedom from the small but constant dull tasks which the settlement boys were set to, his natural inquisitiveness, sharp eye and brain could not stay idle.

He fast became a good herdsman and long before high summer saw the yellow flowering of bog asphodel and the sloughed skins of adder and grass snake on the granite rock slabs; he could pick out from three bow shots away the sick animal in a flock or, running his eye over a herd of cattle, know at once which one was missing since to him they all had personalities as well known as the settlement boys for whom he now had little time. In the evening when he came back and had fed and watered and hobbled the pony, he would sit with Garmon over a meal and then, enjoying his ration of two beakers of mead if any remained, would regale the man with highly coloured stories of his day's doings – mostly to the accompaniment of Garmon's drunken snoring.

There were other times when, doing the rounds alone, if Arturo should find the herd harboured close to Garmon's hut he would use the spare time on his hands by riding southwards across the heathland and moor to a lonely tor from whose summit he could look down on to the dusty, rough road which ran from Isca in the east through the old Roman outpost of Nemetostatio and so westwards to link hamlet and settlement all the way down to Antivestaeum and the great land-ending promontory of Belerium where, so old Galpan had told him, a man could stand on a clear day and see the dancing mirage of the Blessed Isles, beyond which the seas ran away into the endless mystery of time and space. But Arturo's young eyes turned mostly to the east for that way lay the world of which his mother had told him so much, the world of fighting men, of great woods full of wolf and bear, and the high mountains beyond the Sabrina river and the rich lands of the Catuvellauni and the Coritani where great chiefs ruled and fought, and where a man who could handle spear, sword and bow could gather others to him and find adventure.

Sitting astride the dun pony he would watch the road and the small bands of travellers raising a trail of dust as they moved on foot, mounted or by cart. Sometimes they would see him perched on the tor and often would give him greeting by the long clear call of a horn to show that they passed in peace.

One day Arturo watched a small party coming along the road, travelling eastwards. A man walked at the head of a horse which was pulling an open cart in which sat two cloaked figures pressed close together against the bluster of wind and rain squalls which were sweeping the moorland. Tethered to the rear of the cart was a milch cow and a spare horse. When the party was directly below Arturo, no more than half a mile away, the cart lurched in one of the deep road ruts and the sudden movement alarmed the tethered horse.

It reared on its hind legs, tossed up its head and broke the halter rope. The animal galloped off the road and took to the moor ground in alarm. Faintly on the wind Arturo caught the sound of the shouts and cries of the party and for a moment or two he sat his pony, grinning at their plight. Before they could unhitch the cart horse to go in chase of the escaping animal it would be well away into the moor and – the thought was suddenly strong in him – an easy prize for him to capture.

Impulsively he kicked his heels into the flanks of his pony and began to ride fast down the tor slope on a line to bring him to the escaping animal. Behind him, barking and losing ground, came Cuna. Excited now at the easy prize which lay before him Arturo, as a squall of wind and rain beat into his face, cried, '*Aie! Aie!* The gods give and Arturo takes!'

Thighs and legs gripping tight on the pony's sides, Arturo swung the animal around rocks and heather and gorse clumps and fast overhauled the horse which had now dropped to a slow canter, flinging up its head once and neighing as though celebrating its escape. On the far ridge of the tor Arturo drew level with the horse and pulling the pony back to match its gait he rode alongside, talking and calling to it until, either from his cajoling or the presence of the pony, it dropped to a slow amble. Arturo leaned over and caught the free-flying halter rope and drew horse and moor pony to a halt

Flushed with his prize, he sat back and looked down at the road party. The man was making no effort to unhitch the horse from the cart to follow him. But one of the two people in the cart had jumped to the ground and was running quickly up the long slope towards him. Arturo grinned as he watched. He had but to turn and canter away with his prize and none could stop him. Mischief rising in him, he waited, planning to hold his ground tantalizingly until the figure neared him before riding away. The runner was a bowshot away when the passing of the fierce rain squall allowed him to see clearly. He saw that the pursuer had thrown off his cloak and now came towards him wearing only a rain damp red tunic, and carried no arms. Then, as the gap between them narrowed, he saw more – that the pursuer was no man or youth, but a girl with long black hair and that she ran faster than he had seen anyone run before and with the sure-footedness of a deer. He was on the point of turning away with his prize in escape when the impulse to kick his pony into action died in him. He sat and waited for the girl to come up to him.

She drew up before him and stood, squaring her shoulders as she took deep breaths before speaking. She was, Arturo guessed, little older than himself and more beautiful than any of the settlement girls. Her hair was as black as a raven's wing and lay now plastered to her head and neck with wet like a sleek helmet, and the same rain had drenched her tunic so that it clung to her body like a skin, firming into bold prominence her apple-small young breasts. Her legs were bare except for light leather sandals, the thongs between big and second toes cross-gartered high up her bare legs. But more than the boldness of her young body which Arturo covered unbashfully with his eyes, was the beauty of her face. Her skin had the soft, dull polish of a hoarded hazel nut, her eyes were a bright, clear, piercing blue and her lips were red as the wild rose-hips which grew on the banks of the lower combes of the moor. Arturo had never seen a girl so beautiful and the sight made him clear his throat with a grunt as though his gullet were dry with sudden thirst.

Her breath recovered, the girl stepped forward and laid her hand on the halter of the escaped horse. In an accent which told him that she had never been born or bred in Dumnonia she said, 'I thank you stranger for catching our horse.'

Tempted by some demon of mischief, Arturo answered, 'And

I say no thanks are needed since I do not mean to give him up!'

The girl laughed and tugged gently at the loop of the rope that curved between horse and Arturo's hand. 'Then you must get down and fight for him – but watch as your feet touch the ground lest I fairly slit your gullet with this.' As she spoke she pulled up the long hem of her tunic and drew from a sheath held by the top-gartering of her sandals against her thigh a long single-edged knife. Seeing the look of surprise on Arturo's face as he still sat his pony, she laughed and said, 'I see you have no stomach for knife work!' With the last word she jerked the free end of the halter from Arturo's unresisting grasp.

Arturo, confused and suddenly no master of himself, said, 'You are not of these parts?'

'No, nor wish to be if it is peopled with horse thieves.' She spoke harshly and then as though from her mastery she had decided to be magnanimous, went on, 'We come from Gaul and landed two days since in the bay which is named after the island of Ictis and we make our way to Lindum.'

'Where is that?'

The girl smiled. 'To hear my father tell it – where every other spring flows wine instead of water, where the birds on the trees have golden wings, and the cattle grass grows knee-high and lush through winter. You want to leave your bog hut or beach shelter and come? You would be welcome, less for the company of yourself than the gain of your pony and the friendship of your dog.' She stooped and fondled the ears of Cuna who sat at her feet.

Arturo slowly mastering the unusual confusion which had spread quickly through him said with a return of spirit, 'One day I will come to Lindum and seek you out. You shall see – when I am grown I shall come and woo you and we shall lie in the long grass, listen to the golden birds sing, and drink the new wine. This I promise you.'

The girl laughed, shaking her head so that the rain drops sprayed from her long black hair, and said, 'You have a boy's build but a bard's tongue. How will you ask for me since you know not my name?'

Enjoying himself now, excited by her presence and the day's adventure, Arturo grinned then spat like a man over his pony's neck and said, 'I need no name for I shall ask for one who has eyes like the blue bellflower, lips redder than the thorn berry and hair like polished black serpentine.'

The girl rubbed the back of her hand across her nose as the rain, which had begun again, ran down it and said, 'There could be many such.'

'*Aie* ... so. But not any who can lift a tunic skirt to take knife and show a red birthmark like a swallow's gorge on her thigh.'

The girl was silent for a moment then shook her head and asked, 'How many years have you got, boy?'

'Ten,' lied Arturo.

She shook her head, and said, 'I doubt the truth of that – but one thing is true, your tongue outruns your years.'

As she finished speaking there came through the wind and the rain from the road below the high, winding sound of a horn.

'Your father calls,' said Arturo.

'Then I go. But –' she grinned impishly, '– to save you trouble in the years to come I give you my name for I would not have you wandering the streets of Lindum lifting the skirts of every dark-haired girl looking for a swallow's gorge birthmark. Tis Daria, daughter of Ansold, the swordsmith.'

She turned from him, as the horn blew again, leapt to her horse's back, kicked him with her heels and set him at a canter down the slope.

'And mine –' shouted Arturo after her, though the rain and wind drowned his words, '– is Arturo, son of Baradoc, chief of the people of the Enduring Crow and ... and ... and ...' He spluttered into silence as a sharp squall burst into his face.

He sat then, still on his pony, watching Daria rejoin her father, seeing the escaped horse re-tethered to the cart, and unmoving still sat on, watching, until the slow-moving party disappeared over a far crest of the moor.

Two days later Tia walked the river path from the cave up to the long hall. She was smiling to herself because Arturo had returned from the moor that morning with Garmon and had come straight to her in the cave where she worked, stuffed himself with two of the fresh-baked wheat cakes, and had insisted that she draw a map in the sand of the cave's floor to show him where Lindum lay. But when she had asked him why he wanted to know he had been evasive and she had not pressed him. In the last few months, since he had spent less time with boys of his own age, and had frequented first the priest and then the herdsman she had sensed a growing impatience in him, a restlessness of spirit and body, and a precocity which far from pleased her. When he slept at home now it was no longer to share her bed platform but to lie in the long empty bed of Mawga's father. The children of the tribe grew faster and matured earlier than the Roman and Romano-British boys and girls of her own childhood. Since most of the youths and maidens of the tribe moved about in the good weather half-naked it was a development to be expected – but it was an early ripening which, she felt, needed the control more of a father than a mother so far as Arturo was concerned. Had she a daughter she could have dealt with her, but Arturo was fast slipping beyond her grasp. He needed the firm hand and sharp tongue of a father to guide and school him. For a moment or two her heart was full of fierce longing for the return of Baradoc. By all the gods she needed him for Arturo's sake and for her own . . .

When she entered the long hall Inbar was sitting alone at the table lashing the three-tined head of a fish spear into the socket of a new ash pole with waxed leather thongs. To one end of the table was set the customary mead jug and by its side two beakers. He rose as she came in, holding the door wide to let her pass with the great rush basket of new bread, and stood watching her as she carried it through to the store room. When she came back, without any word or greeting, he motioned her to sit at the table. He went to the door, glanced around as she sat with her back to him, then closed the door and with a flick of his fingers drew the leather latch thong inwards through its hole so that none could open the door from outside. He came back round the table and sat facing her. He lifted the jug and filled the two beakers and Tia saw at once that instead of pouring mead he was pouring wine. Seeing that she had noticed this Inbar smiled.

'There is a reason,' he said.

'And for these, too?' Tia touched her beaker with a finger. Like the other it was not the usual earthenware beaker but two fine glass drinking cups each engraved with the snake-wreathed head of the gorgon Medusa. Such glass work, she guessed, could never have been made in this country.

'For those too,' said Inbar. 'In his time my father traded for and hoarded much treasure. But he seldom used such things as these – unless someone as important as the Prince of Dumnonia or his high steward came this way.'

'Then who is honoured today?'

'You.'

'Why?'

'Because this is the day of my birth.' He smiled. 'That is if Galpan, the priest, in his keeping of the calendar is to be believed. So I make you my birth day guest, and for this meeting plague you not about marriage, but ask in its stead that you pledge my health.'

Tia smiled. When he was in this mood, despite all he had done to Baradoc, she could find herself easier with him. She took the glass and breathed in the bouquet. How many years had it been since she had last drunk a fine Falernian? Besides his treasures old Aritag had hoarded wine, too; wine bartered for in the peaceful days when the trading ships came coast creeping all the way from the Mediterranean.

Tia said, 'In return for a truce to marriage talk, I drink willingly.'

'You do me honour. Tis but a small glass, so drink deep.'

Tia nodded, raised the glass higher in salute to him, and then drank. As the sweet wine caressed her palate she remembered vividly the last time she had tasted it. It had been with old Truvius in his Aquae Sulis villa on the first night that she and

Baradoc had arrived there. The memory was sharp, but curiously without poignancy and the sudden conviction flowed through her that there might soon come a day when, for her sake and Arturo's and from the slow-dying of hope of Baradoc's return, she might forgive this man the sin she held against him, forget the past since it was blighting her future, and marry him. She drank deep and as she put the glass back on the table Inbar raised his own glass.

He said, 'From this day I ask no more that you should be my wife, but wait only for the time when you shall look into my eyes and I shall know that the thirst I have for you lives also in the woman who for me is the woman above all women.'

He drank, emptying his glass, and as he set it back on the table he touched its rim against the rim of Tia's glass and a small, silvery note rang high and then died through the silence of the long hall. Then he stood up and moved slowly round the table to come to Tia's side. As he did so Tia's head began to swim and, smiling at the conceit, she fancied that suddenly there was not one but three Inbars who approached her, three that swam first apart and then merged into one and then broke again into three, and then, as almost uncaringly she began dimly to know what had happened, the middle Inbar came to her and lifted her from her seat. As he drew her to him, knowing now that the wine had been drugged, she tried to push him from her. His arms encircled her and his lips came down to hers and took them, and he held her until there was no resistance left in her.

He lifted her from her feet and carried her, kissing her face and neck as he walked, to his sleeping booth at the end of the hall. He laid her down on the great white spread of bearskin, the pelt of one of the northern monsters which dwelt among the icebergs and frozen seas which only the Viking sea raiders knew, and rested her head on the red of the damask cushion stuffed with the nesting down of eider ducks. She lay there, breathing gently, with her eyes shut and her fair beauty fogged his eyes with tears of joy.

Yet to himself, as his hands began to unlatch the buckle of

his deerskin surcoat, he said, the edge of regret in his voice, 'A little more of patience and gentleness, good Inbar, and she would have come to you freely, tamed by her own desire. Now loving itself must be the shy mare's gentler.'

His belt dropped to the floor, but as he moved to slip free of his surcoat there came from outside the distant sound of people running and calling, the noise growing louder with each second.

Then clearly through the still summer air came the fierce, insistent clarion calling of Bada's horn, beating and searing and wailing, as he heralded the first shoaling of the year.

As the sound of shouts and racing footsteps came nearer and the horn's clamour grew fiercer and fiercer, Inbar looked to the indrawn latch thong of the door and then down to Tia. Slowly a wry smile spread over his face. A man could plan, he thought, but there was no escaping the intrusion of the gods. As Chief of the people of the Enduring Crow there was no escape from honouring the great gift from the sea.

He picked up his belt, rebuckled it, and then went to the wall and took down the great shield. He opened the door as Bada and a gathering of tribespeople swarmed across the forecourt. Seeing him they rushed forward and eager hands began to pull him away, across the court and down the valley while the horn blower paraded before him, waking the cliffs to wild echoes and setting the seabirds awing and awailing.

Only one of the tribe loitered and turned back to the long hall. Mawga, before the opening of the door, had seen that the latch thong had been pulled inside. She went in and saw the wine glasses and jug on the table, and Tia lying clothed and untouched on the bed.

A Chaplet of Purple Vetch

Inbar guessed that Mawga had helped Tia to escape. Two nights later he took her to the long hall, dismissed the old woman from the cooking quarters and the other house servant. Then he flung her on the bed and beat her until she confessed (which she did soon enough) that she had brought a moor pony to the long hall, set the partly recovering Tia on it and had led her until long after nightfall across the dark upland until they had reached the Isca road. Here, recovering fast, Tia could manage the pony herself. Wearing the Epona brooch of Ricat, she had ridden off eastwards.

Four days later Inbar had married her, and Mawga, despite her weals, was well content. To Arturo he said nothing for long since there had been no lack of boys and gossips to tell him the story. But he took Arturo into his household and treated him as his ward. Arturo, behaving himself and docile, took advantage of being lodged in the hall and the ward of the Chief to avoid any task which displeased him. Within himself he nursed the promise that he would leave the settlement as soon as he had grown to self-sufficiency and, if chance could be wrought, would kill Inbar before he left for attempting the dishonour of his mother.

In Isca Tia was met by Ricat, the horse-master, as she rode down in the pearl-haze of a summer morning to the shallow ford across the river. Beyond the river rose the great Mount of Isca topped with the long-abandoned Roman fortress. It had been beyond the memory of most men since any cohort commander had made the night rounds of legionary sentinels, and the fortress now was slowly lapsing into ruin as the townspeople robbed it for its quarried stone, its well-wrought woodwork and the great red tiles which had roofed stables, barracks and officers' quarters. Beyond the Mount at the foot of its slope was spread out the British town, a huddle of squalid reed and straw-thatched dwellings. A haze of cooking smoke rose in the still morning air, cattle grazed in the water meadows, and pigs rooted and foraged through the middens that spread around the skirts of the lower town. Above all, flying from the topmost rampart of the old fortress, the scarlet standard of the Prince of Dumnonia hung from a stout pine flagpole like a lazy flame as the idle wind now and then unfurled it to show the Dumnonia symbol of a great oak tree.

Ricat greeted Tia warmly and then, without asking her for any explanation of her coming, he said, 'One of my horse handlers saw you wearing the Epona brooch as you came down from the moor at first light, and the signal was passed from watch post to watch post.' He took her right hand and pressed it to his forehead briefly. 'You are welcome, Lady Tia.'

He took her to his house which was stone built and tile roofed and stood at the side of the old Forum. Its entry was through a small courtyard where roses grew in red earthenware urns, and across its front struggled an ancient vine which held now small clusters of green grapes. He led her into the house and showed her around and told her that the top room, which was approached by an outside flight of stone steps, was hers. He handed her the key bolt to its great wooden lock, and said, 'You shall do such work as you wish, but each day there comes Berna, an old woman from the lower town, who will help you. I am often away on the Prince's business, but when I am a night watch will keep the courtyard.'

Tia, her spirits still in slow turmoil from her escape from Inbar, took his hand and kissed it. As he stirred with embarrassment, she said, 'You are good to me, Master Ricat. The day will come when you shall be rewarded for your goodness.' Then unpinning the Epona brooch she held it out to him, saying, 'I thank you for the loan of this.'

Ricat shook his head, smiling. 'Keep it as a gift, Lady Tia. A gift to welcome you in my house.' Before Tia could protest he had gone.

Touched deeply by his kindness she went up to her room and, putting the cloth-wrapped bundle of her few belongings which Mawga had hastily packed for her on the low table which stood in the centre of the room, she sat at the window and looked out over the untidy sprawl of the town beyond which the slow curves of the river shone like a silver ribbon. In a niche at the side of the window stood a bronze bowl which held fresh sprays of large white ox daisies and meadowsweet. Though he could have had but little time to order their gathering she knew that they came from Ricat. The thought of the goodness which was in the man laid the beginning of a slow balm over the misery of her own feelings. Arturo stayed with Inbar, but she had no fears for his safety. Some strange god, she fancied, watched over Arturo. From the moment that his small baby hands had clasped the silver chalice and the water in it had been suffused with the red flush which would come for no other she had known that he was marked for greatness. He would live to be and do whatever her own gods, or the Christian god of the old hermit Asimus, had already foreseen for him. For herself, stronger now since she had known how close she had come to abandoning it, lived only one faith, one conviction – that someday Baradoc would return to her. Never again would her woman's body or weak woman's mind ever waver from that belief.

Ten months after her marriage Mawga gave birth to a girl-child which was given the name Sabele. By this time Arturo was well into his ninth year and grown taller and thinner as though his strength and bulking were hard-pressed to keep pace with him. Inbar showed no impatience that the child had not been a boy. There was time and plenty for that. Eleven months later, when Arturo was into his tenth year, Mawga gave birth again and this time to a man-child who was called Talid.

Inbar gave a feast in the long hall to celebrate the birth and long before he and the other men were too drunken to talk or understand sense he called for silence and then told the men of the tribe the changes he was going to make in the running of the settlement. He had now, he said, a son to follow him and a man of wisdom and goodness had a duty to lay up, not only treasure for the son's future, but a future which should be peaceful, industrious and well-ordered. This was the duty of all men. He then told them the changes which were to be made in the settlement life. All the middens were to be cleared away and one main midden set up on the beach verge where the high spring tides would scour it away periodically. The river would be rock-dammed at the foot of the valley beyond the last of the huts and there and only there should the women do the washing. There would be cattle and pig pens well-fenced for the winter-folding. Crops and cattle were to be held in common and each family to draw meat, fish and flour according to their size and their standing. Every youth would be trained to arms for defence against raiders, but no man or youth was free to take leave of the settlement without his permission. If any did so his family would be punished in his stead. When traders came whether by sea or land then a council of elders from the settlement would negotiate the bartering and there would be a fair division of all the goods purchased. There was talk, he said, of war and raiding and the rise and fall of new war lords throughout the land beyond Isca and as far as the shores of all the Saxon seas, but such trouble was no concern of the people of the Enduring Crow. If such trouble did eventually come then the Prince of Dumnonia would call the levies from each settlement and lots would be drawn among those of fighting age to determine who should go.

There was more he said, but in truth few of the men paid much attention for not only had they heard most of it before, but they knew in their hearts that many of the things would not be done and that life would go on much as before. It was idle to speak against him and delay the moment of feasting and full drinking.

Some time after this Inbar's manner to Arturo began to change. When Arturo approached Inbar one morning after the

Chief had spent most of the night drinking to ask permission to go out with one of the fishing boats Inbar refused him. Arturo began to argue and in the midst of his protest Inbar struck him and knocked him to the floor. Arturo, tight-lipped, picked himself up and left the long hall. He went down to the beach and sat on a rock staring at the sullen grey sea of late autumn. He was no fool and knew that Inbar's changing manner towards him came from good reason. He was held now in the settlement always under the eye of one of the tribe, be it man or older boy. He was allowed no more to the cattle and horse grounds on the moor, nor even permitted a visit to old Galpan, the priest. Although no one had ever said so, he was a prisoner in the settlement.

As he sat there, brooding, and watching a handful of black-headed terns diving for fry in the shallow water, Mawga came across the sands with two other women and, seeing him, left them and came to him. In the crook of one arm, wrapped in the loose folds of her gown she carried her babe, Talid. The gown was of good stout linen, dyed blue and sewn with black beads around the hem and throat. Mawga now wore such clothes as she had never known in her life before. She gave him greeting and sat beside him.

After some idle talk she said to him, 'Arturo, you are grown now enough to know better how to approach Inbar. When he drinks and after drinking is no time to ask him for favours.'

Arturo was silent for a while and then he answered, 'There is no proper moment for me to ask anything of Inbar. Every time he sees me he thinks of the shame he would have done my mother. *Aie* ... and more than that. He sees that I am the son of Baradoc and the rightful one to be Chief of this tribe when I reach full years.'

'Nay. There is goodness in Inbar. Speak him fair and hold yourself proper to him and one day he will name you to be Chief after him.'

Arturo looked at her, his eyes widening a little and the line of his lips slanted wryly. Mawga was good, but she was simple. He said with a nod to the babe in her arms, 'You know not Inbar.

He waits but to see that Talid grows into sturdiness and health. *Aie* ... maybe he waits for more than that. For the time when you bear him another healthy boy-child. Then will come the thing he wishes for me.'

Mawga's face clouded with anger. 'Speak not so. You are his ward. The gods would mark him if he harmed you.'

'Tis a small point. He will not kill me himself – any more than he could boldly kill my father. But I can be killed by the chance fall of a rock from the cliffs. Or the mischance of a badly aimed hunting arrow. *Aie* ... or from the sudden movement of a boat as I help haul the nets while fishing.' He leaned forward and placed the tip of his forefinger on the soft nose of Talid, and went on, 'He is pink and soft and helpless like a new-born harvest mouse in a straw nest. And so, for the moment, am I.'

Mawga shook her head. 'Your mind is full of black images. Inbar is a good man.'

'That you must say – for he is to you. But if he is so good, then ask him for permission for me to go and join my mother in Isca.'

'That I cannot do for it is not my place to meddle in Inbar's affairs.' Then seeing Arturo grin broadly, she went on, 'Why do you smile so?'

'Because –and I do not blame you – you did not draw back from meddling the day you helped my mother. Tether me a pony in the thorn scrub at the valley bend and one night be careless with the lock of the great hall. Inbar would never suspect you, though he might beat you for carelessness with the key.'

'You ask too much – and without reason. But for love of your mother what I have heard I have not heard.'

Mawga rose and walked away, and Arturo watched her without emotion. He had not expected her to help. Nobody would help him for none was rash enough to meddle in the affairs of Inbar. Raising his eyes from watching Mawga, he saw that on the high cliff behind him one of the older youths was sitting on an outjutting crag looking down at him. So they watched, he thought, day by day, and the night saw him safe within the long hall. Well, then he must use the cunning of the cliff fox, the patience of the fishing heron, and find his own way out, for to Isca he would go. He picked up a piece of dried bladder-wrack and began to pop the black blisters in its strands. As he did so it seemed to him that suddenly the gods were speaking to him and giving him the sign which would show him the way to escape. He lay back on the rock, watching the grey scud of clouds sweeping eastwards up the coast and began to chuckle to himself. Yes, the gods had spoken and given their sign. Yes, he would go to Isca, but not to stay for long since even the Prince might for his own reasons send him back. What matter that he had so few years? The years would come, and there were always travelling parties that would take him as horse or mule boy. He would find his own way, make his mark and when manhood was with him he would come back. *Aie! Aie! . . .* the whole world lay to the east and a man should see it before he came back to his own people to settle down.

That evening in the long hall Inbar was good to him, sat him at his right hand to eat and allowed him an extra beaker of mead and Arturo showed a due gratitude and cheerfulness which he did not feel. He knew quite well that Mawga must have spoken to Inbar on his behalf and urged him to show more kindness to him.

The next morning Arturo set about gathering the things he wanted to make good his escape and since he did not stray from the settlement area little notice was taken of him. Not that he would have cared if he were watched closely for none could have drawn suspicion from his movements. Not once did he go down to the beach or beyond the settlement bounds for the next week. He loafed about the cave, watching and talking to the women baking bread and grinding corn. He spent time each day to sit and talk to Bada who, apart from being the horn blower, was a skilled bowmaker. Arturo took delight in the man's adroitness in shaping and fashioning the layers of wood to make bows, and learning from him how to tell by look, feel and hand-tensing the best lengths of gut and sinew for use in finely plaiting drawstrings. Since autumn would soon pass into winter, and selected cattle and swine were now being taken to the slaughter pen for killing and curing against the hard days to come when fresh fish would be scarce and corn and flour would only by tight rationing last through to the next year's crop, he would sit atop the fence of the killing pen and watch and talk with the tribesmen working at the skinning and quartering of beasts. He was polite, ever cheerful with everyone and willing always to humour Inbar and to serve him. But though this, he knew, pleased Inbar, he noticed that always someone, man or boy, and different every day, watched him.

Only at night lying on his bed did his face show his real thoughts, stubborn thoughts that matched the stubborn lines of his face and which made him clench his teeth and grind them slowly. But when everyone else in the hall was asleep, he would sit up quietly and, by the dim light of the red glow of the turf and peat fire, he would draw from inside the straw-stuffed palliasse of his bed the things he had quietly filched during his loafing days. He needed little light to work by for his preparations were simple.

By the near end of October when the new moon was passing to its first quarter and the bright evening star Venus showed only briefly in the south-western sky after the setting of the sun, Arturo had everything ready, and waited now only for the right conjunction of time, and tide and chance. For chance, he needed Inbar to sit after Mawga, himself and the servants had retired to bed, as he did sometimes, warming himself at the night-piled fire and drinking a last beaker of mead or wine before retiring. For time he had to have the tide on the turn, and setting on an easterly course up the coast.

When the right moment came he was favoured by the weather. As though he thought, as he lay abed, fully dressed and with his needs for escape concealed under his tunic, the gods were on his side and wished to harass all pursuit until he should reach the safety of the cliffs, and even there, confuse the sight and hearing of the cliff and beach patrols.

Through his partly open bed curtains he watched Inbar sitting on a stool by the peat fire, leaning forward with his elbows on his knees and a great beaker of mead cradled in his hands as he warmed it. The thought had been in his mind during his planning that he could kill the man, but he had decided against it. Inbar could engineer some accident to kill him and there would have been no trouble. But if he killed Inbar without honour like some assassin, then the blood-mark would have been put on his name by the Prince of Dumnonia and no man in the west would have given him aid or shelter. No matter, he thought, as he watched Inbar raise the beaker and drink, the time for an honourable killing of Inbar would come. This was no moment to use the knife which he carried bound to his right leg under his long trews.

Inbar coughed and hiccoughed as he swallowed his drink and his body swayed a little as he was lulled between part sleep and part intoxication. Arturo slipped from his bed platform and with no attempt to quieten his movements walked towards the fire.

Inbar heard him and half turned. In a good mood from warmth and drink, he smiled and said, 'What, not abed and fully dressed, my Arturo?'

'I was cold and couldn't sleep, my lord.'

Inbar said nothing for a moment or two, but the smile stayed on his lips. He held out the beaker and Arturo took it and drank a little of the mead and then handed the beaker back.

'It puts warmth in the gut,' said Inbar.

'And dreams in the head,' said Arturo, thinking that if the opportunity he needed did not come then he would try again some other night and there would, because of this night, be no suspicion in Inbar.

Inbar belched gently and said, 'And what dreams does my Arturo dream?'

Humouring him, Arturo answered, 'That the days between me and manhood were gone.'

'And if they were?'

'Then my lord I would ask your leave to take my arms and go east to fight against the Saxons now that the troubles have started again.'

'How do you know that?'

'From every pedlar and packman who passes. Ambrosius and Vortigern are in arms again.'

'More likely against one another than against the long-keel men.' Eyeing him for a moment in silence, Inbar gave a sudden laugh. 'And which would you serve? Vortigern, who to save his life once married the harlot daughter of Hengist? Or Ambrosius, who, like his father once, dreams of wearing an Emperor's purple?'

'Ambrosius is of our race. I would serve him and, by serving well, do honour to the people of the Enduring Crow.'

Mellowed by the mead, Inbar handed him the beaker and said, 'Here, cool your hot blood with this and wish not your young years away so readily.'

'Nay, my lord. I have had enough.'

Inbar nodded his head and withdrew the beaker. 'And so have I. Enough so that my bladder calls for relief.' He rose slowly and putting his hand on Arturo's shoulder said, 'Go to bed, and dream not of fighting.'

'Ay, my lord.' As Arturo began to turn away Inbar stopped him.

He said, 'You are a good youth, Arturo, and I would not have you think I bear you any ill. Firm I am with you for your own good as with any other youth in the tribe. But more, I would have you know that never in my life have I ...' – he swayed a little and cleared his throat noisily – '... offered your mother any disrespect for all that malicious gossips may say. We drank wine together to honour my birthday and she from overtiredness and the wine grew faint so that she lay on the bed to recover ... Yes, no more. So harbour no bad thoughts. Now get to your bed.'

Arturo nodded and showed nothing on his face of the swift upsurge of contempt in him for the man, knowing that the mead was speaking in him strongly and fogging his thinking. Had he forgotten that his mother had taken flight to Isca to escape him?

As Arturo began to walk to his bed Inbar moved to the main

door and drew from his belt pouch the long key of the heavy wooden lock. He unlocked the door and went out. The night air swept in and sent the grey fire ashes swirling. The door swung almost closed behind him. As it did so Arturo turned quickly and went to the fire. He picked up the stout length of oak plant which lay there for prodding the turves and ran to stand against the wall so that the inswinging door would hide him.

Outside he heard the sound of Inbar relieving himself, and from the far end of the hall came the light sound of Mawga snoring. Without harming Inbar he could have slipped out and run for liberty, but Inbar would have raised the alarm and every man, boy and dog in the settlement would have been soon hunting after him. Such a shift would have served him nothing. He needed time. And too, although he could not use his dagger on Inbar, there was pleasure in the use he could make of the oak post.

Holding it two-handed Arturo waited. He heard Inbar belch outside and then the shuffle of his feet as he turned to enter. As the door swung open slowly Arturo raised the oak plant, stepped forward to clear the swinging door and crashed the long post down on to the man's skull.

Inbar collapsed to the ground and lay still, and the door swung back to be held by his prone body which sprawled across the threshold. Arturo, moving now without excitement or clumsy haste, bent over Inbar and pulled him free from the threshold and then took the key from the lock. He went out and locked the door from the outside and began to run towards the scrub and bracken growths that grew up the side of the valley. When he reached the first of the bracken he sent the key flying deep into the now dying growths.

Reaching the crest of the valley side, keeping well below the skyline to avoid being seen by any of the settlement patrols, he dropped his pace to a steady trot heading always east and on a parallel line to the cliffs. Although he had long discarded the temptation of striking inland and making a bid overland for Isca, he was momentarily tempted to try it for the escape he had planned was not one he relished. Commonsense told him, however, that he had no alternative. Inbar would soon recover and when he did the pursuit would begin on foot and on horse and the chances of his reaching the river Tamarus and making the crossing were remote. His best chance of escape was by a route which none would dream that he would risk.

He moved steadily along the line of a wide gully that ran parallel with the sea on his left. There was light from the stars and the thin slip of the new crescent moon. After a time the gully sloped upwards and was lost in a maze of rocks and broken ground not far from the cliffs' edges and here Arturo followed a narrow path which took him out along a headland which he knew well. When he reached its point he climbed down its face, disturbing the roosting seabirds, until he finally stood on a flat rock at its foot. Some way below him the rock foot disappeared into deep water, the sea heaving and swinging as the tide which some time before had been at full ebb was now setting in flood eastwards along the coast. Under the light of the stars and the moon Arturo could see the dark line of current streaming away from the headland out to sea. It was a current which the men of the settlement used in their fishing for one could work the tides to go west or east on the ebb and return on the flood. Arturo knew that many, many miles away to the east the current swung inshore again and would carry a man with it if he humoured it. To fight it was to ask for an early drowning, and to ride with it for the long swing out and back called for the strength and endurance of more than most men since the body weakened fast with just the effort of keeping afloat.

But, as Arturo had realized when his bursting of the bladders of sea-wrack had set him thinking of escape, that which a man could not achieve by strength he might well, with some risk, bring to fruit by artifice.

He sat down and began to work fast. From beneath his tunic he pulled out three pigs' bladders stolen from the slaughtering pens and, blowing them up, trapped the gut ends with thin but strong lengths of old Bada's bowstring sinews, leaving small loops in the thonging through which he ran a long length of thickly braided gut to fasten the three bladders together so that he could slip them over his head and secure them under his armpits to keep him afloat without any effort on his part. Inside his tunic he had, wrapped in a large piece of pig bladder, two flat rounds of hard bread and a slice of smoked neat's flesh. The tidal current would eventually bear him safely to shore but, although the sea lacked yet its biting winter cold, it could sap strength and the body's warmth. Against this the blood's fire must be stoked with food. As for thirst ... well, that must be endured if there were not juice enough in a handful of small crab apples which he carried with the other food in the blouse of his belted tunic.

His preparations complete, the bladders securely about him, he went to the rock edge, waited a while to judge the surge of the slowly heaving seas, and then jumped as a great swell rose below him, keeping his arms stiff at his sides to hold the braided thonging that joined the bladders from slipping. He landed backside first and as he went under felt the fierce tug of the thonging cut into his armpits as the bladders dragged above him. Then he surfaced, riding high and comfortably, and the current took him and bore him away from the cliff point seawards, swinging him gently up and down in its long-paced swell.

In Isca, living in the house of Ricat, Tia had found, if not happiness, at least a form of contentment which bolstered the patient faith she had in Baradoc's return. Although the old woman servant kept the small house clean and did the marketing and cooking, there was plenty for Tia to do in making Ricat's bachelor quarters more homelike for him. She made new cushions for the benches, repaired his sheets or renewed them, kept his clothes in good order and, against his protests, restuffed the old palliasse on which he slept. She polished the silver and bronze ware and, as time went on, took over some of the accounting for the Prince's buying of fodder for the horses against the winter and brought up to date the parchment pedigree rolls of the bloodstock mares and stallions.

But there were two things she loved most of all to do. One

was when, through sickness or absence, there was a lack of hands to exercise the horses and she, wrapped warmly in loose tunic and baggy, cross-gartered trews, would ride through the water meadows, the autumn air sharpening to near winter's bite blowing in her face and setting her long golden hair streaming behind. She loved horses and, though Ricat was not one to fashion fine compliments to a woman, he praised her for her riding and for the silent communion she seemed at once to establish with even the most difficult beasts for there was much mixed blood in some of the mounts and they could be as wayward and unexpected as sudden April showers. The other thing Tia enjoyed was the entertaining of his frequent guests when they came to eat with him.

Most of them were horse dealers and traders, some rough, some polished, who came to buy or sell, men of all tribes and some of mixed nationality who, despite the unsettled state of the country, travelled the old Roman roads north of Glevum to Eburacum, west as far as Moridunum in Demetae and over the wild Cymrian mountains to far Segontium facing the shores of the island of Mona. None, though, went so far east as the Saxon lands, for the men of the long keels had no way with or need for horses. Thus, it was from their talk at table – where she always sat as hostess for Ricat, leaving only for her own quarters when she sensed that wine and mead were loosening their tongues to unguarded frankness of speech – that she began to learn for the first time of some of the things (though many of them meant little to her) that had happened in the days which had passed since she had taken the babe, Arturo, to the people of the Enduring Crow.

Ambrosius the Elder was long dead and his son, Ambrosius Aurelianus, reigned now through all the northern lands west of the Sabrina river and had refused to give any aid to the despised Vortigern in the past years when the Saxon folk had broken out of their holdings in the east. There were many mixed opinions about Ambrosius; a braggart and a poltroon, said some, who sat safe in the marches of his own land while the rest of the country slowly tore itself to pieces; a dreamer and a man of courage, said others, who, now that Valentinian, the last legitimate Roman Emperor of the West was dead, bided his time before coming down on the Saxons and, through victory, would claim right to wear the purple. Men, young and thirsting for battle, flocked to him, but many soon wearied of waiting for action and turned away either to freeboot for themselves or to join smaller captains who took joy in deep raiding down the valley of the river Tamesis or making swift forays as far east as the margins of the Saxon Shore lands once proudly held by the Iceni and the Trinovantes.

There was, too, speculation among the guests of the mind of Gerontius, the Prince of Dumnonia, who sat patiently here in the far West, holding men and horses enough and slowly enriching himself with a growing trade to Gaul, where many now of his fellow Britons had emigrated to serve under Aegidius. Emissaries had come to woo the Prince, but none so far had been given more than a soft answer, to which criticism Ricat gave reply that he could not speak for the Prince's true thoughts since he was only keeper of his horse and not his mind or heart. But he always said it with a sucking in of one cheek as though he were enjoying some private joke.

Back in her own room while the men talked and drank late below, Tia would lie on her bed and watch the slow movement of the stars through the rough window glass and wonder where at this moment her Baradoc lay, Baradoc who carried so much hatred of the Saxons in his breast and so much pride in his own people that he would not have long sat brooding and enigmatic like Gerontius, or have watered down by inaction the fire in the bellies of fighting men so that they turned from him. Thinking of him she would sometimes raise a hand to her face and find that without her knowing a tear had wetted her cheek; and there was no escaping then a spasm of self-pity for her sadness at being bereft so long of Baradoc and parted now from Arturo.

It was on such a night, long after Ricat's guests had departed, that Arturo came to her. She had dozed off to light sleep when she awoke to hear voices in the courtyard. One of the voices was Ricat's but – dulled with sleep still – the other meant nothing to her. Then came the sound of footsteps on the outside stairs, a knock on her door, and Ricat's voice called: 'Mistress Tia, you have a visitor.'

Throwing a cloak over her shoulders Tia went to the door and opened it. Silhouetted against the star-stippled sky stood Ricat and Arturo.

'Arturo!'

Tia reached out her hands for him and Ricat with a chuckle pushed the boy forward and said, 'When you have finished with him – send him down. There is food and drink enough on the table board still.' He turned away and clattered down the steps.

Tia drew Arturo into the room and embraced him. Even in her joy she smiled briefly to herself, for he stood within the embrace patiently like a well-schooled pony and his lips only briefly and shyly touched her cheek.

Their greeting over she stood back from him, fetched a pine wood taper spill and from her bed light set the wall sconce lamps to flame. Turning back to him she asked. 'You are well?'

'Yes, my mother.'

'Thank the gods for that.'

'*Aie* ... they helped somewhat. But we must not forget the pigs.' He said it solemnly, but the lamp lights marked a familiar and brief ironic smile.

'Pigs?'

'Forget them, mother. I am safe and sound and have been well fed these last five days since I came ashore.' Then, with a touch of maturity and command, he reached forward, took her arm and led her to the bed. 'Sit down, my mother, and I will tell you all.'

Tia sat down on the bed and Arturo straddled himself across a stool and began to tell his story. As she listened Tia had it borne into her that despite his lack of years, not yet in his twelfth year, he was fast outstripping boyhood. Close about him hung the shadow of the man to be, fairly setup, holding himself with quiet pride and sureness. Ay, she thought, maybe too sure, too proudful. His rough tunic and loose trews were torn and dirty and about his waist he carried a tightly buckled leather belt in which, without benefit of scabbard, he wore a short double-edged sword, its cutting edges keenly honed.

Without hurry he told her the story of his escape and again, despite her joy in his presence, she hid a smile now and then as he fell victim to garnishing truth with fancy.

'. . . so I was cradled by the tide and carried safely far up the coast beyond the Point of Hercule. As I went I ate crab apples and neat's meat and the mermaids sang to me to while the night away and with the rising of the sun the pearl-bellied dolphins made a ring about me and amused me by their sports.'

Coming ashore on the estuary sands close to the mouth of the Two Rivers he had gone inland, walking the high divide between the rivers southwards towards Isca and had found no lack of food or friendship.

'. . . Most gave me food gladly for I told them that I had been taken for slave in a Scotti raid and seized my chance to jump overboard to escape in bad weather. At other times, if I could not eat by charity, I filled my belly by theft, mostly by taking eggs from the hen roosts and sometimes a hen for roasting over the embers of a friendly charcoal burner's fire. And one night, as I sat by a river pool, a dog otter came up from the dark waters carrying a salmon. It killed the fish with a bite across the neck, feasted but briefly and left the rest for me. The taste of raw salmon curd and its red-berried spawning seed is in my mouth still.'

'And the sword you carry – which here you must not wear for none of your age may openly bear arms?'

Enjoying himself and genuinely glad to have arrived for, in truth, his travels had been far less than comfortable, Arturo grinned and was momentarily all boy, the shadow of manhood gone from him. He asked, 'Would you have the truth or some comforting fable, my gentle mother?'

Delighted with his coming Tia said, 'No matter which I ask you will give me the tale of your own choosing.'

'Then hear the truth. Two forenoons gone I sat in the sun by the river and, lo, this same dog otter came from the water and laid the sword at my feet and for gift fee accepted one of my stolen eggs. And if you doubt there is enchantment about the sword see the finely sharpened, bright cutting edges. In a day and a night of rain they took no rust to mar their keenness. It is a sword of magic and shall ever be with me awaiting the day when I shall cut the dog's throat of Inbar with it and send him to the Shades.'

'Arturo! Enough! Either tell me the truth or say nothing.'

'I have told you the truth, but now I would eat and then sleep.' He stood up, reached for her hand and kissed it, and went on, 'I will go down to Master Ricat.' Then for a moment or two he paused, his face slowly clouding and, in an uncertain voice asked, 'When the Prince knows I am here, will he take Inbar's part and send me back to the settlement?'

'The Prince is a man of honour. Through Master Ricat he has given me sanctuary, and the same will be done for you – but you will get sharp punishment if you walk Isca carrying that sword. Give it to me.' As Arturo hesitated, she repeated sharply, 'Give it to me. I will guard it until you are of age even though I shall never know the truth of your gaining it.'

Arturo shrugged his shoulders and then, drawing the sword from the hanging loop on his belt, handed it to her hilt first. Tia sat with it on her lap as Arturo clattered down the outside steps whistling gently to himself. He needed, she knew, a man's hand on him and a father's authority to curb him for he grew too fast and fanciful despite his courage and mounting strength. Ricat would give him some curb and direction, but she had an uneasiness in her that soon no man would be able to hold or control Arturo for long. He was built of dreams and fancies ... liar she could not call him for she knew that a boy's imagination was shaped of finer stuff than common deceit. The flushing of the clear water in the silver chalice to the soft pink of a swallow's gorge, the pale stain of blood, had marked his destiny. Maybe to achieve it, for it must needs be great if Asimus were to be believed, then the coming years would put him beyond any man's control, the manipulated puppet of the gods. For a while her mother's heart grieved for him. Then she put the thought from her for there was no human standing against the gods if they in their wisdom took one from so many to be their chosen instrument in this world.

She gently touched the keen edges of the sword and then rose and put it away in the ash wood chest under her window.

Though Inbar of the people of the Enduring Crow sued for the return of Arturo, Gerontius, the Prince of Dumnonia, refused to send the boy back and made Ricat – who had spoken strongly in his favour – his ward and responsible for his sober behaviour.

But first Arturo was taken before the Prince and left with him in solitary audience. Arturo stood straight and manly before him and listened to his words with a serious face, though in truth he paid little heed to them. They held mostly only a due formality, and he guessed that had Gerontius a real friendship for or need of Inbar he would have been sent back under escort. More interesting to him were the man and the room in which he stood.

Once the audience room of the Roman Commander of the Isca garrison, its floor was clean and cool with black and red tiling. A long window flanked by tall wall niches which had once held statues looked out from the castle heights over the town and river. The wooden shutters were wide open now and the fine kidskin curtains were drawn back to let in the light of the westering sun that slowly marked the dying of a mild late autumn day. A long table held bowls of fruit and a silver tray on which rested a blue glass flagon of wine and silver drinking cups. A fresco ran round the walls in a running design of stiffly prancing and galloping horses. A silk-covered couch held some papyrus reading rolls and a sleeping black-and-white tom cat. At the foot of the couch stood a great marble vase which was full of tall spikes of reed mace, some of the heads already aburst to show the pale spume of breaking seed.

Gerontius sat in a high-backed throne chair. He was a man in his late forties, dark-haired and with dark eyebrows that merged with one another over the high bridge of his hawklike nose.

His eyes were half-hooded as though burgeoning sleep sat waiting full capture of him. He wore a long tunic of fine white wool and over it an open toga of green linen under the hem of which showed a pair of soft red sandals fastened with gold cord laces. He looked, Arturo thought, as though he had no interest in the world except to fall gently into sleep, a look which Arturo knew must be deceptive, otherwise in these times he would never be sitting where he was.

The Prince, after Ricat had retired from presenting Arturo, stared at him for a while from half-hooded eyes and then taking a slow, deep idle breath said, 'You are?'

Arturo said, for in truth Ricat had warned him of some of the Prince's manner, 'I am, my Prince, Arturo, son of Baradoc, chief of the people of the Enduring Crow.' He touched his left shoulder and went on, 'And bear their tattoo mark here.'

'Your father could be dead.'

'Then, my Prince, I am rightful chief of my tribe and not my uncle Inbar.'

Without any change of expression Gerontius said flatly, 'Then why not thrust a knife in his gut and settle the matter?'

For a moment or two Arturo was confused by the man's sudden bluntness. As his face showed it the Prince chuckled slowly to himself. He rose from his chair and walked across to the table and poured himself a cup of wine. Behind Arturo's back, he went on, 'Don't tell me that one who had the courage to escape as you did – though I gather the sea maids and the dolphins helped you and even the otters of the river provided you with fresh salmon and a fine sword – lacks the wit to use a knife in the dark?'

As the Prince came back to the chair Arturo said, 'It could easily have been done, my lord – but it would not have been fairly done, face to face. And more, my lord, if my father lives and returns it is for him to do. When there is no more hope of that and I am youth no longer then I shall do it.'

The Prince nodded and asked, 'You believe that your father still lives?'

'It's enough for me, my lord, that my mother believes it and has the word of the wanderer Merlin for it.'

'Ah, the words of Merlin are well known for being so cunningly shaped that whatever he prophesies comes true, though it is not always the truth that one has expected.'

'Maybe so, my lord. But for my mother's sake I pray that the words of Merlin about my father bear only one shape and one truth.'

The Prince nodded, sipped at his wine and then said, 'Well spoken. Now go to Master Ricat who will set work for you. But for two hours each day before sunset you will come here and be tutored by the good priest Leric.' He waved a hand in dismissal and Arturo touched his forehead in homage and left the chamber.

So began for Arturo a period of hard work and happiness that was to last until he was almost fourteen, and his eyes were lifted skywards each morning to seek the first sign of the returning swallows – the birds of his birth month – and, as he worked at the schooling of horses in the river meadows, his ears were cocked for the first notes of the cuckoo.

Ricat and his overseers worked him hard and after a few months had grudgingly to admit that he had the true gift of the Epona-marked. When he sat a horse they were no longer man and beast, but one entity. Iron-thighed, gentle or masterly handed, he could bring the most wayward steed to obedience, and there were many horses which were so for their blood lines were long mixed from the days when the first Roman cavalry units had come to the country. The old priest Leric (who worshipped horses a little less than his country's gods, and seldom lost a wager on a horse match on fair days) explained to him (strictly in his history lessons) that the blood of the mounts of the cavalry wings of such units as the *Ala Hispanorum Vettonum civium Romanorum* stationed as far back as the time of Trajan in Cymru at Brecon Gaer and the *Cohors I Nerviorum*, mounted by Gallic auxiliaries, had often escaped or badly guarded mares had been covered by the wild hill pony stallions. Wild blood, pedigree blood, pack horse to war horse, hill pony to the high-blooded eastern mounts which many a young *tribunus* or *praefectus* had brought to Britain on his first cavalry command, the blood lines were a maze which no man's memory could now thread. But in Isca, with Prince Gerontius and Ricat and men like them who acknowledged the special divinity of the horse, a new breed was slowly being evolved. The itinerant traders and the Iscan townsfolk who laid their wagers on fair days and lay in the sun on the grass banks above the river watching the horses turned out to pasture, closely guarded and contained, thought that Prince Gerontius followed but a fancy and a princely whim, having no more than a lust in his dark, beetle-browed eyes for horses where other men carried the glint for gold or women. But there were some who thought differently yet kept their counsel, and there were a few who knew the truth and schooled themselves to patience.

Of all this Arturo had no knowledge. He was content with his work and his station. He was content, too, for the first time with the comradeship he found with the youths of his own age who also worked for the Prince. Like himself they had been handpicked for one quality or another, though there was one trait – apart from their skill with horses – which they all shared and which often brought them a flogging or a week's stay in a cell on bread and water. They knew no fear so could not resist a challenge which might put their courage or ribald sense of humour in question.

For Leric – a lapsed Druid priest with tentative leanings towards Christianity who had escaped from Gaul and been given sanctuary within the bounds of Isca by the Prince for reasons known only to the two of them – Arturo had an odd mixture of high regard, occasional contempt and, rare for him, pity. Leric was far more learned than Galpan in the Druidical mysteries, far wider travelled and educated in the Roman and Greek tongues, but he was plagued by doubts still over the religion he had abandoned and, too, over the one he lacked the courage yet to embrace fully. To escape this dilemma he often sought comfort in drink, and then became so pitifully besotted and pathetic that orders had been given by the Prince that once he took to the mead he was to be shut in his room and guarded until he was sober. This was a duty that neither Arturo nor any of his friends relished. Nevertheless from him Arturo learned more fully his mother's tongue and enough Greek to cope with the exercises that Leric set him. But of far more interest to Arturo were the lessons in the history of his own country which Leric gave him; a history going back far beyond King Cunobelinus and the great Queen Boudicca, and the days when the Emperor Claudius invaded Britain or the first Saxon Shore fort was built on the island of Tanatus. He taught him, too, some of the songs and stories handed down from the days wrapped now forever in myth when Rome herself had yet to exist.

As for Tia, she was well content with Arturo's progress and paid not over-much attention to his occasional lapses into bad behaviour because on the whole he worked hard and his company was a joy to her. He was attentive to her and she was proud when she walked the streets with him, or watched his mastery of horses in the meadows. On the day he was fourteen and the swallows and house martins had returned she gave him a hound puppy which had many of the markings and much of the build and stance of old Lerg.

To her surprise, although he thanked her and showed pleasure as he stood in her room cradling the puppy to his chest, she could tell from the brightness of his eyes and a restlessness in him that his mind was far from presents. It was evening and still light and he had just come from his lessons with Leric.

He said, 'Put on your cloak, my mother, and come with me. *Aie* ... I know well 'tis my birth day, but it is also a day of other importance. And ask no questions, for I give no answers.'

They left the house and walked down the hill to the river and then took the road southwards. A little outside the town the land rose. At the top of the rise stood an old oak, its branches blasted long ago by lightning. Arturo stopped at the foot of the hill, and said, 'Go to the tree. There is one there who would speak to you.' His face which he was holding solemn broke suddenly into an impish grin. Then, without another word, he turned and left her, making his way back to the town.

It was then that Tia knew the truth as surely as though it had been announced with a fanfare of trumpets and a proclamation by the Prince himself. She hurried forward through the growing twilight, her heart beating rapidly, her lips and mouth drying with excitement.

A wiry pack pony was tethered to a bole sapling of the oak and a man stood by it. He was tall, with a lean, strong body, wearing a short-trimmed tawny-red beard, his clothes dusty from travel, his belt carrying a scabbarded short sword and a dagger. For a moment or two he watched her coming. Then, the impatience in him matching Tia's, he moved forward swiftly down the slope and, without word on either side in that first ecstasy of reunion, took her in his arms and kissed her.

From a distance, Arturo watched them, his heart pounding with excitement and his mind active with speculation about this man, Baradoc, chief of the people of the Enduring Crow ... his father, who, mindful of his own safety and the courtesies due to his Prince, had halted outside the town and sent message asking for a yea or nay to a free and unmolested entry to Isca. While Arturo had been at his lessons with Leric the Prince had come into the room, told him the news and said, 'Go now to your mother and lead her to your father, and when their greetings are made tell him there is welcome here for him.'

That night as Tia and Baradoc lay abed, the pale sky showing through the window cut with the erratic movement of hawking bats and distantly the occasional screech of hunting owls breaking the silence, Tia said, 'Oh, my love, the moment you landed you should have sent a messenger ahead of you and I would have made a feast and a great preparation for you.'

Baradoc, holding her in his arms, kissed her eyelids gently and said, 'I came as swiftly as any messenger and for feasting what needed I more than to glut my eyes on your beauty and to feel beneath my hand the joy throb of your heart.'

When she woke the next morning to find herself alone, but hearing his voice and that of Arturo as they spoke in the courtyard below, she found beside her on the old wax stylus pad she used for making household notes the same lines which Baradoc had written for her in the hut on Caer Sibli when he had been taken from her :

> The gods raise the door-latch of night
> To let the silver morning in
> Sleep veils the brook-lime blue of your eyes
> The gay bird of love in my heart begins to sing
> Returning, I will lay a chaplet of purple vetch about your hair
> And, kneeling, call you queen.

At that moment the voices in the yard ceased. She heard his footsteps on the stairs and the door opened to show him, framed in sunlight, smiling, and holding in his hands a circlet of purple vetch which he had gathered from the river meadows.

Between Sword and Sea

For nearly two months Baradoc and his family stayed in Isca. Each day for the first week Baradoc was closeted for hours with the Prince, who had a hunger for the tales of his long years of wandering and slavery; and when the telling was done a friendship had sprung up between the two men and their talk passed to other matters, though of these Baradoc said nothing to Tia or Arturo.

But at night as they all sat around Ricat's table eating, Baradoc gave them the story of his wanderings, which not only held Arturo spellbound but slowly excited his envy and longing for such adventures. Lying in bed at night he would fancy himself in the place of his father ... captured at sea by the Northern long boat men, those who had no hunger for land like the coast-creeping Saxon keelmen, but sought only quick plunder or slaves for marketing and knew the world's oceans far beyond the bounds of shipborne traders and merchants.

Passing into the Mediterranean through the Pillars of Hercules, Baradoc had been sold as a slave on the African shore to a band of desert traders and had passed through the hands of many masters, escaped and been recaptured often, but in the end had become a mercenary soldier in the service of the Eastern Empire under Marcian. Later, since he was always seeking to return home (though Arturo and certainly Ricat guessed, if Tia did not, that as there was so much to see and hear there had been times when the call of hearth and family had given way to his passion for learning and lust for experience) he had made his way to Rome and fought with the forces of Ricimer, captain of the German federates who had overthrown the Emperor Avitus. Eventually he had found his way into Gaul and finally back to Britain.

Listening to him talk Tia waited at times for some sign of his youthful flaming hatred of the Saxons, for some show of his old ambition to raise men and take arms against the barbarian keel-men. That he gave no sign of these passions, however, did not deceive her and she guessed that his long sessions with Prince Gerontius must have held more than an account of his adventures. Time, she guessed, and maturity had taught him not to wear his ambitions openly. When he learned of the treachery of Inbar, his face showed nothing except a thin tightening of the lips and he said, 'Soon the Prince will give me leave to return and then Inbar shall be made to answer. Arturo did well to run from him for as soon as his own sons had grown to health and years he would have killed him.'

'And now that you have had time to learn something of your own son – how like you him?' asked Tia.

Baradoc smiled, his dark brown eyes lit with a teasing light. 'He is a brave and kind youth, and the Prince reports well on his learning, his skill with horses and his training at arms. But there is a wilfulness at times in him which needs schooling. For that I am to blame by my absence. But it shall be remedied. There are times too when almost unknowingly he speaks fable for truth. That, too, must go for it will serve him ill when his full manhood comes. Men follow faithfully a leader who talks plain of hardship, danger and chances. The marsh of destiny cannot be crossed safely by the flame of a dancing bog light.'

Tia smiled to herself. Baradoc had changed but there was much about him that remained the same. Fine phrases he kept for his love and his heart stirrings, but for the harsh business of life and the cold press of his ambitions and love of his country only the crystal hard words of truth would serve.

She said, 'What you say is true. But treat him gently at first for through your absence he comes late to the breaking pens.'

And so, in the first of the two months they spent at Isca before returning to the settlement, Baradoc after his own manner was forbearing with Arturo, but the past years of his own slavery and then the iron disciplines of soldiering had made him readier to punish than to forgive.

Three times in that month was Arturo flogged by Baradoc (though if his father had not been there the flogging would have been carried out by one of the Prince's men). Once it was for taking horse and spear on his free day without permission and riding with three of his working companions, who had been given permission, to hunt boar in the low hills to the north of Isca; and another time for spending an evening in a drinking house in the poorer part of Isca and being too fuddled to do his work properly the next morning, and a last time for brawling with the son of a trader from Lindum in the castle yard in broad daylight. When asked, after the guards had separated them, to explain the reason for the fight, in which Arturo had suffered most, Arturo refused. When explanation was demanded from the trader's son, he had shrugged his shoulders and good-naturedly said, 'If this young cock is silent – then so I am. But –' and here he had turned to Arturo and said, '– to him I say this truly. I spoke but in ill-mannered jest and without truth.' Nevertheless Arturo was beaten for breaking the peace within the precincts of the Prince's household. Even so, Tia could see no sign of resentment in Arturo for his punishment by Baradoc. The beatings done, he forgot them, though to his working companions he boasted, 'In a dream long ago the god of healing, Nodens of the Silver Hand, revealed to me a magic word which, chanted to oneself during a flogging, makes the hardest swipes but feather strokes and all wounds to heal without pain.' Offered payment for revealing the word, he had explained, 'Nay. To do so at once kills its magic.' Though most laughed at this, there were some who wondered, for whenever Arturo was beaten his face betrayed never a wince or grimace of pain. Neither was there any resentment in him against Baradoc. His father was right to beat him. It was a simple matter of weighing the punishment against the pleasure of forbidden actions. Within an hour he would be sitting at his father's feet, eagerly pressing him on to further and more exact descriptions of his adventures and hardships, and Baradoc, though he was careful not to show it, took now a rare delight in the company of his son. There was time and enough he knew for the young tiercel to be weathered and manned as he had seen the desert hawks brought to true hunting skills and obedience by the handlers who served in the courts of the Vandal chiefs of his African captivity. Since his long talks with Prince Gerontius, he knew now that the time would come when he would need a skilled and disciplined Arturo at his side to help him with the labour and fighting which should bring his country back to greatness again as it was in the days before Vortigern in his cravenness and the now dead first Ambrosius in his stiff pride gave land grants and privileges to the Saxon mercenaries and so fed their greed for more and more territory and power. Arturo would serve him well, but first he must grow and there was time enough for that since the plans of the Prince needed time too. The Saxon chiefs and commanders for some years now had pressed no farther forward, since they were busy fighting and quarrelling amongst themselves. Time at the moment was on their side, and time was needed for the calling together of men, to train and arm them, and also for the raising and schooling of horses.

They rode back to the settlement of the people of the Enduring Crow in high summer weather. There were four of them; Baradoc, Tia and Arturo, and Ricat who went as the Prince's surrogate. The Prince would have sent more men, but Baradoc disclaimed need of them. From reports which had already come from his people Baradoc knew that they waited his appearance with loyalty and that Inbar stood his ground from pride and the knowledge that his one hope of escaping being an outcast from his people was to stand and contest by arms Baradoc's right to the chieftainship.

Except for Tia, they all rode armed and Arturo was proud of his right, now that he was free of Isca, to wear on his belt the keen-bladed short sword which Tia had held in keeping for him. The larks sang high in the warm air currents over the moors and the tall grasses, ripening to seeding, swayed like a restless sea in the westerly wind. At the heels of his mount Anga, Arturo's hound puppy, now growing fast to legginess and strength, loped until tired when he was lifted to couch between Arturo's thighs.

They passed one night on the road, taking lodgings at a homestead by a ford across the river Tamarus. Although they could have reached the settlement by the following nightfall they stopped on the high moor above the settlement valley and passed the night in the open camped near the hermit refuge of the priest Galpan.

As they rested here Bada the horn blower came up to Baradoc with a message from Inbar. Baradoc and Bada walked apart from the camp and sat on a rock close to the stream's source, the bank behind them thick with whortleberry growths over the pale flowers of which the night moths hovered. From the high tor behind them a vixen screeched and was answered distantly by her mate.

Bada said, 'Inbar says that he will stand and give you answer only by arms. By your long absence he declares you have forfeited the right to lead our people.'

'And what do the people of the Enduring Crow say?'

Bada smiled. 'Had they been for Inbar they would have taken sword and spear and you would not have rested peacefully here tonight, no matter that you come with open warrant from the Prince. Inbar will await you on the fighting ground and gives you choice of weapon, spear or sword.'

'I take the sword.'

'So be it.' Bada was silent for a moment or two and then with something like a sigh shrugged his shoulders and went on, 'You were good friends once and shared many trials before he wronged you. Should it come to it, there is a strange goodness in him which might stir you to mercy.'

Baradoc's face muscles tightened. 'No ... When he lies disarmed his heart shall know my blade.'

'So be it.' Bada rose, touched his forehead in farewell and began to move down the stream side.

Later as Baradoc lay by Tia's side under the rough canopy

which made their shelter she said quietly to him, 'You remember Mawga?'

'A little. But her father more. He taught me the art of braiding horse-hair to make fishing lines.'

'She was good to me when I needed help.'

'For that she shall have a reward and high place among us.'

'What reward or high place will heal the grief in her heart if you kill Inbar – as kill him you know you can with all your years of fighting skills such as I have seen you display at practice with the guards in the Prince's yard?'

Baradoc said coldly, 'He and a companion strung me to an oak to die. He would have dishonoured you and killed my son in the fulness of time. Only his pride and the shame of being branded coward makes him stay to stand against me. For that, at least, the gods may give him some small regard when I send him to them. Sleep now, and trouble yourself no more.' But it was long before Tia found sleep.

Not far away Mawga lay on her bed in the long hall with her children sleeping near her and she knew that there would be no sleep for Mawga this night or many nights to come. Love Baradoc as she did, and still cherish undiminished her joy at his return, she knew that once his mind was made up there was no turning it by any plea she could make. A man's pride was beyond the knowing of a woman, shaping Baradoc to mercilessness and ... *Aie*, the gods help him ... Inbar to stay and stand against him without hope of victory. For all the shame he would have done to her there was no stilling the hope that had been in her that Baradoc would find some pity once it lay within his gift to kill or spare ...

Unsheltered under the stars against the dew Arturo lay sleeping with Anga curled between his drawn-up knees and arms and his sleep was untroubled by dreams for Arturo rarely dreamed by night since his days were oversurfeited with them. Long before the first sunflush in the east roused the larks to rise and sing he came awake and walked with the hound puppy to the stream. He stripped himself and washed in the cold water and then sat on a boulder and stared down the long valley whose turns and twists hid the settlement and the sea from him. Proud he was, he thought, to be coming back with his father to the settlement; a father who had travelled far, seen many wonders, and fought under many commanders, a father who spoke now the tongues of Romans, Greeks and the dusky-skinned men of the African Vandals' lands, a father whose skill with sword and spear, aye, and throwing axe had amazed him when he had seen him (not without pride) display them in the Prince's yard. The only fault he could find in him was that adequately as he sat a horse, man and steed were never completely one. Though today held the coming excitement of the fight between his father and Inbar (and Inbar would fight well but must finally be overcome) he wondered what excitements could really exist for him in the settlement when all was put in order under his father. He had the feeling strongly that he would soon miss the work with the Prince's horses, the smell of the stables and the blood-stirring gallops and tussles with wild, unruly mounts in the breaking pens ... *Aie*, and the good companions of his own age with whom he worked. Here, his father could school him to the chieftainship which would eventually be his, a future which held no relish for him unless first he had proved himself in lands and countries far beyond this Dumnonia. There was, out there, to the east, north, west, and south, so much to be seen and tried, a feast of adventures and discoveries and challenges of all kinds to test him into full manhood. No, something told him that, patient as he might try to be, his father could never succeed to shaping him into ways that would chafe his spirit. The tattoo of the red-legged chough on his shoulder was no brand to mark ownership. No, when the time came he would go so that men everywhere would know his mark and think deep before they stood in his way.

Footsteps sounded behind him and he turned to see Galpan carrying his drinking bowl to take water from the stream. The old priest dipped and drank and then, squatting on his hunkers, the edges of his rough robe trailing in the water, looked up at him and said, 'How was my once good friend Leric?'

Arturo grinned. 'Scholarly and in good health when sober,

but unruly as a drunken pig when not. He sent you greetings.'

'Which I may not welcome.' Galpan spat into the clear
stream.

To tease him Arturo said, 'He taught me about the Christ
religion. I did not know that once it was so strong in this
country.'

'Aye, with the strength of bindweed which under a canopy of
white, innocent-seeming flowers throttles all that grows. Now
the land is hoed clear of it in most places. What did you think of
its teaching?'

Arturo shrugged his shoulders. 'Nothing. It is a religion for
women, not men.'

'Aye, and Rome learnt that too late.' Galpan rose, rested a
hand briefly on Arturo's shoulder and added, 'You are a good
youth, though a little too full of spirit. It may be that our gods
have marked you for great things, but let that not blind you to
small things. Your hound dog's ears carry sheep ticks which
suck its blood and you have not seen them. In the days which
may come make sure that before you venture into great affairs
or affrays you have not been blind to the small galls and frets
that fill life. There is no trust or truth to be found in the line of
an arrow with worn flight feathers.'

He moved away and, after watching him for a while, Arturo
called to Anga and began to nip free the swollen sheep ticks in
his ears, whistling gently to himself. Priests were all the same
. . . Galpan and Leric . . . full of mysteries and prophecies which
he was sure they invented to mark their own importance.
Sometimes he had wondered whether they had not invented all
the gods themselves, too, in their imaginations. Anyway, he
had known before they left Isca that Anga, moving through the
moor grasses, would get sheep ticks, had pinched them clear
before setting out on the morning of their second day, and had
been on the point of doing so when Galpan had come to him.
As he finished clearing Anga's ears the voice of Baradoc called
to him from up the slope. He rose, stretched himself, and went
to him. Today, he thought, Inbar would die. For a brief moment

the stir of some emotion disturbed him ... there had been things about Inbar that he had liked. One thing at least had to be said for him, evil at most he might be, but he did not lack courage to stand and face his father. The gods would show him some kindness for that, maybe, when he went to the Shades.

Baradoc and his party rode down the valley to the rock-paved open space before the long hall. The sun from a cloudless sky gilded all with its brightness, and charged with changing colours the spray of the stream's falls. Baradoc drew rein before the silent tribespeople who had lined themselves in a great cres-cent between him and the path to the sea. They gave him no greeting or raised arm welcome. For the moment Inbar's chal-lenge lay between them and the joy in their hearts at his return. Why, too, should they greet the one they loved with noisy acclaim if in a little while the Fates should throw their knuckle bones against him and so leave them to the wrath of a vic-torious Inbar? Baradoc understood this and tightened his lips against the turn of disdain in him at their waiting on chance to save them venturing their own skins by any show of favour to him. Over the heads of his people he could see the sharp cleft that opened the view to the beach and the sea, the beach from which, boys still, he and Inbar had by the treachery of visiting traders been snatched to slavery. He watched for a moment or two the white, combing curl of the breakers and his eyes fol-lowed the flight of the seabirds, low coasting shags and puffins breasting the waters and the gulls screaming high while on the dark cliff crags he caught the quick, restless foraying of his tribe's bird, the black chough with scarlet legs. High above all a pair of sea eagles circled on an air current. *Aie* ... he thought, he had been long away, gone as boy and returned now as man. These people were as children to him. There was much they would have to learn ...

The horse party dismounted and a group of boys and youths came forward and took their mounts. Bada came from the crowd to Baradoc and said, 'Inbar waits on the trying ground.'

Baradoc nodded and, as Bada turned, he followed him. The

crowd parted before them as they took the path to the clifftops and then followed behind them. They climbed the track through gorse patches where bees and flies feasted on the golden pollen, across the sheep-bitten grass fragrant with milk-wort and marjoram to the high headland which thrust its steep fall into the restless waters below like the prow of a questing sea-raider's craft.

On the flat turf, his back to the sea, Inbar waited for Baradoc. He wore short leather breeks and his feet were bare to give him true fighting grip of the ground. From his waist upwards he was bare, his torso and arms brown by the sun, the wind stirring his dark hair and beard. He held himself tall with a new dignity which came strange to all who marked him now, and although his lean, thoughtful face was firm set there was the twist of a bleak smile about his lips.

A few paces in front of him there lay on the grass two broad-bladed long swords and two small fighting shields, wooden framed and covered with layers of stiff, hard-cured leather. In the centre of each shield the sun struck dull fire from the high rounded bronze bosses. As the tribespeople made a wide cres-cent behind Baradoc to enclose from cliff-edge to cliff-edge the fighting space, Bada went forward and stood over the swords and shields. But for the moment Baradoc was unaware of Bada. He halted a couple of spear-lengths from Inbar and looked at him. If there were to be speech between them he knew that by tribal custom it could not come first from the man who claimed to have been wronged. At first, since no word came from Inbar, Baradoc slowly stripped himself of his belted tunic and the coarse shirt he wore below it. As he tossed the shirt away Inbar's eyes marked his naked, weather-tanned and hardened body and saw too the puffed lines and pale furrows of battle and slave-whip scars.

Seeing these, there was a strange, sudden stirring in Inbar that roused the sharp memory of their old friendship when as youths they had served as slaves to the same wise master who had been butchered to death by the axes of drunken Saxons at Durobrivae long ago, and in his heart he felt regret at the shifts of his own ambitions and greed which had finally brought him to this trying ground. Raising his eyes he saw beyond Baradoc on the edge of the waiting crowd, the figures of Tia and Mawga, standing close together. His eyes passed quickly from Tia to Mawga. The golden-haired beauty of the Roman girl who had once stirred him to lust meant nothing now for over the years Mawga had moved into his heart, and Mawga, her eyes moist with waiting tears, lowered her head as though she would not with her womanly fear dull the edge of his courage.

Inbar's gaze came back to Baradoc and in a steady voice he said, 'It is long since we met last. The gods ruled that day as they rule all days and gave its outcome. Now I am content that they shall judge this day and give life to rest with him who shall be proved to hold their favour.' He stepped back a pace and nodded to the weapons which lay between them.

Baradoc said evenly, 'So be it.'

He stepped forward, picked up one of the small shields, slipped his left forearm through the thonged loop on its inner side and grasped the wooden hand-hold on the far side. Then he took up from the ground the sword nearest to him, swung it once or twice to get its feel and balance, and then stepped back and watched Inbar ready himself with shield and sword.

From the edge of the crowd, his throat drying already, Arturo watched them, saw them raise their swords high to one another and then spring back and half-crouching begin to circle warily. The shock of their first meeting took him by surprise for suddenly they were closed and the clash of their swords struck fire sparks in the bright air and the thud and hiss of sword against shield seemed to fill the morning with a noisy venom and anger which seized his own body and tensed every muscle in his limbs.

They came apart from that first clashing and, holding fighting distance, swung and cut and lunged as though they sought now only to test and prove each other's qualities and courage. Their breath grunted and sobbed from their lungs as they circled and stamped and parried and slowly over their naked torsos the sweat rose and lacquered their skin so that every movement was marked with the fierce ripple of sunlight running like fire over them.

Suddenly, without any eye keen enough to mark the swiftness of the blade that scored it, a crimson line of blood marked Inbar's left cheek. As suddenly again, as though the gods would match their favours, a great chip of leather flew from the edge of Baradoc's shield and the glancing blade of Inbar turned course and cut into the soft under flesh of Baradoc's sword arm. From then, as he fought, his forearm grew red with the blood that came from him to seep over his hand and the pommel of the heavy sword. But from the moment of his wounding it seemed that Baradoc, resenting even such a minor injury, lashed himself with some inner chastisement for under-valuing the prowess of his adversary. He became as a man demented with cold contempt for Inbar, and as a man exalted and so much at one with his weapon and so much in accord with the skills that had come to him over the years that fighter and sword were one whirling, probing, taunting, invulnerable singleness, and a low sigh of wonder came from the watchers as they saw plainly now and again as Inbar left himself open that the slashing edge of Baradoc's sword was turned at the last moment to strike flat-faced in brutal arrogance. Again and again, for further humiliation, Baradoc forced Inbar step by step back to the cliff's edge and held him there while all knew that he had the power and mastery now to send him toppling and spinning to the sea below with a thrust to his body. Yet, each time, Baradoc drew back and stood with sword point lowered while Inbar held his ground, shoulders heaving, his mouth gaping and sucking at the salt air to give him breath for fresh fight.

At such times Tia was forced to turn her head away to shut the sight from her until she heard the clash of swords again ring clear above the cries of the seabirds below. At her side Mawga had no power to turn away. She prayed to the gods either to give Inbar quick end or the gift of their favour to soften Baradoc's heart when Inbar finally lay at his feet.

Then as the swaying, breath-hungry Inbar, blind now to all but the craving to fight while he kept his feet, came forward in weakening attack, Baradoc gave ground until they were in the centre of the open space.

There, in a gesture of contempt, Baradoc slipped his left arm free, tossed his shield from him, and leapt forward. His sword drew two fine blood lines across the man's chest within his laggardly guard. As Inbar winced with the pain and his head jerked skyward with muscle shock, Baradoc smashed the flat of his sword down viciously across the knuckles of his opponent's fighting hand so that his weapon was beaten from it to drop at his feet. Inbar swayed, then fell to the ground and lay there, lost for the time from the world by fatigue and humiliation.

A great cry went up from the watching tribespeople. Baradoc, his body gleaming with sweat, unheedful of the blood that coursed down his sword, darkening the dull gleam of its blade, stepped forward and put his broad swordpoint to Inbar's chest above his heart. Then, for the first time did Mawga turn away to find Tia's arm wrapped around her and Tia's hand pressing her face gently to the comfort of her breast. By Tia's side, while the tribe sent up cry after cry for the kill, Arturo stood woodenfaced watching, loth to move or speak or by any sign betray a strange shame for his father who, despite his wound, must have known that he was always more than Inbar's match and had played with him like cat and mouse and who now, in easy victory, would show no mercy for this humiliated man in whom much that was good outweighed the bad.

Inbar, lying at Baradoc's feet, opened his eyes, felt the small bite of the sword's point against his chest, and saw the red-bearded muscle-taut face of Baradoc above him, the deep brown eyes still and dark as the darkest bog pool. Then with a slow sigh he said, '*Aie* . . . you have learnt fine skills and feints in your wanderings. But before you press home the sword and send me to the gods I pray one charity from you. Take my wife Mawga into your house and treat fairly my sons who had no part in my doings.'

Looking down at him as he spoke Baradoc felt no pity for the man. No matter the companionship of their boyhood and the slavery of their youth this man would have left him to a slow death to make pickings for the carrion birds and the scavenging beasts. Behind him he heard the stir and low voices of the tribe and he said aloud so that all should hear clearly, 'Though you would have dishonoured my wife, yours shall live under my roof in peace. Though you would have killed my son when yours were well-set, your sons shall live and serve with the tribe without fear of me.'

Inbar said, 'I am content. So now, send me on my way.' As he finished speaking he closed his eyes and lay waiting.

Baradoc stood above him and his hand firmed on his sword to make the thrust true and clean. But it seemed to him then as though some power beyond his control was slowly possessing him, staying his sword hand and, against his will, invading his whole mind and body. Through their dead fathers they shared blood, he and this man, and their fathers had only known love and comradeship with one another. Then, as though not he but some other voice now lodged in him spoke, as though not he moved but some inexorable will commanded him, he knew himself to raise his sword point. He stepped back from Inbar to the close-by Bada and said, 'I rest it in the hands of the gods who suddenly move within me. Let him make the cliff run, but if he have not courage for it, let him be stoned for he is not worthy of my blade.'

Almost before he had finished speaking, a great shout went up from the crowd. 'The run! The run! Let him take the run!' While they still shouted Baradoc turned away from Inbar and moved through his people, seeing for a moment Tia's face, her eyes moist with tears, and by her side Mawga who would have moved to him but was restrained by the hand of his wife. He walked alone down the cliff path, hearing the shout of voices and the stamping of feet behind him as all was prepared for Inbar's run. He climbed the stream-side path to the long hall and entering called to an old, half-crippled woman servant who served the cooking booth to bring him water and cloths to clean and dress his arm wound. As he sat and was tended by her he heard distantly a great shout arise and he knew that Inbar had taken the cliff run. Once, as a boy, he had seen a tribesman take it and go to his death. In the living memory of the tribe out of a score of men to make the run no more than two or three had been known to live and escape to banishment from all the tribal lands of the Cornovii here or with their cousins in the far north of the country.

Some time later when Tia and Arturo returned to the long hall and Tia was insisting on re-dressing his wound after her own fashion with a salve of healing herbs and the whites of fresh eggs, he said, 'He took it. I heard the great shout.'

When Tia made no answer, Arturo said, 'Yes, my father. He took it. But though we waited he did not show.'

Tia, finishing his fresh bandaging, said, raising his right hand to her lips and kissing it, 'I was glad in my heart that you found that mercy for him.'

Baradoc grunted. Small mercy it had been and that never lodged knowingly in his own heart. He said, 'Where is Mawga?'

'For tonight she keeps her place with her children on the cliff to mourn Inbar. She will come here in full time.'

That night, lying on his bed, the window slit above him un-boarded to let the cool air in, Arturo lay thinking about Inbar. The crowd had formed a long open lane which led to the cliff's edge. Inbar had stood at the end of it while two tribesmen stood a spear's length behind him armed with the broad-bladed fighting swords. Once a man began the run along the lane to the cliff brink from there to take the outward jump and the long drop to the sea below there was no holding back except to be overtaken by the following swordsmen and to be hacked to death. There had been no hesitation in Inbar. He had run out-pacing the followers and had leapt clean and far out. Arturo could see him now ... dropping feet first and then, as the wind took him, cart-wheeling and sprawling while the dark sea rushed up to meet him and the cliff birds rose from their roosts in their hundreds, their cries drowning the shouts of the tribe as they lined the cliff and watched. Far below as Inbar had hit the water a plume of foam had spouted and been ragged and teased to nothingness by the wind. Inbar had gone under and had not shown again. Had he shown none would have helped or hindered him. The tribal law was that he must go where sea and tide took him, but seek the shore he must not until darkness came. If the gods gave him that grace then he must pass out of the tribal lands, out of all Dumnonia and never return. But Inbar had not shown. Few men ever had, though often their broken and battered bodies had been recovered days after when the tide washed them ashore.

That night, too, as Tia lay alongside Baradoc it was long before sleep came to her as she thought of Mawga with her children keeping vigil on the clifftop. The grief which she knew clouded Mawga's mind took from her the secret joy which she, herself, had come to know in the last few days. She was with child again. Although she had waited to be certain before telling Baradoc she knew that it would be many days yet before she would speak to him. He had been as merciful as tribal law allowed him to be towards Inbar and for that she honoured him, but she wanted no telling of her joy while Mawga dwelt in the first dark shadows of loss and despair from Inbar's death.

At her side Baradoc mumbled in his sleep and then, groaning a little, clutched at his bandaged arm with one hand as the pain of his wound invaded his dreams.

During the next two years Arturo never left the tribal lands. He grew in strength and height and in longing for the life which he had known at Isca. On the few occasions when Baradoc went to see Prince Gerontius he was refused permission to go with him. There were times when he sat alone on a cliff top staring out to sea, brooding over his grievances and the dullness of life in the settlement. Even the Scotti raids had now grown few and far between so that there were only rare times when, sword in hand, he could join the tribesmen in their stand on the beach at night or early morning to beat off the sea attacks. Sometimes he wondered whether Baradoc's firm refusal to allow him to go back to Isca came from his own, though never expressed, bitterness at the loss of his fighting powers. The wound which Inbar had given him which he had at first treated as of little account had refused to heal properly. It had festered and sent him into a fever for many weeks. Tia and Galpan had treated him, but when with the passing of the months the wound had finally healed it was only to reveal that the arm muscles had wasted so that he could no longer wield a heavy sword. Baradoc had made light of it, no matter what his inner feelings might be, and had trained himself to use his sword left-handed but with only a shadow of the dexterity and skill he had known before.

A man so burdened, Arturo guessed, must always know bitterness or regret, and – he was honest enough with himself to see this – would want to keep a growing son, his heir, close to him, to fight at his right hand against the Scotti. *Aie* ... he thought, watching a peregrine stoop from on high above the cliffs to take a rock dove, but what of the son? Each day here, except for the changes of weather and season, was the same as another and his body and mind itched for the excitements and adventure of Isca and all the lands beyond.

So it was that out of boredom and restlessness as he reached his seventeenth year Arturo began to find himself more and more in trouble with his father. He would steal out at night to meet a girl and then have to face Baradoc and an angry father. If one of the other youths spoke to him carelessly he would waste few words but take to blows and then accept stoically a beating from his father for brawling. Once he stayed away for three days high up on the moors, hunting and roaming with only the now full grown Anga for company. When he came back he stoutly maintained that he had been bewitched and held captive in a cave, and went on to invent some fanciful story which even made Baradoc secretly smile to himself. Of words and inventions to excuse or defend himself Arturo never had any lack.

One day as he sat on the cliff, brooding over his pinioned life, Tia came to him. She sat beside him, holding in her arms the girl-child, Gerta. Arturo leaned back on his elbow and stroked the warm cheek of Gerta and said, 'She has your eyes, my mother, like the blue flower that grows among the corn, and your hair, brighter than the bunting's breast. One day she will marry a great chief and men will sing about her beauty and her goodness.'

'That she be a good wife to some man is all I ask,' said Tia.

'And what do you ask for me?'

'That you pleased your father more.'

'So I would if he gave me liberty to do what I must. And if he does not give me that liberty then soon I shall take it for the gods command more obedience than any father.'

Tia laughed. 'Now you begin to talk in your riddles again.'

'No. I say only what has been said. In the cave where I was held on the moor by enchantment the gods spoke to me plainly.'

'Arto!' Tia shook her head, smiling. 'You dreamt with your belly empty from hunger.'

'No. I have few night dreams. I saw and heard. The gods have put their mark on me and, when the time comes, I must obey them.'

'And do they tell you to chase the maidens here and brawl with your companions and –'

'No.' Arturo sat up. 'They tell me only that when the sign is given I must go.'

'And what is the sign?'

'I shall know it when I see it.' He plucked a grass stalk and began to tickle the nose of Gerta, making her crow with pleasure. With a glance at his mother, he said, 'You do not believe me? You think I am no more than a fledgling whose growing flight feathers begin to itch and make it long to take the air? No. It is more than that. There are things for me to do.'

'What things?'

'The gods will show.' He rolled over on his back and stared at the sky. 'You have all power over my father. Ask him to give me leave to go ... back to Isca and then when the sign comes to where the gods will.'

For a moment Tia said nothing. She was thinking of the old Christian hermit, Asimus, who had placed the sacred silver chalice in her hands and told her that one day held by the right hands it would blush crimson within to mark one – the words of Asimus rang clearly in her memory – *who is marked for*

316

great and noble duties, someone whose name will live for ever,
to be praised by all true and just people ... Often, since he was
now grown almost to manhood, she had thought of telling Arturo this but had decided against it for it would have only increased his longing to be away from the settlement. Yet now
that he had begun to talk of signs from the gods himself, and
she herself had once seen the chalice cup blush pink as his baby
hands held it, she wondered whether there was not a duty in
her to tell him. The temptation was strong in her this moment,
but she suppressed it for she knew that it would only strengthen
his discontent and, maybe, push him to some rashness which
would bring down on him the anger of his father and the Prince
of Dumnonia.

Standing and cradling Gerta in the crook of her arm, she said,
'Carry yourself patiently and keep from all wildness until the
winter comes and I will speak to your father for you. But expect nothing from me if you once play the hellion or the bully
or –' her lips tightened to hide an impulse to smile, '– seek to
frolic with any maiden in the bracken.'

Arturo jumped to his feet, seized her hand and kissed it and
cried, 'I shall be as patient as the plodding ox, as forbearing as a
priest ... aye, and as untouched by any maiden's charms.'

So, through the rest of that summer and autumn until the
first of winter's gales pushed great curling combers far above the
summer drift line on the beach, Arturo was of good behaviour;
though sometimes to give ease to the pent-up longing and excess
of natural spirits in him he would get leave to ride on herd duty
on the moor. Then, with Anga at heel, he would set his pony to
wild galloping among the tors, and sing and shout to himself like
a madman. But also, too, when he was on the moor he would
spend time with old Galpan and make him tell all he knew of
their country and draw maps with a stick in the heath sand of
all the tribal lands that divided the country. So great was his
demand for knowledge that there were times when Galpan,
squatting with his back against a rock in the sun, would lose his
words in a mumble and drop off to sleep. Then Arturo would
lie back and stare up to the sky and watch the great clouds

drift in from the west and, of all the places of which Galpan had spoken, his mind would go flighting northwards to Lindum and he would remember Daria, the black-haired daughter of Ansold the swordsmith. One day, he told himself, he would ride into Lindum and find them and Ansold should make him a sword that all men would fear. Then he would take Daria to be his wife and somewhere carve himself a domain and a kingdom so that all men should call her queen and bow their heads to him for permission to speak just as all men did to Prince Gerontius and that old windbag Ambrosius and to ailing Vortigern. *Aie*, and maybe the day would come when the long kennelled Angles, Jutes and Saxons of the East should have their days numbered and be driven into the sea. That, at least, would give his father pleasure.

On a night of hard frost when the stars seemed fixed like chips of ice in the sky and the winter grasses were so hoared with rime that the clifftops looked as though they were snow-covered, Tia spoke to Baradoc about Arturo. She had chosen her time well. That day she had told him that she was certain that she was with child again, and also a messenger had arrived from the Prince of Dumnonia calling him to a counsel at Isca.

Baradoc listened to her patiently, watching the firelight play over her face and draw sharp glints from her fair hair, and sometimes took no heed to her words as he remembered the early days of their meeting in the forest of Anderida. Their love now was mature and abiding and he knew that she spoke as she always had done from their first meeting with common-sense that came from careful consideration.

She finished, 'He has curbed his ways and shown all patience. To be a man among men he must now go from here. Take him with you to Isca and leave him with the Prince. Things are afoot there and I ask nothing about them. That you show openly now little of your old hatred of the Saxon kind means only that your anger is now appeased by some great hope for the future. Make Arturo part of that future. Although I think he talks too easily of signs and miracles which live only in his

318

imagination, maybe that is how the gods work. But with my own eyes I saw the water in his silver bowl turn crimson as he held it.'

Baradoc smiled. 'It was but the reflection of the red sunset.'

'No. It was mid-morning, and you know so for I have told you the story often.'

'I tease you.'

'Then please me also. Take Arturo with you.'

Baradoc reached out and took her hand. 'It was already in my mind. He shall go.'

So Arturo rode to Isca with his father. But before he went Tia took him aside and told him of the silver bowl and the words of the good Asimus and how, as a babe, he had held it and the water had flushed with crimson from the blood of the Christ who had died on the cross, and she gave him the bowl to take with him since it was rightfully his.

Looking at it as he held it in his hands he said his thanks and then added thoughtfully, 'I would it had been one of our country's gods.'

'There are many in this country who claim him as the only god.'

'So I know. But for my taste there is over-much gentleness and forbearance talked about him unless, of course –' he gave her a quick grin, '– he uses that as a cloak to hide his real strength and power. *Aie* . . . maybe that is it. He waits for the day when, perhaps through me, his true majesty and power shall be shown to all. Maybe, too, this is the sign the other gods have chosen to test me. Instead of Badh I have this Christos for they know that one day he will be even greater than Badh.'

When Arturo was alone he filled the bowl with water and cupped it in his hands. He held it until the silver was warmed by his palms but there was no flushing of the water. He gave a careless shrug of his shoulders, tipped the water to the ground, and then stowed the chalice away in the baggage pack he was making ready for his trip to Isca.

The Road to Corinium

Arturo sat at a bench in the tavern courtyard, elbows on the rough table, staring at the sparrows which quarrelled over a scattering of scraps which Ursula, the tavern keeper's daughter, had just thrown out of the door. Spring sunlight filtered through the leaves of the ancient elderberry tree which grew against the courtyard wall. Anga lay in the shade under the table snapping at the flies which teased his muzzle. Discontent and boredom showed plainly on Arturo's face. If anyone, he thought, had told him almost three years ago when he came here that he would be tired of Isca so soon he would have laughed in their face. He was, too, he knew, out of favour with the Prince for his occasional bouts of brawling and outspoken comments on military affairs. The Prince, he felt, with all the men and horses at his command should have moved east long ago. The minds and spirits of the cavalry men yearned for action and being denied it they grey bitter and sullen – though not so outspoken with their discontent as he.

Ursula came from the tavern and set before him a jug of beer and a beaker. She was a dark, tall girl of his own age, her cheeks the colour of ripe spindle berries, a strong, large-breasted girl who knew how to look after herself when the young men of the Prince's household grew over bold from drinking. But with this Arturo she had never had trouble ... more the pity for everything about him found favour with her. In his twentieth year, broad-shouldered and tall with a closely cropped beard and his pale hair fired with red glints, a young man to make any girl's mind flower with romantic fancies, he had it seemed only two loves, the ageing hound which lay at his feet and the horses of the Prince's pastures.

Arturo fumbled in his belt pouch and dropped a small silver piece on the table. It was one of the coins which the Prince had started to mint in the last year for the use of his household in Isca and the surrounding country. Because he pretended to be or really was – no man could say for sure – descended from the old Belgae people who had come to the country now held by the Atrebates and the Dumnonii and had spread north to colonize the Sabrina basin, Prince Gerontius had copied a pattern from their old coins. On one side was a barbaric design of a horse with a triple tail and on the other a primitive shape of a thorn tree which the townsfolk said resembled more the skeleton of a flat fish.

As Ursula picked up the coin Arturo said, 'Bring another cup. Durstan joins me soon.'

Durstan came into the courtyard before Ursula returned with the extra beaker. Thickset, dark-haired, sharp yet smiling brown eyes deepset in his weathered face, he was dusty from exercise in the schooling pens. Of the same age as Arturo, he was much shorter and seldom given to brooding. Life for Durstan was a brightly moving pageant which gave him constant delight. It was said that where others sometimes groaned and talked in their sleep Durstan always laughed.

He sat down opposite Arturo, reached for Anga's lifted head and briefly fondled and teased the hound's ears. Then he filled the single cup and drained it in one long draught, his adam's apple working against the throat.

Putting the beaker down, he said cheerfully, 'You look like a crow in moult, Arto.'

'Who would not when life here is the same thing every day?'

'Nay, the day will come.' Durstan turned and grinned at Ursula as she brought the second beaker and pinched her bottom as she turned away, though ducking swiftly to avoid the backhand swing of her arm.

'The day has come and gone. How many times has the Prince sent the Count Ambrosius's plea-men – who came to ask for more men and horses – away with an empty answer? I think he means not to join any fighting but to make all secure here and stay within his bounds until – and then it may be too late – the fighting comes to him. Meanwhile, what do we do? We breed and break horses and drill and sharpen up our men – and then give them nothing but exercises in mock attacks and battle skills. And when we have finished with one lot we send them back to their tribes where they soon forget what they have learnt while we go to work on a new lot of levies. Do we sit here for ever, fighting imaginary battles?'

'And is this the feeling of your good father, Baradoc?'

'I know nothing of his thoughts. He keeps them as secret as does the Prince. Once it was well known that his hatred of the Saxon kind was like a fire in his belly. And now, so Leric has told me in confidence, the Prince has sent for him. He arrives in a few days, and it is in my mind he comes to take me back to the settlement.'

'Why so?'

'Because I have asked the Prince to give me a horse in return for my services here and leave to ride to join Ambrosius – and have been refused.'

Durstan laughed. 'Then go without a horse.'

Arturo frowned at him. 'How could I? I am the son of the chief of the tribe of the Enduring Crow –'

'Now in full moult.' Durstan laughed.

'Aye, maybe. But Ambrosius would do me no favours if I arrived without horses and without men. He would do me no honour since the Prince has refused him more help to take arms against the Saxons.'

'The news is that they sit quietly, content with what they have. Why stir up the hornet's nest?'

'No Saxon sits quietly – except to let his wounds heal – when over the hill there is plunder and land to take. In this, for all his vanities, Ambrosius is right. Do you tell me that you are happy to be here, sweating and riding and shouting all day at sour-faced tribesmen who come only because the Prince has ordered their levy. Not one of them but longs to get back to his home grounds.'

Durstan shrugged his shoulders and filled his beaker. 'No, I am not happy. But I take care not to show it openly. But I am patient, where you are not. Here there is good living, horses and work, and drink and girls in the evening. When the gods will it, then things will change.'

Arturo smiled suddenly, and said, 'Sometimes the gods feign sleep, I think, to give us the chance to arrange our own lives for a while.'

Durstan was silent, but his eyes were on Arturo. He had the same discontent as his friend, but more patience and, for all his carefree manner, more caution since, where Arturo was the son of a chief who was close to the Prince, his own father was long dead and had never been more than a horse trader from neighbouring Lindinis in the country of the Durotriges. Only his eye for and skill with horses had brought him to the Prince's service.

Finally he said quietly, 'So the gods sleep. How would you have us arrange our lives?'

'We have our own arms and the right to carry them. We buy two horses at the next trading fair and then go north to Ambrosius.'

'But he would give us no welcome. This you have said.'

'Not us alone – but with men well mounted he would. Twelve men, nay six, well horsed and armed he would accept.'

'And where would we find these others and their mounts?'

Arturo sipped at his beer, and then said, 'The gods must wake some time and give us a little fortune. You think that between here and Corinium or Glevum there are none such as us waiting for the prick of comradeship to bring them forward? No horses to be found or plunder to be taken to pay for them? We shall come as no ragged band. You and I between us can train them and when Count Ambrosius sees us there will be no heart in him to turn us away. He needs fighting men.'

'The next trading fair is but three days hence. When we have these horses where do we keep them so that none knows they are ours?'

Arturo nodded to the tavern. 'Ursula's father, Durno, will stable them and say he has bought and holds them for resale. Which he often does at fair times.'

'The Prince will make trouble for him when we are gone.'

'No. He will say that we stole the mounts.'

'You speak as though you had already arranged all this with him.'

'I have, Durstan.' Arturo grinned.

'And he does this out of friendship for you alone? Or maybe you have promised to marry his daughter?'

'I make no promises, nor does he deal in them. You go to the fair with him. You pick the two horses and he buys them and holds them until we are ready.'

Durstan shook his head. 'All this is wild talk, Arto. You live in a dream. With what are these horses to be bought? Here in Isca the Prince's demand for good mounts sets the barter price high.'

'I have that which will get us two good horses and also leave enough to pay Ursula's father for his trouble.' As he spoke he reached into the loose front of his tunic and brought out the silver chalice which his mother had given him. Seeing the look of astonishment on Durstan's face, he said, 'It was a gift from my mother and is mine to do as I wish with. Take it and hide it until fair day.'

Durstan picked it up and turned it about, examining it. Then whistling gently as he put it under his short cloak, he smiled at Arturo and said, 'For this we should get two good mounts and Durno be well satisfied with the barter balance.'

'Aye, he can use it as a dowry for Ursula.'

'For myself I would take her without dowry.'

'For yourself, Durstan, there will be no marriage for many years. A little love-making in the bracken or heather now and then, but no marriage. I want no men with me who are thinking always of home and wife and children. Such thoughts clog the eyes and make the shield arm slow to drop to counter a sword thrust to the gut. All those who join my company must be free to fight without care except for themselves and their comrades . . .'

Durstan said nothing, but his eyes grew round and a smile faintly touched his lips. Arto was away again . . . and without benefit of a beaker too much of beer or Gaulish wine. He turned away to seek Durno and briefly found himself wondering whether for all their friendship he was wise to link himself with this venture. For all that the Prince refused at the moment to give Count Ambrosius any help there was a bond between such men that held them in smaller matters. Neither would give sanctuary in their lands to any man the other had outlawed. And for all he knew it could be that both of them let it be known that the Prince refused all help to Ambrosius purely to tempt the Saxons into some advance which, by the unexpected intervention of the Prince, would bring disaster on them. Men like Ambrosius and the Prince followed high and secret policies that few were privy to. The one thing he was sure about, no matter what Arto said, was that all that went on in Isca and its surroundings was not concerned simply with the protection of their own lands alone. The levies and tributes laid on the merchants, traders and common people were too high for that.

As he went through the tavern kitchen to find Durno, Ursula, bare-armed, was mixing flour in a great bowl on the table, her back to him. He pinched her bottom and darted through the far back door to the rear courtyard and the stables where he knew he would find Durno.

On the first day of the horse fair Durstan went with Durno and the two horses were bought. One was a black stallion of seven or eight years, well schooled, which had been shipped from Gaul two years before, and the other a grey mare, older than the stallion but smaller with a touch of dun and mealyness about the ears and muzzle which showed some not far distant moorland strain.

They were lodged in the big courtyard behind the tavern and kept there for three days. Arturo and Durstan made their preparations to leave on the night of the fourth day. Since the tavern was well outside the fortress area and on the southern side of Isca, the two had decided against the risk of riding north through the town. They would go south down the river road and, when they were well clear of Isca, begin to make a wide semi-circle to the east which by daybreak would bring them around to find the north-easterly road running up to Lindinis. They left their lodgings in Ricat's house just before curfew. Not risking a noise on the stairs they dropped from the window of the room in which Tia had once been lodged to the softness of the freshly turned rose bed below. Both wore their long cavalry cloaks over their leather tunics and trews and their thick belts from which hung their swords and side daggers. The weather had blessed them by bringing an evening of soft rain with a fair breeze so that there was nothing odd seeming in being abroad heavily cloaked.

But if the weather had blessed them the gods – perhaps waking from their sleep – had not. Durno had betrayed them, following the prompting of his own fears and wisdom. He was a prosperous tavern keeper, but the worm of anxiety had eaten into his mind, growing more active as with each hour he foresaw the strain that would be his when the Prince's men began to question him and the horse trader who was still in Isca. Maybe the worm would never have stirred had it not been for a remark of Durstan's when he had handed him the silver chalice. When he had admired it Durstan had told him – there was never any subtle bridling of his tongue for his nature was too open – that it had been a gift from Lady Tia to her son. The horse trader, under questioning, would produce the chalice and he knew that the Prince, or Ricat or one of Arturo's companions would recognize it. So that morning he had gone to the castle and told all and in return had been given his part to play.

When Arturo, with Anga at his heels, and Durstan came into the darkened yard Durno was waiting for them, holding the two horses. The only light came from a pine faggoted torch thrust into a wall bracket, its flame flattening and swirling in the breeze.

Durno held the stallion while Arturo mounted. But, as Arturo settled to his mount, three men came swiftly out of the stable, all armed with drawn swords. Two of them moved to Durstan who was still unmounted and the other came swiftly to take Arturo's horse by the reins while he held his drawn sword ready to strike. His back to the others the man said, 'Sit firm, my master, and no harm comes to you. It is the Prince's order.'

As he spoke there came the first clash of swords as Durstan was backed against the stable wall and faced the two other guards. Arturo sat firm, knowing that one movement to reach his sword would set his guard free to strike. Helpless he watched as Durstan, back to the wall, fought the two guards. Durstan gave no cry for help, no look towards Arturo. He was a good swordsman and for a time kept the guards at a distance, but for Arturo watching it became clear as the courtyard danced with the leaping shadows from the wall torch that the two were taking their time and enjoying themselves a while before finishing their business. If became clear too to Arturo that Durstan was to be sacrificed because he was nothing, the son of a dead horse trader, a man of no importance. Durstan was marked for death – but he, since he was Baradoc's son, would be spared, and sent back in disgrace to the tribal lands. In that moment, also, he realized that only because the Prince needed his father was he being spared. A black fury suddenly possessed him. He drew breath and shouted angrily, 'Saheer! Anga – Saheer!'

From the courtyard shadows behind the stallion which suddenly curvetted and moved nervously came Anga, his hound, like a great shadow, swifter and truer than any of the dancing torchlight shadows, rising in a long curve from the ground beneath the guard's raised sword arm to take him in the throat. Man and hound rolled to the ground together and the scream in the man's throat was brief lived.

Arturo swung the stallion round, drew his sword from under his cloak, and rode down on the two guards who turned to meet their death at the noise of his coming, one from a thrust in the back from Durstan and the other from the sweep of Arturo's blade slashing into the side of his neck.

Holding in the stallion only for time to see Durstan swing himself on to his horse, Arturo called to Anga and rode hard for the open yard gate. He went sweeping out into the rain and wind, riding fast through the maze of hovels and huts that fringed the southern side of Isca. Behind him he could hear the sound of Durstan's mount following hard.

They galloped in single file without halt or speech between them and took the road along the left bank of the river which led to the sea, but three miles from the town Arturo swung his horse off the road to the left. Dropping pace a little, he began to thread his way through a broken country of small, stream-lined valleys and over the rises of the sparsely forested hill tops to make a half circle which should take them round well to the north and east of Isca.

They both knew this country for they had ridden over it at exercise many times and on their free days had hunted boar and deer here with the Prince's hounds. As he rode Arturo carried in his mind a picture of the maps which old Galpan had drawn for him in the sand and, more accurately, those which Leric treasured in the Prince's chambers limned on faded and brittle papyrus. Lindinis was forty miles from Isca on the old legionary road which ran north-east through Aquae Sulis and on to Corinium and further Glevum, and beyond, if fortune and the Prince's and Count Ambrosius's displeasure forced them to it, there were roads that ran north to Lindum and Eburacum. But there was no wisdom in taking the Lindinis to Corinium road yet for they had killed two, maybe three, of the Prince's men and the warrant against them would be passed from post to post quickly.

Pulling up to breathe their mounts, they sat side by side, the steam and sweat of horse hide strong in their nostrils, and for the first time they spoke. Their cloaks were heavy with the soft rain and their baggage rolls lashed behind their thick felt saddles hung limp and bulky like badly made hogs' puddings.

Durstan wiped his face and eyebrows with his hand and said lightly, 'Arto, my thanks.'

Arturo nodded at the ageing Anga who lay flat on the wet ground panting. 'Give me no thanks, but you owe a cut of good venison to Anga.'

'He shall have it.' Durstan sighed slowly, shook his head and went on, 'By the gods, the Prince is a fox.'

'And Durno a serpent.'

'Nay, a frightened man, tempted by silver and then made sleepless by fear. Your true villain makes a bargain and sleeps sound. There will be no welcome for us from Ambrosius.'

'That is to be tried.'

Durstan shook his head. 'No. It comes to me that there is something between the Prince and Ambrosius which they only know. Against it, you and I are nothing. The Prince would have had me killed and you sent back to your people. Now the word will be out against us. I am for death and you to go back and serve your people and stay fast within the tribal boundaries.'

'Be the Prince what he may. The gods serve those who serve themselves. If there is no welcome for us at Glevum then we will find a welcome elsewhere. But for now you are right about the Lindinis to Corinium road. We go farther east to Sorviodunum and then north through Cunetio and Durocornovium. For a time we ride by night and rest by day.'

'And draw our belts tight when our bellies grow empty.'

Arturo laughed. 'That never while we have Anga.' He pulled his horse's head around and began to move off at a walk, heading more sharply east. There was no need for hard riding or haste for they were going into a wild, thinly peopled country of few roads, a country valleyed and moulded by the headwaters of the rivers that ran south and finally found the sea between Durnovaria and Vindocladia, the main townships of the Durotriges.

The next morning Baradoc, long since summoned by the Prince, arrived in Isca. Tia had come with him and they were lodged in Ricat's house. He stood now in the sunlight by the open window of Gerontius's audience room and the anger in him against Arturo smouldered still. Smoke rose in the still air from the homesteads below the castle. A skein of swans came in heavy flight from the river and the jackdaws quarrelled over their nesting sites along the broken ramparts.

He turned to the Prince who, red robed, heavy-eyed, sat in his chair, one hand drooping to scratch at the head of the hound which crouched at his side.

Baradoc said, 'Withdraw the warrant. Have him back here. Have them both back. They have had their lesson and will come to heel.'

The Prince shook his head. 'Two of my men are dead. The warrant stays. The word has gone to Count Ambrosius. Against Durstan I would withdraw it and he would stay kennelled. But there is no taming Arturo. Time or the gods must do that. There is no place for him in the matter we both cherish while he stays as he is.'

'And if he is killed and someone claims the head price?'

'He shall have it.'

'How then shall he free himself from the warrant?'

'Can I read his future? If there is a way, then the gods will show it. That two of my guards are dead is nothing – but too many of the young men are restless against the discipline and the long wait. Many of them have felt as Arturo did, but would have stayed content. But now they have to be gentled again to a patience which is not in their true natures. There is no place for Arturo in this matter. For you, my good Baradoc, I would do much. But two men are dead, and their price must be paid or I shall have my hands full of further trouble from their comrades.'

Baradoc's lips tightened. Behind the firmness in the Prince's voice was also the echo of arrogance. Not for the first time Baradoc found himself wondering which of the two men, Ambrosius or Gerontius, held mastery and called the tune for their followers to dance. At this moment his feeling was hard in favour of Gerontius. Ambrosius was older, and vain for the day when a campaign could be fully carried against the now quiet Saxons who, except for a few marauding, plundering bands that forayed the border lands, kept to their own enclaves in seeming peace. Ambrosius looked only for the day when his dream of wearing the purple of an emperor should come. On that vanity Gerontius played with skill, he was sure, but this Prince had his dreams too, though he babbled them to no man in the way Ambrosius did. For the time being Gerontius gave service and precedence to the older man while here in Isca and the western lands he built slowly to a strength in men and horses that could come to his call and be made ready in weeks when the time was right.

Now, once more, for the sake of his son, he said stubbornly, 'Count Ambrosius can refuse you nothing. Call back the warrant. Banish Arturo from your lands for a term, but let the Count Ambrosius know that he can take my son into service. He will weather in time and he is the kind men will follow when the years have steadied him.'

Gerontius shook his head. 'No. To do so would encourage others into impatience and rashness. But for you, out of my love – aye, and also my need of you, good Baradoc – for there is only frankness between us – I make the warrant of outlaw for a term of three years. After that your Arturo, if he lives, is free to come and go and serve either here or with Ambrosius. More I cannot do.'

'And Durstan?'

'Is he then also your son from some happy chance?' The thin lips curved slightly.

'No. But he is Arturo's man, and Arturo will not accept for himself that which is denied his comrade. This I know.'

'Then Durstan shall be given the same grace.'

'I thank you, my Prince.'

Gerontius nodded and then, rising from his seat, walked across the room and took from the long table on which stood a great bowl of pink apple blossoms a cloth-wrapped bundle. He came to Baradoc and handed it to him.

'You have someone who will find Arturo?'

'Yes, my Prince. Myself.'

'Then take this to your son and give him this message. In three years' time if he brings me the bowl which is wrapped in that cloth he is a free man. Until then death waits for him in my lands and those of Count Ambrosius. Also, since you are his father, you will pay the death price to the families of my two guards who were slain.'

'So shall it be.'

Baradoc slipped the wrappings from the bundle, but already he knew well what lay within, the silver Christos chalice which old Asimus had given to Tia and himself over twenty years ago.

On his return from the Prince to Ricat's lodgings where Tia waited for him. she said, 'Who will you send to find Arturo?'

'I go myself with two of my men.'

'How will you find him?'

Baradoc smiled and reaching for her hand said, 'He is my son and though wild and without sense his mind when his skin is at stake works as mine would. I shall find him.'

'The gods protect him.'

Holding down a sudden movement of bitterness, Baradoc said softly, 'Why should they not? Already he talks with them like a familiar. The otters will feed him with fish and the ravens bring him meat and the sparks from his flint will kindle wet tinder to give him fire and warmth . . .'

Two days later in the early forenoon, while Arturo and Durstan rested their horses just off the old track that ran up to the north from Sorviodunum to Cunetio, Baradoc rode up to them, leaving his two companions on the track below. Both Arturo and Durstan had long since seen the party approaching but when Durstan had looked inquiringly at Arturo he had merely smiled and shaken his head, saying, 'It is my father.'

'How can you know?'

'The gods told me as I lay awake last night with my belly rumbling from half-cooked pig meat.' But the truth was that he could pick out his father riding a horse from a far distance because of his stiff right arm which he liked to ease by thrusting it into the front of his tunic to hold it like a sling.

Durstan grinned. 'Did the gods tell you how he would find us and why?'

'They had no need. He would read my mind and know we would never take the Lindinis road. Each day it has rained and the tracks of two horses and a hound have given him our line.'

They stood at their horses' heads as Baradoc rode up to them. When he halted Arturo gave him greeting and Baradoc acknowledged it, grim-faced, with a nod. He said, 'For two who have a blood-price on their heads in all the lands of Prince Gerontius and Count Ambrosius you travel leisurely.'

'A man without destination has no need of hurry, my good father. That there should be a blood-price is unjust for arms were drawn against us and we had the right to protect ourselves.'

'I am here for no dispute. The warrant runs for three years. If you are alive then you are free of the now forbidden lands.'

His face tightening with sudden stubbornness Arturo said, 'We are free of them now if we care to take the risk. There are many who live so . . . aye, both Saxon and British.'

'I give you no counsel but this. To live you will need companions. Pick them well for the blood-price is high and a temptation. Your mother's heart sorrows for you. Mine knows only stiffness. The Prince from some fancy of his own sends this.' Baradoc tossed a cloth-wrapped bundle to Arturo. 'At the end of the three years there is no pardon unless you return it, so guard it well.'

Arturo loosened the cloth and took from it the silver chalice. Then, seized by pride and deep anger, he said with deliberate contempt, 'Your Prince, my father, is a man of windy fancies and little action. He plays at war with his horses and men but sweats with fear at the thought of a wound. For him even the quick buzz of a wasp is too like the feathered hiss of an arrow for comfort. Against him pompous Ambrosius is Mars himself. So speak thus to him from me – for the gods have said so – that one day he will sue me to return. Aye, the day will come when this country will cry for Arturo and his voice and that of Ambrosius shall not be the least among them in clamour.'

For a moment or two Baradoc said nothing. Emotion played within him like summer lightning. Anger, despair and bewilderment and the faint flicker of pride possessed him. There was a madness, he felt, in Arturo that made him stranger not son, and against all common-sense he wondered whether there was not some other creature inhabiting him deeply who now and then woke and rode him to wildness.

Then, in a weary voice, Baradoc said, 'If I live to see the day that Gerontius or Ambrosius sue for your return, then I shall have lived into the age of miracles. Yet, because you are my son, and for your own sake, I pray the gods to bring you to reason.' With a jerk at the reins with his left hand Baradoc wheeled his horse away and called over his shoulder, 'Until today I had a son. Now I have none.'

Arturo said nothing. He watched as his father rode away to join his companions on the trackway and they turned and put their horses to a steady trot, and he watched still, his face grim, until they disappeared over the smooth shoulder of the chalk downs. He knew quite clearly that he had been boastful, arrogant and vain with his father and there was no pleasure in him from it. He knew, too, that the warrants of outlawry would make life hard and dangerous for himself and Durstan. But there was no turning back now. He was in the hands of the gods who would show him no favours unless they saw him proving himself ... *Aie*, and maybe then not give their help too readily at first for they knew too well that the early spring of courage could be the false growth of anger and pride. No, he and Durstan were with each day in peril of their lives. To survive would call for the patience of a stalking wildcat, the cunning of the hunted hill fox and the bravery of the cornered boar that savages a way to freedom through armed men and blood-lusting hounds. More too he would need – the wisdom and the exemplar of a true leader to bind men to him in loyalty and service without question so that he could make good his hastily flung vaunt that one day both the Prince and the Count Ambrosius would call for his aid as an equal and without condition. For a moment, as brief as the flick of an eyelid, he wished he were safely back in Isca, dust and dung and horse flesh smells about him as he rode to exercise or drill. Then the wish was gone, leaving a dying ripple on his mind like the fading water ring where a swallow stoops its breast to the stream in swift flight.

Behind him Durstan said quietly, 'And did the gods truly say that one day our lords of the West would sue for your return?'

334

Arturo turned, smiling, and shook his head. 'No. But they will.'

They turned their horses' heads northwards, moving towards the distant sanctuary of the forest and marsh lands about the headwaters and upper valley of the river Tamesis, a lawless land between the Saxon East and the sprawling enclaves of the West, a land of low-caste men of both sides who tilled their patches, tended their cattle and when times or seasons grew bare took to plundering their neighbours Here, forest and downland and meagrely cultivated valleys had been fought over again and again in the last sixty years, and was now a refuge for robbers, outlaws, traitors . . . hard, vicious men who would cut a good man's throat to rob his hen roost and then the throat of his wife when they had dishonoured her.

As the light began to pale in the western sky they came over a smooth curve of the downs and saw before them the great ring of standing henge stones which men called the Circle of the Gods. They came to it unexpectedly for neither of them knew this country except by repute, but Arturo recognized the place at once from his mother's stories of the great journey she and his father had made over twenty years ago when the country had been torn with civil strife following the ravaging westward movement of the Saxon armies.

They spread their pack blankets and made camp outside the circle and ate what remained of their cold pig meat. They lit no fire for the night was mild and they had nothing to cook and no desire to draw attention to themselves. Lying on his back, staring up at the brightening pageant of the stars, Arturo found it strange that he should be here where all those years ago his mother and father, not so old then as he was now, had made a shelter and slept. A little way from him Durstan lay with his head cushioned on Anga's flank and played on the small elder-wood pipe he always carried with him the slow, lazy tune of a stable-yard song. He broke off as Arturo suddenly stood up and began to rummage in the loose pack at his side.

Arturo took the silver chalice from the pack and then drew his dagger from his belt. When Durstan raised an eyebrow questioningly he said, 'Where we go and what we do – how long should we keep a silver bowl safe?'

'There are those who would slaughter a handful of homesteaders for it. Aye, or murder their mothers, fathers and brothers.'

'This place is under the protection of the gods. Come.'

Durstan rose to his feet and, followed by Anga, they moved between two of the great cross lintelled henges into the cricle. At the foot of one of the great stones against whose side a fallen lintel leaned half propped Arturo buried the chalice, cutting a square of turf clean from the chalky soil and then digging the hole deep with his dagger and hands. When he had finished and stamped the turf back into place Durstan said, 'The gods have it in their keeping. Would that they could name to us the day of îts recovery.'

'No matter the day. It will come in good time. I ask the gods only that on the day we shall both be together.'

Arturo looked up into the star-scattered sky and Durstan smiled to himself, knowing that his companion looked for a sign from the gods of their approval. *Aie*, he thought, the smallest of shooting stars would do, or the slow drift over the stones of a pale winged owl, that bird of omens. For his friend's comfort of mind he hoped that chance would favour him. But there was no open sign from the gods.

The Villa of the Three Nymphs

From the Circle of the Gods the two went north-eastwards, travelling slowly, following the line of the old road to Cunetio but keeping some distance from it wherever they could, though they were forced to take to it to pass through the great forest to the south of Cunetio. The town, lying on the far slope above a tributary of the river Tamesis, was largely in ruins, and almost uninhabited. Only a handful of old people existed miserably among the abandoned and despoiled houses.

As they left the town and began to climb the slopes of the downs beyond it on a line which would take them to the river Tamesis, Arturo fell into a silent mood, riding ahead of Durstan with Anga at his horse's heels. Durstan made no effort to break into his companion's solitariness. There had been a time when he had sought to break through these periods of withdrawal by talking cheerfully or playing his pipe, but he knew now that there was nothing to be done but to keep silent and wait for the mood to pass. Out of loyalty to him and to save his life Arturo had altered the whole fashion of his own life. He, Durstan, had little to lose for he had never had much to protect or treasure, but Arturo was the son of a chief who was close to Prince Gerontius. He was high born and, from his father's closeness to the Prince, would in time have come to rich honours and important commands in the Dumnonian army ... though the gods knew that there had been little sign of the Prince ever wanting to commit his men to any eastward move against the Saxons. And now, Arturo was outlawed, which made him prey to any man eager for his head price. Arturo had spoken defiantly to his father, but now he was digesting his rashness – not regretting it, Durstan was sure, for when Arturo committed himself he accepted all the consequences and soon found reason or excuse or the spur of divine intervention to justify his acts. But now he was concerned with the shaping of the life that lay ahead of him and the common-sense way of dealing with it. This he must do by himself because only so would the gods still keep him in favour. A whine of self-pity grated on their ears, and a turmoil of regrets in a man's heart left them unmoved.

So they rode for a long time while the midday sun began to slide down the sky. Then, as they crested the long curving shoulder of the downs, Arturo pulled up his horse and waited for Durstan to come up with him. Without a word he pointed to the valley below where from a clump of thorn trees a billowing of thick black smoke rose into the air. Some of the land around the trees had been cleared and was now bright with the green of growing crops. As they watched an old man came stumbling and running from the thorns pursued by another man who in a few paces overtook him and felled him to the ground with one sweep of the sword he carried. The old man screamed and the noise carried faintly to them on the wind. Then the noise was gone as the swordsman thrust his blade into the man's throat.

Arturo said, 'To help others in trouble is the best way to forget one's own. Come.'

He drew his sword and began to ride fast down the valley side, and Durstan followed him. The swordsman below saw them coming and ran back into the thorn trees. With Anga racing at their heels the two swept down to the trees and, dividing, went one round each side of them to come galloping into a small hollow in which flames and smoke roared up from the burning of a brush-thatched hut. Beyond the hut two men, with their backs against a small cart, were fighting off the attack of four other men, using spears against the swords of their attackers.

As Arturo and Durstan rode into the fight from either flank the men turned to face them. They were Saxon outcasts, wearing sheepskin tunics, short trews, and armed with scramaseax swords and daggers. As Arturo bore down on his man, the Saxon began to run quickly, hoping to get under Arturo's sword and find a way to take him in the groin. Arturo wheeled away to escape the threat and flat-bladed him with a backhand sweep that sent him to the ground. One of the men who were being attacked jumped forward and thrust his spear into the man's heart. Another Saxon ran at Arturo, seeking to get under his guard and chop at the horse's forelegs to unseat him, but this time, anticipating the move, Arturo levelled his sword at the man's throat, riding hard down on him until the man was almost under his guard and then, thrusting the sword point into his throat, sent the man toppling away, screaming in a strangled death agony.

In a few moments the whole affray was over. Two of the Saxons lay dead on the ground and the others were racing fleet-footed up the downside, choosing the steepest scarp where the horses would have been hard put to follow them. Arturo watched them go, but his attention was less on them than on the significant and always to be remembered fact that he had killed his first Saxon.

From behind him a voice said, 'The good Lord give you thanks for coming to our help.'

Arturo turned as the man, one of the two whom they had rescued, finished speaking in time to see him cross himself and knew that he was one of the Christos followers. He was a young man, lightly bearded, wearing a long shirt whose ragged hem fell well below his knees. He had a pleasant, open face, the deep brown of his eyes the same colour as his long hair.

Arturo said, 'Who are you? And why do the Saxon men attack you while the crops are still in the ground?'

'My name is Marcos. And this is my brother Timo.' He nodded towards the other man who was the shorter of the two and looked also the younger. He had the same hair and eyes as his brother, but his face was solemn and tight-lipped. Marcos went on, 'He, too, would thank you, but he has no speech though he understands all that is said.' At this Timo nodded though his face remained unchanged. 'As for the Saxons . . . there is one crop they can gather all the year round. They came to take us for slaves. Many of our kind have been taken down the river and sold to the people of King Hengist. They need slaves since for the barbarians the only work worthy of a man is fighting. To follow a plough and raise crops is the work of slaves and women.'

Arturo looked at the now smouldering remains of the thatched hut. 'This is your home?'

The lips twisted ruefully in the pleasant face. 'Was.'

'And the old man who lies dead beyond the thorn trees?'

'Our father.'

Arturo nodded and then said quietly, 'We remain here to-night. Go bury him.'

Marcus nodded and then turned to his brother and said, 'Come.'

Still sitting their horses Arturo and Durstan watched the two brothers go to the rough cart to which a small, sturdy pony was yoked. They took a well-worn wooden spade, its blade iron tipped, and an axe from the back of the cart and made their way to the thorn trees.

As they disappeared Durstan said, 'We have given our help. Why stay here tonight? The Saxons will not return.'

For a moment or two Arturo said nothing. He watched a kestrel wind-hovering above the downside. It had been there when they had ridden down to attack the Saxons and it was still there. It was an inhabitant of another world than the world of men; and above and beyond the world of the kestrel was the world of the gods who marked and controlled all life ... the movement of a vole in the short grass below the kestrel and the movement of chance and time which had brought them to the aid of Marcos and Timo. But only men of small vision called it chance and time. Life was patterned more intricately than the interknotted serpentine designs of a jewelmaker's brooch and the gods ordained the pattern of men's lives.

He smiled suddenly and said, 'These two are homeless and dispossessed. So are we. A single stick breaks in the hand easily. Bind ten together and they defy the strength of most men. They owe us their lives so they would never sell ours for a handful of blood money.'

'True – but what can you offer them? This is their home. We have nothing.'

Arturo smiled. 'But we shall have, Durstan. If they agree we shall be four bound together . . . the gathering of strength begins. First men and then –' he nodded towards the dead Saxons, '– their arms and their clothing, though the gods know it will take hard washing to clean the stink from it. And in the cart there I see tools, hoes and axes and homesteading gear. The pony, too, is young and well-fed so they are no men to neglect their animals. With all this we need but a place to settle and soon others will come to us.'

'And you will tell them who we are and why we are without any true state?'

'Is there any enduring companionship and faith built on other than the truth?'

Durstan smiled and shook his head. 'And, so, in the end you will have a comitatus, a gathering of companions, that will grow into an army which will one day bring both Count Ambrosius and Prince Gerontius to sue for your help? You dream, Arto – but I like the dream.'

'Everything in life begins as a dream. That is how the gods speak to us. First the dream and then the reality. Believe that and work for it and then the gods are on your side. Today I have killed my first Saxon. It is a day of portent. I should ignore it at my peril. Now let us go strip the carrion there of their arms and clothes and leave them to the foxes and kites. Later I will talk to Marcos.'

They ate that evening with the two brothers who produced eggs, cheese, cabbages and two chicken from their cart, and a bronze cauldron for cooking with water that came from the still running source of a winter bourne that flowed away down the valley from the edge of the thorn brake. When they were done Arturo spoke frankly to Marcos, first of the state in which he and Durstan found themselves and then of their need for comrades, of a great company of comrades which should eventually grow into a great army to be the envy and the awe of all men.

At first, Durstan noticed, the two men were plain-faced,

showing nothing of their feelings, but slowly the spell of Arturo's words began to touch them. For the first time, too, Durstan found himself listening to an Arturo he had never heard before. Although he stayed quiet-voiced there slowly grew an enspelling magic about him, an undeniable display of his utter belief in the destiny which the gods spelled out for all men who were ready, without questioning, to follow the gods' beckoning and make their faith work for them so that dreams should become life. Never in all their time in Isca had he known this Arturo and never before – since there had always been an edge of amused disbelief (not frankly revealed) in him for Arturo's flights of fancy – had he found himself, as now, won over to the slow, powerful faith which Arturo had in his own destiny ...

When Arturo had finished speaking Marcos said, 'Our father is dead and neither Timo or myself are married. Living here grows more dangerous for –' he nodded to the distant bodies of the dead Saxons, '– more and more small parties of the men of the South Saxons come up the river valleys since they can find neither living space nor good plundering in their own kingdom. When you arrived our cart was loaded for we were going to abandon our young crops and move away. But where we move and whom we serve rests not with me. My brother and I are as one. I go nowhere nor accept any service unless we are together. For myself I would join you.' He looked at Timo and said, 'You have heard the words of this Arturo How do you find them?'

For a moment or two Timo gave no response, but slowly the corners of his solemn mouth moved to a wry smile. Then suddenly his hands came to life, fingers touching palms, fingers playing against each other, and sometimes a hand flighting to make some expressive movement about his forehead, and all done so rapidly that to Durstan watching it seemed like a flight of two wide-winged birds steepling and playing together in some intricate courtship display. Then, abruptly, his hands collapsed and lay still on his knees.

Arturo said, 'What does he say?'

Marcos smiled. 'That we are fatherless, and you shall be our father. That we now seek a home and a new life and the bond of comradeship, and that he is ready to serve you. But he says also, and so do I, that we serve only one god, while you serve many. We are Christos men and must remain so.'

Arturo answered, looking directly at Timo, 'In my camp all men shall be free to serve their gods, be they one or many. We swear but one oath. That of comradeship. He who breaks it shall himself be broken.'

So Marcos and Timo joined Arturo and Durstan. They slept that night in the open close to the warmth of the slow-dying embers which were all that remained of the hut. But Arturo lay awake for a long while before sleep came to him. Today was a beginning, but he was wise enough to know that the passage of a dream into reality would be a long slow birth. Before men could be drilled and shaped into a fighting force they must eat to live and not all the hunting skills of a band of comrades could feed them. Both Timo and Marcos were good husbandmen and with time their fighting skills could be sharpened. But it was for now as sowers and reapers of crops that he needed them most; and before any ground could be turned or cattle herded a place had to be found where they could dwell securely. From talking to Marcos he knew that only in the nomansland around the source waters of the Tamesis far south and east of Corinium and Glevum, where Count Ambrosius's mandate did not yet fully run nor the slow up-river creep of small Saxon bands yet reach, hope lay of some haven which would give them and, with the help of the gods, others to come, shelter and time to grow into an ever-increasing company.

At his side Anga growled softly, catching the scent of the marauding foxes about the bodies of the dead Saxons on the hill slope. From the thorn trees a little owl shrieked suddenly and, for a moment, the noise echoed the dying scream of the Saxon he had killed. Everything about this day, the thought as sleep began to take him, had been touched by the gods. In the years to come when the story of the companions of Arturo came to be told, the seed and growth of their renown, springing from this day, would be hailed as the work of the gods.

*

Two days later having crossed the weed-grown, slowly breaking-up Londinium-Calleva-Corinium road close to Durocornovium they found a ford over one of the tributaries of the Tamesis. Some miles to the north of the ford in a small valley they discovered an old abandoned Roman villa. It lay at the head of the valley, screened by a new growth of trees and bushes. Its large courtyard was surrounded on the west side by the ruins of the steward's office, the kitchens and the latrines. Linking this on the north side to the east wing were the weed- and bush-covered remains of the foundations of the hot and cold bath houses. Only the east wing with the old reception room and a series of private rooms fronted by a covered corridor remained partly roofed. Here from time to time travellers or temporary settlers had made a home. Much of the villa had been pillaged for building stone and roofing tiles and all the wooden and iron piping long since taken.

At the side of the courtyard a spring – the source of the stream that ran away down the valley – broke from the steep hillside to cascade into the overflow from a circular basin of marble. This was backed by a pillared and arched shrine holding the figures of three nymphs.

Riding into the courtyard, followed by his companions, Arturo drew up and looked around him. Broken stones and burnt rafters lay about the weed-covered courtyard. The villa was hidden from the lower valley to the south by screening trees and from the north by forest land which came right up to the back of the old bath houses. As he sat on his horse, his eyes going over the litter of shattered red tiles, the rubble of broken masonry, the air full of the sound of the spring water flowing from the marble basin, he saw not the ruin before him, but the villa as it must once have been, and the thought came to him that this was the kind of dwelling place which his mother's people had once known. All over the country lay such ruins, shabby, broken and despoiled reminders of the now faded and shrunken Roman Empire. Well, empires flourished and died, but empires could spring again from their own ruins. Greatness was never dead. It languished here still and all over the country waiting for the restoring hand and the undying spirit of man to bring it back to the glory it had once known. Surely it was for this that the gods had directed his steps this way? Here was a refuge and a beginning, here was a place and a moment opened to him as a challenge from the gods. Bracing his body proudly as he sensed the truth and significance of this moment, he looked for the sign which he surely knew the gods must make him.

And the sign came. The black stallion he sat suddenly moved restlessly under him, curvetted, and called for all his strength to hold it. The horse threw up its head and neighed, setting the echoes beating back from the surrounding trees. From the trees beyond the ruined line of bath houses came an answering whinny and out into the sunlight, stepping proudly, her head turned towards them, came a white mare, neck arched and mane flowing as she broke into a gallop across the tree front and then, with another whinny, disappeared into the forest.

Calming his restless mount Arturo turned to his followers and said, 'This is our place for the goddess Epona has marked it with her sign. There is water for all our needs, wood in the forest for our fires, sun-facing ground in the valley to break for our crops and –' he smiled, '– a roof over our heads from the simple task of picking up these fallen tiles.'

So, the villa of the three nymphs became their home. Although it was growing late in the season they broke the ground on the south facing slope with the simple plough of Marcos and Timo and sowed the little that remained of their barley seed. They all worked through the lengthening days from morn till night re-tiling and refurbishing the east wing into living quarters and a secure stable for their mounts. At night they stood guard duty in turn, but for two months none disturbed them. Arturo and Durstan set up a small shrine at the end of the pillared corridor to Epona and welcomed with grace the homage Marcos and Timo made to their own god when they carved the Greek letters *Chi Rho* above a niche outside the door of their room and kept the niche adorned through the seasons with wild flowers. And their gods seemed to favour them for the crop lines showed quickly and they were lucky enough, or godgraced, to round up four sturdy winter lambs and a milch cow which they found straying in the forest. A hen they had brought with them, squired by a great black cock, sat a clutch of twelve eggs and brought off eight chicks. There was pasture in the valley for their hobbled horses and the rich promise of hay to be made which would see the beasts through the coming winter. In Marcos and Timo they found two men of skills which they envied. Marcos made a turf-covered charcoal burning stack in the forest and a pair of deerskin bellows to fuel and work a small forge where with heavy hammer he repaired broken plough shares and hoes and grubbing picks and mattocks. In the rubble of building material he found an old sharpening stone so that their weapons and the Saxon seax knives and scrama-seax swords they had brought with them never lacked a bright keen edge. Timo, too, had his skills for he made hunting bows and knew the right wood to shape fire-hardened throwing spears and he was a true herdsman maybe because his dumbness reached out and gentled the dumb animals in his care. His hands, too, with which he spoke – and whose language Arturo and Durstan began slowly to read – had a deftness with which he shaped fish hooks from bones to take trout from the broadening valley stream and horse-hair lines not only for fishing but to fashion bird-nets which they hung like a fine, faint mist between trees to take pigeons and doves and wild geese and ducks in the marsh at the far end of the valley. So, as the days passed, they moved from short to good commons and from poorly to well lodged, and their beasts and poultry thrived and the milch cow proved to be in calf which, dropping at high summer, brought milk for all and a store of cheeses to set against the coming of winter.

All this time they lived without going far from the villa. They had their own small world to make before there could be any far venturing beyond it – though there were times when the itch of impatience took Arturo like a fever and he longed for the blood stir of a more manly work than careful husbandry. When these moods came on him he would go through the forest to its limits and sit overlooking open country and the dim shape of the hills that lay to the northwest knowing that there lay Corinium and Glevum and men and horses and weapons without which the design of his life which the gods were slowly patterning could never be completed. Though it was hard for one of his nature, he schooled himself to patience, telling himself that these days were being set for him by the gods to temper the iron of his ambition.

Then, on a day when autumn was whitening the forest glades with the fronding curls of willow herb seeding and the red squirrels worked the hazel branches collecting the loose capped nuts to store against the coming winter, Arturo came into the courtyard in the early morning as his companions readied themselves for the day's work. He was dressed in rough cross-gartered trews, wore open shabby sandals on his feet and a long, belted tunic which had belonged to one of the dead Saxons, a dagger in the belt, and a short cloak caught at the throat with a rough circular brooch which Timo had found in the ruins and repaired. Over his shoulder he carried a small store of provisions in a knotted cloth.

Seeing him and marking his dress and provision sack Durstan said, smiling, 'So the time has come?'

'Yes. Last night the gods spoke to me in a dream.'

'You – who so seldom night-dream? They must have waited long for the chance. What did they say?'

'Go north to where the hills fall away into the great valley of the Sabrina. There one waits for you.'

Durstan would have smiled more broadly but he deemed it wise, sensing Arturo's stiff mood, to keep his face unmoved.

'Just that?'

'No more.'

'You take your horse?'

'No. Nor Anga.'

Marcos said, 'There is a price on your head and men may recognize you.'

'No. I ride no horse. I dress like a peasant. Who is to recognize Arturo, son of Baradoc of the tribe of the Enduring Crow and a troop leader in Prince Gerontius's cavalry? Besides, I fancy that after all these months men will long have marked us as dead or murdered by Saxons. There will be none who watch still with hawk-eyes for Arturo and the chance of blood money.'

Timo stirred and looking at Arturo moved his long thin hands in a brief flutter of his finger play.

Arturo, his mood changing suddenly, laughed and said, 'Good comrade Timo, if by ill-fate I am killed then that is the will of the gods and this place will be yours for the grace of a prayer for my soul. But that time is not for now since the gods in my dreams, though they spoke no more than I have said, held up before my eyes a red banner on which was blazoned a white horse and the white horse carried a rider, fully armed and capped with a war helmet, and the face of the man was my own face. Would they have shown me this if I am to die in the near future?'

Marcos said, 'There is no doubt in my mind that your gods have spoken so and shown you this sign. But you go into bad country. So I tell you this. If he still lives my father's brother, Paulus, who is a carpenter, settled in Corinium. He lives near the east gate. If you should need help or shelter go to him and say that you are the good comrade of Marcos and Timo, the children of his brother. You will not be turned from his door.'

Arturo nodded. 'This I will remember.' He bent and fondled the ears of Anga who stood at his feet, then gave the hound a word of command. Anga hesitated and then moved from him and went to Durstan. With a farewell movement of his hand Arturo turned and made for the forest boundary beyond the west wing of the villa. As Arturo disappeared into the trees Durstan, with a shrug of his shoulders, turned and followed the others who were already moving to their work.

When he caught up with them Marcos said, 'I have nothing but honour and gratitude to Arturo – but do you believe the gods truly speak to him and show him their signs?'

Durstan shrugged his shoulders. 'You saw the white horse when we first came here?'

'Aye, and have seen the mare since for often she grazes in the lower valley. She is as wild as a hawk and no man could come near her. What has she to do with the gods?'

'Does your god never give you a sign?'

'Yes, but it is nothing that the eye can see. When I pray I feel him move in my heart and thoughts, and I feel his strength comforting my weakness.'

'From each god his own way of revelation. And for each man his own way of marking the shadow which his god casts.'

For a moment or two Marcos was silent. Then casually, he said, 'A white horse on a red banner. White and red, those are the true colours of Christos.' He nodded to the villa. 'It would look well flying from the roof-top yonder.'

'But better carried before a well-armed host.'

Arturo travelled for five days without haste, and each day he moved into more settled country where men worked their fields and tended their herds in peace. Seeing him come, armed only with a dagger and poorly dressed, he was given welcome and food and shelter for the night. None asked him from whence he came or where he was going for if a man made no move to explain himself then all knew that he remained silent out of good reason.

He passed through the deep valleyed country well south-west of Corinium and on the morning of the fifth day came out of a thick wood that covered a valley ridge to find before him a great fall in the land. The ridge side plunged steeply away from him, dropping almost sheer in places to a wide plain far below. Through the clear air of the autumn day a vast panorama was spread before him and he saw it as though from the eyes of an idling falcon borne up on a steady air current. Beyond the plain ran the broad, snaking ribbon of the Sabrina river in full tide, the sun taking the silver of its waters with a keenness which hurt the eyes. Far to the north-east it ran until it was lost in the encroaching folds of the long ridge line on which he stood. To the south-west it broadened slowly and was swallowed by the sun sparkle from the waters of the sea into which it ran. Beyond it, purple and mist-hazed, rose the hills and mountains of Cymru and Demetae. He stood for a while, letting his eyes rove over the great spread of river and country, seeing clearly in his mind the sand maps drawn by old Galpan and drunken Leric. Beyond the river lay Venta and the Isca of the Silures, and far away up the river on his right hand, hidden from his sight, the Sabrina waters came down through Glevum. For the first time, since he now saw it as a high-pitched falcon would see it, he became aware of the vastness of his land, and the immensity moved him, drying his throat and waking an unnameable stir of emotion in him. All this, and more and more to the north and the east was Britain ... a country torn and divided by the quarrelling of the tribes of his own kind, harried by Scotti and Pictish raiders, and threatened by the slow, barbarian march of the Saxon warriors and settlers from the West.

He sat down and began to munch on one of the wild apples he had gathered in the wood, melding their sharpness with goat's cheese and flat bread which he had bought from a homesteader with one of the silver coins from his still-remaining store of Prince Gerontius's money. As he ate he was slowly seized with a dullness of mind and lack of spirit, rare for him, and which he would never have confessed to any man. For the truth was that now he was here he knew that he had come, not at the bidding of the gods, but because he had girded at the tedium which had grown with him week by week at the villa of the three nymphs. Homesteading gave him no joy, no fulfilment. When he had lain awake there at night there had been a confusion in his mind which had made it easy for him to imagine, or to wish, that the gods would speak to him or make some sign that would give him their sanction to leave his comrades. But the truth, sharp in him now, was that he had gone a-wandering for his own pleasure and relief. If the gods held any favour for him, then truly it would be a miracle if watching him they should trick time and chance and make real what was only a self-wrought fancy in his mind. True, he had dreamt of the white horse on the red banner. But such a dream could easily have arisen from his longing for warlike action.

With a sudden spate of self-disgust he threw his apple core out into space and heard the sharp click of bursting seed-pods as it fell into a broom bush. As he reached for another apple, a long shadow fell across the grass at his side. He looked round to see a short, strongly built man, dark-eyed and with long black hair, who wore a rough, long brown robe girdled with a thin belt of plaited leather thongs and carried a well-seasoned ash stave.

The man smiled at him and said, 'Greetings. 'Tis a long time since we last saw one another.'

Frowning slightly Arturo said, 'We know one another?'

The man sat down, placed his stave across his knees and reached out for one of Arturo's apples. 'I know you. I knew you from the time of your birth until I last saw you as a bare-bottomed infant splashing in the sand at my feet on the day I left your mother and your people. My name is Merlin.'

'Merlin? Ah, yes, of course .. My mother often spoke of you. You are the –' Arturo broke off for fear of offending the man.

'I am the ageless, the wandering one. Or so men say. But then it is seldom that I agree with what men say. And what do you do, brooding here like an eagle on its eyrie?'

Arturo hesitated for a moment or two. He had heard many tales of this man, knew too that he had been overkind to his mother and had brought her and himself as a babe from Caer Sibli to the settlement of the people of the Enduring Crow. But mostly he knew that it was said that Merlin spoke like a brother to the gods.

He said bluntly, 'I was outlawed with a companion by the Prince of Dumnonia with whose cavalry I served. I have been hiding for many weeks in a small homestead with my companions – but my feet began to itch for better occupation than following the plough and my eyes to smart for sight of new country. To the others I lied that the gods had told me to come here where I should meet a man who waited for me.'

'And what will you say when you return to them?'

Arturo smiled. 'No doubt I shall lie again, though what the lie will be must rest unknown until the moment comes.'

Merlin laughed. 'At least your frankness should please the gods. You could say, of course, that you had met me.' He reached out, broke a piece from Arturo's cheese round, put it in his mouth, and mumbled as he chewed, 'And that I had a message from the gods for you – which I have not, of course. Nor am I here by their direction. Our meeting is pure happenchance. I am on my way to Glevum from Aquae Sulis and often take this way along the ridge. So you are young Arturo who sent message to the Prince Gerontius and the Count Ambrosius that one day they would sue for your return?'

'How do you know that?'

'The message was given in full counsel by your father. Many heard it and the tongues of man wag faster than any woman's when a Prince is so defied that he hurls a full wine cup from him in anger at the words. The discomfort of the great is ever a delight to the small. From Dumnonian Isca to Deva and Lindum the story runs ... Aye, and to Saxon Cantawarra and the island of Tanatus to make the barbarians roar with laughter over their rude mead. My young captain Arturo, the country knows you and –' he stood up and brushed cheese crumbs from his robe, '– now for any who pledges beyond his performance call it an Arto promise –'.

'Then the gods damn them!' Arturo was quick on his feet, standing now, his face stiff with anger. 'They shall see the truth of it one day.'

Merlin shrugged his shoulders. 'Such a truth would not be unwelcome to many. Now cool the fire of your anger. There is a foolishness about your boast that warns me, and for this I give you my own message – for sadly,' his mouth moved to a mock mournful twist, 'I am out of humour with the gods this long time and they favour me with little of their dispositions. You know the Roman tongue?'

'At my mother's knee and by the hammering of old Leric's fist between my shoulder blades.'

'Then know you suffer not alone from acedia. There are many such in the growing army of Count Ambrosius, and none

more bored than in the Sabrina cavalry wing which he has
stationed near Corinium. Many there grow stale with drills and
manoeuvres and might be tempted from their barracks and the
taverns of Corinium with an Arto promise – even if at first the
promise showed no more warlike gain than petty raiding against
the Saxons down the Tamesis. But remember this, speak not
your heart to any man until you have proved him.'

'And how should I do that?'

'If you know not that, then you are not one to command
men. Now, I thank you for the apple and cheese. I would have
thanked you more had you carried a wine skin. The gods be
with you.'

As he turned to go Arturo said, 'It is in my mind, for all your
talk, that the gods did indeed send you to me. How else could
you have recognized me whom you last saw as an infant just
able to stand and walk?'

Merlin smiled. 'You could have answered that for yourself
were your mind not idle. You sprawl on the grass cuddling your
cheese, your tunic flung wide open to cool yourself from walking. Need I say more since I have seen you naked many times in
your mother's arms?'

Arturo smiled ruefully, and said, 'No.' With one hand he
rubbed the strawberry coloured birthmark below his left ribs.
Then with a frank, friendly smile, he went on, 'I thank you for
chiding me. Your words will stay with me.'

He stood for a long while watching the receding figure of
Merlin move away along the tree-edged ridge. When the man
was finally lost to sight he turned and gathered up his gear. A
glance at the westering sun gave him the direction he wanted
and he set out, following Merlin's path until he should be clear
of the forest edge and could make his way across country to
Corinium in the east.

He reached Corinium on the evening of the next day while
there was still a couple of hours of daylight left. The streets
were crowded with people and the troops from the nearby
camp. Market booths and stalls were open and the rutted roads

were busy with the carts of country folk and packhorse-trains carrying army supplies. As he made his way towards the east gate he was with other people pressed back to make way for a patrol of cavalry moving through the city. A young man who led the party was wearing a leather war helmet, plumed with dyed horse-hair, a bronze plated cuirass taking the dying sunset light dully, knee-length boots, and was armed with a scabbarded broad sword. About his neck was knotted a blue scarf with its ends swinging freely to the motion of his horse, and the similarly coloured scarves were worn by all the men in the patrol and, too, by the dismounted cavalry men who walked the streets on leave. Arturo had no need to ask about the scarves for he knew that they were the mark of the men of the Sabrina wing of Count Ambrosius's army. He decided that when his day came all the men of his army should wear the white and red scarves of the banner he had seen in his dream ...

A small boy, his skin as brown as sun-dried earth, wearing only a ragged pair of short trews, directed him to the house of Paulus the carpenter. It was a dwelling place that stood with its back hard against a section of the ruined city wall and was no more than one large living room and cooking quarters with a rough ladder that led to a communal bedroom above. The workshop was a faggot-thatched open shed to one side of the house.

He introduced himself to Paulus, a white-haired man in his sixties, wearing a leather working apron, the stubble of his face hoared with sawdust and all about him the sweet smell of worked wood and shavings, and told him that he came on the urging of Marcos and Timo. He was accepted at once and with few questions. Paulus lived by himself, but a neighbour's wife came in once a day and cooked a meal for him in the evening. The old man made a place for him at the table and while they ate questioned him about the welfare of his nephews. When he heard of the death of his brother at the hands of the Saxons, he said, 'God rest his soul.'

Arturo said, 'You, too, are of the Christos people?'

'Yes, and there are many in this city. It is said, too, that Count Ambrosius is one of us, but I doubt it more than pretence for the Count is ready to be all things to all people so long as they will serve his ends.'

'And those ends?'

Paulus paused from dipping a bread crust into his stew and said, 'He dreams of a conquest of all Britain with himself wearing the purple of emperor.'

'And what is wrong with such a dream?'

Paulus shrugged his shoulders, poured ale into Arturo's cup and said, 'Nothing – except the man who dreams it.'

'Men say that openly here?'

'Go into any tavern or drinking court and you will, as the night lengthens, hear many of his own soldiers and cavalrymen say it. They long for action and he gives them drills and marches and mock battle – and now that autumn is well with us it is clear that there can be no campaigning this year. This winter many men will drift from him back to their homes It is two years since the army marched east and south. Two years – and that is a long time for warriors to content themselves with sword and spear drill. Go into the country to the villas and the farms and you will hear strong words against Count Ambrosius. Although the land is rich and is tilled in peace the crop levies to feed his men are high. I ask nothing of your business here, but take heed of your speech in this city. In drink a soldier speaks freely and nothing is done. But if a freeman, craftsman, or a farmer says aught that same soldier will whip his back bleeding raw. You like this stew? 'Tis hare ... I have a friend who passes through often who always brings some fine gift ... So, my brother Amos is dead, uh? And by a barbarian. Thank god they come not this way. Hare stew, I like it well. But not so well as venison – though 'tis seldom my friend brings that. Such game gets rarer the longer the army stays ...' The old man suddenly broke off, leaned back and smiled, saying, 'I ask your forgiveness. I rattle away like a gossip from the pleasure of company for I am much alone.'

Arturo raised his cup to the old man and said, 'Talk, my friend, for there is much that I would like to know about this place and the cavalrymen here.'

Chuckling with pleasure Paulus drank with Arturo and began to talk again, never flagging, but always ready to take a new line when Arturo put a question to him.

That night Arturo lay long awake while the old man snored gently in his cot. He was in Corinium and here, and in the country around, were cavalrymen, many of them owning their own mounts, who longed for action. With money or rich barter men and horses could be bought to his side. But he had nothing to offer except a share in his dream to create a company whose fame and success would eventually bring the Prince Gerontius and Count Ambrosius to sue for his help. How many men, he wondered, would have the vision to see what he dreamed and for the sake of it go into the wilderness with him? Not many. *Aie*, probably not any – unless he found a way to play on their boredom and trap their minds with the promise of high rewards. Few men would accept the reward of simple comradeship. That was a growth which must come later. He groaned gently to himself. If ever a man needed the help of the gods to direct him he was that man.

The next morning he left Paulus to his work and wandered abroad in the city. It was market day and the old ruined Roman forum was crowded with stalls and benches on which vegetables, game and meat, crockery and pots and pans, and woollen cloths and belts and buckles and leather goods were laid out for sale. Wandering through the crowd Arturo noticed that there were few army men about. Most of them were held at stables and cavalry drills until late in the afternoon . . . the same training exercises which he, as a troop commander, had known endlessly at Isca.

Walking now from stall to stall it was clear to see that there was more for sale here, and a richer variety of goods, than had ever appeared in the Isca markets. The penned poultry and cattle were plump, the cloths and fabrics rich, and much of the pottery and bronze and iron pans and cauldrons of a finer work than the people of Dumnonia knew. Count Ambrosius, whose writ ran from the Sabrina plains north to Glevum and beyond to Deva, held in his power a fat and rich land to which tradesmen and craftsmen flocked and where farmers and settlers worked their ground and tended their cattle in peace. Maybe because of all this the Count had grown over content and was loath to stir away – but among his men there had to be those who suffered from a restlessness and a lust for war and action which full bellies could not assuage.

As he turned from a stall hung with loops of gaily coloured clay beads his eye was caught by the bright blue of a long, belted robe worn by a young woman who worked her way through the crowd, a straw-plaited basket hanging from the crook of her right elbow. A stallholder shouted some pleasantry to her and as she turned her head to reply her eyes were briefly met by Arturo's. For a moment or two, like the sudden gleam of sun between racing clouds, she smiled at him, a warm, friendly and, he imagined, a beckoning smile. Meeting it the whole purpose of his business here in Corinium was reft from him. The sharp thought went through him that it was long since he had held an Iscan girl in his arms, or felt the warmth of full red lips beneath his own. Hardly aware that sudden impulse was moving him to action, he moved forward through the crowd to follow the young woman. But at this moment the market throng pressed back upon him, trapping him against the side of a stall, to make ground for the passage of a herd of cattle being driven to the slaughterhouse on the far side of the Forum.

When he stepped free from the press at last the young woman had gone and he made no attempt to search for her. He needed no woman. Men and horses were his need. He turned away towards the north gate and left the city. A little way along the Glevum road he climbed a grassy knoll crested with two beech trees and sat down, looking across at the camp of the Sabrina cavalry wing through the air which was hazed with the dust kicked up by three troops of horse at drill. He was angry with himself for even momentarily being stirred by the sight of a pretty face. The gods had brought him here for matters of far higher import.

Horses and Men

Arturo sat on his knoll for over an hour watching the cavalry drills. He had heard that Count Ambrosius had formed his cavalry in the old Roman fashion into wings – the Roman *alae* – of sixteen troops with each troop holding thirty-two men and had even named the commander of a wing in the old style of Praefectus. From the size of the camp and the number of mounted men drilling he guessed that this Sabrina Wing was no ordinary *ala* of around five hundred strong. This seemed more like an Ala Milliaria of twenty-four troops each of forty-two men – around a thousand men in all – and no doubt commanded by a Tribunus. Maybe it was yet far from its full complement of men and horses, but it was a larger force by far than any that Prince Gerontius could muster. Clearly the ambitions of the Count ran high and matched his pride in the ancestry he claimed for himself. He was a man, full of nostalgia for the great days of past Roman glory, of Roman blood himself (though that was common enough now in this country), who longed to restore the glory of the old Empire. A hopeless dream, thought Arturo – but was it any more hopeless than his own?

Tired of watching the cavalry and over-warm under the midday sun, he slipped off his tunic, made a pillow with it for his head, and lay back, staring up at the sky. Men there must be, he thought, drilling out there on the plain who longed for real not mock action and must know that it could not come this year for it was far too late for campaigning. To tempt any of them to his side he had nothing to offer. Watching the small clouds slide across the blue his face muscles tautened with frustration. Now, if ever before, he needed help from the gods or some sign from them that there should be no death of hope.

He shut his eyes and silently called on them, willing them to hear him, his teeth grinding with his fervour as he mutely named them ... Epona, Nodens, Coventina, great Dis, father of all ... great gods and small gods he named, battle gods and household gods ... Badh and his brothers, and was tempted to call, too, to the Roman gods for surely they held lien and interest still in this land, but turned away from the thought for fear of offending his own native deities.

He was brought from his silent, almost rigid fervour, by the sound of horses' hooves behind him. He sat up to see a man riding one pony and leading another come up the knoll and, after a brief nod to him, dismount and hitch the ponies to a beech branch.

He came across to Arturo carrying a drinking skin and sat down by him. Without a word he drew the stopper from the skin, drank, wiped his lips with the back of his hand then the mouth of the skin and handed it to Arturo saying, 'A gift is the best greeting. Drink.'

Arturo took the skin and drank Expecting mead he found that it was wine. Handing the skin back he said, 'I thank you.' Then prompted by a wry sense of humour, he went on, mocking his own newly passed fervour, 'If you bring a message from the gods then I will give you double thanks.'

For a moment or two the man eyed him without replying. He was small of stature with a pear-shaped face, brown as a ripe chestnut and, as Arturo had noticed when he had walked across to him, bow-legged as though he had come into this world riding a pony and had seldom set foot on ground since. His eyes were as dark as polished sloes, his hair darker and tightly curled, his cheeks cleft with deep wrinkles and his thin lips, at this moment, drawn back tight over firm white teeth in an amused, houndish smile. Driving the wineskin stopper home with a quick smack of his palm, he said, 'And what kind of message wants young Arturo, son of the chief of the tribe of the Enduring Crow?' He nodded at Arturo's bare shoulder as he spoke. 'Nay, look not surprised. You would not know me, but many a time I have seen you at drill in the river meadow below Isca town. And many a mount your old friend, Master Ricat, has bought from me.'

Arturo pointed a finger at the long knife which the man wore in the belt about his hide surcoat and said, 'What charity stayed your hand as I drank? You could have slit my throat and claimed my blood-price.'

'I deal in horses, not men's lives, no matter the price. If I come from the gods then they send me without my knowledge. If they do, I thank them because it pleases me to meet one who has spoken with open challenge to Count Ambrosius and Prince Gerontius for they have often had my back laid thick with weals for horse stealing, and a few other trivial matters. But you would do well when you take the sun to keep your tribal sign and the birthmark below your ribs hidden.'

Ignoring this, Arturo asked, 'What do men call you?'

The man shrugged his shoulders. 'A hundred names, mostly vile. But seldom my own, which is Volpax.'

'Then Master Volpax — and I have indeed heard of you — the gods sent you. Knowing or unknowing by you makes no matter. They know I need horses.' He nodded towards the beech trees. 'Not mixed breed ponies like your dun-coloured mare there with a black tail.'

'You shame my mare. On a long march she would outlast many of those overstuffed, over-cosseted cavalry horses out there.' He nodded to the plain where the last of the dust was settling as the troops rode away to quarters. 'She will go six days on a handful of corn and her own foraging and meet the seventh fresh as the day she started. So you need horses? Aye, from Deva down to Isca the whole country knows that. Have you found some silver hoard that you can afford to buy them?'

'We have no need to buy them.'

'We?' Volpax's eyes widened and he grinned wolfishly.

Arturo smiled. 'The gods have sent you to an honest and reliable partner. There are hundreds of horses quartered around the barracks of the Sabrina Wing. You could work alone and take a few, or you could work with some rogue helper who would betray you when you trimmed his share – which you would.'

'It is always a temptation, I agree.'

'With me it would be different. I can betray no man without betraying myself. And we would draw no daggers over sharing for out of every three horses we take I would keep one. Remember this, too. I know a horse from an overstuffed hay bag. And, as you can, I can talk their soft language at night to gentle them and cut their hobbles or head ropes while you ride a mare in season down the lines for them to follow.'

Volpax chuckled. 'You know the tricks.'

'Why not. You probably played them at Isca against us and then sold the mounts to Count Ambrosius, only to do the same thing to him and sell them back to Prince Gerontius or some northern chief. I say, although you do not know it, that the gods have sent you.'

Volpax pursed his lips, his eyes hooding with thought and then said, 'I would not quarrel with that – for it is a sign of distinction and I gladly take your word for it. But if the gods have sent me it is beyond their power to make up my mind for me. I will think on what you say.' He stood up, the wineskin swinging from his left hand. 'You stay in Corinium?'

'I do. At the house of Paulus the carpenter.'

Volpax shook his head. 'You are too open – even with me. There is a blood-price on your head. Every man knows the taunt you have flung at Gerontius and Count Ambrosius.'

'I am open with you alone – for the gods sent you.'

'Let us from now keep the gods out of this. I have an affair which takes me to Glevum. I shall pass this way again in three days' time. Be here then at midday and I will give you an answer. Until then keep well away from this place. There are those among the blue-scarfed Sabrina men who have sharp eyes for a loitering stranger.'

'You have my promise. And I thank you for your answer, Master Volpax.'

For a moment Volpax seemed on the point of protest. Then

with a slow shake of his head he turned and went to his ponies. But as he mounted the dun, he called, 'Stay close to Master Paulus. Keep away from the drinking places and wenches, and forget that you ever met me or heard my name, comrade Arturo.'

Arturo sat and watched him ride away down the Glevum road. He could have wished to be going with him for he would like to have seen the city. Then he rose and began to make his way back to Corinium. The gods were with him. There was no doubt of that. One horse in three. That meant stealing sixty to gain twenty mounts. And three hundred to have a hundred ... *Aie*, but that was looking too far ahead. All great matters began small. Twenty mounts and then twenty men ... almost a troop, drilled and hardened for action, red-scarfed and white-bannered and the nomansland eastwards beyond the villa of the three nymphs waiting to be claimed and ordered and tribute gladly paid for the security from up-river creeping Saxon bands which he would give to all honest folk who now lived in fear.

He began to whistle gently to himself. The gods had truly marked him. But for all that, they were stern and devious masters. Had they not momentarily tempted him that morning with a glimpse of a young woman in blue? He could have pressed after and searched for her and never have met Master Volpax. No, until he came again to the beech knoll in three days' time he would keep close to old Paulus.

For the rest of that day and the one following Arturo stayed close to old Paulus and never went beyond the workyard where the man was content to have him either helping or sitting on a stool as he worked and gossiped. Towards sunset on the evening of the second day, while Arturo helped Paulus to stack a pile of rough-cut planks which had been ordered by one of the market officials for the repair of broken stalls, a voice from behind them called, 'Master Paulus!'

Arturo and Paulus turned. Standing in the open front of the thatched shed was a young woman and one glance told Arturo that it was the girl in the blue robe whom he had seen a few days before in the market. Unaware almost that he did it, Arturo ran his fingers through his sweat-tousled hair and then drew his open tunic about him and belted it.

'Mistress,' said Paulus shuffling past Arturo, 'if you come with a complaint from your father about his tool racks tell him that they will soon be ready.'

The young woman shook her head and said, 'He sends no complaint. But a summons to a meeting of the city's tradesmen and craftworkers called now because of a new demand by the Count's warden to raise the levy once again on the free work you and my father and all honest craftsmen must give to the cavalry camp.' She smiled. 'They meet now and will talk until dark and drinking time and it will all come to nought.'

'Aye, that is so. And my supper will be ruined with keeping, and I shall wake with a sore head in the morning from drinking. So be it.' He shrugged his shoulders and moved away to his house.

But when he had gone the young woman still stood her ground, her dark red lips curved in an almost mocking smile which, for some reason that baffled him, suddenly irritated Arturo so that he said, ignoring courtesy and ceremony, 'Some mornings since you smiled at me in the market place, and now you stand as though there was something you expected from me.'

Her smile broadened, and she said, 'And why should I not? Or are your promises like blowing thistledown to be carried away and lost? Have you forgotten then that once you said to me that one day you would come and woo me; that we should lie in the long grass, listen to the golden birds sing and drink the new wine? That seeking me you would ask only for one who has eyes like the blue bellflower, lips redder than the thorn berry and hair like ... *Aie*, now that escapes me –'

'Like polished black serpentine,' said Arturo suddenly, for now memory was back with him like the sudden sweep of light from the sun breaking free of dark clouds.

'True, that was it. So why should I not smile at you in the market place – since I would know your face anywhere, or so

I thought until you greeted my smile with a face as blank as a mouse-stuffed owl's? But now I know you as all folk who have heard the blood-price called against you would know you with your tunic drawn back to show your tribal tattoo and birth-mark. Would you, too, have me immodest enough to lift my robe and show you the swallow's gorge mark on my thigh?'

'There is no need,' said Arturo quickly, recovering from his confusion. 'I would have known you at any time except this when – as you must know – there are other matters which bear heavily on me. You are Daria, daughter of Ansold the sword-smith. But it was to Lindum, not Corinium, that you were trav-elling.'

'True – but my father changed his mind when he saw the work which was here with Count Ambrosius's army. As for the matters which weigh heavily on your mind, I think you give them too little thought. You are a fool to work with old Paulus half naked for all to see your marks and so make a high blood-price an easy picking for any man who passes. Such heedless-ness will never bring you the years to make good your boast to Gerontius and Count Ambrosius. Perhaps those who called that an Arto promise were wiser than I thought. None will ever sue you to come with your army to their aid. And, too, without a head how will you ever lie in the long grass and hear the birds sing and drink the new wine?'

As she finished speaking she began to turn away, but Arturo, anger rising in him, stepped forward and held her by the arm and said pugnaciously, 'You do right to mock me. But you do wrong to taunt me with talk of empty promises. They shall sue me for help for the gods have ordained it.'

Daria frowned down at the hand which held her arm and, as Arturo released her, she said, 'And the golden birds and the new wine – when shall they be heard and drunk?'

Arturo smiled. 'There will be time and place for them. You think you stand here and talk to me out of chance? Nay, even though I had forgotten you the gods had not. I take my shame for a misty memory, and accept your chiding. But it is written that on the day of my triumph you shall come riding into

Glevum with me on a white mare wearing a cloak of scarlet with a lining of blue silk and about your waist a golden belt with a clasp of two singing birds. And when Count Ambrosius comes out to greet us he shall hand to you a silver goblet full of new wine, and then –'

'And then, and then,' Daria interrupted him, mockingly, 'will be the day when pigs shall be flying and the salmon coming up the Sabrina shall wriggle ashore, their mouths full of sea pearls to lay at my feet. But for now, be wise – keep your tunic drawn and your god dreams to yourself.'

Without other word or look she turned from him and walked away. Arturo watched her go, knowing now that he would never again lose her from his mind, and wondering how he ever could have forgotten her and that rain-drenched day on the high moors when she had slipped a quick hand to the dagger in the garter sheath beneath her tunic.

He lay awake that night, long after old Paulus had come stumbling back from his meeting and the drinking which had followed it, thinking about her, knowing that he would like to seek her out at her father's house but firming himself not to do so. The gods had sent her to him and they would mark the time when either he or she would have their feet set true on the paths that led to a meeting place. *Aie* ... and for the future he really would keep his tunic close-belted.

At noon on the following day Arturo waited for Volpax under the trees on the little knoll that overlooked the cavalry training grounds. When he arrived it was as before, riding the dun pony and leading another. He came over to Arturo carrying his wine-skin and a knotted cloth in which were six cold roasted quails.

He set the food between them and this time offered the wine-skin first to Arturo and began talking as though there had never been any break in their conversation.

'The affair is settled. I have a friend who keeps cattle in a valley far to the south of Corinium. He will lodge and find fodder for up to thirty horses. No more. We take no more than four horses a night – and that at long intervals – and never

travel the same path to my friend's valley. Nor when the
ground is soft from rain to show the hoof marks. When we
have the thirty, you take your ten and I take my twenty and we
go our own ways. When you have the men and need for more
mounts all you have to do is to pass a message to my friend and
I will come to you.'

'And how will I travel ten horses back to my homestead?'

Volpax smiled wolfishly, flicked his hand at a bluebottle
which buzzed above a roasted quail, and said, 'That, Prince Arturo – for so I call you to give you heart – is your problem.
Our bargain is for horses. Also from today you see no more of
Corinium. We stay together, not from lack of trust on my part
– but for each other's safety.' He lifted the wineskin and drank
deeply.

Speaking almost to himself, Arturo said, 'We shall steal our
horses. Would that it were as easy to steal men.'

Rubbing a hand over his wine-wet lips Volpax shook his head,
and then, grinning, said, 'You could – since you are so close to
them – ask the gods for their help. If they remain silent then
you must find your own way. You and I are in the business of
horses. No more. But this I say – once it is known that you need
men and can promise them what they want they will find a way
to you.'

Arturo lay back on the grass, staring at the slow march of the
heavy clouds above, and felt a heaviness, too, in his heart. Now
that the moment was on him for action he suddenly felt helpless
and undecided and astray. So far he had done no more than
make Arto promises. Now was the beginning of the time when,
gods or no gods, he had to work and scheme and make a beginning to bring to truth the words and dreams which had com-
forted him for so long. He sighed suddenly. 'Well, tis with one
step after another that a long march is made. We will take the
horses and then I will think about the men.'

'So be it.' Volpax flung a picked quail carcass into the grass.
'Be here at nightfall, fair weather or foul, and we will walk
around the camp. Then tomorrow night, if the weather is kind,

we will take our first horses. For now you can go for the last time to Corinium. Tell Paulus you travel back to your friends. Then, without his knowing, steal charcoal from his fire pot to blacken your face and hands for tonight.' He stood up, taking the wineskin and went on, 'I leave you the rest of the quails. But stay not overlong here. When you come back tonight give me a curlew's whistle three times. If I do not answer, then you must find some other to help you with mounts.'

Frowning, Arturo asked, 'It could happen that you won't be here?'

'Why not? I have many enemies. Is there any man who can be certain that he will see tomorrow?' He turned and walked away, rolling on his bowed legs.

Arturo stayed until he had finished the quails and then went back to Corinium. Crossing the Forum he was tempted to ask the way to Ansold the swordmaker's workshop but held down the desire firmly. His business here was with horses and men.

That night, with blackened faces and hands, he and Volpax made themselves familiar with the cavalry horse lines. Some of the beasts were penned inside wooden palisaded yards but more were hobbled and tethered to picket lines. Guard fires burned at intervals around the camp and sentries patrolled each sector of the great space which the cavalry wing occupied. They made the circuit of the camp twice to familiarize themselves with it and then, withdrawing to a safe distance, they sat in a patch of low broom scrub and watched the movement of the patrolling guards. As the night began to wear away they saw that the guards often hugged their fires and missed a patrol, and saw, too, that the guard officers were lax in their duty rounds. In-action, Arturo knew, bred carelessness and indifference in the best troops.

Long before first light the two withdrew to their ponies which they had left tethered in a wood far up the Glevum road and Volpax led the way to a small bothy made of hazel boughs and roofed with dead bracken in a small dell deep into the wood. They slept and ate their way through the long day and there was little talk between them and no passing of the wineskin. A nearby stream gave them water to drink. When Volpax was about his business he remained sober.

The next night they took the first of their horses. Volpax left Arturo near the picket lines and went to the far end of the camp. Here, between midnight and dawn, standing in the cover of some trees he drew his bow and shot four arrows at the three guards who sat around the watch fire. The first struck the three-legged iron brazier and sent sparks and burning wood high in the air. The others thudded into the ground about the guards. The men scattered, shouting and drawing their swords. Expecting an attack, one of them blew the alarm on his horn. The blowing of the alarm brought the main guard turning out from their hut and they ran towards the danger spot. Arturo smiled to himself as he saw the two men guarding his length of picket line jump to their feet and hurry towards the alarm call. Crouching low, one hand holding his dagger and the other two stout rope halters, he went quickly to the line of horses where the animals moved restlessly. Talking softly and soothingly to the disturbed animals he slashed the hobbles from two of them and slipped the halters over their necks. Then standing between them, gentling them, crooning the love talk and caressing noises which bond all good cavalry men to their mounts, he waited. In a few moments Volpax, running low, crablike on his bowed legs, came scuttling across to the line and freed another two horses. He swung himself on to the back of one of them and rode, leading the other, out into the darkness of the night and away from the pandemonium and shouting from the far end of the camp. Close behind him rode Arturo.

By daybreak they were well south of Corinium in wooded, steep valley country, each man now riding his own pony with a haltered stolen horse on either side of him.

As the sun, glowing red through a misty autumn sky, climbed high Arturo rode with a light heart. Here, by the gods, was a beginning. Horses first and men later. And if the men were to prove more difficult than the horses, then he was content for the gods were with him. Impatience on his part would be an insult to the gods.

A week later they took four more horses, and this time without causing any disturbance since it was a night of thin brume, lying waist high over the ground under clear starlight. They worked their way on their bellies to the lines while the guards huddled about their braziers, cut the horses free and mounting galloped them away, separating and twisting and curving through the mist to defy all hopeful pursuit.

On the next foray, two weeks later, and now there was the nip of sharp frost in the air and the camp drinking troughs were plated with a thin layer of ice, Volpax and Arturo wormed their way to the pens at the northern end of the camp where un-hobbled horses were quartered. Volpax surprised the single guard at the gate, laid him low with a blow from a wooden club and then freed the horses to stampede them through the camp while he and Arturo roped two horses each and rode off with them. After that they kept away from the camp for three weeks, and then made another raid using the same strategy as they had employed on their first raid.

By the time the year was well on the turn they had taken twenty horses. Since a fall of snow then made raiding unwise Arturo took two of the six horses which had fallen to his lot and riding a pony borrowed from Volpax led them back to the villa of the three nymphs where he found all in order but his friends becoming over-anxious about him.

When he returned to Volpax he brought Durstan with him so that his companion could take by turns his remaining four horses back to the villa. Now, because the weather was worsening, snow and rain often making raiding impossible for fear of their tracks being followed, Volpax and Arturo spent many a long day lodged in their bracken-roofed bothy waiting for the right conditions to favour them. Once or twice, since tedium was an enemy which Arturo was least fitted to combat, he left Volpax sleeping or nursing his wineskin and wandered off through the woods by himself, close wrapped in his cloak against the cold or the rain. Once or twice he stood at the edge of the wood and looked across to the smoke of the cooking fires rising above far Corinium. The day came when, the impulse strong and irresistible in him, he made his way there. If a man's feet itched, he found excuse for himself, then might not that be a sign from the gods? If they could colour his mind with visions why should they not as surely direct his footsteps past denial?

Avoiding the main gates he entered the city through a gap in the broken walls. A heavy squall of rain made him draw the cape of his cloak over his head. He ran across the Forum and took shelter under the colonnade which fronted the Basilica. There were very few people abroad and those that were hurried about their business. Arturo sat on a stone bench and watched the puddles forming between the broken paving of the Forum square. As he sat there his eye was caught by some graffiti marked with the soft edge of a slate on one of the colonnade pillars. A long inscription amongst them ran vertically down the length of the column. As he read it anger grew suddenly and sharply in him.

> Between the empty promise of Arto and the
> sloth of Ambrosius where shall a warrior
> blood his lance?

Impulsively, heedless of any who watched, he stood up, fumbling inside his cloak for his belt pouch and went to the pillar. With a piece of the charcoal which he carried for night raids he wrote:

> Arto has taken your horses. Are all the
> warriors of Ambrosius dormice to sleep
> through winter? Come south with your swords
> and claim your mounts.

A few minutes later, careless of whether he had been seen, he left the city and made his way across country in the gathering gloom and rain towards the forest shelter. As he went there was a sureness in him, lifting his spirits, that the gods had truly sent him to the city to read the inscription.

A few nights later with the ground iron hard from frost he and

Volpax took another lot of horses, but this time things went wrong for them. As Volpax crouched, cutting the hobbles of a horse, the animal, frightened by the noise of the alarms sounding, reared and a fore hoof struck Volpax to the ground. A guard came running through the darkness, saw the two men and threw his spear from a distance. It struck Volpax in the side of his neck as he rose, tore deeply through his flesh, and then fell away from him. Abandoning the horses he would have taken, Volpax ran from the picket lines and caught up with Arturo who, ignorant of what had happened, was leading his two horses away at a fast trot. As Volpax called to him he pulled the horses up, saw the blood streaming from Volpax's neck, and without word – the night behind them loud with the cries of men and the blowing of horns – he hoisted Volpax to the back of one horse and swung himself on the other and they rode hard into the darkness. When they were well clear of the camp they pulled their mounts up and Arturo, ripping lengths of cloth from his cloak, tied them about Volpax's neck to stop the bleeding from the wound.

Choking over his words, Volpax said, "Tis nothing. A glancing blow that will leave but a ragged scar and –'

He swayed and Arturo held him on his feet. From the way the blood had run and spurted from the wound he knew that it was far from nothing. The life was pumping fast from his friend.

He said, 'Save your words to spare your breathing.'

Suddenly Volpax's eyes closed and he fell heavily against Arturo and, before he could be held, collapsed to the ground. After a moment as Arturo tried to staunch the blood flow Volpax opened his eyes. They shone dully in the starlight and Arturo knew with a heavy heart that the death look was on the face of his friend.

With his next words Volpax showed that he knew it, too. He raised a hand and held Arturo's, gripping it tightly, and said, fighting for breath, 'There is an end to every road. Mine stops here, Arto. *Aie* . . .' A weak smile touched his lips, '. . . and I go without the comfort of a wineskin. May the gods be kind and greet me with one . . .' He coughed and swallowed violently as the blood gorged his throat. Then, in a moment of ease, he went

371

on, 'Leave me. Take the horses – they are yours now ... all of them. A parting gift from Volpax. In return say a prayer for me when you ride to Ambrosius to make your promise good...' Then, with the faintest of sighs, his head dropped and he lay still in Arturo's arms, his dead eyes staring up to the frost-bright stars. As though in salute to his passing, from the depth of the forest about them a dog fox barked three times sharply.

Because of the comradeship which had been between them Arturo wrapped the body of Volpax in his cloak and bound him crossways on the back of the second horse. He had no means of burying him and would have thought it scant respect to have left him to be picked clean by scavenging birds and beasts. He rode the rest of that night leading the spare horse on its halter. The dun-coloured and the other pony they had abandoned near the camp in their flight. There was nothing in him now but sorrow for the loss of his friend. Horses he might have now in plenty, but for the first time he knew the measure of the loss of a friend. If the gods granted him his wishes he knew that the time would come when he would mourn other friends, but none, no matter how dear, would cloud his mind with the blackness of the sorrow he felt for Volpax.

At daybreak he stopped by a small forest pond to rest and water the horses and to eat the hard bread and cold meat which he carried in his pouch. The night had brought a thick hoar frost which now, as the sun strengthened, dripped from the bare tree boughs. A moorhen foraged among the sere tangle of dead rushes on the far side of the pool and a robin came timidly to pick at a crust of bread he threw it. Winter was fresh on the land and iron fast in his heart. The gods had given him horses ... and now, as though to mock him in his need for men, they took from him Volpax.

Deep in his own misery, sitting with his elbows on his knees staring at the black surface of the pond, he was taken by surprise when from behind him a voice said, 'Reach not for your dagger. I come in friendship.'

Arturo swung round and half rose. His hand went for the knife

372

in his belt, gripped it, and then was stayed from drawing it by the sight of a young man who stood on the fringe of the trees. He was on foot, a sword hanging from his belt, his hands held wide and free from any weapon. He was bare-headed, his hair, the rich colour of a polished chestnut and fired with sharp red glints from the rising sun, ran down the sides of his cheeks to a small, bushy beard. He wore a close-fitting surcoat and tightly gartered trews while about his neck was tied a blue Sabrina Wing cavalry scarf. He smiled as Arturo now stood slowly upright.

Arturo said, 'Why should one of the Sabrina Wing offer me friendship?'

The man came forward a few steps, his eyes going from Arturo to the two calvary horses standing by and then to the cloaked body of Volpax on the ground. He said slowly, 'Because if you are, as I truly think you to be, that Arturo of the famous promise, and also that same one who has set Corinium and all cavalry men talking about your message written on the basilica pillar, then I am no longer of the Sabrina Wing.' He raised a hand to the knot of the blue scarf, tugged it free and threw the cloth from him to rest pinned on the thorns of a leafless briar.

'I am that Arturo.' As he spoke Arturo's eyes went from the man to the thickness of the trees and scrub behind him. Soft words and friendship's appearance could be the forerunners of treachery.

As though he had read his mind the young man said, 'There is none behind me. I come alone, riding your dun pony and leading the other. 'Twas my comrade's spear that sent your friend to the Shades – the gods celebrate his coming. I followed on foot and found your ponies which you dared not stop to untether. *Aie* ... and then there was another trail plain to follow ... wet and shining on grass and leaf under the stars. And when that went the gods gave a quick night frost to bear your marks. The gods have grieved you with one loss, and now – if it is your will and you are truly the man I seek – offer you the gain of myself and others like me. If I talk overmuch be not surprised. My father was a bard in Lavobrinta in the country of the Ordovices and I would have become one but that I loved horses more. My name is Gelliga.'

'You would offer me service and bring others of the same mind?'

Gelliga shrugged his shoulders. 'Why not? Three weeks past you stole my mount, a grey mare. We were both tired of empty drills and empty words. I come to join her. And there are others like me.'

For a moment or two Arturo said nothing, but there was in him now, growing fast, a rising exultation. The gods took and the gods gave. But in loss or in gain a man should never cease to honour and trust them. Volpax was gone. But was it not true that the very life blood he had shed on grass and leaf had brought one to stand in his place and he, a man from whom trust shone without flaw, one who should bring others.

He said, 'I am Arturo, and the gods have been kind. Go back to your friends. Tell them of this place and be here with them at the next full moon. I shall come to greet you and lead you to those who have already sworn service.'

'You will come alone?'

Arturo smiled 'Why should I not? The gods have marked me, and now they have marked you. I give you and your comrades my trust. To do other would shame me before the gods.'

Comrades of the White Horse

Arturo found Durstan waiting for him at the horse-keeper's steading. Between them they led ten of the horses back to the villa of the three nymphs through two days of wind and rain. On hearing of the death of Volpax and the promise which Arturo had made to go back and meet Gelliga and such men as would follow him, Durstan tried to argue Arturo out of such foolishness. But after a while, when he saw that Arturo was adamant, he shrugged his shoulders and said, 'So be it. May the gods protect you.'

Arturo, heavily cowled against the driving rain as they rode side by side, said, 'The gods have willed it through the death of Volpax. While I am gone there is work for you to do. Ride eastwards down the river. Talk to the farmers and the headmen of the villages. Take a good horse, dress well and carry a sword, and tell them Arturo sends his greetings, and that soon he will be riding with his comrades to clear the banks, the swamps and the woods of the upriver lands of all Saxon bands.'

Durstan's eyes widened in surprise. 'In mid-winter?'

'Aye, in mid-winter. Is it not then that Saxons find their bellies empty and begin to raid our people to rob them of their corn and root stores? I shall have a company which has long itched for true action, already drilled and sharp-set for fighting. Within three days' ride of the villa there is fighting and enough to pleasure them. Tell our river people that we come to protect them and to clear the headwater valleys of the Saxons.'

Despite himself Durstan smiled, recognizing the note of exultation in his friend's voice. Arturo was flighting again on god-given wings of daring, and he knew that it would be useless to say that the Saxon riff-raff – criminals and outcasts mostly from

375

the lands of King Hengist – would withdraw to their swamps and riverside thickets where no horse could follow them. He said, 'And in return you will take tribute for your protection?'

'That would be to do as the Saxons do. I take nothing, but accept whatever is offered freely for the service and protection we give.'

Durstan made no reply. The river settlers lived a hard life. Since they seldom if ever found any willing to help them the habit of gratitude was almost lost to them. With the extra horses and men Arturo would bring the winter fodder and supplies at the villa would soon be gone. To point this out to Arturo, he knew, would only bring the reply that the gods would provide.

Twelve days later Arturo rode down the forest path under a full moon to the pool where he had first met Gelliga. He had dressed himself as proudly as he could from the meagre possessions of himself and his friends at the villa. He wore a woollen cloak caught at the throat with a bronze brooch donated by Timo, long trews crossgartered with deerskin hide thongs, his own tunic and belt from which hung his sword, sharply honed by Marcos, and on his head a leather cap with a stiff plume of white and red goose quills – the red quills so dyed by Durstan in the dark blood of a winter hare which had been trapped for the pot. He rode a chestnut stallion, the best of the stolen horses, and carried for lance a seasoned length of ash, the tip fire-hardened and capped with a sharp iron point fashioned by Marcos from a piece of scrap metal scavenged in the villa's ruins.

The moon threw ebony tree and branch shadows across his path, the stallion's breath plumed in the frost-sharp air and the ground rang iron hard under its hooves. Arturo came openly, armed and alert, but fearing no mischief for this night, this meeting, he knew had been long ordained, and the knowledge – whose provenance he never questioned nor thought to prove – was in him with a noble certitude and filled him with a controlled but commanding arrogance. Openly he rode down to the hollow and came out of the cover of the winter-stark trees and brought the stallion to a halt at the side of the white rimed reeds of the black, star-mirroring waters of the pool. He sat and waited, curbing the horse firmly as it fidgeted. An owl called from the trees far up the valley side and the star reflections on the water were shattered into a maze of shifting silver as a water rat swam across its breadth. He sat there facing across the clearing, his eyes on the path by which Gelliga had first come to surprise him.

The owl called again and the waters of the pool grew calm, holding the reflections of the stars firmly fixed in its dark mirror.

A voice from behind him said quietly, 'Greetings to Captain Arturo.'

Arturo wheeled his steed about to find Gelliga standing at the foot of the pathway which had brought him into the clearing. Touched with a moment's irritation at the conceit of the man's manoeuvre, Arturo said, 'Greetings, good Gelliga. You come alone – and without horse?'

Gelliga shook his head. 'No, my captain. There are six others with me and we bring four horses. There is a high wind of suspicion blowing through the camp now. Guards have been doubled and a curfew keeps all men in barracks after nightfall. There were those who would have come but could find no way. But they will with time.' Then with a slow movement he drew aside his long cloak, pulled his sword from its scabbard and thrust it upright into the hard ground before him, saying, 'Here is my sword which I, Gelliga of Lavobrinta in the country of the Ordovices, pledge to you in true comradeship.'

He stepped back a few paces from his sword. As he did so another man moved out of the trees to his right. Heavily cloaked, tall and with a deeply wrinkled face, he too drew his sword and fisted it into the ground and said in a voice which was like the low growl of a bear, 'My captain, I, too, Garwain from Moridunum on the banks of the river Tuvius in the country of the Demetae, pledge myself to you.'

After him, and before Arturo could stir or say a word, another man stepped out from further along the ring of the trees and stabbed his sword into the ground. Short, lean and bow-legged he said in a high voice, 'Lacto of Calcaria in the country of the

377

Parisi, my captain, gives his sword to you.' Then, clear in the moonlight, his face broke into a broad grin as he went on, 'My horse you have already for you sit upon it now.'

Arturo answered, 'It is yours again when we reach the villa of the three nymphs.'

Then from beyond Lacto another man moved into the moonlit circle and announcing himself gave his sword and pledge to be followed by four others so that Arturo sat the stallion within a crescent of swords. After Lacto came Bovio from Deva, fresh-faced and big-handed, Tarius from Olicana of the Brigantes, lean, hardbitten of face and older than all the rest, and then Netio of the Catuvellauni with a hawkish, hook-nosed face marked to one side by an old sword scar; and last of all the youngest of them all, Lancelo, short, broad-shouldered and with a round moon of a face set with smiling eyes who came from Corinium.

Arturo sat his horse and let his eyes swing from one to another and slowly there rose in him the beginning of a deep pride. Great oaks, he thought, from little acorns grew ... *Aie*, but the coming of such greatness would cover the life span of many men. But here was the seed which would grow fast to bring him a great company of men, a *comitatus*, a firm brotherhood which in a few years could become an army. Truly now he was poised on the brink of a god-marked destiny, and he saw now that the drama staged for his benefit by Gelliga must surely have been put into the man's mind by the gods. Seven men to pledge their seven swords. There was magic in the number, and magic in this moment which he must meet appropriately. Brothers they might be truly, but captain and commander he must remain to create an army from what otherwise might become a rabble.

He dropped his horse's reins, holding it firm and controlled by the clamping pressure of his knees alone, and he drew his sword with one hand, holding it upright before his face, and raised his lance with the other hand and began to speak without thought because he knew the gods would put the right words into his mouth.

His face tight drawn from the fervour which stirred in him, he said boldly, 'With this lance I give you welcome and will be with you as straight and true in comradeship, in valour and in faith.' Then drawing his up-pointed sword to his lips he kissed the broad, cold blade, and went on, 'On this blade I make the oath-kiss and swear that I shall never ask of you that which I would not dare myself. I shall be your true captain and you my beloved brothers. Neither in distress nor want, nor in courage nor in victory shall there ever be shadow or stain on the love and duty which I hold dear towards you. Swear then to accept but one destiny, to rid this island of all those who do now and would further oppress us, to bring back the glory and the peace which once were lodged with our fathers and their fathers. Swear this by the god or gods who rule your hearts!' He kissed his sword again and raised it high.

Before him in one movement seven swords were drawn from the ground, flashing in the bright moonlight; seven swords were raised as one to take on their cold blades the oath-kisses, and as though in one voice the seven cried, 'We swear! We swear!'

Then began, in the raw and savage days of mid-winter, the first of Arturo's true time as a captain of men. Durstan had returned to say that while he had been received with friendship by their own people none of them would move to help them or freely provision them. They had been left alone so long without help that the poverty and hardships of their life and the sudden attacks of raiding Saxons formed a pattern of their days which they met now with a practical stoicism. They hid in storage pits, cliff caves and woodland dells most of their harvest corn and lodged their lean cattle in secret pastures. When the Saxons came they withdrew to the woods and hills and the raiders took what they would from their poor huts and when they were gone the homesteaders came back to repair the damage and to mourn wife or child or the aged who had been butchered by the Saxons. They lived in fear on the knife-edge of want and prayed only for the coming of spring when they could open their furrows and sow what seed corn was left and look to the farrowing and calving of what swine and kine they still held. Spring and summer were the easeful seasons for the

barbaric Saxon robbers had enough sense to leave them undis-
turbed to their cropping and folding against the fat ·time of
autumn harvests and full cattle pens.

For a few days while his new comrades settled into the villa,
and Durstan and Gelliga saw them mounted and in mock battle
drills they learned to move and know one another, Arturo sat
for long periods in his room planning his first move against the
Saxons. More men would soon come to him, of this he was sure.
But to hold a company of any size together he knew that he
needed not only the friendship of the settlers, but a supply of
stores and services from them. What the Saxons needed they
took by force. That way could never be his. He had to find some
shift by which, swiftly and surely, he could bring the settlers to
his side and gain from them a confidence which would turn
them to him in true gratitude. For the first time, although his
band of brothers was small, he found himself with the beginnings of the weight of true command. Slowly he came to a decision, but once reaching it he threw all doubts from his mind
and moved to action.

Leaving Durstan and Lancelo with Timo and Marcos to guard
the villa, he took the rest of his men and they rode out, scantily
provisioned, on a morning of heavy, cold rain. They rode down
the left bank of the river, skirting the swamps and the low-
lying, winter flooded pastures and when darkness came they
turned their horses into the marshes and swam them across the
river. For the rest of the night they moved down the right bank
of the river. When dawn came they made camp in the shelter
of a tree-covered knoll. That evening as early dark fell they left
the knoll, each man knowing now the moves to be made.

The river Saxons, unlike those in the settled lands who preferred to build their huts apart in widely scattered communities,
lived in small groups by the water side where they moored their
boats for upriver raiding. At midnight, circling around such a
Saxon village, Arturo's men took it by surprise from the east.
Arturo rode at their head and with a great cry of 'Arturo comes!
Arturo comes!' he lowered his lance as they swept by the rough
log-built and reed-thatched huts and speared from the heart of

the watch fire a burning brand and lodged it in the roof of a hut. Behind him came Gelliga and his iron lance tip caught the throat of the startled, bemused Saxon on watch as he rose from sleep beside the fire. Behind Gelliga came the other comrades, spearing brands to fire the thatched hovels of the Saxons and then to wheel, following their captain, and with drawn swords cut down the Saxon men as they came tumbling, hands groping for seax and fighting axe, from their sleep into the flame-lit circle of huts. The victory was swift and bloody. No fighting man was spared. Most of them stood and fought, back to back, and died from lance point or sword's edge almost before the sleep which fogged their minds had time to clear. Spared only – and this long ordered by Arturo – were the women and children and the young boys whose chins had yet to know the roughness of a growing beard. These survivors were marshalled to the river bank where the raiding boats were drawn up. There were seven boats and four were put to the flames. Into the others were hustled the women and children and two old men. Before these were pushed out on to the dark bosom of the racing stream Arturo spoke to one of the old men who, like many of them, understood his tongue and said, 'Know well that I am Arturo and hold my words firm in your memory. This night has begun the cleansing of the valleys of all your kind. Go down the great Tamesis and to all your race give warning that, under the gods, I, Arturo, begin now the purging of the upper river lands . . .'

Listening, watching the fire-lit faces of the people in the boats, Gelliga smiled quietly to himself. He was content – for, this night, he and his comrades had tasted action which had long been denied them, and this night, too, Arturo had begun to make good his promise. But there was this about Arturo which all his comrades now understood and were content to accept – in all things Arturo saw the hands and the will of the gods and believed without any shadow of doubt that he had been chosen to foster their work and their dreams for this country. At times he could be stiff and pompous in his role, but at no time could any man watching and listening to him fail to mark the sincerity of his conviction. Such men, Gelliga knew, were the stuff of great commanders, and those who followed them, as he and his comrades followed Arturo, knew well that behind the high words lay the iron will which took men into battle ready to give their lives for him and his god-touched passion. He looked across at Netio, his hawk-face wet with sweat, the blaze from the burning huts shadowing the great scar on his cheek, his blooded sword resting across his knees and there was no surprise in him as the warrior gave him the winking flick of an eyelid and his tongue ran slowly along the underside of his top lip. Aye, he thought, they had found a man who would give them all the battle and bloodshed so long denied them by Count Ambrosius. One thing was certain now, there were many men who would, if this were a true beginning, come eagerly to Arturo. This night, gods or no gods, Arturo had committed himself to a dream which would either bring him to quick death or to lasting life in the memory of all men; and despite himself the bard in Gelliga jostled aside the warrior and he knew that before they reached the villa a song would have been born in him, polished and repolished like a sword blade, and be sung without reproof from Arturo around the camp fires of his comrades...

They watched the three boats move downstream and slide from the light of the leaping flames into the murky curtain of night. Then they searched the houses and grain pits for all they could bundle and carry. They took plunder of bronze and silver armbands, and brooches and torques. They stripped the dead of their weapons but touched none of their clothes for the Saxon men with no love of cleanliness stank like polecats. Then in darkness they made their way up river. They swam their steeds across it at dawn, laden like pedlars and baggage men.

At midday they rode up the slope of a wide valley through which ran a narrow tributary of the Tamesis. Just below the crest a poor stockade of thorns and loosely piled turves enclosed a group of huts. Seeing them coming the villagers ran to the ridge crest and there halted to watch them.

Arturo, his men following, rode into the stockade and there unloaded the stores and plunder which they had taken from the Saxons. As they did so an old man came limping from one of the huts and approached Arturo. He was dressed in patched skins and loose woollen trews.

Greeting him, Arturo said, 'You come without fear, unlike the rest of your kind. Look at us, do we seem like Saxon robbers to you?'

The man shook his head. 'No, my lord. But know that had I the full use of my old legs I would have run too. It is not only by the Saxon kind that we are plundered and robbed and killed. In these parts there are men of our own race who do the same.'

'The times are changing. Know now, that all the valleys of the river from here to the high wolds are the domain of Captain Arturo who now speaks to you. These last days we have taken war to the Saxons and this is our booty –' he nodded at the corn sacks and baskets and the piled Saxon plunder and weapons, '– which we now give to you and your people. In return we ask for nothing which you cannot find a willingness in your hearts to give. We are to be found at the villa of the three nymphs.'

Without waiting for the old man to reply, Arturo wheeled his horse and led his companions from the village. Riding at his side Gelliga said, 'No forced levies, no pressed labour – they will think us witless, my captain. We should at least have taken a pannier of seed corn.'

Arturo shook his head. 'No. We are not as Saxon robbers, or some thieving band of cut-throats who have forgotten their own race. The gods will touch their hearts with the finger of faith to rouse them to new hope and true generosity.'

Whether indeed the gods did this or, more likely, the villagers acted from a policy of caution scantily endowed with good will, the upshot was that four days later a pony-drawn cart on wooden runners came up the snow-covered valley to the villa attended by two youths whose curiosity showed clearly through their fears. In the cart were two earthenware pots full of flour, a basket of flat bread cakes, two skins of beer and half a deer carcass.

After Arturo had thanked them the two youths stood awkwardly by the cart without making move to leave the villa yard. Seeing their hesitation to go, Arturo said, 'You would eat and drink before you go?'

One of the youths shook his head and then answered hesitantly, 'No, my lord ... We are to say that pony and cart are yours and ... and, we go with it. To stay here and serve you.'

For a moment Arturo said nothing but he knew that in the most wretched of men there was always one heart spot which the gods could touch. For slaves he had no use since forced labour was the seeding ground of treachery. But a willing man was without price. Now, smiling at the two, he said, 'You look alike.'

'We are brothers, my lord. We will stay and work for you ... and ...' the taller of the two who was speaking, hesitated and then smiled, 'and perhaps one day you will arm and horse us to fight against the sea people.'

'For which we are impatient, my lord,' said the other with a sudden grimness, 'for the Saxons killed our father and carried away our sister.'

His face forced to severity to hide the sudden joy in him, Arturo said commandingly, 'So be it. Work hard and drill hard and the day will come soon.'

From then on through the slowly lengthening days until the first primroses began to push pale buds from their green leaf rosettes and the rooks in the leafless trees began to bicker and fight over their winter-ruined nesting sites and the trout rested thin with spawning in the valley stream, Arturo and his companions carried war against the river Saxons.

They struck in short fierce raids mostly by night. When they attacked a Saxon village by day it was always just as the light was going and the men were settling to their eating and drinking and the cooking fires flamed high and made the flinging of fire brands on to the hut roofs easy. Old men and women and children they spared but all able-bodied men were killed; and it must be said of them that the Saxons, once they knew there was no escape, stood and fought, facing the companions, ready to go to Woden's hall without the coward scar of a sword or lance thrust in the back.

Of his own men Arturo lost two. Lacto of Calcaria in the country of the Parisi was killed by the thrust of a scramaseax into his groin, and Tarius of the Brigantes, the oldest of his companions, had his horse ham-stringed, to be stabbed to death as earthbound he tried to fight off his enemy. But against these losses there came fresh cavalry men to join them for innocent-looking, moon-faced Lancelo returned secretly to his family home in Corinium and there recruited willing men from the Sabrina Wing and brought them through the high wolds and forests to the villa.

Since the death of a comrade was to Arturo like the death of a brother, he sought all ways to protect them. He took from the Saxon war booty their small round shields which were easier to handle than the large, cumbersome shields that Ambrosius's men were drilled to use. The Saxons facing mounted men came in fast and ducked the lance to make a great stabbing thrust at the rider's groin; but the small buckler could be quickly dropped to turn away the upward jab and leave the comrade free to ride the man down. Later, too, the lances were discarded. In a set battle charge they would have their use, but in quick night-raiding they were more dangerous nuisance than they were worth. Sword and small round shield were enough. Fortunately, too, the Saxons made no attempt to combine their scattered forces. The men of one village or marsh settlement gave no trust to the men from other communities. They lived in suspicion towards one another and, because of this, never once assembled in force to meet Arturo and his men.

In two months Arturo had cleared five miles of the upper river valley and the closely adjoining lands. Tribute came now willingly from the British villages and farms that knew a peace and safety long absent. In far Glevum Count Ambrosius had heard of Arturo's exploits and for a while had considered sending two troops of cavalry against him but had discarded the idea since he feared the men might desert from him and join Arturo and their comrades who had already gone to his side. At the moment Arturo was no more to him than the bite of a flea in his sleeping blanket. When the fine weather returned he promised himself that he would move against him. Now was not the moment to risk the ridicule of an open desertion of a troop of cavalry to the outlawed son of the chief of the tribe of the Enduring Crow. Already enough of his men had gone over to Arturo to make him quick with anger when his name was mentioned.

So it was that as spring broke over the land, Arturo could look with pride at the force he commanded at the villa of the three nymphs. He had enough men for a full troop of horse and, beyond fighting men, there were another dozen who worked and serviced the villa and the warriors. The villa itself was fast being repaired and warmed again to human life. The stables had been extended for the horses and a smithy set up for the repair of tools and arms, worked by a friend of Marcos from Cunetio who had sought him out. A wandering Christian monk, too, called Pasco – who would give no details of his life, though he spoke their tongue with the heavy brogue of a Scottus – had settled with them unasked and finally welcomed because of his skill with wounds and ills and his reluctance to preach or proselytize.

Among the comrades there were occasional small quarrels and jealousies but none so troubling that they went beyond the usual barrack life jealousies and mead or beer stirred sudden resentments at imagined slights. One bond held them all firmly together, their love and admiration for Arturo. Though this was not so reverent that it stopped the quick wink or sly grin when their captain, in the exultation following a successful raid, or some felicitous turn of events which brought them food or services when sorely needed, spoke pompously of the great shield of the gods which covered them in battle and the all-seeing eyes of the deities which watched over them zealously each day. Smile though they might, and joke amongst themselves at their captain, there was none who would deny that Arturo's sure knowledge of being god-touched and god-directed was not as real to him as the sword he carried and the horse he rode. Unmarked by them, legend was slowly growing about him and the full truth behind his own words escaped even Gelliga when at night in the long eating hall, full of food and flushed with drink, he would sing:

> The knife has gone into the meat
> And the good wine fills the horn
> In Arturo's hall . . .
> Here is food for your hound
> And corn for your horse
> In Atruro's hall . . .
> But none there shall enter unless he be
> Swift with a sword and comrade to all

But with the passing of the evening and the drink Gelliga's and the other comrades' moods would change and then he sung of the yearning that not even battle and the chance of death waiting at the opening door of each day could smother.

> Take my true greeting to the girl of thick tresses
> The sweetheart I lay with in the glen of green willows . . .

It was of this sentiment that Pasco, the priest, spoke to Arturo one morning when the land lay iron-bound in hard frost and the horses were stayed from exercise by the iciness of the ground.

He said, 'You dream a dream, my son, for this country which I, too, hold dear in my heart. But that dream must be made real by men of human clay. Your comrades are cloistered here without the full and fulfilling submission to God's love alone which men of my kind know. Already now when the people around send tribute there are women who find reason to walk with the carts. As fox fight over vixens in the spring and the gentle doves grow fierce in courtship so stirs the same passion in the hearts of men.' He smiled, rubbed the tip of his nose, his eyes quizzical, and went on, 'The gods you worship may have made you in a different mould from your comrades – though I doubt it. You order things well here. Now you must order this, not as Count Ambrosius does with loose camp followers at Corinium, nor as your own Prince Gerontius with the stews of Isca. You are the captain of a brotherhood – but not a brotherhood of monks.'

Acknowledging the wisdom of Pasco's words Arturo talked the matter over with Durstan and Gelliga. Each week now two or three men filtered through the valleys and woods to the villa from Ambrosius's forces. Some brought horse and weapons, and some came on foot with nought but a dagger in their belts. But with these reinforcements, all of them well-trained, there were now more men than mounts. So, since for the time being the immediate river lands had been almost rid of Saxon bands, and Arturo was now nourishing a dream of action which would carry his name far beyond the domains of Gerontius and Count Ambrosius, he announced to his comrades that some of those who came from far lands could return to their people to visit sweethearts and wives. They would be chosen by the drawing of lots so that the main force of the brotherhood was not depleted beyond the number of horses they owned. For those whose homes lay around the westward side of the Sabrina basin permission was given for their womenfolk to visit the villa for limited periods. Quarters would be set up in the west wing of the villa, but at the first sign of discord or quarrelling then all the women would be banished.

Over all these concessions Arturo laid one adamant condition. All men would be back by the feast of Beltine, which was the first day of the month of Damara, the goddess of fertility and growth. At the end of this month – though Arturo kept this secret between himself and his two closest comrades, Durstan and Gelliga – he meant to move from the villa for this was a time when he guessed that Count Ambrosius might be tempted to strike at him. But more to his concern it was also the time when he meant to make his own move which would send his name echoing widely over the country and bring even more men to his side.

Among those who were unlucky in the first drawing of lots was Lancelo. But one of the comrades, who had neither wife nor sweetheart, nor immediate wish for either, had set his lot up for bid and Lancelo had gained it in exchange for a pair of old but serviceable bronze grieves taken as plunder in a Saxon raid.

Seven days later Lancelo rode out of the forest and into the

courtyard of the villa. There were only two men in the courtyard at that moment for the rest were either at their work or
exercising and drilling their mounts in the lower valley pasture.
One of the men was Arturo who sat in the sunlight on the edge
of the fountain of the nymphs with old, grey-muzzled Anga at
his feet.

Lancelo rode up to him and dismounted. He saluted Arturo
and said, his face grave, 'I bring no sweetheart or wife, my captain. Sweetheart I had, but on my second night in Corinium she
betrayed me to Count Ambrosius's men. But one of the Sabrina
men, an old friend, sent me warning in time so that we were
able to escape.'

'We?'

'My family, my captain. Had I left them they would have been
butchered by the troopers in their anger at my escape. I ask your
permission for them to stay here until such time as they can
move on to a fresh place of safety.'

'Where are they now?'

'They wait in the wood for a signal from me.'

'Then make it, good Lancelo.'

Lancelo's face beamed with pleasure. He put two fingers to
his mouth and blew a piercing whistle. A few moments later an
elderly man rode out of the wood on a small pony. He was
small, bare-headed, and almost bald and wrapped in a great
square cloak of sewn furs. Across the withers of his mount hung
two bulky, awkward packs of stained and patched cloth At his
side on another pony rode a woman wearing a cloak and cowl
of red wool and her mount carried two slung panniers of plaited
withy branches.

They rode up to Arturo and as they halted the woman pushed
the folds of her cowl free of her face and a pair of clear blue
eyes regarded Arturo solemnly. In that instant Arturo knew
with a certainty that this moment was god-touched. At three
different times in his life he had looked into those eyes, and
now, this time, he knew that here was no capricious play of
time and chance but the deliberate hands of the gods as they
moved their pieces on the playing board of his destiny. For

reasons he gave not a straw since all would be revealed to him in full time by the gods. Although he would have returned the smile he kept his face calm and turned to the man.

Smiling now, he said, 'I did not know that the father of Lancelo was Ansold the armourer and smith for here we ask nothing of a man's past or family so long as he brings loyalty and a ready sword. But you, good Ansold, are more than welcome. *Aie* ... and would be even without your hammers and tongs.' He nodded to one of the packs from which protruded the handle of a long pair of forging grips.

Ansold blinked happily and rubbed a worn, charcoal-grained hand across his chin, saying, 'Your welcome warms my heart, Captain Arturo, for the truth is that, although the lying will be harder here than at Corinium, I would rather serve you than Count Ambrosius who pays poor for good work and that only after long waiting.'

Pushing the cloak cowl free of her dark hair, Daria, straight-faced except for a slight curl at the corners of her berry-red lips, said, 'And what welcome does my lord Arturo give me?'

Arturo, smiling, speaking without thought as though the words flowed from elsewhere through him to her, said, 'You have no need of welcome for my heart has given it before to you. Once on the rain-cloaked moors when you would have taken a dagger to me. Again with the fleeting flash of your eyes in the Corinium market place and then lastly bowered with a scolding frown at my rashness in showing my tribal mark in old Paulus's workshed. And now – although you speak teasingly – I know there is a true kindness to me in your heart since the faces of your father and Lancelo tell me that they have never known until this moment that we had met before. Though I count that caution not needed.'

Daria laughed and shook her head. 'Then you count wrong. Give my good father too much mead and in some moments his tongue grows too loose. As for Lancelo I wanted for him no more favour than rested in his own body and skills. Nor now do any of us ask for undue favours. So long as we are here we are at your commands, knowing that they will always be just.'

Before Arturo could reply, Ansold said gruffly, 'She is right about the mead loosening my tongue. But smithying is hot work and hard and a man's throat gets parched.'

When Lancelo led them away to find quarters for them, Arturo went back to the fountain and sat, one hand teasing at Anga's ears. The gods had sent him a master swordmaker ... a man who could wander the breadth and length of the land and always find a welcome in any camp. And the gods had sent him Daria. In so doing there was no doubt in him that they moved him and the dark-haired, blue-eyed young woman in some pattern of destiny not given yet to the eyes or mind of man to know.

A Gift from the Gods

The winter, which had been hard, spent its strength at last and spring began swiftly to spread its coloured mantle over the land. The woods grew green and primroses and white and purple violets studded the mossy alder thickets along the valley stream and the gold of daffodil blooms was spread like largesse over the meadow banks. Blackbirds and thrushes sat their early clutches in the thorn tangles and the tall tree tops were noisy with the clamour of rook colonies. Buzzard pairs moved as they climbed in lazy spirals on the rising warm air currents and, as the sun rose higher each day, adders and grass snakes stirred from their winter sluggishness and sought their basking places on the warm-faced rocks and ledges of the old quarry behind the villa. Man, beast and bird . . . all living things began to move to the rituals of spring, to the divine dance of courtship, mating and increase which each year the gods decreed.

Although the affairs and the ordering of his small but growing command filled much of his days, there were times when Arturo, quick with the restlessness of the season, found himself turning away from the ordering of men and horses, from drills and cavalry exercises, to forsake the villa and walk by himself in the surrounding woods. Here, he found his mind full with two things. The first was the pattern of his own destiny which he was convinced now was god-ordained and to be of great moment – though that only if he himself could through his own skills, courage and imagination prove always worthy of the gods' favour. Sitting alone in a wood clearing he would become lost in a dream of the campaign which he meant to start as soon as the first days of summer came. Ill-provided and rash he knew it had to be, but there was no doubt in him that the gods would approve his daring. With a handful of men he would do what Gerontius with all his forces had talked long of doing but still had not found the will to effect. Active though his mind was with this dream, there were the times when its place was usurped by his second passion. From thoughts of coming renown and glory, he found himself slipping into thoughts of Daria.

Again and again the gods had put her in his path. He was in love with her and knew that she, for all her challenging and teasing spirit, looked with more than ordinary kindness on him. Yet one doubt tangled his thinking about her. Through her the gods might be tempting and testing him. Many men in history had been drawn from the path of greatness by their love for a woman; men who, as they stood poised on the edge of some great matter, as he did now, had by passion allowed themselves to be drawn away from the divine love of country to lose their favour with the gods who so tempted them to prove their worth. Brooding over this he knew himself to be poised on the blade edge of choice, to be left alone in his dilemma to read the mind of the gods, and to read it rightly or suffer. Because of this uncertainty in him he had more and more in the past weeks avoided the company of Daria.

Sitting late one afternoon in a small glade above the villa, idly stripping the young bark from a hazel wand with his thumbnail and frowning to himself as he teased his mind with the dilemma which Daria posed for him, he saw her come out of the trees on the far side of the glade and walk towards him. She sat down close to him. He gave her no greeting and kept his eyes from her.

Smiling, Daria said, 'There was a time when you had no lack of words boastful or bard-like to greet me. *Aie* . . . even in my first weeks here. Does the beginning of greatness which all your men claim for you begin to move you away from ordinary courtesies?'

Throwing the hazel wand from him, Arturo said, 'You are right to chide me. But do not think because I lack words that there is no greeting in my heart. You know what is in my heart as I know what is in yours. The gods have brought us together, and for purpose.'

'But you cannot read that purpose, is that it?'

'Can you?'

'I do not try.'

'But I must.'

'Why?' She leaned forward and cradled her brown arms around her knees and her dark hair fell about her cheeks.

'That I cannot tell you.'

'Then I can give you no help. But when the feast of Beltine is over and the women go from here I shall go with them. There is one who has offered me a place with her people.'

'Your father goes with you?'

'I cannot speak for him. Nor he for himself until the moment comes. I think that you, too, are much like him. You do not know what you will do until the moment comes. But when it does you find good reason for your actions. It is clear to me that you do not know your mind or your body's actions until you stand on the edge of unalterable circumstances. Like a hare disturbed from its form you bound away and even when you are moving you do not know why you have taken your line.'

Despite himself Arturo smiled, and said, 'What need to know till then – since the gods will have put it in my mind?'

'The gods control us, true. But not every moment of the day. There are times when they are too full of their own affairs.'

'For most men, yes. But not for me.'

To his surprise Daria threw back her head and laughed. 'Oh, Arturo . . .! You have such faith in the gods. And true – there is that about you which speaks of greatness. Your men mark it and respect it. But the gods cannot be with any man for every minute of his life. Would you have them decide for you whether to eat fish or meat, to take this path or that, to sing one song or another?'

'The gods are always with me when the moment is of great importance. Since no man would talk to me as you do, then I will talk to you as no man would to a woman without shaming himself. I love you and would make you my wife – but this I

394

cannot do unless I know it is in the will of the gods that it should happen.'

For a moment or two Daria was silent. Then in a low, angry voice she said, 'My lord Arturo, you forget one thing. Gods or no gods, when a woman takes a man for husband it is a matter of her will, and hers alone.' Then standing up, her dark eyes narrowed, her cheeks flushed with emotion, she went on, her voice almost contemptuous, 'I am no woman to wait on the will of the gods for a husband. *Aie* . . . I would have been wife to you if you had asked me frankly out of your own true love for me. But now I am as far out of your reach to master and to cherish as is the wild white mare that roams these woods!'

She turned from him and walked away through the trees and Arturo, watching her go, was suddenly filled with a great elation and joy which almost made him call out to bring her back for he knew that through her the gods had spoken and given him the sign he needed.

For the next two weeks he spent much of his time away from the villa camp. He went on foot into the woods, by day and by night, and the only company he had was Anga. He searched the valleys and dales, the remote clearings made by long-dead charcoal burners, the places at streams and pools where deer, boar, fox and other forest animals came to drink. On the high meadows and swampy river pastures he marked the hoof marks and the cropped patches of sweet new grass that told of the passing of the white mare. He followed the trails which she used, found the resting places where she couched at night, and the bare sand patches among the wild heath lands where she rolled in the dust, and from fresh and stale dung droppings he began to have a clear picture of her movements about the country around the villa. Sometimes he heard the distant thud of her galloping as she scented him and Anga and hurried away. Once he saw her break free from a copse of young beech trees and canter away from him down a valley side, her long tail and full mane floating in the wind of her passage like silk, the sun turning her white coat to moving, polished ivory and her beauty made him catch his breath with its wonder. A joy rose in him at the sight of her which was known only to true horse-masters, to men like Master Ricat, himself, and most of his companions, such joy that there were those who would murder and rob without pause for thought in order to possess such a beast. She was a fit steed for a great commander and she was god-marked to be his. When the first days of summer came he would ride out on her at the head of his company. But before that he would come astride her, her master, into the villa courtyard and Daria seeing him would need no words to know his mind, and to know that he came to claim her as wife, the wife the gods had ordained for him.

Knowing now the ways of her coming and going to places of grazing and drinking he waited three nights running for the breaking of dawn when she would move from her couching place to find food or water. Above a narrow forest track he lay stretched out on a stout overhanging oak branch, a rope halter thrust inside his tunic, and Anga hidden at his command in a thicket a little way ahead of the oak at the track side. For two dawns the mare kept away from the track, but on the third as the sun lipped the eastern sky and the birds began to greet the morning with song, the mare came down the track, trotting gently and tossing her noble head so that her mane was wide flung like a floating web. When she was almost under his branch Arturo spoke his will silently to Anga with the art which belonged to all men of the tribe of the Enduring Crow.

Anga came out of the thicket and stood in the trackway. The mare shied a little and halted. Then seeing that she faced no bear or wolf she moved forward and stamped her right foreleg on the ground. At this moment Arturo rolled from his branch, twisted his body, and dropped squarely on to her back. As she began to rear with fear and surprise under him, he jerked the halter from his tunic, slipped it over her head and held its loop in either hand as he clamped his legs and thighs iron hard to her sides.

From that moment Arturo was translated into a world which held only himself and the wild movement of the white mare. There was no thought in him except to follow the will of the gods and make himself master of the white horse, and no art in him except the savage skill of muscled purpose which inhabited legs and knees and thighs and hands to make him one with the racing, plunging, rearing animal beneath him. Neighing with anger and panic the mare, blind to open track or glade, raced through the forest. Thorn and branch ripped at Arturo's hands and face and raked great swatches of cloth from his clothes, and the blood from his cuts and wounds dripped and ran from him to stain the white hide of the mare. Time and place lost their meaning. He lived in a world of savage motion as the mare sought to unseat him. She came out of the forest, bursting through a great bank of gorse thicket like a wind devil to set the new bloom scattered high in a golden drift. She thundered down a valley side and, as though with deliberate malice and intent, raced with long neck outstretched under the low branches of an old yew to sweep him from her back so that Arturo, laid low across her back, his face pressed close into the sweet horse smell of her wild mane, felt the slash of scaly branches rip and tear the cloth of his tunic's back. They went, man and horse like one beast, through copse and pasture, hooves throwing sand clouds high across wild heathland, and the mare's wild neighing filling the bright morning air. He knew the great gathering and surge of her muscles as she jumped brake and stream and when she reared and plunged and swung round on her hind legs the world spun before him in a mist of green and blue chaos. Then, as no sign came of let or stop to the mare's wild panic and anger, there slowly crept over Arturo the black humiliation of knowing that his strength could never outmatch hers. His body was bruised and battered and his hands and thighs grew weaker. He found fresh anger and determination to fight his growing weakness, but only for a while. Silently within himself he cried out to the gods to be with him, but all that rested with him as the mare raced plunging and kicking beneath him was now the certain knowledge that she would master him. The gods were with her and not with him.

The moment of defeat came when the mare galloping wildly through a forest clearing which held a sedge-ringed pool suddenly from full pace, her hooves scoring great marks in the soft ground, pulled up to a violent halt such as Arturo had never known horse to make before. His body slid forward with its own momentum, but before he could fall the mare reared suddenly to full height and, as her forelegs pawed and threshed the air, twisted herself in violent pirouette and flung Arturo from her.

As he fell, and in the few moments before his head struck the ground to send him into oblivion, Arturo knew that the gods had truly deserted him. They had given him the sign and he had gone gladly to the task to prove himself – and he had failed.

He lay on the ground close to the pool's edge, face and hands bloodied and cut, his clothes ripped, and he was lost to the world. The old hound, Anga, long left behind, came loping into the clearing and sat near him, panting with exhaustion, his great tongue lapping free over his jaws, and whined when Arturo made no move. Time passed and the moorfowl which had taken cover in the new sedge growth came out on to the waters of the pool. Chiff-chaffs sang in the tall trees. Distantly a cuckoo called from the forest depths, and a rust-red hare, moving into the clearing, saw Anga, leaped high and raced back into the trees. Anga moved closer to Arturo, sniffed at his face, and then settled beside him and snapped at a fly which teased his muzzle. The sun climbed higher, clearing the tree tops, and a shaft of light began to warm Arturo's face. He groaned and moved, came slowly back to his senses and knew only two things, a great aching in all his limbs and his mouth parched raw with thirst.

Slowly he sat up and, seeing the pool, crawled towards it on all fours and like a dog lowered his head and lapped at the water. With the easing of his thirst memory came back to him. He sat back on the grass and, resting his aching head in his hands, knew that he was truly forsaken of the gods. They had seen his pride and arrogance and had set him to a task which would break and humble him For a moment or two he was near to weeping but before his manliness could be breached a new pride suddenly flared in him, starting him to anger and the fire of bitter challenge. This country, his country, torn and parcelled by warring tribes and ravaging Picts and Scotti, knowing no true leader or destiny except the greed and self-seeking of petty princelings like Gerontius, Ambrosius and the discredited, ageing Vortigern, was at the mercy of the growing strength and arrogance of the Saxon Hengist. His own proud boast which had sustained him for so long that Count Ambrosius should one day sue for his help suddenly meant nothing to him. In the mire of his humiliation, a new and fuller cause was born in his heart. Gods or no gods, from this moment he was dedicated to the cause and the great matter of Britain and would follow it and master it and all his country's enemies so that as the name of the great warring Caesar could never die from men's minds nor should his. Forsake him the gods might, but there was that in him which forced him to scorn their desertion.

He pulled himself to his feet and turned away from the pool but, as he raised his eyes across the glade, he saw that which was a humble and a wild joy in him and a never to be forgotten sign. Henceforth he could pursue his dream held up always by the truth which a few moments before he had named in anger to be a lie. The gods had tried and tested him, humbled him in misery, but from that misery they had sparked a fire to kindle in him the life flame of his destiny. Never again would he deny them for clear against the bright green of new forest leaf stood their sign of favour. Cropping peacefully at the lush spring grass was the white mare, her briar and thorn-raked hide flecked with her own and his blood, the halter hanging slack from her lowered neck, and the long white tail switching across her quarters to break the tease and bite of worrying flies.

Sure of himself, Arturo walked slowly across to the horse and the mare stopped cropping, raised her head and looked at him from her dark-pooled eyes and showed no sign of fear or flight. He stood by her, put out a hand and stroked her muzzle, and she took his touch with a gentle blowing of breath through her nostrils. He spoke to her gently then and called her white one, called her queen of all horses, breathed and crooned the low love talk of a horse-master and ran his hand along the proud line of her neck and promised her cherishing and honour for all the days of her life.

He took her halter and led the white one back through the forest paths to the villa. He could have mounted and ridden her but would not on this day for he knew her pride was like his own. They came together down the slope to the villa of the three nymphs. And when his people and his comrades came running and hurrying to gather about him, the mare stood quietly and without fear and Arturo knew with an enduring and passionate truth that he and the white one were god-fingered.

He said to the crowd about him, 'She is the White One, the Shining One, and wherever we ride against the enemies of this country she shall be known and seen as the White Horse of Arto and all the shields that follow shall be marked with her emblem and all our scarf and helmet colours shall be the white of her shining hide and the crimson of her blood and mine which dapple it now.'

Then, from the crowd, he called a small boy who had come with one of the visiting families and he handed the loose halter end to him and said proudly, 'Lead her to the stables and remember always that after Arturo you were the first to have her gentle obedience.'

The boy led the White One away and she followed without let, stepping like a queen along the lane which the crowd fell back to make for her passage. As she went Arturo turned away from his people and walked across the yard to the ruined steps which led up to the colonnaded open way which ran across the face of the west wing of the villa where Daria stood, the morning breeze flicking free the tendrils of her dark hair and moulding the soft wool of her blue gown about her tall, full body.

He took her right hand and said humbly, 'You know what is in my heart, and I know what is in yours. Although I have mastered the White One, to you I say I would take you for wife and between us for all our days there shall only be cherishing.'

Daria was silent for a while. Then, raising a hand and brushing her dark hair from her face she said, smiling, 'You do me honour, my lord Arturo, in the asking. *Aie* . . I will gladly and lovingly be wife for you. But though we shall lie in the long grass and listen to the golden birds sing and drink the new wine, those times will be few and far spaced for I know that there will be often the loneliness of longing for you when the White One takes you away. And now –' she smiled broadly, mocking and teasing him with her eyes, '– you must do grace to my father and go ask him for leave to make me your bride. I doubt that he will refuse you, but should he then make him a gift of a jar of beer and ask again when he has drunk it.'

Inbar of the tribe of the Enduring Crow had been well drilled by the captain of the guard on how he should behave before Count Ambrosius. Stiffly drawn up to his full height he stood before the low wooden table at which the Count sat on a folding stool and waited for the man to raise his head to mark his awareness of his presence. All he could see at the moment was a bald head with fluffy wings of greying hair over the ears bowed low over a sheet of new parchment covered with writing. On a bed against the far wall of the room lay an old but well polished cuirass, a red cloak, and a horse-haired plumed bronze helmet as old as the cuirass. Count Ambrosius, all knew, kept to the old Roman ways and ordered his army so. The word from some was that he was a fool who lived in a dream, but there were many more who knew the real truth of the commander. It was that truth of the man which Inbar was hoping to use for his own advantage now. *Aie* ... and many a long week it had taken him to get this audience.

After a while (and Inbar, whose judgement of men was shrewd, gauged the waiting imposed on him to be deliberate) the Count pushed the parchment to one side and raised his head. As their eyes met Inbar lifted his right hand in a military salute but said nothing, remembering the words of the guard officer who had been one of the last he had bribed to get this interview. A pair of shrewd, narrow-lidded, pale blue eyes fixed themselves steadily on him and a bare arm was raised to jerk the folds of a white toga to comfort about the thin shoulders. A small, hard man, thought Inbar, with no comfort in him for others and need for none himself ... a shadow Roman, dreaming of the past, but a weasel of a man, swift and deadly. And on that he was placing his hopes.

'Name yourself and your business.' The voice was low but gritty like the rub of sandstone on sandstone.

Inbar said, 'I am Inbar of the tribe of the Enduring Crow, cousin to Baradoc its chief, and uncle to Arturo, the son of Baradoc.'

At the mention of Arturo's name Ambrosius's lips thinned and from his hands which he held locked together as his elbows rested on the table came the crack of his knuckles as his fingers tightened. He said, 'I have heard of you from Prince Gerontius and know you to be a dead man for shaming the wife of Baradoc.'

'Shame there was none, my lord, for the woman would have been willing and I would have made her my wife. Dead I should be, but am not for the gods were on my side when I took the long run and the death drop. Out of their bounty I hit the water cleanly feet first, sank deep and then swam underwater to the cover of the cliff foot where that night my wife came –'

'Yes, yes, the gods were with you, but spare me the rest and come quickly to your matter with me.'

'Arturo has taken men and horses from you, my lord, and his company grows.'

'You tell me what I already know, man. Come to your point.'

'I would kill Arturo for you.'

Ambrosius raised his head and the cold blue eyes widened in surprise. With an impatient wave of his hand he said, 'What need to come to me and waste my time? Any man is free to kill Arturo for he is outlawed and then the blood-price will be paid.'

'So it would seem, my lord. But beyond the seeming is now the truth that there is not a man in this land who would kill Arturo for a blood-price that he could not live long to enjoy. The blood-price must be claimed openly before you or the noble Prince Gerontius and proof given of the deed. Such openness would mark a man for life, but that life would be short for there are those among his companions who would make it so.'

Count Ambrosius was silent for a while, the thin fingers of one hand fidgeting with the neck yoke of his toga. Then quietly he said, 'It is true that must be the manner of the paying of the blood-price. It is true, too, that I would have him dead. At the moment he is a gadfly but others begin to gather with him. So, what is in the mind of Inbar of the Enduring Crow?'

'Much, my lord, which I would wish to rest secretly between us. Alone, unmarked, and unknown to any, I will kill Arturo for you. As return I ask little. First I would have a small command in your army for I am tired of wandering like a lone wolf. After that, and I can be patient over the years, I ask that when his father Baradoc dies you should through your friendship with Prince Gerontius have me named as Chief of the tribe of the Enduring Crow.'

'Baradoc's death would not clear the road for you. He has another son by the Roman woman Gratia he married, and could have others.'

'No, my lord. From my own wife who still lives with the tribe I know that the woman Tia is now barren since the birth of a fourth child, a girl-child.'

Ambrosius gave a thin smile. 'And it is to your wife – since you are forbidden to go west of Isca – that you would look for the end of the second son ... a wasting disease, a destroying fever? So, so, and if needs be – for barrenness is no more a certainty in a woman than her affections – she would see that no future man-child lived long?'

'Yes, my lord.'

Count Ambrosius lowered his head on one hand and with the other fingered the edges of the parchment on the table. Arturo and his companions were an annoyance to him. He was a young man of spirit and wild dreams and loud boasts with thirty or forty men at the most (but *his* men and *his* horses). For a moment or two he was on the point of dismissing Inbar. He had greater worries on his mind than Arturo. Vortigern, sunk in senile debauchery in Demetae, had sent no levies this spring and Prince Gerontius, growing in power and ambition, but unwilling yet to move, had cut his levy heavily. The great sickness over the eastern lands was passing, though slowly; and wily Hengist, who had once fought as a Roman auxiliary, was fast drawing fresh men from across the northern sea and would soon begin to move, for no Saxon warrior sat content in camp for long. Warfare and plunder was their only contentment. Feasting, fighting and looting was barbarian joy. Against all this, while he sat there, lacking men still to make his move, waiting on promises, Arturo surely was a single gadfly. He was at the point of dismissing Inbar when the thought quickened in him that even the great Caesars and conquerors were ever at the mercy of time and chance. The sting of a single gadfly could make a mount rear or stumble and a noble captain fall to his death.

Raising his head he said curtly. 'Let it be as you promise, and it shall be as you wish.'

'I thank you, my lord.'

As Inbar went out through the ante-room the captain of the guard said, 'How was the old lizard?'

Inbar smiled and said, 'In the mood for taking flies.' He reached into his belt pouch and handed the man a worn and clipped silver piece of the reign of the Emperor Gratian which had been in the baggage of a trader whose throat he had cut for loot on the Salinae-Glevum road coming south. So, too, would he cut the throat of young Arturo, striking suddenly and without warning.

During the handful of days which led up to the feast of Beltine which was on the first day of the month dedicated by the Romans to Maia, the goddess of growth and fertility, Arturo lived in two worlds. There was the world of his love for Daria and hers for him, and the world of the passion in him to set out on his first campaign – though he knew in his heart that with the forces at his command it must needs be more a demonstration of audacity to make his name widely known and bring more men to his side than one of military worth.

In the world of men and horses he passed most of his time, and this without chiding from Daria for she knew the temper of the man she was marrying and secretly approved it. The companions now numbered nearly fifty, all of them mounted. With them were the retainers and craftsmen and workers at the villa who attended the crops, the stores, the cattle, the repair and making of weapons and the care and fashioning of all the horse gear. At first Arturo was here there and everywhere, attending and supervising to all he could, but as time went by he gave way to the common-sense of leaving many things in the hands of his two chief companions, Durstan and red-bearded Gelliga. He learnt fast that the art of command was to have eyes and ears for everything and everyone, but to turn from wearying himself and worrying his troop leaders by his unnecessary presence and concern at activities and with matters which they could handle as well as himself.

The other world was the one into which he rode most afternoons with Daria on a hide saddle before him and old Anga trotting at the heels of the White One. They went to a withy bower on the far fringe of the water meadow below the forest which the companions had made for them. There they lay in the long grass, and drank, not new wine, but the fresh stream water, yet they listened truly to the golden birds sing, for the hawthorn thickets on the forest edge were full of yellow-hammers in full song. It was there that they talked and caressed one another and between the long sweetness of kisses learned those things of one another which makes the sturdy frame and sheltering roof to house the heart and strength of true love.

One afternoon Pasco the priest came to them and, sitting down on an old grass-covered anthill, spoke to them of marriage.

He said to Arturo, 'The lady Daria has told you that she is of the Christian faith?'

Arturo nodded. 'Yes, but not long since.'

Daria said, 'Why should I talk of something which, in good time, Pasco could talk of far better than me?'

Pasco said, 'It is logic – of a womanly kind. Which means, contrary to most people's thinking, that it is wise. So, my lord Arturo, you know that I cannot marry a follower and worshipper of Christos to one who worships all the heathen gods?'

Arturo nodded, unconcerned. 'Yes, I know that, but it seems to me that you threaten to close a gate against a young ram when he is already within the pen. I worship my country's gods and those of my race. Are not your Christos and his great father gods like other gods?'

'They are indeed, and more so than any other gods.'

'That is no uncommon thing among gods. Some are greater than others. So I am happy to worship your Christos and his father for they are gods and I worship all gods. How else can a man live in grace and under heavenly protection unless he gives homage to all gods? From my mother and my teachers I learned long ago that all the gods the Romans worshipped were but our gods with a different name. Great Bellenus was their Apollo. Our great Credne, who made the silver hand for the god Nodens, was their Vulcan, and so with all of them to the highest. Our all-powerful Dis was their Jove. A name is nothing. There must be as many names for the gods as there are races on this earth with different languages. Have no worry, good Pasco. You can marry me to the lady Daria with a clear mind since I will happily worship this Christos and his great father.'

Pasco rubbed his chin and sighed. He had much admiration for Arturo and knew the goodness and driving passion in him, though there was much about him which gave him doubt. To argue with him further was to invite a spreading of confusion and trouble. In truth he had some sympathy with Arturo's attitude for his own Christian beliefs were touched with paradox and schism which had brought his departure from his own land. The lady Daria would have Arturo for husband for she loved him. For that, if need arose – since her faith was not well-tempered – she would unhesitatingly declare herself no longer a Christian. It was better he gauged to keep the lamb in the fold than lose it forever to a young ram from a strange flock. And was it not true that Christos often chose to bring the heathen by strange paths to grace?

Seeing Daria's eyes attentive on him and her hand holding Arturo's in a union which his common-sense told him, since the season was spring and young blood was young blood, must soon be celebrated, he said, 'Then I will marry you. But there is one small rite of the Christian god you must make.'

Arturo smiled. '*Aie* ... I know of that, too. You would have me stand in the fountain of the three nymphs and duck me under in baptism? So be it. Cold the water may be, but what could be colder than a heart denied of its love? And know, too, good Pasco, that I shall take pride in being a follower of your Christos. Many of my men are such. Was it not the great Christian Bishop Germanus who gave our people the miraculous Alleluia Victory over the Saxon and Pictish forces of the young Hengist when he first came to these shores?'

So it was that, in a courtyard crowded with all his followers, Arturo – stripped to a loin cloth – was baptized in the great stone bowl of the fountain of the three nymphs. The water which he had expected to be ice-cold seemed warm to him and he gave thanks, as Pasco spoke his ritual words over him, to the goddess Coventina for her favour.

They were married and feasted and then taken in procession by torchlight to the bower in the water meadow, and all that night the forest and stream edges of the meadow were guarded by his companions to watch over their safety, and as the first slip of a late rising moon paled the sky the nightingales began to sing from the hazel beds. The next morning, when the two came out from the bower to face a morning lively with a fresh breeze from the south, Arturo was greeted by the sight of a tall lance fixed firmly in the turf. From it, its folds curling and uncurling in the wind, flew a red war banner which had emblazoned on its centre the device of a rearing white horse, mane and tail flaring as though the breeze itself were giving the animal life.

Daria said, 'This night you have had my bride's gift. This morning I give you my first gift as your wife. May the gods protect you whenever you go into battle with it.'

Arturo, putting his arm around her, his eyes fast on the waving banner said, 'If ever I bring dishonour to it or to you may all the gods desert me.'

*

407

Three days later in the early afternoon came the high warning call of the horn of the watchguard on duty at the southwestern edge of the camp lands. The call was three high-pitched blasts which told of the approach of strangers. As the guard men of the day came running from their quarters and the companions working and training about the villa grounds began to muster to arms the horn called again. But this time it was the long high sustained note which told that the strangers came in peace.

Shortly afterwards a small party rode into the villa courtyard where Arturo and his men stood waiting to greet them. Arturo's face lit up as he watched them approach. At their head rode his father, Baradoc, with his mother, Tia, at his side. Behind came three of Prince Gerontius's men as bodyguards followed by two youths leading heavily laden baggage ponies. They greeted each other affectionately and Arturo presented Daria to them as his wife and saw the quick gleam of pleasure and approval in his mother's eyes. Tia, now in her fortieth year, had grown matronly. Time had not flawed her beauty, but the years had given her the noble bearing of a queenly woman. Her hair was still corn gold and her eyes quick and all-embracing as she looked around her. His father, though little older than his mother he knew, looked much older and there were iron grey streaks in his russet hair. His sword arm which had been injured in his fight with Inbar had grown stiffer and when he embraced Arturo it was only with a clasp of his left arm around his shoulders. His face was stern but more, Arturo guessed, now from habit than mirroring any immediate emotion. But his directness of manner was still the same. Daria led Tia away to the women's quarters, and the guard of the day took charge of the comfort of their mounted guard and baggage men. Baradoc, left alone with Arturo, walked to the edge of the fountain basin and sat down. He accepted the cup of wine which one of the camp women brought to him, touched his lips to it and handed it back. When the woman had gone, he said to Arturo evenly, 'We stay not the night for we are in Count Ambrosius's country and that would be a discourtesy to him.'

Arturo, smiling, answered, 'This is my country – but I take no issue with you, father. That you are here, and my mother, too, is a joy to me. But I would be foolish to think that you come simply as father to greet his son.'

Baradoc nodded. 'That is the truth. I would it were otherwise.' Then looking around him, he went on, 'You have things well-ordered here. Your horses in the pastures are a delight to the eye. The crops show fair, and your men walk and hold themselves with dignity and pride. You and your time here are wasted, though. You live in a dream of defiance.'

'I live to make a dream come true. And the gods are with me.'

Baradoc smiled and, rubbing his stiff right shoulder, said wryly, 'You are as ever, I see, a familiar of the gods and enjoy their favour. Well, I will not argue with you about that. I come from Prince Gerontius on other business. He has entrusted to me a task of great importance – I go now, in fact, to persuade Count Ambrosius of this. For this task I would have one at my side whom I can trust. Someone to take the place of this . . .' he half-raised his stiff right arm.

For a moment or two Arturo said nothing. From the companions who had come to him recently he had heard of the great fortress which Prince Gerontius planned to raise in the country of the Durotriges, west of Lindinis, an armed camp to be a bastion against any future westward move of the Saxons. Then seeing his father's eyes shrewdly watching him, he said, 'I have heard something of this work. But to me . . .' He shrugged his shoulders. 'Well, my father, it is one thing for a hedgehog to roll itself into a ball of spikes until the fox walks away, but Hengist and his Saxon kind are not to be so easily baulked. They will sit themselves down around your hedgehog and wait for it to starve to death.'

Baradoc shook his head. 'There is more to it than that. I would have you know it and work for it with me. That is why I am here. Prince Gerontius will withdraw the warrant of outlawry on you. When I have seen Count Ambrosius he will do the same – for in return he will get a levy of troops he thinks not to have. The Prince expects no humbling of yourself before him.

You give him your allegiance truly. In return, you are free, and you can come with me to help in this great work and you bring your men and horses and all your people as your command.'

Arturo, tight-lipped, shook his head. 'In a fashion he sues for my help. But now the wind blows from another quarter. I have men here who have only one thought in mind – and that is not to sit them down and protect the building of this great fort which you would raise in the country of the Durotriges. Nor have I such thought. Within a month I would have no men. They are hungry for war and defiance – and so am I. We begin small, true, my father. But after the flowering of one blood-red poppy who can count the seeds that burst from the pod? To turn aside now would shame me before my men, and – greater evil – be a betrayal of the bounty which the gods have given to our company. With the gods we can dare all. But sitting on our backsides about a great fort would invite their mockery.'

Baradoc shook his head and sighed. 'You think too much of the gods – but, remember this, there are those they touch with madness in order to destroy them. Still I make no further argument with you about this matter. Your answer is what I expected. Nor, in truth, would I have pursued it this far were it not for the urging of your mother.'

Before the little party left Tia walked alone with Arturo along the terraced plots below the villa where now the young bean shoots grew high and the spring cabbage fattened to say her farewell to her son. Another son she had and two daughters, but this one was the marked one. For him, not long after his birth, the water in the silver chalice had fired to crimson and she had known then and still knew that his destiny was his own to make and – no matter the wish in her heart which had brought her here – she had never had any true hope of turning him from the perilous path which he so strongly believed the gods had set before him. He was Baradoc's son, but where the fire of steady purpose burned evenly in Baradoc, the blaze of destiny in Arturo was like the wild, wind-swept flaming of a heath fire. Her sole joy was to have seen him again and to know an increase in that joy in learning that he was married to Daria to whom her heart had warmed so immediately that, putting aside any thought of a last plea that he should join his father, she said to him now, 'The woman you have taken to wife pleases me. I know that she shares the dream you have. But remember this, Arturo, for I speak to you as a man, not my son, the constancy of a woman's heart-troth for her man is no polished jewel to be untouched by time and absence. It is a living plant which can wither under the killing frosts of long absence while her lover dedicates himself to an all-consuming love of his country – or selfish glory. If you love her truly then find at times the strength to turn aside from your dreams. The gods were never truly jealous of any man's hearth with wife and children round it.'

Arturo took her hand fondly and said with a present honesty and passion, 'I shall never cease from cherishing Daria, nor ever give her true cause to turn away from me. Do I not remember how it was with you during the years my father was away? Your virtue was a sword which went before you.'

Tia made no answer for she knew that he spoke as he would want things to be and, knowing only the strength of his young manhood, had yet to learn how weak and barren the spirit and body of a woman could be who lived in loneliness. Later, as she rode away in the party with Baradoc, the memory came back sharply to her that Daria might not ever have even the comfort of children for Merlin had long ago written of Arturo before his birth on the grey rock of a Caer Sibli cliff face –

> Name him for all men and all time
> His glory an everlasting flower
> He throws no seed

Under the Banner of the White Horse

After the feast of Beltine all sweethearts, wives and children left the villa, except for Daria and Ansold who were to go to the nearest forest settlement when Arturo and his men left. Of all the men who had gone away to visit their homelands and their families only two never returned and it was known much later that of these one had been killed in a drunken quarrel and the other had died of the slow sickness in his home town of Ariconium west of the Sabrina river. This sickness had been spreading now for over two years from the north. It came slowly and unevenly. It left great areas of the country untouched, worked up some main river valleys but left the tributaries untouched, broke out in one village and left its neighbour unplagued, and turned one town into a desert while another a few miles away went unscathed. Against it there was no defence. It began as a mild heating of the body that sent a man gently sweating and gave him a thirst which slowly grew with the passing of the days until within a few weeks his body was a furnace and his strength burned away until the day came when he died, his body unmarked by any blemish. It was no new thing. The oldest of men could remember it in their boyhood and held the memory of their fathers' memories of it. It was accepted as the seasons were accepted, and this year it was being said that it was as bad as any could remember and was the cause of Hengist and his fellow chieftains showing no signs yet of moving their warbands westwards across its direct path.

Arturo gave it little importance. Disease was the lot of man and beast. A beast was at the mercy of the good keeping and feeding of its master, but a man was his own master. He should drink clean water, eat good meat and bread, and – in his camp –

keep the privies clean and, except in the coldest of seasons, wash the body thoroughly every two weeks. So far there had been no sickness in his camp, nor any sign of it in the neighbouring country.

The slow sickness held no part in his thoughts for they were full of the move which he was poised to make with his companions. Each day now was filled with preparations for the march eastwards, and although he knew that it would be no great army he led he was fired with the thought that from the exploits and daring of his handful of men an army would grow and, with its growth, the renown of his name. From its victories must come the approval and favour still further of the gods.

On the night before the morning of his leaving the camp with his company of comrades he lay awake on the bed in their chamber at the villa with Daria. The wall sconces were alight still, the wickering flames giving life to the birds, beasts and flowers of the shabby, peeling wall paintings. Holding Daria's hand, he leaned over her and kissed her and then said, 'I say my farewell to you now. Tomorrow morning will be too full of affairs. While I am gone, pray to your God for me, and know that everywhere I go I carry you in my heart. I shall sleep with my shield at my shoulder and my sword at my side, but in my dreams I shall walk with you beneath the sweet yellow apple tree by the stream and there shall be no sadness in the voice of the storm thrush, nor melancholy in the call of the blackbird from the bower of the white blossomed thorn tree. I shall see your bright cheeks, red lips, eyebrows as black as a chafer and your teeth pure as the noble colour of snow . . .'

Daria made no answer, though she smiled at his words, knowing that with the comrades in his hall he had feasted and drunk the last of the over-winter mead. But her heart was full with her love for him and she needed no words to show it. She drew him down to her and held him in her arms. When he slept she lay awake and kept him harboured within her embrace all night.

They rode out the next morning to leave the villa of the three nymphs to the foxes and the birds, to the basking lizards and snakes, and their growing crops to the care and mercy of the surrounding settlements. At their head rode Arturo on the White One, wearing a leather war cap from which the red and white horse plumes swayed in the morning breeze. About his neck was knotted a red and white scarf and tight around his leather tunic a studded belt which carried sword and knife, his trews cross-gartered with braided deer-hide thongs, his legs guarded by a pair of old bronze greaves. Over his shoulder he carried, as did all the companions, a small round buckler painted red with the device of the rearing white horse on it, and he held himself proudly, his head high so that the low sun set dull fire flecks amongst the growth of the campaigning beard he had grown. At his side rode Daria's brother Lancelo, red and white plumed and scarfed, armed with shield and sword, and carrying high the war banner of the White One. Behind them came the companions, all plumed and scarfed and armed and bucklered, but clothed for war variously. Some wore the clothes of the Sabrina Wing from which they had come. Some were cuirassed fore and back with padded leather plates, and a few proudly bore old bronze cuirasses which had seen service nearly a hundred years before in the days of Stilicho and Constantine, the sad days when the Second Legion had been withdrawn from Isca and the Twentieth from Deva to strengthen the defences of the great Shore Fort at Rutupiae as the Western Empire crumbled and the lights of law and order and prosperity guttered low in Britain.

They mustered near sixty horses, and Arturo had divided his force into two troops of twenty-four horse each. The first troop was commanded by his closest friend Durstan with Garwain of Moridunum on the river Tuvius as his second-in-command. The second troop was led by the bearded, sweet-singing Gelliga from Lavobrinta in the country of the Ordovices who had for his deputy the young fresh-faced giant-handed Borio from Calcaria in the land of the Parisi. Behind them came the remount section of six horses, ridden by two other companions, the brothers dumb Timo and Marcos and the two young men – Barma and Felos – who had first come to the villa bringing tribute from the surrounding Britons. Behind them came a string of pack ponies, led and ridden by the priest Pasco and other workers who had attached themselves to the community of the companions over the months.

It was a small force but a brave one, well trained and disciplined, and now fully aware of what was in Arturo's mind. The only man who travelled unarmed was Pasco, and as the column rode out of the courtyard he intoned in a loud voice a prayer – to which for Arturo's sake he added a few unorthodox touches –

> O chaste Christ well-beloved, and all the native
> gods of this great country, to whom every verdict
> is clear, may the grace of the Sevenfold Spirit
> come to keep and protect these thy servants.

> Let neither sword nor spear restrain them, nor the
> enemy slip from their grasp like an eel's tail, so
> that under Thy banner neither barbarian, bond,
> fortress or bare waste can stop their course.

> O powerful Creator, and Protectors, rule our hearts,
> that Thou mayest be our love, and that we may do
> Thy will.

And so they went down the hill slope to the pasture and into the water meadows to follow the streamside which would take them by midday to the valley of the young Tamesis river. Here, they would turn eastward until they came to the ford which carried the Corinium road that ran to Spinis and Calleva and beyond into the heart of the waste lands waiting yet to be fully claimed and held by Briton or barbarian. As they moved along the stream the feeding mallards rose in flight and their young broods scattered to hiding in the reeds and sedges and the kingfishers fled before them like moving tongues of flame.

High up the valley side, on their right flank and hidden in the woods, Inbar watched them move, sitting his horse which switched its tail lazily against the summer flies. He wore a long brown woollen cloak which hid the sword he carried from his belt. Across his back was slung a hunting bow and a plaited-straw sheath of arrows, and lashed behind him was a roll of baggage to serve him in the slow hunt which was now beginning. Only the gods could number its days, but he knew that it would be long. Of patience he had no lack, but he prayed, his thick lips twisting wryly at the irony, that the gods would protect Arturo from Saxon sword or spear so that his death should come at his hands, that he could cut the young head from its broad shoulders and carry it secretly to Count Ambrosius to claim his due.

Two days later Arturo and his company rode into Calleva of the Atrebates. In their progress, riding along the old road, its ditches ruined, its surface broken and long despoiled in places, they had met no travellers. In the crop fields their fellow countrymen watched them from a safe distance, offering them no friendship, and the cattle-minders seeing the cloud of dust that rose about them drove their beasts fast to distant safety. They trotted in over the old earthworks, the setting sun rose-tinting the ruined walls, and through the west gate opening, bare now of the great portals which had once swung close to protect the town at night.

Except for a few old people, spinning out their handful of days, left in misery and hunger, the town was a place of the dead. There was nothing of value left. Here no man pursued his craft, no merchant his barter, no housewife her marketing. No children played and even the sparrows and kites had deserted the place. Between the Saxons of the East and the Britons of the West and North the country was a nomansland where safety lay in forest and river marsh or the openness of the high downs. If a town were visited by the people scattered in the surrounding country it was done in strength and then only for the pillage of masonry and wood or metal water pipes.

They slept that night in the old, almost ruined *mansio* close to the south gate. The horses were quartered in the inner courtyard and the company slept either in the surrounding lodging rooms of this old official inn of Roman days, or lay rolled in their blankets under the balmy night sky. A courtyard well held good water still for men and horses. Doing his rounds that night to the sentries he had posted, Arturo, his footsteps echoing through the ruins, could imagine the days when travellers and staging Roman officers and officials had made the place a hive of warmth and talk as they passed through on their way to new postings in distant legions or to seek fresh markets and trade as far north as the Antonine Wall. His lips tightened as he thought of those ordered, prosperous days and of his country now. A country which was being torn apart by so many forces and made a ruin and a desert to offend the eyes of man and the hearts of the gods. That night he swore that his companions should never be quartered again in any town so long as this campaign lasted. *Aie* ... he thought, grinning ruefully, if campaign it could be called with none it seemed ready to stay the way of his handful of companions.

Yet despite this moment of self-doubt, the next morning he had his men round up all the miserable people who still stayed in the town, bringing them limping and halting into the old Forum through the ruins of its monumental east entrance to be greeted by his companions, mounted on parade and drawn up in line along the front of the shell which had once been the basilica.

Riding out from the centre of his companions, the White One curvetting and restless beneath him, and with Lancelo holding the red banner of the white horse behind him, he spoke first in his own tongue and then in the tongue of his mother to them. Listening, Pasco smiled to himself for it amused him to recognize that in the warrior a great preacher had been lost. The smile went as he wondered why it was that war and bloodshed could silver a man's tongue so readily where love of God and one's neighbour so often left him dumb.

Arturo spoke as though he were addressing a crowd of able-bodied, just-minded citizens and seeking recruits and support to his cause which he called the Great Matter of Britain and for which, he proclaimed with sincerity, the gods of his country had fingered him as the chosen one to achieve. To his side must come the warring and jealous princes and kings and warriors of his own country, all men of good intent, to revive the greatness of the past, to restore peace and prosperity, and to order justice and free passage for all. But to this end there could be only one beginning – the barbarian Saxons of the East must be swept away, driven to the sea to seek their ships and the safety of their own countries.

Although his companions had heard it all before when he had told them of his dream of this great progress which would give them fighting enough and also carry his message abroad, and had mostly latched their minds to the prospect of battle, there was something in his manner this morning, as he spoke to the miserable handful of old crones and broken men before him, that kindled a new fire in their spirits. A horse and a sword, the dust and sweat and blood of war had been promised and would be given them. But now they began to see the shape of a greater glory than their passion for battle had ever promised. They saw themselves now, each according to his faith, the picked of the gods or God. From that moment, though none showed it openly, there was a new dignity of the heart and a bolder, nobler edge to their allegiance to Arturo which they would take with them into battle counting the loss of their life for a comrade's safety no loss but a gain to be rewarded in Heaven or the Shades.

As they rode out of Calleva, Arturo, loosening his neck scarf against the morning's growing heat, turned to Pasco, who had come trotting up to give him company on his right side, and said, 'And what does the good Pasco think of my preaching in the Forum?'

Pasco smiled, wetting his lips with his tongue, and said, 'The preaching was good. But the congregation was poor. What gain will you have for your cause in such few and wretched hearts? There was not a man among them with strength to raise a sword nor any woman with her mind on aught but the hope of good pickings to fill her supper pot.'

Arturo nodded his head. 'Aie ... that is true. But they have that which I need. Each mouth has a tongue and when they go into the countryside to steal or beg amongst the scattered country people they will talk of the strange company in Calleva this day. And since country people are hungry for news and gossip they will listen, and the story will pass and pass until it begins to blaze like a summer fire through dry glasslands. Though I have sworn to quarter no more in towns, for their ruin and misery sickens my heart, there is none we shall pass without a herding of its wretched people to hear my words.' He paused for a moment and then added slyly, 'Does it not say in your religion that in the beginning was the Word?'

Pasco, surprised, raised an eyebrow and asked, 'How do you know the disciple John so well?'

Arturo laughed. 'From a Druid priest who taught me well when he was sober enough to sit his stool without falling.'

'Do not forget that since you have been baptized it is your religion as well.'

'Nor shall I. A man cannot have too many gods to watch over him.'

Pulling up his horse sharply Lancelo said, 'Then let us hope they are all with us now.'

From the top of the gentle hill which they had just crested he pointed ahead down the slope. At the bottom of the broad valley where the road crossed a small stream a body of about thirty men on foot barred the way in three ragged ranks.

Arturo, reining in, said, 'They would have done better to have chosen this hilltop than the valley bottom. Sound the horn for Gelliga's troop.'

From inside his cloak Lancelo pulled his bull horn and blew the four sharp battle notes and then a long fifth which was the call for Gelliga's command.

Without looking back Arturo sat the White One and watched the men at the valley bottom. Many a time the manoeuvre which must come now had been made in mock attack from the forest hill down to the stream at the villa of the three nymphs. Many a time this situation and others had been drilled and re-drilled into men and horses. But now across his path stood his first real enemy, and on this bright morning there awaited him his first real attack. His breath quickened a little with pleasure.

The moment had come sooner than he had thought, but it was more welcome for that. He looked back and saw Gelliga leading his men at a gentle trot away from the road and up the hill slope to the left to stop just short of the skyline. Keeping to the road came Durstan's troop to ride openly on to the crest and halt in four ranks of six behind Arturo. Farther back the remounts and baggage horses were being taken well away to the right flank.

Durstan rode to Arturo's side and said, 'They cannot know our strength or they would not stand so bunched and ready for plucking.'

'There are many things they will learn and those that live will tell. Now let us see what days and nights of aching backsides and sore thighs have done for us.'

Pasco, steadying his restless, sturdy hill pony, sat and watched. The men were Saxons and were a rabble, though well armed. They were, he guessed, the war party of a scattered community of outcasts or adventurers who had moved away or been banished from the settled lands of the Saxon shore. There were many such pockets along the line of the valley of the river Tamesis and those communities often lived in uneasy peace with the native British of the district. The rumour of Arturo's coming must have spread ahead of him. They stood now to dispute his way unless he chose to make a detour around their lands – which he well knew was not in the character of Arturo whom he had come to love well, to regard highly and – from a religious point of view – to indulge gently for he knew well that Christ chose His servants with a wisdom and understanding beyond the minds of men.

The skirmish was brief and to be repeated with variations dictated by ground and chance many times to come in their advance eastwards. Lancelo's horn sounded the long, high, wickering call to advance. Durstan's troop put their horses to the gallop and charged down the slope towards the Saxons who awaited their coming with heavy, sharp-pointed, single-edged scramaseax swords drawn and their small round shields raised, not for defence so much as for striking at the face of their enemy once he was brought to ground to fight foot to foot. Arturo and Lancelo stayed on the hilltop.

Seeing him restraining the impatient White One, Pasco smiled to himself. He knew well what was in his mind. This was no full battle that needed him at the head of his force. Both Durstan and Gelliga knew his mind, and he would take away no part of their pride of command. Also, too, Pasco guessed, more than the pleasuring blood-surge of moving into action, he would be drawing a greater pleasure from seeing the long hours of cavalry attack drills at the villa now pass into reality itself where a ham-stringed horse could send a man to the ground to meet the swinging scramaseax, the face-smashing shield and – if the gods were unkind – have a ready seax dagger sharp-slit his throat.

The dust clouds rose behind Durstan's troop as it swept down on the Saxons, and the unruly barbarians, eager for fight, broke ranks and ran to meet it. But the moment that the troop was within a spear's length of the foremost Saxons every horse swung to the right and raced across the front of the enemy as though their riders had suddenly lost heart. A great shout of triumph went up from the Saxons as they turned and chased them, calling taunts and bellowing their derision.

It was then that Gelliga's troop came over the hill top and charged at full gallop down the slope to take the Saxons in the rear. Hooves thundering, tails and manes flying, the morning sunlight bright on drawn swords and helmet crests and streaming crimson and white scarves, the troop, with Gelliga and the great-handed Borio leading its centre, the companions' line spread out into a horned crescent and scythed its way into the rear of the Saxons. Some turned to meet their foe and died with wound in throat or chest, but most were killed from behind and went to their end not knowing they carried the death mark of those who die with their backs to the enemy to be banished forever from Woden's hall.

In a short while the attack was over and the few Saxons who had survived were running away from the road and along the stream and over the marshy ground where they were left free from pursuit. Amongst the companions there were few injuries. One had taken a spear thrust in the shoulder, another a slash from a seax which had cut through the hide cross-gartering of his leg and scored his calf with a long, though shallow wound, and others had cuts and bruises of no importance. But one horse had had its windpipe and neck artery slashed with a sword and died as Gelliga's troop reformed. It was left for the crows and kites and foxes and rats to pick clean. None said a word to the companion who had ridden it, for there are no words that can pass with any comfort to a man who has lost a loved mount. He sat by it, stone-faced, until the party moved on and then took his remount and cantered to his place in his troop column. Behind the troop came the baggage party, its cart and pony packs loaded with the pick of sword and knife and axe and the meagre plunder taken from the bodies of the dead Saxons.

From that day they moved no longer directly to the east. Staying south of the Tamesis, which hereabouts took a great loop northwards, they travelled in zigzag fashion, meeting little opposition, but when they did having scant trouble with it for the Saxons, hating village or town life, lived separately in single huts in the woods and hills, and had no firm leader or trust in their own kind to band together often to oppose them. Wherever he could find a British village or settlement, no matter if it only contained a handful of people, Arturo would stop and, with his companions on full parade behind him, make his declamation as he had done at Calleva, so that the news of his presence and progress ran before him. To his delight now and again men of worth who had long deserted Count Ambrosius and Vortigern to return to their homes came to join him. Welcome they were when they came mounted and armed, but those who carried only the clothes they stood in and the itch for action were mounted and supplied with arms and such war gear as Arturo's force took from the Saxons in their path.

By the time that Arturo reached the town of Pontes and the now south-curving Tamesis he had almost the makings of a third troop of horse under his command. He stayed three days in camp on the banks of the river outside the town and was pleased to see small groups of local people come close to the camp to watch and – he knew full well – to go back to their settlements and homes to talk about him and his men.

Sitting that evening on the river bank by the side of the ford which they would cross the next morning, for the old wooden bridges had long been wrecked and pillaged for the sake of their timbers, he knew that far and near now the name of Arturo and his companions was working in the minds of more and more of his countrymen like a ferment in the honey and water of new mead. On this progress he commanded no force large enough to fight great battles, but he would have blazed his name and intent across the country to catch the eyes and ears of every man who longed for true leadership and an end to his present misery, and so bring many of them to his side. With that for this year he would be content.

As he sat there a thin summer drizzle began to fall and suddenly from the smooth surface of the rolling Tamesis a great salmon, running the river to the spawning beds of the headwaters, leaped like a great bow of silver into the air. Seeing the fish he remembered the story of the goddess Latis who wept and brought the rains to fill the rivers to bring back her warrior lover who deserted her each year to go to the sea as a salmon. Remembering this, he thought suddenly of Daria who sat now and waited for him, Daria who grew more and more absent from his mind if not from his heart.

He had then a black sense of shame that he, whose eyes watched always for signs from the gods who controlled his destiny, saw now a sign from the peaceful, gentle Latis which should not have been necessary.

He rose and with the Latis rain dewing his face went into the camp and found the youth Felos.

Arturo, the shame still clouding him, said, 'Go to Marcos. Tell him to give you a horse, weapons and food. Ride back to the lady Daria and give her all the count of our days and progress. Then, returning, bring with you all her news.'

'Yes, my lord.'

'Say that I am well and bear her always in my thoughts and heart.'

'Yes, my lord. And where will I find you, my lord?'

Sharply, Arturo said, 'Only the gods can say. But ...' he smiled, to ease his tartness, '... find me and from that day you and your brother Barma shall ride as companions.'

Felos, beaming, raised his hand in salute and was gone at a smart trot to find Marcos.

Three weeks later they rode out from the great elms which crested the high ground to the north-west of Londinium. They were now a company of two troops of 32 horse, each still commanded by Gelliga and Durstan, and a reserve troop of fifteen horse commanded by one of the new companions, Cuneda, from Lactodorum in the country of the Catuvellauni, a man of forty, built like an ox, black-bearded but without a hair on his head. Their camp servants had increased and they now had two carts, the second taken from a burnt-out farmstead which they had repaired and fitted with runners to carry their food supplies and grain for their horses – though the grass being abundant and sweet at this time of the year their mounts needed no more than a few handfuls of corn a day. Five of the companions bore wounds which, under Pasco's care, were fast healing, and two companions had been killed the day after leaving Pontes when riding ahead of the column as scouts they had been ambushed by a band of robbers and cut-throats who stripped them of clothes and weapons and disappeared into the thickness of the surrounding forest where none could follow them. They were buried where they lay and, as Pasco finished his prayers for them, Arturo turned aside and rode alone with his grief, knowing it to be the beginning of a burden of the soul which he must from now on learn to endure as the never-ceasing lot of a commander of men.

Below them now the silver loops of the Tamesis snaked away eastwards to the sun-blazed spread of its estuary, and at their feet lay the once great city of Londinium. Only a few wisps of smoke rose from its houses. It was a dead city for these days, without true commerce or trade, there was no gain or security to be found in it. People in these times drew away from towns and settled where a living was to be found, in their hovels and sparse communities close to their poorly cropping fields and cattle grounds.

Arturo sent two of the companions to ride down to the city gate close to the ruined fort at the north-west corner of the walls to bring him back news of the place. When they returned they reported that the two western gates, though unmanned, were open and in good repair, that the fort was empty and that the great wooden bridge over the river was broken and gapped in many places and would give no crossing. There were people in the half-ruined city still, but they were a miserable set of wretches who lived by pillage which they bartered to the surrounding country folk, and there was scarce an able-bodied man or woman amongst them. Where there had been greatness and the noisy bustle of commerce and trade, and the ring of horses' hooves and the clank of armour as well-furbished and well-ordered troops had garrisoned the great fort and the walls, there was heard now only the scavenging cries of the kites and the carrion birds and the barking of dog packs that roamed the alleyways and deserted houses. And that they were there was due to one thing. The slow sickness had swept through the city since the beginning of summer and, although it was now almost abated, the streets and houses still held the corpses of the dead, lying as they had fallen to make a feasting for all the city's carrion.

Hearing this Arturo was for a while in two minds whether he should risk his company in such a place, but then the conviction came strongly to him that since the gods had led him thus far under their favour, that favour would still run only if he entered the place and raised the white horse banner for all to see so that the report of his coming would spread like a great ripple across the country. This was Londinium Augusta, once sacked and burnt by the great Queen Boudicca, greater than Camulodunum or any other city, the capital of the great Roman province of Britain. Through him, he knew with unquestionable conviction, this capital and his country would one day become great again.

He left the reserve troop of horse to guard the baggage train and with the rest of his companions, Lancelo carrying the white horse banner before them, he rode down to the city and entered it through the most southerly of the two western gates. Men, women and children, dull-eyed from the slow sickness, lay in the gutters and doorways and gave them no greeting as they waited for death. Hooves clattering on the broken paving and rubble of the streets, the crows and kites rising in wild flight from the bodies that here and there littered their way, the dog packs retreating from them, snarling and barking, they moved along the Tamesis side, past the ruined warehouses and collapsed river stockades, the gulls and river birds, disturbed from their low tide feeding, flighting from the beaches. Past the broken and burnt and pillaged Londinium bridge and the ruin of the great river palace they went, and then swung north to breast the rising ground and finally rode in proud formation into the old Forum and drew up in a long line of horse across the face of the ruined and derelict basilica. With them came a growing drift of miserable human flotsam and jetsam, men and women with nothing to lose but their lives which for most would be a happy release, ragged, half-starving and moving like famine-weary cattle.

Arturo rode forward a little and to these, as though they were proud, well-set citizens, he made his declamation. When he had finished there was for a while a low muttering among them and then it died as the sound of a slow flurry of passing rain dies before the wind. Arturo and his men rode away and the crowd stayed where they were, no strength or curiosity in them to fire their wasted limbs and weak spirits. Helmet plumes tossing, the white horse banner before them, the companions passed from the city, splashing over the summer-low river which flowed down through the heart of the city, past the ruined Baths, past the shells of once noble buildings with their broken statues and defaced and cracked tablets of dedication, and out into the clean air and the green grass of the hill slopes where the rest of the company awaited them.

At Arturo's side Lancelo said, 'Can such a city ever live again?'

Arturo, stiff-faced, moved by all he had seen, said with curt emotion, 'Under the gods, some day, it must and will.'

The next day, at low tide, they forded the river well above the city and the column turned south to begin a great sweep which should bring them westwards to move along the fringes of the great forests that rolled northwards from the shore line of the country of the Regnenses, from the sea towns of Anderida and Noviomagus.

Twelve days later they fought their first and only battle of the progress. In the early hours of the morning as they were camped below the crest of a steep scarp of the hills it started to rain heavily. Since they lay in the open, rolled in their blankets without cover, Arturo gave the order to break camp and move. Every campaigner amongst them knew that the misery of rain soaking through blankets and clothes is abated if it can be met marching rather than lying on wet ground.

The companions formed into their two troops and moved off while the baggage train followed them more slowly with the half troop of reserve horse in their rear to prevent surprise attack from behind. But as the morning wore on the ground became soaked and soft and slowed up the movement of the two baggage carts and the rearguard screen of cavalry. Little by little the leading troops gradually drew out ahead. Two troopers rode wide on each flank of the column as scouts, their cloak hoods drawn close about their heads against the still driving rain. At mid-morning as they rode along the crest of a broad upland sheep run, the turf studded with gorse and broom bushes and clumps of wild hawthorn and bramble thickets, the two leading troops dropped down into a great dip in the land and disappeared from the sight of the reserve troop and baggage column following.

At this moment, from the bushes well to the left flank, there arose a party of fifty or sixty Saxons which came running hard, howling and shouting and brandishing their weapons, to drive a wedge between the head of the baggage train and the forward two troops of horse now lost to sight. Then, too, from the right flank more Saxons ran from their hiding places and raced to the rear of the train to form a barrier between it and the following guard troopers.

Long before Cuneda, the rear guard commander, could reach for his horn and call the alarm the two parties of Saxons had swept round and among the baggage carts, killing all those who had not escaped at the sight of their coming. As the first notes of Cuneda's horn wailed the alarm the Saxons formed a circle about the carts and stood firm in three ranks to defend their position and their plunder.

That morning as Arturo, the alarm horn sounding in his ears, forced the White One hard back up the slope to the down top and saw the Saxon force surrounding his baggage carts, he learnt a lesson he was never to forget. Hard rain makes a man seek what comfort, even on the move, that he can. His scouts had ridden with their cloaks cowling their heads, their eyes part blinkered, their minds on their discomfort rather than on the country around them. But, more important, and this came from instinct rather than deliberate thinking, he knew that any hesitation now would only feed the wild temper of the Saxons who ringed the baggage carts while others of their comrades were already pillaging them. The situation before him now was none that had ever been faced in mock attack at the villa of the three nymphs. He acted from impulse and instinct without time even for a prayer to the gods to be with him, for anger and humiliation at being so surprised possessed him completely.

He shouted a command to Lancelo at his side and as his horn began to sound, he drove the White One forward into a gallop with the troops of Gelliga and Durstan following him in a combined wedge-shaped formation.

Pasco, who had been riding his pony with the leading troops, came back up the slope on to the level ground in time to see the tight wedge of flying horses, great scuds of turf flung up behind them by their pounding hooves, burst into the ring of massed Saxons, the swords of the companions swinging and flashing in the rain.

But the Saxons, shouting insults, held their ranks as the cavalry swirled round them on either side, the horses neighing with excitement and others squealing with pain as they were cut down or ham-stringed, leaving their riders to fight on foot. Around the baggage carts men and horses circled like a great whirlpool. The air was full of the shouts of the Saxons who stood their ground; and the bright and bloody flash of sword and axe and swinging scramaseax. Watching, Pasco realized – for he had travelled far and seen much in his time – that these were no cut-throat, outcast, plunder-hungry men such as harried the valley of the Tamesis. They stood and fought like warriors and there was one among them, towering head and shoulders above the rest, who wore an iron-banded leather helmet and a short white sheepskin cloak that fell to his waist and was caught there by a sword belt with a silver clasp, who was clearly the leader. These men were Hengist's men from the settled Saxon lands to the east, seasoned men who would stand their ground so long as the faintest flicker of victory burned for them.

Lancelo's horn blew and the two troops drew back and re-formed, and then the horn blew again to send in the rear-guard troop under Cuneda and then Durstan's. Arturo watched Cuneda's attack break against the Saxon ring, swirl about it and pass by, and then, his anger passing and his brain clearing, he realized that cavalry could only do so much against men who stood and fought and kept their ranks.

Durstan's troop followed Cuneda's to the attack. As it went in Arturo dismounted followed by Gelliga, Borio and all their men to attack on foot. The cavalry swung left and right of the Saxon ring to harry its flanks and the dismounted companions flung themselves against its front. Leading them was Arturo, sword swinging, his buckler held low to prevent the swift Saxon thrust to the groin, cutting and hacking his way into the ring of men, forcing his way towards their leader in the sheepskin cloak. The Saxon chief, seeing him come, recognizing he must be the leader of the companions, pressed forward through his men to meet him. They met with a great clash of sword and scramaseax, Arturo silent while the Saxon shouted taunts and insults at him. In the few moments before the lust of battle claimed him Arturo called silently to the gods to be with him, and then all thought deserted him as he became one with the flash and hiss of his sweeping, jabbing sword.

Pasco, watching them fighting face to face in the confused and bloody throng of men, saw the swing and thrust of cavalry sword and scramaseax flash above the sea of heads and straining bodies, lost them, saw them again while the air rang with the fierce shouting of men and the screams of those who fell. Then suddenly, the white-fleeced cloak was gone. A great shout went up from the companions and, like the concerted movement of a raiding flock of crows taking wing in alarm from a field of young corn, the Saxons broke and ran. Pasco, who had seen battle against the Saxons many times, knew their mind and their temper. With hope of victory they would fight and stand and die, but when hope or strong leadership went, they would turn and run. Only if they were hopelessly surrounded would they bunch and face their enemy and fight to the end, taking their wounds from the front and going gladly to their death to claim a warrior's welcome from Woden.

As the Saxons ran, the cavalry reformed and harried them along the down top until Lancelo's horn blew the recall. Pasco, riding up on his pony into the carnage and destruction that surrounded the baggage train, found Arturo standing over the dying Saxon chief.

Blood running over his white fleece cloak from a great sword thrust into his chest, he lay with his eyes closed. But after a few moments he slowly opened his eyes, looked up at Arturo and said something in his own language. Then his head dropped to one side as life passed from him.

Arturo, leaning on his sword, said to Pasco, 'You know their tongue?'

Pasco nodded. 'Yes, my son. He said that now in Hengist's

hall the name of Arturo of the White Horse will no longer make men laugh in scorn.'

Arturo, after a moment's pause, said solemnly, 'May his gods honour him, as this day we humbly honour ours for the victory they have given us.'

That evening they camped beside a muddy, slow-flowing stream and Arturo, after eating, sat by himself on the bankside in a brooding mood which kept his companions from him.

The day which was passing had taught him many things and among them those which he knew he should have long marked from his own understanding. Ten of his troopers had been killed, and six of the baggage train, among them Timo the dumb one. Six wounded horses had had to be destroyed. If his name were not now to be held in scorn in Hengist's hall there was much about his own conceit of himself which gave him self-scorn. The gods, though they had kept his side, had given him lessons which he would never forget. Chief among these was that cavalry by itself was useless against men who would bravely stand and fight on foot. He had to have such men, men who would march and fight afoot, to come behind the cavalry and hold the ground or pour through the breaches made by his horse. He knew now that he had fed too long on his dreams. From this day the hard work began. He had made his progress and the name of Arturo had spread and was spreading. Behind the Word now he had to work and build and shape the reality of a great command.

Then, looking up into the evening sky, pearl-streaked and as lustrous as the inside of a mussel shell, he saw a peregrine stoop from its high pitch and heard the hiss of the scarred air as it came down to take a teal duck which was planing down to the river for its evening feeding. But the teal, seeing the peregrine coming, swung aside in alarm and dropped like a stone into the safety of the streamside flags to leave the peregrine to fly down the river calling angrily, and he knew that it was a sign from the gods to him. Swift and deadly might be the cavalry, but when the prey went to ground there must be means to flush it from its place.

Dawn Meeting

For more than a month Arturo and his company moved westwards and wherever there was town, hamlet, settlement or village to be found they would stop and Arturo would draw up his companions and address the people. The news of the manner and purpose of his coming running ahead of him, there was now no fear of him so that on the high downs when they rested for a night the cattle and sheep minders would come from their runs to see and hear him, and in the wooded valleys he drew the lonely charcoal burners and swineherders wonderingly from the trees into the clearings. Now, when he called for men to join him, there were those few who stayed after their fellows had left. He went south down the river valley to the outskirts of Venta which, although a shadow of its former self, was more prosperous and inhabited than most towns, and although the gates were closed against him there were those who came over the walls secretly by night to hear and see him. He moved like a man in a dream and spoke like one possessed and there were many of his companions who were hard pressed to keep patience and face with him. But others, like Durstan, Gelliga, Lancelo, Garwain and Borio, who knew his mind and purpose and read them right, knew, too, that he had long forsaken his old vow that he would only return to the banners of Prince Gerontius and Count Ambrosius when they should sue him for his help. That fire was dead ash now. Arturo meant to raise his own army and own no master but himself. When the day came to league himself with Gerontius and Ambrosius it would be as equal and with his own troops. Pasco, firm though he was to his own religion, had times when he could not but believe that the old gods lived still and, from first touching Arturo with their fire, now claimed and possessed him wholly.

From Venta they turned north-west and at the end of that day's march Felos rode into camp. He found Arturo grooming the White One after feeding and watering her for he would let no one serve her but himself.

Arturo said, 'Greetings, good Felos. You have been so long gone that I had thought never to see you again, that some danger had taken you.'

Felos, smiling, shook his head. 'I would have been with you sooner, my captain. But your lady Daria kept me many weeks at her side.'

'She is well?'

'She is, my lord, and full of deep content.'

'Then why should she keep you so long and deny me the happiness of this news?'

Felos grinned. 'Because she would be certain that I might bring you the happiest news you could have.'

Arturo, stroking the neck of the White One with his hand, knowing that for days on end his mind had held no place for Felos or Daria, said, 'What news could I have greater than to know she is well?'

'That of which she would be doubly certain before my return. She bids me tell you that she carries your child and all is well with her.'

Arturo's hand dropped from the White One's neck and his face stiffened with the quick spasm of his inner joy and pride. Then, with an impulsive movement, he reached into the pouch of his sword belt and drew from it the silver buckle which he had taken from his first true Saxon foe and gave it to Felos, saying, 'Such a great gift as you give me with your news deserves a return. Take this in token of my joy. And now go attend to your horse first and then yourself.'

Felos moved off happily, and smiled to himself at his master's last words . . . *your horse first and then yourself.*

When he was gone Arturo stood alone in thought for some time, and there was a mixture of emotion in him which tinged his joy with shame. His love for Daria was deep and true, but it was of a different nature from his love of his country and his desire to see it become great again. This love the gods had given him to nourish and it could never be absent from him since it burnt in him constantly like a flame. But now Daria carried his child ... *Aie*, more than that, his son it must be if the gods were truly with him; and as though they were and would have him know it there came to him the bright conviction that without delay he must ride to their place and give them his thanks; and more than that, to show no disrespect to the god of Pasco, in whose name he had been baptized, he would take from the place of the gods a gift for the child from this other god to bear home with him.

Impatient now, he called for Durstan and said, 'I saddle and ride this night to the Circle of the Gods for there is a thing I must do to set my mind at peace.'

'Alone?'

'Alone, yes. Our company moves that way tomorrow and I shall be waiting for you. Give me no talk against it for my mind is set. Felos will give you the news he brought me and from that you shall, since our thoughts keep pace together, know my reasoning.'

For a moment or two Durstan hesitated, but the look on Arturo's face told him there would be no shifting him. He said, 'There is a moon tonight and you ride through peaceful country. Go, and the gods watch over you.'

'They will – for I go to give them all thanks.'

Losing no time Arturo saddled the White One, armed himself, and rode out of camp. The night was still and balmy and the full moon was passing to its last quarter. He rode north away from Venta to the high ground and then swung westwards. Fox and fowl marked his passage. The hares on the grassland held their place as he passed while above him the hawking bats called thinly as they hunted the high-summer moths. But well behind him, trailing on his left flank, another marked and followed him, a man on a dark horse, heavily draped in a cloak which had grown ragged and torn and hid the sword he carried. Behind him was slung a bow and a sheaf of arrows hung at his side. The man's face, under its unkempt growth of beard, was drawn and haggard, but there was a dark gleam in his eyes which seen close would have told his joy. Many a time had Inbar in the past been on the point of turning from his hunt, but now he was joyful that hunger and thirst and hard lying and the perils of following the companions had not drawn him from his quest. Why Arturo should leave camp and ride into the night alone he did not know nor care. One desire only burned in him and he waited now only for the meeting of time and place to give him the reward and the reformation which his manhood demanded.

Towards dawn with a light ground mist rising knee high over the land Arturo came from a belt of trees out on to open ground and saw ahead of him on the sheep-bitten slopes of the down the great circle of henge-stones silhouetted blackly against the westward dying moon. As he had ridden through the night his thoughts had been full of Daria and the coming child, and of Daria and his days with her. Sparse though they had been, each one now seemed like a wondrous jewel inlaid with precious stones and enamelled with flaming colours. He saw her riding up to him as a girl on the rain-swept moors, Daria of the blue eyes, brighter than the periwinkle flower, smiling at him across the market place, and Daria lying in his arms in the meadow bower while the larks sang and the scent of fresh-cut hay filled the air with perfume and her heart beat under the palm of his hand so that the joy in her moved like a slow fire into the depths of his being. The gods had marked him for greatness to serve his country and he would make her by the grace of the gods a queen for all men as she was now queen for him.

He rode into the great circle of stones and, slipping from the White One's back, took his knife from his belt and walked towards the fallen slab where long before he had hidden for safe-keeping the silver chalice which had once held the blood of Pasco's god. As he moved away the White One lowered her head and began to graze on the sweet downland grass and herbs.

Kneeling, Arturo dug into the turf and quickly unearthed the chalice. He brushed it free of soil with his hands and the moonlight touched it so that it gleamed dully. At this moment Inbar, on foot, his horse left tethered to a thorn bush out of sight, stepped noiselessly from behind one of the tall stones. In his hands he held the drawn bow and the goose-feather flighted arrow, armed with its sharp iron tip. There would be no honour in this killing, and he needed none since honour had been long lost to him. To his right the White One raised her head from cropping and looked at him. The sun, yet to show itself over the edge of the eastern land, already paled the sky with light and touched the underbellies of the low morning clouds with red and gold wash. The kneeling figure of Arturo was clear against the growing light, and already overhead a lone lark sang and the meadow pipits looped their way in morning flight across the juniper-tufted downland.

As Arturo slowly began to rise to his feet, the White One whinnied gently and uneasily. Arturo, knowing her moods and manners, swung round, suddenly alive with an instinct of coming danger. The arrow, meant to take him below the left shoulder blade, sped true across the stone-encircled grass, the hiss of its feathered flight one long, low note against the morning quiet, and the deadly point sank deep into his body below his right ribs. He cried aloud with the sudden shock of pain and staggered backwards, the silver chalice dropping from his hands. He would have fallen but the great stone behind him held him up and through the mist of pain which briefly dimmed his eyes he saw Inbar racing towards him with his sword drawn.

They fought then, without shield or buckler, sword-armed, and no words passing between them while the blood ran dark over the linen shirt under Arturo's open tunic. The sparks leapt blue and gold from the clash of their swords and the White One, disturbed and frightened, raced round the great inner circle and whinnied high. In a moment of withdrawal Arturo reached down with his left hand to the hampering shaft of the arrow lodged in his side and snapped it short. His hand came back, dark as ebony with the spurt of his own blood, and he prayed to the gods, if it were his destiny to die, to give him life blood enough and strength to kill Inbar before he fell himself.

And the gods were good to him and gave him this boon. He fought with the blood-veil fast clouding his eyes and fighting he remembered how his father had faced and fought this man, and of the dishonour which had been planned for his mother. From memory of time long-passed but now sharply recalled, he drew the last of fighting strength from within himself. They fought without words in the growing light of the burgeoning morning. The grass about them was trampled and scarred and blood-stained and, when the moment came that his sword slashed across the neck of his foe and Inbar fell with his death cry bubbling from his blood-filled throat like the wailing cry of an upland curlew, all reality passed from him. He fell to the ground and passed from violence into the calm of a dream of fair days and love's delights. He walked with Daria in the river pasture and plucked for her the scent-heavy meadowsweet plumes. He rode the forest paths with her lodged between his arms, riding before him on the White One, her dark hair in the wind making a moving lattice before his eyes and the sweet warmth of her woman body filling his nostrils with a headier perfume than any that could come from the flowering summer blooms. With time out of joint, he walked with her through the villa court-yard to the fountain of the nymphs and she held in her arms the man-child which was his, and the child, seeing the splashing waters fling a veil of drifting, jewelled spray to trap the sun-light in rainbow colours, stretched out his hands to take them and crowed with delight; and with the sound of his son's voice in his ears and the sight of Daria's red lips parted to touch the child's warm cheek with a kiss, lips redder than the breast of any spring-fired robin's, he drifted further into the dark shades of oblivion.

A long-haired, shaggy moorland pony grazed close to the White One within the circle of great standing stones. The pack which had been on its back lay open on the ground beside the body of Arturo which was half-propped against a fallen lintel, his head cushioned by his own blood-stained cloak and tunic, and his body naked above his trews except for the tight binding of torn strips of cloth that circled his body below his ribs and held, tight pressed, a great moss wad which blocked and staunched the flow of blood from his wound.

At his side sat the man Merlin whom he had last seen on the high scarp above the Sabrina river, the dark-haired, stocky, brown-robed man known as the ageless, the wandering one. On the ground lay a half-empty water skin and a piece of old cheese resting on a great dock leaf. The man ate and, from watching Arturo's face, he turned now and then to look at the body of Inbar lying a little way off, the flies and bluebottles crowding the wound in his neck, the eyes upturned and open, staring sightlessly at the mid-morning sky.

A pair of grey-polled jackdaws, scavenging and eyeing the cheese below, sat atop one of the great stones and called noisily. At the sound Arturo slowly opened his eyes. He lay without moving for a while and there was a weakness in him that made him feel without body or contact with the turf and stone which supported him. But that he lived he knew, for slowly there grew in him a raging thirst which fired his throat and brought him to an awareness of his own flesh and blood. Seeing the man, his mind clearing, he said weakly, 'I live.'

Merlin smiled 'And will for it is the wish of the gods. Why else would they have set my steps this way? Once by happen-chance we met. But now they stir themselves and begin to meddle with my affairs and give me dreams to plague my path. Yes, you will live. While you rested in limbo I cut the broken arrow head from you.'

'You have my thanks.'

'The years ahead may turn them to reproaches.'

'You talk in riddles. Thanks I give you, and more thanks would for a drink. My . . . my throat is like a smithy's furnace and my body burns.'

Merlin reached for the water skin and then took from the ground at Arturo's side the silver chalice. He filled it and, with an arm around Arturo's shoulders, lifted him a little so that he could drink in comfort.

Arturo took the chalice in his weak, trembling hands and

drank. The water went into him with a coldness that suddenly made his body shake. He half-lowered the chalice and coughed, holding it in his cupped hands against his breast, and closing his eyes against the shock. When the spasm passed he opened his eyes, felt strength stirring in him and moved to raise the chalice to drink again, but slowly stayed his hands. Within the silver bowl cradled between his palms the clear water was slowly flushing with a crimson hue that deepened and, as the water stilled, took the morning light and glowed with a high brilliance to show his own bearded, fight-sweated face mirrored in it.

He raised his eyes in wonder at the sight and saw that Merlin, too, had seen the colouring. They looked at each other without words and then Merlin smiled gently. Above them the jackdaws suddenly screeched and took to wing, and the White One, raising her head, whinnied high and fiercely and cantered across the marjoram and thyme-laced turf.

From the dip in the land to the east there rose then the sharp, echoing call of a horn. Over the crest of the land came the leading troop of Arturo's companions with Lancelo at its head, the white horse banner streaming in the rising morning breeze, and behind him cloaked and scarfed and helmeted moved the ranks of the companions with scarlet and white plumes tossing and swaying.

Merlin, speaking almost as though to himself, said, 'Your people come and there is no more need of me. But there will come a day when I shall be with you in an hour of your own choosing when the war horns shall blow neither for victory nor defeat, but to set echoes rolling for evermore over this land to give your name everlasting life while you take the long sleep which the gods have decreed for you.'

But as he spoke, and scarcely hearing him, a great weariness and weakness seized Arturo and the chalice fell from his hands as he passed into the first sleep which would stage him well on the road to full force and proud intent again.

The Immortal Wound

– With love –
'To the one who wept
when the dream ended'

The Coin of Hadrian

In full company they came riding across the flat headwater meadows of the infant Tamesis river and breasted the growing slope to the wide mouth of the wooded valley at the head of which lay the Villa of the Three Nymphs. It was a day of high summer, the blue sky cloudless. Early morning rain had lacquered the beech and ash trees and brought the valley stream into a foaming spate above which dragon and damsel flies hawked and hunted the gnats. At the head of the company rode Arturo on the White One, the mare's long mane and tail swirling in the strong breeze, her hocks mud-splashed, while at her side loped the great hound Anga.

Arturo held himself stiffly in the saddle to ease the slow-dying pain in his left side and to lessen the chafing of the tight bandages of coarse linen strips that bound his midriff. But for him the nag of the arrow wound meant little against the growing pride and joy which filled him at this time of triumphant return. Behind him rode Lancelo carrying the wind-streamed red and white banner of the White Horse, and following them came the full company of Companions, their red and white scarves and war helmet crests tossing and swinging. Every man among them was straight-backed with pride and tight-lipped with deep pleasure at the thought of the long, hard weeks of the progress they had made down the Tamesis river to Londinium and then of the long return which had taken them, fighting and triumphant, through the lands of the Regni to give taunt and despite to the Saxon people of the south-east. There was not a man among them who did not give thanks to their God or gods or find silent prayer for bosom friend or stout flankman in cavalry charge who rode no longer with them. And not a man among them now who, with the prospect of ease and leisure so near, would not have turned at Arturo's command and ridden east again to harry the Jute and Saxon men. Yet with the prospect of comfort and rest so near in this friendly territory there was no relaxing of their hard-taught discipline. The slow-moving baggage train was shielded by two ranks of protecting horsemen and along the rising valley sides flanking patrols threaded their mounts through the thinning trees. Arturo came in triumph but with no lessening of care.

Arturo himself, glancing skywards, seeing there for the first time a slow circling of hawks and kites, frowned as he watched them. The bite of sharp instinct born of grim campaigning suddenly roused him. He reined-in and called a command to Lancelo.

A command horn blew, the sharp notes wickering and echoing from side to side of the valley. The company halted and its flanking troops formed a herisson about the baggage train. The outriding patrols on the valley sides changed formation and strung themselves in a wide protective bow across the front of the company.

At Arturo's side, now, Lancelo, his eyes skyward, said, 'When the carrion birds gather they come for feasting.'

Arturo nodded. 'Stay here. I go forward with Gelliga and his troop.'

Lancelo raised the command horn to his lips and at its call the dark-bearded, sweet-singing Gelliga with his second-in-command, fresh-faced, giant-handed Borio, came riding up with their men.

With a glance at the far sky and its circling birds of prey Gelliga said, 'Maybe the wolves have taken but a single cow somewhere and the carrion wait for the pickings.'

Arturo said nothing. He put the White One to a trot and rode forward through the thinning wood and the troop followed him. After a while they came out of the trees into the wide, sloping bowl of the valley which rose to the Villa of the Three Nymphs from whose goddess-protected fountain rose the source of the stream that watered the valley. He reined-in his mount and raised a hand. The troop spread behind him in a half moon and, as they did so, the feasting carrion birds rose in alarm from the slaughtered cattle and swine whose carcasses littered the stock pens. A thin plume of smoke rose still from the smouldering ruin of a thatched cart shed. The dead thorn fences around the crop strips were gapped and the high standing barley and bean vines lay trampled and flattened where horsemen had rampaged wantonly through them.

Tight-lipped, Arturo raised his eyes to the villa itself. Long days of restoration he and his fellows had laboured to make the old Roman villa inhabitable again. The red tiled roofs were gapped and the gaunt fire-blackened timber frames of eating hall and sleeping quarters still smouldered. Sword-sharp anxiety coursed through him. For the crops and the cattle and the wanton destruction of the villa he cared little. He had come riding back in triumph, waiting for the moment when free of the forest he would raise his eyes to the villa and see standing at the top of the wide steps that led down to its lower terrace the figure of his wife Daria, the woman whom the gods had gifted him, Daria of the bright eyes of the blue bell flower, of the lips redder than any thorn berry and hair like polished black serpentine ... Daria who carried his child. As he would have kicked the White One into a gallop he was halted by the appearance of two horsemen who came round the eastern edge of the villa, picking their way over the rubble of the long eating hall, and began to ride down towards them.

Behind him Gelliga said, 'They come in peace, my captain.'

The two men rode down to them slowly. One was elderly and the other a young man. They carried their shields slung over their shoulders, their swords were at their sides. They were war-capped, their tunics and gartered hose worn and marked with rough living, their hair long and lank over their shoulders.

Lancelo said, 'They are Cymru men and they ride the cavalry crossbreeds of Ambrosius but wear not the blue scarves of the Sabrina squadrons.'

Arturo said nothing. The destruction he saw before him he knew could be at Ambrosius's orders. For that, slaughtered cattle, spoiled crops and sacked villa, he cared nothing. But if harm or death had come to Daria, he swore to the gods that Ambrosius should pay the debt with his own blood.

The two men came down to them and now Arturo saw that the cloth of their belted tunics was crudely striped in greens, yellows and reds. The elder man – who was much the same age as Arturo's own father, Baradoc – wore a bronze torque about his neck, partly hidden by his unkempt beard. The young man at his side carried the other's features with a faithfulness that marked him as a son.

Reining-in before them the elder man raised a hand to touch his brow in friendly greeting. Then, smiling, he said, 'Arturo, son of Baradoc of the tribe of the Enduring Crow, let my first words be of happiness. Your wife, Daria, is safe and well and awaits you at the villa.'

'May the gods be blessed for that. And you, too, if it is so because of your protection.'

The man smiled. 'The gods it seems have fated me to bring happiness of this kind first to your father and now to you. You do not know me?'

Smiling now from the joy which was in him Arturo said, 'Aye, I know you now. My father has spoken often of you and of the time when you would have carried off my mother into slavery when you raided her uncle's villa in Aquae Sulis many years ago but since you were of the Ocelos tribe, all of whom are distant kin to his own, he denied you the right since he claimed that my mother was already betrothed to him.'

'Aye, he tricked me to save her, not knowing that he spoke the truth then of their love. Yes, I am Cadrus of the Ocelos.' He pulled aside the front of his tunic and showed, tattooed on the brown skin of his shoulder, the symbol of the goose with the golden feet. 'And this is my son Anwyl who would take service with you. He brings with him my blessing and ten good men, mounted and armed who wait in the woods beyond the villa. For myself I go back to my own lands in the hills west of Gobannium and Eurium beyond the Sabrina for I campaign no more with Count Ambrosius.'

'Whose work this was?' Arturo waved a hand over the dead cattle, stricken crops and the ruined villa.

Cadrus smiled. 'You should have foreseen it. You are not only banned from all his lands and those of your own Prince Gerontius, the blood price on your head for any man's taking – but you have made Ambrosius a figure of shame by drawing some of his best men from him. Aye, and now you have marched your warriors east to Londinium and south about to taunt and fight the Saxons while Ambrosius has stayed close to Glevum and Corinium and seen his own men grow restless for action and loud with complaint. To ease their grumbles a little . . .' He half turned and held out a hand towards the ruined villa, '. . . he sent a wing of the Sabrina cavalry to destroy all you have created here and to take your wife captive. And would have taken her if we had not ridden ahead and saved her.'

'For which you have my thanks yet may well suffer from the hands of your own king Vortigern with whom he is leagued.'

Cadrus shook his head. 'Vortigern is dead. There will be no levies from his lands beyond the Sabrina until Ambrosius or some other proves his worth –'

'And that man.' Anwyl, despite his father's frown, broke in sharply, 'is you, my lord Arturo. The news of your great progress has run fast before you. Men speak openly in the barracks of Corinium that now there is only one way to manliness and true action against the Saxon kind, and that with the companions of Arturo. And I . . .' He stopped suddenly and looked at his father.

Cadrus smiled and with a cock of his head towards Arturo said, 'My wolf cub has much to learn, not least that he steps out of place from over-eagerness. But take him and his men and see them blooded. They are all of the Ocelos and will serve you well when you have schooled them.'

'I take them willingly. But now I would go to my wife wherever you have lodged her.'

Cadrus wheeled his horse about and pointed up the long valley slope. 'She waits for you.'

Looking upwards Arturo saw that Daria now stood at the

top of the courtyard steps waiting for him. He gave an order to Lancelo and then urged the White One into a canter towards the villa.

Standing on the steps, the sound of falling water from the spring that filled the broad basin of the fountain of the three nymphs making quiet music for her ears, Daria waited for the coming of her husband. The eager breeze moulded the soft stuff of her blue woollen gown about her body and, against the constraint of the yellow band about her head, lifted and toyed with the fall of her ebony hair. One hand ran nervously with pleasure along the amber beads which strung her neck and the sun dully fired the bronze clasps which ringed the dusky skin of her arms. Gown, beads and armlets were all tokens of his love, all plunder spoil sent ahead of his coming, but none so dear or precious as the gift which she held now for him, that life which in the last few days had begun to move with increasing vigour beneath her heart, the child of his begetting.

As Arturo rode towards her a command horn blew below, the notes long and compelling. The company broke line and formation and moved to make camp in the lower meadow, men and mounts moving with an ease and assurance which had never been there during the long training days of the past, a sureness never to be perfected by drills, a sureness which only came from campaigning.

At Daria's side, Ansold, her father, seeing the companions disposing themselves below, said, ' 'Tis battle that puts the final temper to a sword. Born of hammer, fire and water it may be, but true virtue it must find against its own kind.' He spat with the wind and grunted something else to himself.

Daria smiled to herself, knowing his envy. Great swordsmith though he was, he had longed to follow Arturo as had done Lancelo, her brother and Arturo's banner-bearer and righthand man. Arturo reined-in at the foot of the steps and the horse tang of the White One came to her on the breeze as her eyes marked Arturo's bearded face. He had lost weight and his skin was dark and tight-stretched like the leather of a worn belt. Yet the shine in his eyes was the old shine and for a moment his lips showed pale and pink in the purse of a private smile for her. But she knew the pain and wound stiffness in him as he dismounted, came to her and took her hand and kissed it, saying, 'You wear my gifts.'

Remembering sharply the boasting boy she had long ago first met on a rain-swept Dumnonian moor, she smiled with the happiness that flooded her and answered him in the teasing manner which was always open love play between them.

'There is no gift, man of the tribe of the Enduring Crow, greater than your safe return. So – you have moved against the Saxon kind at last. May the gods make you content enough to stay by my side until you are whole again.'

'The wound is clean and heals fast.'

'That I would see for myself.'

She took him by the arm and led him across the courtyard, through the rubble and desolation, to her room in the south wing of the villa, the walls fire-scorched, the roof gapped and its beams roughly propped with newcut timbers, and then out to the open portico. Here, untouched by fire, a great growth of yellow roses rambled up the pillars, surviving still from the days, long distant now, of the peace and prosperity of the villa before Rome had withdrawn its last active legions from this its most northern province, budding and blooming through the days when the ill-starred Vortigern had made federation with Hengist and Horsa to aid him against Scot and Pict only to find them with the passage of years not allies but land and plunder-hungry pirates. Close to the roses stood a table and two stools, the table bearing an earthenware jug of wine and drinking beakers.

Daria poured wine for him, but before she could pass the beaker, he put his arm around her and kissed her and the trembling in her body was matched by the shaking of his own hard frame.

Releasing her, Arturo said, 'Now tell me that you and the boy are well.'

Smiling against the certainty in him, she said, 'The child and I are well, my lord. To know that it is a boy you must –' the

451

tip of her tongue flicked teasingly between her full red lips,
'– as usual have had private word from the gods.'

Soberly Arturo said, 'It is a boy. In a dream the gods have
promised it.'

'*Aie* ... those dreams of yours. Then there can be no doubt.
Now drink and then strip. Your wound to me is of more account
than anything else.'

Arturo hesitated, then grinning and shrugging his shoulders,
he began to strip to humour her, saying, 'From Sorviodunum I
rode ahead alone to the Circle of the Gods one night. There
after Prince Gerontius had outlawed me I buried beneath one of
the standing stones a gift from my mother which I would make
a gift on his birth to my son. As I dug in the dawn light one,
whom I thought to be a homeless wanderer, took bow and
arrow to me for the sake of plunder. The arrow missed its true
mark. I killed the man with my sword to find he was my uncle
Inbar, long cast out of the tribe for his villainies ... a wanderer
who would have killed me, less for the blood money, than for
the joy he would have taken in the grief of my mother and
father.'

'And the gift?'

Dropping his short cloak to the portico balustrade Arturo
reached within his shirt and pulled out the silver chalice which
his Roman mother, Tia, had given him when he had left the
tribe as a youth to go to Isca Dumnonia to serve with the
cavalry of Prince Gerontius. As Daria took it, he said, 'There is
a story to it which I will tell you the day that our son is born
and I place it between his hands.'

Daria smiled. 'A story, no doubt, of gods and magic.'

Running the back of his hand down the soft bloom of her
cheek, Arturo grinned. 'In truth, yes. But not one of my dreaming. Would you doubt the word of my mother Tia?'

'Never. But yours often.' As she spoke Daria turned the silver
chalice in her hands. It was little larger than a drinking goblet
with handles each side curved and worked in the shape of rams'
horns. One of the handles was badly bent and the bowl was
marked with dents and had become tarnished from burial in

the ground. Around the outside rim ran a continuous key pattern and on one side, in bold relief, was a large round boss in the shape of a circular wreath of bay leaves enclosing the outline of a human eye. As she turned it in her hands Daria was thinking that although she had often said she doubted his words there was in them a passion and conviction which could not be ignored. There could be no doubt of his belief that he was marked for greatness by the gods to whom he always looked for signs of approval – and found them, though others might not be so convinced – before taking any great action. This belief was a flame in him which burned strongly, never wavering or dimming. But for her he was her husband and man. The wish was suddenly strong in her that the child should be a boy. For that she would pray, but to her own God.

At the sight of the wound she was relieved to see that it had begun to heal cleanly. As she washed and fresh salved it, Daria gave him the news of Count Ambrosius which old Ansold had gleaned by secret visits to nearby Corinium. Ambrosius would have marched eastwards at mid-summer against the Saxons. But Prince Gerontius at Isca had sent only scant and poorly trained levies, and from the now dead Vortigern had come no levy but a straggling of small chiefs and independent young warriors. So Count Ambrosius had sat tight, too wise and cautious to mount a great campaign with a doubtful force.

Sipping his wine and listening Arturo felt at once contempt and compassion for the man. Ambrosius dreamt still of the past glories of the Empire and was impatient to rid this country of Pict and Scot and Saxon kind and call himself Emperor. He lacked no passion for that end, but the glory would be forever denied him. Caution inhabited the centre of his heart like a frightened harvest mouse huddled in its grass nest high in the summer corn, scenting the rank of hunting marten or polecat. There was scorn in him at the pettiness of the man who, hearing of his own small progress with a handful of men, could give vent to it by raiding the villa and destroying crops and cattle. There would be no joy in the hearts of the gods at such smallness of spirit. *Aie* ... already, he knew without arrogance, that they looked elsewhere to place their favours. Although his own progress had been from lack of men no great affair, he knew that their eyes were on him. They had fought no great battles for he lacked men as yet for these. But the men would come, and come quickly now as the noise of his name spread and the story of his long-spanned foray was told and re-told and carried far and wide, from hearth to hearth and town to town. And what bard or traveller was there who would not add his own wonder touches? Then let it be so. There was a power in the sword which showed only in the heat of battle. But there was a power in the word which worked without let and spread fast like bright morning over the land.

At his side Daria said, 'You smile. But I doubt it is from the pleasure of returning.'

For a moment he would have told her the truth of the smile, but then not wanting the gentle mockery which she alone had the privilege of offering, he said affectionately, 'Then you are wrong. I smile because the gods have been good to me in linking your life with mine. As lovers we lay in the uncurling bracken together and the high larks sang our happiness. As man and wife I have lain at your sleeping side and your soft breath has touched my cheek like a silk-winged moth. I smile because each day I have wakened beside you the morning light borrowed brightness from your opening eyes. And I smile now because –'

'Because, my Arto –' Daria interrupted him, '– you have finished your wine and it fills your head with fancies.' She leaned forward and kissed him on the brow, and went on, 'My lord, I am content to see you back. You will rest and recover, and that will be all my happiness.'

Arturo said nothing, but the smile went from his face and slowly he shook his head and then said flatly, 'No, there is no rest for me, not for many a long year.' With a gesture of his hand down the valley to the ruined crop strips and to the carrion birds that still fought and bickered over the dead cattle, he said angrily, 'The gods arranged this welcome for me. You think it was to daunt me? No – it was to show me clearly their will. Tomorrow at sunset we ride for Corinium. No man now, not even Count Ambrosius, can offer injury to Arturo and his companions without knowing that it will be returned in full measure ... fire brand for fire brand, slaughter for slaughter.'

Eyes widening Daria said, 'You would move against Corinium where Ambrosius numbers a hundred and more men for each one of yours?'

'Against Corinium, no. I have no quarrel with honest citizens and work folk. But against Ambrosius and the Sabrina cavalry which are camped outside it. Their food stores and their cattle shall know fire and slaughter. Their barracks and their eating halls shall be gutted and left roofless. And when all is done there will be those of the Sabrina squadron who will hide their smiles and their joy and will ride to join me. Under the sky nothing happens by chance. The gods rule the world. Mark their signs, read their message and obey it, and their favour is with you until the day they justly decree the last grain of sand has fallen to the bottom of the hour glass.'

Tight-lipped Daria held back the protest within her. When the madness of the gods touched this man, her lover, husband, father of her child to be, she knew that there was no crossing his purpose. She lifted the wine jug and refilled his beaker.

When they had ridden out long weeks ago to make their progress down the Tamesis river into the Saxon lands they had numbered two troops of twenty-four horse each and a remount section of six horses – scarce sixty horses and fighting men. They had lost and won men and horses along the way and now mustered three troops of thirty horse and a remount troop of ten horse. The company of companions had grown and with it, too, had the baggage train and the men who manned it. The growth would continue almost each day.

At sunset the next evening they paraded for their foray against Count Ambrosius. Arturo took with him but two troops, and there was not a man among them who did not know the hard country ahead of them, and knew, too, the cavalry camp of the Sabrina Wing at Corinium. Many of them had come from there to join Arturo, discarding the blue neck scarves of Am-

brosius for the red and white scarves and war helmet plumes of
Arturo. Durstan, the first of the companions who had been
outlawed with Arturo by Prince Gerontius, led one troop with
Garwain as his second-in-command. Black-bearded Gelliga with
Borio as his second-in-command led the other. The rest of the
companions stayed to guard the villa camp with Anwyl, son of
Cadrus, and his ten men. Cadrus himself went with Arturo,
not claiming the honour as a return for the service he had rendered him, but pointing out that Corinium lay on his route to
Glevum where he must cross the Sabrina to reach his homelands. Before they set out Pasco, the broad-minded priest who
had shared all their past campaigning, sitting on his sturdy dun
pony, made prayer for them and kept it short for one of his
virtues was never to give warriors more measure of admonition
than he sensed their mood would take.

'You fight now,' he called in his high voice, 'to free this land
from the tyranny of strangers and the covetousness and pride
of those of your own race who see only in victory a bloody
licence to oppress their own people. To be such is to be less in
the eyes of the gods, and the Father of all gods, than the creatures of this earth – for where is there fowl or fish or four-
legged beast that makes war to enslave its own kind? In victory
be merciful. Be less than that and when you die your spirits
shall wander unshrived for evermore in limbo.' He touched his
brow and raised a hand in blessing, piping loudly, 'Holy Christos
and His great Father and timeless Dis and fierce Badb and gentle
Coventina give you protection and comfort as long as you move
in the ways of truth and honourable brotherhood and companionship.'

As he finished speaking Lancelo at Arturo's side blew the
command horn and the horsemen moved away to flanks and
centre and breasted the steep slope behind the villa.

Standing beside the courtyard steps Daria watched them go.
Arturo had given her his love and protection. But neither to her
nor to any other woman had she not come into his life could
he ever truly give himself. The gods had claimed him long be-

fore she had met him on the rain-swept Western moors beyond the Tamarus river, the old, fierce gods of this country – not hers to whom out of respect for her and others like her among his company he paid respect. Ambrosius dreamed of the past glories of the Empire and ached to clear this country of its foes and then take to himself the imperial purple ... Aye, and then maybe turn his eyes southwards to Gaul and beyond, brooding in a dream of restoration of all the provinces that Goths and Vandals now held. The dream was void of reason for time could not be turned back. Only Arturo held the true dream; to clear this land of its invaders, to make it one country and to give its peoples peace and prosperity under the sign of the White Horse. For this end the old gods had claimed him. With any woman or man who loved him and gave him their companionship and trust but did not read his heart aright there must always be the fierce, intermittent ache of loneliness. There was no doubt in her mind that though he loved her she was less to him than his love of country, than his love of the gods who, he had no doubt, shaped his destiny, and – the truth of this more easily borne – less than his desire for their child to be a boy. The dream the gods gave him called for a son to follow him and to make fast the bright future for which he laboured now. With this she was content, but she knew she would be less than a woman truly in love not to have grieved in the dark stretches of night when she lay alone for that part of him which was forever beyond her understanding and cherishing.

Three nights later as she lay on the furs of her couch while the quiet of the valley was broken now and then by the call of nightjar and owl, Arturo and his companions raided the cavalry camp which lay a little off the Glevum road to the north of Corinium.

They had waited in the thick woods some miles from the camp, the woods which had once sheltered Arturo and the now dead horsetrader Volpax in the days when they had made horse stealing raids on the cavalry picket lines for mounts. They came down on it in the hour when sentries and guards yawn and rub their eyes and nod with sleep, when the fighting men off duty were filled with dreams or sunk in the lingering stupor of the past evening's wine and mead drinking, when the brazier fires of the picket watches along the horse lines burn low; and they came, spread wide across the heath and meadow land in a great front of two lines of horses shaped like a crescent moon. They bore down on the camp, with no shout or war cry, with only the pounding beat of hooves drumming the hard ground in a rolling tattoo of endless growing thunder. They came, the extended double rank of horses and warriors, sweeping from the north like the onward rush of a great tidal wave, fiercer and swifter than any of the great bores which from time to time swept up the broad channel of the not far distant Sabrina river, and they overwhelmed the camp in a wave of destruction. But no companion killed unless to protect his own life. Arturo had given this order for among his own men were many who had come to him from the Sabrina cavalry wing. They lit the heath and straw torches they carried from the picket fires and took flame to huts and brushwood stockades. They stampeded the picket lines, setting the hobbled and tethered Sabrina horses rearing and kicking and squealing with panic so that they broke free from their tethers to run or stumble or roll loose into the camp to add confusion to confusion. They fired corn sheds and stores and set ablaze the year's new hayricks and burst through the folding pens of sheep and cattle to send them stampeding into the night and the surrounding countryside from which – since town and country folk never hesitated to take the gifts the gods sent – less than a third of them were ever recovered. They swept round the great blue tent of the Praefectus of the Sabrina Wing (Praefectus because Count Ambrosius clung to the names and ranks of the old Roman formations) slashing the guy and straining ropes so that it collapsed like a stricken monster over the cavalry commander as he lay in his bed and trapped him there until long after the great crescent of Arturo's men and horse had wheeled at the far end of the camp and swept back and through the camp again as the fires of destruction now turned night to day. As they went the horns of the crescent curved more sharply inwards and the charge took ahead of it all loose and stray mounts herding them northwards into the night as booty.

They left behind them firmly planted in the earth, so that it was the first thing the Praefectus saw when he wormed his way out from under the loose tent cloth, a tall standard pole driven into the ground by Lancelo as he galloped by. From it in the freshening night breeze flew the banner of the White Horse, snow white and blood red, streaming in the wind. Tied to it was an old piece of vellum on which Arturo had written – in the Roman tongue as a touch of mockery to the imperial dreams of Ambrosious – this message :

Arturo and his Companions of the White Horse thank Count Ambrosius for the courtesy of his virtuous concern for the well-being of all those at the Villa of the Three Nymphs who do now humbly return it in somewhat fuller measure – Arturo, War Duke of Britain.

Later the following afternoon in the fortress at Glevum which was Ambrosius's headquarters the Praefectus of the Sabrina Wing stood stiff-faced before his commanding officer and watched him as he read the message. Ambrosius, wearing a red cloak over a well-polished cuirass, raised a hand and smoothed one of the greying wings of hair which tempered his growing baldness. After a moment or two he lifted his head. From the large, severely lined face a pair of narrow-lidded faded blue eyes fixed the Praefectus coldly. He raised a hand and eased the cloak more comfortably on his left shoulder and then said in a quiet, bitter-edged voice, 'So, he calls himself Dux Bellorum. In jest or in earnest?'

'I know not, my lord.'

'And maybe neither does he. But no matter. He has made a fool of you, a laughing stock of the Sabrina Wing, and a mockery of me. More than that wherever men sit and drink and gossip, wherever pedlar or packman stops to beg crust or drink at farm or hovel, the story of this night's work will run and grow and grow and grow!' With each repetition of the word 'grow' he thumped the table before him angrily with his fist, his face stiff with anger.

'Maybe, my lord. But he should not live long to enjoy the pleasure of it. I wait but your order to take my men to the villa.'

Thumping his fist on the table Ambrosius almost shouted, 'You are a fool, Corbulo! By the time you get there he will be long gone. No, go back to Corinium and I wish you joy of the looks and laughter of the townsfolk – which you have well earned. Go!'

Without a word Praefectus Corbulo saluted and left the room to seek the staff officers' quarters and the ease of a large goblet of wine which, whether earned or not, he badly needed.

Alone in his room Count Ambrosius picked up the tattered piece of vellum and read the message once more. Then slowly he began to smile to himself and shake his head. Dux Bellorum, he thought ... and all the message in the Roman tongue. That at least was courtesy ... By Mars, the man had spirit to match his courage and arrogance and he dreamed high. Well, that were no failing given the right schooling to go with it. What should he do? Smoke him out wherever he might now seek to lodge himself? Or let him run under whatever favour the gods might show him? And then use him? More and more men were beginning to be drawn to him. Did they sense that he had that divine afflatus, that magic which he himself had never known? Well, then why not let him run until his power and his followers had grown and then cut him down and step into his place, grieve for his loss, honour him in death, and then gather into his own command the army which he would have created ... Aye, even leave his men the White Horse banner under which to fight for him still, every man going into battle knowing that his ghost rode ahead of them, that his magic armoured and protected them still.

He reached forward and beat with his bare knuckles on the hanging gong which stood on the table. When the guard outside the room came he gave him an order. Then he rose and went to the window. Looking westward over the partly refurbished Glevum walls he could see a great loop of the Sabrina river and beyond the rise of the wooded hills that rose and died in the mist haze of summer, a mist that hid the mountains of Cymru . . . mountains and valleys which were full of fighting men who could be drawn across the Sabrina by a leader with the magic and appeal of an Arturo.

He turned as the guard came to the door and announced the Decurio Aulus Venutius, the troop commander of Ambrosius's personal mounted bodyguard, a Roman of full blood still although his family had been domiciled in Britain for eight generations, a proud young man who shared Ambrosius's imperial dreams and served him faithfully without questioning or seeking for the reasons behind any order given to him.

Ambrosius sat down while Venutius stood before him, a young man in his early thirties, sandy-haired, clean shaven, a pink and white complexion which the sun never affected, something a little plump and boyish about his face still, the pale jade-coloured eyes frank and marking a seeming guilelessness which masked, as Ambrosius knew well, a ruthless devotion to him and his aspirations. Venutius sensed – though no open words had ever been spoken between them about it – that his fate and the promise of future power and position would wax or wane with his master's. Like a good cavalry man he never questioned orders, nor would he tolerate any questioning of his own. He wore now a short off-duty white tunic waisted with a soft leather belt dyed blue with woad, the colour matching the neatly tied cavalry scarf about his neck, a pleasant-seeming young man who could be trusted under the greatest stress never to show the full truth of his real nature.

Gently Ambrosius said, 'You know my faith in you?'

'Yes, my commander.'

'Three nights from now you will desert from your command here in Glevum. You will take your horse and arms and ride south and find Arturo of the White Horse. You will join him as so many of the Sabrina Cavalry Wing have done. You will give him faithful and loyal service. Aye, if it comes to it you will die at his side in battle as any of his other companions would do. You will love and honour and obey him in all things.'

'Yes, my commander.'

'All this you will do – until one comes to give you my wishes.' Ambrosius leaned back a little in his seat and felt beneath his toga for the belt which he wore around his under tunic. His hand came free from the belt pouch and he tossed on to the table between them a coin. It lay on the boards, shining dully in the sunlight which came through the window. 'Whoever comes will bring the coin with them so that you will know he comes from me. You will do whatever is ordered. And think not that my messenger will come only once. Time will show how long my need for an ally in Arturo's camp will last. But when that time is past you will come back to stand first at my right hand.'

'Yes, my commander.'

'Good. Take up the coin now and look at it for I would have you know it well.'

Venutius reached out and picked up the coin. He knew it already, though not in detail, for when Count Ambrosius was in counsel he often absently took it from his belt pouch and toyed with it as though the play of his fingers over it aided his thoughts and decisions. It was an aureus of the Emperor Hadrian, a gold coin much worn. Still clear on one side was the head of the great Emperor and on the other a seated goddess figure wearing a Phrygian cap and holding in her left hand an upright spear with the words – *Roma Aeterna* – encircling her, and the rim was marred in one place by a deep nick in the soft metal.

Venutius handed the coin back and said quietly, 'I shall remember it and wait for it, my commander.'

Ambrosius took the coin and, fingering it in thought for a moment, suddenly smiled, and said, 'Then go and become a good Companion.'

'Yes, my commander.'

Decurio Aulus Venutius saluted and left, and Ambrosius sat slowly fingering the gold coin of Hadrian and said quietly to himself, 'Rome Eternal . . . Rome Eternal . . .'

The Camp above the Cam

Four days after the raid on the Sabrina cavalry camp they left the Villa of the Three Nymphs. They took with them the few cattle which had escaped slaughter and the small supply of food and grain which was left to them. The ruined crops, so near to the point of harvest, meant that they faced a lean winter. They loaded the wheeled carts and the few pack animals with the most vital and precious of their household and warfare gear. What they could not carry they left to the settlers and the people of the district who had befriended them. Arturo rode ahead with Durstan, his friend of the old Isca days who had been outlawed with him by Prince Gerontius, and Gelliga was left in command of the progress of the slow baggage train and the full complement of cavalry troops. Daria pressed to be allowed to ride ahead with Arturo but he forbade it. She was near four months gone with child and rode a quiet pony. When she tired of that, she was carried on one of the baggage carts and always close to her hand were her brother, Lancelo, and her father, Ansold.

They went south over the Tamesis river and then across the country of the headwaters of the Abona river which flowed through Aquae Sulis and finally found the sea at the mouth of the Sabrina estuary. They crossed the lands of the old Belgae tribes to reach the northern limits of the territory of the Durotriges. Here they swung sharply due west. As he rode Durstan smiled to himself for they were now retracing almost exactly the path he and Arturo had taken in the days when they had escaped from Isca Dumnoniorum after being outlawed by Gerontius.

He said now, 'This place you have chosen will bring you no

favour with Gerontius, nor that of King Melwas of the Summerlands in whose country it lies.'

'We shall see. But since – no matter how remote it is at the
moment – they both fear the threat of any Saxon approach
from the East they will take some comfort from knowing that
we stand first in their path.'

'It will be many a long day before the Saxons thrust so far
West.'

Arturo smiled. 'Long days become long years. But well within
our lifetime you will see it. The gods will favour them to give
us the trial of proving our manhood and right to hold what is
our own.'

'The gods have told you this?'

Unexpectedly Arturo grinned. 'They had no need. Hengist
and the other Saxon leaders might now be content to sit and
hold what they have south and east of Londinium and northwards along the Saxon shores – but each spring more of their
countrymen arrive in their long keels. And they are land and
plunder-hungry men. A bucket can only hold so much water.
The Saxon bucket is almost full and must soon overspill.'

'This place we go to has already been marked by Gerontius.
Your own father works on it still?'

Arturo shook his head. 'The work was hampered by Melwas.
He wants no fortifications overlooking his country.'

'What greeting then can you expect from him?'

Arturo shrugged his shoulders. 'All those who stand against
me – even in good conscience – must know that the gods are
with us. All that is needed is courage and patience. The rest is
in the hands of the gods.'

Durstan said no more. There was no man in the company of
the Companions now who would say or argue more once Arturo said that the gods were with him. The gods of his country
had Durstan's reverence but he sometimes wondered ... aye,
occasionally felt sure ... that the will of Arturo was more often
than not remote from any dictation of the gods. Arturo lived
in a dream of his own creation, the great dream of a Britain
freed from the faintest taint of Saxon intrusion. But, by the

gods, one had to admit that once set on course there was no stopping him. The thought occurred to him that although – perhaps unknowingly – Arturo took the name of the gods in vain they looked kindly on his presumption and, so far, had given him their favour.

Late in the afternoon of the fourth day of their travel they came to the borderlands of the Summerlands held by King Melwas. Here the country was gentler. For the most part men worked their plots in peace, game was plentiful and when the gods gave good harvest only the improvident had to pull the drawstrings of their trew tops tight in winter to still their bellies' grumbles. But the roads were still broken and ruined for the days were long past since the last Roman *mensor* travelled them with a surveying detachment of legionaries to keep them in good state by the enforcement of local labour. Men now used the old tracks and ridgeways and the ancient pathways over down and through deep forest. Long before sunset they reached the edge of the smooth downland and following it saw slowly rise from the green country ahead a great hill which stood on its own in a sweeping bight of the downs. A long loop of a river called the Cam curved around the foot of its westward flanks to run away to the north through the heart of the Summerlands on its way to the Sabrina sea. They rode up the mount, following a track from the north-east, through the thin skirting of trees around its base. Finally they came out on to the great ridge-backed plateau of its crest, the whole of whose perimeter was enclosed by a triple line of ancient earthworks and ramparts long neglected and falling into ruin.

On the top of the plateau ridge, where stood the remains of a Roman shrine to the god Mars, raised there to mark the conquest of the hill fort by the westward thrust of the legions when they had first come to the country over five hundred years before, Arturo and Durstan sat their horses, slacking their reins so that the mounts lowered their heads and grazed the sweet grass. To the north-west lay the Summerlands, the country of King Melwas. In the still lucid light of early evening they could pick out the green slopes of Ynys-witrin, the glass isle, at whose foot Melwas had his summer quarters for he delighted in the abundance of game and fish which filled the rivers, streams and meres and the wide spread of marshlands. And far beyond the glass isle, backed by the sun sparkle on the waters of the sea, there stood up, too, the great knoll of the raven god Bran.

That night, as Durstan slept rolled in his heavy cloak, Arturo kept watch with Anga at his side, and he was full of content. This hill above the river Cam would serve all his wants for some time to come. The plateau too was large enough to house more men and horses than he would have under his command for a long time to come. There was room too for the growing of crops and the building of shelters for which there was plenty of timber to be cut from the steeply wooded western side of the hill. For water there were two spring-fed wells, one within the perimeter and the other a little way down the slope on the north-east side. As he sat there listening to the call of a little owl from the wooded slope and the steady cropping sound of the hobbled horses as they grazed in the warm night, he knew that the coming winter would be hard, and made harder if he found turned against him the anger of Prince Gerontius and King Melwas. They could harry and plague him at a time when the real hardships up here would be hunger and the fast need for warm quarters. There was nothing he could do to appease Gerontius, but the Prince would never move against him into King Melwas's lands unless Melwas gave leave. The first thing he had to do was to make some sort of peace with the King – and a man who came suing for peace, no matter for how short a period, must bear gifts and the promise of more. The main body of the Companions would not arrive for at least another three days. The peace must be made before they arrived. To ride with only Durstan as companion to King Melwas was to offer the man the chance of treachery. Chewing on a sweet grass stalk he considered the wisdom of this move. Should he wait for his people to come and then lodge here in open contempt of Melwas or should he sweeten the man by riding without companions to seek his peace? As he pondered this the sky to the north-west was suddenly and fiercely afire with the burning streamer of a falling star which curved earthwards and finally burnt itself away high over the summit of Ynys-witrin. Without doubt he knew that the gods had spoken.

They rode into Ynys-witrin the next morning over the long causeway which spanned the marshes at its foot and were halted by the guard at the stockade which blocked the entrance to the small settlement. Arturo asked for an audience with King Melwas. A messenger was sent to the King and after a long delay – deliberately prolonged, Arturo was sure, to stamp upon them his authority and power – they were conducted through the settlement to the edge of a wide mere on whose bank had been built of withy poles and rush thatch a long hall which Melwas used as his hunting lodge. Children played and frolicked about the water's edge and a guard of long-haired, half-naked marsh warriors armed with swords and spears formed a half circle about a rough wooden table outside the hall. Here Melwas sat, bareheaded, the sun firing the red tints in his fair hair, wearing a short cloak of otter skins across his shoulders, his chest, tanned brown, bare to the top of his trews. The man wore no finery, and carried no mark of kingship; a man who had twice Arturo's age, a man powerfully built with a large, pock-marked face, whose eyes were hidden as he bent over a fishing net spread on the table and his fingers worked skilfully with waxed thread repairing a hole in it.

Arturo and Durstan dismounted and Arturo, standing at the head of the White One who blew gently through her nostrils not liking the smell of rotting fish and offal that came from the midden at the nearby water's edge, dropped a hand and touched Anga's head, as the hound, sensing some stress in the air, began to growl low and deep in its throat. The growling stopped at Arturo's touch and Melwas raised his head to show grey-green eyes, the skin about them deeply creased from years of sun glare on the waters and marshes of the Summerlands.

Unexpectedly Melwas smiled and said, 'So at last I meet Arturo of the White Horse, son of Baradoc, outlaw of Prince Gerontius, thorn in the side of Count Ambrosius and –' his tongue flicked between his lips like a lapping cat's – 'the scourge of the Eastern long-keel men. All these to so many. And what are you to me?'

'One who comes in friendship and asks for sanctuary on the hill above the Cam until such time as I can turn against the Saxons again.'

'And if I refuse, and hold you now to send to Prince Gerontius?'

Arturo smiled. 'Would I have come, King Melwas, had that thought held truth in my mind?'

'But it may be the truth in my mind.'

Arturo shook his head. 'No, for last night the gods spoke to me and gave sign that I should come to you. I could have stayed on the hill until my company arrived and defied you – but I am here and make you the gift of friendship.' Arturo stepped forward, ignoring the tensing of the Melwas warriors who stood around, and drew from within his surcoat a cloth bundle which he put on the table before King Melwas. He un- wrapped it to display the gifts he had brought, all of it plunder taken from the Saxons; an old Roman gold chain, two bronze arm bands with their bosses intricately worked in enamels that flashed with kingfisher brilliance, a silver ring fashioned in the form of a snake, its coils studded with small emeralds and its eyes two bright rubies and, last of all, a small bronze wine flagon whose handle was shaped in the form of a hunting dog which stalked a pair of finely modelled duck which adorned the spout. It was no surprise to Arturo when Melwas picked up the flagon first and ran his fingers over the moulding of the dog and the ducks.

Melwas looked up at Arturo and his eyes were suddenly shrewd beneath their busy, sandy brows. 'Fine gifts ... aye. Well then, you shall have my leave to stay on the hill if you add to them one other.' He glanced from Arturo to Anga who sat on his haunches at his side, and went on, 'Two days ago I lost my best hound to a boar. Give your hound the word to come to me and serve me and, even though Gerontius and Am- brosius give me commands and threats to deny you winter sanctuary, I will defy them. *Aie* . . . give me the hound and you can take back these other gifts.'

For a moment or two Arturo said nothing. The noisy, happy cries of the children bathing and playing by the mere filled the air. A heron flapped low and clumsily across the water and at his side Anga snapped at a bluebottle which teased his muzzle. Then slowly shaking his head Arturo said, 'No, my lord. There are three things which the gods deny any man the right to gift to another, a virtuous wife, a horse which was the first to carry him into battle, and a hound which would stay by his dead body till death for itself gave it release to follow him into the Shades. No, my lord – you ask too much.'

Melwas was silent for a while and then, with a shrug of his shoulders, he said indifferently, 'Then my young warrior, Arturo, it seems that the gods have betrayed you and have sent you here to rid themselves of you.' He raised his right hand and pointed his forefinger at Arturo. With the movement, each of the men in the half circle about him lifted his spear and held it poised ready to throw. Melwas went on, 'They wait but one word from me.'

Arturo dropped a hand so that it rested on Anga's head and he answered in a level voice, 'There may come a day when the gods will desert me, King Melwas. But this is not the day. Give the word and you shall see the spears turned aside from me in full flight.'

Melwas's lips tightened and his brows almost hooded his eyes as he faced Arturo's defiance, then suddenly he gave a great shout of laughter and smacked the table before him with his fist and cried, laughing, 'Lower your hackles, you fighting cock. You think I would tempt the wrath of the gods by the death of one they love so much? But know this, for a hound such as yours I would trade any of my wives – though to be fair none of them are virtuous. The hill is yours and we will drink to it.' He turned and shouted to his womenfolk who stood bunched about the doorway of the long hall to bring wine and at this his body-guard lowered their spears.

As they rode back to the hill fortress through the early afternoon Durstan said to Arturo, 'The gods were truly with you.'

Arturo nodded 'As they always are. But also a man has his own wits. Gifts are made freely as we gave our plunder. But no man of pride names the gift he wants. The mind of Melwas was open to read. He did but follow a humour to test me.'

Durstan said no more. Close though he was to Arturo, the first of the companions, he knew that there would never be any man with a true reading of his nature. Well, it would be a story to tell the others when they arrived, and in his mind he began to hear the telling as he would give it . . . nay, sing it, for it deserved the rise and fall of rhythm and the stamp of rhyme. Arturo and the Spears of Melwas The spears that were thrown only to be miraculously turned aside in mid-air by the gods . . . when the mead flowed the stamp of feet and thumping of fists on the boards would set the wonder alive to spread through all the land long after all that lived today were dead and dust.

Within the week the full company had arrived at the hill and every daylight hour was spent in establishing itself there. Trees were felled to make living quarters, stables and cattle pens. Furrows were turned to make crop strips across the gentler slopes of the hilltop and the little of seed corn left was sown. They cut late hay and carted it from the free land to the south and each day game was hunted along the downs and river valleys for fresh meat and also for salting against the winter. Deer, boar and small herds of escaped or abandoned kine, swine and sheep roamed in the woods and heaths.

There was a small settlement of King Melwas's people nearby and Arturo gave strict orders that none of them was to be molested nor the goods or cattle taken. As the weeks passed traders and pedlars were to learn of the camp on the hill above the Cam and found that they could come and go freely to offer their wares. But even so, it was clear that the winter would bring lean times. Leave was given to any man who asked to go back to his own people so long as he returned well before spring. Few asked for most preferred to tighten their belts and stay with Arturo. If there were any doubts in Arturo's mind about the near starvation they would have to face as the months passed he showed none of it. The future was in the hands of the gods and there would be no favours from them for any man who doubted their powers. And already the gods were on their side for warriors hearing of the camp began to drift to them and most of them came carrying a grain or roots sack across their horses' backs. But of all the men who gathered to him Arturo was most content with the first to ride up the hill only a few days after his company had come to rest there. This was Decurio Aulus Venutius, the commander of Ambrosius's personal mounted bodyguard.

He was escorted to Arturo by Gelliga who still could hardly believe that such a high ranking Sabrina officer should choose to join them. Arturo was sitting on a rock outside the rough shelter which had quickly been made for himself and Daria. Daria, refusing to over-cherish herself, was away with some of the other women gathering hazel nuts from the hill slopes to be ground into flour for the winter.

When Gelliga had left them, taking Venutius's horse to be watered and fed in the lines, Arturo said, 'And what brings Aulus Venutius to my side?'

The plumpish, fresh-complexioned face of the man creased into a smile. 'Aulus Venutius grew tired of being barrack-bound and bodyguard to Count Ambrosius. I am a cavalry man and, like my horse, have grown stale and restless for the need of action.'

'All I can give you here is a tight-belted winter of hard and cold lying.'

Venutius shrugged his shoulders. 'After the winter comes the spring. I am tired of keeping sword and armour bright for ceremonial parades.'

'No matter your rank in Glevum you will serve here as a trooper.'

'That will be no hardship. There are many here who have known me as such. Although I am of full Roman blood this is my country and my family have served it faithfully for many generations. I have no more love for the Saxons than you, my lord.'

'You know the mind of Count Ambrosius and the working of his thoughts?'

'Yes, my lord.'

'Then we will talk about this soon. But for now go to Gelliga and he will assign you to a troop and your duties.'

That night, as Arturo lay by Daria's side in the darkness, she said, 'Your Venutius gives up a good deal to come here. Your name and your force grow. Ambrosius could have sent him.'

'All things are possible. But had I been Ambrosius I would have sent someone of lesser rank and importance.'

'Maybe that is how Ambrosius has reasoned.'

'Then I will keep that in my mind too.'

Smiling to herself Daria went on, 'Maybe the gods will give you a sign to prove him faithful.'

Arturo laughed gently. 'They have no need for I have already decided to put him to the test. If he comes to kill me – and what else could Ambrosius wish? – then he shall have his chance, and soon.'

Four days later on a day of great heat, as though summer were making a last gesture in defiance of the onthrust of autumn, Arturo rode down from the hill to the river Cam with a party of men to set osier traps in the river to take the eels which with the coming of autumn were now beginning to run seawards. He took with him Venutius. When he had seen the men set to their work Arturo rode up the river to a spot where it broadened into a wide pool, its far side thickly matted with tall mace reeds and beyond them a tangled scrub growth of willows and thorns.

Pulling up the White One Arturo nodded at the pool and said to Venutius, 'It is too long since I had a proper washing.' He dismounted and began to strip free his clothes. 'Keep guard on me.'

Naked he dived into the pool and swam for a while. Then he came back to stand below the bank where he reached to the pool bed and began to scrub himself with handfuls of sand and small gravel as he had used to do in the moor streams of his own tribelands in the far west. Above him Venutius sat his horse, sword hanging from his belt and his long cavalry lance held upright, and said, 'In Glevum the Roman baths are still in use for as far as he can Count Ambrosius keeps all the old observances.'

Arturo laughed as he stepped naked out of the water and began to dry himself on his under shirt. 'Aye .. but he puts the cart before the horse. First there must be fighting to bring peace – then with peace a man has a just need for comforts.' As he spoke – naked and defenceless, an easy mark for the swift dipping and thrust of Venutius's lance, a quick heart blow and then an easy escape for the man – he heard Anga snap at a worrying fly and his eyes held his companion's.

Green and guileless were Venutius's eyes as they watched Arturo and he said, 'The wound in your side, my lord, has healed clean. Is it true it came from your uncle Inbar?'

'It is. He was a man of many parts, courage and craft and greed. The gods twisted his nature at birth.' He turned away from Venutius and bent to recover his clothes, knowing that he was fair mark for a swift downward thrust of the lance to spit him through the heart if the nature of this man, too, had been twisted at birth But no thrust came.

As they rode away and began to breast the rising ground to return to the camp Durstan, bow in hand, the arrow still strung in it ready for use, stepped free of the scrub on the far side of the pool and watched them. His brow was beaded with sweat but not from the heat of the day. One muscle movement of Venutius's spear arm and the arrow would have been winging towards him ... *Aie*, but even so, the risk had been great. He could hear Arturo saying, 'If he raises his lance and your hands are not steady and the arrow flies not true – then the gods are no longer with me.'

That night as they lay together Arturo told Daria of the testing of Venutius, and she said, 'And you mean to try him no further?'

'No. To do so would be to doubt the gods. If he is here for mischief it is not against my person. Maybe he comes to read my mind and plans and then to return to Ambrosius. But I think not.'

A month later, when the first of the fierce autumn gales blew hard to set the browning tree leaves spinning and flighting through the air and the first prick of green from the winter corn began to stipple the worked soil of the crop strips, a party of pedlars and traders came into the camp to barter their salt and seed and cloths and their leather hides and rough pottery wares for the few young foals already dropped by the mares of the cavalry mounts and the little that now remained in the companions' war-chest of their Saxon plunder. Venutius, who had been made horse-master and put in command of the fodder stores for all the cavalry mounts – and was proving hard and demanding of any companion who grew idle or careless over the care of his beast – was wrapping a dressing of strong herbs over a festering cut in the right forehock of a stallion. As he squatted at his task he heard someone come up behind him and glancing over his shoulder saw one of the pedlars. He gave the man a nod and bent again to his task. The pedlar stood watching him until he had finished his work and then, as Venutius faced him, smiled, and said, 'The bellies of horses and companions will be full of loud grumblings before this winter is out.'

Venutius grinned. 'Maybe, but the remedy is tight belts, tight girths and a patient notching away of the days to spring.'

Looking down the picket line of horses the pedlar, who was middle-aged, thick-bearded and warmly clad in a heavy woollen surcoat over strong leather trews, said, 'It is known that you have more mounts than men. I have done well this year and have a mind to change from shank's pony to a good beast to carry me comfortably. Sell me one of your spare mounts and I will pay well.'

Venutius laughed and shook his head. 'We part with nothing but the foals . . . aye, and with those reluctantly.'

The pedlar said, 'I can pay you in coin which will buy you corn and fodder to keep a dozen horses from dying through winter lack.'

As he spoke he reached into the wallet of his surcoat belt and flicked a coin through the air for Venutius to catch. Looking down at it Venutius's face stiffened as he saw the sun-glitter rise from the golden face of the aureus of the Emperor Hadrian, one edge of which was deeply nicked. Then, without a word he tossed it back to the pedlar. They faced one another in silence while about them the air was full of the sound of the bartering going on in the camp. A horse whinnied high, and there was a sudden bright burst of laughter from a handful of the few women who still stayed with their men in the camp. For a few seconds it was in Venutius's mind that he could have wished that he had come to the companions as a free man for he had grown to admire and respect the spirit of them all. He said sharply, 'Speak that which you have come to speak!'

The pedlar, scratching at his thick beard, said, 'The lady Daria carries the child of Arturo. He longs for a boy and, if it is true the gods favour him, then it will be a boy.'

'Boy or girl, what matters it to Count Ambrosius which she drops?'

'I am not in his counsels. Like you I do his bidding. But his mind is not difficult to read sometimes.' He waved his hand around the hill top. 'This is a beginning. Come spring Arturo will move again and more men will come to him and suddenly a handful of deserters becomes an army. Armies have leaders, and given enough victories the leaders become kings. Kings have sons so their deaths solve no problems when a line of inheritance is secure. When Arturo dies –' he winked, '– god-willed or Ambrosius-willed – then our noble Count would have none alive with right to claim his place.'

'Then why not have Arturo killed now – before there is any army to win victories?'

The pedlar shook his head. 'Even a simple man like me can read that riddle to its end. At this moment Count Ambrosius knows that none of the tribes and their leaders will fully rally to him. His military caution offers them no glories, no plunder – only drills and exercises and, for the most part, the irksome rub of camp life. Warriors will not come to him, and those he has grow rebellious and many desert him. But if he lets Arturo run until all this country knows his name and the bards sing the renown of his victories ... You do not see it? Then there is a rich tree in full bearing to be cut down for the fine ripe harvest of its fruit to be easily gathered. Aye ... he will mourn Arturo and praise him – and then take his place for there will be no son to follow him. Believe me – Count Ambrosius will let no woman, be she wife or concubine, come to full term with any child seeded by him.' As he finished speaking he felt again in his wallet and pulled out a small alabaster amphora no larger than a pigeon's egg, its top thickly sealed with green wax, and handed it to Venutius. 'Guard it well, and when the right moment comes – which must be soon for the lady Daria is already, so 'tis said and so her belly shows, near six months gone – see that the liquid it holds goes into her wine or water beaker. It has neither taste nor true colour.'

'To kill the child but not the mother?'

For a moment the pedlar frowned, puzzled at what he took for the other's stupidity – or naivety. He said shortly, 'Why kill the foal and leave the mare to be served again? Both will die, but slowly so that it will have the look of nature.'

Venutius was silent, his lips tight. He had known that at any time he might have been ordered to assassinate Arturo and save himself as best he could. A sharp coil of disgust tightened his guts at the thought of becoming poisoner of a mother and child.

He said, 'And this being done I will stay at Arturo's side?'

The pedlar, though he gave no sign of his thoughts, wondered at the innocence of Venutius's thinking, and doubted whether Count Ambrosius had made a good choice of this spy in the camp of the companions. He said, 'You would leave when she is dead and so sharpen all men's minds to the truth? No, Venutius, you are bound to Arturo for many a long year. You will become one of the noblest and most fearless of the companions. Aye, in truth you will come to love Arturo as a brother and when you kill him you will truly grieve him, but the tides of time will slowly wash away the stains of your dishonour. Believe me, it is so, for I have known many men, myself not least among them, who have passed through the sad vale of self-disgust and found high fortune or great command a quick balm to ease the raw bite of a troubled conscience.'

He raised a hand in parting and moved away into the heart of the crowded camp to join the other traders. Venutius slipped the amphora into his tunic breast and as the sick horse turned its head and nuzzled at his shoulder he put up a hand and gently stroked its muzzle, relishing the softness of its skin under his palm and the sweet body smell of its sleek hide in his nostrils. So be it, he thought. Until this moment he had never truly known himself. But now the truth was locked firmly in his heart. He was a man whom the Fates had fingered. He prayed then that in the turbulent times ahead he might find honourable and gallant death in battle and so never know the shame of seeing the aureus of the Emperor Hadrian again.

Two weeks later he poured the liquid from the amphora into Daria's drink. The ease with which he was able to do it he felt might have been arranged by the dark gods. It was a night when he was guard commander, a night of sharp frost and a cloudless sky which blazed with bright stars. As he made his rounds in the late evening, he could hear the singing of some of the companions in the open hall which lay beyond the ridge of the plateau. He picked out the sweet voice of Durstan and the lusty bellow of Gelliga and, suddenly at some bawdy turn in the song, the high, neighing laughter of Lancelo. He knew and loved them all now, troopers and troop commanders, hard men, many of whom, since there were too few shelters to roof them all, wrapped themselves in their cloaks and slept in the open or huddled close packed under skin-covered lean-tos.

As he moved from post to post along the perimeter he felt the soft rub of the leather pouch, hung by a thong around his neck, against his breast. In it was the small amphora. As he crossed the far neck of the plateau from high above him came the distant calling of geese and he looked up and saw the wedge-shaped skein of flying birds against the great stippling of stars. He moved on and spoke briefly to the guard who kept watch at the foot of the small rocky rise on which Arturo's quarters had been built.

The guard, a stocky tribesman, bow-legged from riding almost before he could walk, was from the country of the Ordovices far south of Segontium. Looking up at the geese he said, 'By morning, they could be harbouring on the flats of the Tisobis river where I have taken many of them with bow and arrow as they cropped the eel grass.'

Venutius smiled. 'You would you were there now?'

'Nay, my commander, not for my sake.' He grinned and leaned on his lance. 'But for my wife's, yes. A woman needs a man to keep her warm at nights. Cold nights try a woman's virtue hard.'

Venutius laughed and moved on. As he came to the front of Arturo's hut a figure, heavily cloaked, moved out of the doorway and he recognized the lady Daria.

He saluted her and said, 'You should be warmly asleep, my lady.'

Daria smiled and said, 'So I should, good Venutius, except for two things. There is too much noise from the men's hall and I have a raging thirst from the salt meat at table this night.' Her hand lifted to show him a bronze beaker. 'I go to the spring.'

Venutius reached out for the beaker and said, 'You stay here, my lady. This is no time for you to be scrambling down the path.'

Without waiting for a reply, not wanting to see the starshine in her dark eyes, he turned away. As he stood at the thin overflow from the small well he pulled out his breast pouch and took from it the amphora. With his knife he cut off the wax stopper and then pierced the tough goatskin cover of the amphora's mouth. He filled the beaker and then poured the liquid from the amphora into it. He turned back to the path to the hut and felt his teeth clench tight and his face muscles stiffen as he drove from himself all thought.

Daria took the beaker from him and drank. She paused with the beaker half empty, gave a little sigh of contentment and said, 'You come from Glevum, don't you?'

'I do, my lady.'

She gave a soft chuckle. 'Once Arturo said to me that one day he would ride into Glevum in triumph and I should ride beside him on a white mare wearing a cloak of scarlet with a lining of blue silk and about my waist a golden belt with a clasp of two singing birds, and that Count Ambrosius should come out to greet us and hand me a silver goblet full of new wine.' She raised the beaker and drank, finishing the water, and then went on, 'You warriors throw your promises about as lightly as you venture your lives.'

Venutuius shook his head. 'My lord Arturo breaks a given promise to no one. When the day comes you shall ride so beside him.'

Daria's white teeth shone in the starlight as she laughed and said, 'Aye, that I shall, my kind Venutius – for I shall remind him.'

Gone from her, Venutius finished his round of the camp sentries and then went back in the shelter of the little lean-to of hazel poles and bracken thatch he had long made for himself. He put the amphora between two cloths and with the heavy pummel of his sword smashed it into chips which he flung out into the night. He did all this as he had done everything from the moment he had taken the beaker to fill from Daria without thought or emotion, his heart and mind frozen.

That night as Arturo lay at Daria's side and her breath warmed the side of his face she took his hand and placed it below her breasts and said, 'Feel, the child moves.' Underneath his hand he felt the faint kick of his son. Aye . . . son it had to be for certain. Placing her hand over his Daria went on, teasingly, 'It will be another mouth to feed this winter but there shall be no lack for the babe for already I begin to grow as well-stored as the finest milch cow.'

'But lack there will be for all others, you think?'

'There must be. We are here without full corn bins or pits well stored with smoked fish or meat. The time will come and,' her voice changed to a serious note, 'I say this, my lord, because you will not say it to yourself – when horses will be put to the slaughter and men, before they will starve, will leave you for their homelands or to forage for themselves.'

Arturo stirred angrily and said, 'None shall starve and none shall so leave. We have come here under the gods who turned aside the spears of Melwas to name this our sanctuary. Tight belts we shall have, but for the rest the gods will provide. It is written.'

Daria said no more, but she smiled in the darkness to herself. It was written. The gods had spoken. Always it had been so with him and always would it be so, and his belief suddenly warmed her with a sweet flush of love so that she slid her hand about his neck and pressed her lips to his and made silent prayer to her own God that out of His charity the child she carried should be a son.

Two weeks later, when the sun rose to show the hilltop covered with a first and thin fall of early snow, Daria woke to find her body heavy with a lassitude which with the passing of the days was to grow to a weakness that finally held her to her couch and slowly began to waste her body. Within a month she was dead, passing away with her hand in Arturo's as the first owl-call of night echoed through the wood on the western slope of the hill. They cut a deep grave for her in a dell of the hillside, bowered by young beeches which still held their brown leaves against the winter gales. Pasco the priest spoke the burial rites of her own religion and old Ansold, her father, and Lancelo, her brother, filled the grave, and after them the companions piled stones and rocks to a cairn over her while all the time Arturo stood by with his face graven and speaking no word. When all was done Arturo turned and took the reins of the White One being held by Durstan. He mounted and rode slowly away down the hill, followed by Anga, armed but unprovisioned. None doubted that he would return, and a few like Pasco and old Ansold and some of the older companions moved with him in spirit for they knew that with the death of true love a man must move for a while into the wilderness and seek solitude before he can return to the world and live again.

The Return to Isca

It was five days before Arturo returned. He came back leaner
and with his beard grown matted and shaggy and with a hard,
tempered look in his blue eyes which he was never to lose even
when making merry with his companions, a look which, when
he wished, seemed to throw an icy veil between himself and all
others and, when it was there, make all men choose their words
to him with care. Only when he laughed and played with children or spoke to the camp women did the look become remote.
And on his return he began to organize the camp for the winter
ahead with a grim and inflexible ordering of life on the hill
which none questioned and none ever evaded. The daily mess
issues were cut to a point where no porridge bowl was left until
licked clean and no bone tossed to a hound until it had been
picked bare and the marrow sucked from it. The dogs foraged
for themselves and as the game around the hill grew scarcer so
dogs and men foraged wider afield, the hunting parties often
being away for days on end. Only the horses were treated with
a more generous hand.

Every night before Arturo went to his bed in the hut on the
rocky outcrop of the plateau he would walk with Anga to the
head of the small dell which held Daria's grave. He would sit
with Anga beside him and his eyes seldom left the rock-piled
cairn. There was no inner rebellion in him against the bereave-
ment which had been placed on him. He understood it and
accepted it. The gods had gifted him and great things lay ahead
of him. In return they had schooled him with this loss less there
should have arisen in him any unwarranted arrogance or pre-
sumptuous pride to make him forget that he and all those he
loved and cherished were mortal.

481

By the turn of the year the camp was a place of lean men, lean women and lean children and of rib-straked horses. Prayers and hopes for a mild winter went unfulfilled for the snows came early and stayed and the nights were either clear with iron frost or wild with the blanketing and drifting of snow. In the mornings crows and owls could be found dead and frozen stiff to their perches and the river Cam was quietened by a covering of thick ice. These were mornings when men, women and children found it no shame to gather the fresh dung in the horse lines and wrapping it in old cloths hugged it under their clothes to their bare bellies to give them heat and the false relief of food warmth in their guts. None, not even the hardiest, washed their bodies, and hair and beards were let grow long to protect faces and necks from the white patching of frost bite. Men and women in the sharp unending agony of cold and hunger called on their gods and goddesses for help, to Belenus and Dagda and Lug, the fair-haired one, to Nodens of the Silver Hand, to Taurus the bull, Epona the horse, to Artio the bear, to Cernunnos the stag and to Dis, the god of the underworld, from whom all mankind had descended – all those, that is, who were true to their country's gods. For the followers of Christos prayers were made to Him and His Father. And Pasco, the outcast priest of the divided heart and faith, called on them all for he knew that all were one and the same God.

In the middle of the first month of the new year when, in a night sky of pale ice-blue, the moon was passing to full and Orion's great belt hung high near the meridian, Lancelo came to Arturo's hut where he sat outside, cloak-wrapped, before retiring. It was near midnight and a bitter wind was sweeping across the hill, whirling spinning snow devils low across the ground, and now and again from the wooded slopes there came the clear cracking of some frost-split branch or tree trunk.

Lancelo, who next to Durstan could speak most informally to Arturo, said, 'I have just made the round of the sentry posts. Cuneda is dead. He was lying where he fell – struck through the heart by the cold.'

For a while Arturo said nothing. Cuneda had been one of the

companions who had joined him at Pontes whe he had been making his great progress to Londinium. He was from Lactodorum in the land of the Catuvellauni, a man of forty, built like an ox, black-bearded but without a hair on his head. Just as the winter's killing frost could rive the stoutest oak so had sturdy Cuneda been riven That there would be others he had no doubt. The gods were testing him. Daria had been taken because they were jealous of his love for her, wanting him single-minded in his great resolve to restore freedom and greatness to this country. For him there would be no woman in his life until he had proved himself – and none ever that could truly take Daria's place in his heart. So would be the loss of any of the tried companions who stood with him now on this bitter, winter-plagued hill, these men of courage and similar vision to his own. Their going would mark his spirit with a grief which he could never know in same full sorrow for any of those who would take their place and swell the ranks of the army to come. He said :

'Bury him in the beech dell.'

'The ground is iron and will not yield.'

'Take iron to iron. The gods have his spirit. The wolves and foxes shall not feast on his proud heart or bones.'

'It shall be so, my lord.' Lancelo was silent for a time and then went on, 'No man living can remember a winter like this. A man on his own or with wife and child would fare better in his homelands or tribal town.'

'Have they asked to leave ?'

'No, my lord. They would die first. But if you gave the word ...'

Arturo stern-faced said, 'The gods are with us and in the time of our greatest want they will provide. No battle is lost until the standard falls. When the moment of cruellest pinch-belly comes you will see ... the gods will send us a winter harvest. But any who wishes is free to leave.'

Going back to the companions Lancelo said to them wryly, 'Without leave from you I have spoken to Arturo about our state here. He says two things. Any who asks is free to leave and seek warmth and food elsewhere. Against this the gods have told him that at our moment of greatest need they will turn winter want to summer bounty. The trees shall fruit, the corn shall grow and ripen overnight, the wild duck shall fly in and lay their eggs for us and then submit to killing and roasting. The gentle does shall climb the hill to be slaughtered and the white hares lollop to our cooking places and wait their turn to take the pot —'

Durstan gave a great roar of laughter. 'My mouth waters. And who would miss such a time? Have I not seen the spears of Melwas turned aside? Why then miss the sight of the sky clouded with quail and pigeon falling ready plucked and drawn to the waiting cauldrons?'

When the laughter died Lancelo said soberly, 'Who would ask to leave?'

Speaking for all of them black-bearded Gelliga from Lavo-brinta in the country of the Ordovices said firmly, 'There is no leaving for any of us except by the hard road already taken by Cuneda.'

So the next morning they took mattock, pick and spade and before the early sunset reddened the sky above distant Ynys-witrin they buried Cuneda alongside Daria and raised a cairn of ice-coated rocks above him and Pasco who knew him for a Christos man commended his soul to the mercy of God.

Within the next three weeks a woman died in childbirth, and another companion, wrapped in wolf skins and huddled deep in a bed of bracken under his lean-to shelter, died in his sleep. The same night, a roving lone wolf broke into camp and attacked the horse lines and, before it was killed by a spear thrust from Venutius, so badly mauled a bay stallion that the beast had to be killed and so provided meat for the pot for a handful of days. When the last of the horse meat was gone, the snows came again to lay a fresh mantle over the pocked and broken surface of the old snow and ice on the plataeau top. Venutius, thinking of the winter quarters of Ambrosius at Glevum with its glowing charcoal braziers and the hypocausts at full heat warming floor and wall ducts, knew that although all contentment was for ever denied him he was nearer to it here than he ever could be elsewhere. The gods had truly marked him and that day on which he gave death to Arturo – far ahead though it might be – would also bring him the dark comfort of death at his own hand. But in these days he was a true companion, eating and drinking less than his meagre share and giving all his care and concern to the horses.

After the snow the days were clear and bright as though the sword-sharp sweep of the frosty air had forever purged the skies of all cloud Hunger and cold each day took toll of some living thing on the hill, a hound, a child, a woman, a camp servant and, twice, a companion. Although Arturo by word and manner held them firm and denied the death of hope and confidence, he hid the growing heaviness of spirit within himself until it could be borne no longer. There was no trial the gods could put on him which he would not accept. But the death and misery of others now defeated him.

He called Durstan and Lancelo to him and said, 'Tell the others that I go away for two or three days. When I return it will be with plenty for all.'

After a moment or two of surprise from them both, Lancelo said, 'You journey where, my lord?'

Arturo answered, 'To seek the charity of the gods. They have tried us hard and. for my part, could try me harder. I take no shame in becoming supplicant to them for others.' He smiled and there was a swift glint of his old teasing spirit in his eyes so that Durstan at least knew that what was to follow would be no truth. 'Last night I dreamt that the gentle goddess Coventina spoke to me and said, "Since great things are destined for you and your pride grows stiff and iron-bound I tell you for the sake of the others with you that the gods wait for you to become a humble beggar. Before they grant you a kingdom you must come begging for a crust".'

'You ride alone?' asked Lancelo.

'Yes.'

'And where?'

'I shall give the White One loose rein and the gods will govern her going.'

For a moment Durstan would have spoken. Always the nearest to Arturo he could read him in a way hidden from all the others. There would be no loose rein, he knew, for Arturo would head for Ynys-witrin and ask for charity from Melwas and the answer of Melwas no man could predict. He kept his own counsel. But one thing he knew, and knew, too, the cost to Arturo's spirit and pride, was that to go a-begging to either gods or men was to diminish his own manhood.

When the White One was saddled Arturo led her, slithering and slipping, down the steep hill path for none could dare it mounted, and with him went the now ageing Anga, gaunt-framed, and his coat staring with hunger-roughness.

At the bottom of the hill Arturo mounted and gave the mare slack rein so that she moved towards the river, but Arturo knew that soon the reins would come firmly into command of his hands for indeed he knew no other place to go nor other charity to seek than that of Melwas, and knew, too, that all the king's people would be on tight belly-strings for this winter had spared no one, and knew further that if the gods gave him any bounty there would never again be woman or child in any camp or army train of his. A man could gnaw the ice-cold ash bark in winter ... *Aie*, and even take a handful of earth to his mouth and cud it for comfort, but women and children were gentler creatures. For each dead mother and child that lay on the hill he grieved because their death and misery before death came from his own arrogance in not forcibly sending them away in good time with their men. Light-headed a little from his own deprivation it seemed to him now that gentle Coventina had truly spoken to him in a dream for her heart had been moved where his had remained untouched. . .

As they reached the Cam, he took the reins firmly and turned the mare's head downstream and he knew that all these troubles came from the sacking of the Villa of the Three Nymphs, where all could have lodged without lack this winter. One day Count

Ambrosius should be given back in double score the misery and loss which he had heaped on the companions ... And so he rode on towards Ynys-witrin knowing that he would get from Melwas not even a handful of oats enough to make a bowl of porridge. For this he could make no grudge against the king. A man must look after his own people when want held the land as hard and iron-fast as did the snow and frost.

A white-coated hare got up from the frost-rimed sedges at the river's edge and moved wearily away over the river's ice and Anga, seeing it, growled but gave no chase for the hound was wise in his weakness and knew that he could never overtake it.

For two hours Arturo travelled slowly, letting the White One pick her own gait. Man, mount and hound all harboured and conserved their little reserve of strength, and for Arturo the day passed into the substance of a dream. His eyes, narrowed against the blinding sunglare on the snow-covered earth, now and then played him tricks, creating the vision of things long forgotten and of desires long now unfed. A willow tree seemed suddenly to be loaded with a crop of fat yellow plums. A hollow in the ground ahead was a coolness to the eyes with a rich spread of now spring grass but as he rode down into it there was only the hard crunch of the frozen snow drifts under the White One's hooves. He talked to himself and also talked as though there were others with him. The waters of the Cam were suddenly free of ice and he thought he saw a fish leap high in the ecstasy of a fast spring run from the sea, just as he had seen the salmon leap in the Tamesis river at Pontes on the day when Cuneda had joined him. But all the while there was a detached presence in him which understood all mirage and held firm to the burning truth of his real state. The gods, for their own purpose and his future greatness, were humiliating him, putting him to the trial of asking charity for himself and his people from a man who would give none. When that was done the story would run with him always. Arturo, the great one, the outlawed defier of Count Ambrosius and Prince Gerontius, went a-begging to a fish-reeking marsh king. *Aie* ... the gods were demanding that so that in all the days of whatever greatness came to him it would be a never healing sore on his pride to remind him of his puniness below the gods.

It was then, as he sat his saddle, head drooping as the head of the White One drooped, that he heard Anga growl. He looked up and another mirage danced before his eyes and he watched it, wondering at the power of the mind to create fantasy from the weakness of his body and the loss of his pride.

A man, heavily cloaked and cowled, was riding towards him on a sturdy moorland pony, fat flanked and making light of the hard going. His robe was belted and from his right side hung a leather scabbarded sword. In the midst of his vision Arturo smiled weakly to himself, touched with the arbitrariness of the mirage which sent him a left-handed man. He lowered his head and shut out the hallucination, seeing only the White One's dipping head before him and hearing only now the slow bite of her hooves into the crisp snow crust.

Then clearly through the frost-purged air a man's voice said to him, 'You would pass without greeting one who holds you most dear?'

Arturo raised his head as the White One came to a stop to see that the horse and rider mirage now blocked his path. The man drew back the loose edges of his head cowl and Arturo knew then that the gods put further mockery on him. The other rider, lean-faced and his beard a rusty tan colour, was a man well in his forties with eyes the colour of ripe hazel nuts, and he was smiling with his face full of welcome. Arturo knew him, though he had not seen him for more than a year, and he knew too that this other lived only in his fancy as had done the ripe plums and the sweet meadow grass, and he marvelled at the truth of the mirage which had made this visionary man left-handed.

He said, 'If you were true man and not my brain's fancy I would give you the warm greeting of a son. Aye ... and for all that you do not in flesh and truth smile at me from your pony I give you greeting and even hold my hand out as though to feel yours in mine and be warmed by the blood which we both share.'

As he spoke he held out his hand and the other took it and said, 'I am Baradoc, and I am flesh and blood and your father.' As their hands were clasped it was as though Arturo had been struck a sudden blow, for beyond all doubt of mirage or the mind's deceit, he knew his own flesh to be grasped by true flesh and blood and knew that his hard palm and calloused fingers were held by the like of his father's without shadow of doubt.

In that moment of truth before the gods gave him release from their trial they abased him with a final chastisement. He swayed in his saddle, his hand slipping from his father's, to topple to the ground in a fit of oblivion, and as he lay there Anga stood over him growling, the soft skin of his mouth drawn back to bare the ageing teeth and fangs. But when Baradoc dismounted and squatted on his hunkers alongside his son, he spoke gently to the hound in the speech which all men of the Enduring Crow used with their beasts and, slowly, the growling died in Anga's throat like the passing away of distant thunder.

There were his father and two other men whose ponies were heavily pack laden. He lay propped against the bole of a great oak close to the river. Above him the bare branches were hung with great daggers of icicles. They would have built a fire and made a meat and barley soup for him, but he refused for he knew now, though nothing had been said as yet by his father, that the days and weeks of starvation were over, and there was nothing which could make him fill his belly until he saw his own companions and camp people succoured first. He accepted only a pull at the mouth of a mead skin and the honey bite of it went through him like fire, a warmth that cleared his head and waked his weak body to the stir of new vigour. A little way from him the two men fed oats to the White One from an osier skep and Anga lay full length chewing at a piece of smoked deer meat.

Baradoc squatting at his side said, 'You would have had nothing from King Melwas for he is not at Ynys-witrin. He has taken his people over the marshes to the hills where they live warm in the old lead workings but eat poor because the ice holds rivers and marshes hard bound and all the marsh fowl have gone south to Gaul or the open sea. If the gods sent you this way then it was to me. Half a day's march behind us comes a pony and sledge train with supplies for you from Isca.'

'Why should Prince Gerontius give me, whom he outlawed, such charity from his store?'

'He gives nothing. He is dead and now his son reigns, young Prince Geraint and I am made Pendragon of all the tribes of the Dumnonian lands and stand at his right side.'

'And knowing of our wants you begged for me?'

Baradoc laughed. 'Damp the fire of your pride a little. I begged nothing. Prince Geraint remembers you and was ever trying to persuade his father to pardon you. Now that he is Prince he has given the pardon himself – though since his writ does not run with Count Ambrosius at Glevum you are still outlaw under his mandate.'

'From Ambrosius I would accept nothing. Neither pardon nor provisions.'

Baradoc shrugged his shoulders. 'Time brings changes. But we live now and there is this winter lack on the camp hill which must be met. But Prince Geraint has more in his mind than present charity. He would meet and speak with you.'

'To what end?' As he spoke Arturo was remembering Geraint. He could give him a handful of years and there were many times when he had schooled and drilled the cavalry horses of Prince Gerontius when the boy had first watched and then ridden with him, a quiet youth with a pleasant manner who spoke little but clearly thought much of matters beyond his years for he sought seldom the company of those of his own age. And now he was Prince of all Dumnonia though in years he could scarce be yet twenty.

'That rests with him. As Pendragon I am his counsellor but I am far from knowing his true mind. But I know that he speaks fair and is a man of his word and favours you where his father knew only wrath for you. The pony train that follows us comes from him out of his good bounty, a charity which carries no threat to your liberty or your ambitions for this country.'

Arturo nodded. This news and the presence of his father already refreshed his body and spirit and he began to feel a new man and to know now with thankful conviction that his trial by the gods had always carried this fore-ordained end. He took another pull through his cracked lips at the mead skin and let its fire seep through him like a slow peat burn. 'How,' he asked, 'did Gerontius die? He was a man in good health.'

'He was trying a new mount that had been shipped from Gaul with other of its kind .. an over mettlesome creature which threw him so that he struck his head on the ground. It seemed no more than a bruise a man would rub and forget but he was found dead on his couch the following morning.'

Pulling himself upright slowly Arturo said, 'For all those who love horses death is the distance between the saddle and the ground. May the gods keep him.'

As he began to move towards the White One with the clear intent of mounting Baradoc said, 'You ask not of your mother and the rest of your kin?'

Arturo paused with his hands on the reins, ready to mount, and he smiled. 'No harm can have touched them for the gods this day have done with trying me. But I take your scold with humility, and I ride now to take good news to my people on the hill of the Cam. They have become my kin, tied to me by bonds as fast as any blood sharing.'

'You still dream your dream?'

'Aye, my father. A dream that was once yours. You once told me that you would turn the hill camp into a great fortress against the day the Saxons moved west. I see no signs of new work there.'

'My dream lives, but before I could assemble the workmen Gerontius and Melwas quarrelled and the marsh king closed his lands against our passage. Aye, the dream lives still but only as a sorrow in my heart.'

Mounting the White One Arturo said, 'The day will come when you shall do it.'

Baradoc laughed. 'A while ago you were a half-delirious and near to dead man, and now you talk like the arrogant son whose bare rumps I birch-marked often for insolence and waywardness. One would think it was the nectar of the gods I gave you to drink not the thin brew of an Iscan tavern keeper.'

Arturo shook his head. 'The mead was good, but my new strength comes from the far greater boon of seeing you and knowing the good fortune you bring. Come, my father – ride with me to give proof to my people of the great bounty the gods have sent.'

The baggage train arrived the next morning. There were twenty sturdy pack horses fully laden and two great sleds teamed by lank-shouldered, long-headed draught mules which Gerontius had bred from Gaulish imported he-asses on his moorland pony mares. The train brought food and stores in no great plenty but of a sufficiency to see the camp through the rest of the winter and early spring no matter how hard the weather should stand. Within a week starvation's marks began to pass from men, women and children and the horses and hounds, and where there had been little chatter and less laughter about the camp fires there came a singing and a gossiping and shouting which filled Arturo's heart with lightness except when he paid his nightly visit to the beech dell. Of Daria's death he had no need to tell his father for the news had reached Isca by one of the camp-visiting pedlars and Baradoc, knowing the nature of true grief, said no more than a few words about her going to Arturo and then talked no more of Daria.

Thin though the commons were they represented feasting to all. The hounds now had vigour to fight and quarrel and forage afield. Wet mash and oats began to put a new bloom on the horses. When Venutius walked the picket lines and pens at night and saw their eyes bright in the starlight and their breath pluming in the sharp air he knew a happiness which brought him for a time forgetfulness of Ambrosius and Glevum. The men of the provision train and mule sleds rode back to Isca, but Baradoc stayed to ride there later with Arturo and they spent much time together walking the old, broken, and overgrown ramparts and defences of the hill. Arturo – man to man now with his father and forging a bond which had never existed before – saw how, from a great warrior who had served south across the seas from Rome and knew all the lands from the Pillars of Hercules to far beyond Byzantium, Baradoc had by the loss of the full use of his right hand turned to new skills and had made himself a master of forts and defences and towers and knew from his own experience of them the art of making *ballistae* which could throw a flight of arrows or flaming iron bolts coated with tarred tow to flare through the air further than any spear could be thrown and knew, too, the setting up of large catapults – the *onagri* which the early Roman legions had used against Britain in the days of the great Queen Boudicca – that slung with ease large boulders to a distance far beyond any arrow flight.

Arturo knew that his father would have made this hill impregnable and many others like it to give a secure base from which the tribes and factions now holding the long spine length of this country could move forward to meet the Saxon's westward creep. But in his heart Arturo knew that the dream could never flower as his father saw it. When the Saxons came in sufficient numbers they would flow around each fortress like the tide round a standing rock. The true answer, he sensed, though the vision was far from clear with him, lay elsewhere. But a well protected winter base when none would move to fight he knew to be wise. Armies that gathered in spring, fought through the summer and then scattered, each man to his own holding and fireside during the winter, were no more than flocks of mad starlings who had lost all sense of due seasons. For himself he knew one thing with absolute conviction. The gods had sent him to this hill above the Cam. On this hill they had tried him and his people with the cruellest winter men could remember and, at the point of despair and disaster, had redeemed him. This hill was his and none should take it from him for already he began to see the glimmerings of the way he would use it. But first he had to bring Prince Geraint and King Melwas to his side.

In the first week of the month of the Roman god Mars, the

great thaw came as a robust and warm westerly wind blew across the land. Every gully and rivulet ran high with water. The ice sheets that had covered the Cam melted and broke into floes which went racing downstream on a growing flood which in two days, as the winds became rain-laden, reached high over the banks and flooded the low-lying lands. All the country which had been a waste of whiteness now delighted the eye with the sweeps of green hillside and the lush growth of the first new grass. The thickets, woods and skies which had been bereft of all creatures now stirred with their return to renewed life. A stormcock sang with high melody each morning in the beech dell. Robins and sparrows and jackdaws and crows came back to the camp to forage for pickings about the cooking fires and middens, and kestrels, sparrow hawks and high-winging kites and buzzards and higher-pitched peregrines took toll of the life below them or tore and gorged themselves at the thawed carcasses of hinds and hares and boar which winter starvation had claimed and the snow and ice had until now held locked fast under its iron pall.

The rain lasted three days and when it passed Arturo and Baradoc left the hill camp and set out for Isca. With him Arturo took one of the first of his camp servants at the Villa of the Three Nympths, Marcos whose dumb brother Timo had been killed in the fighting of the previous year. Marcos now was no servant but a fully trained and seasoned trooper. He left Durstan in command of the camp.

Some days later at noon they rode into Isca. They came along the old road westward from the Fosseway, a road which – now the winter had broken – was, the nearer they came to Isca, busy with the movement of pedlars and traders and drovers herding lean pigs and long-coated cattle towards the town. It was a road which long ago had known the steady tramp of cohorts of Roman auxiliaries beating out their twenty miles a day, their raised standard going before them, gilded and wreathed with their battle honours. They topped a long slope and Isca lay before them, its great Mount crowned with the partly ruined fortress where Prince Geraint had his seat. To the south below the hill lay the wide sprawl of the town itself, hearth-fire smoke wreathing lazily into the still air, and beyond it the curve and sweep of the river and the water meadows where Arturo had broken and trained new horses and learned the elements of his skill as a cavalryman. Seeing it a wry smile touched his lips as he remembered how he and Durstan had ridden from it on a night of storm to escape with their lives and be unjustly named as outlaws for the killing of two men who would have murdered them on the orders of the present Prince's father.

They rode through the town and up to the fortress over which flew the great scarlet Dumnonia standard with a green oak tree in its centre. Arturo and Marcos were shown to their quarters and Baradoc left them to go to the house of Master Ricat, the Prince's horsemaster, with whom Arturo had always been a favourite, though this had never saved him thrashings as a youth for wild conduct.

Before Baradoc left he said to Arturo with a smiling twist to his mouth, 'The Prince is young. Speak fairly to him. To be overbold will serve you nothing. So, keep well bridled –' he grinned openly, '– the arrogance you draw from the gods. At the moment you have more need of him than he of you – and so it is with me. I would see your camp well-fortified, and you need quickly more men and mounts than will come from other parts this spring.' He paused for a moment or two and then said straightly, 'Until now I have thought you a dreamer and a maker of your own myths – god-touched but in the way of men with disordered minds. Now I know better, and now is the time for you to lay the strong foundations of your desire which is also mine – to turn the Saxons back to the sea and heal this country of its long sickness.'

Arturo nodded and said quietly, 'Have no fear, my father. This winter the gods have schooled me well.'

Later that afternoon Arturo was given audience by Prince Geraint. They spoke together in the large room where he had had his first meeting with Prince Gerontius when he had been a youth. Its floor was paved with black and red tiles. A long window flanked by wall niches looked out over the town and river, where the day was dying into the last red glow of sunset. A long couch held a tumbled cloak and a pile of papyrus reading rolls. On the marble floor was a vase full of the long sere stalks of mace reed, their heads split and curled with the bursting of ripening seed. An oak table held a great silver tray on which stood a glass flagon of wine and two drinking cups. At the head of this table sat the young Prince, not yet twenty, dressed in a surcoat of finely cured doeskin over a white linen shirt, and wearing red woollen trews whose bottoms were stained and still wet with mud from riding the water meadows.

He had his father's face and complexion, dark hair, and dark eyebrows that merged with one another over his high-bridged hawklike nose. But whereas the father's eyes had always seemed, under their heavy hoods, to be burgeoning with sleep or suspicion Geraint's eyes were warm and frank.

Ignoring all formal greeting the Prince put out a hand to warm it from the heat of a charcoal brazier which stood near his chair and said pleasantly, 'You remember me?'

Arturo nodded. 'Yes, my prince. The last time I saw you, you sat in a meadow puddle having been thrown there by a bay stallion moor pony that had far to go to be broken.'

'But in the end broken it was.' He nodded to the bench by the table. 'Sit – when I want formality you shall know it – and pour wine for us.'

As Arturo did this, he said, 'The whole land has known a cruel winter. I give you the thanks of all mine and myself for your bounty, my Prince.'

Geraint smiled, shrugged his shoulders, and took the wine cup which Arturo passed him, saying, 'Without it you would have held place The gods would have sent ravens with meat and the corn would have pushed through the ice and snow to come to full ripening between dawn and dusk.' He drank a little of the wine, and went on, smiling broadly, 'Tell me, is it true that the spears of Melwas were turned aside from you in full flight?'

Arturo laughed and said, 'Is there any warrior when the mead flows who does not sing his leader's deeds in bold words, forsaking truth for fancy? No, my Prince. The spears were stayed by the command of King Melwas.'

'There are times when men, weary of the hard truth, look only for miracles. This is such a time. So now, tell me what is in your mind. I have freed you from outlawry where my writ runs, but you have made an enemy of Count Ambrosius and with a handful of men have given Hengist's red beard a more than gentle tweak. Where do you go now?'

'Where the gods lead, my Prince.'

The Prince shook his head and a hint of a frown marked his face. 'Let us now leave the gods from this for a while. They will stay or give their favours. Tell me in plain words what you have in mind.'

Arturo's hand tightened a little around his wine cup. For all his father's warning he found it hard to take the Prince's reprimand. Although he could only give him a handful of years they held all the difference between unfleshed youth and scarred warrior. Then, aware of his own arrogance and the great service the Prince had done him this winter, he said quietly, 'You shall have it plain, my Prince. I have dreamt a dream for this country and shall live in discontent until I have brought it to truth ...'

So, while Geraint sipped his wine now and then and listened patiently, Arturo spoke his mind and clothed his dream in simple words of good sense, and the Prince heard him through without interruption. He heard him, too, without irritation because Arturo, who believed that he had been fingered by the gods, held now to facts, suppressing all fancies or god-predicted certainties. But though this was so there came into Arturo's mind as he spoke of practical things – of levies of men and garrisoning over winter, of stores and the weapons of war, and the need for armourers and smiths and the careful selection of good mounts and foot soldiers – the one prime argument which might hold this young Prince Geraint and all others like him as allies – and that thought he knew came from the gods.

He finished: 'This is a country now of great chiefs, princes and kings, many of whom although they fear the Saxon threat, fear more the loss of their own high states. They give no full levies to Count Ambrosius because in their hearts they know that by giving him victory they would be raising him high above them in full sovereignty. And this is true, for Count Ambrosius – ageing and waning as he is – sees himself as the coming Emperor and will never relinquish that dream.'

'And your dream?'

'I am of no royal blood. With victory in my hands no one has cause to fear tyranny from me. In anger I not long since underscored a message to Count Ambrosius calling myself *dux bellorum*. War duke of this country to give it freedom. When the victory is won and there is no more war then the title, like a morning mist under the rising summer sun, vanishes. I shall be content under my father or as chief myself to return to the people of the Enduring Crow to improve my lands and the lot of my people. You have been kind to me, my Prince. Be kinder. We are both of Dumnonia so it is fitting that you should be the first. And by your example in a few years others will follow.'

For a moment or two Geraint was silent, tapping his fingers against the side of his drinking cup. Then he smiled and said, 'You will find this hard to believe, but not long since I sat where you are and listened to my father speaking and he said much that you have said. More, too, he spoke of you and the things you have done this last year. Hearing you speak now I know that he had read much that was in your mind. Had he lived he would have soon pardoned you and called you to him. That is why you have your pardon and are here now. If this thing is to be done and achieved by you – then it is right that the first to aid you should be the Prince of your own country. Prove yourself in the coming years and the others will follow.'

'Even Count Ambrosius?'

Prince Geraint stood up to show that the audience was over, and said with a sly smile, 'Since the gods are so strongly on your side what need have you to over-concern yourself with him?'

That evening Arturo walked down to the house of Master Ricat, the Prince's horse-keeper, where his father was lodged.

Here to his surprise, for his father had not mentioned her, he found also his mother, Tia. She rose from a couch by the glowing brazier that warmed the room and embraced him. Then stepping back but still holding his hands in hers she looked at him and said quietly, 'I loved Daria and know your grief. I say no more.'

Looking at her, a tall, handsome woman in her forties, her periwinkle eyes bright, her fair hair, caught with a braid of red silk, still untouched by any dull tint of time, he knew that she spoke from her own heartache during the long years when his father had been torn from her to serve as slave and then mercenary in distant lands.

He said, 'To you I can speak of her for you will know the truth in me. There is none ever that can take her place.' Then dropping her hands he said, looking beyond her, 'But who is this?'

On a stool, her lap full of simple embroidery work, sat a girl of about eight or nine years; a dark-haired, brown-skinned child with a solemn face.

The girl without bidding rose, her embroidery work spilling to the ground, and came to him holding out her hand in greeting as she said, 'I am your first sister, Gerta. Is it true that when King Melwas gave the order to spear you they were turned aside by the gods?'

Arturo laughed, his spirits lifting at the pleasure of being with his family, and said, 'Of course it's true, and to feed us on the hill during the snows the ravens brought meat each day.'

'Ah, then that, too, I shall work into my embroidery.'

'Enough,' said Baradoc. 'Once he starts his stories there is no knowing where truth begins or ends.' But when he brought a mead cup to Arturo there was a shine of pride in his eyes which Arturo had never known before.

That night when Arturo returned to the fortress he was summoned to Prince Geraint.

The Prince said, 'Not long since a trader who for years brought news for my father arrived. He travels freely in our lands and the Saxon shorelands because –' he smiled, '– he takes news to both sides though he would deny it to either. But he is a man of true news. He tells that Hengist is dead and that his son, Esc, rules all the lands south-east of Londinium in his place.'

Without thought of any irk it might give Geraint Arturo said, 'Then truly the gods begin to move. They stir you to forgiveness and bounty and now they take away the one man who held the first place over all the chiefs of the Saxon shores from the Ocelli point in the north to beyond Lemanis in the south. Each chief now will struggle and fight for leadership over the others since Esc is not the man his father was. Truly this is the time to begin to harry them. Aye, they will find a leader in time, my Prince, but long before then I shall have an army trained and battle-blooded by harassing them; an army which will, when in the years to come they find unity, meet and break them with bloody slaughter and drive them from our shores. The gods are with us!'

A spasm of irritation reaching near anger touched Geraint as Arturo spoke. The gods, the gods ... always the gods. Aye, he had belief and faith in the gods, too, but was not blind as this Arto seemed to be that they worked their ends, shaping the destinies of men and nations, in a pattern that mortal eyes were slow to pick out. Then, oddly, he remembered the times when he had watched this Arturo school and break horses, had seen his love and care for them and the men in his command, and knew from Baradoc, too, the downing of pride that he had forced on himself to go seeking charity from King Melwas. In this moment he found a truth which he needed to keep countenance and temper with Arturo. He was not one man, but two, a dreamer and a warrior – and the one could not live without the other. So he now said evenly, 'Tomorrow we will talk more about this.'

The Taunting of the Boar

A week later Arturo rode back to the hill camp with Marcos, but on the way he turned off and went to Ynys-witrin. As they rode to the settlement the flood waters lapped over the cause-way still in places. He was escorted to King Melwas who with his people had now returned from their winter quarters in the old lead mines. The air was balmy with the first promise of spring and he found Melwas – who like all true marshmen was most at ease with the sky rather than a roof above – sitting in the courtyard of his palace, which was no more than a long hall built of timber and part stone quarried from the mount behind it.

Melwas, who was having the thick winter growth of his beard plucked and trimmed by one of his women, made him wel-come. He sat at the rough plank table with him and a jug of crab-apple brew was set between them, and as they talked his men and women went about their business in the yard and the hall. Melwas was truly king but he had little love of ceremony or formalities.

As their beakers were filled and Melwas waved away the woman tending his beard so that he could drink, he said, 'So you have charmed the young Prince – and now comes my turn?'

'News runs fast. But I have come to use no charms. Plain speaking serves us both best.'

Melwas laughed. 'Your tail is up. You begin to feel your oats after the winter fast. My answer is – nothing of charity will be found here.'

'Nor do I ask it. I need your leave to keep quarters on Cam Hill and to make the place secure. The need will be with me for many years.'

'You speak plain ... aye, even a little rough for a beggar. Now, to your plain need add the golden tail.'

'One third of all loot we take. From this you pay the fighting men you bond to me.'

'First my land – and now my men! How many men?'

'Fifty.'

Melwas laughed. 'Young of course. And able – able to take bow and shoot the eye from a crow at fifty paces, and to throw a spear that will slit the throat of a bounding deer and so not spoil good carcase meat. This, too, at fifty paces?'

Arturo smiled. 'Is there any marshman who cannot do that?'

'No.' He scratched at his beard. 'But go on – the morning was dull until you came. Did Prince Geraint suffer your humour as pleasantly as I do?'

'He has seen how this country's needs must be served. He supplies horses and men and provisioning and asks nothing in return.'

'He is young and generous with his new inheritance. Even so you will have no great force.'

'Success will bring the growth I want. But I must have a safe stronghold for winter quarters for the next few years to come. This I ask you to provide, not from charity, but on fair terms. If I speak boldly it is because I know the gods will govern your heart.'

'You talk of the gods as though you supped with them on their feast days. People already sing the tale of my spears being turned from you.'

'And will sing it for a thousand years to come. Would your name live so long had not the gods brought us together? And longer still will it live when men sing of your wisdom and fore-sight in giving me Cam Hill for leaguer to begin the great pro-gress against the Saxons.'

Melwas leaned back and roared with laughter and then thumping the rough table boards he said, 'There's a boldness in your begging which puts me on the edge so that I know not whether to smile and say yes – or shout to my men to throw you in the mere. Though, of course, should they do that the gods would see to it that you landed on your feet and walked the surface of the water.'

'Would you have me go elsewhere so that people in years to come will say that Melwas was –'

'Enough! You make my mind itch more than my winter beard does my face. I am a fool to like you and more fool to listen to you, but I have a son your age who shares your spirit and dreams and nags me like a gadfly to be allowed to take service with that old fool Ambrosius. You shall have what you want if he comes as leader of your bow and spearmen and all others of the same like who may join you in the days to come. He dreams of nothing but battle and wastes his days here in fishing, hunting and tupping the marsh maids.'

'He shall have command until the day he proves unworthy of it.'

'If that day comes he is no son of mine. Now go your way before the gods put it into your mind to ask further alms of me. Coroticus will bring his men to you within a few days and the hill is yours and your good father Baradoc can fortify it.'

'I give you thanks, and thank too the gods who sent me to you.'

Melwas shook his head slowly and with a shy smile, his lips wet red through the tangle of his beard, said, 'So, so – but think me not deceived. You would have come gods or no gods.'

Coroticus arrived with his men five days later. He was of much the same age as Arturo, but with a marshman's small, lean figure. Dark-haired with a tightly trimmed beard, his face was grave and brooding and seldom showed any emotion, a dark pool of peat water showing nothing of the depths below. He spoke quietly and pleasantly except when he would be obeyed in exercise or command and then his voice could take on a rasp like the scything of a winter wind through the frozen sedges of his own marshlands. Pride went with him, too, Arturo saw, for all his men came dressed alike. They wore leather skull-caps, their hair bound tightly over the napes of their necks, and soft leather tunics belted over thick woollen shirts. On the left breasts of the tunics copper studs pricked out the rude shape of the Summerland and King Melwas's emblem of a hovering fish eagle. Below the tunics they wore leather aprons over short woollen trews and their legs and feet were bare each year from the first spring thaw until the first winter snow. Each man had a slung bow, a quiver full of arrows, a long knife in his belt and carried a heavy fighting spear. That the men were all dressed alike told Arturo much about Coroticus. Not only pride went with good appearance but the beginning of hard military discipline – and discipline was a rare virtue among the marshmen.

He said, 'You are welcome, Coroticus.'

Coroticus answered quietly, 'We are proud to come, my lord Arturo. There is no man with me not of his own free will. Show us some piece of this hilltop for our quarters and the rest we will do for ourselves. And so it will be on the march and in fighting camps.'

Arturo smiled. 'And will it be the same the day your fifty men become five hundred?'

Coroticus said, 'If I lead them then – yes, my lord. I wish only to serve you and fight against the Saxon men, and in all things to be obedient and faithful to you.'

From that day Coroticus and his men were as he had said they would be. And from that day there was a new beginning for all on the hill. They were days of drilling and exercises, days of training in battle and surprise attacks, when troops of horse went thundering down the long slopes of the neighbouring hills and valleys in mock attack and the marshmen came fast behind them to learn to take advantage of the confusion and panic in the ranks of imaginary Saxons. They were drilled for one long hard month in all the tactics and feints and battle moves which Arturo could devise, and there was not a man from Arturo down who came riding back from a day's training who, fatigued though he might be, did not still sit proud in the saddle or trot lightly, skin sweat-and-dust coated, with long spear at rest on his shoulder. The hill now was a company of men, for Arturo had sent all women and children back to their lands and settlements. He drove the men through all the lengthening daylight hours. When darkness came there was only rest in relay for those who came from guard and sentinel duties for they lived now as though they were camped in hostile country and attack could come at any time. No man grumbled, for it was clear to all that in these days the discipline was building habit and instinct on which their lives would rest when they moved away from Cam Hill to face the killing reality of bloody warfare. Their pride, too, blossomed in pace with the bursting sprays of blackthorn bloom on the hillside. They were Arturo's men, companions and fish eagles, the men of the west and all the other free lands.

One day only they rested – though not from guard duties. This was the seventh day of the week. Then Pasco gave service and preached for those who were Christos men, and later for those who held to their country's gods did equal duty, though far fewer of these came to him because most of those who served the gods gave worship each in his own fashion before one or other of the many little rock-piled altars which had sprung up among the ancient, broken ramparts, altars that showed a bunch of primroses for Coventina, one of the first pale blue eggs of the shy dunnock for Morrigan, the Queen of Phantoms, for remembrance of the winter dead, a little carved warrior on horseback to Andraste, the goddess of victory, and plaited hair rings taken from the manes of the camp's mounts to Epona, the horse goddess.

At the end of the first month there came from Prince Geraint two troops of mounted cavalry volunteers and with them a fresh baggage train bringing supplies. The new horsemen were put to exercise and drills and within a handful of days ten of them were sent back to Isca (though their horses were kept) with the returning baggage train for under the eyes of Arturo and his troop commanders their worth was quickly weighed and found wanting.

Venutius said to Arturo, 'Returning these men, my lord, could anger Prince Geraint.'

'Then angered he must be, Venutius. These are men of good enough nature but there is no true bottom to them. They came because they seek the excitements that come after victory ...

boasting and drinking and raping. Any bright lure of the flesh or appetite would draw them aside from duty.'

'How can you know this?'

'You forget that Durstan and I served with the Isca cavalry. We know these men ... aye, and were friendly enough with them. But they are not what we want. No man rides or marches with me in this great beginning who looks to the spoils and lusts of victory before victory is won. How long would they last? We begin a struggle which will eat up many years. I need none who look no farther ahead than a summer's span.'

Hardly daring, but unable to hold back, Venutius said, 'You can say that of the marshmen, my lord?'

Arturo laughed. 'Not I. But go study Coroticus. He would have none who were other than he.' He paused and then with a smile asked, 'You think me hard?'

'No, my lord. Determined.'

'Then take this for comfort – to each man I have sent back I spoke the truth of his going. You shall see that a half of them will return to find us when they have chewed the cud of their rejection.'

Before the end of April Baradoc arrived at the camp with more provisions and a party of workmen to begin putting the hill defences in order and to raise new ones. The carts and horses he brought were taken over by Arturo to add to his own to make the baggage train for his force. Army it could not be called, nor did he see it as such. This first year, he knew, could only be a probing, proving campaign. The baggage train would travel well in their rear. He was seeking for swiftness and suddenness. Every man would carry with him – in saddle pack or back sack – that which would keep him for a week, dried meat, hard biscuit and, if pack or sack hampered him in fighting, it would be abandoned until the fight was over and then sought afterwards.

That the news of his hill camp and his campaigning intentions must have spread far abroad, he knew. *Aie* ... the very swallows and returning birds would be crying it from south to north of the land, as were the pedlars and traders that visited the hill. But none knew the way of his going or his coming. This he kept to himself for he was determined that for the Saxons the first sight of the companions should be the streaming of the White Horse standard coming over down slope or breaking from wood or rearing above the river mist as dawn broke. No, he told himself, no army yet. But that would come and when it did – remembering his talk with Venutius – he knew that he would draw men of doubt and opportunity and must take them; but none should ever wear the scarlet and white cavalry scarves of the companions or the copper-studded marsh eagle unless they were proved heart- and battle-worthy.

At the beginning of May, two days after the feast of Beltine, and the night before Arturo's men were to move from the fortress of Cam Hill, he walked in the half gloaming to the beech grove where Daria lay. As he sat there a nightingale began to sing from the nearby thickets of elder and was answered by another from the valley of the Cam. The gods he knew held all men and women in the hollow of their hands, and they had taken Daria from him to make the long passage to the Blessed Isles cradled in the Western sea where Cronus slept his long sleep. For himself he knew the years would be long before he followed her, and knew too that this was the ordering of the gods for they had reft him of the full joy of human love so that the seed should spring and flourish of another love far more demanding of his devotion.

As he sat there in the beech dell there was one who at the same moment had Arturo much in his thoughts, and this was Count Ambrosius.

He sat in his command tent at the Sabrina camp outside Corinium. A fair breeze coming over the distant river from the Cymrian hills lifted and flapped the blue folds of the tent cloth above him and set flickering the flames of the two oil lamps that stood in tall holders at each end of his table, the smeech of their burning wicks strong in his nostrils. Standing before him, waiting for his attention while he studied a map drawn on fine parchment, was his Praefectus Castrorum.

Without looking up Ambrosius waved a hand to a chair and said to the Camp Prefect, 'Sit – and take some wine.'

Grinning briefly to himself since Ambrosius was not looking at him, the Prefect sat and helped himself to wine from the flagon and glass on the table. Both flagon and glass were old and each held an engraving of the god Bacchus. The old man, he thought, must be in a good mood, for except on feast days he seldom touched wine.

As though Ambrosius had read his thoughts, he now pushed the map aside and with a thin-lipped smile reached for the flagon and poured wine for himself, and said, 'We make no great campaign this year. Such levies that have arrived can be sent back.'

'There will be no grumbling from them, my commander. They are a poor lot and all forced men. But it will be hard for our regular troops to sit in idleness.'

'There will be no idleness. We go first west through Cymru to show our strength to these hill chiefs and then north to Luguvalium on the Wall.' He sipped his wine and added pleasantly, 'You think we waste a year's campaigning now that Hengist is dead?'

The Camp Prefect shrugged his shoulders. 'Esc is young and not the man his father was. He can never hold the other Saxon warlords together for now they will fight among themselves. Still, I should have thought, my commander, that –'

Ambrosius cut him off with a wave of his hand. 'That this was the time to march against them? No. That would serve us badly. To hunt summer wolves who have all broken pack would gain us little. And neither is there need – for our young Arturo will do that for us.'

'True, my commander. And in so doing will draw more men to himself and new glory to his name.'

'Which serves us well, though he may be long in seeing it. He shall make an army and a name for himself, and in a few years we shall shake the fruit of his growing into our basket. I would have the Saxons finish their quarrelling with the rise of a

new leader – be it Esc or some other – and then we shall have
again a head and heart to strike at.'

'And Arturo and his army?'

Ambrosius flicked a finger nail against the rim of his glass so
that it rang, the high note trembling and then dying. He said
quietly, 'At heart he's a raw western savage, full of courage and
bloodthirsty, but his brains are in his backside and only work
when he sits a horse. I have handled his kind many times, chiefs
of the Brigantes, the Ordovices and the Dobunni in our own
country here. They think only of the glory of fighting and the
triumphs of victory. The building of a great state and the craft
and judgement which that demands is beyond them. When they
meet their limits they come to hand like broken horses. It is for
this that I have called you here. You will send an envoy to him
to say that he is outlaw no longer and more, that I give him free
right of passage for his army throughout the land. A handful
of sweet oats to feed his pride.' He paused for a moment and
pulled from his hand one of the rings he wore, and slid it across
the table to the Camp Prefect. 'Let this go to him with the
pardon.'

Outside the tent the Camp Prefect weighted the ring in his
palm. It was gold, a signet ring with the seal worked into an
intaglio of Ambrosius's head, laurel wreathed. For a moment or
two he wondered whether the Count practised some wisdom
beyond his seeing. Arturo was more likely to throw pardon and
ring back in the face of Ambrosius. But maybe the Count knew
that and wanted it to happen so that a sharp edge should be
honed to Arturo's strong contempt for him ... a goad to prick
him forward to higher and bolder deeds which could be used
by the Count to shape his own destiny. Aye, perhaps so, for
his master could be as patient and cunning as a serpent, and
knew well how to make others work for him without their
being aware of it. Well, so be it until time made it plain. But
on one score his commander was right. There was no gain in
marching against the Saxons this year for they would never
come out to fight in full strength until they had another leader
who could call and gather them to full battle unity.

Some days later a Sabrina cavalry troop leader with an escort of two of his men arrived at Cam Hill. Olipon, the troop leader, left his two men at the foot of the hill and rode the path to the battlements alone to show his peaceful coming. The sight that met his eyes surprised him. Work was going ahead on the great ring of fortifications and inside them was a well-ordered camp, full of bustle and preparation for the coming campaign. The horses were sleek and well-fed, every fighting man moved with a spring and alertness which showed growing zest for the fighting days ahead. Here was no rabble of disorganized tribesmen under an impetuous, plunder-hungry chief. Things moved here with almost as much order as they did in the Sabrina Wing at Corinium. And why not, he thought, since as he was led to Arturo he saw many a former Sabrina man among them? Aye, and was called to and jested with by men who had been his friends and companions in arms so that it was hard for him not to wonder whether they had moved to a wisdom and understanding of this Arturo which escaped him. Momentarily the urge took him to deliver his message and then ask to be allowed to join this company, for nothing but a long dull summer of parades and show-of-strength marches lay ahead of the Count's army.

He was led to Arturo's hut, over which flew the White Horse standard. Outside on guard stood a short, dark-haired, dark-skinned marshman, resting on his spear, the copper studs of his fish eagle insignia burnished to catch the sunlight. Arturo came out to him and he was at once less and more than he had expected: a young man wearing a loose linen shirt belted over his leather trews, smiling, fair brown hair and blue-eyed, his beard tightly trimmed, who could have passed without notice on the Corinium drill grounds until at second look the force of the young face and the depth of the blue eyes suddenly spoke of some tight-bridled passion. It was all there to see if a man had the eyes and wit to see it. There was iron in this man and an age beyond his years.

Olipon raised his right arm in the old Roman salute, announced himself and gave his message and then handed Am-

brosius's ring to Arturo. Arturo nodded, his face unchanging
as he weighed the ring absently in his hand after giving it no
more than a glance, and then said, 'How many days are you
from Corinium?'

'Three, my lord.'

'Hard riding. You would stay the night to rest yourself, your
men and your horses?'

'You are kind, my lord – but no. I give my commander's
message and return with your ... your –' Olipon broke off.

'My thanks, you think, to Count Ambrosius?' Arturo smiled.

Recovering himself, Olipon said, 'I shall speak, my lord, as
you shall command me.'

'Then say this to Count Ambrosius. When I and my good
companion Durstan were first outlawed by Count Ambrosius I
swore a promise that men now call Arto's Promise ... aye, they
still call it so to mark any idle boast.' His smile was frank and
good-natured. 'Tell your commander that promise was made
under the gods and still holds faith with me. I come only to
Count Ambrosius when, as equal to equal, he sues me for help.
On that day I will ride to Glevum and be with him in good
faith to serve this our country.' He handed the ring to Olipon.
'Take back this, too. He wears the laurels of victory well ahead
of due season, but to spare you his anger you need not give
him those words.'

Riding down the hill to rejoin his men there was a moment
when Olipon was half-tempted to turn back and ask leave to
join the companions. Then his good sense prevailed. Plenty of
chiefs had gone their own way before and made fight against
the Saxons, refusing to league with Count Ambrosius. Few
still lived and those that did held to their wild homelands and
sent the Count their spare levies with bad grace.

When Olipon was ushered into the Count's presence some
days later to speak Arturo's words and return the ring – though
he said nothing of his wearing the laurels ahead of season – Ambrosius merely nodded and showed no emotion. But when
Olipon had gone he slipped the ring back on his finger and
smiled broadly to himself. Many a warband like Arturo he had

seen come with promise and go chastened after a few fighting
seasons back into the obscurity of their bogs and mountains.
But now the Fates, it seemed, were truly sending him the man
he needed. Had Arturo accepted the pardon gratefully then he
would have known that there was no hard lasting in him But
last this western hothead and dreamer would until the day
when he should decide on his going and with no mark of infamy
on him gather up his victories and his army for himself. So ..
in due time he would sue Arturo for help and let him come
riding to Glevum in triumph, and in further time, when he gave
the word for Arturo's death, then the full harvest of his victories
and the full strength of his army would fall to him and he
would make himself master of this land and bring it back to
the greatness which it had once known under those other proud
wearers of the laurels and the purple.

On a May morning with the high soaring downland larks
filling the bright air with their song the Companions of the
White Horse left Cam Hill and began their long march eastwards. They numbered three troops of thirty-two horse each.
The first ranking troop was commanded by Durstan, who had
for second-in-command Garwain. The second was headed by
Gelliga with Borio at his side, and the third by Netio, the right
side of his face puckered with an old sword scar, with Marcos
to second him. In reserve, behind the two baggage trains, was
the reserve troop – mostly men and mounts from Prince Geraint
– commanded by Venutius in the place of the dead Cuneda, and
served as next in command by an Iscan trooper called Branta.
Holding the flanks, split into two detachments, were the marshmen of Coroticus. In the baggage train, ridden by the camp servants, were twenty remounts. In all there were close on one
hundred and fifty horse and cavalry men – for no servant rode
a remount unless he could turn fighting man too – and fifty
spear and bowmen.

At their head rode Arturo, and Lancelo carrying the White
Horse standard. Anga, the ageing hound, kept pace at Arturo's
side. It had been in Arturo's mind to leave the hound behind

for the days ahead would be long and hard, but if death were to come to Anga, he decided, then it should not be pining on the hill top. He should die on the march or in battle.

They rode out, red-and-white scarfed and fish eagle studded, all weapons and fighting gear true, the rising Spring-lust in them for action and triumph; and with them went Pasco on a moorland pony, Pasco who had wearied them with a too long sermon and blessing before they left the hill.

Watching them go, Baradoc, stiff-faced with pride in his son, swallowing the gall of his own envy to be fighting fit and to go with them, remembered the day when he and Tia had landed on Caer Sibli where Arturo was to be born, remembered too what the hermit, Merlin, had written of him, scratched on the face of a rock:

> Cronus in the dream spoke thus
> Name him for all men and all time
> His glory an everlasting flower
> He throws no seed

Glory, Baradoc thought, kneading his crippled right arm, was coming to him for over the days he had spent here he had found a new Arturo and, though he tried to deny it in himself at first, had come to accept that he had fathered a man who was to be marked out among other men. Then thinking of Daria lying in the beech dell he wondered if the gods would deny Arturo the common gift of a man's love for a woman because they would keep him bound indivisibly to them for the full length of his days .. *Aie*, Arturo was close to the gods. He accepted that now. But there was always for such men some great tribute to be paid. He raised his eyes to the far down slopes and saw the cavalcade strung out and spread across it and the red and white scarves and banners burned like a slow flame over the new grasses.

In the following days the Companions rode down the old road to Sorviodunum and on to Venta through peaceful country, the news of their coming running fast ahead of them. In Sorviodunum – where the citizens were slowly rebuilding their town, which had been sacked in a raid by sea pirates some years before – they were welcomed and freely provisioned during their stay. At Venta the same greeting met them. They then at Arturo's orders – and none knew what they would be beyond the day's march ahead – turned south-east towards the coast and rode two days to Noviomagus. Here was a strong community of Christos people and also the seat of the bishop of the diocese, an ancient, not fully witted man who believed that the rule of the Great Empire still ran through the southern lands. He gave Arturo and his chief companions lodgings in his palace. Hearing from the priest Pasco that Arturo had been baptized in the Faith before his marriage to Daria, though not that he had done so because he held all gods in reverence and some, because of their greater powers, in more reverence than others, the bishop came out at their departure and gave his Christian blessing to the little army. He also presented Arturo with a rich scarlet sleeveless surcoat embroidered with the blue-robed figure of the Virgin Mary, the halo about her head formed by clusters of small seed pearls cropped from the oysters that flourished in the nearby sea creeks and tidal flats. Arturo wore it until they were out of the bishop's domain. After that it was put with his spare gear on one of the baggage carts.

As they went eastwards between the shore and the rising slopes of the great forest of Anderida to the north, Durstan dropped back to ride with Arturo. After a while he said, 'We ride gently, as though in triumph, all victories won. This way what shall we meet but a handful of raiding sea pirates now that the good season makes fair passage and landing for their keels? The true Saxons from the Cantiaci lands seldom come south through the forest.'

Arturo nodded. 'You speak the truth. This way we ride gently – but far slower than the news of our coming. The forest is full of eyes. The word goes swiftly from charcoal burners' stands to swineherds' huts, and to the boothies of fish- and bird-trappers and so by smoke signal and fast runners to Durobrivae and Durovernum to find Esc and his warriors. Last year we were a warband, no more than a thorn in the side of Saxon pride. Now we come as an army, a sword thrust which must be met. Though it draws not Esc himself, he will send men to meet it. If he would hold his father's inheritance this is no moment for him to lose the smallest part of his valour. The eyes of his people mark him to see whether he is worthy son and successor to his father.'

Two days later, when they were almost on the borders of the lands of Eleutherus, who held the fortified British town of Anderida and called himself King, but stayed in power because he had compounded an uneasy pact with Hengist, they turned northwards up the valley of a sluggish river which cut through the thick forest. Three days later they broke free of the trees and thickets on to the stream-laced high land of the river's watershed. Here, as they marched in battle order, with out-riders ahead and on their flanks patrols of Coroticus's men, a horn sounded loud and clear from the front, giving the warning for the sighting of the enemy.

Riding ahead to the leading troop, Arturo saw that the Saxons had placed themselves well. The land fell away into the narrow mouth of a steeply cut valley. Three lines of Saxons held the valley bottom and its steep sides. No cavalry charge could take the steep valley sides for no horse at speed could safely assault them from the front. The Saxon lines at the valley bottom were equally well protected, for any charge down the sharp slope – if the Saxons opened ranks to let it through – would take men and horses into the marshy quagmire which was the nurturing ground of the stream that flowed north down the valley. The soft ground would hold a man with ease. But horse and man would sink and flounder in the quaking bogland to become easy victims to the long sabre-curved scramaseax swords of the Saxons.

Looking down at the enemy Arturo saw that they were no hurriedly gathered band of undisciplined settlers and townsmen. Although few of them wore any body armour, being clothed in short leather trews and tough skin and pelt surcoats belted tight to carry axes and the sharp, deadly seax knives with which to cut the throats of a fallen enemy, they stood proudly, many of them leather helmeted and all carrying small round shields which they struck into the face of an opponent while their swords went into his guts below. More than a few, he noticed, carried a spear instead of a scramaseax and he guessed that they were local men, no true warriors, pressed into service to swell the ranks. He realized, too, that behind this confrontation, lay the warcraft, if not of Esc himself, then one of his trusted commanders, warcraft which was designed to tempt him to disaster or give him the humiliating choice of turning aside from them. But to turn aside from them would be all the victory Esc needed for the news would run like a summer heath fire and his name would be shamed before the gods and all men.

With Lancelo at his side, the White One moving a little restlessly under him so that Anga stayed away from her, Arturo ran his eyes over the Saxon lines – the warriors unnaturally silent for usually they shouted taunts and abuse – and knew that the gods were putting him under trial. And, under the gods, he knew too that there was no choice for him, nor did he seek it. Now was the time when the long days of drills and exercises back at Cam Hill must be shown to serve them all in bloody reality.

He turned to Lancelo and said, 'Give the call of the Taunted Boar.'

Lancelo put the horn to his lips and sounded the call. It was one among many that had been born of their training days, and all of them were named ... the Taunted Boar, the Coiling Snake, the Wolf Circle ... and there was not a fighting man or a baggage man who did not know as the notes rang out exactly what was demanded of him. The horn wailed, high and screaming, changed to a quick succession of sharp blasts and then was suddenly silent as its echoes rolled down the valley still.

Curbing the restless white mare, Arturo watched the pattern of his men and horses move and swirl and heard the shouts of the baggage train handlers as the end of the column closed up and the reserve troop rimmed it in a double-rowed crescent.

The two forward troops went wide on each flank, well above the valley head, and held their mounts champing and restless in double lines, the forenoon breeze teasing their red and white scarves and helmet crests, the sun striking points of fire from the scabbard-freed swords of each front rank and sparking the lance tips of the second lines.

Then into the forefront of the battle formation came Coroticus and his men, spears slung behind their backs, their bows drawn and arrowed and each man holding three arrows crossways in his mouth. They trotted down the slope in two lines abreast and when they were within easy bowshot of the ranks of Saxons Coroticus called an order. The first line of marshmen dropped to one knee and the second line stood two paces behind.

For a moment or two there was no movement save that of restless horses, no sounds save those of the high chorusing larks. Not even from the Saxon ranks came taunt or shout for they were meeting now a move which puzzled them for they had expected an onrush of cavalry to cut through them and throw them into disorder while the marshmen followed up behind with their spears.

Coroticus, who assumed no commander's privilege in fighting itself and knelt at the right end of the first line of bowmen, gave a low curlew's whistle and, flexing his arrow-charged bow, took aim at the throat of a man on the right flank of the centre line of the Saxon warriors in the valley bottom. The arrow sped true to take the man in the gullet and with a high choking scream he toppled backwards. As he did so the marshman on Coroticus's left sent his arrow through the left eye of another warrior. And then the next marshman, unhurried, following the well-learnt drill, fired another arrow, the goose-feathered shaft sinking deep into a Saxon's left breast. Deliberately, without hurry, a few moments between each shot, the marshmen picked their targets and fired, and not until twenty of their men were down did the Saxons stir and break their silence. The taunting of the boar had begun and Arturo, watching, knew that the Saxons barring the marshy ground would not long hold themselves in check for it was the nature of these men to go to meet the enemy eagerly, filling the air with their battle cries.

So it proved. As man after man went down, now from the middle ranks and now from the valley-side flanking ranks, the cries came and grew louder and angrier, and those Saxons with spears flung them at the marshmen. But Coroticus had gauged his front well and they all fell short. Then suddenly like the onrush of a tidal wave, in a great burst of noise, the three ranks of Saxons, on the steep hill sides and valley bottom, enraged that they should stand like sheep to wait the arrow which would send them to Valhalla, broke ranks and surged forward shields high, scramaseaxes swinging, eager to come to grips with their foes.

Arturo at Lancelo's side smiled as he saw their coming. Thus was the taunted boar goaded to break cover and offer itself to slaughter. He nodded to Lancelo and the horn called, echoing down the narrow valley.

Coroticus's men, as the Saxons rushed for them, turned and ran back and as Coroticus passed Arturo he looked up. There was a gleam in his dark eyes and – seldom seen in a marshman except in drink – a broad grin on his face and the faces of all his men.

As the Saxons raced after them, leaving their boggy ground far behind, Gelliga's flanking troop came galloping down upon them, the heavy swords of the first rank swinging and slashing and cutting into the enemy, killing and maiming. Behind them came the second line of lances to bring death to those wounded warriors who from the ground on their knees or backs tried to hack and stab at the legs and bellies of the horses. Then, after the passing of Gelliga's troop, there came down from the opposite flank, charging through their already blooded companions, the troop of Durstan to hack and hew and carry their killing lances through the shouting rabble of Saxon warriors.

Arturo watched as the two troops wheeled, reformed and charged again. This time the Saxons broke and ran hard for the safety of the lower soft ground from which they had been tempted and kept running even as Lancelo's horn sounded be-

hind them the call to break action. Watching them go Arturo
knew that this was a beginning, a good and god-given beginning,
a gift from Badb, the god of battle, and an offering to Andraste,
the goddess of victory, and proof that – great fighters though the
Saxons were when they saw victory coming to their grasp
– they were no men to stand and die in defeat if any loophole
of escape still offered itself to them.

Close to a hundred men lay dead or dying, their arms to be
plundered, and their small wealth of rings and torques, brooches
and armlets which they wore into battle to be taken into the
war chest of the Companions against the wants of the long campaigning days ahead. The news of this first clash would run
fast and far and wide. Looking up, Arturo saw in the clear
afternoon sky the beginning of the first circling of the prey
birds, kites, eagles, the diamond-tailed ravens and the already
bickering crows mobbing the stately circling buzzards to ease
their impatience to arrive at the waiting feast below.

That night, as Arturo made his round of the sentry posts
with Lancelo, he heard from the downland hollow where his
men sat around their camp fires the voice of Durstan singing:

> The boar in the east does not call
> No more in his bracken lodge does he sleep
> The hornet flight of the arrows of Coroticus
> Have taunted him to rage
> And the swords of Arturo
> Have stayed the strength of his red anger
>
> Under the moonlight his saffron tusks
> Make perches for the ravens who feed on his eyes
> And on the dead pine branches
> The eagles sit heavy from feasting

Girl with a Harp

For the rest of that spring and summer they sat nowhere in camp for long. For the first part they stayed south of the river Tamesis, moving, sometimes in small bands and sometimes in full strength, along the borders of the Saxon lands, harrying and destroying the outlying settlements, of which there were many; for the Saxons were no lovers of town life. They lived mostly in family and kinship groups in the clearings they had made in the forests or on the slopes of the gentle river valleys.

They came and went with no pattern of movement or settled strength which the Saxons could anticipate. They were a wolf pack, marauding now in force and now in small groups. They leaguered their baggage train well to their west and then for a week the cavalry troops of the Companions would disappear to the east with Coroticus's men to attack at dawn or as last daylight faded, until the time came when they mounted a strong assault on the heavily settled outskirts of Durobrivae, the next largest town after Durovernum. They came at night and set fire to the hovels and round huts and squalid log cabins along the river so that the flames turned its waters to blood. When daylight came – for the Saxons had no taste for night marching – and the warriors had gathered in the dawn to pursue them they had melted away, splitting into small parties of eight or ten horse and a few marshmen, each group going its own way back to the baggage train. Then, when at last Esc – who had other matters on his mind – finally gathered a force to overmatch them and marched westwards they were nowhere to be found on the borders of his land for they had gone north around Londinium – which the aftermath of plague had turned into a ghost city, though even without such a scourge there were now few who chose to live and trade there – and were sitting openly and in force on the road to Durolipons which bordered the land of the Trinovantes held by the East Saxons.

Now, too, though Arturo never gave explanation of his over-all strategy, the shape of the design that lay in his mind began to come clear to most of his leading Companions, and – since he had served under Ambrosius as a staff officer – abidingly clear to Venutius. This year and for a few more years the pattern would be fixed. Harry and raid and go. They would stand and fight when the battle was fairly matched, but not otherwise. A man or horse lost in a useless foray or an over-matched confrontation gained Arturo nothing. This was the first sowing of a rich crop to come and the sowing would be not of one year but many. Already fighting men were coming to them, seeking them out and to all of them the answer of Arturo was the same: to ride to Cam Hill, come the autumn, where a wel-come would await them. None joined him now who did not know the ways of the Companions and had not their training and discipline. No man could fight with them until he had learnt their ways, their discipline and proved himself, and Venutius saw readily the virtue of this demand. One man accepted by Arturo would be worth ten reluctant levied men. He saw too – perhaps more than any other Companion – that patience was now yoked with Arturo's warlike, eager spirit. The dream he dreamt was not to be accomplished in a few years. Already he was looking ten, twenty, thirty years ahead. Ambrosius had dreamt and schemed like that, did so still, but time was now against him unless he let Arturo enrich his fame and his power and then, with no sign of villainy, gather them to himself. Venutius tried often to shut the thought of that moment from his mind, but each day it was with him inescapably for he knew that he was trapped. When Ambrosius's messenger came with the nicked golden aureus of the Emperor Hadrian he would have no choice. If he let Arturo live then Ambrosius would make it known that he had poisoned Daria and, no matter the esteem Arturo might have for him through his service as a Com-panion, he would be killed . . .

Against the East Saxons that year they pursued the same tactics as they had done with the South Saxons. Then as summer began to pass they moved farther north through Causennae to Lindum, where the news of their coming had run ahead fast of them. Here, where the city and surrounding country were precariously held by the Coritani, they were welcomed warmly by the townsfolk and the bishop. The Companions made camp on the gently rising ground to the south of the town, but the bishop insisted that Arturo should take quarters in his own palace, and on his first evening they supped together.

The bishop, a small, spare man of fifty, a sparrow of a man, with a dark, cheerful glint in his eyes, entertained him alone, and was full of eagerness to hear of his progress along the borders of the Saxon lands.

He said as they ate a dish of stuffed carp, 'I shall be in bad grace with Count Ambrosius for making you welcome but 'tis long since he was here and may be longer before he comes again. But who am I to deny hospitality to one who brings a gleam of hope for this wretched land – and one, too, who is a Christian. Is that not so, my son?'

'It is, your grace.'

The bishop smiled. 'But have, too, I am told, a great respect for this country's old gods.'

Arturo, who liked the man, and had measured quickly his nature, said, 'This is my country. Without its gods it would be nothing. For love of my dead wife I became a Christos man. For love of my country I also worship my country's gods. A warrior, your grace, needs all the help he can get.'

'I will not argue that point with you. Time will make a better argument than I can.' He sipped wine from his silver mounted glass and went on, 'It is a pity that there is bad blood between you and Count Ambrosius. God knows you are welcome here for we live dangerously and are raided often by the fen Saxons beyond the great Car dyke.'

Arturo shrugged his shoulders. 'The Count is a dreamer of dusty dreams. As dusty as the old ways of Rome to which he clings. He waits for a miracle. I work for an end and, if the gods spare me, will come to it. While the South Saxons are all in disarray he should have gone against them, but I hear that he holds back because he thinks they will not come out against him, lacking a strong leader. Why wait? If I had two thousand men this summer I could have swept through the Cantiaci lands and driven them into the sea from Tanatus round to Lemanis, could have smoked them out of their holes like rats. But the day is coming when I will have those men, and this summer I have made a beginning under the gods ...' he paused for a moment, and then added, '... and under the banner of Christos.'

The bishop nodded, his mouth pursed with a wry smile, and said, 'You have an interesting approach to theology – but a very direct and admirable one to the great matter of this country. In a man who loves his country so ardently many things can be forgiven.' He sighed. 'Ah, me, yes. The good Lord works in a fashion not always easily understood. But we grow too serious. We shall have music to sweeten the rest of the evening.'

He spoke to the servant who was attending them who left the room to come back a few moments later with a young girl who carried a small harp. Sitting herself on a bench by the open window she began to play and sing for them in a sweet, though not oversure voice at first, as though she were nervous. But after a little while she grew confident.

Leaning back in his chair Arturo listened to her as his eyes marked the evening hawking outside of the young swallows who were beginning to flock together for their southerly passage. Already the swifts had gone. Soon the geese and the migrating peregrines would go and the host of small warblers and finches. Summer was fast deferring to autumn and his first campaign was almost done. The stone had been thrown into the still pond and the ripples were spreading. How many summers, how many campaigns before ... ? He sighed, touched for a time by a sudden sense of weariness. In that moment, seeing his return to Cam Hill, he knew a brief and bitter flare of sorrow for the one love who could give him no greeting.

Through that moment of rare self-pity the young girl's voice came to him, clear and sweet. She was singing an old song which he knew well; a song the Companions sang around their camp fires. Daria lay in the beech dell. Ten of his Companions and as many of Coroticus's marshmen would see no return to Cam Hill.

> I have a hut in the wood
> None knows it but my love
> An ash tree this side
> A hazel on the other
> A little hidden lowly hut
> Where waits my flame-haired love ...

For the first time Arturo looked closely at her. She was a girl of twelve or thirteen years, her young breasts scarce challenging the soft material of the short white linen robe she wore. Her bare legs were sun-browned and on her feet were red sandals of soft doe skin. Sensing that the two men were now listening to her song, she raised her head, her fair hair caught with a ribbon of the same colour as her sandals, and smiled at them. For a moment the pink tip of her tongue ran like some small soft animal between her teeth and there was a momentary widening of her blue eyes. Deep, dark blue, Arturo saw, like the flash on a jay's covert feathers.

> The black cock calls from the high heather
> We eat sweet apples under summer's mantle
> Her lips the red of the ripe bog-berries ...

A child still, thought Arturo as he sipped his wine, but with already something of boldness in her eyes. In five or six years' time she would turn the heads of young men and many would sigh for love of her.

When she had finished the song the bishop said to her, 'It is a song fit for a resting warrior. Play once more for us, child, and then away to your couch.'

On the word 'child' Arturo saw the flick of her eyebrows, momentary as the beat of a bird's wing, mark a fast passing frown and remembered the childhood years when, feeling himself more, he had bridled at the same word.

She lowered her head over the harp, her face hidden from them and touched the strings strongly so that the notes came boldly and arrogantly –

> The boar in the east does not call
> No more in his bracken lodge does he sleep ...

Beside him the bishop began to chuckle with pleasure and looked at Arturo for approval.

Arturo smiled too as she played on and when she had finished he said, 'From where do you get such a song?'

Without shyness she said, 'From your men, my lord, who walk the city. I would have liked to have been there to see the taunting of the boar.'

Arturo laughed. 'It was no fit place for a girl.' Then seeing the brief tightening of her face, he went on, 'But you sing sweetly enough to shame the nightingale at dusk and when the words are of war you have all the music of the dark torrent.'

She laughed then and said, 'You tease me, my lord.'

'And I tease you more straightly,' said the bishop, smiling. 'Get you to your couch and be glad you will become a woman and have no part in wars. Away with you.'

The girl rose from her chair, bowed to them and went to the doorway. There, her face full now of mischief and spirit, she drew her fingers across the harp to sound a full, loud run of chords, bowed and went out.

Both men laughed and then Arturo asked, 'Who is she, your grace?'

'She is from far north of Eburacum. Her father, one Loth, is a good friend of mine. She visits here with her mother, who is my sister, for there is some talk of placing her with the nuns here, though ...' he sighed a little, 'I doubt that it will serve her much. She is high spirited and wayward when she chooses. But also full of womanly charms and guile when she needs. I have my own minstrels here, but tonight she cajoled me – no difficult task with a doting uncle – to be allowed to play and sing for you. So you see, your fame begins to run fast before you. Arturo of the White Horse and his Companions are more

to her liking than the sparrow chatter and spartan life of a
nunnery.'

'And her name?'

'It is Gwennifer.'

That night as he lay on his bed Arturo was long in finding
sleep. In a few more days the Companions would turn and take
the road south to find Cam Hill. There were many good wel-
comes to await a returning warrior, but none sweeter than the
woman of his heart. If the gods blessed him with long life and
with victories and the true shaping of his dreams for this
country they had already taken their toll in return for his
triumphs to come. Daria slept in the beech dell with Cuneda
to guard her. True heart and true friend. Without these a man's
life was barren. Thinking this he dropped a hand over the side
of the bed and his fingers found the hoary head of Anga sleeping alongside him. He remembered the day of his fourteenth
birthday in Isca when his mother had given him the hound
puppy as a present to take the place of old Lerg; remembered,
too, his grief when the old hound had died. Some griefs passed
so that memory ran without pain but others endured, their
season unending. An owl called and the rising moon began to
limn the room with pale light. As sleep began to touch him he
remembered his first meeting on the Dumnonian moors with
Daria who travelled north with her father, old Ansold, and her
brother, now his good companion, Lancelo, and how she had
said that they travelled to this town – though they never
reached it – where ... Her voice rang clear in his memory. *To
hear my father tell it – where every other spring flows wine
instead of water, where the birds on the trees have golden wings,
and the cattle grass grows knee-high and lush through winter.*
And he had replied – *One day I will come to Lindum and seek
you out ... I shall come and woo you and we shall lie in the
long grass, listen to the golden birds sing, and drink the new
wine.*

He slept and the memories slept with him.

Two mornings later he woke to hear the lowing of heifers
being driven up the street below, the cries of their drovers and

the ringing of the high towered bell of the nunnery, a bell which rang the alarm when over the green marshes and low willow thickets to the east beyond the great Car Dyke the lookouts marked the approach of raiding Saxon bands. This morning they served as a farewell to Anga for the old hound had died in his sleep during the night. Arturo took him, wrapped in his cloak, and buried him under a mulberry tree in the bishop's garden. Three days later the small army left Lindum marching south-west down the old Imperial road of the legions, a road broken, neglected, but still serviceable that ran in a long diagonal across the land through Crococalana to Ratae to Corinium and from Corinium to Aquae Sulis and then through Lindinis to Isca Dumnoniorum.

Not long after they had left Lindum there were cries and shouts from the rear troop and the baggage trains. Slewing round in his saddle at the head of the long column, Arturo looked back. Coming down the road was a youth on a small skewbald pony galloping fast, and laughter broke through the bright morning air as now and then he was forced by baggage cart or troop formation to veer to the side and take to the rougher going of the roadside vallum.

Arturo, signalling to Lancelo to keep the long strung column moving, pulled aside free of the road to a bank where already the tall spikes of sweet balsam were being harvested by the bees and wasps. The youth rode up to him, his face flushed with sweat and dust He wore a loose cloak that reached to the knees of his short leather trews and a red scarf wrapped like a turban about his head to trap all but a few loose curls of his fair hair.

Arturo smiling, knowing that the deceit of habit was not meant for him but to fool – though it scarce could have done – the gate sentries of Lindum, said jokingly, 'We seek no recruits who are not of age – especially one who rides so awkwardly.' There was no mistaking the deep, dark blue eyes and the fair hair and poppy bright lips of Gwennifer.

The girl was silent for a moment, catching her breath. Then dropping her reins she pulled the scarf from her head and her hair fell in a tangle which the breeze teased so that it was a moving web of gold threads under the sun, and she said solemnly, 'My lord Arturo, I ride not to join you, but to bring you that which may ease a little the sorrow in your heart.'

Then, urging the pony forward a little so that she was at the side of the White One, she fumbled beneath her drawn cloak and drew out a brindle and white-throated puppy which squealed as she held it from her and from fright piddled a little so that the liquid sprayed one of her bare legs. She said urgingly, 'Take him, my lord. He is of the best blood and will be a good hound. The bishop would have none other in his kennels.'

Touched by the gesture, Arturo covered the quick emotion rising in him, and said chaffingly, 'The bishop will give you no thanks for pillaging his kennels and I would not see you in trouble for your kindness.'

Gwennifer frowned and said firmly, 'But he is mine to give. My uncle made present of him to me when I came here with my mother. Take him, my lord.'

Arturo hesitated for a moment, then reached out and took the puppy – which could scarce have had three months since its whelping. Its belly was warm against the palm of his hand, and the sweet hound smell strong from its pelt. He said, 'I take him and give you thanks. What is he called?'

'Cabal, my lord, and he will be a hound above all hounds for the gods have told me so in a dream.'

Cocking an eye in open doubt, Arturo asked, 'The gods speak to you in your dreams?'

'Sometimes. They have shown me many things that will happen. Some I like and some I like not, but then . . . ' she shrugged her shoulders lightly, '. . . there is no changing the fall of the dice they have shaken.'

'You talk old for one so young. The Christos nuns will have their hands full with you.'

She shook her head and laughed. 'I shall make them such trouble, my lord, that they will cry out to be rid of me.' Then eyeing him boldly, she said, 'Why wish them that trouble? I can keep these clothes and come with you to Cam Hill to serve you as well as any other. I can do –'

'Enough.' Arturo shook his head and his lips tightened severely. 'I thank you for your gift and for the gentleness of thought that provoked it. But now you go back to Lindum to your mother and the good bishop. And to make sure you do I send two men with you. Back to Lindum. This I command.'

'Then I shall go – for such I would have done anyway since I came only to lodge Cabal with you. But this I say, my lord, and further risk your anger. One day I shall ride into Cam Hill and you will welcome me since in a dream –'

'– the gods have shown you this,' finished Arturo for her.

'Aye, my lord and more.'

'Then I believe you. Now ride for Lindum.'

He turned from her back on to the road and called for Marcos to give her escorts and handed him Cabal to find place for on one of the baggage carts. Then he rode to take his place at the head of the main column – for one troop of horse rode well ahead even in this peaceful country – alongside Lancelo.

Lancelo grinned when Arturo told him what had happened and said, 'All Lindum and Eburacum, it is said, knows her for her wildness and, although she is a girl, her father has taken the birch to her for some of her doings.'

Lightly Arturo said, 'Some women are born with the hearts of men, and some men with the hearts of women and for the making of trouble there is no choosing between them.' He said no more but as he rode and looked down to where Anga had for so long padded alongside him, he knew gratitude for the gift she had brought. The gods had sent him another hound. Let their gifts to her be always so good . . .

They marched that day to the outskirts of Ratae where they made camp. That evening as Arturo sat outside his small tent Durstan came and joined him, bringing a bowl of goat's milk for the hound puppy. As they watched the puppy drink Durstan said, 'You mean to keep this road for the full march?'

'I do.'

'We march through Corinium?'

'We do. The more we are seen the more will men come to us this winter.'

'And what of the Sabrina Wing? We are no match for them as yet.'

'There is only a small holding force at Corinium. Count Ambrosius is still making his progress, so the bishop told me, and is at Deva.'

'He is well informed.'

'You do not stay bishop long otherwise. I learnt much from him. He is with us, and will make and find friends for us among the chiefs north of Eburacum.' He picked up Cabal and stroked his white throat. 'We are only at the beginning of things. We need the friendship and the help of his kind over the years to come. The Christos bishops and their people grow stronger in this country. The more a country suffers . . . aye, and they with it, the more their strength grows and we have chance to turn it to our advantage.'

Durstan plucked a tall grass stalk, chewed its end for a moment or two and then, even he not knowing what reception his words might provoke, said quietly, 'But you are no true Christos man, Arturo. They will come to know this.'

Arturo frowned 'I am as true a Christos man as any for he is a god with other gods. When you are with fever you do not pray to Epona. You send your prayers to Nodens of the Silver Hand. In battle you cry on Badb not Lug who blesses the seed of man in woman. But when a whole nation suffers then you call on all the gods. I would think it no shame or treason to put on the surcoat given me by the bishop at Noviomagus and go into battle wearing the image of the blessed mother of Christos.'

Durstan said nothing. There were times when the reasoning of Arturo escaped him. He prodded the flank of Cabal and the puppy turned and began to worry at the hard leather of his campaign boot.

The silence between them was broken by the first evening churring of a nightjar and the flames of the bivouac fires from the camp spread around them on the sandy heath they had chosen for the night were cut by the black shapes of the sentries who patrolled the limits of their resting place.

Arturo said quietly, 'What has to be done will be many years in the making. Only if Cronus woke from his great sleep could he speed the years so that they seemed but weeks to bring us to end of the long labours which lie ahead. We are mortal and so must live and fight and build to the measure of our own breathing.'

Four days later they marched through Corinium. The small holding party which Ambrosius had left at the Sabrina Wing camp had advance news of their coming. When the dust of their marching showed the commander called his men to arms and two troops of cavalry were deployed in battle formation along the eastern front of the camp which was flanked by the Ratae–Corinium road. Ambrosius had left him without orders for this happening. But he was a man of good sense and not without admiration for Arturo. When the long snaking column of Arturo's Companions came into view with Coroticus's men and mounted scouts guarding its flanks, he put his horse to the trot and, leaving his men, made to the place in the long column where the White Horse standard flew in the soft breeze.

Seeing him coming Arturo rode away from the road and across the bare, hoof-packed training grounds to meet him.

Reining-in the White One, Arturo said, 'We come in peace. We fight the same battle and follow the same cause as Count Ambrosius.'

The commander's mouth twisted to a wry smile and he said, 'Aye, that is true, my lord Arturo. Then pass peacefully. I can give you no provisioning or quartering here for under the writ of Count Ambrosius you are outlaw still.' He shrugged his shoulders, and with a firm hand gentled his restless horse. 'A pity . . . for otherwise we could have shared wine, and I would have had pleasure in good talk with many of my old friends whom I now see among your ranks.'

Smiling Arturo said, 'A pity, true – but if you feel their loss so much you could join us.'

The commander shook his head. 'Not me, my lord. I am one of the old Ambrosiaci. When you were a boy I fought with the Count in the days of the great raidings of the South coasts. We were young then and fought at Anderida and Noviomagus to tame the sea raiders. My battle scars were suffered under him. I carry them with honour and – though he grows old now like me and, in truth, less venturesome – I am his man. So, pass in peace, my lord. Break it and we shall come against you.'

'We pass in peace, and may the gods give you honour for your loyalty.'

So Arturo and his men passed in peace, over the clear waters of the river that curved gently around the north-eastern side of the city, a river where the trout grew fat on the jettisoned offal from the market slaughterhouses, and the citizens opened the newly built portals of the Verulamium gate. A great crowd lined the streetway that led through the city's heart to the far Aquae Sulis gate and Arturo – now at the head of the column – smiled to himself as they passed the Forum on their left where, on a rainy day now seeming far into the past, he had scrawled with a piece of charcoal, words of defiance at Ambrosius when he had first been outlawed. Over the heads of the crowd he could pick out the very pillar of the Basilica colonnade on which he had written ... *Between the empty promise of Arto and the sloth of Ambrosius where shall a warrior blood his lance?* Bold words, but seeded with truth, a truth which this last year had seen grow and flourish, and there was no hollow ring to his youthful promise now. The gods had set him on his way and he knew that he was in their hands for the rest of his years.

They came to Cam Hill on a day when an early and sharp frost had set the leaves of the riverside willows and the ash trees on the camp slopes falling. His father, Baradoc, was there to greet him, and had been there with his workmen for all the spring and summer months. Work on the plateau fortifications was running fast; a great hall, troop quarters and stables had been built of wood and roofed with reed and hazel-bough faggots and there was now a small set of private quarters for Arturo. New ground had been broken in the valleys, crops sown and harvested, and hay gathered and stacked for the horses against the winter so that they would have to make no great call on Prince Geraint and King Melwas for provisioning. Ansold had set up a smithy and forge for the repair of arms and armour and stores of charcoal had been bartered for with the cutters and burners in the woods to the west. But most pleasing to Arturo was the sight in the valley to the south of a camp where was quartered a force of near a hundred men and horses ... free men and trained cavalry men and their mounts, and two men – sons of a chief of the Durotriges – who had come, provisioned and armed, to beg leave to join the Companions. As the good name and the renown of the Companions ran wider Arturo knew that there would be many a glory-impatient son of a tribal chief pestering or bullying a father for leave to take men and mounts to come and join him.

The following night a great feast was set to celebrate their return. The chief companions filled the long table in the new hall and all the other men sat at rough tables or squatted around the fires that ringed the hall and whose blaze could be seen afar on Ynys-witrin top and the sea-dominating knoll of Brant. They roasted three heifers, two pigs and long spitfuls of trussed wild-fowl taken from the Cam river marshes. Six goatskins of new mead and apple ale matched their thirst, and flat cakes of fine-querned corn flour were spread with sweet thyme-and-marjoram tanged honey which had been brought as a gift by the two sons of the chief of the Durotriges.

Before the feast Pasco said a commons grace, calling on the names of Christos and His Father and others from the crowded pantheon of the country's true gods. He then called for the first filling of cup and beaker and horn and leather tankard with wine and mead to drink to the memory of their fallen comrades and to make plea for their high cherishing in the halls of the gods. The great shout which went up after each beaker and cup was drained at a single draught sent the harbouring starlings into wild night flight from their roosts in the trees so that their high calling sounded like a matching paean of praise. This done, all set to, eating and drinking without stint, heedless of the morning which would bring them thundering wine-pounded heads and the sharp belly cramps of gluttony which could sear a man's guts as cruelly as winter famine.

Much later when the men still held to the long hall tables and the lowering fires, laughing and singing and over-gilding the tales and exploits of their campaigning days, Arturo left them and with Baradoc at his side sat outside his own private quarters, teasing the ears of the sleeping Cabal in his lap.

Baradoc said, 'My son, you have begun what I would have done when I was your age if the gods had been kind.'

'I know, my father. But the gods have marked you for as great a work. There are other hills like this which need your art and provisioning. To campaign is one thing, but when Latis weeps and the rains come and the snow denies passage to man and mount then we must have harbour to hold us through the winter. Although the men sing of our triumph, I know that it has been but a little thing to give me understanding. We must have such places set from south to north across the country, from Lindum down to Noviomagus so that men and arms can at all times bar passage to the Middle, East and West Saxons. We must hold them to the lands they have and strike if they try to break through. When the time comes that they weaken because few come now across the seas to join them because there is no true promise of new land to settle or easy raiding for plunder and slaves ... *aie*, then we shall press against them and send them into the sea and to their long keels.'

'You talk of many years ahead.'

'Aye. Of a full life time. But it will be granted me for the gods have promised it. Next year, if Prince Geraint give you leave, we must find such a place set back from the front between Lindum and Londinium from which in winter and all seasons the Middle Saxons can be held, and then between Londinium and the Gaulish sea to hold the others. And Londinium – still little more than a desert, shunned by traders and not looked to as market place for the Tamesis settlers – must be held and garrisoned to bar all land passages between Esc and the Saxon shoremen to his north. Aye, the thing is a loose tangle in my mind still but with patience and years the yarn shall be spun and the good cloth woven...'

Listening, Baradoc felt the force of the passion that worked in his son and without harsh regret he knew that the dream he had dreamt at Arturo's age had been put into the hands of this fair-haired, lean-faced warrior of his own seeding to accomplish, and that the gods to aid him had given him the gift of foresight so that, as a golden eagle soars high to take the full span of a country in sight, Arturo saw not the year ahead, saw not five or ten years but held in view the years of a lifetime. For the first time then, piercing him so that he felt the hair-prick of awe touch the back of his head like a chilling wind, he gave surrender to the full and new truth that indeed the gods had marked him.

He rose and, touching Arturo on the shoulder, gave him goodnight and walked away, rubbing gently at the stiffness of his injured right arm. As he went laughter and shouting ceased from the long hall and through the sharpening air of the night came the voice of Durstan singing to the clear, vibrant notes of a harp.

> The knife has gone into the meat
> And the good wine fills the horn
> In Arturo's hall ...
> Here is food for your hound
> And corn for your horse
> In Arturo's hall ...
> But none there shall enter unless he be
> Swift with a sword and comrade to all ...

Long after his father had gone but while the singing and playing still made bird and beast uneasy over the hill top and slopes, Arturo rose and, holding Cabal warm under his cloak, went down to the beech dell where Daria lay.

He sat still and brooding for a long time, so still that once a disturbed hare came lolloping past him within spitting distance. The gods had taken Daria from him and the taking had place in the pattern of the life they had marked for him. On the march and in skirmishing and forays a man had no thoughts of women. But when the winter came and there was all to refurbish and peaceful nights to lie abed in warmth a warrior's manhood called for companionship and close harbouring under the warm furs and thick woven covers. Even as he thought this it was as though the mood of his companions matched his own for the sweet voice of Gelliga came clear to him.

> Take my true greeting to the girl of thick tresses
> The sweetheart I lay with in the glen of green willows ...

He sat listening as Gelliga sang on of the hot yearning that not even battle and the chance of death waiting at the opening door of each fighting day could smother. To tumble a willing girl in the high quakegrass, its falling pollen sweetening all kisses, to slake the blood's hot fever in the arms of some milk-breasted matron ... *Aie*, these the gods would permit him. He had paid the full barter price in the loss of Daria. To take another wife and worship her, though her flesh and warmth could never cloud the memory of Daria, would be no affront to the gods now nor stir their jealousy. They had marked him for their own and could justly claim they had given him the only love he needed, constant and life-abiding ... the love of his country. With the passing of years would come the great consummation of that love – freedom from tyranny for all men.

Cabal stirred within his cloak and then the hound's head was thrust free from the folds that cradled him. Cabal yawned, then whimpered and struggled free to the ground. Yawning still, Cabal piddled against a mole hill.

The next morning early Coroticus came to Arturo to take his leave and return with his men to Yyns-witrin. His men were drawn up in line on the plateau grass land and with them were two ponies laden with the share of plunder spoil that went with Coroticus for his father Arturo walked with Coroticus down the double line of men and there was pleasure in him at their appearance. Pride they had always had for few marshmen were born without it, but now they had added to it a sense of brotherhood and a spirit of discipline which he knew would mark them out from all other marshmen and fire more men to join them in the years to come. The past campaign had brought them losses, a sad price that had to be paid for the discovery of an abiding purpose in the seasons of fighting to come. Although their dress was marked, as were their bodies, with the scars and rubs of fighting, they stood proudly, the sun flashing on the copper studdings of their fish eagle emblems. Standing back from them with Coroticus at his side, he spoke to them, giving them his thanks and warming their pride with a fair eulogy of their prowess. When he had finished Coroticus called on them for the marshmens' salute and – all of them moving as one man – they drew their bows, notched their goose and heron feather flighted arrows and with a great shout sent them high into the air above their heads, the song of their flight a great keening through the morning brightness. Then the arrows turned at the top of their flight and came hissing back to earth to form a circle of trembling, feather-plumed wands about Arturo and Coroticus.

Coroticus stepped forward and pulled one of the arrows from the ground and with a quick movement snapped it in half across a raised knee. He handed the feather-tipped half to Arturo and said, 'My lord Arturo – you are the first man not a marshman to be given the royal salute of the House of Melwas. With that broken shaft in hand you are free of the Summerlands and marshes for all time and wherever you show it my people will know it and give you welcome and safe passage for all the years of your life.'

He touched his forehead in salute and then moving to the head of his men led the company of marsh warriors, the proud wearers of the fish eagle, away. Arturo stood and watched them go until the last man had disappeared down the wooded slope of Cam Hill.

The Woman of the High Rocks

For near six years Arturo campaigned, building slowly to the great plan which now lay clear in his mind, to hold the Saxons behind the line that ran from Lindum in the north down to Londinium and thence south-west to the fringes of the great forest of Anderida. Behind this line the Middle and East Saxons – denied any leaguing with Esc – and the South Saxons of Esc himself sat and stirred themselves only occasionally to make token forays. It was as though a great sleep had overcome them from which now and then they waked and, petulant at the disturbance, made a brief show of strength. But Arturo – though he was content over the years to see his forces grow and new camps organized by his father – knew that the day would come when Esc or some leader of the Middle and East Saxons would take the field to try and break him. Nothing could stop this happening because their own kind still came over the seas to them, though in smaller numbers since eastern Gaul and the great prizes lying to the south and beyond the Alps drew most of the land- and plunder-hungry warriors. The Saxon enclaves in the land were like leather water skins which were slowly filling to overflowing point.

During these years Count Ambrosius kept strict intelligence of all he did, and of the growth of his forces to which more and more men flocked. To avoid conflict with him – since Arturo was serving him without knowing it – he limited his own campaigns to the country well north of Eburacum and to the western and southern parts of Cymru where now the Scotti raids and encroachments had to be met and contained. There were times, too, when he acknowledged that the young Arturo, now near his thirtieth year, for all his passion and lust for war, carried a wise head on his shoulders and schooled himself with a patience beyond his years. Where there were small peaceful Saxon outlying settlements to the west of his line he left them untouched and forced tribute and stores from them. If unwisely they took to arms and raiding he rode down on them and there was a burning and a slaughter to signal a flaming and bloody warning to their fellows. But the passing of the years now began to build an impatience in Ambrosius. His years were limited and the past of his beginnings when he had stood against the Saxons at Noviomagus was a misted memory. Each day now the itch for the great triumph, the lust for the day when he could ride, laurel-wreathed and wearing the purple toga, to the full inheritance he claimed in this land, bit and worried him, denying him sleep and forcing upon him an impatience which ate into him with each passing day.

On an autumn evening as he walked in the rose garden of his headquarters at Glevum and his feet sank deep in the first frost-fall of leaves from the great walnut tree which some long forgotten Roman commander had brought from mid-Gaul, his Camp Prefect came to him with the news that Arturo, instead of returning to Cam Hill, was staying with a small army to winter in Lindum. Walking stiffly, aware of the rheumatic ache in his legs which had come over the years from hard lying and campaigning, and from that awareness conscious with a sudden pang of bitterness and anxiety that his years might be fewer than he thought, that the gods even might be tiring of the slow game he played and would turn against him, he decided that the time had come to make the throw which would win him the game which he had played for so long with patience . . . aye, and suffering, for he had taken the arrogance and open contempt of Arturo with a softness which hid his true feelings.

A week later, as Venutius sat in his lodgings in Durobrivae where he had come with Arturo to make an inspection of the small force of cavalry and foot soldiers who were to garrison it for the winter, a travelling horse dealer came to him to make an offer for some of the foals which had been dropped by the mares of the Companions but had been rejected by him as horse-master as unworthy of their winter keep. When the bargain was struck the man, a pleasant-faced, affable fellow, took a coin from his belt pouch and dropped it on the table before Venutius, saying, 'This is payment and more for the foals.'

On the table between them lay the nicked golden aureus of the Emperor Hadrian. Venutius looked without emotion at the coin for he had known for some time now that its coming could not long be delayed. The mind and the emotions of Count Ambrosius were nothing strange or unreadable to him He said, 'Say what you have been told to say and say it quickly.' Just for a moment the spark of hope burned in him that the man's words would not be the final ones from Ambrosius.

'It is to be done, and done quickly and with no loss of honour to your reputation or forfeiting of your standing with the Companions. The room that Arturo's going makes is to be filled by you under the Count. You have proved yourself with the Companions. There is none among them more fitting to take his place than you.'

He spoke the truth for over the years Venutius had slowly come to stand closer to Arturo – not in friendship, but in military worth and the ordering of large commands of men – than any of the Companions who claimed his warmest friendship, and stood now acknowledged as Arturo's right-hand man. He could turn them to Ambrosius and with that done Ambrosius would move Prince Geraint, King Melwas and the ever growing ranks of tribal chiefs and overlords to acknowledge him while doing honour to Arturo's memory and greatness.

He picked up the coin and said, 'Tell Count Ambrosius it will be done.'

After the man had gone he sat on and, pouring himself a beaker of wine, drank absently, his eyes looking into the future which the gods had set for him. There had never been any escape for him from the day when, in all ignorance of Arturo, his loyalty to Ambrosius had sent him on his way to Cam Hill. Nothing now remained to him but that loyalty and its rewards and the slow, enduring stain of his own self-disgust that there was not the courage in him now to fling the golden aureus from him, take his side dagger from his belt, and make an end to his already crippled life. But the power that stayed his hand from the dagger was beyond his changing for it had true place in his nature. Raising his head as he drank more wine he saw that outside the first heavy snowflakes of the onsetting winter had begun to fall.

The snow fell all that night and in the morning lay deep on the ground. Since the road from Durobrivae to Lindum was safe and picketed by winter quartered patrols of Arturo's men, Arturo and Venutius rode it alone with the hound Cabal, now grown to prime, at their heels. No Saxon band ventured westwards to raid the road in winter. A few hours after leaving Durobrivae the snow thickened and with this came a strengthening wind which swept it into growing drifts and white-pelted their tight-drawn riding cloaks. Horses, riders and the great hound moved through it with their heads lowered. After a couple of hours' slow going both men knew that they would be hard put that day to do more than reach Causennae, a small town little more than half-way to Lindum.

Drawing up to breathe their mounts Arturo looked across at Venutius and laughing said, 'Where is road, and where is sky, and where the good earth? We move through the biggest gooseplucking ever made in the halls of the gods on high. They must make some great feast tonight.'

Venutius said, 'We must keep moving. The wind blows from the north and that way lies Causennae. And where is Cabal?'

Arturo looked around and then shrugged his shoulders. 'He will find us. The snow balls up on his pads and he sits to chew and worry them free, but even in this his nose will bring him up to us in time. I would the gods had chosen another day for their feasting.' He stirred the White One to a walk and moved ahead.

Following him Venutius knew that the gods had chosen this day for more than feasting. Although they headed into the wind, they were soon lost to the road. The snow was so thick falling now that there were times when it was hard to make out the shape of Arturo and the White One ahead of him. The thought came to him that a man alone on his horse on such a day could be thrown by a stumble, crack his head against tree or rock and lie unconscious while the snow covered him and froze him to death. That Arturo's death should look natural he had always known. No suspicion must touch him or Ambrosius's treachery would be clear and then not even the meanest camp follower among the Companions would turn to him. Truly the gods were setting to his hand the time and the season for his work. No man would doubt his word that in the blizzard they had become separated.

Ahead of him Arturo pulled up to rest the White One. The snowdrifts now were almost to their mounts' knees. To their right Venutius caught a glimpse now and then of a tall craggy rock face, the wind sweeping the bare falls and slabs free of snow. He rode up behind Arturo, who was leaning forward sweeping the matted snow from the ears and long nose of the white mare. He pulled his sword from its scabbard and raising it struck hard with the flat of the blade at the back of Arturo's head. Arturo cried aloud, made to turn and then fell sideways from his mount. He lay still on the ground face downwards.

Venutius eased his horse into the shelter of the rocks and dismounted. He moved to Arturo and squatted by him and there was a coldness in his mind far greater than the icy bite of the blizzard wind. The only small crumb of grace granted to him was that Arturo's face was pressed into the snow so that he could not see it. Within an hour the freezing wind would have leached all warmth from his body and within the next hour all life would have gone from him. Any who found him would know that his horse had stumbled and when he had fallen to the ground the startled mount had kicked him ... the gods had given him the day and he had done the deed. But at this moment Arturo stirred and, from shame that even for a few moments Arturo should turn his face and see him, he raised his sword and struck with the flat of his blade again. Arturo groaned and lay still and in that moment the gods, needing sport and cruel jest before they feasted, brought savage irony into play.

Limping in the lee of the rocks came Cabal to see the sword blow. Silently the great hound came across the snow and leapt at Venutius to take him by the neck with his strong jaws. Venutius screamed and fell sideways and the scream was fast choked as Cabal clamped his great teeth through his throat, worrying and shaking as though he were holding down an over-run stag. The sword lost from his grasp in the first assault, Venutius beat with his fists at the hound and twisted and rolled to find freedom, but Cabal held him, his life blood running from the hound's ironfast jaws to carmine the snow while the two horses, frightened at the screams from Venutius, stampeded and disappeared into the blizzard.

Growling low now, his jaws set fast, his weight holding down the now weakening struggles of Venutius, Cabal stayed bound to his prey until all movement died in the man. Then he rose and went to Arturo, sniffed at his head and body, nudged him now and again with his iron grey muzzle and then, with a low whining, couched himself down alongside his master, pressing close to him. They lay together as the light went fast from the day and the snow laid a mantle over them and the red stains of Venutius's life blood.

From a cleft at the foot of the rocks a woman watched them, as she had watched from the time the White One had first whin-nied on reaching the rock face. But for the hound she would have shown herself long before, but she feared the animal. Now as she watched, Cabal, who had long scented her and knew her presence, slowly rose from Arturo's body and came towards her. She would have turned and gone back into the rock shelter but Cabal stopped a little way from her and lowering his head whimpered softly. Hardly knowing she did it the woman spoke softly to him and Cabal came forward, whimpered again and swung his tail in friendship. He raised his muzzle to her hand and, taking heart, she stroked his head and spoke to him with soft words. Cabal turned and moved back towards Arturo, stopped and looked over his shoulder and then moved on.

No fear in her now, the woman moved out into the deep snow. Under her belted greasy furs her body was strong and full, and her bare arms and legs were weather-tanned. Her long black hair flared in the strong wind as she came to Arturo. Kneeling by him she turned him over. His eyes were shut, his face grey with cold and his dull copper-coloured beard matted with snow. She knew him and had recognized him and the White One when he had first ridden into the lee of the rocks. She put her hands under his armpits and dragged him across the snow into the narrow cave which was her home. A small peat fire burnt dismally at the back of the cave, the smoke wreathing up through a fissure in the roof. Close to the fire, on a low bed of rough boards, was a thin mattress stuffed with dead bracken that spilled loosely from a slit in its side. At the foot of the bed rested an untidy bundle of hides and furs. She pulled him to the bed and then rolled him on to it with ease for she was strong and hardy. Many a man among those who visited her she had rolled, limp with drunkenness, on to the bed.

Talking to herself and to Cabal who had couched himself by the fire, she stripped Arturo to his under shirt and wondered whether he would live for, apart from the blows to his head, the freezing cold was set into his body, and when she put her ear to his mouth there was no moving touch of warmth from breathing. And this, she thought, was my lord Arturo who rode the White One and had made this part of the country safe for men to travel in peace, and whose name rang through the land like the calling of a great brazen bell. The gods had served him badly this day, but they had set her in his path . . . a worthless woman, trapped long ago by her own wildness and beauty . . . beauty of which only the coarse mockery now remained. Yet woman she was and her body was a fire which could fight off the killing clamp of the death cold which was taking him.

She went to a rock ledge and found a hard corn cake which she threw to Cabal who nosed it but refused to eat, his eyes on Arturo. She dropped the leather curtain over the rock face opening. Then, in the darkness shot only by the dull red eye of the peat fire, she stripped the furs from herself and lay down on the bed with Arturo. She pulled the furs and hides over them and took him into her arms, shivering herself at the first touch of his ice cold flesh and then conquering it with the fierce animal heat of her own naked body and limbs.

She lay awake all that night while the snow fell and the wind screamed and howled and there were times when she knew that she lay with a corpse, cold and stiff, and she mourned the passing of one who above all others would be most mourned in this country. But as dawn put grey fingers through the rented and torn hide curtain and she held him tight, feeling his coldness now begin to overcome the warmth of her own body and legs, her chill cheek was touched by the feathered brushing of his faint breath as he returned slowly from the limbo to which the gods out of their unfathomable reasoning had sent him.

And while that night passed the White One, separated from Venutius's mount, ploughed the drift and found shelter in the open-fronted shed of a reed-cutter But wolves found the other horse and killed it, and towards dawn they came to the high rocks and, while Cabal growled and stood guard at the opening curtain, they found easy prey in the body of Venutius, dragging it away, fighting and quarrelling over it as the blizzard matted their pelts, so that what had been the shape and shame of a man was no more than a butchered, bleeding hideousness, and the golden coin of the Emperor Hadrian, falling from his fang-ripped belt pouch, sank into the trodden snow to find lodging when the thaws came in the moss and reeds of a swamp.

The snow lasted three days. On the fourth the skies cleared and, as though the gods still feasting needed yet another jest to tease men with, a warm thaw set in which filled the air with the running of snow water and swelled the streams and meres with flood while the sun shone with the heat of summer and the birds found song again.

Those days were a dream through which Arturo lived and of which he was never to have clear memory. He knew the warmth of the woman that brought him back to life and sustained his growing strength. Warm broth and porridge made from the black peas of vetch were fed to him and then the mists of delirium passed and clearness came slowly to his mind as strength grew in his body.

He sat now on the edge of the wide bed, wearing his shirt and long leather cavalry trews, and chewed on a corn cake spread with honey while the woman squatted by the fire broiling dried fish in herb-spiced mead. The beauty which had once been hers was clear to him, and he knew that it was her body and warmth which had brought him back to life – but he knew little else.

He said, 'What do people call you?'

She smiled. 'Genara – and much else besides at times, my lord Arturo. My husband is long dead, but I would lie if I said I lack men to comfort me.'

'For saving my life you shall have reward which will take you from this place.'

'No, my lord. I need nothing but your thanks and the truth of knowing that the gods put me here for a purpose. I rest happy here and seldom lack company. You have no need to do me great favours.'

Putting a hand to the rags which wrapped his wounded head Arturo said, 'Then let me call on you for a favour.'

'If it is in my power, my lord.'

'These things you tell me you saw. The way of my wounding and the death by Cabal of my friend Venutius – you would do me favour if you keep silent about them always.'

'That I will, my lord. But what do I say, and you, my lord, about your wounding and being here?'

Arturo smiled. 'That I fell from my horse in the storm and wounded my head and you found me close by. As for Venutius – you never saw him or his death by Cabal. I shall say that we were separated by the blizzard, and the wolves found him.'

'Which they did, my lord – on my threshold.' She stood up and came and took his eating bowl and smiled down at him with a sudden boldness. 'You will go this day, my lord? Causennae is close by.'

'Aye, I go this day.'

'Is one day more lost of great account even to my lord Arturo?'

Arturo laughed and standing began to pull on his long over-shirt. 'No. The days are ours to squander, but I would not cap these last days in which you have served me better than you can ever know with a final one which would not be god-touched. But remember this –' he picked up his riding cloak from the bed '– if you should ever want ought that I can fairly give you in the future you shall come and ask and it will be given.'

Genara, her dark eyes bright with teasing, came to him and drawing the cloak close across his shoulders fastened the holding brooch. 'Maybe my lord in these last days you have already given me the gift I ask and I would but know it again before you leave.'

Arturo took her hand and kissed it. 'It could be, but if it were so then it was of the gods' doing not mine.'

'The gods were kind to you in sending you here. Maybe they were also kind to me. But let it rest so. I will walk with you to the Causennae road. You are still a sick man and should have company at hand.'

And Arturo was still a sick man. A few hours after reaching Lindum and being installed in the bishop's palace he was taken by fever and passed into a delirium which lasted for seven days. When he woke, his head clear but his body still weak, on the morning of the eighth day it was to find Lancelo standing at the room window and to hear the steady fall of rain from outside.

Hearing him stir, Lancelo turned and came to him. He grinned and said, 'Welcome back, my lord. And to give you more heart I tell you that the White One was found four days ago and is now in the bishop's stables.'

'I give thanks for that.' He sat up, shaking his head to stop Lancelo's offered help. 'I've been too long a-dreaming. But in my dreams the gods have spoken to me and now there is work to be done.'

Lancelo shook his head. 'The season is too far gone for campaigning.'

'There are some campaigns served better by pen and parchment than men and horses. Get me the stuff for writing and I would have Durstan and a troop ready to ride at noon for Glevum.'

Knowing all Arturo's moods Lancelo recognized this one as not to be crossed.

When the writing materials were brought Arturo sat up in bed and wrote with the fine goose quill in the Roman language which had been beaten into him by his tutor at Isca, the drunken Druid priest Leric. When he had finished Lancelo brought him braid and wax for its sealing and then wrapped it in a sealskin pouch for protection against the weather.

'Durstan will ride with the white flag of peaceful passage, but fully armed, to Glevum and will himself see the message into the hands of Count Ambrosius and await his reply. If mishap falls on the road and there is danger of the loss of the writing he is to destroy it without looking at it. And now have sent in to me a jug of wine and bread and goat's cheese. I have been absent from this world too long and return with sharp set appetite.'

A little later there came into the room a young woman in her early twenties, fair-haired and tall, wearing a red gown caught about the waist with a silver linked belt, each link fashioned in the shape of some running animal ... hare, wolf, horse and charging boar. She set a large wooden platter of wine and cheese on the table at Arturo's side.

Stepping back, she said, 'If you need ought else, my lord, you have but to call. I am within earshot.' She smiled. 'It is good to see your old force returning to you at last. The priests and nuns of the bishop have prayed for you without let – and to their prayers have been added mine.'

'Then I thank you and them, mistress –' He paused, and then added, 'What do they call you?' He reached for the wine jug, but his hand was stilled as the young woman gave a laugh.

'My lord Arturo, you ask my name? Am I so changed in six years or so?'

For the first time Arturo looked at her with attention. Then, shaking his head, he said pleasantly, 'You ride a few lengths ahead of me.'

'Then I am set down. Why even in your fever sleep you called my name, though there again your memory faulted you a little, but I do not grumble for in these last years there have been many things to crowd your mind. I am Gwennifer, though your swollen tongue could do no better than Genara. Yes, my lord Arturo, I am that pony-riding Gwennifer who brought you Cabal –' she nodded to the window where the hound lay full stretch '– and I am that Gwennifer-Genara who combed and trimmed your rust-red beard while you slept and fed you broth. And when you complained of the cold in your fever and called me I brought you more wraps to heat your body.'

Arturo laughed suddenly and shook his head. 'Of course . . . Ah, mistress Gwennifer you have my apologies and my thanks. The good nuns trained you well in the care of the sick.'

'They trained me in nothing, my lord, for I did not stay long with them.'

'Then what do you do here now?' As he spoke he was thinking that she had grown in beauty but nothing of her spirit had changed. Behind the self-possessed young woman was still the tom-boy, restless and wayward, waiting chance to show.

'My mother is dead these two years and my father stays little at Eburacum for he winters and fights in the north against the Picts to hold the land he owns there. So I am here to run my uncle's household. And rare tedious work it has been until you came. When you leave you should make me master of your household and I will doff these –' her hands plucked at the folds of her gown '– for trews and tunic and serve you well.'

Smiling Arturo shook his head. 'I can find no such service for you. Our ways are rough and the sermon the bishop would preach me for harbouring you rougher.'

'Maybe . . . then marry me and all will be proper –'

Arturo laughed, cutting her short, and the wine in his cup spilled to the bed coverings. 'You talk wild and wilfully and frank – the nuns were well saved from you.'

'Nay – you put me off. Maybe you called not me but some other named Genara in truth, one who claims your love.'

Arturo eyed her in silence for a moment and then said firmly, 'There is no living woman that I love and call for.' Then shaking his head, a smile touching his lips, he went on, 'Where do you find this bold way you think and speak?'

'My lord, that is easily answered. What I feel I show. What I think I speak. So the gods made me, and I have no quarrel with them.' Before he could move she bent over and kissed his forehead lightly and then, laughing, moved from the room.

The room was warm with an even steady heat for the old hypocaust system had been repaired and was fired now with seacoal that came upriver from the mouth of the Sabrina. The wall sconces gave a steady light and on the table in a bronze holder burned a fat tallow candle which threw its full glow on the parchment which held Arturo's letter to Count Ambrosius.

Munching a russet apple which he took every evening with his wine before retiring, Ambrosius, flattening the stubborn creases of the parchment, began to go again through the message from the Dumnonian warrior. In places it was tedious and his eyes skipped the passages of no real intent. The young Arturo wrote as he lived and fought ... often with an undue waste of effort. But the truth of the overall matter lacked nothing in good sense...

... and this Venutius, being your man, served you well and, but for the protection of the gods, would have faithfully worked your purpose. Dead he is now, and no stain against his name for none but I, and now you, know the dark truth ...

Ambrosius sipped his wine. Aye, lost in a blizzard and torn to death by wolves and now, he touched his greying hair and smiled wryly, the young Arturo standing on the advantage of his growing popularity and increase in forces could make the truth known to spread through the country to raise a cry like the howling of wolves against his name and bring an even shorter fall in the raising of levies and a jibing at and cursing of his name. Maybe the old gods truly worked for him. He knew now, too, how to seize his advantage with the smooth shuttle of changing policy.

I will come to you as long ago I said I would when you sue me for return. This done I will serve you faithfully as *dux bellorum* and acknowledge you as *Comes Brittanicus* for I have no wish for king or overlordship of this country – only to fight and win its true liberty under the gods and then return to my people ...

Ambrosius smiled and picked an apple pip from his teeth. Aye, likely so. But the truth in a man of thirty was only one season. In twenty years success would bring on a different fruiting. Still, by then his own seasons would have wintered in to death's unending keep. He smoothed the parchment and re-read the fine hand. The man was no barbarian. He wrote with the smoothness and polish that few now brought to the Roman tongue; and, writing, asked now for that which was to feed the young pride in him.

This is how I would ride to join you at Glevum and this is the manner of your greeting and none shall know that it is other than the true courtesy of a father welcoming a son, none other than the measure due to a well-serving War Duke come to be honoured by his noble Commander ..

Though in truth it was much other ... Aye, but why not so? Few in this country would fail to follow Arturo, where many now grew tired of him and withheld their men and loyalty. Leagued with Arturo he would still hold supreme power. Many Caesars when young had fought in the field and many, when age and success came, had been content to leave the war grounds and work for the peace and prosperity that followed victories. Of one thing he had no doubt. For this country both he and Arturo wished and lived for the same thing, that it should rise to freedom and greatness again. And truth it was that his ageing bones and body found no joy in hard lying and the eating of hard tack, and the supping of cold ale or spring water on the black and windy nights of mountains and bare heathland.

With sudden pleasure and a curt dismissal of all irony he freely gave ground to the run of time and chance. The promise of Arto should be made good. He pulled his purple cloak to proper set over his long sleeved white toga and beat twice on the gong which stood on the table. His Praefectus Castrorum came in, the man Olipon who had once visited Arturo on Cam Hill. He said, 'Send to me Arturo's man.'

When Durstan entered and was alone with him, he said, 'You are the man Durstan?'

Durstan nodded. 'Aye, my lord.'

'Who was outlawed by me with Arturo?'

'That is so, my lord.'

'You are no longer so.'

'I am so, my lord, so long as the writ runs against my lord Arturo.'

For a moment Ambrosius would have been angry. Then he laughed and said easily, 'Aye, you are a stubborn lot, you Arto men. But you have no need to be now. The writ against Arturo no longer runs. There is peace between us.'

'Then I thank you, my lord.'

'Return to your lord Arturo and say from me that all shall be as he wishes and that he shall find true and warm greeting from me.'

When Durstan had gone Ambrosius took the parchment – which could have been washed and scraped clean for further use – and reluctantly burned it in the flame of the big candle, the smell of its burning acrid in his nostrils.

So it was that in the year of Christ four hundred and eighty on a morning when the hawthorn bushes showed scarce green with yet to open buds, and the past year's leaves of the beech were burnished copper and gold on their branches defying the new growth, and the first swallows and martins were yet to come, Arturo made good his promise to his dead wife Daria to ride in triumph with her to Glevum. He came riding the White One, his war cap red and white plumed and wearing – in honour of his wife who had been a true believer – the rich scarlet surcoat with the blue robed figure of the Virgin Mary given to him by the Bishop of Noviomagus, his sword sheathed, his lance raised high and his small red and white battle buckler slung on his back. Behind him in mounted troops came five hundred Companions, red and white plumes and scarves flaring in the robust breeze, and five hundred marshmen with Coroticus at their head, their spears over their shoulders, the fish eagle device on their breasts, their bows slung on their backs and their quivers showing blood-red dyed goose feathers as flights for their arrows. There was no man among them not tried and proved by battle. Behind them on the rising slopes to the south the rest of the army, save for those who still kept winter stations along the far east line, lay in camp and cursed the draw by lot which kept them from place in the proud company on this day that the great War Duke Arturo made good his Arto promise.

But none, except those closest and dearest to Arturo of his first small band of Companions, knew the meaning of the great white mare that, riderless, her hide gleaming like polished ivory, kept place alongside and made pair with the White One. Across the mare's back was laid a cloak of scarlet with a sky blue lining caught about the waist with a golden belt with a clasp of two singing birds and from it hung a soft leather pouch which held three locks of Daria's dark hair which Arturo had taken from her before her burial.

As Arturo rode at the head of the column to the East gate, where Count Ambrosius with a guard of honour waited to greet him, in his memory coursed clearly the words he had long ago spoken to Daria in Corinium while yet his bold promise was a thing of wind and angry boast. *It is written that on the day of my triumph you shall come riding into Glevum with me on a white mare, wearing a cloak of scarlet with a lining of blue silk and about your waist a golden belt with a clasp of two singing birds. And when Count Ambrosius comes out to meet us he shall hand to you a silver goblet full of new wine* ... And then, curbing the smile that touched his lips, came memory of her reply. *And then and then will be the day when the pigs shall be flying and the salmon coming up the Sabrina shall wriggle ashore, their mouths full of sea pearls to lay at my feet ...*

Before him now, a spear's throw away, stood Ambrosius not knowing or caring to know the reason for the coming ritual, knowing only that it was small price to pay for this alliance and that the wagging of tongues in the years to come would give it meaning or myth for this stalwart warrior knew the power of riddle and mystery from the god-touched side of his nature.

Ambrosius waited, helmeted and cloaked, his ancient well-burnished cuirass shining in the sun, purple-cloaked and leather-belted and highly honed heavy legionary marching boots on his feet, studded and unchanged in design from the boots worn by the fighting men of the Twentieth and then the Second Augusta Legions who had first built and held Glevum, *the colonia Nerviana Glevensium*, under the governorship of Julius Frontinius when the Son of the Virgin that Arturo wore on his surcoat had been dead little more than seventy years. And now, mused Ambrosius, here comes one who served willingly any and all gods and was mad – or shrewd? – enough to make his own rituals though there was no denying the sense in him which understood and used the power of mystery to carry his name through the land and bring men to him and enslave the affections and loyalties of those who looked and longed for greatness to return to this country.

As Arturo drew up a few paces from him and the long column halted behind him, Ambrosius went forward with his bodyguard while at his side came, too, his Camp Prefect carrying a great withy-plaited tray on which rested a fresh-run Sabrina cock salmon, its partly open jaws stuffed and overflowing with sea pearls. Beside it couched on its belly, its hide smooth scrubbed, lay a young dead pig with a pair of dove's wings fixed wide-spread to its back and a goblet of wine held between its fore trotters.

The two men gave greetings to one another and then Arturo leaned forward and took the goblet from the tray, half turned and poured in libation some of the wine over the scarlet cloak on the mare at his side and then spilled the rest to the ground.

Arturo raised his right arm high and from the long column of warriors behind him came a great shouting and chanting – 'Ambrosius ... Ambrosius ... Great Count of Britain!'

Erect, shoulders tight-drawn in pride, Ambrosius smiled and drawing his short, broad-bladed, double-edged legionary sword from its wood and bronze scabbard raised it high to return the salute. As he did so he knew that the gods had served him well in sending Venutius's treachery and his own awry, and knew too that in Arturo he had found the first warrior ever in this land who read his mind and guessed his dreams and had the spirit to bury other men's evils if in that way lay true service to his country. Whatever the future held their names would live and for once – touched by a rare humility – he knew that he cared not which name would prove the greater.

Elegy for a Warrior

Arturo and his men stayed ten days at Glevum, and in that time he became convinced that not only had the gods intended this alliance, but that it was meant to show him how much still he had to learn and to understand about the art of warfare which lay behind the straightforward marshalling of men into fighting positions when the enemy, in large or small bands, was sighted. His respect for Count Ambrosius increased when he realized that not only did the man share his dreams for the future of the country but he faced the task with an industry that covered every least aspect of the enemy. He gathered news of the Saxons from a discreetly organized network of pedlars, traders, disaffected Saxon warriors, and from their own countrymen who lived as slaves or worked, barely tolerated, in the Saxon lands.

Sitting in Ambrosius's room until late in the night the Count brought out for him maps and reports which for the first time gave him a picture of his own country to which he had almost been blind before. Seeing and understanding this Ambrosius smiled and said, 'Before the first sword is drawn or spear thrown if an army leader has done his work well then the battle should be half won. Would you waste time besieging a Saxon hilltop knowing that they hold stores and water for a month? No. Pass them by and then they must follow you and somewhere come to equal terms. You know why Esc lets you parade along his borders and only a few glory-hungry bands of his young men come out to find honour or a welcome in Valhalla by swarming like hornets around you? I tell you – because he sits content knowing you have not the force to come to him. So, he farms and harvests his lands and waits to make the move on the playing board which will surprise and defeat you.'

'What move?'

'Of that later, my Arturo. But remember this, Esc iş the true son of his father, and like his father he makes others work for him – as did now dead Vortigern.' He smiled and sipped his wine. 'Now – for he will have had the news – that we are drawn together he will know that time is short for him and the move he would make must soon be played.'

A little roused, Arturo asked firmly, 'Why should I not know of this move now? Tell me so that I can prepare to meet it.'

'And find that nought waits for you to meet? Esc has his men here as I have mine with him. If I seem unduly secretive unfitting our new friendship it is because I wait for more news to be sure of Esc's mind. For now take one half of the men you have with you and go to Cam Hill. Send the others east to Lindum. Draw such extra men as you can from Prince Geraint and – if things move as they should – my Camp Prefect, Olipon, whom you know, will be with you within a few weeks to tell you my mind.' He paused for a moment, watching Arturo's face, and then went on gently, 'So soon after my treachery and our new accord you take this caution well. But – though it give some shame – who is to know that there is not among your men . . . aye, and mine . . . some new Venutius. All great commanders dwell on a peak of loneliness. Until the day comes to march trust no one for there is no man living who has not his price.'

Arturo's mouth tightened as he held down the momentary anger at this cynicism and the shame it held for him to withhold trust in any of his near Companions. But remembering Venutius, he saw the wisdom of it. Nevertheless he said, 'Under the gods then there is no true trusting between man and man?'

'Nor between man and woman – when the man has been marked by the gods for his work. You are now in truth and all honour Dux Bellorum of this country. You will find the wind blows chill on your high peak. When I was your age I had all to learn and none of true wisdom to help me.' He smiled, scratching the tip of his beaked nose. 'Now you have me, and with our coming together a force far larger than I ever had. And more will come. In time we shall be victorious and this country will stay as it is now, the last part of the great Roman Empire never to be overrun by the barbarians.'

'And then you will call yourself what? King? Emperor?'

Ambrosius shrugged his shoulders. 'What matters the name? King or Emperor? It is the power that counts. Since my remaining years are few I may not live to make the choice. That will fall into your hands.'

'I seek no such titles. The work done I would go back to my lands and live in peace.'

Ambrosius shook his head. 'So you think now. The thought does you honour, but you will find that the years you have to spend on that cold high peak will change you. To warm your loneliness you will have need to wrap yourself in the cloak of majesty. There will be no escape for all men will demand it of you. The gods are on your side. Your legend begins and you are already sacrificed to them.'

Arturo rode back to Cam Hill with his men and for a month he sat waiting for word from Count Ambrosius. In that time he drew fresh men from Prince Geraint and put them into training and schooling to the ways of the Companions.

Towards the end of that month Prince Geraint rode into the camp with a bodyguard. Talking to Arturo as they ate together in Arturo's small dwelling, he said, 'I stay with you, my lord Arturo, to march with you and my men.'

Wiping grease off his lower lip from the chewing on a roast wild duck leg, Arturo was silent for a while, studying the man. He was now in his late twenties. He grew each year more like his father, dark-haired, dark-browed, a smouldering warmth in his eyes and a restlessness in his body as though he held down deep impatience.

Quietly Arturo asked, 'Why so, my Prince?'

'For two reasons. One – you wait the coming of the Prefect Olipon. The second – I am young and have sat at Isca too long without true taste of battle.'

'I wait for Olipon, it is true – but how could you know this?'

'Because by direction of Count Ambrosius I come in his place.

Olipon we shall join in good time where he waits for us. For now I speak for him.'

Straight-faced, thoughtful, Arturo said, 'It was to me that Olipon would come, and for me to wait for him by command of Count Ambrosius. I trust and honour you, but –'

Prince Geraint laughed. 'You raise your hackles? There is no need.' He put his hand in his belt pouch and laid a gold ring on the table between them. Arturo knew the ring for Olipon had once brought it to him from Ambrosius and he had in defiance handed it back to him. 'This is from the Count to show that I truly speak for him. Matters have moved fast and Olipon was needed elsewhere. Now will you hear me?'

Arturo nodded, his face easing into a smile, but even so he felt the bite of the truth which Ambrosius had so recently spoken to him. The high peak was lonely. Never would he have believed that he would have spoken so to his own Prince. And in far Glevum Ambrosius had read his mind and sent the ring to ease his caution. Reaching over he refilled the Prince's cup with ale and said, 'You could have given me the rough of your tongue first and the ring after. The ways of the field and fighting I know. Now I begin to learn new arts and observances.'

'It is forgotten. Now listen to the words of Ambrosius.'

For more years than most men could remember, around Noviomagus and to the lands south and close up to Venta and along the shores of the Vectis sea and on the island of Vectis itself, explained Geraint, there had long been settled sporadically small Saxon settlements that gave little trouble and an uneasy truce ran through all these parts. More trouble came from the pirate raiders from the Gaulish seas once the seasons turned fair. At this time there was as leader of this straggling, ever-changing territory a leader called Cerdic, still a young man, whose birth lines were unknown but variously described. His name was clearly British, and British he might have truly been, or as truly – as many claimed – either the son of a Saxon born in or out of marriage with a British woman, or – and his name was strong argument for this – the son of a Briton got with a Saxon woman. Whatever his birth his ambitions had grown with the coming of manhood and his loyalties and ties were all with the Saxons. This man, so Ambrosius's intelligence ran, had been chosen by Esc to lead the first of his moves against Arturo and Count Ambrosius. As soon as the spring brought the right weather Cerdic – who was already secretly marshalling the local Saxon settlers into a fighting force – would be joined by the arrival of a seaborne band of Saxon warriors, five or six hundred strong, all adventurers eager for plunder and land who would sail into the Vectis sea and make a landing somewhere between Noviomagus and Clausentium, on the long broken coastline full of deep inlets and creeks. All this Prince Geraint explained, and finished:

'These sea Saxons will come on the first good wind and tide as the season betters. That cannot be more than a few weeks distant. If Cerdic is successful then Noviomagus and all the lands right up to Venta and the western limits of the Anderida forest will be his. Then will come a linking up with the South Saxons who under Aelle now hold Anderida itself. With the creation of this new territory of West Saxons the whole right flank of this country is open and the way clear right up through Calleva to Corinium. Would you be happy to fight or even hold the line you have now, knowing that Esc would move out against you while Cerdic can march north and take your rear?'

Arturo who had been toying with the bare-picked duck leg frowned and tossed it to Cabal at his feet ... The hound rose and went out into the night with it and the sound came clear of his teeth crushing the fragile bone. So this, he thought, was one more lesson among the many to be learned, the lesson of the value of foreknowledge which gave a commander long sight to prepare his moves. So far, although he had done much and made the country ring with and rise to his name, he had, compared to Ambrosius and his secret gathering of news, been no more than like some lucky, impetuous, feckless raiding son of a tribal chief adventuring the good seasons away to cure the itches of an idle winter.

He said, 'Only a fool would wait for the dagger thrust in his side as he crosses swords with the enemy. Where is Olipon now?'

'He sits with a small party well north of Venta, a handful of men that will cause no tongues to wag and word to run to Cerdic. We go to join him at the full of the moon and march by day through Sorviodunum and take the Calleva road as though making for Londinium, there to move north to Lindum or south to the borders of the Cantiaci lands which Esc holds.'

'Which all men would expect of me.' Arturo said it wryly, though not without a sense of amusement for he was truly being taught a new lesson in the craft of warfare and with it a light touch of the switch from Count Ambrosius to his high mettle by making all this plain to him through another and so – to which he had good and acknowledged right – reminding him that he served a master. He scratched gently at his beard and went on, 'And when we meet with Olipon? Am I still to be under instruction?'

Prince Geraint laughed. 'No. You will hear what Olipon says, take the news of his gleaning about Cerdic and make your own decisions. I come with you from here on my own will. I have two sons now, the elder, Cato, now in his sixth year so the Dumnonian line is secure should aught happen to me. If the gods take me then your father becomes his ward until he is of age and if anything happens to your father before then you will take his place. But I pray the gods spare me for I have that still to do in Dumnonia which one day you shall see and for which you shall give me thanks.'

'You talk a riddle, my Prince.'

'Aye, a riddle of time and blood.' He rose to take his leave and as they walked out into the night for him to go to his own quarters, he put a hand on Arturo's shoulder and said, 'Prince I am but from now on I march with you and take your commands without question as you would those of Count Ambrosius.'

As he walked away in the moonlight Arturo watched him, moving with the ground mist knee high about him, and he knew then that the fashion of all his future days was to be changed. He had come from boasting outlaw to make his Arto promise good, riding in the favour of the gods, and now if he would keep their favour and his ambition for this land bright he had new and hard lessons to learn ... *aie*, and would learn them fast and use them with the years better than any other before him.

He looked up at the moon and an owl called from the trees. The moon was just moving out of its first quarter, the month of Mars and Badb, the gods of war, was with them. In eight days it would be at the full. Calleva was three days unhurried march, and unhurried they would march as though going back to their old lines to relieve the winter stations – for now, although he might never know them, there were eyes that watched him and tongues that would send words running to the ears of Esc and this Cerdic if the pattern of these last years should show change. Unhurried for sleep he made the rounds of the new turf and timber-revetted parapets his father had begun and which were still yet fully to make and, since it was the marshmen's night of duty, met Coroticus coming from his round.

He greeted him and then went on, 'Good Coroticus, you people of the Summerlands know the true coming of the weather – is that so?'

'Some of us, my lord.'

'You?'

'Aye, my lord. All the royal house –' he grinned, '– for they need it most.'

'How will this month of the war gods be?'

Coroticus bit his lower lip gently for a moment and then looked up at the sky and the moon and said, 'Tomorrow a change comes and we shall have wind and rain until the full of the moon. As the moon dies so will the bad weather. The last days of the month will find the wind in the south and the land early ready for sowing.'

'This you will promise?'

Coroticus laughed softly. 'Aye, but it will be a marshman's promise – not one on which he would stake his life. But that it will rain until the full moon is true for neither water ousel nor wild duck have moved to nestmaking, knowing there is flooding to come yet to the rivers.'

The weather until the full moon was as Coroticus had predicted. The rivers ran bank high and the meres and lakes rose until only the tips of the rushes and reeds showed above water. The short turf of the downlands was sodden so that the passage of men and horses turned it into quagmires and even the amadou tinder a man carried safe wrapped in his pouch for firemaking became useless as it breathed and caught the dampness from the air.

Three days after the full of the moon, the rains now ceased, Arturo moved out with his company to meet Olipon. He had with him two hundred mounted Companions, nearly the same number of Coroticus's marshmen and eighty mounted Dumnonian men under Prince Geraint who had yet to prove themselves as Companions. They met Olipon ten miles north of Venta on the Calleva road close to the headwaters of the river which ran south through Venta to find the sea at Clausentium. Olipon had with him a company of sixty odd men, all tried footsoldiers, which was split – for Ambrosius still clung to the old Roman divisions – into self-contained parties of eight men who shared a tent or made their own from brushwood and ash poles, managed their own cooking and provisions and had a horse to pack their gear. They carried heavy spear and either a short broad-bladed gladius sword or the longer spatha and wore mostly heavy leather helmets, surcoats and short trews. A few boasted ancient pieces of chain and scale mail and counted themselves fortunate for their were few armourers left in the land.

That first evening in camp Olipon gave Arturo his report. Cerdic had mustered nearly three hundred footsoldiers from the local settlements and these were lodged halfway between Noviomagus and Clausentium, split into small parties and hidden away in the marshes and along the creek sides, waiting the arrival of the long boats. As he spoke he drew with a stick in the heath sand the dispositions of Cerdic's men. On the high ground north of the Noviomagus–Clausentium road he had placed lookouts to light a smoke fire at the sighting of the long boats and another party on the downland to the east of Venta to make smoke fire when the first signals were seen. When he had given all this information, he looked with a tight-lipped smile at Arturo and added, 'We join forces now, my lord Arturo, and I think that the gods have made it so with clear intent. It was to the east of Clausentium that I fought with Count Ambrosius long years ago when he first began his war. His body grows old but his mind is still blade sharp. The gods have given him you and have chosen this place for your trial.'

'There shall be no failing. How many warriors will there be to a long boat?'

'Since they come as warriors and not as settlers with wives and family there could be fifty to sixty a long keel. With at the most six boats – say, three hundred and sixty men. With Cerdic's army you have rising seven hundred men against you and you have well less than six hundred.'

'It is enough.'

Olipon said nothing, but he knew that the words were not made in boast.

That night Arturo lay long awake. The whole stretch of country from Venta to the sea lay open in his mind, and beyond that picture he could see the long boats coming in on the growing tide so that they could reach and beach their craft at the head of the creeks. The gods were testing him where they had first tested Ambrosius. To meet the keels as they grounded would be a child's folly for Cerdic would long have known his coming and there might be no landing. Even if there were, then he would be fighting with only half his force for the creeklands and marshes were no place for his mounted men. This – no matter what the future held – was his first real testing by the gods. If he were to fail them then they would turn to place their favours elsewhere. Anger flared in him at the thought. Then with its passing he knew that now he faced in truth the real understanding of many of Ambrosius's words to him. The winning of battles must be shaped long before the first spear was flung or the first troop of horse thundered into action.

The next morning he called Olipon to him and said, 'Send word to your smoke fire parties. They are to keep place after the landing and send fresh signals when Cerdic's men and the sea warriors have crossed the Clausentium–Noviomagus road and are well set on their march to Venta.'

Olipon nodded and there was now no tight-lipped smile on his weathered face, but a frank grin as he said, 'You learn fast, my lord, to pick your own ground.' He looked up at the sky which was pocked with the drift of a few light clouds, moving before a southerly wind.

Two days later the first smoke signal billowed and plumed into the air south-east of Venta. The next morning the smoke came again, rising high and flaring away like the streaming of a horse's tail in the wind.

That evening Arturo marched southwards. By the time they were below Venta the sun had long set and they had the light of the dying moon. Coroticus's marshmen went ahead in a wide crescent-shaped screen. None could move faster or with more ease and quiet than a marshman at night. Behind came the troops of cavalry while Olipon's footmen were split to march on their flanks.

Before dawn while the first bird had yet to sing the coming daylight and the last of the beetle and root-grubbing badgers had returned to their holts, they saw below them the dying night fires of the Cerdic forces and, with the first pale wash of light in the eastern sky, could pick out the stir of the Saxons as they rose and began to prepare themselves for the coming day.

That day was one of triumph and bitter sorrow for Arturo. Without the cry of battle horn or wild shouting Arturo led the cavalry of the Companions. They came down with the gathering dawn like a horde of wolves and were on the camp before most of the Saxons could buckle on their sword belts or reach for their scramaseax. Those that were armed stood and fought and made time for their fellows to seek their weapons.

The Companions streamed through them, killing and maiming

and, once through them, turned and splitting into two rode back around the flanks of the camp to re-form on the higher ground as the marshmen ran forward and from a safe distance poured a swarming flight of arrows into the camp. When their quivers were empty the battle horn of Prince Geraint blew and the marshmen drew aside as his company of Dumnonians rode down and carried sword and lance to the Saxons. But by now the Saxons were past their first surprise. They formed a ring about the camp and faced their foe, shouting and crying, their swords finding many a trooper's groin, their seax knives quick to cut the throat of any who fell. The bright morning air was full of the screaming of maimed horses and the last calls and shouts of dying men.

As Prince Geraint's troopers spent themselves and turned away to reform, Arturo led his Companions to the attack again, closely followed by Olipon and his foot men and Coroticus's spear-carrying marshmen.

On this attack, their lances tossed aside for they were of little use now, Arturo's men took the fight to the Saxons with their swords and with their small round bucklers held low to protect their groins. Riding hard, knowing that the surprised Saxons must soon break and run, the air full of the bitter tang of sweating men and horses and sharp with the bite of dust and blood, Arturo saw beyond the camp the first of the enemy to run and knew they would be Cerdic's men, the tolerated settlers who had no real heart for battle.

Again the Companions broke the Saxon ring and rode it through while the footsoldiers came hard behind them. As he fought and hewed with his sword, Arturo knew again what he already knew that, once the fight was joined, a man could see nothing but confusion and know nothing but the shock of iron and flesh, but knew *now* that which had been beyond him before, that each man and trooper in this battle held to his place and to his duty under his commander knowing that the design of battle scratched out in the bare dust and loose sand the day before must be followed and, because they took pride in their training and their god-filled duty, would follow it to death. And many there were who found death, and many more among them who lay open to it and were saved by their comrades. Among these Arturo took company for as he cut and slashed his way free from the heart of the camp a wounded Saxon, lying on the ground, half raised himself and thrust with his heavy spear at the breast of the White One. The mare screamed and reared high, throwing Arturo to the ground where one of the White One's flailing hooves struck him on the side of the head and sent him into oblivion. Lancelo and Durstan jumped from their mounts and stood over him. They were joined by four others of the Companions, tight pressed, fighting off the crowding Saxons, and stood fighting them off until Prince Geraint and his countrymen came again at the charge and broke a great passage through the ring into which Olipon and Coroticus led their men.

They fought while the prey birds began to gather above, spiralling on the soft southerly wind. They fought while Prince Geraint and his men re-formed and charged again, and they fought on when they saw the Prince go down as a great axe broke the left foreleg of his mount. He fell to take a spear thrust through his throat and then, as his dying cry burst from him, the Saxons broke and ran. Those who were Cerdic's men ran, throwing arms and war gear from them, to seek the safety of their marsh huts and wood boothies, and those who were sea warriors ran for their long keels and prayed to Woden that the news of their defeat would not outstrip them and give courage to the country's natives to come out and burn their craft.

Seeing them go, Olipon, who now stood in command, gave orders for the marshmen to gather their arrows and harry the enemy to the coast. The rest of the army re-formed and stayed where they were to make camp, to collect their dead and mourn and bury them, and to shelter their wounded and care for them. As darkness came the cooking pots simmered over the wood fires, the guards were mounted and the horses hobbled and fed and watered, and those that lived blessed their God or gods but, having little stomach for food, took the pack train ale and drank to those who would drink no more on the sweet turf or in the shady thickets of their green land. And Borio who, beneath a warrior's sweat and blood soiled shirt, carried the heart of a bard gave rein to the spirit in him and sang of the day and its triumphs and its sorrows.

His voice was the first which Arturo heard as he came out of the blackness of coma where he lay under a canopy of laced willow boughs with Olipon sitting outside watching the dance of men's shadows around the camp fires. Arturo, his head throbbing, lay still, and Borio's voice coming to him told him of the day's victory and its grim losses.

> At the battle of the men of the Long Boats, I saw
> Arto's men who flinched not from spears
> Under the thighs of the Companions, swift chargers
> Long their legs, wheat their fodder, swooping like eagles
> Men in terror, bloody their heads
> At the battle of the men of the Long Boats, I saw
> Great Geraint, Lord of the land of the West
> Before Geraint, the enemy's scourge
> Loud the clash of swords, bitter the war cries
> Lovely to behold, the glory of the West
> When Geraint was born, the gods touched him
> At the battle of the men of the Long Boats, I saw
> Geraint slain and Heaven's gate open
> The gods give him welcome, the Bright One
> Lovely to behold, the glory of Britain

Arturo closed his eyes and to stiffen himself against the sorrow in him, ground his teeth. The gods gave and the gods took and there was no tracing the pattern of their ways. They gave men friendships and broke them by death and, since the pattern of his days was clear to him, he knew that grief must be a silent thing for there were no words to speak its truth.

Olipon came into him and Arturo sat up. Before Olipon could speak, he said, 'I have heard Borio singing of Geraint. I saw the spear go into my White One.'

'She is dead, my lord, and buried deep where no vermin can touch her.'

'And now tell me the rest.' His voice was level and his hand unshaking as he took a beaker of water which Olipon carried for him.

'Coroticus's men followed to the long boats. Men from Noviomagus had set fire to two of them. Three got away with less than a hundred to crew them. . .' He went on, telling the run of the day and the toll of losses, and finished, 'You have done what Count Ambrosius wanted done. Esc will squat like a broody hen for a long while yet.'

'Cerdic?'

'He was not among the dead. He will lie safe for a long while. The story of this day will run for more years than any child of living man will ever see. I leave for Glevum tomorrow, my lord, with your permission, to give a full account to Count Ambrosius.'

Arturo nodded and sliding his legs from the bed stood up, massaging the back of his head with his palm, saying, 'And I for the East.'

He moved out of the shelter and saw the thin slip of the passing moon above. Borio's voice came again clearly to him.

> At the battle of the men of the Long Boats, I saw
> Men who did not flinch from spears
> Great Arto's men who now drink wine with the gods. . . .

Cabal walked at his side and he dropped his hand to the hound's head. Anga was gone, and now the White One. The White One it had been who had brought Daria to him when, running wild and free in the forest, he had caught and broken it and brought it to her for betrothal gift. True love, though it was mortal, raised a man near to the gods. But it was a once-given gift. All love that followed was no more than the broken reflection on the face of troubled waters of joys past.

That year Arturo took his men north to Lindum and on to Eburacum along the borders of the northern Saxon enclaves. Few came out to meet them. Twice he rode to Corinium to meet Count Ambrosius. At Glevum and Corinium men now came flocking to join the army of Arturo, the great Dux Bellorum, the flame of his name and exploits drawing them from their craggy tribal lands in Cymru and north as far as Luguvalium on the great Wall of Hadrian.

By the end of the good season the men were trained and sent to increase and strengthen the growing line of armed camps and stockades that formed the long stretched frontier against the Saxon East, leaving Arturo free to withdraw the bulk of his cavalry to Cam Hill and the west for the winter so that with the coming of the next war-season he could turn to the clearing of the wild lands of the Tamesis river valley to school or destroy the Saxon outcasts and adventurers from the lands of Esc. These were men who called no man leader and lived by raiding to take crops, plunder and – highly prized – slaves to trade with their fellows in the east. But beyond this clearing which would safely open the approaches to Londinium he knew, for he learnt fast the craft and foresight of an army commander, that when the day came for Esc and his fellow chiefs to break out, the main force must move westwards along the Tamesis for it led to the heartland of Britain.

A week before he and the Companions were to leave for Cam Hill Arturo with Lancelo and Durstan rode into Lindum to take their farewell of the bishop. In the place of the White One Arturo was now mounted on a black stallion which was a gift to him from Count Ambrosius, a beast with a fiery war temper and a wilfulness at times which brought hard bridling from Arturo, and often made him long for the smooth understanding needing no words, no hard mastery, only the pressure of knee or foot to know his will, of the White One.

As they entered the palace courtyard the bells from the monastery and nunnery rang for them and the bishop came forward with his household to greet them. Arturo dismounted and embraced the bishop. After their greetings were made Arturo was shown to the room which stood always ready for him in the palace. A bowl of warm water, scented with the oil of honeysuckle, was brought to him for his washing. As he stood alone, combing his beard after washing, he heard the door open be-

hind him, and he smiled to himself for by now he knew the
ways of the Lady Gwennifer.

Without turning, he said, 'I had been told that you had gone
north to your father.'

'I did, my lord. On two matters of importance. But now I am
here and you grant me only a view of your dusty tunic back.
How could you know it was me?'

Arturo turned slowly. 'When I hear the scolding of a wren in
the wild clematis, the sweet plaint of the nightingale in the
hazels, or the complaint of the chiff-chaff on the poplar top –
do I have to see them to know them? When you move the
silver bells of your bracelet ring – and more, there is none in
this town but you would pass through my door without knocking.' He gave her a little obeisance of his head. 'You should be
schooled to small courtesies.'

'It is of a schooling already done that I come to you.'

The sun through the window burnished the long sweep of her
fair hair, and the blue eyes which seemed to shade or brighten
with her moods now had the depth of the wood-bowered col-
umbine. She stood proudly, of good height to match his own,
the long white gown close collared about her neck, its folds
caught smooth across her breasts with a crossing of red silk
ribbons, its looseness below her waist moulded in the draught
from the open window to caress the run of her legs. She had a
beauty which had been in his mind often this campaigning
season. Seeing his eyes on her, she was caught in a rare moment
of uncertainty and raised her right hand to touch the side of
her sunbrowned face so that the bells of her bracelet broke
again into soft, sweet sound .

With a sudden gruffness that served to cover a rare stir of
desire in him, Arturo said, 'I am in no mood to tease myself
with your riddles.'

She laughed quickly, knowing her power to move him, and
came forward and took his hand. 'Then come, and an end to
riddles. Please come ... humour me, in this, my lord.'

They went down the flights of curving stone steps and she led
him through the bishop's herb garden and into the stable yards.

Standing in the middle of the yard was a white mare, bridled and carrying a red leather saddle and strong braided girths of the same colour. At its head stood her personal manservant, Lacus, a dark-haired, bow-legged, middle-aged man whose right eye sat askew from the healing of a dagger cut underneath it.

Her hand still in his Gwennifer said, 'My lord should always ride the White One for all men know him as Arturo of the White One. My father bred her in the lands below the Wall and would neither sell nor make gift of her to anyone. Mount her, my lord, and see how well she has been schooled. She moves to the whisper of a voice between her ears. The scratch of a finger nail on her proud neck will tell her your mood and her mouth is as soft as the inside of the nest your wren makes in the wild clematis.' Her eyes shone with teasing and excitement.

Arturo went to the White One, holding down the choking in his throat as he thought of the day of the battle of the Long Boats. She stood like a queen and her eyes were pools of peat-stained mountain water, and the curve of her arching nostrils marked her spirit and her pride. He put a hand on her withers and felt the pulse and strength of her body and he caressed her bowed neck as a lover might smooth the white flesh of his beloved, and he spoke to her in the soft language that came from birth to all the Epona-blessed and she tossed her noble head and curled her lips back from her strong teeth and neighed softly.

He took the reins and Lacus knelt and made a cradle of his hands for him to mount. He walked her round the yard and felt the movement in all her muscles which he had known with the White One, and he was thinking how Gwennifer had brought him Cabal to take the place of Anga, and now brought him this god-fired beast to take the place of the White One. Because all good fortune came by threes there was no escaping the impulse that took his eyes to Gwennifer as she stood watching man and mount move over the great flags of the yard.

He rode back to Lacus and dismounted, handing the reins to the groom who said quietly, 'My lord Loth, the lady Gwennifer's father, says her lines go back to the great horses of the Syrians who served on the Walls three hundred years ago.'

'Can history be told so true over so many years?'

Lacus grinned so that his right eye closed. 'History with my lord Loth is known by its horses. Her sires have borne Caesars and now, my lord, she will bear another.'

Laughing Arturo went back to Gwennifer and taking her hand kissed it. 'First Cabal and now the White One. I thank you but there are no words fitting to mark your bounty. But one gift deserves another. Come.'

He took her hand and led her back through the herb garden and up to his room. She went with him without words for she had none to command against the beat of the strong pulse in her neck as her heart raced.

In his room he sat her down and poured wine for them both and asked, 'Who schooled the mare?'

'I did, my lord.'

'And the matters of importance you had with your father?' As he spoke he went to his saddle pack.

From behind him Gwennifer said, 'The first was of the White One. Of the second I cannot yet speak without immodesty.'

Smiling he came to her and laid across her lap the scarlet belt with the clasps of two golden singing birds which had ridden with him to his triumph at Glevum. 'Your present calls for this return. It was my wife's. Now it is yours.'

'I thank you, my lord.'

He raised his wine cup and drank to her and Gwennifer drank too, lowering her head. This, she sensed, was the time when she stood waiting the sweet or sharp turn of her destiny and must keep her eyes from him so that no shadow of change on his face should give her forewarning of his words to come.

Arturo poured the wine which was still in his cup to the ground. 'The wine is spilled and now so freely runs my desire. Two things greatly loved you have given back to me. There is a third still in your gift. If it is in your heart to grant me that gift then there is no need of words. Share your wine with me and I know that the gift is to be given.'

Gwennifer looked up at him then and her eyes were bright

now with the clear blue of the flax flower and she stood proud and radiant before him and slowly held out the wine cup.

'Drink, my beloved lord Arturo.'

Arturo took the wine and drank. Making no move to her, his eyes narrowing with gentle mischief, he asked, 'And now tell me – what was the second matter of importance you had with your father.'

She was silent for a moment, then throwing her head back a little she laughed, and said, 'It was to ask him that if you should speak for me in marriage that he would give his leave.'

'And his answer?'

'That the likeliness was as remote as pigs flying, but if it should happen then he would be proud of the honour done to both of us.'

'You are both wrong. The honour is done to me.'

He reached out and took her hand and drew her gently to him and embraced her. As they kissed, Cabal, who lay by the window, rose, stretched his long body and gave a half-yawn half-whine and then thumped back to the floor and beat his tail against the boards.

The return to Cam Hill was delayed for two weeks.

They were married by the Bishop of Lindum and, to do the God of the Christians honour, Arturo wore the surcoat given him by the Bishop of Noviomagus and a ceremonial sword sent him as gift from Count Ambrosius. At his side Gwennifer wore a white silk robe with a saffron coloured cloak and saffron coloured shoes. Above her hair was a circlet of bay leaves and she stood at Arturo's side as the bishop joined them in marriage and her lips were dark red as the hawthorn berries that grew on the great dike which rimmed the city on the east. Watching them old Pasco, the priest, held down a smile at the sight of the surcoat which Arturo wore. Arto was no man to dedicate himself solely to one god. The more who watched over him the better – but he never lacked a fitting sense of any serious occasion. And the lady Gwennifer . . all had known that in her fixed way she had chased him and lured him with the sparkle of her blue eyes and thrown a net about him in capture as golden and finely spun as her own corn-gleaming hair. She was – he sighed a little to himself at the frailty and fleetingness of human moods – a woman of all weathers, changing like the wayward days from sun to cloud, from the balms of spring to the coldness of winter. It would be long before the beauty with which she blinded Arturo passed.

The night of their wedding Arturo and Gwennifer withdrew early from the feasting and as they lay abed, she full woman now and he no longer lacking manhood's joys, the soft breeze of the warm late autumn day which had favoured them stirred the window drapings through whose opening the full moon, hanging low over Lindum, silvered the floor and tipped the grizzled pelt of Cabal with ivory points. Clear to them as they lay in each other's arms came the singing from the feasting hall and Gwennifer kissed the hard muscle of his shoulder as the words came to them.

Set your strawberry coloured mouth against my lips
O skin like foam; stretch your lime-white arms around me ...

And later, when Arturo slept but Gwennifer lay awake and the singing still lingered :

She's the white flower of the blackberry
She's the sweet flower of the raspberry
She's the best herb in excellence –
For the sight of my eyes

Lying there she knew she had gained that which she had wanted from the first time of setting eyes on Arturo as she had played her harp to him. Her need for him was passionate and absolute. Sensing the glory that with the protection of his gods must come to him she desired no more than to bear his sons and one day be his queen. No woman in the land should have claim on him or issue from him but her. Thinking this there came back to her the stable talk and camp stories freely spread of the woman Genara whose ill-fame was known in Causennae who claimed birth of her son from the fathering of Arturo when

575

she had spread her body over him to drive the killing cold from his heart . . .

Thinking this she stretched her love-eased limbs in the great bed knowing that no woman or child should live to lay claim to the smallest part of Arturo's coming glory or prove blood claim for any male child. She yawned with pleasure and the joy of long-sought possession.

Three days after Arturo rode out of Lindum on the White One with Gwennifer at his side and the Companions raising the dust behind them, Lacus went at night to drink with Genara of the cave. The boy babe whose age was yet to be numbered by years slept under cloths in an old corn pannier. Lacus was good to the woman, drank and ate with her and praised the babe whom she had called Anir. Because there was a mustard-sized grain of compassion in him he waited until dawn while mother and child slept, the one in drunken stupor and the other in innocence, and cut their throats with less noise and little more thought than he would have given to the butchering of pigs.

The Horses of the Gods

They returned to Cam Hill for the winter where now on the plateau top there were stout log-built quarters for men and horses, and the store huts and barns were well stocked with fodder and provisions to take them through to spring. On the low land around the hill the ground had been turned to long ploughed strips and the winter corn sown. Northwards towards Aquae Sulis two more fortified camps were almost completed and here – since the growing army of Companions could not be held at its full strength on Cam Hill – were lodged garrisons of four troops of cavalry each under the separate commands of black-bearded Gelliga and Tarius of the sword-scarred face. To the south-east not far from Vindocladia another camp – under the command of Garwain – had been fortified with the help of the Durotrige people who, thankful for the victory at the battle of the Long Boats, now acknowledged the overlordship of the Prince of Dumnonia.

That Prince was now the six-year-old Cato for whom Baradoc stood ward in Isca. To Isca at the turn of the year Arturo rode with Gwennifer and a small band of his men to be welcomed and lodged in the old fortress. Here Arturo found Baradoc and his mother Tia and his eldest sister, Gerta. Gerta, now seventeen, was six months married to Adipo, the son of the chief of the Durotriges, and in this Arturo saw the hand of the dead Prince Geraint and his father, Baradoc. Blood bonds were the stoutest ties between tribes. But looking at the tall, slim, dark-haired Gerta, seeing the happiness in her face – and the slight burgeoning of her body beneath her green gown that spoke of a child to come – and the pride of young Adipo beside her he knew that matching the diplomatic union was that of love given and love returned.

577

His mother, nearing her fiftieth year, proud of Baradoc's position and her son's fame, held the beauty now no longer of a woman's summer, but the fullness of ripe autumn. Her golden hair was touched with the silvering tints of time, but there was still a defiance of her years in her bright cornflower blue eyes and in the bold vigour of her body. Baradoc had aged and looked more than his years. The hard, weathered face held sometimes a weariness at odds with the vigour of his speech and his actions and his troubled right arm had grown stiffer – but the keenness of his fertile mind and the unslaked passion he held for his country's future and his hatred of the Saxons ran unabated in him.

That first night when Arturo and Gwennifer retired to their chamber, Gwennifer said, 'In your father I see you. And more I see. Your fame is a great joy and a slow bitterness to him. You are doing what he dreamt of doing. Am I right?'

'You are. But there is one thing you do not see. Without him I could never have been what I am. In the long years to come though men may remember my name and forget his there will be no forgetting in the hall of the gods for they know that the victory that comes with the breaking wave crest of a cavalry charge could never be without the abiding strength of the sea behind it.'

Gwennifer laughed. 'Prettily said. You never lack for words.'

'At this moment I lack for sleep and would have the warmth of your body to make it come fast.'

Lying awake beside him as he later slept Gwennifer thought of the beginning of proudness in Gerta's belly and her hands smoothed the flatness of her own. Maybe, she thought, the ache of longing to be full with his child by its own force delayed the fruiting of the wish. If the love of the gods held, king Arto would be of this country and she his queen and she would bear him children so that his blood and glory should live forever. Tight-lipped with sudden impatience she knew that sleep would be long coming.

The next morning as Arturo came down to the fortress courtyard, the jackdaws calling and quarrelling on its ivy-covered walls, it was to find his father and Master Ricat – the horsemaster of the Princes of Dumnonia, now greying and, though crabbed by age, still sitting horse as though he and beast were one – mounted and waiting for him while old Ansold, the swordsmith father of Daria, held the White One already saddled for him.

Without ceremony Baradoc said, 'Mount and ride. We have things to show you.'

For a moment Arturo eyed them all, then knowing his father's humour, mounted the White One. They rode off with Ansold following, his lean legs flapping loose over the back of a moorland pony. Horses Ansold loved, but for their mettle he had no time, preferring a docile mare or a plodding pony.

They rode out of the fortress and down the southern hill slope through the old town and took a path that led seawards along the river Isca. Herons stood among the sere reeds fishing. A pair of otters cruising upstream, whiskered faces and bright eyes turned towards them, left a widening wake behind them. The late salmon were running and they were well-fed and bold. The sky was a pale blue-grey wash with the sun carrying a filmy cloud halo. Nostalgia touched Arturo. Here, in this Isca and on its water meadows, he had come as little more than boy to serve Prince Gerontius and to pass from stable lad duties to trooper and cavalry training. Here, south down this river, he had seen his father make his return after long years to be re-united with his mother, Tia, a father taken by sea raiders first to slavery and then to war service in the lands above the middle seas when Rome was bleeding to death from the wounds of the Goths and the Vandals.

Following a turn in the river he saw now that which had never been here in his time. A small meadow held in the river's bend had been palisaded around with a high stockade fence. Guard platforms marked its perimeter, all manned, and at its only gate, spanned by a log-faced watch tower, other guards stood on duty.

The gates opened as they rode up. Inside the great enclosure was lined about with stalls, stables and storehouses. Piped water ran into the drinking troughs from a small aqueduct that tapped a stream coming down the slope to the east of the stockade. In the centre, shut off by barred rails, was a large tan-bark ring.

At the entrance of the ring they halted. Baradoc, who, Arturo knew well, lacked no sense of the dramatic, nodded to Master Ricat who put two fingers to his mouth and whistled shrilly.

From the far stalls there came then twelve stable servants each leading a horse. They filed into the tan yard, the servants straining back against the leading bridles to curb those mounts touched by mettle.

The prick of surprise and wonder needled Arturo's cheeks as he watched. Roan, black, grey, chestnut, bay, piebald and skew-bald, mares and stallions . . . these he knew were the horses of the gods. Now and again he had seen great horses and the White One he rode could match them, but here were twelve and over the half stable and stall doors around the enclosure he could see the heads of others. In all, his quick glancing eye told him, there were no less than a hundred of these animals.

He turned to Master Ricat, under whom he had served as youth, a man who had used birch and the flat of his hand to him for misdoing, and he said, 'Master Ricat . . . this is the dream of Prince Gerontius come true.'

Master Ricat, lips pursed, nodded his head, and then said, 'Thank the gods he lived to see it. For years he worked at this. Aye, and the secret of it has been well-kept. Until this year the horses were lodged in a well-guarded valley near Nemetostatio. Whenever there came news of a great horse in this country, it was sought out and bought. And not in this country alone. Some of the sires and dams of these you see were shipped from Gaul, bought in the great horse fairs of Hispania. Bred they have been, and mercilessly weeded, for their size and strength and courage. It was horses like these that served in the legions that Caesar brought to this country – the Second and Twentieth Augusta from Argentoratum and Novaesium, the Ninth Hispania from Pannonia and the Twenty-Fourth Gemina from Moguntia-cum and –' he stopped suddenly and smiled. 'I can see that your mind is less on history than the beasts before you.'

Arturo grinned. 'My mind is on history to be made, not that which is dead. These are the horses of the gods. How many is the tally?'

With the precision characteristic of him Master Ricat said, 'One hundred and seven of age and ready for battle, and eighty-five that run from yearlings to four- and six-year-olds. No big increase, but Prince Geraint, like his father, would have none to live not truly thrown to his standard. Of brood mares that have stood to stallions this autumn there are thirty-one.' He sighed a little wearily. 'And sore hard have been the loads for feeding and care and the guarding against robbery.'

'With horses like this one charge against the standing Saxons would be as the fall of a cliff to crush them,' said Arturo softly.

'There is more,' said Baradoc. 'Now, when you charge, you have your lance or spear which you must thrust into your enemy by your own strength and that finely gauged so that the shock does not unseat you from the saddle and with always the thought in your mind that a thrust does not come to your groin if you lower not your buckler. When you abandon or lose your lance and take to your sword with how much of your full strength can you use your blade edge or point since you must clamp knees and legs to your beast to keep your seat? The full vigour of your sword arm must be tempered to the firmness of your seat. Sit astride a thick tree branch and throw a stone. Stand on the ground and throw a stone. Which goes the farther?'

'From the ground to be sure, my father.'

'On the back of the White One now, you are as on a branch. But need be no longer. Ansold with others has made for you that which will turn the White One's back from branch to ground.'

He called to the groom who held a chestnut stallion in the middle of the line. As the man began to lead the stallion to them, Baradoc went on, 'I show you something now that I remembered from my lost days soldiering along the southern and eastern shores of the Middle Sea. Lost, too, from my memory it was until you and your Companions began to grow to strength and triumph.'

The groom halted the stallion before them and Arturo saw that the saddle on its back was of thick leather, plentifully padded on its underside and that fore and aft it rose into a wide high pommel or saddle bow which would cover a man's groin before and the base of his spine behind and thus give protection from the thrust or swing of sword or scramaseax. He saw, too, that hanging from each side of the saddle in line with the girth bands hung thick leather straps to the ends of which were looped heavy iron rings with their lower rims flattened out to fit flush to the sole of a man's boot. At once he understood all and marvelled at the simple good sense of these devices and marvelled more at the blindness that the gods could put on men to stay their fashioning of such devices.

He would have spoken but Master Ricat said, 'Watch, my lord Arturo, and you shall see the power given to a man who rides with his feet on the ground. The man who rides the bay mare wears leathers and stirrup rings. The other rides his saddle with his feet free even as you do now.'

Ricat called to the line of horses and two men carrying heavy swords mounted their horses, one a grey and the other a bay which bore the new saddle and stirrups. They trotted to the far end of the enclosure and then turned. Putting their mounts to a gallop, each man holding his sword free, they came thundering down towards two stout ash posts which had been set firmly and deeply into the ground in front of Arturo and his party. As they swept by each man struck at his post and circled away. The force of the sword blow by the man riding the grey cut deep and sent a great chip flying into the air. The sword blow of the bay's rider swung into his pole and sliced clean through it.

Before the horses could rejoin the lines on parade Arturo, his face stiff with pleasure in him at the vision of power to come, said sharply, 'How many of these new saddles with their hanging irons do we have?'

Baradoc said, 'Ansold and the other craftsmen have made eighty-four.'

'I want one hundred and fifty before the feast of Beltine and as many each month after that as can be fashioned. The increase of the great horses comes slow at Epona's pace, but even the horses we have now will with these saddles give a man double the strength in his sword arm.' As he began impetuously to wheel away, he called, 'The gods give you glory, my father and Master Ricat – for this day, too, they have given the promise of triumph to our arms!'

They watched him as he cantered out of the stockade and Master Ricat turned and looked ruefully at Baradoc. 'I would have told him ... aye, in a pretty speech, that all, horses and new gear, was a gift from Prince Geraint, sworn before he left here to join him.'

Baradoc laughed. 'How many times did you flog him as a youth for impatience and heeding naught but his own desires? You shall see him fret this winter away, eating his heart out for the moment to ride against the Saxons again. I know him. He rides now alone down the river and, maybe, prays to the gods to turn winter to spring in a day. Aye, and though he must wait like all mortals the due change of the seasons he will live this winter with a fury in him to leave only small part of his mind to others.'

Master Ricat shrugged his shoulders and said sourly, 'It seems that those whom the gods touch make poor company for their fellows.'

Baradoc said nothing, but he knew the truth of the words. His son, Arturo, was fated to live apart from other men, for, like a man on a bare, high hill top, his view spread wider and farther than that of those who hugged the comforts and shelter of the valleys.

Later, on the afternoon of that day, when Gwennifer came into their chamber it was to find Arturo seated in a chair with his feet up on the broad ledge of the window opening, brooding and staring out at the great curve of the Isca river far below. She came up behind him and kissed him gently on the neck and he absently reached up a hand and caressed the side of her cheek.

She went and sat at a small table which caught the light from the window and, loosening the braids from her hair so that it fell loose about her shoulders, began to comb it, studying her face in a large polished bronze mirror that stood on the table.

'I have heard, my lord, about the great horses. Some rumour of these had reached my father . . .'

Arturo grunted, his thoughts far away. Knowing his remoteness and its reason, Gwennifer smiled and began to pluck at her eyebrows with a pair of silver tweezers, studying her face closely in the mirror and taking pleasure in her beauty. Now, it was only when she rode with him or they made long progress from one camp to another that she dressed as a man in long trews and tight-belted surcoat. Leaning forward she touched the skin under one of her eyes. It was rough and the lower rim of her eye was a little inflamed and swollen, a common complaint when one rode much and wind and dust blew in one's face. She reached for a silver goblet which she had filled with scented salve and, dipping a finger tip into it, smoothed the ointment close under her eye. A man, she thought, would scarce heed the beauty of a woman's face or body when his mind was full of affairs and dreams of the future. And clearly this was the way with Arturo now. But when the need rose in him like a returning tide for the joy of his beloved and the pleasures of sweet congress, then he marked all of beauty or blemish with the eye of a peregrine falcon. To tease him from his mood, the turn of the new-minted words coming easily from her and making her long for her harp to enrich them, she sang, half-turning to catch his response:

> Proud on the meadow, great horses
> Grey of the winter mists
> Black of the raven god Lugus
> Brown as the new-turned ploughland
> Epona's children, Badb's delight
> Great horses for the Chosen One
> Great horses of all the gods

To her delight the words reached through Arturo's mood and he turned, smiling at her, and rising came towards her. But, as he was poised to bend to kiss her, he halted and a frown darkened his forehead, a cloud over the sun of his smile.

His voice sharp, he said, 'From where did you get that goblet?'

Surprised at his curtness, she looked at the silver goblet in her hand, and then confused said, 'I did my duty to you, my lord, by unpacking your campaign chest and found it. Look –' she smiled, hoping to overcome the anger in his face, '– I have cleaned it for you with fuller's earth and the polishing of my own warm breath.'

'Take the ointment from it,' said Arturo curtly. 'It is not a chalice to be used for any ordinary service. Clean it and put it back in my chest.'

Without another look at her Arturo walked to the door and she, stung by his uncouth manner which rode her high mettle hard, called after him angrily as he went from the chamber, 'Command me to anything, my lord – but not in the voice of master to servant!' She raised the chalice high and flung it after him. It hit the long curtain over the door opening as it fell back on his going and dropped without sound into the softness of trailing folds on the ground.

She sat, hearing the sound of his footfalls on the stone stairs fade away, and then with a shrug of her shoulders, anger quickly gone from her, she got up and retrieved the chalice. She held it, the spilled salve sticky against her fingers, and wondered why Arturo had been so moved because of her found use for it. It was the size of a drinking goblet with handles each side, curved and worked in the form of rams' horns. One of the horns was badly bent and the bowl itself was pocked here and there with dents. Around the outside rim ran a continuous Greek key pattern and on one side of the bowl, worked in relief, was a large round boss in the shape of an almost circular wreath of bay leaves enclosing the simple outline of a human eye.

That night after Gwennifer had retired to her bed, Arturo stayed long below talking with his father and Master Ricat. There was no sleep for her as she lay watching the long shadows cast across the chamber by the tall candles whose flames swayed in the draughts like yellow crocuses in a spring breeze. When at last Arturo came to bed she pretended sleep. But as he lay alongside her he was not deceived. After a time, without touching her, he said, 'I have offended you and rightly you give me no welcome. For this I ask your forgiveness. I was harsh to you who are gentler than the soft-breasted dove on the red rowan trees, but that only because the chalice you used for your salve has a holiness that comes from the blood of the Son of the Great Father in the heavens whom the Christos followers worship. When He was crucified it was this bowl which caught the blood that dripped from the spear wound in his left side – so the story runs from my mother who was given the chalice in return for her goodness by a hermit. It is said that if it is filled with water and held by one marked for greatness the water flushes to the colour of the Christos blood. Twice this has happened to me. First when I was a babe without understanding, and again when I was newly in manhood and near dying from an arrow wound of an enemy. I am the offending lover. Between us lies the winter of hasty speech. Turn then and speed the seasons to the clover-scented warmth of summer.'

In the darkness Gwennifer smiled to herself. When he chose his tongue could drip honey. Hasty he had been and would be again, but that came from the loneliness in him and was no more than the kingfisher play of summer lightning. She turned and put her arms around him and her lips to his.

The following fighting season, during which Arturo began the clearing of the valley of the lower Tamesis to make the approaches to Londinium secure, he made no use of the heavy horses. The Saxons about the river, he knew, would never come out in sufficient force to warrant their use – and, additionally, he was in no hurry to apprise Esc of their existence. The time would come when the Saxons made a real show of strength. Enough horses were drawn from Isca and taken to Cam Hill to form two troops and left under the command of Gelliga, with young Borio and enough men to mount them and to begin their training while Ansold, with other smiths and leather workers, made saddles and stirrup irons to accoutre them.

Nearing the end of the summer the approaches to Londinium were secured and the city – which had long recovered from the plague – was lightly garrisoned by local recruitment. But, as the Romans in the long past years had seen, it was no place to be heavily fortified and manned to stand as a strong point. For the time being it was slowly coming back to its old position as a trading centre and port which even the Saxons of Esc used through the offices of merchants and craftsmen who put commerce higher than patriotism. Nevertheless Arturo left it strongly enough held to stop any movement by land between the Saxons of the South and those of the East and Middle lands reaching up to Lindum. At the end of the season he left a troop of cavalry there under the command of Netio, hawk-nosed, face sword-scarred, who had been one of the first of the Companions to join him from the Sabrina Wing at Corinium.

He rode back in the autumn to Cam Hill and then to Isca where he found that, of his mother's three other children, Gerta, his eldest sister, had given birth to a boy whom she had named Mordreth, that his young brother, Gareth, had died of the summer fever, and that his younger sister, Amla, was fast moving from childhood to girlhood and growing in looks more like her mother every day. His mother's hair was greyer and there was a calm and serenity about her face through which her true feelings seldom showed. Baradoc was alert and vigorous when anyone was near him and still improving the Cam Hill defences and those of the other hill sites running north to Aquae Sulis. But caught when he felt that none observed him the weariness in him and the growing pain of his right arm seemed to mark his face and body with far more years than he could claim. His time, Arturo sensed, was running out too fast for his spirit and there was an honourable disappointment in him that the dreams he had cherished as a young man would stay dreams to be shaped by the hands of himself to true life. That this should be so was the god-sworn duty of Arturo.

For Gwennifer, his wife, there was only wonder in Arturo. The blaze of her beauty and the warmth of her love for him were like the light and heat of a never-setting sun. Her laughter and high spirits, marking her great appetite for life, enchanted him so that he could refuse her nothing and, since he could never find the love in him for her which he had held for Daria but at times wished he could, he sought to humour and grant all her indulgences and wishes. And her wish – which was his, too – for a son, he humbly prayed to the gods to be granted. A son he needed as much as she did for the day would come when all that he should create would, at his going, need his own flesh and blood to take from his hands and build to even greater glory. For this he prayed to the gods, and not always with modest patience.

And Gwennifer prayed too, and while that autumn, as though the march of the seasons had been stayed, ate well into the last months of the year she watched for the signs of the springing of his seed within her and sometimes, in moments of disappointment, alone in her chamber at Isca or in the now comfortable lodge at the top of Cam Hill when none could see or hear her, she would vent her impatience in strong action or words, striking her fists against the top of her toilet table, some-times smashing unguent or salve pot, and once deep denting her polished bronze hand mirror while she swore with the words and fury of any trooper amongst the Companions. Arturo would be king of this country and where was there king who did not yearn for a man child to carry his memory and great-ness forward into the future?

But the day came when this passion of frustration passed from her. Going from their chamber one late afternoon to the eating hall of the Isca fortress she passed the door of the room in which Baradoc and Tia were lodged. The door was ajar but covered on the inside by the long hanging doeskin draught cur-tain which was also partly drawn. Clearly to her came the voice of Baradoc and his words made her halt.

He said, 'There is a recklessness in the Lady Gwennifer which Arturo should curb.'

'Why so?' The voice of Tia was a little absent as though her mind were on her toilet or needlework.

'She took one of the great horses yesterday and insisted on riding it in battle drill with the troop. *Aie* ... and in wildness and indiscipline left them all trailing, riding like one of the Furies.'

'She is high spirited, true. But she rides as well as any man.'

'This I know. But the time could come – or may have come now without her knowing – when she could be with child, and by her wildness lose it. Arturo needs a son, for himself and for this country. Arturo will say nothing to her, even if I ask him – but you could speak to her and she would listen for there must be in her as in us a longing for a man child.'

There was silence for a while and then the quiet, firm voice of Tia said, 'Have you forgotten the words that Merlin wrote on the cliff rock the day we came to Caer Sibli?'

'What words?'

Tia laughed gently. 'You know well, but do not wish to remember. He wrote of Arturo, even yet to be born but carried within me –

> Cronus in the dream spoke thus
> Name him for all men and all time
> His glory an everlasting flower
> He throws no seed

– so there will be no child, no son, no daughter. It is the price which our Arturo has already without his knowing paid to the gods for his coming greatness.'

Baradoc grunted intolerantly. 'Who believes Merlin and his nonsense?'

Tia said quietly, 'You should for he warned you, as you have since told me, that you should not put your boat to water to leave the island until the first swallow had come north. But you did – and were gone from me for many a long year. There will be no child of Arturo born to Gwennifer and my heart aches for her.'

Stiff-faced from the sharp turn of emotion in her, Gwennifer moved on down the stone steps.

*

The year lingered, mild and unseasonable. There was still thin growth in the pasture grass, the great geese that came always from the eastern lands which had been the cradle of the Goths were still to arrive, and the peregrines of the Dumnonian cliffs and the mountains of Cymru still lingered, and the holly trees were almost barren of berries as though they knew the birds would have no need of winter feeding. On a morning when Baradoc's men, still labouring on the defences of Cam Hill, worked stripped to the waist under the sun a messenger, covered with sweat and dust, riding a hard-pressed mount, came to Arturo with a message from Count Ambrosius at Corinium.

The north Saxons who held all the shore lands running south from Petuaria on the Abus river to the great fens and marshes below the Metaris estuary, reinforced by sea from the East Saxons of Esc, had broken out of their enclaves and were besieging Lindum and Durobrivae of the fenlands.

That evening Arturo rode out of Cam Hill with two troops of the great horses and two of his original gathering, and with them went a hundred marshmen with Coroticus. Each man took with him his short commons to last until they reached Corinium. Four days later they rode into Corinium as the sun was dropping low over the distant Cymru mountains and took quarters in the camp of the Sabrina Squadron – a camp which Arturo saw at a glance was held by only a beggarly handful of Ambrosius's cavalry.

As he dismounted and Lancelo took the reins of the White One and led her away Arturo saw Count Ambrosius standing at the opening of his blue-dyed square tent to greet him. The meeting was short of ceremony for Arturo was in a mood of angry bitterness which had built in him as he had ridden these past days. He knew his Ambrosius over well now and had easily filled for himself the gaps in the scanty information brought to him by the messenger.

Ambrosius poured wine for him, but Arturo did little more than touch his lips to it. Seated across the table from his commander, he said without ceremony, 'The weather holds fair still – too good for the season – and if we had been ill-prepared at Lindum and Durobrivae might have tempted the Saxons to break out and breach the line we hold from Lindum to Londinium. But both towns and all the armed camps along the line were left full-manned. What gives them then this sudden courage and hope of success, my lord Ambrosius?'

For a moment or two Ambrosius said nothing. He closed his eyes briefly and breathed deeply. Arturo was all fire and anger and would need careful handling. Even so, he resented his arrogant mood and, but for the tiredness in him, would have bridled it with sharp words. Then, before he could answer, Arturo spoke again sharply.

'I ask, my lord, what gives the Saxons this boldness since between us we had left the line and its cities fully garrisoned and patrolled?'

Smoothing the grey patches of hair over his ears Ambrosius answered, 'The reason, Arturo, lies in the craft of Esc and — I admit it — a lack of foresight in me. He has leagued with the Scotti and they have made landings with many craft from the Mona island as far south as Moridunum and Nidum in Demetia. Without time to warn you I have had to withdraw men from the Lindum line and from here to send west as reinforcements. Would you have done differently?'

'Aye, I would. The Scotti could wait. They have always harried the coasts of Cymru. The mountains would have held them long enough to give time to deal with the Saxons first. You can only hunt one stag at a time. Esc is our stag. The Scotti would take slaves, plunder and cattle and perhaps settle in a few sea valleys to await our coming. What is the last news from the east?'

'That Lindum and Durobrivae are surrounded but still hold. That was seven days ago.'

Arturo stood up 'Then there is no time to be lost. The Companions of the White Horse ride tonight. I pray the gods keep this good weather flowing for us on the ride. What it be when we arrive I care not.' He smiled suddenly, and went on gently, 'There is much to be done, my lord, so I ask your leave to go. We stay but to water and feed our mounts and ride this night.'

For a moment Ambrosius was on the point of finding words to curb the mastery in Arturo and to bring him back under control, and he knew well, too, that the gentleness in his last words held no true respect for him. Then with a tired shrug of his shoulders, he said mildly, 'You will do me one last courtesy before leaving. Drink your wine with me.'

As he reached for his beaker Arturo took his and when they had both drunk Ambrosius said, 'May the gods give you success.'

'If they do not it will be from no lack of manhood in the Companions.'

When Arturo had gone Count Ambrosius poured more wine for himself and sat sipping it. Wine he found more and more these days drove the tiredness of mind and body from him for a short while, but he was under no delusion about the true meaning of its comfort. His days were slipping from him. He had battled and planned and wasted himself in trying to bring unity between so many of his country's chiefs that there was now no true force left in him. He would go soon and Arturo would take his place. No man could escape the toll of his years. He only hoped that the gods would grant Arturo a wide span of life to bring his dream for this country to life.

Then, with a sudden flush of pride, he called for his servant. The man helped him to dress and two hours later as the first stars began to take brightness in the sky, he sat his horse at the great gateway of the Sabrina camp, wearing his plumed war helmet, polished cuirass and greaves, his blue riding cloak over his shoulders and his broad sword held in salute to the Companions as they marched out, near a hundred and fifty horse and a hundred marshmen; the cream of all the fighting men in this country, the pride in them clear as they went under the banner of the White Horse because they knew themselves to be Arturo's men and knew Arturo to be chosen of the gods. But the great gods above, Ambrosius knew, were too remote for man to serve without sight or sound. They needed a man to go before them who was clear to be seen and heard, a god of their own creating.

*

They were four days on the road to Lindum. On the third day the morning broke with a clear sky and a shift of the wind from the west to the east, a wind that blew strong with an icy, biting savagery as though winter, long deferred, was arrived with a freezing fury at its long delay. Within an hour the roadside ditches were surfaced with ice and the breaths of men and horses plumed in the air and set their sweating beards brittle with its cold grip.

On the fourth day as they came down off the high ground before Crococalana and passed through it they could see, far ahead of them across the flat lands, tall plumes of smoke rising from the direction of Lindum. Now, too, they began to meet people who were fleeing from it with their small possessions hastily salvaged and learnt that after a long siege the Saxons had broken into the city five days ago killing all who could make no escape. The garrison had died fighting. The bishop and the monks and nuns had been slaughtered. The Saxons had spent three days ravaging, slaughtering and plundering and then a day and a night of feasting and drinking and were now – three hundred or more of them – moving down the river Dubglas on their way south to join their fellows – some two hundred strong – who were still trying to take Durobrivae.

Arturo drew his forces off the road to the east and made camp. He sent three of Coroticus's marshmen up the river Dubglas to bring back reports on the Saxons' movements. The river which was close by their camp was slow running and heavily reeded along its banks. Parts of it were already iced over and the soft ground of its marshy verges had frozen hard enough to take the weight of man and horse.

Long before dawn the marshmen returned with their reports on the Saxons. Hearing it, Arturo gave the order at once to break camp and move. Now, he blessed the hard times of night riding and marching at Cam Hill during training. With the marshmen scouts leading them they went five miles northwards up the river and then drew away from it and made themselves ready for the morning light to come. Through the darkness they could see the camp fire flames of the Saxons two miles away in the direction of Lindum. All men stood to their arms and their mounts and long before dawn came there was no troop commander or trooper who did not know the part he must play with the full rising of the sun. Coroticus and his men had already moved off into the night which was bitter with the east wind blowing a gale, setting dust and dead leaves and rushes swirling into the air, and numbing bare hands to a stiffness which only the coming heat of battle was to warm

When dawn came, cloudless and biting cold with the wind, the troopers standing to their horses saw that they were lodged in the cover of a thin growth of pines which covered the low summit of a stretch of heathland a mile from the river. Beyond the pines at the edge of the heathland Coroticus's marshmen lay hidden in the trough of an old road that led down to the river. Three bowshots beyond them, on the slightly lower ground by the river, was the Saxon camp. The warriors were already astir, breaking camp to begin their onward march down the river to Durobrivae and the plundering and ravaging of any farm or small settlement that came between.

Coroticus lying on the lip of the road saw that they were well armed and clothed in heavy furs and thick woollen clothes, and unlike most roving Saxon bands moved in a disciplined manner about their business. Clear in their midst, ordering and commanding them, was a warrior, tall for his race, who wore a winged helmet and a surcoat of black sheepskin. None of the Saxons were mounted for they had no use or skills for handling horses in battle, but they had with them ponies and mules now being laden with their supplies and spoils of war. From behind him there came clear to Coroticus the signal he awaited; the high, whistling pipe of a greenshank. He rose, but gave no order for all his near hundred men knew their part in Arturo's battle plan. As he stepped into view clear of the sunken road ten men followed him on either side. They walked without hurry towards the Saxon camp, spears slung over their backs to free their hands for the bows they carried. They were so small a party that they excited no great interest, except for a few shouts and bursts of laughter from the warriors who were now forming up raggedly to begin their march.

Within bowshot of the camp Coroticus and his men knelt to one knee and then one after another they shot their arrows. As the flighting hiss of one arrow died so another whistled to life and followed it, and each arrow found its mark in throat or chest or groin. They shot five arrows each and then as the roars of anger and shouts of the wounded filled the air forty or fifty warriors, like a roused swarm of wasps, came running up the gentle slope towards them with swords and spears poised for action.

Coroticus and his men turned from them and trotted without hurry back to the edge of the sunken road and, on the lip of the bank, knelt again and without hurry string-notched their arrows and sent them flighting towards the Saxons. Stung by this taunting affront from so few men the Saxons came charging up the gentle rise, roaring with anger and filling the air with their oaths, leaving eight of their men on the ground behind them. When they were half-a-bowshot away the rest of the marsh-men rose suddenly over the edge of the road bank with their arrows ready strung to let them fly into the packed ranks of the attackers. The Saxon attack broke and withered like wheat under the sickle. Then, as another flight of arrows thinned their ranks, they turned and ran back down the slope.

Coroticus licked his lips with pleasure as he saw the fresh stir from the far Saxons as the survivors rejoined them, and grinned at the howling and crying and milling movement in the camp as their black-coated leader began to draw them to some kind of order. Here was, he thought, the beginning of the firing of the wasps' nest. He watched as the swarm below took ragged order and then widestrung rank after rank of warriors, led by their wing-helmeted leader, came charging up the road.

The marshmen stood their ground until their last arrow was spent and then, as though content with their wrought havoc, they turned, crossed the road and began to trot for the far cover of the pine-studded heath crest.

Seeing them turn and run the Saxons, breaking ranks and raging to avenge their fallen, came pack hunting after them, swarming across the road.

As the marshmen came through the pines and past the waiting cavalry, Lancelo's horn blew and the long note made the cheek skin of Arturo tighten with joy. Here now was the first day of the Great Horses and the power that came from safe saddles and body-bracing stirrup irons. With himself at the centre, faithful to the White One, they came out of the pines at a growing gallop, Gelliga and his troop to the left and Durstan with his men on his right. Behind them, in a thick driving column, came the long tried smaller horses of the Companions. They burst down on the Saxons who had crossed the road, lances lowered and strongly couched, and Arturo led them, marking the figure of the black-surcoated Saxon leader. The shock of their meeting was like the sudden breaking of an angry sea, and for the first time Arturo and his men knew the real power of their new mounts and horse gear. The Saxon leader ran to meet him and threw up his small shield to hammer aside the lowered lance while the blade of his scramaseax drove hard for Arturo's groin. Arturo dropped the point of his lance and felt the great arm and body shock as it drove through the man's chest. He fell to the ground, screaming, his sword flying from his hand and lay there with the lance spitted through him. As he passed Arturo drew his sword and knew now with certainty that although the lance could only serve but once there was a new strength and sureness in the sword's blade. The battle lust took him and all his Companions as for the first time they knew the bloody, death-giving strength that lay in their sword arms. The swing of the blade which before cut deep, now sheared through flesh and bone like a butcher's cleaver taken to quartering carcasses.

If it was a morning of joy for the Companions in their new-found strength, it was also a morning of blood and relentless carnage, a massacre without mercy to avenge the people of Lindum, a great killing to claim blood price for the murder and rape of the gentle nuns, and a hunt to the death of the sea wolves which would make the memory of the battle of the river Dubglas live for ever. Over the hard, frost-bound river lands they harried the fleeing Saxons, driving them to the water's edge either to turn and meet death or to fling themselves in to sink or swim to the far bank. No mercy was shown. Behind the fast scouring cavalry groups there came Coroticus and his men with their spears and their daggers drawn, seeking the hearts and the throats of wounded and living.

When the killing was done and the last Saxon had found safety across the river, the Companions reformed and buried their dead of which there were few and the march began up-river to Durobrivae, which was to prove luckier than Lindum. The town still held, and the Saxon survivors from the Dubglas battle had reached their comrades with the news of Arturo's coming. The siege was quickly lifted and the Saxons marched in haste to the east and the safety of their flat mere and river-cut lands.

Arturo stayed three weeks at Lindum setting to rights the ordering of the city as the citizens who had escaped came back, reforming the patrols and strong points along the Lindum–Durobrivae line, and pressing to service any youth or man able to bear arms. They would serve until the spring came and then be free to return to farm or settlement; but he knew that there would be no real fighting for them to face. Esc had made his throw and the gods had turned the dice against him. It would be long before he cradled the marked ivories in his palm to make another cast. He left Gelliga in command of the city and the defences of the line with a troop of horse and fifty of Coroticus's men to give heart and fire to the local forces.

He rode back to Cam Hill through Corinium. The news had long been sent ahead of his victory. But there was no welcome for him from Count Ambrosius. He had died of a heart attack two days after receiving Arturo's messenger.

Sitting in the Count's quarters at Corinium with Olipon, the Praefectus Castorum, Arturo asked, 'What was the manner of his death?'

The campaign-hardened Olipon, who now had a real affection

for Arturo, though not greater than his love for his old commander, shrugged his shoulders. 'Some men know when their time comes to die. He had a seizure, but he had known them before and overcome them. But this time ... the wish was no longer in him to live. Two days after your messenger came he died and has been buried at Glevum which was his wish. Long before spring the whole of this country will know of his going.' He paused and grinned ruefully. 'You will then be set high as target for the rivalries and enmities of many chiefs. You must win them by your boldness if you wish for kingship over this country.'

Arturo said curtly, 'There is no lust for kingship in me – only a wish for the return of the greatness of this country and the flowering of peace when we have driven the Saxons from us.'

Olipon shrugged his shoulders. 'True lust or not, my lord – you must assume the shape of it. He who commands must be king for where else does authority rest?' He reached within the loose robe he was wearing and brought out a folded piece of parchment fastened with the seal of Count Ambrosius. 'These are Count Ambrosius's last words to you. Since he wished it I have read them. He speaks as father to son, and he speaks with the wisdom which came with his years and their bitter experience.'

The words of Count Ambrosius, written on the parchment, read:

> I salute you:
>
> Be king and above all men. No throne can
> be shared.
> Give your trust to no one except for a season.
> The summer of a man's loyalty is often followed
> by the mischievous winter of his pride.
> No matter the warmth of your heart, keep the
> cold sword always at your side.
> Treachery respects no blood bonds; look for it even
> seated at your own hearth.
>
> The gods have claimed you for this country and
> freed you from the wrack of conscience.

The Horses of the Gods

I give you the inheritance of Ambrosius.
Enrich it so that in the years to come all men
will shout 'Arto' while my name will be whispered
like a brief echo, the gentle fall of ash from
the fire of your kindling.

The Holly on the Hillside

Arturo rode back to Cam Hill, leaving Durstan with horses and men to stand in command for him at Glevum and Corinium. His course was set by the words of Ambrosius, all that remained was to test the tides and perils of the voyage ahead. King he would be, but the proclamation should come from others. If any stood in his way they should fall for the gods had freed him from conscience.

The man changed and lived no longer for himself but for his dreams. At Isca he talked long and late with his father who, standing ward for the young Cato, held control of the Dumnonian treasury. Baradoc, knowing the change in him, would have tempered some of his demands but saw the darkness of rising frustration in his eyes and gave him his way. Arturo sent messengers to all the chiefs of the far North as far as the Wall of Hadrian, to all the chiefs of Cymru and the ruler of Demetia calling for their presence at Glevum by the feast of Beltine. He rode to see King Melwas at his winter quarters on the slopes of the limestone hills above the great swamp. When he left Melwas – enriched by presents from the Iscan vaults – it was with the firm promise that Coroticus would come to him in the spring with three hundred armed and provisioned men.

After he had gone Melwas said to Coroticus, 'The old wolf has died. Now the pack gets a new leader but there are many who will wait to tear him down.'

Coroticus rubbed his nose and grinned. 'What other leader is there? There is not a man amongst us who does not know his mind and is with him.'

Melwas grunted. 'I am no fool to sit overclose to the fire and burn myself. I give him the men, but for your glory, not his.

Aie ... though, I like him well, and he is no fool to call himself king yet. He will work that royal yeast differently.'

Three weeks after Arturo's return – and he lodged now more often at Isca than Cam Hill – the gods sent him an unexpected gift. A young man who had crossed from Gaul to the estuary of the river Isca with a shipload of horses and returning refugees asked for an audience with Arturo and would name nothing of his business. In the end after much pestering of the fortress guards he was brought to Arturo by Borio who had searched him for hidden weapons.

Arturo saw him in the great chamber where he had once been taken to see first Prince Gerontius and then his son, Geraint. Without opposition from Baradoc Arturo had taken the chamber into his own use.

Alone with Arturo – for he had refused to speak in the presence of any other – the young man said, 'My lord Arturo, I am Oleric, the son of Theodoric from the land of the Visigoths below Gaul.'

'And so?'

'My father's name means nothing to you, my lord?'

'Nothing.' Then seeing the youth's surprise, Arturo smiled and went on, 'In this country we have our own troubles. The Franks, the Goths and the Visigoths are known to me from my studies but of their present men of fame I know little.'

The young man smiled boldly. 'How did you know that I spoke of a man of fame, my lord?'

'Because you stand proudly and speak as would the son of a man of high state. Now give me plain facts and the reason for your coming.'

'I will, my lord. But I should say to you that on crossing from Gaul it was to Count Ambrosius I travelled. Now, since he is dead, I learn, I speak to you who have taken his place, so all men tell me.'

Momentarily Arturo frowned. Then with a shrug of his shoulders he said, 'Speak to me then.'

'Very well, my lord.'

Arturo sat and listened as the youth spoke and, within a very short while, he knew that here being offered to him by this Oleric son of Theodoric was a part of the inheritance from Ambrosius of which he could never have guessed the existence but whose richness made him long for the moment to come when he met the war chiefs of this land at Glevum.

When the youth had finished Arturo said, 'Return to your father and tell him that I accept that which he offers and the first price shall be paid when he comes ashore in this land at the time and the place you have named.'

'I thank you, my lord.'

'My thanks are to you and your father. The gods keep you on your journey back to him.'

A little after Oleric had gone Gwennifer came into the chamber to him. She had been riding and still wore dusty men's clothes, her long hair part-freed from its nape ribbons.

Teasingly she said, 'You look like a cat that has been at the cream bowl, my lord.'

Rising, Arturo went to her and kissed her hand and said, 'I smile because of the sight of you now, as wild and tousled as the morning you first brought Cabal to me. I smile, too, because it is now hard in me that I have had enough of affairs here and the closeness of this fortress and the streets and the midden smells. Tomorrow we ride for Cam Hill and you come with me. We will lie in our hilltop lodge together and hear the fox bark through the frost-thin air to his vixen and walk by the Cam and see the sun take the silver of the leaping salmon as he comes to the call of Latis.'

They went to Cam Hill where all now was well ordered and sound quarters long made for men and beasts. In the hard bright winter weather they rode by the Cam and sitting their horses by the bank could look down through the clear crystal of the waters and watch the hen salmon arching and curvetting their long bodies as they cut their redds for spawning while the great cock fish kept station at their sides, waiting for the berried moments of seeding and milting, and sometimes, unseen by Arturo, Gwennifer's white teeth would bite frettingly at the inner edge of her lower lip from longing for the boon for her body which was still denied her.

They rode the high downs with Cabal and a span of chase hounds and with the setting up of a winter-coated hare they followed hare and hounds, shouting and calling and laughing as though they were youth and maiden charged with the wonder and passion of a first love which gave all the world a freshness unseen before For Arturo this time of a few weeks, though not planned from his known need, was a time that his body and spirit needed to refresh him for the days to come. He put from his mind all cares and turned sharply away from the temptation of brooding meditation over the great matters and affairs which awaited him and with the coming of spring. He was a lover with his beloved and the warmth of her kisses and the bonding of their bodies gave him a kingship at night which pushed all thought of far Glevum and of mistrusting, obstinate, and proud war-chiefs from him. Even as the gods now and then turned away from the ordering of men's affairs in this world to days of feasting and nights of revelry so, he knew now, must a great commander seek forgetfulness of his heart's true passion and his iron dedication to his country's desperate needs to lose himself in a skein of simple days and simple delights and simple sights ... the quick ear-cocking of a wily hare in the moment of sitting upright before breaking to flight, the tolerant complaint in the calling of a diamond-tailed raven as a pack of fork-tailed red kites mobbed it, the rainbow colours the sun's glance gave to an icicle hanging from the lip of a moss-ribbed rock face, the straddled legs and unsteady stance of a new-born winter foal as it rose to face for the first time the new world of light ... and each morning's unlidding of the blue eyes, clear as the colum-bine bloom, of his beloved Gwennifer lying with her corn silk hair all a-tousle on the long goose-down pillow at his side.

On their last night at Cam Hill they sat by the turf fire and drank wine, shared from the same cup, and Gwennifer took her harp and played and sang for him and the words that came from her were, he could believe, a gift from the crook-nosed god Maponus who fired the heat of true-tempered words in the minds of all bards. . .

> Arto the spearhead in battle
> The Saxons will cry woe
> As they flee before the Britons
> Arto will hunt them down
> A pillar of flame, King over men
> High the banner of the White One
> Under its linen border, great Arto
> From Isca in the West
> To the great wall in the North
> King over men, beloved of all

Light-heartedly Arturo said, 'You sing too soon of future things.'

Gwennifer shook her head. 'No, my lord. In men's hearts you are king already. Only the word is lacking and that comes soon. King you will be and sons I shall bear you to be Princes.'

But as the year's shortest day came and went and the feast of the Christos people to celebrate their Lord's birth passed with Arturo joining them in worship – for he would give offence to no god – Gwennifer knew that her deep wish to bear him a child still showed no sign of being granted, and she came fully to believe the truth of the words of Tia which she had overheard. Anger and frustration turned in her like two serpents, so that when Arturo and Baradoc went back to their tribal lands on the north coast below Caer Sibli to order affairs there, she – at her own wish – stayed in Isca There were times then when she paced her chamber restlessly and others when she took her harp and played airs of sweet melancholy so that the tears misted her eyes.

On one such day as the winter-burnished sun hung low, reddening the waters of the Isca in its setting, she sat at her window playing when Borio, now commander of the fortress and its winter garrison, came down the winding stone steps from the broad walks that ran around the fortress walls. Her door was partly open and seeing her playing the harp he stopped and listened. When she had finished and raised her head to see him, he smiled and said, 'You play a sad melody, my lady. But sing no words. Are they then even sadder?'

'Good Borio there are no words to match its sadness.'

'Then it is a tune which must be teased to cheerfulness.'

He came across the chamber, took the harp from her in his big hands, and began to play the same tune in a brighter vein, raising gaiety and liveliness from the same sad notes she had struck, and because the bard's gift was in him and words and music came to him as easily as breathing, he sang:

> Her hand and eye are gentle
> Walking under the vine
> The nightingales salute her
> She will come over the high crag
> To sit with me under the holly
> Until there be no green leaf over us
> So long will be the season of love

When he finished Gwennifer laughed with pleasure and went to the table and poured him a goblet of wine. As she gave it to him she asked, 'And where is the one who waits under the green holly tree for Borio?'

Borio's face puckered with a wry smile. 'If she waits, my lady – which I doubt – then it is beyond Deva by the wide sands of the estuary where the wild geese will now be wintering and where –' his smile broadened, '– the holly trees are few.' He touched the wine to his lips and saluted her and Gwennifer felt that although his eyes rested on her face only briefly there was in them a rise of boldness.

When he was gone she took the wine goblet and, standing at the window, sipped gently. He had been with Arturo from the beginning; one of the youngest of the Companions. When he was campaigning he grew a beard, but during the winter he went clean shaven, a fresh-faced young giant, big-handed yet with fingers that caressed the harp strings with a light and magic touch to match the easy spring of his gift for words. That far away maiden beyond Deva, she thought, would be a fool not to wait and keep herself for him to bear his children ...

That night she lay awake for a long time, her mind twisting

and turning. The conflict in her between her love for Arturo and her own needs for him and his wide ranging ambitions drove sleep far from her, and sometimes, while her face stiffened in the spasms of her resolution, she felt the touch of tears in her eyes. No man she knew would doubt her honour. No man would talk loosely of her for fear of Arto's wrath and the safety of his own life.

Two nights later when Borio, who had his chamber at the top of the tower above Gwennifer's room, retired he found lying on his bolster a sprig of green holly, its dark leaves silvered by the dim light from a single wall sconce. Because of the poetry and music in him and the memory of the parting look which Gwennifer had given him he knew the meaning of the holly and felt at once the stir of loyalty to Arturo move strongly in him, warring against the sharp onset of his manhood's desires.

She came to him long after the watch had called midnight from the fortress gate-tower. Her hair was braided into plaits, the long tresses coiled in a golden wreath about her head. Her long white gown was close-caught about her neck, but her arms were bare and she moved he thought as swift dryness took his throat, like a golden-crowned swan.

Curbing his troubled spirit, he said gently. 'My lady, you would do me a great honour. But this must not be. Many years ago I came to Arto and pledged him my sword and my faith and swore to serve him with all my honour.'

'You do him no dishonour, my Borio. The gods have brewed the draught of this night's drinking. Arto would have a son to match his greatness when he goes, but there is no living seed in him. Since you have sworn all love for him and I carry none but love for him and his desires the gods have marked us thus to serve him and the secret stays between us for all time.' She came close to him and reaching up touched gently with her fingertips the weather-browned firmness of his cheek. 'Arto's Companions are Arto's flesh, and Arto's wife is the vessel that must hold the everlasting wine of his greatness. The gentle breath of a woman's sigh can blow the candle light to death and darkness. But tonight the boon of darkness lies with you, and I ask it of you from my love for Arto.'

For a moment or two Borio stood, unmoving. The gift of words was in her as in him, but the truth of her words and her pleading was like summer lightning, coming and going in proud, many-hued flames, turning the world to brief wonder and blinding him to set free all the coiling desires of his manhood.

He turned, took three steps to the solitary wall sconce and blew the tallowed wick to darkness; but, in that darkness as he came to her and his arms went round her and the stir of her body wakened to full life the desire in him, he knew that he did this alone as Borio and for no other reason than Borio's because Borio was a man and Gwennifer was a woman, and both were caught in the snare of the gods.

They were lovers until Arturo's return which was on the last day of the month of the two-faced god Janus. That evening Borio, with Arturo and Gwennifer, ate in full company in the fortress hall. Borio drank heavily to kill the shame in him, while Gwennifer laughed and drank at Arturo's side and teased him gaily. After midnight when, for all his drinking, the gods had withheld from him the least edge of oblivion's cloak, Borio walked the ramparts on his rounds as the rain fell steadily, and – so it was thought when he was found later, though the truth died with Borio – he slipped on the wet planking bridging a parapet gap and fell sixty feet to the cobbled yard to break his neck. They buried him off the roadside along the Isca, where a side stream ran down to serve the aquaduct for watering the horses in the great stockade and where the sound of their neighing and the thunder of their hooves in exercise would reach him. But it was not with this in mind that Gwennifer had chosen it. He lay beneath an old holly tree, its berries red as the robin's breast, red as his blood which had marked the fortress cobbles. But, as Gwennifer was to find as the weeks went by, the sin and the sacrifice found no pleasure with the gods.

A few days before the feast of Beltine marking the coming of Spring, Arturo, leaving Gwennifer at Isca, rode north with a

full company of Companions drawn from the hill forts and
Cam Hill and with three hundred marshmen under the command of Coroticus and the tramp of their going cloaked the
young leaves of the roadside growths with dust and made those
not in the van of the column draw their scarves across their
mouths to save their throats from parching. When they reached
Glevum the army of Arturo was camped outside the South gate
and close to the river for the watering of horses while the com-
panies and retinues of the war chiefs lay between the West gate
and the river. The tribal chiefs and petty kings were lodged in
the city in the old half-timbered, half-masonry quarters of the
long gone legions which Durstan had put to order during the
winter. Arturo himself had quarters in the old basilica which
Count Ambrosius had long ago turned into his residence and
army headquarters. It was here that the full congress of chiefs
took place in the ancient long hall while the townspeople
crowded the forum and basilica colonnades to see for themselves the coming and going of lords and princes of the far
north-west and north-east and from Cymru beyond the Sabrina,
and – from Demetia in the far south of Cymru – the flamboyant
figure of Difynwal, young and headstrong and heedless of the
distant Saxon threat since his country was still hard-pressed by
Scotti invasions and settlement.

In those first days at Glevum there was much coming and
going and private meetings between all these men both with
and without Arturo. In those first days, too, the magic which already cloaked Arturo and his name grew, flourishing fast among
the townspeople, then with the young warriors from the north
who each in his bold, impatient heart knew himself to be another Arturo and longed for the liberty to escape from tribelands to march and fight and readily to risk any death to snatch
at honour and fame. And, in those days, wherever he went
Arturo – since Durstan and Lancelo had their own affairs to
marshal – took Pasco with him, Pasco the shabby, shuffling
priest whose eyes missed no passing shadow of doubt or shrewd-
ness on a man's face and whose memory held every word
spoken in store to be brought out against a man's turn of spirit

or to prompt a man from hesitation when fear or greed silently possessed him.

Sitting alone late one night, and seeing Arturo lapse into a rare, silent mood of introspection, Pasco smiled and said gently, 'My lord, you told me once that you honour all gods and given them all worship, and true this seems for they have withheld no favours from you. Now comes the moment when you have to draw these little earthy gods of flesh and blood together and gain their favour. I think you find this a greater matter. Favour one above the others and this pantheon of tribes becomes a squabbling family.'

For a moment Arturo said nothing. Then, loosening the scarf about his throat, for the night was warm, he smiled and said, 'Tis no easy matter, but it will be and must be possible since the truth is that they are all of one family, no matter where their lands lie, no matter the blood lines they carry. They are the family of Britain, Britain which has fathered them. Whoever attacks one member of that family attacks them all. The young wolves fight amongst themselves for leadership. But when winter hunger rib-strakes their flanks they hunt as one. So with these men – they still do not see that there is a hunger creeping over this land which must be stayed – the hunger of the Saxons for land and living space. So long as the Saxons hold their own, then time and the years go with them and against us. Their eyes must be opened. So that the light of truth floods in.'

'And you will do that when the gathering of chiefs takes place?'

'By the grace of the gods, yes –and their grace I have, and for it give humble thanks. This is a gathering Count Ambrosius longed to see. Much he did against me but I would for his honour have him living and be in my place at the meeting to come. Aye – though there is the difference between us that he dreamt of seeing himself Emperor – whereas I dream only of one thing, to be Commander of the armies of the kings of Britain in this war.'

For a moment or two it was on the tip of Pasco's tongue to

say that a commander of kings must of right then be the greatest of kings but, seeing the dark intensity of feeling show on Arturo's face, he said mildly, 'And when the great battle is won, what do you do, what will you have become, my lord?'

Surprising him, Arturo grinned and said lightly, 'Why, I shall be my own man again. Free to walk without care through the long summer grasses with my wife, to mark with an untroubled mind the flight of the blue down butterfly, to hold a falcon on my wrist and slip it free to hang high and wait for the flushed wildfowl ... Aye, free to travel any road or track in this land without fear and to see men smile in good will to one another, and free to hold close to my wife and kin with the humble joy of any ploughman or woodcutter. Men were not born for battle. They were born for the good business of enjoying the fruits and blessings of this earth with which the gods have dowered us ...

Quietly but boldly Pasco said, 'The gods have always this in their power yet withhold it, my lord.'

'True – but the gods have their reasons which neither the eye nor the mind of man can read. But good reasons they must be and we must await their revelation patiently.'

Four days later the meeting of the kings and chiefs was held in the hall of the basilica. All the men stood and carried their arms and had at their sides a grown son or trusted warrior. Arturo stood at the top of the steps at the end of the hall and four Companions in full war gear stood on the lowest step as bodyguard. They were Durstan, Lancelo, Gelliga and Coroticus of the Summerlands. Bareheaded, wearing the long surcoat given to him by the Bishop of Noviomagus, sword belted about it, Arturo faced them with Cabal couched at his side. Sunlight coming through the high windows of the hall drew rusty glints in his hair and there was a set to his tall figure into which the waiting men, each according to his temper and his own ambitions, read arrogance and pride, the firmness of true authority, or the boldness of courage sustaining a great dream. But there was none that could truly deny the force in the stance of the man and the magic of personality which against all odds had set him where he was that day.

And that day, as he spoke, there was no denial of the gift of tongue which the gods had given him. When he spoke of the Saxons his words were sword sharp; when he spoke of this country, their Britain, it was now the voice of a lover, now the gentle tones of a son to his mother; when he spoke of the need to hold and further strengthen the long line against the Saxons, to give them no westward freedom so that either they must come out in force and make battle or slowly be pressed to the sea, his words were cold, and iron-hard and relentless with the logic of a far-seeing Caesar, and when he came to name them all, one and separately, with the call to be made on them for men and provisions and the duties which they would have to accept he spoke evenly and without emotion as a commander making clear the ordering of the battle lines for the coming clash with the enemy.

When he spoke of the dream of the dead Ambrosius, which was now his dream, he did so with truth, sparing neither fault on the side of Ambrosius nor the arrogance of spirit on his own, and ended with a plea without weakness, saying, 'The like of this day will not come again. The gods in their wisdom send no new day's tide to order the grains of sand on the shore as they ever were before. The great sea tides of this world march under the gods' design, but the full tide of our country's greatness they will hold back forever while there is one least man amongst us who deceives and plots only to feed his own lust for power and riches. Now is the day when the tide of this great country's glory is at the low. But now is the time, and now rests the power in your hands, if you have the courage and the heart and the wisdom, to give me command and men and arms to make battle to win back what is ours. Tread on the adder and it strikes, the wild boar defends its own . . . aye, put your hand under the breast of the gentle dove to rob its nest and it will draw blood with its blows. Are we then to be less than the beasts and to sit quietly and await the slaughter from the east?

Under the gods I say I am not, and under the gods my heart tells me that you are not, for there can be no man here who would wish to be known by his children and their children to come as one who lived and died a craven. You are the kings and lords of this country. Give me the means to bring it back to its true glory . . .'

As he finished speaking, his hand dropping and touching the rough head of Cabal at his side, there was silence in the hall. From outside came the sound of the sparrows quarrelling along the colonnade roof and the rattle of a cart's wheels over the Forum paving stones.

Looking at the gathered leaders, bearded, weathered of face, and most carrying the open and hidden scars of war, their cloaks and furs and robes and kilts making a field of colour, a field at this moment which knew no breeze to stir it to life, Arturo knew the passing of the moments of destiny when all that was needed for his triumph was for one man to stand forward, draw sword or raise spear and cry 'Arto!' His lips firmed wryly at the thought that there had been in his mind long before that such a man could have been bought by him to play this part and with one shout set to work the great yeasting in men's hearts which he must have. But he had set his face against this. Ambrosius would have had it so, but not he. Either the gods touched these men to follow him or he would turn from them and travel his own path and wear down the years of his life with the same spirit and stubbornness that had wrung from him in new manhood the rash promise of Arto.

Then from the front ranks of the company stepped forward young king Difynwal of Demetia, his long black locks greased so that they shone with the bloom of a raven's wing, a gold torque about his brown neck, his stiff beard cropped short to a hedgehog's bristle, and a great chequered cloak of reds, greens, yellows and white billowing over his shoulders and arms and, from the belt about his waist, a short sword hanging from his side. Behind him stood his young son holding the tall standard from which hung the great round shield of Demetia on which was blazoned the fire-breathing red dragon of their country.

Boldly, his voice echoing in the shadowed roof spaces, Difynwal spoke.

'You call for men and arms to come to your command, great Arto. And there is none here with true heart or mind to refuse you this. But what warrior is there who goes to battle with a red heart and an iron hand if he leaves behind him kith and kin in peril? What victory is there when the returning bow or spearman climbs the crag to mountain home or rides the glen to farm and family – and finds death and fire and rapine have gone before him. You would have us face the east and the Saxons ... *Aie*, that is all our wish. Have you forgotten that your mighty Esc and his chiefs are leagued with the Scotti warriors and shipmen and they raid the coasts of the West from the mouth of the Sabrina river to the headland of Octapitarum in my lands and north to the island of Mona and the straits of Segontium and north again to the Ituna estuary and the shores of the lands of the Novantae? They press us back from our own shores, and when we find strength to press against them they move away in their long curraghs and strike again like a moving swarm of hornets where there are few to make stand against them. The gods have been with you. We all praise your triumphs. We all would cry you Duke of War, Commander of the armies of the kings of Britain, but this cannot be for we have no warriors with the wish to go East to win glory and then coming back to the West find none to share his triumphs, and the nettles and charlock of despair growing through the bones of his loved ones, his hearth cold and open to the sky ... no joy of wife and sweetheart, no red and yellow cattle in the glen, no proud ram to stand and stamp his foot and marshal the ewes and lambs. Rid me of the men from Erin and you shall have the great part of my men. And know this, I speak not alone for myself.' He half-turned to the chiefs behind him, and cried, 'Look and see those who know the truth of my words and have felt and still endure the suffering of their people. Aye, the gods are with you, but the Scotti are with us and our swords demand their blood!' He drew his sword and raised it and, as he did so, from more than half of the men behind him came also a raising of swords and spears and a swelling roar like the call of a high sea comber in the moment of breaking on the shore.

When the noise had died and the last sword had been lowered and sheathed, Arto spoke and Pasco, lost in the crowd, listened to him wondering at the change in his manner of speaking and in the man himself. He spoke now as though from an age far beyond his years, and with a gentle patience, each word well-honed, but, when he needed, there came the soft burr in his Dumnonian touched voice, now a caress and now a sad chiding, and he began :

'The first man I killed ... aye, and that long before I found a taste for kissing and cuddling the maidens of my tribe ... was a Scottus. I cut his throat with a dagger on the sands at night. And when I was youth, I stood and fought the night raiders from the sea with the men of my tribe. With the passing of years, and the growing of my hatred for the Saxon men do you think I have forgotten the Scotti? Do you think I would ask you to give me men to go East and have no care for the West? What great command could I claim from you if I were so stiff-necked and one-eyed that I could not see double danger and turn to meet it? Know this then, without their long-planked and hide-plated curraghs the Scotti are as my Companions would be without horses. When you press them to the sea they take to their boats. But now the days of their boats are numbered. From far Belerium's point there sailed a handful of days ago a fleet of warships, greater in number and size than any the Scotti command, and this fleet will take watch and ward and make battle with the Scotti wherever they be met off our western shores. And the man who commands them has no more love for Saxon or Scotti than we have. Though –' he grinned, '– he is man enough to want payment for his services and the first part of this has already been found from the Dumnonian treasury at Isca. The rest must be met from the war levies laid on us all ... gold and silver and stores for his ships and harbouring for them. No land grants such as Vortigern gave to Hengist and Horsa. This man lives by the sea and his men are of all nations with their homes far to the south in the country of the Goths below

Gaul. This man is Theodoric and he waits now off the mouth of the Sabrina for the beacons on your hills to be fired to bring him into your waters, to scour them free of the Scotti.'

Arto paused and in the silence that held the assembly of chiefs his eyes found those of Difynwal and held them steadily. Then with slow, deliberate words he went on, 'Great Difynwal, I have answered you. I am no beggar to plead with any man for alms for my country. I am no pedlar to haggle over a deal for my country's honour. I seek only the glory which was and must be again hers, and if any in this hall turn his back to me now he turns his back on his country's gods, on his fellows-in-arms against the Saxons. Living there shall be no honour in him and his women and children shall take no joy in him, and dying there shall be no welcome in the Shades for him. I am Arto and have given you my promise. Now, let those who would go tend cattle, lie warm at nights with wives and sweethearts, let them go. I would sooner have a beardless boy with fire in his belly than a grown man whose spirit is a timid hare to send him running at the distant sound of hounds. I am Arto and, with or without you, shall take no rest, nor know any settled hearth until I have done what the gods have commanded me to do.'

For a moment or two none spoke or moved and all eyes watched the two men who had gathered to themselves the ordering of this moment and knew each that the balancing of the future was weighted evenly between them. Against his side Arturo felt Cabal rise to his feet and the soft muzzle came to his hand, while below him Difynwal stood grim-faced and unmoving. Then with a slow movement Difynwal drew his sword, and there were those who thought for bloody work, and he walked up to Arturo and as he came so that only Arturo saw, he smiled, but needed not the smile for Cabal beneath his hand was without sound or stiffening of muscle. At Arturo's side Difynwal turned, raised his sword, and shouted, setting the echoes ringing in the roof, 'Arto! Arto!'

Before the echoes died all men in the hall drew sword or raised spear and the echoes rang again and again, 'Arto! Arto! Arto!'

And Pasco watching, seeing Arturo and Difynwal embrace, remembered the first days of the beginning at the Villa of the Three Nymphs, remembered the marriage of Arto and Daria, the springtime of their love, and the springtime of Arto's manhood; and he knew that now again the season of Arturo's life had changed and, because he gently questioned all God's movements in the affairs of men, yet had no lack of faith, he could find in himself no true happiness for Arturo. From this day he lived apart from men.

The Immortal Wound

There were no doubts in Gwennifer. Arturo was Commander of the armies of the British kings. It was a title as clumsy and shambling as the movements of a crippled beast unable to fend for itself. The title would die. But not Arturo. King he would be and once named it would be forever. Through his sons his glory would live. Borio had failed her, but there were others and now that she was at Glevum and bore herself like a queen to all men there could be no bar to her desire and no mercy shown to any man, no matter his rank, who should smile out of place or boast with or without truth of her brief and long-spaced favours. Always there was with her Lacus, the groom, to use poison or dagger or the turn of designed but innocent-seeming accident.

But while time and time again she remained barren there were those who knew the truth without sound of words or sight of deed, knew just as rain still a day's coming could be smelt in the wind. All kept their counsel. Arturo stood highest in the land and with the full weight of affairs now on him showed a change under which in a few years the old Arturo was buried to all except a few chosen of his Companions. Only when he rode or made camp for night in some small party with a handful of tried friends would he talk of old times for a while.

In public and campaigning affairs he was ruthless with any who failed him, expecting all men to push themselves to the bounds of their strength and faith as he did himself. And for the most part men did this, for the torch which had been fired in the basilica flared high and bright over the land. For those few whose levies or dues to the war chest fell short there was no mercy. No matter the distance and the days it cost, Arturo

would ride with a force of his Companions and there was then
no withstanding his demands for now, as many of the shrewder
chiefs and small kings had seen without fear, for they had no
desire in themselves for it, his power had grown from the day
they had acclaimed him Commander. As the years passed he
gained an ease and assurance from the knowledge that the men
who now served him in the field and garrisons took pride in
him, matching their prowess and dedication with his. They were
part of him and apart from all men who were strangers to his
service. The young sons of tribal chiefs and kings itched to
come of age so that they could join him ... aye, even if it only
meant that they did duty on the Saxon line in idleness during
winter cherishing their memories of the scarce summer days of
sword-blooding when some rash Saxon warrior had led a foray
against them, fretting against the imprisonment of his own en-
clave. Youth and young manhood held to Arto and many a
chief's son shamed his father from trimming his levy or hoard-
ing his wealth when Arto called.

These were years when there were no great battles; these
were the years when the slow turn of fortune in favour of the
Britons began. The weight of Theodoric's ships and men slowly
began to clear the west coasts of the Scotti threat and found
them, losing stomach for fight, moving far north to pillage and
settle along the shores of the land of the Picts. These were the
years when the garrisoning and patrolling of the Saxon line
penned in the warriors of Esc and his chiefs and brought to Esc
the truth that, with the dwindling of the Scotti threat in the
rear of the Britons, the time must come when he would have to
march out in force and drive westwards to break the budding
might of Arturo for ever. And these were the years when many
a night Arturo sat late in his chamber at Glevum or Isca or
Deva pondering the reports and messages that came to him from
paid or willing place men amongst his Saxon foes. Dead Ambrosius had strung this network and now Arturo spread it
wider, and from his gleanings he knew that it would be many
years before the itch in his men for true and full battle would
be eased by any great march west by Esc. But, though he knew

that the time of Esc's coming lay years ahead, Arto lived and planned and worked to strengthen his armies and secure his garrisons and posts as though time were pressing him hard. The gods might at any time ferment the slow yeast to fast rising.

They now had at Corinium near five hundred great horses, manned and equipped and held under the command of Durstan with Gelliga to second him. Lancelo, grown man now, he kept with him as he moved through the country, and it was to Lancelo now, more than Durstan, that he sometimes showed his heart. Towards the end of the year four hundred and ninety as they rode for Isca with a troop of horse Arturo, finding the turning of the leaves as the year died and the soft mists shrouding thinly the countryside moving him to melancholy, felt an unexpected need to ease some of the lone burden he bore. His years were forty now, and with the passing of each year the running out of time seemed to speed ever faster. As a young man a day was an age, giving time for the conquering of a world. Now his days were so hard-pressed that they slipped through his hands like running sand

Riding well ahead of the troop on the White One, the third now of that name, and a new hound Cabal alongside him – for the old Cabal was two years dead, gored to death by a boar at hunting – he spoke to Lancelo without turning to him and said, ''Twas this road from Corinium that you rode with your father, Ansold, and your sister Daria to bring them first to the Villa of the Three Nymphs.'

'Aye, my lord. A day when the young beard on my chin was as soft as goslings' down.'

'You have served well, Lancelo, and have always been true Companion, but more – you are my brother through your sister Daria, my true wife. Have you ever turned the truth from me, Lancelo?'

Puzzled, Lancelo said, 'We ride at different gaits, my lord.'

'Aye, but side by side.'

'There has never been else but truth between us. Am I not your man, your brother?'

'You are – and because you are that you would give me no

grief or pain. But now I speak plainly and would know a truth and you must answer plainly with no trimming of your words. I walked the rounds at Corinium two nights ago. There was a mist and I heard two guards talking about their fire. That I was there they did not know, that they live still comes from the charity of the gods who stayed my hand. They spoke ill of my lady Gwennifer. Tell me, Lancelo – did they speak the truth?'

Lancelo bit his under lip and was tempted to lie for the sake of their friendship. Then, knowing that a lie from him now would serve no purpose, for truth would come some other road, he said, 'It is the truth, my lord.'

Arturo turned and smiled at him 'For that I thank you. Look not so glum. I am in good company for many a man from Caesars down to charcoal burners have worn the horns. You should know, Lancelo, that most often when the gods give greatness they season it in a man with a spice of ridicule to curb him from thinking himself more than mortal. Mortal I am and chafe not against it. That the gods spoke for me and made sign when I was born is enough.'

On his first night at Isca as Gwennifer sat at her mirror combing her long hair before retiring, while a south-westerly roared the long length of Dumnonia and shook the closed wooden shutters of the window and the flames of the tall candles swayed in the draughts Arturo, cradling a glass of wine in his palms, spoke to Gwennifer, his eyes on her and no anger in him.

'It was written by Merlin before my birth that I should throw no seed to flower. Merlin whom I have met a few times is a man whose words should always be marked with care. The truth in them is as hard to tell as the counting of the scales on a salmon or the numbering of bubbles in a beaker of cider.'

Gwennifer turned slowly to him. 'You talk in riddles, my lord.'

'No, I talk frankly and without anger. Seed I have and it is good seed and it grew in the body of Daria – but the gods denied it flowering.' He smiled. 'Good Merlin is always a little less than exact and a little more teasing than truthful. The gods have marked me for greatness but for long now I have understood that in their wisdom they will give me no heir in flesh to hold and increase my heritage. Would you know why?'

Firming mind and body now against the unexpectedness of this talk, but grateful for the lack of anger in him, Gwennifer said, 'Yes, my lord, I would. If greatness is your part why should there be none of your blood to inherit and increase it? There is shame in me, but that it was done, this thing I did, then it was done to cheat the gods and glorify your name when you were gone. In that lies all my love for you.'

'Your love for me is clear but ill designed. That you have not borne a child to foster on the world as mine lies in your own barrenness. My seed is good but at its first shooting the gods would wither it and the womb that held it. You wonder that I am not angry with you and send you from me?'

'Yes, my lord, I do, for I have deserved both.'

'No. What you did was out of love for me. But now there must be an end of it for there is no ripeness in you. Wife you are, but never mother ...' He stood up and went to her and she rose from her stool to him. Facing her, he saw the slow start of tears in her blue eyes and his nostrils were full of the perfume of her tall, slender body and the candlelight streaked her hair with soft shadows. He took her in his arms and held her to him and against his cheek he felt hers touched now with the dew of her falling tears and her body shook with the slow rack of her sobs.

Later in the darkness, as they lay abed with the night full still of the great shout of the gale winds, Gwennifer said, 'You would have told me why the gods who give you greatness give you no heir to inherit, my lord.'

'And tell you I will, but you must mark my words as you would those of a Merlin. I am not born in this land for the first time. This country has known me before in its hour of need and I have given it peace and greatness, and shall give it that again during this life and then dying shall rest in chaos until I am called again to restore its glory ...' He was silent for a while and then, with a little grunt, went on, 'You think that both a puzzle and a dream? Well it may seem so, but it is also a truth beyond explaining. Some men there are who are marked by the gods with an immortal wound. They die the death of this earth but not the death of the gods .. and they sleep a while until the gods call them from darkness to know the joy again of the rising sun, to hear the neighing and tramp of the waiting war horses in the meadow, and the cries of misery from their oppressed countrymen whose ills they must set to flight again ...' He yawned suddenly and then laughed. '*Aie* ... I was long a-seeing it – but true it is.'

He put out an arm and drew her to him and kissed her tenderly and then as he felt the tips of her fingers caress his forehead, he went on, 'So take no fear from me. Tomorrow you are born again and we shall ride out on the water meadows into a new world to watch the fall of the red and brown leaf, the flick of the white scuts of the moorfowl in the sedges, see the great oaks wrought black like shaped iron against the rising sun, and I shall be your love and you mine and we shall both be content to live under the will of the gods whose judgement is beyond any man's knowing.'

In the year that followed, old Ansold the swordmaker, the father of Daria and Lancelo, died sitting at a tavern bench in Isca after a heavy day at his smithy. He finished his mead sitting among friends and then, as though the drink had fuddled his head, he bent forward and rested his forehead on his arms. Thinking him sleeping his friends laughed and talked teasingly to him until one touched his shoulder a little roughly and the old man slid sideways from the bench to the ground. He was buried not far from Borio above the horse grounds and close to his smithy where the sound of hooves on the ground and hammers shaping the iron for stirrups kept him company. Two months later Lancelo married a young woman from Corinium called Hylda whom Gwennifer took as a companion and found no envy against her when she was soon pregnant, took pride in all knowing it, and had no shame when the child was born six months after the marriage.

In that year as the campaign season opened with the firming of the ground and the dying of floods from the valleys, Adipo, the son of the chief of the Durotriges and the husband of Arturo's sister, Gerta, came to Corinium with the levy of warriors from his father. With him came Gerta and their ten-year-old son Mordreth, who spent his days with the troopers on the cavalry grounds of the Sabrina Wing, learnt fast all barrack talk and oaths, and loved horses with a passion untouched by fear. He worshipped his uncle Arturo and found quickly a way to his heart and favour for he was the nearest to a son, Arto knew, that he would ever have. He set him up on the broad back of the White One with a wooden sword in his hand and let him circle the tan bark ring, shouting and calling. When the White One half bucked playfully from the laughter and the cries of the troopers he fell heavily only to pick himself up, his small dark face straining to hold back cry or tear, and demanded to be remounted. Arturo came to love the boy as near son – and shrugged off the sharp talk from Gerta at his indulgence of the boy.

In that year too, beginning with the lesser chiefs who had favours to seek for the placing of their sons or, since the times were quiet, asked leave to stay men from their levies for sowing and cropping and cattle-minding, there were those who addressed him as 'Royal Arto' and – since they were seldom refused their wishes – the habit spread. Arturo kept his pleasure to himself and was content to let the gods shape the weather of his ambitions, knowing that king he would be since they were willing it and the country – as Ambrosius had long ago seen – needed a man to stand above all others in sovereignty.

In that year too Cerdic of the West Saxon settlements stirred again and Arturo sent word to the Bishop of Noviomagus and the Chief Citizen of Venta to keep him supplied with all they could find of Cerdic's thinking and planning, and was content to wait until that tree was in full bearing before he should cut it to the ground. He knew, too, that Cerdic was in full league with Esc and could be watched as a weather gauge to the coming moves of the Saxon leader. That the move would not now be long delayed, he knew to be true for in all the Saxon enclaves men were restless and called for an end to their penning and craved the liberty to move west to the days of fighting and plunder and the nights of drunken boasting.

In that year, too, Oleric, the son of Theodoric, married a daughter of king Difynwal and was given a land grant in Demetia, and many of Theodoric's men married girls from the towns and settlements of the sea coast of Cymru so that the fleet was slowly being bonded to the land with ties stronger than any stout hempen hawser The valley of the Tamesis was peaceful except for a few small bands of cut-throats and outlawed men, both Britons and Saxons, who gave sport and good training to the unblooded and untried young men of the levies who were sent there. Londinium began to prosper but few men chose to live within its broken walls except merchants and traders and craftsmen and that these made trade with Esc's people gave Arturo no worry. That the Saxons should buy where before they had robbed was no pleasure to Esc or his chiefs and must shorten their tempers and the days to come before they moved in strength.

In the summer of that year Baradoc, now near his sixtieth year, took Tia with him to Aquae Sulis where he was working on the defences of an old hill fort to the east of the town and they were lodged in the old villa of her uncle, the long dead Chief Centurion Truvius. They would eat in the courtyard under the shade of the great sweet chestnut tree, the courtyard in which they had been married. One evening sitting there Tia looked across at Baradoc, weathered, stiff-armed, hair now greying fast, and teasingly she said:

> 'Over the silver stream hunts the four-winged fly
> Each eye holds a thousand eyes
> But he sees not your beauty'

Baradoc spooning up from his bowl wild raspberries laced with sweet wine smiled. 'Prettily said. After a day in the sweat and labour of digging, with one's ears deafened by shouts and hammerings, there is no balm like the music of poetry.'

Tia ran the tip of her tongue between her lips to stay her laughter and found more words for him :

> 'I would have built for you a house with a
> roof of green rushes and a flower-pied floor.
> A thousand seabirds would have greeted the
> golden girl with a brow like a lily, the
> young queen who rode the perilous paths
> without harm or hurt.'

Baradoc looked up, his face a little puzzled, and wiped fruit juice from his mouth with the back of his hand. 'I praise the man who made the words. I would like to have shaped them myself and spoken them for you ... *Aie*, there was a time in my youth when I could sweet-talk my love.'

Tia hid her smile behind her hand for the words were his and belonged to the days when they had travelled to Aquae Sulis and had stayed in this villa. But they were gone from his memory. Man wooed and spoke love words but when the wooing was done the years took their words from them. The past was a load which could not be carried forever by them, unlike a woman who hoarded its rare treasures never to lose them. Yet, as the thought ran with her, Baradoc suddenly shook his head, laughing, and he rose and came to her and kissed her on the forehead and said, 'Aye, now I remember. The last of the words I wrote here in this yard by moonlight for you ... on ... on, yes, the wax of your uncle's old ivory tablet.'

The next morning as she lay abed by herself, Baradoc having ridden away to work before dawn, she listened to the screaming of the swifts as they hawked over the river below the terrace slopes and the calm joy on her face moved suddenly to a tightening wince of pain. Her hand went to her right side, pressing against it to ease the sharp bite which with the passing of this last winter had begun to assault her more and more. The gods, she knew, had nearly marked the full tally of her days and she would share the secret with no one. She died in the autumn while she made visit with Baradoc to his tribal lands on the north coast of Dumnonia, moving to sleep in his arms at night and passing to the Shades before dawn broke.

She was buried on the clifftop under a high cairn of boulders in sight of distant Caer Sibli where she had brought Arturo into the world, buried with the purple bloom of the heather moorland behind her and before her the tall cliffs rising over the gold and white sands where the seabirds wheeled and called and the red-legged choughs scavenged and quarrelled along the rock faces. She was of full Roman blood, rare now in the land, and her only living son was Arturo to whom the news came a month later as he rode south from Eburacum to winter at Glevum.

That night in camp on the road, Arturo walked through the willows of the riverside grove where they rested, alone except for Cabal, and knew the regret that all men have for the passing of a loved mother, and regret, too, that time and affairs had forced them apart. Daria and his mother he had now lost. Loneliness and loss was the constant lot of all god-touched men for they had a greater family to serve. There was a shame in him, too, that evening as he walked by the riverside, his face brushed by the passing of the night moths, his eyes and ears aware of all sound and stir. the splash of a foraging water rat, the brief gleam of a glow-worm under a dock leaf and the screech of a little owl, for there was a part of his thoughts which rode free of his grief because with the news of Tia's death had come also news from his spies who served him from the lands of Esc. With the coming of spring Esc meant to move out against him, but not with a full force, to test his readiness and the quickness with which he could marshal and move men against him. To crush such a move ruthlessly he knew would defer Esc's full effort for years. The Saxons should be encouraged to think that for all his strength he lacked the skill to manage it quickly. Esc should be encouraged.

That winter at Isca the young Prince Cato, not much older than Mordreth, began to show a rebellious, imperious nature, resenting the wardship of Baradoc. He had the courage of his father but not his understanding, and the arrogance of his grandfather but an ambition which was far narrower, seeking only pride and pleasure and power for himself. Mordreth was brought to Isca to keep him company and there were few weeks when they were not in disgrace. They were young hawks eager for the onset of their moult to adult plumage. For only one person were they gentle and obedient to hand, and that was Gwennifer who saved them many a beating and days of sour bread and water for their escapades. It was, too, through the unruly boys that Gwennifer met Merlin for the first time.

She was riding down the river towards the horse enclosure one afternoon of frost-bright sunshine when she heard cries coming from ahead. Breaking from a small alder growth on the river bank she saw Mordreth and Cato shouting and laughing as they danced around a brown-cloaked man with long black hair and an unkempt beard. They were pelting him with addled eggs from an ancient and spring-deserted swan's nest which they had found in the reeds. As soon as the man rushed at one, striking out with his staff, the other attacked him from behind, and both the boys were too nimble and alert to take any harm from him.

Setting her horse to a canter she bore down on the boys who, seeing her coming and recognizing her, ran away up the hill-slope and disappeared over the road towards Isca. As she pulled up in front of the man he plucked a handful of browned dead grasses and began to wipe egg mess from the front of his robe. Looking up at her as he did this, he grimaced wryly and said, 'You came at a good time, my lady Gwennifer. A few more moments and I would have lost patience with their antics and cracked their skulls with my stave.'

'You would have needed their nimbleness.'

'And could have found it. But I was content to mark them and make some study of them.'

'Why so?'

'Time will show why.'

'You talk in riddles.'

'When I need, my lady. But I can beg alms or a night's lodging boldly like any homeless man. Nay, reach not for your belt purse. I need no alms from you, my lady.' He picked broken egg shell from his beard, wiped his messy fingers on his robe and went on, 'You are fortunate to stand up wind of me, my lady Gwennifer.'

'To right the ill done to you, you shall come to Isca and be given fresh clothes and lodgings – and the boys shall be whipped.'

Merlin laughed. 'I need neither clothes nor lodging. But see the boys whipped. It is time their hides were seasoned. And give my good remembrances to your husband, Great Arto.'

'How shall I name you?'

'You know not that already, my lady?'

The truth came slowly to Gwennifer and with it she felt the mantling of blood in her cheeks. 'You are the one who wrote – His glory an everlasting flower ... He throws no seed.'

Merlin smiled. 'With a fine pointed slate in his hand and a bare rock face before him ... aye, why then I am the kind of man who itches to fill its smoothness with words. I could have as easily written – Fish with a feathered hook in these waters and the gods will give you jade-flanked mackerel.'

'But you did not.'

'All poetry comes from the gods and we must abide their choice of the moment. Time is a succession of small accidents arranged by the gods.'

'And why have they arranged this time and chance to bring us together?'

'Could it be that, no matter the truth of the words on the rock, you would have cheated them?'

Angry, Gwennifer said, 'You talk over boldly now, master Merlin. Yes, I would have cheated them, and if there were new hope to show him my love would cheat them again. Men have many gods but a woman has only one – the man she loves.'

'Well spoken, and true.'

'Against all the gods I say that Arto will be Great King of this country and should have sons to harvest the fruits of his victories.'

Merlin put a hand up to the muzzle of her horse and gentled it as it stirred restlessly under her. 'There are no fruits of victory with the sword. Seasons of quiet, yes. The real conquest comes not from the men who invade a country or the men who defend it. The good earth of the country, shaped by the rains and rivers and the seasons, is always victor. It is the land and the seasons over it which conquer – not the warriors.'

'Now you talk in riddles again.'

Merlin shrugged his shoulders. 'It is a simple one, my lady – except that you would have to live all the years of your life and a thousand more to know it.'

Angry still and now impatient with the man, Gwennifer said sharply, pique strong in her voice, 'I think you are no more than a fool who makes idle play with the first words that come into your head. So be it – and now, go tell the gods, who made me barren for their sport, that they have my curses!' Then, as she wheeled away and was poised to set her mount to a gallop, she called back over her shoulder, 'And the boys shall not be beaten!'

Smiling, Merlin watched her go and disappear down the road to Isca. Then holding his nose to shut out the stink of addled egg he went to the river to wash, chuckling to himself at the flash of fire there had been in Gwennifer's eyes. No matter her deeds she was true wife to Arturo and the gods would take her curses indulgently.

The Breaking of the Saxons

In the early spring Arturo went north to Glevum leaving Gelliga in command of very much reduced forces both at Isca and Cam Hill and the other fortified camps. Before he went he spoke alone with Gelliga at Cam Hill, the two of them sitting in the strengthening sunshine outside his quarters where none could overhear them. Gelliga's face grew doleful as he listened.

'They will come this year, and long before summer. Esc's men from the east, keeping south of the Tamesis and there will be a joining with them by Aelle and Cerdic from the south. You will call your men together from the forts. But make no great haste in the matter, as though the surprise of their coming has left you in doubt whether you should make full battle with them or wait until you can get help from me from the north.'

'That gives me a bitter taste in my mouth even now, my lord.'

'Then swallow it. I want Esc to think that these past years of success have turned us too confident and slow to act. Harry them and harass them, but make no stand to block their way. They will only come so far to test us – and I want them to find us surprised and slow to act. By the time I come south they will be on their way back to their own lands, and Esc will think that in a few more years he can come again in full strength and overrun the whole length of the Tamesis valley ... aye, and press on to Aquae Sulis to split the country in two and so gain the rich southern half for himself. Where the young wolves wanton this season, the whole wolf pack will come in later years – and we shall then make the full killing.'

Gelliga sighed. 'You live ahead of me, my lord. I am still in the old days when if the Saxons moved we went to meet them with the sword and lance.'

Arturo plucked a young grass stalk and chewed on it. 'No more. In these days if a commander has true cunning the battle must be won before the first sword is drawn and the great horses put to the gallop. All I say here is between us. If men speak against me saying I left you ill prepared and came late to your help . . . well,' he grinned, sliding the grass stalk to the side of his mouth, 'agree with them and grumble a little with them. There will be much spoken against me and I want the sound of it to reach Esc.'

Gelliga laughed. 'Arto the bear, men call you. But you have learnt the cunning of a serpent. Aye, I will make hard words against you my lord, but only from my mouth, not my heart.'

There were a few others to whom Arturo spoke as he had done with Gelliga; Difynwal of Demetia, Loth the father of Gwennifer who was marshal now of the far northern forces, Baradoc his father, and the father of his brother-in-law Adipo, the chief of the Durotriges who held the country west of the Vectis sea . . . all men in whom he had trust.

And that year the Saxons marched as he had known they would. They came three hundred strong from Esc and were joined by two hundred men from the West Saxon shore, and they spread death and took plunder and slaves along the Tamesis. Aelle and Cerdic, ignoring Noviomagus and Venta, went close about the western end of the forest of Anderida and joined Esc's men at Calleva and rumours and tales of bloody slaughter went winging like black crows over the country. Among Gelliga's men as they rode and shadowed the Saxons, harrying and harassing them when they could but too weak to oppose them boldly, there was grumbling at and some scorn for Arturo who was slow in coming down the old road from Glevum, through Corinium and Spinis to Calleva with the great horses and his foot troops. When he arrived, to find the Saxons long on their way back to their lands and no hope left of catching and bringing them to battle, there were even those among the most faithful of the Companions – Lancelo and Durstan and others – who found their loyalty to his good name and leadership hard pressed. This Arturo suffered for he knew it would pass. It was better to lose a little of their love and faith for a few years than to give them the truth to spill when the drink ran in the halls at night and so find its way to Esc.

With Prince Cato and Mordreth, youths now, there was anger in the one and disappointment in the other. Sunning themselves one afternoon on the Isca fortress parapet walk Cato said angrily, 'He grows lazy and too content with the thought of his coming kingship. Aye, and look how he bears himself here. Am I the Prince of Dumnonia or is he? Dumnonia's money, not his, has paid for Theodoric and for the breeding and manning of the great horses.'

Mordreth said loyally, 'All money well spent. And I think you talk too soon – like a cock deceived by a late moonrise. There is more in all this than can be openly read.'

'You share his blood and so you stand for him.'

Pugnaciously Mordreth answered, 'Aye, I do. And if you call him badly without truth – then I will spill yours!' He moved towards Cato, his fists raised ready for fight.

'Then try it – for I tell you blood he will spill in time. And that mine. With me gone he will call himself Prince of Dumnonia, name his blood royal, and so use me as footstool to climb to kingship.'

Moving close to Cato, Mordreth, his body taut with anger, said, 'You speak so because you itch for your wardship to be ended. So now take back the words for nobody to my face links Arto's name with murder.'

For answer Cato spat in Mordreth's face. They fought, rolling and tumbling on the parapet, their angry shouting sending the jackdaws skyward and eventually bringing a guard and Master Ricat, old now but far from lacking strength and authority, to pull them apart and clout their heads. Of their quarrel Ricat asked nothing for scarcely a week went by without a fight between them or the two of them falling into mischief.

Gwennifer knowing the murmurings against Arturo understood his mind without need for telling from him. In some ways she had the mind of a man and could guess the thinking of Arto. Knowing his love of his country and its people she knew, too, the hardship of his feelings and the depth of his compassion for the men and women who had been exposed to the Saxon march and who had been pillaged and killed to make the coming bait for the trap he would set. Battle was in Arturo's blood but beyond this he was, unless the gods called for it, a hoarder of the lives of his warriors. That autumn when he came to her at Isca there were times when she woke late at night and knew him to be lying alongside her untouched by sleep. Without need of words she would rest her cheek against his bare shoulder and his arm would go round her taking the voiceless comfort she offered.

The next year as though he feared that Esc would strike again, Arturo moved the main part of his forces eastwards, splitting it to stand in readiness in the south below Londinium and in the north based on Ratae and Durovigutum. But no move came except for a few small raids and attacks made by wayward and venturesome Saxon parties. The following year he did the same as though to stamp on Esc's mind that he had learnt the lesson of unreadiness and would not be caught again. But that winter he set the trap for the taking of the Saxons.

Through the merchants, traders and people of Londinium he started the rumour running that the Picts in the far north were massing to move south with the Spring. By packman and pedlars and paid agents he fed the tale of the coming of the Picts to the Saxon enclaves, and long before the turn of the year he began to send men and horses north to Glevum, stripping forces south of the Tamesis ruthlessly from the march line which Esc must take to gain a lasting hold on the country. Men and horses went north. They were raw levies, barely trained, but they made a marching show for men to see, and the news of their going ran fast to the Saxons. But at Glevum he held the Companions and their great horses. over a thousand of them, and Coroticus with his marsh bow and spear men numbering near another thousand. They camped south of Glevum spread down the river Sabrina below the high scarp to the east. At Glevum Arturo sat and waited for the coming of Esc and for the first smoke and flame of the warning beacons that stretched from the heights above Londinium to run from hill and scarp and downland crest westwards to the last great beacon of piled brushwood and resin-sapped pines on the lip of the scarp south of Glevum. A pillar of smoke by day, or a great finger of flame by night; when the sign came Arturo would know that Esc and all his confederates were on their way to split Britain apart, to butcher it and to flay it like a heifer in a slaughterhouse. But if the grace of the gods ran true then Esc would find that the butchers were to become the butchered.

Six days before the feast of Beltine Arto was sitting in his room at Glevum, the window shutters open to the mild evening air so that he had sight of the southward curving river over which swung a long skein of winter geese disturbed from their feeding on the flats by some hunter. The long sharp scarp of the hills was warm-lit by the light of the setting sun when Gwennifer, who had lodged with him that season at Glevum, came into the room.

With a shadow of a smile touching the corners of her mouth, she said, 'My lord, there are two young warriors who would speak with you.'

Looking at her and sensing her half-teasing near to laughter mood, he asked, 'And should I see them?'

'I think you should, my lord. They come to ask service with you.'

'Then send them down the river to Durstan.'

'They ask for you, and I think they have claim to that right.'

'And since you ask for them they are fortunate. I will see them.' Before she could move away he stretched out his hand and, taking her by the wrist gently, he looked into her clear blue eyes touched now by the finest web of lines in their corners and he knew that she was one of the rare women whose beauty, though changing with the years, would never diminish. The gods had taken Daria from him and given him her in place. This wisdom and kindness of the gods he had long come to know. They had set him to live a life apart, given him grief to try his faith in his dream and then sent him Gwennifer to test his compassion, a compassion which had long ago turned to true love

634

and worship. He kissed the palm of her hand and then said, 'I think these warriors will be no surprise to me – for I was of their age once and know their feelings.'

'Then be good to them for my sake.'

She left him and a few moments later Prince Cato and Mordreth came into the room. They had grown from boys now to well-set youths who held themselves with the fast-coming stance of manhood. They were dressed in tunic and trews without distinction and belted with short swords and side daggers and as they stood there Arturo caught from them the smell of sweat and horse. He welcomed them and then said, 'You should both be at Isca working in the schooling pens.'

For a moment they were silent, each waiting for the other to speak, then Prince Cato said, 'I have but two years of wardship to go, but am only a few months short of the right to bear arms. For the sake of standing on the order of those few months, my lord, would you have me miss the great battle which comes?'

Not answering him, Arturo turned to Mordreth and asked, 'And you – who lack even more months?'

Mordreth smiled. 'My lord, I lack any good reasons except that I would serve with you as groom, servant, or ride messenger and if call arise draw sword to defend myself. Hard words have been said against you, my lord, in these past years, and said by Prince Cato and myself – but now we know the truth. We would be with you in the day of your triumph.'

Knowing the feelings which ran in these two because he had known them himself long ago, he said, 'Men go to battle but the gods ordain which side triumph shall bless . . .' Then with a grin and a shrug of his shoulders, he said, 'Let it be so, then. Ride down river to Durstan and tell him to give you service fit for your years.'

'Fighting service, my lord?' asked Cato.

'Can it be avoided if the gods throw it your way?'

A week later, a little before sunset, the beacon high up on the ridge flared into life, its flames rivalling the glow of the setting sun, its long tail of resinious smoke rolling westwards across the river in ragged plumes. Then began the long wait which, although all now knew its reason, set men itching for the move to come against the Saxons. Soon fast-riding messengers, covering the country in relays, began to arrive at Glevum and on the great war map long ago painted on the wall in Ambrosius's counsel chamber the fine-pointed charcoal sticks marked the slow movement of Esc and his warriors.

They came westwards through the country south of the Tamesis and when they were at Calleva they were joined from the south by Cerdic and his men. Here, under the deliberately scant forces of Gelliga, they were met. Before their strength Gelliga could do nothing and turned away from them, riding west, drawing the Saxons on and convincing them of the weakness of the forces in the south. When they reached Spinis, and it was clear that they were driving for Aquae Sulis to reach the Sabrina river beyond it at Abona and so split the country, Arturo moved.

He sent Durstan with five hundred horse and two hundred of Coroticus's men to move down to the headwater lands of the Tamesis and the Abona rivers north of the Cunetio–Aquae Sulis road. With the rest of his army he went south from Glevum down the Sabrina river road to Abonae and then turned back east to Aquae Sulis. Beyond Aquae Sulis he drew off the road to Cunetio into the wooded slopes and waited for the coming of Esc.

In the years to pass the men who fought in the great battle of Mount Badon which crushed the power of the Saxons for a hundred years to come each told the story they knew. But there is no man in battle who knows its full shape and the terrors and triumphs of all its movements. Each man fights his own battle, lost in a small world of violence and death and maiming. To a Coroticus marshman, arrows ready notched, lying screened by the thickets of the slope above the road, there was nothing at first except the distant cloud dust from the marching, unwary Saxons. The droning of the honey bees working the blooms of gorse and harvesting the pollen from the clumps of purple marjoram and the pink-flushed flowers of the convolvulus rose

higher than the distant stir of tramping warriors. When the
dust cloud became men – axed and sworded, unkempt from
days of marching, sunlight flashing from spear tips and bronze
armbands, a great snake of warriors crawling towards him, men
without care, victory under their belts, and a greater victory to
come – then he picked a man, worked his left hand fingers
gently on the smooth mole-skin grip of his bow and lightly
began to flex the drawcord, his eye never leaving his mark, his
lips drawn back over his teeth which held his second and third
arrow, and waited for the low whistle of command to sing
down the line of his hidden comrades. And when the signal
came and his arrow sped high and curving, flighting now with
a hundred others, searing the air with sharp-honed tip and stiff
flight feathers, his battle had begun and the gods would give
him either the mercy of safe sleep that night or the ease of the
gentle voyage to the Isles of the Blessed.

In the trees on the slope above the marshmen, each trooper
and Companion sat his horse, the great beasts' heads tossing
against the summer flies and the quiver of muscles, nerved by
the communion with their riders, twitching their smooth hides.
The same tremor held the body of each waiting trooper, lance
lowered and cloak belted back to free the quick drawing of
sword from its scabbard when the lance had done its work.
Then was the moment when the Saxons halted under the rain
of arrows and confusion held them briefly and each trooper
lost all thought of gods or sweethearts or family and, hearing
the high call of the battle horns and trumpets, pushed horse to
gallop and went streaming down the hillside, leaving marshmen
to lie flat and let them through while ahead went the White
One with Arturo and at his side rode Lancelo. Following them
to join the marshmen came the foot levies from Cymru and
Demetia, from the tribes of the north and the south of the
land, a moving hillside, an avalanche of Britons to sweep the
Saxons back. Red were the swords that day and swift the
horses and fierce the spear and lance thrusts and bright under
the sun the coloured surcoat of Arto carrying the figure of the
Blessed Mary.

The Saxons stood and fought but when they saw the great crescent of Durstan's horses thundering down the far slope to take them from behind hope went from them. They scattered like a vast flock of crows disturbed from a new sown corn field and, seeking escape from the cavalry, turned south away from the road and climbed the steep scarp of Mount Badon to seek the sanctuary of its ramparts which still waited final ordering at the hand of Baradoc. But there on the level land beyond the summit lay Gelliga and his horse to pen them back or to ride down any that looked for escape. Lucky were those Saxons who broke through to pass back along the road to Cunetio, and luckier still those few who pony-mounted rode into brake and woods and found escape, among them Esc and his son and the bastard Briton Cerdic.

Unlucky were those who found the shelter of Mount Badon's ramparts for there was no water hole or spring to slake their thirst, and the bite of thirst is harsher and speedier felt than that of hunger and soon drives a man to desperation. For three days the sun was brazen in a cloudless but not barren sky for the eagles and kites and the crows and ravens swung in a dark circus above them waiting in patience for the feasting to come.

At sunset on the third day the Saxons broke in force from the hill top down the steep scarp and the Britons hunted and harried them on foot and on horse through the long night and the following day. When the sun went down that day the Saxon might and threat was broken and tamed for a lifetime and more. Victories and conquests when all who lived that day were dead would take strange and wayward paths which unborn men would follow not knowing the shape of the destiny the gods were slowly working for their land.

During the days and nights of the battle and the siege of Mount Badon and the harassing of the retreating Saxons many things happened the memories of which would either be lost or changed by time. Prince Cato and Mordreth killed their first Saxons and with each telling the count rose a little higher. Mordreth's horse stumbled as he tried to force it up the steep scarp to the hilltop in pursuit of the Saxons and youth and beast fell and Mordreth broke his right leg which being set badly always afterwards marked him with a limp. Prince Cato riding hard down the Cunetio road reined-in to lance a wounded Saxon lying on the ground and gave chance to a gut-ripped Saxon lying by to throw with his last strength an axe and mark the youth's face with a long scar from the side of his mouth to his ear.

On the evening when the penned Saxons on the hilltop, made bold and desperate by thirst, broke out, Baradoc, fighting on foot on the steep scarp side, wielding his sword in his left hand, was beset by four Saxons and killed three before the fourth ran him through with his scramaseax and sent him to the gods to join Tia, granting him the only death which he would have wished. He was buried on the vine slope outside old Truvius's villa at Aquae Sulis where the four winged dragon-flies hovered and darted over the yellow flags and the kingfishers flew low like moving fire over the clear waters.

In those days of battle and siege nine hundred and more of the Saxons died, and two hundred of the Companions, troopers and marshmen and foot soldiers of Arturo, among them Marcos who with his long dead brother, the dumb Timo, Christos men both, had been the first to join Arturo and go with him to the Villa of the Three Nymphs. Garwain died when his horse was cut down, and many others long tried by service to Arturo. Among those that buried and mourned their dead were few without wounds to show as small price for the victory which the gods had sent them.

In the first charge down the hill slope to the road Arturo took his own wound. a spear thrust that glanced off his saddle bow and took him above the groin on his left side, a wound ignored until the evening of that first day when Pasco bound it with cloth strips while Arturo made light of it. But men said in the years that followed – though not to Arto's face – that the wound reopened always on the morning of the day of remembrance for Mount Badon and ran blood until sundown.

Three days after the battle Gwennifer came from Glevum to Aquae Sulis to Truvius's villa where Arturo had made his head-

quarters and where there came to him the news of the con-
tinuing eastward flight of the Saxons, harried and hounded by
the forces under Durstan and Gelliga. Gwennifer dressed his
wound and as they sat under the covered way above the courtyard she played her harp for him. Knowing the turmoil in his
mind, the lasting heat of victory in him still, and the strengthening of his dreams for the years to come, she sang:

> The great horses of Arto have broken the sea-men
> Now he is king of the star-bright Kingdom
> A lamp to outshine them, an eagle screaming above the crags
> Over this land now the brown leaves that fall are gold
> The white waves are silver on the shore
> The mist rises from the meadows of red clover
> And the misery of years lifts from the hearts of men

Arturo, hearing her words, remembered the first time she had
played for him at Lindum and how, though he had taken pleasure in her and her music, he had not known then that she
would be wife to him. The gods held the future from men, to let
men dream their own future and labour to create it. At Mount
Badon the work and dreams of years had been brought to fruiting, and each year had levied its own cruel cost. But there was
with him at this moment a wisdom deeper than any he had
known before. The Saxons were broken, and would lick their
wounds for years. But some small part of this country they had
made their own and he knew that there could be no pushing
them into the sea. They must sit where they were and slowly
the seasons and the slow shuttle of daily affairs would mould
their ways and loyalties to the great shape of this land. Warriors
took victory by the sword, but the gods guided a slower and
secret battle. He was now in his forty-fifth year and knew that
the temper of freedom in a land called for more than the simple
acts of warfare which brought peace. War had bonded this land
together by the sword. Under the gods he must find the means
to hold it so in peace. If the gods still loved him he would find a
way and already in his heart he knew that it was a way which
he would walk alone. Men needed gods no matter how they

named them, but a land and a nation needed a man to be seen and to act like a god.

Cold with a sudden loneliness he put out a hand gently and stayed Gwennifer's playing by touching her arm. He said, 'My lady Gwennifer, play me no song of war and kings. In this courtyard my father and mother were married. She lies by the sea and he by the river so there is always the blue water path of joining between them. Play me a song of small delights.'

Gwennifer smiled and took his hand and kissed it. 'I have no great gift with words, my lord.'

'Then give me a small gift.'

She sipped her wine for a moment and then took the harp and played:

> I ask the gods small bounties
> A secret hut in the wilderness
> A moss-lined well beside it
> And a thicket for the singing birds
> Within a row of tall, bright candles
> And under their light the face of my love
> Her eyes the twin stars of constancy
> Drawing me to the smooth haven of her arms

As she played the thought came to her that long dead Borio would have shaped the words with truer pace and sweetness and there was a quick wonder in her that the woman of those days was long dead too. The gods could be cruel in their brief designs but once the due course was run they could sweeten life with new joys. Arturo would be king, but she was content to know that she had long been his queen. The coming years would change him, but nothing in her would alter for her constancy and love was hard set against any change of season.

The Dream and the Dreamer

Arturo rode down the Cam Hill with six mounted Companions behind him. Autumn sunshine was mellow over the land. The White One now and then tossed her head to shake away the teasing flies. Cabal, the last of the great hounds to bear the name, moved at the mare's side, limping a little from the stiffness in his right foreleg from sinews torn by a dog otter's bite in his younger days. From the high branches of a great poplar a red squirrel scolded their passage, and hearing the sound Arturo smiled to himself, for the squirrel had been in the dream of this day to come, the dream which the gods had sent him seven nights before. It had possessed him with a living, undeniable truth and there was no flaw in his memory of it, and no turning from it to find escape. The will of the gods would run its course this day and there was a weariness in his body and heart which gave welcome to it.

In the dell on the hilltop the willow herb flowered between the cairn stones of Daria's grave, and the stones were thick mossed and almost hidden by the spread of ivy growth. Great hart's tongue ferns grew in the shade of a white thorn tree, bird-seeded years ago. The gods had given him the love of two women to comfort and ease the march of his years. Daria lay beneath the berried thorn and Gwennifer, spared the sharing of this day with him, rested at Eburacum to spend the winter with her aged father. The gods had worked the weaving of her days with kindness to take her from his side on this day of golden fruitfulness which was to die into the long darkness of the rest they decreed for him. There was no flaw in the memory of the dream. The flashing of the white rump of a bullfinch flighting across the path had been there, and the rustle of a grass snake through the new fallen leaves that carpeted the bottom of the dry ditch at his side.

In the twenty years since Mount Badon he had given himself to this country and had learnt the art and cunning of being many men, and finally no fixed man to himself. Emperor he had called and made himself to give no rankle to the country's kings. He smiled to himself hearing the name coming from Difynwal's tongue in the old language of the tribes ... Amerauder. In twenty years the Scotti were tamed, the whole of the North recovered. Londinium and other cities flourished, though not fully as they had in the last days of the legions. He had forced formal treaties on the Saxons and they lived like docile cattle in their shrunken enclaves. And he had taken great Camulodunum, the first city of the Romans, to split the North and Middle Saxons from the South. Cerdic and his West Saxons lived on sufferance in their land, and all the provinces of the country had their governors and law givers and suffered sharply if they failed him or their duties. To bring peace to a country had been the first part of his life work, to keep that peace he had had to shape himself anew and found many times when the iron of his pitilessness seared him more sharply than his victims. Men told and sang the stories of his deeds and his wonders and coloured them bright and let truth lie unseen like a mouse in a corner while legend flew high like a red dragon over the land. He let the silvered tongues of bards and singers run free for he knew that, while the gods were always above men, men had need to make of one of their own a god of flesh and blood. He had long ago lost the pathway of true life and rode the shining way of myth. This the gods had decreed for his life, and now they had marked him for a death as unreal as the last great span of his life had been.

They came down the scarp slope to the water meadows of the Cam that ran its crooked way seaward and they rode its bank westward to find the road to Isca. But as he moved to the easy motion of the White One, a man deep in his sixties, tawny beard grizzled with the frosts of the years, the lean face weathered and furrowed, and his body held a little bent to ease the old and constant bite of the wound he had taken at Badon, his eyes were soft with a rare joy. He knew that this day of the coming true of the dream was the one which would take him to the long rest of body and spirit and to the peace at heart which had gone from him on that day on the downs above Cunetio when he had killed his first Saxon. He reached his right hand across and touched the hilt of his scabbarded sword and slipped it a little free to prove its readiness for many a brave but careless Companion had died on hard weather campaigning from the tight grip of rain-swollen wooden scabbard on the wanted blade at the moment of peril.

On a rise in the ground as they left the river the twin green hills of Ynys-witrin showed jewel clear through the bright air. Coroticus reigned there now and called himself Melwas after his dead father, and Coroticus had lost three fingers of his right hand at the battle of Celidon Wood in the far north, long after Badon; Coroticus who had always been true to him and read a fuller understanding of his ways than any other. After this day there would be bitter blood between Coroticus and Prince Cato.

Breasting the rise Arturo marked ahead the pine wood that stood above the road to Isca. It stood now as it had in his dream, even to a kestrel hovering to one side above the harvest stubble of a corn plot and a tethered goat with three free kids watched by an old woman who sat teasing and spinning wool from her hand spindle. A blue skein of smoke rose from a hollow that hid a settler's hut.

After his death peace would slowly die like a great tree being eaten away by rot and beetles; after his death, for his honour and glory, the bards would call this day a day of battle for although many emperors had died by poison and assassination the gods would have for him the glory of death in battle. In the affairs of the gods and emperors truth might serve for a day but the bright, ringing falsehood would quickly flower to ennoble for all time the way of his going.

As Durstan rode silently at his side he was tempted not for the first time since the coming of the dream to turn to him and the other Companions and send them away for their deaths, too, had been marked in it. But there was no power in him to speak the words for he rode under the gods as he had done all his life and was their creature.

He looked ahead at the pines again and saw the kestrel slip sideways down the breeze to hover over the trees and then turn away in rapid flight. He knew that the bird had taken alarm at the men and horses hidden within the wood. Prince Cato would not be there with his envy and malice and fears for the curbing of his gluttony for power. There were others like him in the land and there would be feasting when he was gone. Man's nobility under oppression and peril grew feeble after victory. Those who worshipped him after Mount Badon would now see him gone and the gods for their own reasons would not stay their hands. Mordreth, poisoned from long service and boon-ship with Cato, would ride with the sword drawn to lead the handful of men behind him, Mordreth who through his mother Gerta was part of that flesh of Baradoc and Tia which framed and filled his own body in full descent, Mordreth, whom he had banished in perpetuity to the lands of the people of the Enduring Crow for trying to lay hands in drunken lust on the lady Gwennifer at Isca, would come to give him death and to meet his own and forfeit all reward from Prince Cato.

Durstan at his side looked up and said, 'The sky clouds and there is the smell of rain coming from the West.'

Arturo nodded and said, 'Aye ... Latis will begin her weeping and the lakes and rivers of the Summerlands will rise and over-run their banks.' The rain would fall on him, but not on the living Durstan for there was half a day to go yet before the first heavy storm drops would fall to mark the end of the dream and the onset of the long darkness which awaited him.

Mordreth and his men came when they were within a bow-shot of the pines, but before they showed he knew their coming for the old woman untethered her goat and led it away with the young kids following, and so earned her handful of coins for making the signal of his arrival. They rode without haste to raise no alarm, ten mounted men with Mordreth at their head and no hand lying ready on sword pommel to signal ill intent.

It was then that he turned to Durstan and spoke the last words to him which had marked his dream.

'My good Durstan, stay by me this day as you have stayed by me since the night we rode from Isca into outlawry. Dumnonia which claimed our beginnings now goes to brand itself with lasting shame at our ending, but it is an ending which shall bring you into the everlasting glory and companionship of the gods.'

Then as the horsemen coming to them broke into a gallop and the drawing of swords flashed like the soft play of lightning, Durstan smiled and said, 'I am with you, my lord, and without sorrow for from this day on there is finer and truer company to be found in the shaded halls of the gods than here among mortal men.' Then he grinned and spat and, drawing his sword, went on, 'But let us give ourselves the pleasure, dear Arto, of colouring our blades with the blood of traitors ... *Aie*, tis a far better way to end than by poisoning or midnight dark strangulation.'

They fought without give or flight, the seven against the eleven, numbers which men's pride and the warping and swelling of memory and time would mount twentyfold. They fought stirrup to stirrup, knee to knee, and their movement was the dark swirl of a whirlpool encircling violence, sucking to its centre men and horses. Hooves trampled the fallen and dying. Blood ran down the fair quarters of the White One, shone like dew on the proud neck of Durstan's black stallion, and was trampled beneath hooves to give a darker hue to the red earth of the rich western soil.

They fought from the high pitch of their saddles, and when their horses were cut down or threw them in the rising panic which took the beasts, they fought on foot and no side showed mercy and no man sought flight. It was a time of blood and death under the slow clouding sky and none marked it to live save the old woman and her husband who lay low behind the brushwood fence of their steading and peered through the dead twigs and wished themselves dead for they had not known that the riders from the east would be Arto and his Companions.

Durstan died of a sword slash across his throat from behind for his body to fall and be trampled by the hooves of the horses. The call of a raven, the first of the birds of prey to arrive overhead, gave him farewell. Unmanned horses swirled in the circle until they were spun off like sparks from a grindstone to canter away or stand with their heads lowered in heavy breathing. And when to the raven overhead had gathered the first of the kites and buzzards, there rested living only Mordreth and the last man of his band and Arturo. Then the two rode him down, passing each on either flank of the White One, and as Arturo took the blade of Mordreth's man on his own and swept it aside to free his sword point to drive true into the man's throat to give him death, so Mordreth's sword drove into his left side at the place of his Mount Badon wound. But the pace of his mount, and the sudden swing of the White One's haunches as she bucked free of the fallen man under her rear legs, broke Mordreth's hold on his sword and it fell from Arturo's side to the earth.

Knowing it must happen, the dark strung moments of the dream sliding by under the casting hands of the gods, Arto pulled the White One round and rode against Mordreth who had jumped from his mount to take a sword from the side of one of the dead. He rode him down, driving the full weight and run of the White One into him, and as he lay on the ground Arturo turned and rode him down again, the pounding hooves of the White One battering his body and breaking his bones and his screams came wailing back in dying echoes from the tall stand of the close-by pines.

Arturo rode back to Mordreth and dismounted. Standing over the son of his sister, blood of his blood welling from the slack mouth, he took his dagger – for there was no honour in the man to warrant the nobility of the sword – and mercifully slit his throat and gave his slipping spirit easier and faster passage to the darkness of the limbo which waits to meld into nothingness the souls of those whom the gods reject. Then he mounted the White One, scabbarded his sword, kicked her into slow gait and then dropped the reins loose about her neck and let her have her own way.

She moved and turned her head to the north to follow the

path of the dream. As she went Arto took from around his neck his red and white scarf of the Companions. Wadding it he thrust it under his tunic and held it tight against his wound to stem the steady flow of blood.

When he came to the edge of the marsh lake, through which the river Cam ran, the light was going from the sky and the rain was drifting over the land in thin, soft veils, shrouding close by Ynys-witrin, and pocking the smooth face of the water with its gentle touch. He dismounted, loosed his sealskin travelling pack from behind his saddle, and sat on it to await the coming of the man who had saved his life from bleeding away in the Circle of the Gods from his first wounding by a kinsman. Inbar of his own blood, who had lived between good and bad, now lay dead many a long year; and now Mordreth was shapeless flesh and bone to make quarrel among the birds of prey. The man would come but there would be no saving; Merlin who had said long ago ... *there will come a day when I shall be with you in an hour of your own choosing when the war horns shall blow neither for victory nor defeat, but to set the echoes rolling for evermore over this land to give your name everlasting life while you take the long sleep which the gods have decreed for you.*

From the fringing lake reeds a bittern boomed and through the veiling rain a marsh harrier drifted over the waters like a lost spirit. A frog croaked a slow complaint and a shoal of minnows broke through the water like a silver cloud as they leapt to escape a marauding pike. The White One, unscathed, her smooth hide stained with the running scarlet of his own blood, cropped the sweet turf. There was a slow weariness working over his body that numbed him against all pain. The blood ran slowly over his hand that held the wadding to his side and he knew that as it ran so would run his dream, and knew more, that the ending of the dream he had dreamt was no ending for it had faded on a moment bereft of death's last ease ...

Cabal came and sat by him, pushing his muzzle fretfully against the back of his free hand. He teased the hound's ears, thinking of the puppy hound that Gwennifer had ridden from Lindum to present to him. In Eburacum now she was safe. There were many sides to love and no man or woman could claim to know them all. She would move in beauty through the years left to her and find strength to bear the sorrow of his going.

The soft rain thickened and fell hard now to beat the lake water into a hissing froth. Through it came a narrow flat-bottomed boat of the kind which the marshmen used for duck hunting and fishing. A man sat in the stern and paddled it gently, a brown-robed man, black-bearded, his head uncovered to the fast falling rain. The prow of the craft drove through the reeds and grated on the gravelled bank. The man stepped ashore and then sat on the prow with his feet resting on the gleaming stones of the lakeside. He nodded his head to Arturo, smiling gently, but said nothing.

Arturo said wearily, 'So here the dream comes to an end. What lies beyond it?'

Merlin rose then and coming to him answered, 'Latis weeps for you. She is the gentle-hearted one among the gods, but seldom knows the full truth of her sorrow. The waters are rising for you to make a moving pathway without beginning or end.' He wiped his hand across his beard to free it of rain and fingered his dark eyebrows to clear them of their heavy dewing. 'But you will not lack for company. There are others who move on it. The good and the bad. Some long distant Caesar, a drunken poet with a head full of Spring music and words that touch the heart before the mind. Maybe a few priests who have come close to knowing the purity of the God who stands above all other gods, and some great bishops who handled charity as though it were a sword. The gods stock the pens of time with all sorts of human cattle.'

'Cattle?' The twist of a smile touched the corners of Arturo's mouth.

'Aye. Men are but cattle of a kind and the gods herd them.'

Arturo rose and would have walked towards the boat, but Merlin held up his right hand. 'There is no moving out on to the waters until you have done the two last things of the dream.'

'My dream ended with your coming.'

'But the dream runs on through all time and now you must shape it for yourself. Before you move on the waters you must finish the earth dream from your own fashioning.'

Arturo closed his eyes and swayed a little from the weakness in him growing from his wound. Then he turned and walked to the White One. She raised her head and he stroked the velvet of her mouth and he remembered the first White One, she whom he had caught and tamed from the great woods above the Villa of the Three Nymphs. Blood from the tearing of his flesh as he had ridden her through thorn and briars and the thick lattice of brakes and undergrowth had streaked her hide that day. His own blood this day stained this mare's hide with a ragged poppy bloom.

Moving from her with Cabal limping at his heels, the hound whining, sensing strangeness and distrusting it, he walked to the water's edge and drew his sword from its scabbard. Holding the bloodied blade before his face he kissed it and then threw it far out on to the waters. Its great splash disturbed a feeding mallard and the bird took flight through the rain, trailing feet and wing beats marking a foam-flecked path into the growing darkness.

Behind him Merlin, with laughter in his voice, said, 'Tis no great loss. Until mankind reaches true manhood there will be no lack of swords in this world.' Then, as Arturo turned from the lake and went to his rain-sodden campaigning pack on which he had been sitting while he awaited Merlin's coming, the man rose and joined him.

Arturo knelt, swift pain unexpectedly scything across his left side, and unfastening the strapping of the pack took from it the silver chalice which had always travelled with him since the day that golden-haired Gwennifer had used it for her salving ointment. It was tarnished and dull but the falling rain fast pearled and dewed it with clinging drops which broke and ran to puddle thinly within it. He was tempted to cup it in his hands to see if the growing water within would turn to the blood colour he had known at the Circle of the Gods. But Merlin reached out and took it gently from him, saying, 'Nought will happen, my lord Arturo. On another age and in another's palms the turning will be seen again.' Chalice in hand he went to the boat.

Arturo followed him. Merlin pushed the boat free to rock on the waters which were now loud with the pulse of the heavy rain. Arturo stepped into the boat and sitting took the paddle. Cabal would have jumped in with him but Merlin touched the hound's head and Cabal sat, shivering and whining. Looking at the man Arturo, eyes half-closed with pain, said, 'So the dream goes. But before the waters take me, I ask you one last grace.'

Merlin smiled. 'There is no need for asking. From here I shall go to Cam Hill and make simple prayer for you and Daria. And when I come to Eburacum I will give comfort to your lady Gwennifer.'

'My gratitude. And the gods go with you.'

Merlin's face twisted wryly. 'Aye, I fear they will. But I would give much for the long sleep into which you now drift.'

He put his foot to the prow of the boat, sent it free on the waters, and stood watching in the rain as Arturo with his left hand made stroke or two with the paddle to send it out into the river current that now ran with growing vigour through the lake. Arturo dropped the paddle and sat without movement. He drifted on the surge of the growing current into veils of rain and darkness which slowly enshrouded him and hid him from the sight of Merlin.

At his going the White One raised her head high and whinnied loud. Merlin laid his hand gently on the neck of the shivering hound, speaking softly to it as the rain gathered fast in the bowl of the chalice on the ground at his side.

List of Place and Tribal Names

Abona R. Avon

Abonae Bristol

Abus R. Humber

Anderida Pevensey

Antivestaeum Land's End

Aquae Sulis Bath

Ariconium Weston-under-Penyard

Atrebates Middle Thames Valley tribe

Belerium Land's End

Belgae West Country tribe

Brigantes Tribe holding lands north of York from coast to coast

Caer Sibli Lundy Island

Calcaria Tadcaster

Calleva Silchester

Camulodunum Colchester

Cantawarra Canterbury

Cantiaci Kent tribe

Catuvellauni Essex tribe also holding lands north-west of London

Causennae Ancaster

Clausentium Bitterne

Corinium Cirencester

Coritani Lincoln-Leicestershire tribe

Cornovii Cheshire-Staffordshire tribe

Crococalana Brough

Cunetio Mildenhall

Cymru Wales

Demetae South-West Wales tribe

Deva Chester

Dubglas R. Witham

Dumnonia Cornwall and Devon

Durnovaria Dorchester

Durobrivae Rochester

Durocornovium Wanborough

Durolipons Cambridge

Durotriges Somerset-Dorset tribe

Durovernum Canterbury

Durovigutum Godmanchester

Eburacum York

Erin Ireland

Eurium Usk

Glevum Gloucester

Gobannium Abergavenny

Iceni Norfolk-East Anglia tribe

Ictis St Michael's Mount

Isca Exeter

Ituna Solway Firth

Hercules Promontory Hartland Point

Lactodorum Towcester

Lavobrinta Forden Gaer (Wales)

Lemanis Lympne

Lindinis Ilchester

653

List of Place and Tribal Names

Lindum   Lincoln
Londinium   London
Lugovalium   Carlisle
Lutetia   Paris
Metatis   The Wash
Mona   Anglesey
Moridunum   Carmarthen
Nemetostatio   North Tawton
Nidum   Neath
Novantae   Dumfries tribe
Noviomagus   Chichester
Ocelli   Flamborough Head
Olicana   Ilkley
Octapitarum   St David's Head
Ordovices   North Wales tribe
Parisi   East Yorkshire tribe
Petuaria   Brough (Humber)
Picts   The Scots
Pontes   Staines
Portus Adurni   Porchester
Ratae   Leicester
Regnenses   Hampshire-Sussex tribe

Rutupiae   Richborough
Sabrina   R. Severn
Salinae   Droitwich
Scotti   The Irish
Segontium   Caernarvon
Sorviodunum   Old Sarum
Spinis   Speen
Tamarus   R. Tamar
Tamesis   R. Thames
Tanatus   Thanet
Tisobis   R. Glaslyn
Trinovantes   Essex-East Anglia tribe
Turius   R. Towy
Vectis   Isle of Wight
Venta   Winchester
Verlucio   Sandy Lane
Verulamium   St Albans
Vindocladia   Badbury Rings
Vindolandia   Chesterholm
Ynys-witrin   Glastonbury